Empire of the Sun

The Kindness of Women

J.G. BALLARD

HARPER PERENNIAL
London, New York, Toronto and Sydney

Harper Perennial
An imprint of HarperCollins*Publishers*
77-85 Fulham Palace Road
Hammersmith
London W6 8JB

www.harperperennial.co.uk

This omnibus edition published in 2006 by Harper Perennial

Empire of the Sun Copyright © J.G. Ballard 1984
The Kindness of Women Copyright © J.G. Ballard 1991

J.G. Ballard asserts the moral right to
be identified as the author of this work

A CIP catalogue record for this book
is available from the British Library

ISBN-13: 9780007777747
ISBN-10: 0007777744

Printed and bound in Great Britain by Bookmarque Ltd, Croydon,
Surrey

Empire of
the Sun

Empire of the Sun draws on my experiences in Shanghai, China, during the Second World War, and in Lunghua C.A.C. (Civilian Assembly Centre) where I was interned from 1942–45. For the most part this novel is based on events I observed during the Japanese occupation of Shanghai and within the camp at Lunghua.

The Japanese attack on Pearl Harbor took place on Sunday morning, 7 December 1941, but as a result of time differences across the Pacific Date Line it was then already the morning of Monday, 8 December in Shanghai.

J. G. Ballard

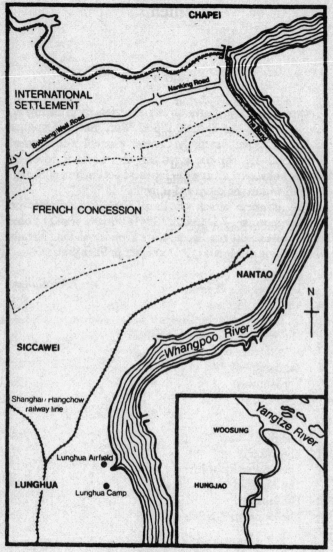

Shanghai in 1941

Contents

Part I

1

The Eve of Pearl Harbor

Wars came early to Shanghai, overtaking each other like the tides that raced up the Yangtze and returned to this gaudy city all the coffins cast adrift from the funeral piers of the Chinese Bund.

Jim had begun to dream of wars. At night the same silent films seemed to flicker against the wall of his bedroom in Amherst Avenue, and transformed his sleeping mind into a deserted newsreel theatre. During the winter of 1941 everyone in Shanghai was showing war films. Fragments of his dreams followed Jim around the city; in the foyers of department stores and hotels the images of Dunkirk and Tobruk, Barbarossa and the Rape of Nanking sprang loose from his crowded head.

To Jim's dismay, even the Dean of Shanghai Cathedral had equipped himself with an antique projector. After morning service on Sunday, 7 December, the eve of the Japanese attack on Pearl Harbor, the choirboys were stopped before they could leave for home and were marched down to the crypt. Still wearing their cassocks, they sat in a row of deck-chairs requisitioned from the Shanghai Yacht Club and watched a year-old *March of Time*.

Thinking of his unsettled dreams, and puzzled by their missing sound-track, Jim tugged at his ruffed collar. The organ voluntary drummed like a headache through the cement roof and the screen trembled with the familiar images of tank battles and aerial dogfights. Jim was eager to prepare for the fancy-dress Christmas party being held that afternoon by Dr Lockwood, the vice-chairman of the British Residents' Association. There would be the drive through the Japanese lines to Hungjao, and then Chinese conjurors, fireworks and yet more newsreels, but Jim had his own reasons for wanting to go to Dr Lockwood's party.

Outside the vestry doors the Chinese chauffeurs waited by their Packards and Buicks, arguing in a fretful way with each other. Bored by the film, which he had seen a dozen times, Jim listened as Yang, his father's driver, badgered the Australian verger. However, watching the newsreels had become every expatriate Briton's patriotic duty, like the fund-raising raffles at the country club. The dances and garden parties, the countless bottles of Scotch consumed in aid of the war effort (like all children, Jim was intrigued by alcohol but vaguely disapproved of it) had soon produced enough money to buy a Spitfire – probably one of those, Jim speculated, that had been shot down on its first flight, the pilot fainting in the reek of Johnnie Walker.

Usually Jim devoured the newsreels, part of the propaganda effort mounted by the British Embassy to counter the German and Italian war films being screened in the public theatres and Axis clubs of Shanghai. Sometimes the Pathé newsreels from England gave him the impression that, despite their unbroken series of defeats, the British people were thoroughly enjoying the war. The *March of Time* films were more sombre, in a way that appealed to Jim. Suffocating in his tight cassock, he watched a burning Hurricane fall from a sky of Dornier bombers towards a children's book landscape of English meadows that he had never known. The *Graf Spee* lay scuttled in the River Plate, a river as melancholy as the Yangtze, and smoke clouds rose from a shabby city in eastern Europe, that black planet from which Vera Frankel, his seventeen-year-old governess, had escaped on a refugee ship six months earlier.

Jim was glad when the newsreel was over. He and his fellow-choristers tottered into the strange daylight towards their chauffeurs. His closest friend, Patrick Maxted, had

12

sailed with his mother from Shanghai for the safety of the British fortress at Singapore, and Jim felt that he had to watch the films for Patrick, and even for the White Russian women selling their jewellery on the cathedral steps and the Chinese beggars resting among the gravestones.

The commentator's voice still boomed inside his head as he rode home through the crowded Shanghai streets in his parents' Packard. Yang, the fast-talking chauffeur, had once worked as an extra in a locally made film starring Chiang Ching, the actress who had abandoned her career to join the communist leader Mao Tse-Tung. Yang enjoyed impressing his eleven-year-old passenger with tall tales of film stunts and trick effects. But today Yang ignored Jim, banishing him to the back seat. He punched the Packard's powerful horn, carrying on his duel with the aggressive rickshaw coolies who tried to crowd the foreign cars off the Bubbling Well Road. Lowering the window, Yang lashed with his leather riding crop at the thoughtless pedestrians, the sauntering bar-girls with American handbags, the old amahs bent double under bamboo yokes strung with head-less chickens.

An open truck packed with professional executioners swerved in front of them, on its way to the public strang-lings in the Old City. Seizing his chance, a barefoot beggar-boy ran beside the Packard. He drummed his fists on the doors and held out his palm to Jim, shouting the street cry of all Shanghai:

'No mama! No papa! No whisky soda!'

Yang lashed at him, and the boy fell to the ground, picked himself up between the front wheels of an oncoming Chrysler and ran beside it.

'No mama, no papa . . .'

Jim hated the riding crop, but he was glad of the Packard's horn. At least it drowned the roar of the eight-gun fighters, the wail of air-raid sirens in London and

13

Warsaw. He had had more than enough of the European war. Jim stared at the garish façade of the Sincere Company's department store, which was dominated by an immense portrait of Chiang Kai-Shek exhorting the Chinese people to ever greater sacrifices in their struggle against the Japanese. A faint light, reflected from a faulty neon tube, trembled over the Generalissimo's soft mouth, the same flicker that Jim had seen in his dreams. The whole of Shanghai was turning into a newsreel leaking from inside his head.

Had his brain been damaged by too many war films? Jim had tried to tell his mother about his dreams, but like all the adults in Shanghai that winter she was too preoccupied to listen to him. Perhaps she had bad dreams of her own. In an eerie way, these shuffled images of tanks and dive-bombers were completely silent, as if his sleeping mind was trying to separate the real war from the make-believe conflicts invented by Pathé and British Movietone.

Jim had no doubt which was real. The real war was everything he had seen for himself since the Japanese invasion of China in 1937, the old battlegrounds at Hungjao and Lunghua where the bones of the unburied dead rose to the surface of the paddy fields each spring. Real war was the thousands of Chinese refugees dying of cholera in the sealed stockades at Pootung, and the bloody heads of communist soldiers mounted on pikes along the Bund. In a real war no one knew which side he was on, and there were no flags or commentators or winners. In a real war there were no enemies.

By contrast, the coming conflict between Britain and Japan, which everyone in Shanghai expected to break out in the summer of 1942, belonged to a realm of rumour. The supply ship attached to the German raider in the China Sea now openly visited Shanghai and moored in the river, where it took on fuel from a dozen lighters – many of them, Jim's father noted wryly, owned by American oil companies. Almost all the American women and children had been evacuated from Shanghai. In his class at the Cathedral School, Jim was surrounded by empty desks. Most of his friends and their mothers had left for the safety of Hong Kong and Singapore, while the fathers closed their houses and moved into the hotels along the Bund.

At the beginning of December, when school ended for the day, Jim joined his father on the roof of his office block in Szechwan Road and helped him to set fire to the crates of records which the Chinese clerks brought up in the elevator. The trail of charred paper lifted across the Bund and mingled with the smoke from the impatient funnels of the last steamers to leave Shanghai. Passengers crowded the gangways, Eurasians, Chinese and Europeans fighting to get aboard with their bundles and suitcases, ready to risk the German submarines waiting in the Yangtze estuary. Fires rose from the roofs of the office buildings in the financial district, watched through field-glasses by the Japanese officers standing on their concrete blockhouses across the river at Pootung. It was not the anger of the Japanese that most disturbed Jim, but their patience.

As soon as they reached the house in Amherst Avenue he ran upstairs to change. Jim liked the Persian slippers, embroidered silk shirt and blue velvet trousers in which he resembled a film extra from *The Thief of Bagdad*, and he was eager to leave for Dr Lockwood's party. He would endure the conjurors and newsreels, and then set off for the secret rendezvous which the rumours of war had prevented him from keeping for so many months.

By way of a happy bonus, Sunday was Vera's free afternoon, when she visited her parents in the ghetto at Hongkew. This bored young woman, little more than a child herself, usually followed Jim everywhere like a guard

15

dog. Once Yang had driven him home – his parents were to stay on for dinner at the Lockwoods' – he would be free to roam alone through the empty house, his keenest pleasure. The nine Chinese servants would be there, but in Jim's mind, and in those of the other British children, they remained as passive and unseeing as the furniture. He would finish doping his balsa-wood aircraft, and complete another chapter of the manual entitled *How to Play Contract Bridge* that he was writing in a school exercise book. After years spent listening to his mother's bridge parties, trying to extract any kind of logic from the calls of 'One diamond', 'Pass', 'Three Hearts', 'Three No Trumps', 'Double', 'Redouble', he had prevailed on her to teach him the rules and had even mastered the conventions, a code within a code of a type that always intrigued Jim. With the help of an Ely Culberston guide, he was about to embark on the most difficult chapter of all, on psychic bidding – all this and he had yet to play a single hand.

However, if the task proved too exhausting he would set off on a bicycle tour of the French Concession, taking his airgun in case he ran into the group of French twelve-year-olds who formed the Avenue Foch gang. When he returned home it would be time for the Flash Gordon radio serial on station XMHA, followed by the record programme when he and his friends telephoned requests under their latest pseudonyms – 'Batman', 'Buck Rogers', and (Jim's) 'Ace', which he liked to hear read out by the announcer though it always made him cringe with embarrassment.

As he flung his cassock to the amah and changed into his party costume he found that all this was threatened. Her head muddled by the rumours of war, Vera had decided not to visit her parents.

'You will go to the party, James,' Vera informed him as she buttoned his silk shirt. 'And I will telephone my parents and tell them all about you.'

16

'But, Vera – they want to see you. I know they do. You've got to think of them, Vera . . .' Baffled, Jim hesitated to complain. His mother had told him to be kind to Vera, and not to tease her as he had done the previous governess. This moody White Russian had terrified him as he recovered from measles by telling him that she could hear the voice of God in Amherst Avenue, warning them from their ways. Soon afterwards Jim had impressed his school friends by announcing that he was an atheist. By contrast, Vera Frankel was a calm girl who never smiled and found everything strange about Jim and his parents, as strange as Shanghai itself, this violent and hostile city a world away from Cracow. She and her parents had escaped on one of the last boats from Hitler's Europe and now lived with thousands of Jewish refugees in Hongkew, a gloomy district of tenements and faded apartment blocks behind the port area of Shanghai. To Jim's amazement, Herr Frankel and Vera's mother existed in one room.

'Vera, where do your parents live?' Jim knew the answer, but decided to risk the ruse. 'Do they live in a house?'

'They live in one room, James.'

'One room!' To Jim this was inconceivable, far more bizarre than anything in the Superman and Batman comics. 'How big is the room? As big as my bedroom? As big as this house?'

'As big as your dressing-room. James, some people are not so lucky as you.'

Awed by this, Jim closed the door of the dressing-room and changed into his velvet trousers. His eyes measured the little chamber. How two people could survive in so small a space was as difficult to grasp as the conventions in contract bridge. Perhaps there was some simple key which would solve the problem, and he would have the subject of another book.

Fortunately, Vera's pride made her rise to the bait. When

17

she had left for her parents', setting off on the long walk to the tram terminus in the Avenue Joffre, Jim found himself still pondering the mystery of this extraordinary room. He decided to raise the matter with his mother and father, but as always they were too distracted by news of the war even to notice him. Dressed for the party, they were in his father's study, listening to the short-wave radio bulletins from England. His father knelt by the radiogram in his pirate costume, leather patch pushed on to his forehead and spectacles over his tired eyes, like some scholarly buccaneer. He stared at the yellow dial embedded like a gold tooth in the mahogany face of the radiogram. On a map of Russia spread across the carpet he marked the new defensive line to which the Red Army had retreated. He stared at it hopelessly, as mystified by the vastness of Russia as Jim had been by the Frankels' minute room.

'Hitler will be in Moscow by Christmas. The Germans are still moving forward.'

His mother stood in her pierrot suit by the window, staring at the steely December sky. The long train of a Chinese funeral kite undulated along the street, head nodding as it bestowed its ferocious smile on the European houses. 'It must be snowing in Moscow. Perhaps the weather will stop them . . .'

'Once every century? Even that might be too much to ask. Churchill must bring the Americans into the war.'

'Daddy, who is General Mud?'

His father looked up as Jim waited in the doorway, the amah carrying his airgun like a bearer, this member of a volunteer infantry in velvet blue ready to aid the Russian war effort.

'Not the BB gun, Jamie. Not today. Take your aeroplane instead.'

'Amah, don't touch it! I'll kill you!'

'Jamie!'

His father turned from the radiogram, ready to strike him. Jim stood quietly by his mother, waiting to see what happened. Although he liked to roam Shanghai on his bicycle, at home Jim always remained close to his mother, a gentle and clever woman whose main purposes in life, he had decided, were to go to parties and help him with his Latin homework. When she was away he spent many peaceful hours in her bedroom, mixing her perfumes together and idling through the photograph albums of herself before her marriage, stills from an enchanted film in which she played the part of his older sister.

'Jamie! Never say that . . . You aren't going to kill Amah or anyone else.' His father unclenched his hands, and Jim realized how exhausted he was. Often it seemed to Jim that his father was trying to remain too calm, burdened by the threats to his firm from the communist labour unions, by his work for the British Residents' Association, and by his fears for Jim and his mother. As he listened to the war news he became almost lightheaded. A fierce affection had sprung up between his parents, which he had never seen before. His father could be angry with him, while taking a keen interest in the smallest doings of Jim's life, as if he believed that helping his son to build his model aircraft was more important than the war. For the first time he was totally uninterested in school-work. He pressed all kinds of odd information on Jim – about the chemistry of modern dyestuffs, his company's welfare scheme for the Chinese mill-hands, the school and university in England to which Jim would go after the war, and how, if he wished, he could become a doctor. All these were elements of an adolescence which his father seemed to assume would never take place.

Sensibly, Jim decided not to provoke his father, nor to mention the Frankels' mysterious room in the Hongkew ghetto, the problems of psychic bidding and the missing soundtrack inside his head. He would never threaten Amah again. They were going to a party, and he would try to cheer his father and think of some way of stopping the Germans at the gates of Moscow.

Remembering the artificial snow that Yang had described in the Shanghai film studios, Jim took his seat in the Packard. He was glad to see that Amherst Avenue was filled with the cars of Europeans leaving for their Christmas parties. All over the western suburbs people were wearing fancy dress, as if Shanghai had become a city of clowns.

2

Beggars and Acrobats

Pierrot and pirate, his parents sat silently as they set off for Hungjao, a country district five miles to the west of Shanghai. Usually his mother would caution Yang to avoid the old beggar who lay at the end of the drive. But as Yang swung the heavy car through the gates, barely pausing before he accelerated along Amherst Avenue, Jim saw that the front wheel had crushed the man's foot. This beggar had arrived two months earlier, a bundle of living rags whose only possessions were a frayed paper mat and an empty Craven A tin which he shook at passers-by. He never moved from the mat, but ferociously defended his plot outside the taipan's gates. Even Boy and Number One Coolie, the houseboy and the chief scullion, had been unable to shift him.

However, the position had brought the old man little benefit. There were hard times in Shanghai that winter, and after a week-long cold spell he was too tired to raise his tin. Jim worried about the beggar, and his mother told him that Coolie had taken a bowl of rice to him. After a heavy snowfall one night in early December the snow formed a thick quilt from which the old man's face emerged like a sleeping child's above an eiderdown. Jim told himself that he never moved because he was warm under the snow.

There were so many beggars in Shanghai. Along Amherst Avenue they sat outside the gates of the houses, shaking their Craven A tins like reformed smokers. Many displayed lurid wounds and deformities, but no one noticed them that afternoon. Refugees from the towns and villages around Shanghai were pouring into the city. Wooden carts and rickshaws crowded Amherst Avenue, each loaded with a peasant family's entire possessions. Adults and children bent under the bales strapped to their backs, forcing the wheels with their hands. Rickshaw coolies hauled at their shafts, chanting and spitting, veins as thick as fingers clenched into the meat of their swollen calves. Petty clerks pushed bicycles loaded with mattresses, charcoal stoves and sacks of rice. A legless beggar, his thorax strapped into a huge leather shoe, swung himself along the road through the maze of wheels, a wooden dumb-bell in each hand. He spat and swiped at the Packard when Yang tried to force him out of the car's way, and then vanished among the wheels of the pedicabs and rickshaws, confident in his kingdom of saliva and dust.

When they reached the Great Western Road exit from the International Settlement they found a queue of cars on both sides of the checkpoint. The Shanghai police had given up any attempt to control the crowds. The British officer stood on the turret of his armoured car, smoking a cigarette as he gazed over the thousands of Chinese pressing past him. Now and then, as if to keep up appearances, the Sikh NCO in a khaki turban reached down and lashed the backs of the Chinese with his bamboo rod.

Jim gazed up at the police. He was fascinated by the gleaming Sam Brownes of these sweating and overweight men, by their alarming genitalia that they freely exposed whenever they wanted to urinate, and by the polished holsters that held all their manliness. Jim wanted to wear a holster himself one day, feel the enormous Webley revolver press against his thigh. Among the shirts in his father's wardrobe Jim had found a Browning automatic pistol, a jewel-like object resembling the interior of his parents' cine-camera which he had once accidentally opened, exposing hundreds of feet of film. It was hard to imagine those miniature bullets killing anyone, let alone the tough communist labour organizers.

By contrast, the Mausers worn by the senior Japanese NCOs were even more impressive than the Webleys. The wooden holsters hung to their knees, almost like rifle-scabbards. Jim watched the Japanese sergeant at the check-point, a small but burly man who used his fists to drive back the Chinese. He was almost overwhelmed by the peasants struggling with their carts and rickshaws. Jim sat beside Yang in the front of the Packard, holding tight to his balsa aircraft as he waited for the sergeant to draw his Mauser and fire a shot into the air. But the Japanese were careful with their ammunition. Two soldiers cleared a space around a peasant woman whose cart they had overturned. Bayonet in hand, the sergeant slashed open a sack of rice which he scattered around the woman's feet. She stood shaking and crying in a sing-song voice, surrounded by the lines of polished Packards and Chryslers with their European pas-sengers in fancy dress.

Perhaps she had tried to smuggle a weapon through the checkpoint? There were Kuomintang and communist spies everywhere among the Chinese. Jim felt sorry for the peasant woman, whose sack of rice was probably her only possession, but at the same time he admired the Japanese. He liked their bravery and stoicism, and their sadness which struck a curious chord with Jim, who was never sad. The Chinese, whom Jim knew well, were a cold and often cruel people, but in their superior way they stayed together, whereas every Japanese was alone. All of them carried photographs of their identical families, little formal prints, as if the entire Japanese Army had been recruited only from the patrons of arcade photographers.

On his cycle journeys around Shanghai – trips of which his parents were unaware – Jim spent hours at the Japanese checkpoints, now and then managing to ingratiate himself with a bored private. None of them would ever show him their weapons, unlike the British Tommies in the sandbag-

23

ged blockhouses along the Bund. As the Tommies lay in their hammocks, oblivious of the waterfront life around them, they would let Jim work the bolts of their Lee-Enfields and ream out the barrels with the pull-throughs. Jim liked them, and their weird voices full of talk about a strange, inconceivable England.

But if war came, could they beat the Japanese? Jim doubted it, and he knew that his father doubted it too. In 1937, at the start of the war against China, two hundred Japanese marines had come up the river and dug themselves into the beaches of black mud below his father's cotton mill at Pootung. In full view of his parents' suite in the Palace Hotel, they had been attacked by a division of Chinese troops commanded by a nephew of Madame Chiang. For five days the Japanese fought from trenches that filled waist-deep with water at high tide, then advanced with fixed bayonets and routed the Chinese.

The queue of cars moved through the checkpoint, carrying groups of Americans and Europeans already late for their Christmas parties. Yang edged the Packard to the barrier, whistling with fear. In front of them was a Mercedes tourer emblazoned with swastika pennants, filled with impatient young Germans. But the Japanese searched the interior with the same thoroughness.

Jim's mother held his shoulder. 'Not now, dear. It might frighten the Japanese.'

'That wouldn't frighten them.'

'Jamie, not now,' his father repeated, adding with rare humour: 'You might even start the war.'

'Could I?' The thought intrigued Jim. He lowered his aircraft from the window. A Japanese soldier was running the bayonet of his rifle across the windshield, as if cutting an invisible web. Jim knew that he would next lean through the passenger window, venting into the Packard's interior his tired breath and that threatening scent given off by all

24

Japanese soldiers. Everyone then sat still, as the slightest move would produce a short pause followed by violent retribution. The previous year, when he was ten, Jim had nearly given Yang a heart attack by pointing his metal Spitfire into the face of a Japanese corporal and chanting 'Ra-ta-ta-ta-ta . . .' For almost a minute the corporal had stared at Jim's father without expression, nodding slowly to himself. His father was physically a strong man, but Jim knew that it was the kind of strength that came from playing tennis.

This time Jim merely wanted the Japanese to see his balsa aircraft; not to admire it, but to acknowledge its existence. He was older now, and liked to think of himself as the co-pilot of the Packard. Aircraft had always interested Jim, and especially the Japanese bombers that had devastated the Nantao and Hongkew districts of Shanghai in 1937. Street after street of Chinese tenements had been levelled to the dust, and in the Avenue Edward VII a single bomb had killed a thousand people, more than any other bomb in the history of warfare.

The chief attraction of Dr Lockwood's parties, in fact, was the disused airfield at Hungjao. Although the Japanese controlled the open countryside around the city, their forces were kept busy patrolling the perimeter of the International Settlement. They tolerated the few Americans and Europeans who lived in the rural districts, and in practice there was rarely a Japanese soldier to be seen.

When they arrived at Dr Lockwood's isolated house Jim was relieved to find that the party was not going to be a success. There were only a dozen cars in the drive, and their chauffeurs were hard at work polishing the dust from the fenders, eager for a quick getaway. The swimming-pool had been drained, and the Chinese gardener was quietly removing a dead oriole from the deep end. The younger children and their amahs sat on the terrace, watching a troupe of

Cantonese acrobats climb their comical ladders and pretend to disappear into the sky. They turned into birds, unfurled crushed paper wings and danced in and out of the squealing children, then leapt on to each other's backs and transformed themselves into a large red cockerel.

Jim steered his balsa plane through the verandah doors. As the adults' world continued above his head he made a circuit of the party. Many of the guests had decided not to appear in costume, as if too nervous of their real rôles to cast themselves in disguise. The gathering reminded Jim of the all-night parties at Amherst Avenue which lasted to the next afternoon, when distracted mothers in crumpled evening gowns wandered by the swimming-pool, pretending to look for their husbands.

The conversation fell away when Dr Lockwood switched on the short-wave radio. Glad to see everyone occupied, Jim stepped through a side door on to the rear terrace of the house. He watched the line of weeding women move across the lawn. There were twenty Chinese women, dressed in black tunics and trousers, each on a miniature stool. They sat shoulder to shoulder, weeding knives flashing at the grass, while keeping up an unstoppable chatter. Behind them Dr Lockwood's lawn lay like green shantung.

'Hello, Jamie. Cogitating again?' Mr Maxted, father of his best friend, emerged from the verandah. A solitary but amiable figure in a sharkskin suit, who faced reality across the buffer of a large whisky and soda, he stared down his cigar at the weeding women. 'If all the people in China sat in a line they would stretch from the North to the South Pole. Have you thought of that, Jamie?'

'They could weed the whole world?'

'If you want to put it like that. I hear you've resigned from the cubs.'

'Well . . .' Jim doubted if there was any point in explaining to Mr Maxted why he had left the wolf-cubs, an act of

26

rebellion he had decided upon simply to test its result. To his disappointment, Jim's parents had been surprisingly unmoved. He thought of telling Mr Maxted that not only had he left the cubs and become an atheist, but he might become a communist as well. The communists had an intriguing ability to unsettle everyone, a talent Jim greatly respected.

However, he knew that Mr Maxted would not be shocked by this. Jim admired Mr Maxted, an architect turned entrepreneur who had designed the Metropole Theatre and numerous Shanghai nightclubs. Jim often tried to imitate his raffish manner, but soon found that being so relaxed was exhausting work. Jim had little idea of his own future – life in Shanghai was lived wholly within an intense present – but he imagined himself growing up to be like Mr Maxted. Forever accompanied by the same glass of whisky and soda, or so Jim believed, Mr Maxted was the perfect type of the Englishman who had adapted himself to Shanghai, something that Jim's father, with his seriousness of mind, had never really done. Jim always enjoyed the drives with Mr Maxted, when he and Patrick sat in the front seat of the Studebaker and embarked on unpredictable journeys through an afternoon world of empty nightclubs and casinos. Mr Maxted drove the Studebaker himself, a trick of behaviour that seemed exciting and even faintly disreputable to Jim. He and Patrick would play the untended roulette wheels with Mr Maxted's money, under the tolerant smiles of the White Russian bar-girls darning their silk stockings, while Mr Maxted sat in the office with the owner, moving around other piles of banknotes.

Perhaps, in return, he should take Mr Maxted on his secret expedition to Hungjao Airfield?

'Don't miss the film show, Jamie. I rely on you to keep me up to date with the latest news in military aviation . . .'

Jim watched Mr Maxted sway along the tiled verge of the

empty swimming-pool, curious to see if he would fall in. If Mr Maxted was always accidentally falling into swimming-pools, as indeed he always was, why did he only fall into them when they were filled with water?

3

The Abandoned Aerodrome

Pondering the answer, Jim stepped from the terrace. He ran across the lawn past the weeding women, sailing his aircraft over their heads. The women ignored him, their knives stabbing at the grass, but Jim always felt a faint shiver of horror when he strayed too close to them. He could visualize what would happen if he fainted in their path.

At the south-west corner of the estate was Dr Lockwood's radio mast. A section of the wooden fence had been displaced by the stay-wires, and Jim stepped through the gap on to the edge of an untended field. A burial tumulus rose from the wild sugar-cane at its centre, and the rotting coffins projected from the loose earth like a chest of drawers.

Jim set out across the field. As he passed the tumulus he stopped to peer into the lidless coffins. The yellowing skeletons were embedded in the rain-washed mud, as if these poor peasants had been laid out on pallets of silk. Once again Jim was struck by the contrast between the impersonal bodies of the newly dead, whom he saw every day in Shanghai, and these sun-warmed skeletons, every one an individual. The skulls intrigued him, with their squinting eye-sockets and quirky teeth. In many ways these skeletons were more alive than the peasant-farmers who had briefly tenanted their bones. Jim felt his cheeks and jaw, trying to imagine his own skeleton in the sun, lying here in this peaceful field within sight of the deserted aerodrome.

Leaving the burial mound and its family of bones, Jim crossed the field to a line of stunted poplars. He climbed a wooden stile on to the floor of a dried-out rice-paddy. The

29

leathery carcass of a water buffalo lay in the shade under the hedge, but otherwise the landscape was empty, as if all the Chinese in the Yangtze basin had left the countryside for the refuge of Shanghai. Holding the balsa aircraft over his head, Jim ran along the floor of the paddy towards an iron building that stood on a ridge of higher ground a hundred yards to the west. Overgrown by nettles and sugar-cane, the remains of a concrete road passed a ruined gatehouse and then gave way to an open sea of wild grass.

This was the aerodrome at Hungjao, a place of magic for Jim, where the air ran with dreams and excitements. There was the galvanized hangar, but little else remained of this military airfield from which Chinese fighters had attacked the Japanese infantry columns advancing on Shanghai in 1937. Jim stepped into the waist-high grass. Like the water in the sea at Tsingtao, below the warm surface was a cool world touched by mysterious currents. The bright December wind buffeted the grass, patterns swirled around him like the slipstreams of invisible aircraft. Listening carefully, Jim could almost hear the sounds of their engines turning.

He launched the balsa model into the wind, and caught it as it returned to his hand. Already he was bored with this model glider. Where he now played, Chinese and Japanese pilots had stood in their flying suits, fastened their goggles over their eyes before taking off for the attack. Jim waded through the deeper grass that rose to his shoulders. The thousands of blades seethed around his velvet trousers and silk shirt, as if trying to identify this miniature aviator.

A shallow ditch formed the southern edge of the airfield. Lying in the deep nettles was the fuselage of a single-engined Japanese fighter, perhaps shot down while trying to land on the grass runway. The wings, propeller and tail section had been removed, but the cockpit remained intact, the rusting metal of the seat and controls blanched by the rain. Through the open radiator shutters Jim could see the

30

cylinders of the engine that had pulled this aircraft and its pilot through the sky. The once burnished metal was now as rough as brown pumice, like the hulls of the rusting U-boats beached in the cove below the German forts at Tsingtao. But for all its rust this Japanese fighter still belonged to the sky. For months Jim had been trying to devise a way of persuading his father to take it back to Amherst Avenue. At night it could lie beside his bed, lit by the newsreels inside his head.

Jim rested his balsa model on the engine cowling, climbed over the windshield and lowered himself into the metal seat. Without the parachute that provided a cushion for the pilot, he was sitting on the floor of the cockpit, in a cave of rusting metal. He gazed at the instrument dials with their Japanese ideograms, at the trim wheels and undercarriage lever. Below the instrument panel he could see the breeches of the machine-guns mounted in the windshield cowling, and the interrupter gear that ran towards the propeller shaft. A potent atmosphere hovered over the cockpit, the only nostalgia that Jim had ever known, the intact memory of the pilot who had sat at its controls. Where was the pilot now? Jim pretended to work the controls, as if this sympathetic action could summon the spirit of the long-dead aviator.

Below one of the clouded dials a metal tape bearing a row of Japanese characters had been punched into the dashboard, a list of manifold pressures or pitch settings. Jim peeled the tape from its worn rivets, then stood up and slipped it into the pocket of his velvet trousers. He lifted himself from the cockpit and climbed on to the engine cowling. His arms and shoulders were trembling with all the confused emotions that this ruined aircraft invariably set off in his mind. Giving way to his excitement, he picked up his model glider and launched it into the air.

Caught by the wind, the model banked steeply and soared

across the perimeter of the airfield. It skidded along the roof of an old concrete blockhouse and fell into the grass beyond. Impressed by the model's speed, Jim jumped from the engine cowling and ran towards the blockhouse, arms outstretched as he machine-gunned the flitting insects.

'Ta-ta-ta-ta-ta . . . Vera-Vera-Vera . . . !'

Beyond the overgrown perimeter ditch of the airfield was an old battleground of 1937. Here the Chinese armies had made one of their many futile stands in the attempt to halt the Japanese advance on Shanghai. Ruined trenches formed zigzag lines, a collapsed earth palisade linked a group of burial mounds built on the causeway of a disused canal. Jim could remember visiting Hungjao with his parents in 1937, a few days after the battle. Parties of Europeans and Americans drove from Shanghai, and parked their limousines on country roads covered with cartridge cases. The ladies in silk dresses and their husbands in grey suits strolled through the debris of a war arranged for them by a passing demolition squad. To Jim the battlefield seemed more like a dangerous rubbish tip – ammunition boxes and stick grenades were scattered at the roadside, there were discarded rifles stacked like matchwood and artillery pieces still hitched to the carcasses of horses. The belt ammunition of machine-guns lying in the grass resembled the skins of venomous snakes. All around them were the bodies of dead Chinese soldiers. They lined the verges of the roads and floated in the canals, jammed together around the pillars of the bridges. In the trenches between the burial mounds hundreds of dead soldiers sat side by side with their heads against the torn earth, as if they had fallen asleep together in a deep dream of war.

Jim reached the blockhouse, a concrete fort whose gun slits let a faint light into their damp world. He climbed on to the roof and walked across the open deck, searching the nettle banks for his aircraft. The plane lay twenty feet away, caught in the rusting barbed wire of an old trenchwork. The paper was torn from its wings, but the balsa frame was still intact.

He was about to jump from the blockhouse, when he noticed that a face was looking up at him from the trench. A fully armed Japanese soldier squatted by the broken earth wall, his rifle, webbing and ground sheet laid out beside him as if ready for inspection. No more than eighteen years old, with a passive and moon-like face, he stared at Jim, unsurprised by the apparition of this small European boy in his blue velvet trousers and silk shirt.

Jim's eyes moved along the trench. Two more Japanese soldiers sat on a wooden beam that protruded from the ground, rifles held between their knees. The trench was filled with armed men. Fifty yards away a second platoon squatted under the parapet of an earth bunker, smoking cigarettes and reading their letters. Beyond them were groups of other soldiers, their heads barely visible among the nettles and wild sugar-cane. An entire company of Japanese infantry was resting in this old battlefield, as if re-equipping itself from the dead of an earlier war, ghosts of their former comrades risen from the grave and issued with fresh uniforms and rations. They smoked their cigarettes, blinking in the unfamiliar sunlight, their faces turned towards the skyscrapers of downtown Shanghai whose neon signs flashed across the empty paddy fields.

Jim looked back to the fuselage of the fighter aircraft, expecting to see its dead pilot standing in his cockpit. A Japanese sergeant was walking through the deep grass between the blockhouse and the aircraft. His strong legs left a yellowing gully behind him. He finished the stub of his cigarette, drawing the last of the smoke into his lungs. Although the sergeant ignored him, Jim knew that he had decided what to do next with this small boy.

'Jamie . . . ! We're all waiting . . . there's a surprise for you!'

Jim's father was calling to him. He stood in the centre of the airfield, but could see the hundreds of Japanese soldiers in the trenchworks. He wore his spectacles, and had thrown away his eye-patch and the jacket of his pirate costume. Although out of breath after running from Dr Lockwood's house, he forced himself to stand still, in the way that least unsettled the Japanese. The Chinese, who would cry at moments of stress and wave their arms, never understood this.

Nonetheless, Jim was surprised that this small token of deference seemed to satisfy the sergeant. Without a glance at Jim, he threw away his cigarette and jumped the perimeter ditch. He plucked the balsa aircraft from the barbed wire and threw it among the nettles.

'Jamie, it's time for the fireworks . . .' His father walked quietly through the grass. 'We ought to go now.'

Jim climbed from the roof of the blockhouse. 'My plane's down there. I could get it, I suppose.'

His father watched the Japanese sergeant walk along the parapet of the trenchworks. Jim could see that it was an effort for his father to speak. His face was as strained and bloodless as it had been when the labour organizers at the cotton mill threatened to kill him. Yet he was still thinking about something. 'We'll leave it for the soldiers – finders keepers.'

'Like kites?'

'That's it.'

'He wasn't very angry.'

'It looks as if they're waiting for something to happen.'

'The next war?'

'I don't suppose so.'

Hand in hand, they walked across the airfield. Nothing moved except for the ceaselessly rippling grass, rehearsing itself for the slipstreams to come. When they reached the hangar his father tightly embraced Jim, almost trying to hurt him, as if Jim had been lost to him forever. He was not angry with Jim, and seemed glad that he had been forced to visit the old aerodrome.

But Jim felt vaguely guilty and annoyed with himself. He had lost his balsa plane and lured his father into a dangerous meeting with the Japanese. Solitary Europeans who strayed into the path of the Japanese were usually left dead on the roadside.

When they returned to Dr Lockwood's house the guests were already leaving. Rounding up the children and amahs, they climbed hurriedly into their cars and drove in convoy back to the International Settlement. Wearing the trousers of his Father Christmas suit and a beard of surgical cotton Dr Lockwood waved to them as Mr Maxted drank his whisky by the drained swimming-pool and the Chinese conjurors climbed their ladders and transformed themselves into imaginary birds.

Still grieving over the loss of his plane, Jim sat between his parents in the back of the Packard. Were they frightened that he might get up to some new mischief if he sat in the front beside Yang? He had managed to spoil Dr Lockwood's party and make it unlikely that he would visit Hungjao Aerodrome again. He thought of the crashed fighter in which he had invested so much of his imagination, and of the dead pilot whose presence he had felt in the rusting cockpit.

Despite the setbacks, Jim was delighted when his mother told him that they would leave the house in Amherst Avenue for a few days and instead would stay in the company's suite at the Palace Hotel. The end-of-term examinations at the Cathedral School began the next day, with geometry and scripture. Since the cathedral was only a few hundred yards from the hotel he would have ample time the next morning for revision. Jim was keen on scripture, especially now that he was an atheist, and always enjoyed receiving the Reverend Matthews' traditional accolade ('The first, and the biggest heathen of the lot, is . . .').

Jim waited in the front seat of the Packard while his parents changed and their suitcases were loaded into the trunk. When they set off through the gates he looked down at the motionless figure of the beggar on his frayed mat. He could see the pattern of the Packard's Firestone tyres in the old man's left foot. Leaves and shreds of newspaper covered his head, and already he was becoming part of the formless rubbish from which he had emerged.

Jim felt sorry for the old beggar, but for some reason he could think only of the tyre patterns in his foot. If they had been driving in Mr Maxted's Studebaker the pattern would have been different: the old man would have been stamped with the imprint of the Goodyear Company . . .

Trying to distract himself from these thoughts, Jim switched on the car radio. He always looked forward to the evening drives through the centre of Shanghai, this electric and lurid city more exciting than any other in the world. As they reached the Bubbling Well Road he pressed his face to the windshield and gazed at the pavements lined with nightclubs and gambling dens, crowded with bar-girls and gangsters and rich beggars with their bodyguards. Six thousand miles away, across the International Dateline, the Americans in Honolulu were sleeping through the early hours of Sunday morning, but here, a day ahead in time as in everything else, Shanghai was ready to begin a new week. Crowds of gamblers pushed their way into the jai alai stadiums, blocking the traffic in the Bubbling Well Road. An armoured police van with two Thompson guns mounted in a steel turret above the driver swung in front of the Packard and cleared the pavement. A party of young

Chinese women in sequinned dresses tripped over a child's coffin decked with paper flowers. Arms linked together, they lurched against the radiator grille of the Packard and swayed past Jim's window, slapping the windshield with their small hands and screaming obscenities. Hundreds of Eurasian bar-girls in ankle-length fur coats sat in the lines of rickshaws outside the Park Hotel, whistling through their teeth at the residents who emerged from the revolving doors, while their pimps argued with the middle-aged Czech and Polish couples in neat, patched suits trying to sell the last of their jewellery. Nearby, along the windows of the Sun Sun department store in the Nanking Road, a party of young European Jews were fighting in and out of the strolling crowds with a gang of older German boys in the swastika armbands of the Graf Zeppelin Club. Chased by the police sirens, they ran through the entrance of the Cathay Theatre, the world's largest cinema, where a crowd of Chinese shopgirls and typists, beggars and pickpockets spilled into the street to watch people arriving for the evening performance. As they stepped from their limousines the women steered their long skirts through the honour guard of fifty hunchbacks in mediaeval costume. Three months earlier, when his parents had taken Jim to the première of *The Hunchback of Notre Dame*, there had been two hundred hunchbacks, recruited by the management of the theatre from every back alley in Shanghai. As always, the spectacle outside the theatre far exceeded anything shown on its screen, and Jim had been eager to get back to the pavements of the city, away from the newsreels and their endless reminders of war.

After dinner, as Jim lay in his bedroom on the tenth floor of the Palace Hotel, he tried not to sleep. He listened to the drone of a Japanese seaplane landing on the river at the Nantao Naval Air Base. He thought of the crashed fighter at Hungjao Aerodrome, and of the Japanese pilot whose seat he had filled that afternoon. Perhaps the spirit of the dead aviator had entered him, and the Japanese would join the war on the same side as the British? Jim dreamed of the coming war, of a newsreel in which he stood in his flying suit on the decks of a silent carrier, ready to take his place with those lonely men from the island nation in the China Sea, borne with them across the Pacific by the spirit of the divine wind.

4
The Attack on the Petrel

A field of paper flowers floated on the morning tide, clustered around the oil-stained piers of the jetty and dressed them in vivid coloured ruffs. A few minutes before dawn Jim sat at a window of his bedroom at the Palace Hotel. He wore his school uniform and was keen to start an hour's revision before breakfast. As always, however, he found it difficult to keep his eyes from the Shanghai waterfront. Already the odour of fish heads and bean curd sizzling in peanut oil rose from the pans of the vendors outside the hotel. Tung-stained junks with eyes painted on their bows sailed past the opium hulks beached on the Pootung shore. Thousands of sampans and ferry-boats were moored along the Bund, a city of floating hovels still hidden by the darkness. But between the factory chimneys of Pootung the first sunlight was diffusing across the river, illuminating the square profiles of the USS *Wake* and HMS *Petrel*.

The American and British gunboats were anchored in midstream opposite the banking houses and hotels of the Bund. Jim watched a motorboat carrying two British officers back to the *Petrel* after their parties ashore. He had met the captain of the *Petrel*, Captain Polkinhorn, at the Shanghai Country Club, and knew all the naval ships on the river. Even in the pearly light he noticed that the Italian monitor *Emilio Carlotta*, which had been berthed beside the Public Gardens on the Bund, provocatively in front of the British Consulate, had slipped anchor during the night. Her place had been taken by a Japanese gunboat, a squat and war-stained craft with dirty guns and stark camouflage patterns on the funnel and superstructure. Rust leaked from the anchor vents on either side of her bows. The steel shutters were still locked over the bridge windows, and sandbags protected the barbettes of the forward and rear gun turrets. Looking at this powerful ship, Jim wondered if it had been damaged during its patrol of the Yangtze gorges. Sailors and officers moved about the bridge house, and a signal lamp flashed a message across the river.

Two miles upstream, beyond the Naval Air Base at Nantao, was a boom of sunken freighters which the Chinese had scuttled in 1937, in an attempt to block the river. The sunlight shone through the holes in their steel masts and funnels, and the incoming tide washed across their decks, swilling through the staterooms. As he rode back in the company launch after visiting his father's cotton mill Jim always longed to climb aboard the freighters and explore their drowned cabins, a world of forgotten voyages overgrown by grottoes of rust.

He watched the Japanese gunboat by the Public Gardens. The signal lamp flickered insistently from the bridge. Was this weary gun-platform about to sink on to its own anchors? Although Jim had a deep respect for the Japanese, their ships were always being disparaged by the British in Shanghai. The cruiser *Idzumo*, moored alongside the Japanese Consulate at Hongkew half a mile downstream, looked far more impressive than the *Wake* and the *Petrel*. In fact the *Idzumo*, flagship of the Japanese China Fleet, had been built in England and served in the Royal Navy before being sold to the Japanese during the Russo-Japanese War in 1905.

The light advanced across the river, picking out the paper flowers that covered its back like garlands discarded by the admirers of these sailors. Every night in Shanghai those Chinese too poor to pay for the burial of their relatives would launch the bodies from the funeral piers at Nantao, decking the coffins with paper flowers. Carried away on one tide, they came back on the next, returning to the waterfront of Shanghai with all the other debris abandoned by the city. Meadows of paper flowers drifted on the running tide, and clumped in miniature floating gardens around the old men and women, the young mothers and small children, whose swollen bodies seemed to have been fed during the night by the patient Yangtze.

Jim disliked this regatta of corpses. In the rising sunlight the paper petals resembled the coils of viscera strewn around the terrorist bomb victims in the Nanking Road. He turned his attention to the Japanese gunboat. A launch had been lowered and was setting out across the river towards the USS *Wake*. A dozen Japanese marines sat facing each other, their rifles raised like oars. Two naval officers in full formal dress stood in the bows, one with a megaphone in his gloved hands.

Puzzled that they should be paying a ceremonial visit so early in the morning, Jim climbed on to the window ledge and pressed himself against the plate glass. Two picket-boats had set out from the *Idzumo*, each carrying fifty marines. The three craft met in the centre of the river and cut their engines. They wallowed among the paper flowers and old packing cases. A motorized junk powered past them, the bamboo cages on its deck loaded with barking dogs on their way to the Hongkew meat market. A naked coolie stood at the helm, drinking a bottle of beer. He made no attempt to alter course as the junk's wash drenched the launch from the gunboat. Ignoring the spray, the Japanese officer called to the *Wake* through his megaphone.

Laughing to himself, Jim drummed his palms against the window. None of the American officers were on board, as everyone in Shanghai well knew. All would be sleeping soundly in their rooms at the Park Hotel. Sure enough, a drowsy Chinese crewman in shorts and vest emerged from

41

the fo'c'sle. He shook his head at the Japanese picket-boat coming alongside, and began polishing the brass rail as the marines clambered on to the gangway and moved swiftly to the deck. Carrying rifles with bayonets fixed, they ran the length of the ship, searching for any American members of the crew.

Followed by the second picket-boat, the motor-launch approached HMS *Petrel*. There was a terse exchange with the young British officer on the bridge, who dismissed the Japanese in the offhand way that Jim had seen his parents refuse to buy the Java heads and carved elephants from the dugout salesmen who surrounded the cruise ships in Singapore harbour.

Were the Japanese trying to sell something to the British and Americans? Jim knew that they were wasting their time. Standing against the window with his arms outstretched, he tried to remember the semaphore he had learned so reluctantly in the cubs. The Japanese officer in the launch was signalling with a lamp to the gunboat by the Public Gardens. As the light stuttered across the water Jim noticed that hundreds of Chinese were running past the British Consulate. Billows of smoke and steam pumped from the gunboat's funnel, as if the ship was about to burst.

The barrel of the forward gun turret exploded in a single flash that scorched the bridge and deck. Six hundred yards away there was an answering explosion as the shell struck the superstructure of the *Petrel*. The pressure wave of this detonating round cracked against the hotels of the Bund, and the heavy plate glass hit Jim on the nose. As the gunboat fired a second shell from its rear turret he jumped on to the bed and began to cry, then stopped himself and crouched behind the mahogany headboard.

From its moorings beside the Japanese Consulate the cruiser *Idzumo* had also opened fire. Its guns flashed through the smoke that rose from its three funnels and curled along the water like a black feather boa. Already the *Petrel* was hidden within a pall of steam, below which a series of raging fires were reflected in the water. Two Japanese fighter aircraft flew along the Bund, so low that Jim could see the pilots in their cockpits. Crowds of Chinese scattered across the tramway lines, some towards the quayside, others sheltering on the steps of the hotels.

'Jamie! What are you doing?' Still in his pyjamas, his father burst barefoot into the bedroom. He stared uncertainly at the furniture, as if unable to recognize this room in his own suite. 'Jamie, keep away from the window! Get dressed and do what your mother tells you. We're leaving in three minutes.'

He seemed not to notice that Jim was wearing his school uniform and blazer. As they shielded their eyes from the point-blank shellfire there was a huge explosion from the centre of the river. Like rockets in a firework display, burning pieces of the *Petrel* soared into the air and then splashed into the water. Jim felt numbed by the noise and smoke. People were running down the corridors of the hotel, an elderly Englishwoman screamed into the lift shaft. Jim sat on the bed and stared at the burning platform that settled into the river. Every few seconds there was a steady flicker of light from its centre. The British sailors on the *Petrel* were fighting back. They had manned one of the guns and were returning fire at the *Idzumo*. But Jim watched them sombrely. He realized that he himself had probably started the war, with his confused semaphores from the window that the Japanese officers in the motor launch had misinterpreted. He knew now that he should have stayed in the cubs. Perhaps the Reverend Matthews would cane him in front of the whole school for being a spy.

'Jamie! Lie on the floor!' His mother knelt in the communicating doorway. In a pause between the salvoes of shells she pulled him from the vibrating windows and held him to the carpet.

'Am I going to school?' Jim asked. 'It's the scripture exam.'

'No, Jamie. Today there'll be a school holiday. We're going to see if Yang can take us home.'

Jim was impressed by her calm. He decided not to tell her that he had started the war. As soon as his parents had dressed they set out to leave the hotel. A crowd of European and American guests surrounded the lifts. Refusing to take the stairs, they pounded on the metal grilles and shouted down the shafts. They carried suitcases, and wore their hats and overcoats, as if deciding to take the next steamer to Hong Kong. His mother joined them, but his father took her arm and forced their way to the staircase.

Knees knocking with the effort, Jim reached the entrance lobby before them. Chinese kitchen staff, guests from the lower floors and White Russian clerks crouched behind the leather furniture and potted palms, but Jim's father strode past them to the revolving doors.

All firing had ceased. Throngs of Chinese ran along the Bund between the stationary trams and parked cars, old amahs hobbling in black trousers, coolies pulling empty rickshaws, beggars and sampan boys, uniformed waiters from the hotels. A pall of grey smoke as large as a fogbound city lay across the river, from which emerged the topmasts of the *Idzumo* and the *Wake*. By the Public Gardens clouds of incandescent soot still pumped from the funnel of the Japanese gunboat.

The *Petrel* was sinking at her moorings. Steam rose from her stern and midships, and Jim could see the queue of sailors standing in the bows, waiting to take their places in the ship's cutter. A Japanese tank moved along the Bund, its tracks striking sparks from the tramlines. It swivelled jerkily around an abandoned tram, and crushed a rickshaw against a telegraph pole. Sprung loose from the wreckage, a warped wheel careened across the roadway. It kept pace with the Japanese officer who commanded the assault troops, his sword raised as if whipping the wheel ahead of him. Two fighter aircraft streaked along the waterfront, the wash from their propellers stripping the bamboo hatches from the sampans and exposing hundreds of crouching Chinese. A battalion of Japanese marines advanced along the Bund, appearing like a stage army through the ornamental trees of the Public Gardens. A platoon with fixed bayonets raced to the steps of the British Consulate, led by an officer with a Mauser pistol.

'There's the car . . . we'll have to run!' Taking Jim and his mother by the hand, his father propelled them into the street. Immediately Jim was knocked to the ground by a coolie striding past. He lay stunned among the pounding feet, expecting the bare-chested Chinese to come back and apologize. Then he picked himself up, brushed the dust from his cap and blazer and followed his parents towards the car parked in front of the Shanghai Club. A group of exhausted Chinese women sat on the steps, sorting their handbags and choking on the diesel fuel that drifted across the river from the capsized hull of the *Petrel*.

As they set off along the Bund the Japanese tank had reached the Palace Hotel. Surrounding it were the fleeing staff, Chinese bellboys in their braided American uniforms, waiters in white tunics, and the European guests clutching their hats and suitcases. Two Japanese motorcyclists, each with an armed soldier in the camouflaged side-car, pushed ahead of the tank. Standing on their pedals, they tried to force a way through the rickshaws and pedicabs, the horse-carts and gangs of coolies tottering under the bales of raw cotton hung from yokes over their shoulders.

Already a sizeable traffic jam blocked the Bund. Once again the crush and clatter of Shanghai had engulfed its invaders. Perhaps the war was over? Through the rear window of the Packard, itself now stalled in the traffic, Jim watched a Japanese NCO screaming at the Chinese around him. A dead coolie lay at his feet, blood pouring from his head. The tank was trapped in the press of vehicles, its path blocked by a white Lincoln Zephyr. Two young Chinese women in fur coats, dancers from the nightclub on top of the Socony building, struggled with the controls, laughing into their small jewelled hands.

'Wait here!' Jim's father opened his door and stepped into the road. 'Jamie, look after your mother!'

Machine-gun fire was coming from the Japanese marines who had captured the USS *Wake*. Riflemen on the bridge were shooting at the British sailors swimming ashore from the *Petrel*. The ship's cutter, loaded with wounded men, was sinking in the shallow water that covered the mud-flats below the quays of the French Concession. The sailors slipped to their thighs in the black mud, arms streaming with blood. A wounded petty officer fell in the water, and drifted away towards the dark piers of the Bund. Clinging to each other, the sailors lay helplessly in the mud, as the quickening tide rippled around them. Already the first funeral flowers had found them and begun to gather around their shoulders.

Jim watched his father push through the sampan coolies who crowded the wharf. A group of British men had run from the Shanghai Club and were taking off their overcoats and jackets. In waistcoats and shirt-sleeves they jumped from the landing stage on to the mud below, arms swinging as they sank to their thighs. The Japanese marines on the USS *Wake* continued to fire at the cutter, but two of the Britons had reached a wounded sailor. They seized him under the arms and dragged him towards the mud-flat. Jim's father waded past them, his spectacles splashed with water, scooping the black ooze out of his way. The tide had risen to his chest when he caught the injured petty officer drifting between the piers of the wharf. He pulled him into the shallow water, dragging him by one hand, and knelt exhausted beside him on the oily mud. Other rescuers had reached the sinking cutter. They lifted out the last of the wounded sailors and fell together into the water. They began to swim and crawl towards the shore, helped on to the mud-flat by a second party of Britishers.

The cloud of burning oil from the *Petrel* crossed the Bund and enveloped the stalled traffic and the advancing Japanese. As Jim wound up his window the Packard was thrown forward, and then shaken violently from side to side. Broken glass fell from the windshield and showered the seats. Jim lay on the rear floor of the passenger cabin as the door pillar struck his mother's head.

'Jamie, get out of the car . . . Jamie!'

Dazed, she opened her door and stepped on to the road, taking her handbag from the swaying seat. Behind them the Japanese tank was forcing its way past the Lincoln Zephyr abandoned by the Chinese dancers. The metal tread crushed the rear fender around its wheel and then rammed the heavy car into the back of the Packard.

'Get up, Jamie . . . we're going home . . .'

A hand to her bruised face, his mother was pulling at the warped rear door. The tank stopped, before making a second pass at the Lincoln. Japanese marines moved between the cars and rickshaws, lunging with their bayonets at the crowd. Jim climbed on to the front seat and opened the driver's door. He jumped into the road and ducked below the shafts of a rickshaw laden with rice bags. The tank moved forward, smoke throbbing from its engine vents. Jim saw his mother pushed into the throng of Chinese and Europeans whom the marines were forcing across the Bund. A second tank followed the first, then a line of camouflaged trucks packed with Japanese soldiers.

A final rifle shot rang out from the USS *Wake*. The last of the wounded British sailors were pulled on to the mud-flat below the Bund. Oil leaking from the swamped *Petrel* lay in an elongated slick across the river, calming this place of battle. The British civilians who had helped to rescue the sailors sat in their greasy shirt-sleeves beside the wounded men. Jim's father was dragging the injured petty officer on to the mud-flat. Exhausted, he lost his grip and collapsed in a shallow stream that ran through the oily bank from a sewer vent below the pier.

The Japanese soldiers on the Bund were driving the crowd away from the quay, forcing the Chinese and Europeans to step from their cars and rickshaws. Jim's mother had disappeared, cut off from him by the column of military trucks. A wounded British sailor, a sandy-haired youth no more than eighteen years old, climbed the steps from the landing stage, hands outstretched like bloody ping-pong bats.

Straightening his school cap, Jim darted past him and the watching sampan coolies. He ran down the steps and jumped from the landing stage on to the spongy surface of the mud-flat. Sinking to his knees, he waded through the damp soil towards his father.

'We brought them out – good lad, Jamie.' His father sat in the stream, the body of the petty officer beside him. He had lost his spectacles and one of his shoes, and the trousers of his business suit were black with oil, but he still wore his white collar and tie. In one hand he held a yellow silk glove like those Jim had seen his mother carrying to the formal receptions at the British Embassy. Looking at the glove, Jim realized that it was the complete skin from one of the petty officer's hands, boiled off the flesh in an engine-room fire.

'She's going . . .' His father flicked the glove into the water like the hand of a tiresome beggar. A hoarse, throttling explosion sounded across the river from the capsized hull of the *Petrel*. There was a violent rush of steam from the risen decks, and the gunboat slipped below the waves. A cloud of frantic smoke seethed across the water, surging about as if hunting for the vanished craft.

Jim's father lay back against the mud. Jim squatted beside him. The noise of the tanks' engines on the Bund, the shouted commands of the Japanese NCOs and the drone of the circling aircraft seemed far away. The first debris from the *Petrel* was reaching them, life jackets and pieces of planking, a section of canvas awning with its trailing ropes, that resembled an enormous jellyfish, dislodged from the deep by the sinking gunboat.

A flicker of light ran along the quays like silent gunfire. Jim lay down beside his father. Drawn up above them on the Bund were hundreds of Japanese soldiers. Their bayonets formed a palisade of swords that answered the sun.

5

Escape from the Hospital

'Mitsubishi ... Zero-Sen ... ah ... Nakajima ... ah ...'

Jim lay in his cot in the children's ward, and listened to the young Japanese soldier call out the names of the aircraft flying over the hospital. The skies above Shanghai were filled with aircraft. Although the soldier knew the names of only two types of plane he found it difficult to keep up with the endless aerial activity.

For three days Jim had rested peacefully in the ward on the top floor of St Marie's Hospital in the French Concession, disturbed only by the young soldier's furtive smoking and his amateur plane-spotting. Alone in the ward, he thought about his mother and father, and hoped that they would soon come to visit him. He listened to the seaplanes flying from the Naval Air Base at Nantao.

' ... ah ... ah ...' The soldier shook his head, stumped again, and searched the immaculate floor for a cigarette end. In the corridor below the landing Jim could hear the French missionary sisters arguing with the Japanese military police who now occupied this wing of the hospital. Despite the hard mattress, the whitewashed walls with their unpleasant icons above each bed – the crucified infant Jesus surrounded by Chinese disciples – and the ominous chemical smell (something to do, he surmised, with intense religious feelings), Jim found it difficult to believe that the war had at last begun. Walls of strangeness separated everything, every face that looked at him was odd.

He could remember Dr Lockwood's party at Hungjao,

and the Chinese conjurors who turned themselves into birds. But the bombardment of the *Petrel*, the tank that had crushed the Packard, the huge guns of the *Idzumo* all belonged to a make-believe realm. He almost expected Yang to saunter into the ward and tell him that they were part of a technicolour epic being staged at the Shanghai film studios.

What was real, without any doubt, was the mud-flat to which his father had helped to drag the wounded sailors, and where they had sat for six hours beside the dead petty officer. It was as if the Japanese had been so surprised by the speed of their assault that they had been forced to wait before they fully grasped any sense of their victory. Within a few hours of the attack on Pearl Harbor the Japanese armies which encircled Shanghai had seized the International Settlement. The marines who captured the USS *Wake* and occupied the Bund celebrated by parading in force in front of the hotels and banking houses.

Meanwhile, the wounded survivors of the *Petrel* and the British civilians who had helped to rescue them remained on the mud-flat beside the sewer. An armed party of military police stepped from the landing stage and walked among them. Captain Polkinhorn, wounded in the head, and his first officer were taken away, but the others were left to sit under the sun. A Japanese officer in full uniform, scabbard held in his gloved hand, moved among the injured and exhausted men, peering at each in turn. He stared at Jim as he sat in his blazer and school cap beside his exhausted father, obviously puzzled by the elaborate badges of the Cathedral School and assuming that Jim was an unusually junior midshipman in the Royal Navy.

An hour later Captain Polkinhorn was taken in a motor-launch to the site of the sunken *Petrel*. Before abandoning ship the captain had been able to destroy his codes, and for days afterwards the Japanese sent divers down to the wreck in an unsuccessful attempt to retrieve the code-boxes.

Soon after ten o'clock the Japanese reopened the Bund, and thousands of uneasy Chinese and European neutrals were ushered along the quay. They looked down at the wounded crew of the *Petrel*, and stood silently as the Rising Sun was ceremonially hoisted to the mast of the USS *Wake*. Shivering beside his father in the cold December sun, Jim gazed up at the expressionless eyes of the Chinese packed together on the quay. They were witnessing the complete humiliation of the Allied powers by the empire of Japan, an object lesson to all those reluctant to enter the Co-Prosperity Sphere. Fortunately, some hours later a party of officials from the Vichy French and German embassies forced their way through the crowd. They protested volubly about the treatment of the wounded British. Impelled by one of their abrupt changes of mood, the Japanese relented and the prisoners were on their way to St Marie's Hospital.

Once there, Jim's sole thought was to leave the hospital and return to his mother at Amherst Avenue. The French doctor who mercurichromed his knees and the sisters who bathed him saw immediately that Jim was a British schoolboy, and tried to have him released. The Japanese, however, had taken over a complete wing of the hospital, cleared out the Chinese patients and installed a guard on each floor. A young soldier was posted outside the children's ward on the top floor, and passed the time asking the nuns for cigarettes and calling out the names of the aircraft overhead.

A Chinese nun told Jim that his father was with the other civilians in a ward below, still recovering from the effects of heart strain and exposure, but would be ready to leave in a few days. Meanwhile, for reasons of their own, the Japanese High Command had begun to eulogize the bravery of Captain Polkinhorn and his men. On the second day the commander of the *Idzumo* sent a party of uniformed officers to the hospital, who paid tribute to the wounded sailors in the best traditions of bushido, bowing to each one of them. The English-language *Shanghai Times*, British-owned but long sympathetic to the Japanese, carried a photograph of the *Petrel* on its front page, and an article extolling the courage of its crew. The main headline described the Japanese attack on Pearl Harbor and the bombing of Clark Field at Manila. Pencil drawings supplied by a neutral news agency showed apocalyptic scenes of smoke rising from the slumped American battleships.

Now that the Japanese had won the war, Jim mused, perhaps life in Shanghai would return to normal. When the young soldier showed him the newspaper he carefully studied the photograph of fighter-bombers taking off from the Japanese carriers, scenes that he seemed to remember from his own dreams in his bedroom at the Palace Hotel on the eve of the war.

Lounging on the bed beside him, the soldier pointed to the assault aircraft, keen to impress Jim with this staggering feat of arms.

' . . . ah . . . ah . . . '

'Nakajima,' Jim said. 'Nakajima Hayabusa.'

'Nakajima . . . ?' The soldier sighed deeply, as if the subject of military aviation was far beyond the grasp of this small English boy. In fact Jim recognized almost all the Japanese aircraft. British newsreels of the Sino-Japanese War openly derided the Japanese planes and their pilots, but Jim's father and Mr Maxted always spoke of them with respect.

Jim was wondering how he could see his father when the guard corporal bellowed a command up the stairwell. The young private was terrified of this small and unpleasant corporal, clearly the most important rank in the Japanese Army. He put away his cigarette butt, picked up his rifle and dashed from the ward, waving a warning finger at Jim.

Glad to be alone, Jim immediately climbed out of bed.

Through the window he could see a group of convalescent Chinese orphans on the balcony of the adjacent wing. In their European dressing-gowns – like Jim's, donated by a local French charity – they spent all day staring at him. A metal fire-escape linked the two wings, blocked by heaps of sandbags packed against the windows in 1937 to protect them from stray shells fired across the river.

Bare-footed, Jim crossed the ward to its rear door. A narrow catwalk led between the sandbags, and the loose sand was littered with hundreds of cigarette ends thrown down by the bored French doctors. Picking his way through the pieces of broken glass, he set off along the fire-escape. A metal staircase ran to the opposite wing, linked by a rusting bridge to the ward below Jim's.

Jim moved swiftly down the steps and crossed the bridge. Somewhere on this floor were his father and the survivors of the *Petrel*. The windows of the wards overlooking the gangway had been painted with blackout tar. Watched by the wide-eyed orphans, he followed the gangway around the wing. The rear door into the ward was bolted, but as he pulled at the handle the Chinese children ducked below their balcony. An armed Japanese soldier stood on the roof, shouting down into the well between the wings. Soldiers with fixed bayonets ran across the courtyard of the hospital, and a motorcycle with armed side-car swung through the entrance. Jim could hear boots and rifle butts ringing on the stone stairways, and a French nun's voice raised in protest.

He crouched between the sandbags outside the locked door. Soldiers were moving along the gangway of the children's ward, and sand poured through the rusting grilles. A klaxon sounded in the Avenue Foch, and Jim was convinced that the entire Japanese occupation forces in Shanghai were searching for him.

A bolt clattered, and the door opened into the darkened ward. In the brief glare of sunlight Jim saw the cave-like room crowded with bandaged men, some lying on the floor between the beds, and the nuns being pushed aside by Japanese soldiers with rifles and canvas stretchers. As the blanched faces of young British sailors turned towards the sun, a stench of sickness and wounds emerged from the dark chamber and enveloped him.

The Japanese corporal stared at Jim, crouching in his pyjamas among the cigarette ends. He slammed the door, and Jim heard him shout as he slapped one of the Japanese soldiers with his fist.

An hour later they had all gone, leaving Jim alone in the children's ward. As the klaxons sounded from the Avenue Foch, he watched a military truck reverse into the hospital compound. The crew of the *Petrel* and the eight British civilians who had helped to rescue them were bundled down the staircases and loaded into the truck. Wounded men on stretchers lay under the legs of others barely able to sit.

Jim did not see his father, but the French sister told him that he had walked to the truck taking them to the military prison in Hongkew.

'This morning one of your sailors escaped. It's very bad for us.' The sister stared at Jim with the disapproving gaze of the Japanese corporal. She was angry with him in that new way he had noticed in the past weeks, not for anything he had done but because of his inability to change the circumstances in which he found himself.

'You live in Amherst Avenue? You must go home.' The sister beckoned to a Chinese nun, who laid Jim's freshly laundered clothes on the bed. He could see that they were eager to be rid of him. 'Your mother will look after you.'

Jim dressed himself, fastened his tie and carefully straightened his school cap. He wanted to thank the sister, but she had already left to look after her orphans.

6

The Youth with the Knife

Wars always invigorated Shanghai, quickened the pulse of its congested streets. Even the corpses in the gutters seemed livelier. Throngs of peasant women packed the pavements of the Avenue Foch, outside the Cercle Sportif Français the vendors locked wheels as they jostled their carts against each other, lines of pedicabs and rickshaws ten abreast hemmed in the cars that edged forward behind a continuous blare of horns. Young Chinese gangsters in shiny American suits stood on the street corners, shouting the jai alai odds to each other. In the pedicabs outside the Regency Hotel the bar-girls sat in fur coats with their bodyguards beside them, like glamorous wives waiting to be taken for a ride. The entire city had come out into the streets, as if the population was celebrating the takeover of the International Settlement, its seizure from the Americans and Europeans by another Asian power.

Yet when Jim reached the junction of the Avenue Pétain and the Avenue Haig a British police sergeant and two Sikh NCOs of the Shanghai police force still directed the traffic from their cantilever bridge above the crowd, watched by a single Japanese soldier standing behind them. Armed Japanese infantry sat like sightseers in the camouflaged trucks that moved along the streets. A party of officers stood outside the Radium Institute, adjusting their gloves. Pasted over the Coca Cola and Caltex billboards were fresh posters of Wang Ching-Wei, the turncoat leader of the puppet regime. A column of Chinese soldiers overtook Jim in the Avenue Pétain, shouting slogans into the noisy air. They stamped away, clumsily marking time below the baroque

56

façade of the Del Monte Casino, and then ran on past the greyhound stadium, a coolie army in pale orange uniforms and American-style sneakers.

Outside the tram station in the Avenue Haig the hundreds of passengers were briefly silent as they watched a public beheading. The bodies of a man and woman in quilted peasant clothes, perhaps pickpockets or Kuomintang spies, lay by the boarding platform. The Chinese NCOs wiped their boots as the blood ran into the metal grooves of the steel rails. A tram crowded with passengers approached, its bell forcing the execution party aside. It clanked along, connector rod hissing and throwing sparks from the overhead power line, its front wheels a moist scarlet as if painted for the annual labour union parade.

Usually Jim would have paused to observe the crowd. On the way home from school Yang would often drive by the Old City. The public stranglings were held in a miniature stadium with a scrubbed wooden floor and rows of circular benches around the teak execution posts, and always attracted a thoughtful audience. The Chinese enjoyed the spectacle of death, Jim had decided, as a way of reminding themselves of how precariously they were alive. They liked to be cruel for the same reason, to remind themselves of the vanity of thinking that the world was anything else.

Jim watched the coolies and peasant women staring at the headless bodies. Already the press of tram passengers was pushing them aside, submerging this small death. He turned away, tripping over the charcoal brazier in which a pavement vendor was frying pieces of battered snake. Drops of fat splashed into the wooden bucket, where a single snake swam, thrashing itself as it leapt at the hissing oil. The vendor lunged at Jim with his hot ladle, trying to cuff his head, but he slipped between the parked rickshaws.

He ran along the blood-smeared tramlines towards the entrance of the depot.

He pushed through the waiting passengers and squeezed himself on to a concrete bench with a group of peasant women carrying chickens in wicker baskets. The women's bodies reeked of sweat and fatigue, but Jim was too exhausted to move. He had walked over two miles along the crowded pavements. He knew that he was being followed by a young Chinese, probably a pedicab tout or a runner for one of Shanghai's tens of thousands of small-time gangsters. A tall youth with a dead, boneless face, oily black hair and leather jacket, he had noticed Jim outside the greyhound stadium. Kidnappings were commonplace in Shanghai – before his parents learned to trust Yang, they insisted that Jim always drove to school with the governess. He guessed that the youth was interested in his blazer and leather shoes, in his aviator's watch and the American fountain pen clipped to his breast pocket.

The youth stepped through the crowd and walked up to Jim, his yellow hands like ferrets. 'American boy?'

'English. I'm waiting for my chauffeur.'

'English . . . boy. You come now.'

'No – he's over there.'

The youth reached forward, swearing in Chinese, and seized Jim's wrist. His fingers fumbled at the metal strap, trying to release the watch-clasp. The peasant women ignored him, chickens asleep on their laps. Jim knocked away the youth's hand, and felt fingers grip his forearm. Inside his leather jacket he had drawn a knife, and was about to sever Jim's hand at the wrist.

Jim wrenched his arm away. Before the youth could seize him again, Jim hurled the wicker basket from the knees of the peasant woman on his right. The youth fell back, flailing with his heels at the squawking bird. The women jumped to their feet and began to scream at him. He ignored them and put away his knife. He followed as Jim ran through the queues of tram passengers, trying to show them his bruised wrist.

A hundred yards from the depot Jim reached the Avenue Joffre. He rested in the padlocked entrance to the Nanking Theatre, where *Gone with the Wind* had been playing for the past year in a pirated Chinese version. The partly dismantled faces of Clark Gable and Vivien Leigh rose on their scaffolding above an almost life-size replica of burning Atlanta. Chinese carpenters were cutting down the panels of painted smoke that rose high into the Shanghai sky, barely distinguishable from the fires still lifting above the tenements of the Old City, where Kuomintang irregulars had resisted the Japanese invasion.

The youth with the knife was still behind him, skipping and side-stepping through the crowd in his cheap sneakers. In the centre of the Avenue Joffre was the police checkpoint, its sandbagged emplacement marking the western perimeter of the French Concession. Jim knew that neither the Vichy police nor the Japanese soldiers would do anything to help him. They were watching a single-engined bomber that flew low above the racecourse.

As the plane's shadow flashed across the road Jim felt the Chinese youth snatch his cap and grip his shoulders. Jim pulled himself away, and ran across the crowded street towards the checkpoint, ducking in and out of the pedicabs and shouting: 'Nakajima . . . ! Nakajima . . . !'

A Chinese auxiliary in a Vichy uniform tried to strike him with his stave, but one of the Japanese sentries paused to glance at Jim. His eye had caught the Japanese characters on the metal tag that Jim had taken from the derelict fighter at Hungjao Aerodrome and was now holding in front of him. Briefly tolerating this small boy, he continued his patrol and waved him away with the butt of his rifle.

'Nakajima . . . !'

Jim joined the crowd of pedestrians moving through the checkpoint. As he guessed, his pursuer had vanished among the beggars and loitering rickshaw coolies on the French side of the barbed wire. Not for the first time Jim realized that the Japanese, officially his enemies, offered his only protection in Shanghai.

Nursing his bruised arm, and angry with himself for having lost his school cap, Jim at last reached Amherst Avenue. He pulled his shirt-sleeve over the dark weals that marked his wrist. His mother worried constantly about the danger and violence in the streets of Shanghai, and knew nothing of his long cycle rides around the city.

Amherst Avenue was deserted. The throngs of beggars and refugees had vanished. Even the old man with his Craven A tin had gone. Jim ran up the drive, looking forward to seeing his mother, sitting on the sofa in her bedroom and talking about Christmas. Already he assumed that they would never discuss the war.

A long scroll covered with Japanese characters had been nailed to the front door, the white cloth stamped with seals and registration numbers. Jim pressed the bell, waiting for Number Two Boy to open the door. He felt exhausted, as worn down as his scuffed shoes, and noticed that the sleeve of his blazer had been slashed from the elbow by the thief's knife.

'Boy, hurry . . .!' He began to say: 'I'll kill you . . .' but checked himself.

The house was silent. There was no sound of the amahs arguing over the laundry vat in the servants' quarters, or the clip-clip of the gardener trimming the lawn around the flower-beds. Someone had switched off the swimming-pool motor, though his father made a point of running the filter all winter. Looking up at the windows of his bedroom, he saw that the shutters of the air-conditioner had been closed.

60

Jim listened to the bell drill through the empty house. Too tired to reach again for the button, he sat on the polished steps and blew on his bruised knees. It was difficult to imagine how his parents, Vera, the nine servants, chauffeur and gardener could all have gone out together.

There was a muffled explosion from the bottom of the drive, the coughing exhaust box of a heavy engine. A Japanese half-track had entered Amherst Avenue, its crew standing among their radio aerials. They moved along the centre of the road, forcing a Mercedes limousine from the German estate to climb the pavement.

Jim jumped from the porch and hid behind a pillar. A high wall faced with terracotta tiles ran around the house, topped with broken glass. Gripping the tiles with his fingertips, he climbed the wall below the barred cloakroom window. After pulling himself on to the concrete ledge, he crawled on his knees through the glass blades. During the past year, unknown to the gardener and the nightwatchman, he had climbed the wall a score of times, always removing a few more of the sharp spears. He lowered himself over the edge and jumped into the dark branches of the cedar tree behind the summer house.

In front of him was the enclosed and silent garden, even more Jim's true home than the house itself. Here he had played alone with his imagination. He had been a crashed pilot on the roof of the rose pergola, a sniper sitting high in the poplars behind the tennis court, an infantryman racing across the lawn with his airgun, shooting himself down into the flower-beds and rising again to storm the rockery below the flagpole.

From the shadows behind the summer house Jim looked up at the verandah windows. An aircraft overhead warned him not to run too suddenly across the lawn. Although undisturbed, the garden seemed to have darkened and

61

grown wilder. The uncut lawn was beginning to billow, and the rhododendrons were more sombre than he remembered them. Ignored by the gardener, his bicycle lay on the terrace steps. Jim walked through the thickening grass to the swimming-pool. The water was covered with leaves and dead insects, and the level had fallen by almost three feet, draping a scummy curtain on the sides. Cigarette ends lay crushed on the white tiles, and a Chinese packet floated under the diving board.

Jim followed the pathway to the servants' quarters behind the house. A charcoal stove stood in the courtyard, but the kitchen door was locked. He listened for any sound from within the house. Beside the kitchen steps was the enclosed hood of the garbage compactor. A chute ran from the compressor into the kitchen wall beside the sink. Two years earlier, when he was younger, Jim had terrified his mother by climbing through the chute as she arranged a dinner party menu with the houseboy.

This time there was no danger of the motor being switched on. Jim lifted the metal hood, climbed between the scythe-like blades and edged his way through the greasy chute. The metal flap swung back to reveal the familiar white-tiled kitchen.

'Vera! I'm home! Boy!'

Jim lowered himself on to the floor. He had never seen the house so dark before. He stepped through the pool of water around the refrigerator and entered the deserted hall. As he climbed the staircase to his mother's bedroom the air was stale with the smell of strange sweat.

His mother's clothes were scattered across the unmade bed, and open suitcases lay on the floor. Someone had swept her hairbrushes and scent bottles from the dressing-table, and talcum covered the polished parquet. There were dozens of footprints in the powder, his mother's bare feet whirling within the clear images of heavy boots, like the patterns of complicated dances set out in his parents' foxtrot and tango manuals.

Jim sat on the bed, facing the star-like image of himself that radiated from the centre of the mirror. A heavy object had been driven into the full-length glass, and pieces of himself seemed to fly across the room, scattered through the empty house.

He fell asleep at the foot of his mother's bed, rested by the scent of her silk nightdress, below this jewelled icon of a small exploding boy.

7
The Drained Swimming-Pool

Time had stopped in Amherst Avenue, as motionless as the wall of dust that hung across the rooms, briefly folding itself around Jim when he walked through the deserted house. Almost forgotten scents, a faint taste of carpet, reminded him of the period before the war. For three days he waited for his mother and father to return. Every morning he climbed on to the sloping roof above his bedroom window, and gazed over the residential streets in the western suburbs of Shanghai. He watched the columns of Japanese tanks move into the city from the countryside, and tried to repair his blazer, impatient for the first sight of his parents when they returned with Yang in the Packard.

Large numbers of aircraft flew overhead, and Jim passed the hours plane-spotting. Below him was the undisturbed lawn, a little darker each day now that the gardener no longer trimmed the hedges and cut the grass. Jim played there in the afternoons, crawling through the rockery and pretending to be one of the Japanese marines who had attacked the *Wake*. But the games in the garden had lost their magic, and he spent most of his time on the sofa in his mother's bedroom. Her presence hung on the air like her scent, holding at bay the deformed figure in the fractured mirror. Jim remembered their long hours together doing his Latin homework, and the stories she told him of her childhood in England, a country far stranger than China where he would go to school when the war was over.

In the talcum on the floor around him he could see the imprints of his mother's feet. She had moved from side to side, propelled by an over-eager partner, perhaps one of the

Japanese officers to whom she was teaching the tango. Jim tried out the dance steps himself, which seemed far more violent than any tango he had ever seen, and managed to fall and cut his hand on the broken mirror.

As he sucked the wound he remembered his mother teaching him to play mah-jong, and the cryptic coloured tiles that clicked in and out of the mahogany walls. Jim thought of writing a book about mah-jong, but he had forgotten most of the rules. On the drawing-room carpet he heaped a pile of bamboo stakes from the greenhouse, and began to build a man-lifting kite according to the scientific principles his father had taught him. But the Japanese patrols in Amherst Avenue would see the kite flying from the garden. Putting it aside, Jim ambled about the empty house, and watched the water level almost imperceptibly falling in the swimming-pool.

The food in the refrigerator had begun to give off an ominous smell, but the pantry cupboards were filled with tinned fruit, cocktail biscuits and pressed meats, delicacies that Jim adored. He ate his meals at the dining-room table, sitting in his usual place. In the evenings, when it seemed unlikely that his parents would come home that day, he went to sleep in his bedroom on the top floor of the house, one of his model aircraft on the bed beside him, something Vera had always forbidden. Then the dreams of war came to him, and all the battleships of the Japanese Navy sailed up the Yangtze, their guns firing as they sank the *Petrel*, and he and his father saved the wounded sailors.

On the fourth morning, when he came down to breakfast, Jim found that he had forgotten to turn off a kitchen tap and all the water had flowed from the storage tank. The pantry was amply stocked with siphons of soda water, but by now he had accepted that his mother and father would not be coming home. He stared through the verandah windows at the overgrown garden. It was not that war changed everything – in fact, Jim thrived on change – but that it left things the same in odd and unsettling ways. Even the house seemed sombre, as if it was withdrawing from him in a series of small and unfriendly acts.

Trying to keep up his spirits, Jim decided to visit the homes of his closest friends, Patrick Maxted and the Raymond twins. After washing himself in soda water he went into the garden to fetch his bicycle. During the night the swimming-pool had drained itself. Jim had never seen the tank empty, and he gazed with interest at the inclined floor. The once mysterious world of wavering blue lines, glimpsed through a cascade of bubbles, now lay exposed to the morning light. The tiles were slippery with leaves and dirt, and the chromium ladder at the deep end, which had once vanished into a watery abyss, ended abruptly beside a pair of scummy rubber slippers.

Jim jumped on to the floor at the shallow end. He slipped on the damp surface, and his bruised knee left a smear of blood on the tiles. A fly settled on it instantly. Watching his feet, Jim walked down the sloping floor. Around the brass vent at the deep end lay a small museum of past summers – a pair of his mother's sun-glasses, Vera's hair clip, a wine glass, and an English half-crown which his father had tossed into the pool for him. Jim had often spotted the silver coin, gleaming like an oyster, but had never been able to reach it.

Jim pocketed the coin and peered up at the damp walls. There was something sinister about a drained swimming-pool, and he tried to imagine what purpose it could have if it were not filled with water. It reminded him of the concrete bunkers in Tsingtao, and the bloody handprints of the maddened German gunners on the caisson walls. Perhaps murder was about to be committed in all the swimming-pools of Shanghai, and their walls were tiled so that the blood could be washed away?

Leaving the garden, Jim wheeled his bicycle through the

verandah door. Then he did something he had always longed to do, mounted his cycle and rode through the formal, empty rooms. Delighted to think how shocked Vera and the servants would have been, he expertly circled his father's study, intrigued by the patterns which the tyres cut in the thick carpet. He collided with the desk, and knocked over a table lamp as he swerved through the door into the drawing-room. Standing on the pedals, he zigzagged among the armchairs and tables, lost his balance and fell on to a sofa, remounted without touching the floor, crash-landed into the double doors that led into the dining-room, pulled them back and began a wild circuit of the long polished table. He detoured into the pantry, swishing to and fro through the pool of water below the refrigerator, scattered the saucepans from the kitchen shelves and ended in a blaze of speed towards the mirror in the downstairs cloakroom. As his front tyre trembled against the smudged glass Jim shouted at his excited reflection. The war had brought him at least one small bonus.

Happily . Jim closed the front door behind him, smoothed the Japanese scroll and set off towards the Raymond twins in the nearby Columbia Road. He felt that all the streets in Shanghai were rooms in a huge house. He accelerated past a platoon of Chinese puppet soldiers marching down Columbia Road, and swerved away showily as the NCO let loose a volley of shouts. Jim sped along the suburban pavements, in and out of the telephone poles, knocking aside the Craven A tins left behind by the vanished beggars.

He was out of breath when he reached the Raymonds' house at the German end of the Columbia Road. He freewheeled past the parked Opels and Mercedes – curious, gloomy cars which gave Jim all too much of an idea of what Europe was like – and came to a halt outside the front door.

A Japanese scroll was nailed to the oak panels. The door opened, and two amahs appeared, dragging Mrs Raymond's dressing-table down the steps.

'Is Clifford here? Or Derek? Amah . . . !'

He knew both the amahs well, and waited for them to reply in their pidgin English. But they ignored him, and heaved at the dressing-table. Their deformed feet, like clenched fists, slipped on the steps.

'It's Jamie, Mrs Raymond . . .'

Jim tried to step past the amahs, when one reached out and slapped him in the face.

Stunned by the blow, Jim walked back to his bicycle. He had never been struck so hard, either in school boxing matches or in fights with the Avenue Foch gang. The front of his face seemed to have been torn from the bones. His eyes were smarting, but he stopped himself from crying. The amahs were strong, their arms toughened by a lifetime of washing clothes. Watching them with their dressing-table, Jim knew that they were paying him back for something he or the Raymonds had done to them.

Jim waited until they reached the bottom step. When one of the amahs walked up to him, clearly intending to slap him again, he mounted his cycle and pedalled away.

Outside the Raymonds' drive two German boys of his own age were playing with a ball as their mother unlocked the family's Opel. Usually they would have shouted German slogans at Jim, or thrown stones at him until stopped by their mother. But today all three stood silently. Jim cycled past, trying not to show them his bruised face. The mother held her sons' shoulders, watching Jim as if concerned for what would soon befall him.

Still shocked by the anger he had seen in the amah's face, Jim set off for the Maxteds' apartment house in the French Concession. His whole head felt swollen and there was a loose tooth in his lower jaw. He wanted to see his mother and father, and he wanted the war to end soon, that afternoon if possible.

Dusty, and suddenly very tired, Jim reached the barbed-wire checkpoint on the Avenue Foch. The streets were less crowded, but several hundred Chinese and Europeans queued to pass the Japanese guards. A Swiss-owned Buick and a Vichy French gasoline truck were waved through the gates. Usually the European pedestrians would have gone to the head of the queue, but now they took their turn among the rickshaw coolies and peasants pushing handcarts. Gripping his cycle, Jim barely held his ground as a barefoot coolie with diseased calves laboured past him under a bamboo yoke laden with bales of firewood. The crowd pressed around him, in a sweat of stench and fatigue, cheap fat and rice wine, the odours of a Shanghai new to him. An open Chrysler with two young Germans in the front seat accelerated past, horn blaring, the rear fender grazing Jim's hand.

Once through the checkpoint Jim straightened the front wheel of his cycle and pedalled to the Maxteds' apartment house in the Avenue Joffre. The formal garden in the French style was as immaculate as ever, a comforting memory of the old Shanghai. As he rode the elevator to the seventh floor Jim used his tears to clean his hands and face, half expecting Mrs Maxted to have returned from Singapore.

The door to the apartment was open. Jim stepped into the hall, recognizing Mr Maxted's leather overcoat on the floor. The same tornado that had whirled his mother's bedroom in Amherst Avenue had swept in and out of every room in the Maxteds' apartment. Drawers full of clothes had been thrown on to the beds, ransacked wardrobes hung open above piles of shoes, suitcases lay everywhere as if a dozen Maxted families had been unable to decide what to pack at five minutes' notice.

'Patrick . . .' Jim hesitated to enter Patrick's room without knocking. His mattress had been hurled to the floor, and the curtains drifted in the open windows. But Patrick's model aircraft, more carefully constructed than Jim's, still dangled from the ceiling.

Jim pulled the mattress on to the bed and lay down. He watched the aircraft turning in the cold air that moved through the empty apartment. He and Patrick had spent hours inventing imaginary air battles in the sky of that bedroom above the Avenue Joffre. Jim watched the Spitfires and Hurricanes circling above his head. Their motion soothed him, easing the pain in his jaw, and he was tempted to stay there, sleeping quietly in the bedroom of his departed friend until the war was over.

But already Jim realized that it was time to find his mother and father. Failing them, any other Britons would do.

Facing the Maxteds' apartment building on the opposite side of the Avenue Joffre was the Shell Company's compound, almost all of its houses occupied by British employees. Jim and Patrick often played with the children, and were honorary members of the Shell gang. As Jim pushed his bicycle from the Maxteds' drive he could see that the British residents had gone. Japanese sentries stood in the entrance to the compound behind a box fence of barbed-wire. Supervised by a Japanese NCO, a gang of Chinese coolies were loading furniture from the houses into an army truck.

A few feet from the barbed-wire box an elderly man in a shabby coat stood under the plane trees and watched the Japanese. Despite his threadbare suit, he still wore white cuffs and a starched shirt front.

'Mr Guerevitch! I'm over here, Mr Guerevitch!'

The old White Russian was the Shell Company caretaker, and lived with his aged mother in a small bungalow beside the gate. A Japanese officer now stood in the front room, cleaning his nails as he smoked a cigarette. Jim had always liked Mr Guerevitch, although the elderly Russian remained unimpressed by him. Something of an amateur artist, in the right mood he would draw elaborate sailing ships in Jim's autograph album. His grey cupboard of a kitchen was filled with starched collars and their miniature front panels, and Jim was sorry that Mr Guerevitch could not afford a real shirt. Perhaps he would come back to live with him in Amherst Avenue?

Jim checked this thought as Mr Guerevitch waved him across the road with his newspaper. His mother might like the old Russian, but Vera would not – the Eastern Europeans and White Russians were even more snobbish than the British.

'Hello, Mr Guerevitch. I'm looking for my mother and father.'

'But how could they be here?' The old Russian pointed to Jim's bruised face and shook his head. 'The whole world is at war and you're still riding your bicycle around . . .' As the Japanese NCO began to abuse one of the coolies, Mr Guerevitch drew Jim behind a plane tree. He opened his newspaper to reveal an extravagant artist's sketch of two immense battleships sinking under a hail of Japanese bombs. From the photographs beside them Jim recognized the *Repulse* and the *Prince of Wales*, the unsinkable fortresses which the British war newsreels always claimed could each defeat the Japanese Navy single-handed.

'Not a good example,' Mr Guerevitch reflected. 'The British Empire's Maginot line. It's right that you have a red face.'

'I fell off my bicycle, Mr Guerevitch,' Jim explained patriotically, though he disliked having to lie to defend the Royal Navy. 'I've been busy looking for my mother and father. It's rather a job, you know.'

71

'I can see.' Mr Guerevitch watched a convoy of trucks speed past. Japanese guards with fixed bayonets sat by the tailboards. Behind them, their heads resting on each other's shoulders, groups of British women and their children huddled over their cheap suitcases and khaki bedrolls. Jim assumed that they were the families of captured British servicemen.

'Young boy! Ride your bicycle!' Mr Guerevitch pushed Jim's shoulder. 'You follow them!'

'But Mr Guerevitch . . .' The shabby luggage unsettled Jim as much as the strange wives of the British privates. 'I can't go with them – they're prisoners.'

'Go on! Ride! You can't live in the street!'

When Jim stood firm by his handlebars, Mr Guerevitch solemnly patted him on the head and set off across the road. He resumed his vigil behind his newspaper, watching the Japanese strip the houses in the compound as if itemizing his lost world for the Shell Company.

'I'll come and see you again, Mr Guerevitch.' Jim felt sorry for the old caretaker, but during his return journey to Amherst Avenue he was more concerned about the two battleships. The British newsreels were filled with lies. Jim had seen the Japanese Navy sink the *Petrel*, and it was obvious now that they could sink anything. Half the American Pacific Fleet was sitting on the bottom at Pearl Harbor. Perhaps Mr Guerevitch was right, and he should have followed the trucks. His mother and father might already have arrived at the prison to which they were being taken.

So, reluctantly, he decided to give himself up to the Japanese. The soldiers guarding the Avenue Foch checkpoint waved him on when he tried to speak to them, but Jim kept his eyes open for one of the corporals in charge of everything.

For some reason, that day there seemed to be a shortage

72

of Japanese corporals in Shanghai. Although he was tired, Jim took the long route home, along the Great Western and Columbia Roads, but no Japanese at all were there. However, when he reached the entrance to his house in Amherst Avenue he saw that a Chrysler limousine had parked outside the front door. Two Japanese officers stepped from the car and surveyed the house as they straightened their uniforms.

Jim was about to pedal up to them and explain that he lived in the house and was ready to surrender. Then an armed Japanese soldier stepped from behind the stone gatepost. He seized the front wheel of the cycle with his left hand, his fingers gripping the tyre through the spokes, and with a coarse shout propelled Jim backwards into a heap on the dusty road.

8
Picnic Time

Unable to surrender, Jim returned with his broken bicycle to the Maxteds' apartment in the French Concession. From then on he lived alone in the abandoned houses and apartments in the western suburbs of the International Settlement. Most of the homes had been owned by British and American nationals, or by Dutch, Belgian and Free French residents, all of whom had been interned by the Japanese in the days after the attack on Pearl Harbor.

The Maxteds' apartment house was owned by rich Chinese who had fled to Hong Kong in the weeks before the outbreak of war. Most of the apartments had been empty for months. Although the family of Chinese janitors still lived in their two basement rooms beside the elevator well, they had been completely cowed by the squad of Japanese military police who had seized Mr Maxted. As the uncut lawns grew deeper and the formal gardens deteriorated, they spent their time cooking small meals on a charcoal stove which they set up beside the cement statuary on the floor of the ornamental pond. The smell of bean curd and spiced noodles drifted among the disrobing nymphs.

During the first week Jim was free to come and go. He wheeled his cycle into the lift, rode to the seventh floor and let himself into the Maxteds' apartment through an un-latched mosquito window on the servants' balcony. The front door was fitted with a spyhole and a complex set of electrical locks – Mr Maxted, a prominent member of the pro-Chiang China Friendship Society, an organization of local businessmen, had once been the victim of an assassination attempt. Once Jim closed the door he was unable to open it again, but no one called apart from an elderly Iraqi woman who lived in the penthouse. When she rang the bell Jim watched her grimacing into the spyhole, parts of her ancient face semaphoring a mysterious message. She then stood thinking for ten minutes in the stationary lift, immaculately dressed and bejewelled in this abandoned apartment house.

Jim was glad to be left alone. After being knocked from his bicycle by the Japanese soldier he had barely managed to return to the Maxteds', and he slept on Patrick's bed for the rest of the day. He woke the next morning to the sound of trams clanking down the Avenue Foch, klaxons hooting from the Japanese convoys entering the city, and the thousands of continually blaring horns that were the anthem of Shanghai.

The bruise on his cheek had begun to subside, leaving his face thinner than he remembered it, his mouth a tighter and older shape. Looking at himself in the mirror of Patrick's bathroom, at his dusty blazer and grimy shirt, he wondered if his mother and father would still recognize him. Jim wiped his clothes with a wet towel – like Mr Guerevitch, many of the passing Chinese stared at him in a curious way. Nonetheless, Jim realized that there were certain advantages in being poor. No one could be bothered to cut off his hands.

The Maxteds' pantry was filled with cases of whisky and gin, an Aladdin's cave of gold and ruby bottles, but there were only a few jars of olives and a tin of cocktail biscuits. Jim ate a modest breakfast at the dining-room table, and then set about repairing his bicycle. He needed the machine to get himself around Shanghai, to find his parents and surrender to the Japanese.

Sitting on the dining-room floor, Jim tried to straighten the twisted forks. His hands fretted at the dusty metal, unable to clench themselves. He knew that he had been

75

badly frightened the previous day. A peculiar space was opening around him, which separated him from the secure world he had known before the war. For a few days he had been able to cope with the sinking of the *Petrel* and the disappearance of his parents, but now he felt nervous and slightly cold all the time, even in the mild December weather. He dropped and broke crockery in a way that he had never done before, and found it difficult to concentrate on anything.

Despite all this, Jim managed to repair his cycle. He unscrewed the front wheel and straightened the forks by bending them against the balcony railing. He tested the cycle in the drawing-room and then took the lift down to the foyer.

As Jim rode along the Avenue Foch he saw that Shanghai had changed. Thousands of Japanese soldiers patrolled the streets. Sandbagged sentry posts had been set up within sight of each other down the main avenues. Although the streets were filled with pedicabs and rickshaws, with trucks commandeered by the puppet militia, the crowds were subdued. The Chinese who thronged the pavements outside the department stores in the Nanking Road kept their heads down, avoiding the Japanese soldiers who sauntered through the traffic.

Pedalling fiercely, Jim followed a heavily laden tram that clanked along the Avenue Edward VII. Morose Chinese clung to its sides, and a crop-headed youth in a black mandarin suit spat at Jim, then leapt down and ran into the crowd, nervous that even this small act would set off a train of retribution. Bodies of Chinese lay everywhere, hands tied behind their backs in the centre of the road, dumped behind the sandbag emplacements, half-severed heads resting on each other's shoulders. The thousands of young gangsters in their American suits had gone, but at the Bubbling Well Road checkpoint Jim saw one youth in a blue silk suit being beaten by two soldiers with staves. As the blows struck his head he knelt in a pool of blood that dripped from his lapels.

All the gambling parlours and opium houses in the side-streets behind the racecourse had closed, and metal grilles sealed the entrances to the pawn shops and banks. Even the honour guard of hunchbacks outside the Cathay Theatre had deserted their posts. Their absence unsettled Jim. Without its beggars the city seemed all the poorer. The sullen rhythms of the new Shanghai were set by the endless wailing of the Japanese klaxons. The roads felt harder than he remembered them from his previous jaunts around the city, and already he was tired. His hands felt colder than the handlebars. Trying to keep up his spirits, he decided to visit all those places in Shanghai where his parents were known, starting with his father's office. The senior Chinese staff had always made a great fuss of Jim, and would be eager to help him.

However, the Szechwan Road had been closed by the Japanese. Barbed-wire barricades sealed off both ends of the street, and hundreds of Japanese civilians moved in and out of the foreign banks and commercial buildings, carrying typewriters and boxes of files.

Jim cycled down to the Bund, dominated now by the grey bulk of the cruiser *Idzumo*. It was moored four hundred yards from the quayside, its antique funnels freshly painted, canvas awnings flared over its gun turrets. A short distance upstream was the USS *Wake*, now flying the Rising Sun, with vivid Japanese characters on its bows. An elaborate christening ceremony was taking place in front of the Shanghai Club. Scores of senior Japanese civilians in frock coats, Germans and Italians in extravagant fascist uniforms, watched a march past of Japanese sailors and officers. Two tanks, several artillery pieces and a cordon of marines ringed the temporary parade ground on the tracks of the tramways terminal. The circling steel rails rang beneath

77

their boots, the diagram of their victory over the British and American gunboats.

Resting his chin on the handlebars, Jim looked at the soldiers with fixed bayonets guarding the entrance to the Palace Hotel. None of them would speak any English, or have any idea that this European boy with his twisted bicycle was an enemy national. If he approached them in full view of the press-ganged Chinese audience the sentries would throw him to the ground.

Jim pedalled away from the Bund and began the long journey back to the Maxteds' apartment. By the time he crossed the Avenue Joffre checkpoint he was too tired to cycle, and pushed the small machine through the begging peasant women and the dozing rickshaw coolies. After climbing into the apartment he sat at the dining-room table and ate a few cocktail biscuits and olives, washed down with soda water from the siphon. He fell asleep on his friend's bed, under the endlessly circling aircraft that swam below the ceiling like fish seeking a way out of the sky.

During the next days Jim again tried to give himself up to the Japanese. Like his school friends, he had always despised anyone who surrendered – he accepted without question the stern morality of the *Chums Annuals* – but surrendering to the enemy was more difficult than it seemed. By now Jim was tired most of the time, as he cycled around the uncertain streets of Shanghai. The Japanese soldiers guarding the Country Club and the forecourt of the cathedral were too dangerous to approach. In the Bubbling Well Road he chased the Plymouth car belonging to a Swiss driver and his wife, but they shouted at him to go away and threw a coin on to the road, as if he were one of the Chinese beggar boys.

Jim went in search of Mr Guerevitch, but the old Russian caretaker was no longer watching the Shell compound –

perhaps he, too, was trying to surrender. Jim thought of the German mother who had watched him leave the Raymonds' house. She had seemed worried for him, but when he cycled all the way down to the Columbia Road he found that the gates of the German estate were closed. The Germans were drawing into themselves, just as nervous of the Japanese as everyone else. Jim was almost knocked from his cycle in the Nanking Road by two Japanese staff cars which swerved across the street. They stopped a truck filled with Germans from the Graf Zeppelin Club on their way to beat up the Jews in Hongkew. The Japanese NCOs ordered the Germans from the truck. They took away their clubs and shotguns, ripped off their swastika armbands, and sent them packing.

A week after his arrival at the Maxteds' apartment the electricity and water supplies were switched off. Jim bumped his cycle down the stairs to the foyer, where he found the old Iraqi woman arguing with the Chinese janitor. They both turned on Jim, screaming at him to leave the apartment house, though they had known all week that he was there.

He was glad to go. He had eaten the last of the cocktail biscuits, and his only meal the previous day had been a musty packet of Brazil nuts which he found in the sideboard. He felt tired but curiously light-headed – the last trickle of water from the bathroom taps had made him almost drunk, the same sensation he had known before the war when he was about to go to a party. He reminded himself of his mother and father, but already their faces were beginning to fade in his memory. He was thinking of food all the time, and he knew that there were a great many unoccupied houses in the western suburbs of Shanghai, with unlimited supplies of cocktail biscuits and soda water, enough to last him until the war ended.

Mounting his cycle, Jim left the French Concession and

pedalled along the Columbia Road. Quiet residential avenues ran between the trees, and the empty houses stood in their overgrown gardens. The rain had washed the ink from the Japanese scrolls, and the scarlet streaks ran down the oak panels, as if all the Americans and Europeans had been murdered against their front doors.

The Japanese occupation forces were too busy with their takeover of Shanghai to bother with these abandoned houses. Jim chose a crescent-shaped cul-de-sac hidden from the main road, where a half-timbered house rose behind high walls. A fading scroll hung between its brass coach lamps. Jim listened to the silence within the house, and then hid his cycle in the unswept leaves beside the steps. On his third attempt he climbed the wall of the Tudor garage and scaled its gabled roof. He lowered himself into the dense foliage of the garden, which clung to the house like a dark dream refusing to be woken.

Carrying a loose tile from the garage roof, Jim walked through the deep grass to the terrace. He waited until an aircraft flew overhead, and then broke the glass pane of a window housing the air-conditioning unit. He let himself into the house, opening the shutters of the air vent in order to hide the broken pane.

Quickly Jim moved through the shadowy rooms, a series of tableaux in a forgotten museum. The house was filled with photographs of a handsome woman posing like a film star. He ignored the framed portrait on the grand piano, and the huge globe of the earth beside the bookshelf. In the past Jim would have stopped to play with the globe – for years he had nagged his father for one – but now he was too hungry to waste a moment.

The house had been the property of a Belgian dentist. In his study, below the framed certificates, were white cabinets containing dozens of sets of teeth. Through the darkness they grimaced at Jim like ravenous mouths.

Jim walked through the dining-room to the kitchen. He side-stepped the pool of water around the refrigerator, and expertly ran his eye over the pantry shelves. To his annoyance this Belgian dentist and his glamorous companion had developed a taste for Chinese food – something his own parents rarely touched – and the pantry was hung like the store-room of a Chinese compradore with lengths of dried intestines and shrivelled fruit.

But there was a single can of condensed milk, of a richness and sweetness Jim had never remembered. He drank the milk, sitting at the desk in the dentist's study as the teeth smiled at him, and then fell asleep in a bedroom upstairs, between silk sheets scented by the body of the woman with the face of a film star.

9
An End to Kindness

Ever searching for food, Jim left the dentist's house the next morning. He found another temporary home in a nearby mansion owned by an American widow whom his parents had known before her departure for San Francisco. From there he moved on, staying for a few days in each house, shielded from the distant, ugly city by the high walls and deepening grass.

The Japanese had confiscated all the radios and cameras, but otherwise the houses were intact. Most of them were far more lavish than his own home – although a rich man, Jim's father had always been spartan – and were equipped with private cinemas and ballrooms. Abandoned by their owners, Buicks and Cadillacs slumped in the garages on their flattening tyres.

Yet their pantry cupboards were bare, leaving Jim to feed on the few leftovers of cocktail food from the fifty-year-long party that had been Shanghai. Sometimes, after finding an intact box of chocolates in a dressing-table drawer, Jim would revive and remember his parents dancing to the radiogram before lunch on Sunday, and his bedroom in Amherst Avenue now occupied by the Japanese officers. He played billiards in the darkened games rooms, or sat at a card table and laid out hands of bridge, playing each one as fairly as he could. He lay on the oddly scented beds, reading *Life* and *Esquire*, and in the house of an American doctor read the whole of *Through the Looking Glass*, a comforting world less strange than his own.

But the toy cupboards in the children's rooms made him feel ever more empty. He leafed through photograph albums, filled with images of a vanished world of fancy-dress parties and gymkhanas. Still hoping to see his parents, he sat by the bedroom windows, as the water drained from the swimming-pools of the western suburbs, draping their white walls with veils of scum. Although he was too tired to think of the future, Jim knew that the small stocks of food would soon be exhausted, and that the Japanese would turn their attention to these empty houses – already the families of Japanese civilians were moving into the former Allied premises in Amherst Avenue.

Jim scarcely recognized his long hair and grey cheeks, the strange face in a strange mirror. He would stare at the ragged figure who appeared before him in all the mirrors of the Columbia Road, an urchin half his previous size and twice his previous age. Much of the time Jim was aware that he was ill, and often he would have to lie down all day. The mains supply to Columbia Road had been turned off, and the water dripping from the roof tanks had an unpleasant metallic tang. Once, as he lay sick in an attic bedroom in the Great Western Road, a party of Japanese civilians spent an hour walking around the downstairs rooms, but Jim had been too feverish to call to them.

One afternoon Jim scaled the wall of a house behind the American Country Club. He jumped into a wide, over-grown garden and was running towards the verandah before he realized that a group of Japanese soldiers were cooking a meal beside the empty swimming-pool. Three men squatted on the diving-boards, feeding sticks to a small fire. Another soldier was down on the floor of the pool, poking through the debris of bathing caps and sun-glasses.

The Japanese watched Jim hesitate in the deep grass, and stirred their boiled rice, in which floated a few pieces of fish. They made no attempt to pick up their rifles, but Jim knew that he should not try to run from them. He strolled through the grass to the edge of the pool and sat on the leaf-strewn tiles. The soldiers began to eat their meal, talking in low voices. They were thickset men with shaven heads, wearing better webbing and equipment than the Japanese sentries in Shanghai, and Jim guessed that they were seasoned combat troops.

Jim watched them eat, his eyes fixed on every morsel that entered their mouths. When the oldest of the four soldiers had finished he scraped some burnt rice and fish scales from the side of the cooking pot. A first-class private of some forty years, with slow, careful hands, he beckoned Jim forward and handed him his mess tin. As they smoked their cigarettes the Japanese smiled to themselves, watching Jim devour the shreds of fatty rice. It was his first hot food since he had left the hospital, and the heat and greasy flavour stung his gums. Tears swam in his eyes. The Japanese soldier who had taken pity on Jim, recognizing that this small boy was starving, began to laugh good-naturedly, and pulled the rubber plug from his metal water-bottle. Jim drank the clear, chlorine-flavoured liquid, so unlike the stagnant water in the taps of the Columbia Road. He choked, carefully swallowed his vomit, and tittered into his hands, grinning at the Japanese. Soon they were all laughing together, sitting back in the deep grass beside the drained swimming-pool.

For the next week Jim followed the Japanese on their patrols of the deserted streets. Each morning the soldiers emerged from their bivouac at the Great Western Road checkpoint, and Jim would run from the steps of the house in which he had spent the night and attach himself to them. The soldiers rarely entered the foreign mansions, and were concerned only to keep out any Chinese beggars and thieves who might be tempted into this residential area. Sometimes they climbed the walls and explored the overgrown gardens, whose ornamental trees and shrubs seemed of more interest to them than the lavishly equipped houses. Jim ran errands

84

for them, hunting for the bathing caps that they collected, chopping wood and lighting fires. He watched silently as they ate their midday meal. Almost always they left a little rice and fish for him, and once the first-class private gave him a piece of hard candy which he broke from a strip in his pocket, but otherwise none of them showed any interest in Jim. Did they know that he was a vagrant? They would stare at his scuffed but well-made shoes, at the woollen cloth of his school blazer, perhaps assuming that he lived with some rich but feckless European family that no longer bothered to feed its children.

Within a week Jim was dependent on this Japanese patrol for almost all his food. More of the houses in the Columbia Road were being occupied by Japanese military and civilians. Several times, as he approached a deserted house, Jim was chased away by Chinese bodyguards.

One morning the Japanese soldiers failed to appear. Jim waited patiently in the garden of the house behind the American Country Club. Trying to calm his hunger, he broke twigs from the rhododendron bushes, ready to light a fire beside the drained pool. He watched the aircraft flying through the cool February light, and counted the three liqueur chocolates in his blazer pocket which he had saved for the emergency he knew would soon come.

The verandah doors opened behind him. He stood up, as the Japanese soldiers stepped on to the terrace. They were waving to him, and Jim had the confused idea that they had brought his parents with them, and so were making a formal entry through the house rather than climb over the wall.

He ran towards the Japanese, who were shouting at him in a surprisingly brusque way. When he reached the terrace he saw that they were members of a new patrol. The corporal cuffed him and pushed him around the flower-beds, then made him clear away the sticks beside the pool. Shouting a few words of German, he threw Jim into the drive and slammed the wrought-iron gate on his heels.

The houses stood around him in the sun, sealed worlds where he had briefly returned to his childhood. As he set out on the long journey to the Bund he thought of the Japanese soldiers who had fed him from their cooking pot, but he knew now that kindness, which his parents and teachers had always urged upon him, counted for nothing.

10

The Stranded Freighter

Cold sunlight shivered on the river, turning its surface into chopped glass, and transforming the distant banks and hotels of the Bund into a row of wedding cakes. To Jim, as he sat on the catwalk of the funeral pier below the deserted Nantao shipyards, the funnels and masts of the *Idzumo* seemed carved from icing sugar. He cupped his hands into a pair of make-believe binoculars and studied the white-suited sailors, as busy as lice, who moved around the decks and bridge. The cruiser's gun turrets reminded him of the candied decoration on the Christmas cakes whose overripe flavour he had always hated.

All the same, Jim would have liked to eat the ship. He imagined himself nibbling the masts, sucking the cream from the Edwardian funnels, sinking his teeth into the marzipan bows and devouring the entire forward section of the hull. After that he would gobble down the Palace Hotel, the Shell Building, the whole of Shanghai . . .

Steam throbbed from the *Idzumo*'s funnels, calmed itself and drifted across the water in a delicate veil. The cruiser had drawn its stern anchors and was swinging on the tide, bows pointing downstream. Having helped to impose Japanese rule upon Shanghai, it was about to sail for another theatre of war. As if celebrating, a regatta of corpses turned on the tide. The bodies of scores of Chinese, each on a raft of paper flowers, surrounded the *Idzumo*, ready to escort the cruiser to the mouth of the Yangtze.

Jim kept watch for the Japanese naval patrols. Across the river, on the Pootung shore, were the galvanized roofs and modern chimneys of his father's cotton mill. Jim vaguely remembered his visits there, embarrassing occasions when the Chinese managers paraded him under the expressionless gaze of thousands of mill girls. Now it was silent, and what concerned him was the boom of the sunken freighters. The nearest of the wrecks, a single-funnel coaster, sat in the deep-water channel only a hundred yards from the end of the funeral pier. Its rusting bridge, like a crumbling brown loaf, still held all its mystery for him. War, which had changed everything in Jim's world so radically, had long since left this forgotten wreck, but he was determined to go out to the ship. Rejoining his parents, giving himself up to the Japanese, even finding food to eat, meant nothing now that the freighter was at last within his reach.

For two days Jim had wandered along the Shanghai waterfront. After being discovered by the Japanese patrol he set off for the Bund. His only hope of seeing his parents again was to find one of their Swiss or Swedish friends. Although the European neutrals drove through the streets of Shanghai, Jim had not seen a single British or American face. Had they all been sent to prison camps in Japan?

Then, as he cycled along the Nanking Road, he was overtaken by a military truck. A group of fair-haired men in British uniforms sat behind the guards.

'Speed up, lad! Let's see you look lively!'

'Faster than that, lad! We won't wait for you!'

Jim crouched over the handlebars, feet whirling on the pedals. They were cheering and waving to him, clapping their hands as the Japanese guards frowned at this absurd British game. Jim shouted at the disappearing truck, and there was laughter, and a last thumbs-up when his front wheel locked itself in a tramline and pitched him under the feet of the pedicab drivers.

Soon after, he lost his bicycle. He was trying to straighten the front forks when a Chinese shopkeeper and his coolie came up to him. The shopkeeper held the handlebars, but Jim knew that he was not trying to help. He stared into the matter-of-fact eyes of the two Chinese. He was tired and had been slapped enough.

Jim watched them wheel the cycle through the crowd and vanish into one of the hundreds of alleyways. An hour later he reached the Szechwan Road on foot, but the entire financial sector of Shanghai was sealed by hundreds of Japanese soldiers and their armoured cars.

So Jim went down to the Bund to look at the *Idzumo*. All afternoon he wandered along the waterfront, past the mud-flats where the injured sailors of the *Petrel* had come ashore and he had last seen his father, past the sampan jetties and the fish market with its pallid mullet laid out between the tramlines, to the quays of the French Concession where the Bund ran out in the funeral piers and shipyards of Nantao. No one molested Jim there. This area of creeks and waste tips was covered with the timbers of opium hulks, the carcasses of dogs, and the coffins that had drifted ashore again on to the beaches of black mud. In the afternoon he watched the Japanese seaplanes moored to their buoys at the Naval Air Base. He waited for the pilots to come out in their flying goggles and stroll down the slipway. But no one except Jim seemed interested in the seaplanes, and they sat on their long pontoons, propellers irritated by the wind.

At night Jim slept in the back seat of one of the dozens of old taxis dumped on to the mud-flats. The klaxons of the Japanese armoured cars wailed along the Bund, and the searchlights of the patrol boats flared across the river, but Jim fell asleep quickly in the cold air. His thin body seemed to float on the night, hovering above the dark water as he clung to the faint human odours that rose from the taxi's seats.

* * *

It was high water, and the seaplanes had begun to circle their buoys. The river no longer pressed against the boom of freighters. For a few moments the surface congealed into an oily mirror, through which the rusting steamers emerged as if from their own reflections. Beside the funeral piers the sampans swayed forward, loosened from the mud-flats even as they filled with water.

Jim squatted on the metal catwalk, watching the water slap at the grille between his feet. From his blazer pocket he took one of his last two liqueur chocolates. He studied the cryptic scrolls, like the signs of the zodiac, and carefully weighed them. Saving the larger, he placed the smaller in his mouth. The fiery alcohol stung his tongue, but he sucked on the dark sweet chocolate. The brown water swelled glassily around the pier, and he remembered that his father had told him how sunlight killed bacteria. Fifty yards away the corpse of a young Chinese woman floated among the sampans, heels rotating around her head as if unsure in what direction to point her that day. Cautiously, Jim decanted a little water from one palm to the other, then drank quickly so that the germs would have no time to infect him.

The liqueur chocolate, and the swilling rhythm of the waves, made him feel giddy again, and he steadied himself against a waterlogged sampan that bumped against the pier. Looking up at the decaying freighter, Jim stepped without thinking into the sampan and pushed out into the jelly-like stream.

The rotting craft was half-filled with water that soaked Jim's shoes and trousers. He tore away part of the freeboard, and used the pulpy plank to paddle towards the freighter. When he reached the ship the sampan had almost submerged. He seized the starboard rail below the bridge and climbed on to the deck, as the waterlogged hulk drifted on its way to the next freighter in the boom.

Jim watched it go, then walked through the ankle-deep water that covered the metal deck. The river had begun to shift slightly, and the waxy surface was unbroken as it entered the open stateroom below the bridge and ran out through the port rail. Jim stepped into the stateroom, a rusting grotto that seemed even older than the German forts at Tsingtao. He was standing on the surface of the river, which had rushed from all the creeks and paddies and canals of China in order to carry this small boy on its back. If he stepped on to the waves by the port rail he could walk all the way to the *Idzumo* . . .

Towers of smoke shuddered from the cruiser's funnels as it prepared to raise anchor. Were his parents on board? Aware that he might now be alone in Shanghai, on this steamer he had always dreamed of visiting, Jim gazed from the bridge towards the shore. The tide was beginning to run, and the flower-decked corpses were following their heels to the open sea. The freighter leaned in the stream, and its rusty hull creaked and sang. The plates sawed against each other, and the trailing hawsers swung across the foredeck, the halyards of invisible sails still hoping to propel this ancient hulk to the safety of some warm sea a world away from Shanghai.

Happily, Jim felt the bridge shudder under his feet. As he laughed to himself at the rail he noticed that someone was watching him from the shipyard beyond the funeral piers. A man wearing the coat and cap of an American seaman stood in the wheelhouse of one of three partly constructed colliers. Shyly, but captain to captain, Jim waved to him. The man ignored him, and smoked the cigarette concealed in his hand. He was watching, not only Jim, but a young sailor in a metal dinghy which had cast loose from the next steamer in the boom.

Eager to welcome his first passenger and crewman, Jim left the bridge and made his way down to the deck. The sailor drew nearer, rowing in strong, short movements, careful not to disturb the water. Every few strokes he looked over his shoulder at Jim, and peered through the portholes as if he suspected that this rusty freighter was infested with small boys. The dinghy sat low in the water, weighted down by the sailor's broad back. He pulled alongside, and Jim saw a crowbar, spanners and hacksaw between his boots. On the bench seat were the brass rings of porthole mounts prised from the ships' hulls.

'Hello, kid – going for a run up the coast? Who else is with you?'

'Nobody.' For all the hope of safety that this young American offered, Jim was not eager to leave the ship. 'I'm waiting for my mother and father. They've been . . . delayed.'

'Delayed? Well, maybe they'll come later. You look like you need some help.'

He reached out to climb aboard, but as Jim took his hand the sailor pulled him roughly into the dinghy, jarring his knees against the brass portholes. He sat Jim upright and fingered his blazer lapels and badge. His loose blond hair framed an open American face, but he scanned the river in a furtive way, as if expecting a Japanese naval diver in full gear to break surface alongside the dinghy.

'Now, why are you trying to bother us? Who brought you out here?'

'I came by myself.' Jim straightened his blazer. 'This is my ship now.'

'Some kind of crazy British kid. You've been sitting on that pier for two days. Who are you?'

'Jamie . . .' Jim tried to think of something that would impress the American; already he realized that he should stay with this young sailor. 'I'm building a man-flying kite . . . and I've written a book on contract bridge.'

'Wait till Basie sees this.'

As they drifted from the freighter the American drew on his oars. With a few powerful strokes he pulled the dinghy towards the mud-flats. They entered a shallow creek between the funeral piers, a black and oil-stained channel that wound past the shipyards. The American stared morosely at an empty coffin that had jettisoned its occupant. He spat into it for good luck, and fended it off with an oar. Expertly he steered the dinghy behind the white hull of a mastless yacht lashed to a beached lighter. Hidden below the swan-like overhang of the yacht's stern, they tied up at a wooden stage. The American looped the porthole mounts on to his arm, gathered his tools together and beckoned Jim from the dinghy.

They crossed the floor of the shipyard, past stacks of steel plate, coils of chains and rusting wire, towards the shabby hulls of the three colliers. Jim scurried along, imitating the American's aggressive gait. At last he had met someone who could help him find his parents. Perhaps the American and his companion in the wheelhouse had also been trying to surrender? The three of them together would be too many for the Japanese to ignore.

An antique Chevrolet truck was parked under the propeller of the largest collier. They stepped through a missing plate into the hull. The American lifted Jim on to a bamboo platform laid along its keel. They climbed a companionway to the next deck, walked across the wheelhouse and ducked through a narrow hatch into a metal cabin behind the bridge.

Faint with hunger, Jim swayed against the door frame. A familiar scent hung in the air, reminding him of his mother's bedroom in Amherst Avenue, the odours of face-powder, cologne and Craven A cigarettes, and for a moment he was sure that she would emerge from this dark cubby-hole like the Christmas fairy and tell him that the war was over.

11
Frank and Basie

A charcoal stove burned softly in the centre of the cabin, its sweet fumes lifting through an open skylight. The floor was covered with oily rags and engine parts, brass portholes and stair-rails. On either side of the stove were a deck-chair with 'Imperial Airways' stitched into its fading canvas, and a camp-bed covered with a Chinese quilt.

The American flung his tools into the heap of metal parts. His large head and shoulders almost filled the cabin, and he slumped restlessly in the canvas chair. He peered into the saucepan on the stove and then gazed gloomily at Jim.

'He's getting on my nerves already, Basie. I don't know whether he's hungrier or crazier . . .'

'Come in, boy. You look like you need to lie down.'

A small, older man emerged from beneath the quilt and motioned to Jim with the cigarette he was holding in his white hand. He had a bland, unmarked face from which all the copious experiences of his life had been cleverly erased, and soft hands that were busy powdering each other under the quilt. His eyes took in every detail of Jim's mud-stained clothes, the tic that jumped across his mouth, his pinched cheeks and unsteady legs.

He dusted the talc from the bed and counted the pieces of salvaged brass. 'Is that all, Frank? That's not a lot to take to market. Those Hongkew merchants are charging ten dollars for a bag of rice.'

'Basie!' The young sailor drove a heavy boot into the heap of metal, exasperated more with himself than with the older man. 'The boy's been sitting on the pier for two days! Do you want the Japs in here?'

'Frank, the Japs aren't looking for us. Nantao Creek is full of the cholera – that's why we came here.'

'You practically put up a sign. Maybe you want them to look for us? Is that it, Basie?' Frank dipped a rag in a can of cleaning fluid. He began to rub vigorously at the grime that covered a porthole mount. 'If you want to work so hard try going out there – with that kid watching you all the time.'

'Frank, we've got my lungs, you agreed that.' Basie inhaled a little smoke from his Craven A, soothing these delicate organs. 'Besides, the boy didn't even notice you. He had other things on his mind, boy's things that you've forgotten, Frank, but I can still remember.' He made a warm place for Jim on the bed. 'Come over here, son. What did they call you, before the war started?'

'Jamie . . .'

Frank threw down his rag. 'All this scrap isn't going to buy us a sampan to Chungking! We'd need the *Queen Mary* out there.' He treated Jim to a dark glare. 'And we don't have enough rice for you, kid. Who are you? Jamie – ?'

'Jim . . .' Basie explained. 'A new name for a new life.' As Jim sat beside him he reached out a powdered hand and gently pressed his thumb against the hunger tic that jumped across the left corner of Jim's mouth. Jim sat passively as Basie exposed his gums and glanced shrewdly at his teeth.

'That's a well-kept set of teeth. Someone paid a lot of bills for that sweet little mouth. Frank, you'd be surprised how some people neglect their kids' teeth.' Basie patted Jim's shoulder, feeling the blue wool of his blazer. He scraped the mud from the school badge. 'That looks like a good school, Jim. The Cathedral School?'

Frank glowered over his heap of portholes. He seemed wary of Jim, as if this small boy might take Basie from him. 'Cathedral? Is he some kind of priest?'

'Frank, the Cathedral School.' Basie gazed with growing interest at Jim. 'That's a school for taipans. Jim, you must know some important people.'

'Well . . .' Jim was doubtful about this. He could think of nothing but the rice simmering on the charcoal stove, but then remembered a garden party at the British Embassy. 'Once I was introduced to Madame Sun Yat-Sen.'

'Madame Sun? You were . . . introduced?'

'I was only three and a half.' Jim sat still as Basie's white hands explored his pockets. The watch slipped from his wrist and vanished into the haze of cologne and face powder below the quilt. Yet Basie's attentive manner, like that of the servants who had once dressed and undressed him, was curiously reassuring. The sailor was feeling every bone in his body, as if searching for something precious. Through the open hatch Jim could see a flying boat about to take off from the Naval Air Base. A Japanese patrol boat had closed the channel, giving a wide berth to the currents that formed huge whirlpools around the boom of freighters. Jim returned to the cooking pot and its intoxicating smell of burnt fat. Suddenly it occurred to him that these two American sailors might want to eat him.

But Basie had removed the lid from the saucepan. A flavoursome steam rose from a thick stew of rice and fish. Basie produced a pair of tin plates and spoons from a leather bag under the bed. Still smoking his Craven A, he served portions for himself and Jim with the deftness of a waiter at the Palace Hotel. As Jim wolfed the hot fish Basie watched with the same wry approval that the Japanese soldier had shown.

Basie tucked into the stew. 'We eat later, Frank.'

Frank rubbed at a porthole, his eyes on the saucepan. 'Basie, I always eat after you.'

'I need to think for us both, Frank. Besides, we have to look after our young friend.' He wiped a grain of rice from

96

Jim's chin. 'Tell me, Jim, have you met any other Chinese big noises? Chiang Kai-Shek, maybe . . . ?'

'No . . . but his name isn't really Chinese, you know.' The hot food made Jim's brain swim. He remembered a word his mother had used, which he had always tried to work into his conversations with adults. 'It's a corruption of Shanghai Czech.'

'A corruption . . . ?' Basie was sitting up now. Having ended his meal, he began to powder his hands. Are you interested in words, Jim?'

'A bit. And contract bridge. I've written a book about it.'

Basie looked doubtful. 'Words are more important, Jim. Put aside a new word every day. You never know when a word might be useful.'

Jim finished his stew and sat back contentedly against the metal wall. He could remember none of his meals before the war and every one of them since. It annoyed him to think of all the food in his life that he had turned away, and the elaborate stratagems which Vera and his mother had devised to persuade him to finish his pudding. He noticed that Frank was staring at a few grains he had left in the spoon, and quickly licked it clean. Jim glanced into the saucepan, glad to see that there was enough rice for Frank. He was sure now that these two merchant seamen were not going to eat him, but the fear had been sensible – there had been rumours at the Country Club that British sailors torpedoed in the Atlantic had taken to cannibalism.

Basie served himself a small spoonful of rice. He made no attempt to eat this second helping, but played with the plate under Frank's burning gaze. Already Jim could see that Basie liked to control the young sailor and was using Jim to unsettle him. Jim's entire upbringing could have been designed to prevent him from meeting people like Basie, but the war had changed everything.

'What about your Daddy, Jim?' Basie asked. 'Why aren't you at home with your mother? Are they here in Shanghai?'

'Yes . . .' Jim hesitated. All his experience of the previous weeks told him not to trust anyone, except perhaps the Japanese. 'They're in Shanghai – but they're sailing on the *Idzumo*.'

'The *Idzumo*?' Frank jumped from his deck-chair. He seized a mess-tin from his haversack and helped himself vigorously to the saucepan of rice. Between mouthfuls, he shook his spoon at Jim. 'Kid, who are you? Basie . . . !'

'Not the *Idzumo*, Jim.' With his white hands Basie selected a piece of charcoal from a bag under the bed. 'The *Idzumo*'s heading for Foochow and Manila Bay. Jim's having you on, Frank.'

'Well, I think they're on the *Idzumo*.' Jim decided to fan the small doubt still in Basie's eyes. 'My father often goes to Manila.'

'Not on a Japanese cruiser, Jim.'

'Basie . . . !'

'Frank . . .' Basie mimicked the sailor's voice. 'Some day you'll want to trust me. I imagine Jim's folks had themselves picked up with all the other Britishers, and now Jim's looking for them. Jim . . . ?'

Jim nodded, taking the last liqueur chocolate from his blazer pocket. He unwrapped the silver foil and bit into the miniature chocolate bottle. Then, remembering what Vera had drummed into him about the need to be polite, he handed half the chocolate to Basie.

'Curaçao . . . Well, things have been looking up, Jim, since you arrived. All these new words, and now this fancy candy, we're getting a little of that Palace Hotel style.' As Basie sucked at the chocolate cup with his sharp teeth he resembled a white-faced rat teasing the brains from a mouse. 'So you've been living at home, Jim, all by yourself. Down there in the French Concession?'

'Amherst Avenue.'

'Frank . . . Before we leave Shanghai we ought to take a ride out there. There must be a lot of empty houses, Jim?'

Jim closed his eyes. He was very tired but awake, thinking of the rice he had just eaten, retasting every fishy grain. Basie talked, his devious voice circling the fume-filled air with its scent of cologne and Craven A. He thought of his mother smoking in the drawing-room at Amherst Avenue. Now that he had met these two American sailors he would be seeing her again. He would stay with Basie and Frank; together they could go out to the boom of freighters; sooner or later the Japanese patrol boats would notice them.

A hot, fishy breath filled his face. Jim woke with a gasp. Frank's huge body leaned across him, heavy arms on his thighs, hands feeling in his blazer pockets. Jim pushed him away, and Frank calmly returned to his deck-chair and continued to polish the portholes.

They were alone together in the cabin. Jim could hear Basie on the bamboo catwalk below. The door of the truck slammed, and the elderly engine began to throb, then stopped abruptly. There was a distant blast from the *Idzumo*'s siren. With a meaningful glance at Jim, Frank buffed the faded brass.

'You know, kid, you have a talent for getting on people's nerves. How is it the Japs haven't picked you up? You must be quick on your feet.'

'I tried to surrender,' Jim explained. 'But it isn't easy. Do you and Basie want to surrender?'

'Like hell – though I don't know about him. I'm trying to get Basie to buy a sampan so we can sail upriver to Chungking. But Basie keeps changing his mind. He wants to stay in Shanghai now the Japs are here. He thinks we can make a pile of money once we get to the camps.'

'Do you sell a lot of portholes, Frank?'

Frank peered at Jim, still unsure about this small boy. 'Kid, we haven't sold a single one. It's Basie's game, like a drug, he needs to keep people working for him. Down in the yard somewhere he has a bag of gold teeth that he sells in Hongkew.' With a knowing smile, Frank raised an oil-stained spanner, and touched Jim's chin. 'It's a good thing you don't have any gold teeth, or – ' He snapped his wrist.

Jim sat up, remembering how Basie had searched his gums. The sound of the truck's motor vibrated through the metal cabin. He was wary of these two merchant seamen, who had somehow escaped the Japanese net around Shanghai, and realized that he might have as much to fear from them as from anyone else in the city. He thought of Basie's secret bag of gold teeth. The creeks and canals of Nantao were full of corpses, and the mouths of those corpses were full of teeth. Every Chinese tried to have at least one gold tooth out of self-respect, and now that the war had begun their relatives might be too tired to pull them out before the funeral. Jim visualized the two American seamen searching the mud-flats at night with their spanners, Frank rowing the dinghy along the black creeks. Basie in the bows with a lantern, prodding the corpses that drifted past and exposing their gums . . .

12
Dance Music

This fearful image dominated the three days that Jim was to spend with the American sailors. At night, as Basie and Frank slept together under the quilt, he lay awake on his pile of rice sacking beside the charcoal stove. Reflected from the portholes and brass handrails, the embers gleamed like gold teeth. When he awoke in the mornings Jim would feel his jaw, to make sure that Frank had not removed one of his molars out of cussedness.

During the day Jim sat on the funeral pier and acted as lookout while Frank rowed to the scuttled freighters. When he began to shiver Jim returned to the cabin and lay under the quilt as Basie sat in the Imperial Airways deck-chair and made wire toys from old pipe cleaners. Basie had served as a cabin steward on the Cathay-American Line, and he treated Jim to the same patter and parlour tricks with which he had amused the young children of his passengers. He made the same effort to ensure that Jim ate his morning and evening meals, while endlessly questioning him about his mother and father. To a large extent Basie had modelled himself on the women passengers he had served, forever powdering themselves in the heat as they lit their cigarettes.

Every afternoon they set off together in the truck and toured the Chinese markets in Hongkew. Here Basie would haggle for a sack of rice and a few pieces of fish, trading packets of French cigarettes from the store of cartons under his bed. At times he would tell Frank to bring Jim over to the vendor's stall, where the Chinese trader would soberly inspect Jim before shaking his head.

It soon became clear to Jim that Basie was trying to sell him to the traders. Too tired to resist, he sat in the truck between the two Americans, like one of the chickens which the Chinese women carried beside them on the seats of the trams. Already he felt unwell most of the time, but his potential value at least assured him of the meals of boiled fish. Eventually the Chinese traders would realize that a few yen could be made by reporting them to the Japanese.

Meanwhile he avoided Frank's heavy hands, ransacked his mind for the unusual words which Basie liked to hear him use, and regaled the cabin steward with tales of the grand houses in Amherst Avenue. Jim invented lives of wholly imaginary glamour which he claimed his parents had led. Basie never ceased to be fascinated by these accounts of Shanghai high life.

'Tell me about their swimming-pool parties,' Basie asked as they waited for Frank to start the engine before their last visit to Hongkew market. 'I imagine there was a lot of . . . gaiety.'

'Basie, there certainly was gaiety.' Jim remembered the hours he had spent alone trying to retrieve the half-crown, gleaming at the bottom of the pool like one of Basie's teeth. 'They had liqueur chocolates, a white piano, whisky and soda. And conjurors.'

'Conjurors, Jim?'

'I think they were conjurors . . .'

'You're tired, Jim.' As they sat in the truck Basie put an arm around Jim's shoulders. 'You've been thinking too much, all those new words.'

'I've used up all my new words, Basie. Is the war going to end soon?'

'Don't worry, Jim. I give the Japs three months at the outside.'

'As soon as that, Basie?'

'Maybe a little more. It takes a long time to start a war,

people have a big investment to protect. Like Frank and me and this truck.'

It had never occurred to Jim that anyone might want the war to continue, and he puzzled over the bizarre logic as they set out for Hongkew. They bumped along the dirt road behind the shipyards, through a desolate area of empty godowns, garbage tips and burial mounds. Beggars lived beside the canals in hovels constructed from truck tyres and packing cases. An old woman squatted by the foetid water, scrubbing out a wooden toilet. Gazing down from the safety of the truck, Jim felt sorry for these destitute people, though only a few days earlier his plight had been even more desperate than theirs. A strange doubling of reality had taken place, as if everything that had happened to him since the war was occurring within a mirror. It was his mirror self who felt faint and hungry, and who thought about food all the time. He no longer felt sorry for this other self. Jim guessed that this was how the Chinese managed to survive. Yet one day the Chinese might emerge from the mirror.

When they crossed Nantao Creek into the French Concession they saw the first Japanese patrol, guarding the checkpoint on the northern end of the steel bridge. But Basie and Frank seemed unafraid of the armed soldiers – Americans, Jim had noticed, were not easily impressed by anyone. Frank even sounded his horn at a Japanese soldier who strolled into the road. Jim crouched below the dashboard, expecting them to be shot, but the Japanese waved them on with a surly stare, perhaps assuming that Frank and Basie were White Russian workmen.

For the next hour they toured the Hongkew markets, past the hundreds of barking dogs in their bamboo cages, not only the Chinese table-mongrels but spaniels and dachshunds, red setters and airedales released into the hungry streets of Shanghai by their allied owners. Several times they stopped for Basie to get out and approach a Chinese stall-holder, talking in his fluent dockside Cantonese. But no portholes or gold teeth changed hands.

'Frank, what's Basie trying to buy?'

'It looks like he's more interested in selling.'

'Why can't Basie sell me?'

'Nobody wants you.' Frank flicked the half-crown he had stolen from Jim's pocket, and snapped it in his heavy hand. 'You're worth nothing. What do you think you're worth?'

'I'm worth nothing, Frank.'

'You're skin and bone. Soon you're going to be sick all the time.'

'If they did buy me, what would they do with me? They couldn't eat me, I'm skin and bone.'

But Frank declined to answer. Basie climbed into the truck, shaking his head. They left Hongkew and crossed the Soochow Creek into the International Settlement. They drove along the main streets, losing themselves in the traffic on the Avenue Foch, following the slow, clanking trams through the wheel-to-wheel tide of pedicabs and rickshaws.

Jim tried to guide them towards the residential suburbs in the west of Shanghai, telling them about the fine houses filled with billiard tables, whisky and liqueur chocolates. But he guessed that Basie and Frank were killing time before dusk. Soon after six o'clock the light withdrew from the façades of the apartment houses in the French Concession. The two sailors wound up their windows. Frank left the Bubbling Well Road and set off into the unlit Chinese districts of north Shanghai.

'Frank, you're going the wrong way – ' Jim tried to point out. But Basie pressed the back of his powdered hand against Jim's mouth.

'Quiet, Jim. Silence is a good friend to a boy.'

Jim rested his swaying head against Basie's shoulder. They embarked on a rambling journey through the narrow streets. Hundreds of Chinese faces pressed against the windows as they edged between the rickshaw and buffalo carts. Jim felt hungry again, and the endless bumping of the wheels over the disused tramlines made him giddy. He wished that they would return to Nantao, to the charcoal-stove with its pot of rice.

An hour later, Jim woke to find that they had reached the western suburbs of Shanghai. The last of the sun touched the rooftops of the Columbia Road. As they cruised past the parked Opels and Buicks of the German compound Basie pointed to the unoccupied houses.

Jim revived, and blew into his hands to warm them. They had completed a pointless circuit of the city, but he realized that he had tempted these devious men with his chatter about the grand life. Like a courier with a party of gullible tourists, he began a commentary on the houses in which he had camped during the past two months.

'That has whisky and gin, Basie. That has whisky and gin and a white piano – no, just whisky.'

'Never mind the alcohol. Frank and I aren't planning to open a bar. Were you a choirboy, Jim? We'll stand you on the white piano, you can sing "Yankee Doodle Dandy".'

'That has a cinema,' Jim continued. 'And that one is full of teeth.'

'Teeth, Jim?'

'It belonged to a dentist. Maybe there are gold teeth, Basie.'

They turned into Amherst Avenue and drove past the deserted mansions. The electricity supply to the street was still disconnected, and the houses in their overgrown gardens seemed even more sombre in the early evening, stranded here like the scuttled freighters in the boom. But Basie stared at them with obvious respect, as if his years as a cabin steward on the Cathay-American Line had taught him the true worth of these beached hulks. Clearly he was glad to be associated with Jim.

'You had good sense, Jim, being born here. I admire a boy who appreciates a good home. Anyone can pick his own parents, but to have the sense to see beyond that . . .'

'Basie . . .' Frank interrupted this reverie. They had stopped under the trees two hundred yards from the entrance to Jim's drive.

'Right, Frank.' Basie opened his door and stepped into the road. There were no Japanese patrols, and the Chinese bodyguards had retreated behind their walls for the evening. Basie pointed to a narrow cul-de-sac that ran between uncut privet hedges towards one of the houses.

'Jim, time to stretch our legs. Take a stroll up there and see if anyone's playing that white piano.'

Jim listened to the low but stressed sound of the truck's engine. Frank sat back in a casual way, but his huge foot was poised above the accelerator. Basie's pallid face hung like a lantern below the trees. Jim knew that they planned to leave him there. Having failed to sell him to the Chinese traders, they would abandon him to the avenues of the Shanghai night.

'Basie, I . . .' Frank had placed a hand on his shoulder, ready to hurl him into the road. 'Could we go to my house? It's even more luxuriant.'

'Luxuriant?' Basie savoured the word in the grey air. He gazed at the houses around them, at the Tudor gables and white modern façades, at the replica chateaux and the haciendas with green tiled roofs.

He climbed aboard, and held the door to the frame without engaging the lock. 'All right, Frank, we'll look at Jim's house.'

They moved forward under the trees, and turned into the unguarded drive. As they approached the silent house Jim could see that Basie was disappointed. He eased open the door, ready to seize Jim and throw him out on to his own steps.

Jim clung to the dashboard, and at that moment two figures stepped from the entrance porch. They wore white gowns, with deep sleeves that floated from their arms. Jim was sure that his mother had come home and was greeting one of her guests.

'Basie! They're Japs . . .'

Jim heard Frank shouting, and saw that the two figures were off-duty Japanese soldiers in their military kimonos. The soldiers had seen them, and were bellowing at the open door. A uniformed sergeant emerged from the kerosene light that filled the hall. He stood on the top step, a Mauser holster against his stocky thigh. Frank was trying to reverse the truck when the soldiers in the kimonos jumped on to the running boards and struck with their fists at the glass. Two more soldiers carrying bamboo staves ran down the steps of the porch.

As the engine stalled, Jim felt himself pulled from the truck and hurled to the ground. Japanese in kimonos were running from the house, like a party of outraged women fresh from their baths. Jim sat on the sharp gravel between the polished boots of the Japanese sergeant, whose angry thighs rapped against his holster. The soldiers had trapped Frank within the cabin of the truck. His legs kicked out as they lunged at him with their bamboo staves, striking his bloody face and chest. Two soldiers watched from the steps of the house, taking turns to punch Basie who knelt at their feet in the drive.

Jim was glad to see the Japanese. Through the open doorway he could hear, between the heavy blows and Frank's cries, the scratchy sounds of a Japanese dance band playing on his mother's picnic gramophone.

13
The Open-Air Cinema

His arms warmed by the spring sun, Jim rested comfortably in the front row of the open-air cinema. Smiling to himself, he gazed at the blank screen twenty feet away. For the past hour the blurred shadow of the Park Hotel had been moving across the white canvas. After a long journey through the godowns and tenement blocks of Chapei, the shadow of the neon sign above the hotel had at last reached the screen. The immense letters, each twice the height of the young Japanese soldier patrolling the stage, moved from left to right at a brisk pace, incorporating the silhouette of this slim sentry and his rifle in a spectacular solar film.

Delighted with the display, Jim laughed behind his grimy knees, feet up on the slatted teak bench. The afternoon diorama staged in collaboration by the sun and the Park Hotel had been Jim's chief entertainment during the three weeks he had spent at the open-air cinema. Here, before the outbreak of war, cartoons and adventure serials made by the Shanghai film industry were projected at night to audiences of Chinese mill-girls and dockyard workers. It often occurred to Jim that Yang, the family chauffeur, might have appeared on this very screen. He had already carried out a full reconnaissance of the detention centre, and in a disused office above the projection room were reels of dusty film. Perhaps the Japanese corporal from the signals corps who was now trying to dismantle the projector would show one of Yang's films?

His giggles brought a sour glance from the soldier on the stage. He clearly mistrusted Jim, who kept out of his way. Shielding his eyes, the soldier scanned the wooden benches, where a few detainees sat in the afternoon sun. Three rows behind Jim was the grey-haired husband of the dying missionary woman who lay on her mat in the concrete dormitory under the seats. She had not moved from the former store-room since her arrival, but Mr Partridge looked after her patiently, bringing water from the tap in the latrine and feeding her the thin rice gruel which two Eurasian women cooked once a day in the yard behind the ticket office.

Jim felt concerned for the old Englishman with his patchy hair and deathly skin. At times he seemed unable to recognize his wife. Jim helped him to erect a screen around Mrs Partridge, who never spoke and had an unpleasant smell. They used Mr Partridge's English overcoat and his wife's yellowing nightdress, suspending them from a length of electric flex that Jim pulled from the wall. If he was bored Jim went down to the women's store-room and chased away the Eurasian children who ran in to play.

There were some thirty people in the detention centre, to which Jim had been sent after a week at the Shanghai Central Prison. Compared with the damp dormitory cell which he shared with a hundred Eurasian and British prisoners, the open-air cinema seemed as sunny as the resort beaches at Tsingtao. Jim had seen nothing of Basie since their capture by the Japanese, and was glad to be free of the cabin steward. None of the prisoners in the Central Prison, most of whom were contract foremen and merchant seamen from China coasters, had heard of Jim's parents, but the transfer to the detention centre was a move towards them.

Soon after his capture Jim had fallen ill with an aching fever, during which he vomited blood. He guessed that he had been sent to the detention centre in order to recover. Apart from several elderly English couples there were an old Dutchman and his adult daughter, and a quiet Belgian woman whose injured husband slept next to Jim in the men's store-room. The rest were Eurasian women who had been abandoned in Shanghai by British husbands in the armed services.

None of them was much fun to be with – they were all either very old or sick with malaria and dysentery, and few of the Eurasian children spoke any English. So Jim spent his time in the open-air cinema, roving around the wooden seats. Despite his headaches, he tried unsuccessfully to make friends with the Japanese soldiers. And every afternoon there was the shadow film of the Shanghai skyline.

Jim watched the letters of the Park Hotel's neon sign blur and fade. Although he was hungry all the time, he was happy in the detention centre. After the months of roving the streets of Shanghai he had at last managed to give himself up to the Japanese forces. Jim had pondered deeply on the question of surrender, which took courage and even a certain amount of guile. How did entire armies manage it?

He was aware that the Japanese had seized him only because he had been with Basie and Frank. He felt frightened when he thought of the soldiers in kimonos attacking Frank with their staves, but at least he would soon see his parents again. Prisoners were constantly coming and going at the detention centre. Two British people had died the previous day, a heavily bandaged woman whom Jim had not been allowed to see, and an old man with malaria who was a retired Shanghai police inspector.

If only he could discover to which of the dozen camps around Shanghai his mother and father had been sent. He left his place and tried to speak to Mr Partridge, but the old missionary was sunk inside his head. Jim approached the two Eurasian women sitting a few benches behind him. But as always they shook their heads and brusquely waved him away.

'Disgusting . . . !'

'Dirty boy . . . !'

110

'Go away . . . !'

Invariably they snapped at Jim, and tried to keep their children from him. Sometimes they mimicked his voice during his fevers. Jim smiled at them and returned to his seat. He felt tired, as he often did, and thought of going down to the store-room and sleeping for an hour on his mat. But a meal of boiled rice was served in the afternoon, and the previous day, when he had felt feverish, he had missed his ration. It surprised him how these old and sick people could manage to rouse themselves at meal times. No one had thought of waking Jim, and nothing was left in the brass cong. When he protested the Korean soldier had cuffed his head. Already Jim was certain that the Eurasian women who guarded the bags of rice in the ticket kiosk were giving him less than his fair share. He distrusted them all, and their strange children, who looked almost English but could speak only Chinese.

Jim was determined to have his share of rice. He knew that he was thinner than he had been before the war, and that his parents might fail to recognize him. At meal times, when he looked at himself in the cracked glass panes of the ticket kiosk, he barely remembered the long face with its deep eye-sockets and bony forehead. Jim avoided mirrors – the Eurasian women were always watching him through their compacts.

Deciding to think of something useful, Jim lay back on the teak bench. He watched a Kawanishi flying boat cross the river. The drone of its engines was comforting, and reminded him of all his dreams of flying. When he was hungry or missed his parents he often dreamed of aircraft. During one of his fevers he had even seen a flight of American bombers in the sky above the detention centre.

A whistle shrilled from the courtyard by the ticket kiosk. The Japanese sergeant in charge of the detention centre was holding another of his roll-calls. Jim had noticed that he

111

seemed unable to remember the prisoners' names for more than half an hour. Jim took Mr Partridge's hand, and together they followed the two Eurasian women. A military truck had stopped outside the entrance to the cinema, whose high brick walls had concealed its films from the Chinese in the nearby tenement blocks. In the intervals between the sergeant's whistles, Jim heard the crying of a British child.

A new group of prisoners had arrived. Invariably this meant that others would leave. Jim was sure that he would be on his way within minutes, probably to the new camps at Hungjao or Lunghua. In the store-room he and the old men still able to stand waited by their mats, mess-tins in hand. He listened to the new arrivals being herded from the truck. Annoyingly, there were several small children, who would cry continuously and distract the Japanese from the serious task of deciding where Jim should be sent.

Followed by two armed soldiers, the Japanese sergeant stood in the doorway. All three men wore cotton masks over their faces – there was a foul smell from the young Belgian asleep on the floor – but the sergeant's eyes inspected each of them in turn and counted the exact number of mess-tins. The daily ration of rice or sweet potatoes was allocated to the mess-tin and not to the person attached to it. Often, when Mr Partridge was tired after feeding his wife, Jim would collect the old man's ration for him. Once, without realizing it, he had found himself eating the watery gruel. Jim had felt uneasy, and stared at his guilty hands. Parts of his mind and body frequently separated themselves from each other.

Masking the tic in his cheek, he smiled brightly at the Japanese sergeant, and tried to look strong and healthy. Only the healthier people tended to leave the detention centre. But as usual the sergeant seemed depressed by Jim's cheerful gaze. He stepped aside as the new arrivals reached the store-room. Two Chinese prison orderlies bore a stretcher carrying an unconscious Englishwoman in a stained cotton dress. She lay with her damp hair in her mouth, while her two sons, boys of Jim's age, held the sides of the stretcher. A trio of elderly women hobbled past, unsure of the smell and the grey light. Behind them came a tall soldier wearing lumpy boots and British army shorts. He was bare-chested, and his emaciated ribs were like a birdcage in which Jim could almost see his heart fluttering.

'Well done, lad . . .' He gave Jim a rictus of a smile and patted his head. Quickly he sat down against the wall, his cadaverous face turned to the damp cement. A second team of orderlies lowered a stretcher on to the floor beside him. From the cradle of roped straw they lifted a small, middle-aged man in a bloodstained sailor's jacket. Strips of Japanese rice-paper bandages were stuck to the wounds on his swollen hands, face and forehead.

Jim stared at this derelict figure, and raised his forearm to his mouth to shut out the unpleasant smell. Several of the Eurasian women were leaving the detention centre with their children. Looking round at the sick and dying men in the store-room, and at the orderlies and Japanese soldiers with their cotton face-masks, Jim began for the first time to grasp the real purpose of the detention centre.

Mr Partridge and the old men stood by their mats, shaking their mess-tins at the guards, rattling for their evening meal. The wounded sailor beckoned to Jim with his bandaged hands, beating his empty tin with the same rhythm that the dying beggar had used outside the gates of Amherst Avenue. Even the emaciated soldier had found the lid of a mess-tin. With his face pressed to the wall, he banged the lid on the stone floor.

Jim began to rattle at the Japanese watching behind their white masks. Yet, at that moment when he was about to despair of ever finding his parents, he felt a surge of hope.

113

He knelt on the floor and took the mess-tin from the injured sailor, aware of a faint scent of cologne and certain now that together they could leave the detention centre and make their way to the safety of the prison camps.

'Basie!' he cried. 'Everything's all right!'

14
American Aircraft

'The war's going to be over soon, Basie. I've seen American planes, Curtiss bombers and Boeings . . .'

'Boeings . . .? Jim you're – '

'Don't talk, Basie. I'm working for you now, just like Frank.'

Jim squatted by the American sailor, trying to remember the amahs of his early childhood. He had never looked after anything before, except for an angora rabbit that had died tragically within a few days. He tilted the mess-tin and tried to pour a little water into Basie's mouth, then dipped his fingers in the murky fluid and let Basie suck them.

For three weeks Jim had devoted himself to the cabin steward, bringing his ration of boiled rice and sweet potatoes, fetching water from the tap in the corridor. He sat for hours beside Basie, fanning the sailor as he lay on his mat below the transom window. The stream of fresh air soon revived him, and one by one he pulled away the paper bandages fluttering on his face and wrists. Helped by Jim, he moved his mat from the English soldier dying against the wall. Within a week he had recovered enough of his strength to keep an eye on the Japanese guards and the comings and goings of the Eurasian woman who cooked for the prisoners.

As he cleaned Basie's mess-tin Jim wondered if the sailor really recognized him. Did he know that Jim had managed to trick him? Perhaps he would report Jim to the other prisoners, but there was little that they could do. Relieved that at last he had an ally in his struggle with the Eurasian women, he rested his head on his knees.

He felt Basie nudge him with the mess-tins.

'Chow time, Jim. Get in line.' As Jim sat up, hoping that he had not talked in his sleep, Basie wiped some of the dirt from his cheek. The steward's canny eyes took in every detail of Jim's shabby state. 'Make yourself useful to Mrs Blackburn, Jim. Ingratiate yourself a little. A woman always needs help with her fire.'

Somehow, during his visits to the latrine, Basie had learned the Eurasian woman's name. Jim ran from the store-room with the two mess-tins. The other prisoners followed, the old men stirring from their mats. Mr Partridge took the mess-tin from the hand of the English soldier who sat in a pool of urine by the wall.

Smoke rose from the courtyard behind the ticket kiosk. The Eurasian woman fanned the briquettes in her stove, but the rice and sweet potatoes in the congs had gone off the boil. A Japanese soldier stared gloomily at the tepid swill, and shook his head at the hungry prisoners. They shuffled among the teak benches of the cinema, sat down and stared at the smoke drifting across the empty screen.

Holding the mess-tins, Jim hovered around Mrs Blackburn and treated her to his keenest smile. She disliked Jim, but allowed him to chop the basket of firewood. He pushed the spills into the stove and blew hard to ignite them. He fanned the embers until the briquettes caught light again. Half an hour later, with the Japanese soldier's approval, Jim was rewarded with his first fair ration.

Basie was satisfied but unimpressed. After finishing his meal he propped himself on his elbows. He gazed at his fellow prisoners, some too exhausted to eat their rations, and tore the last of the paper bandages from the cuts over his eyes. Whatever had befallen him in Shanghai Central Prison – and Jim never dared to ask about Frank – he had once again become the ex-steward of the Cathay-American Line, ready to assemble a small part of a ramshackle world around himself. He surveyed Jim again, taking in his ragged clothes and scarecrow appearance, his deepset and yellowing eyes. Without comment, he gave Jim a piece of potato skin.

'Say, thanks, Basie.'

'I'm looking after you, Jim.'

Jim devoured the shred of potato. 'You're looking after me, Basie.'

'You helped Mrs Blackburn?'

'I ingratiated myself. I made myself very useful to Mrs Blackburn.'

'That's it. If you can find a way of helping people you'll live off the interest.'

'Like this piece of potato . . . Basie, when you were in Shanghai Central did anyone talk about my mother and father?'

'I think I did hear something, Jim.' Basie cupped his hand conspiratorially. 'Good news, they're in one of the camps and looking forward to seeing you. I'll find out which one for you.'

'Thanks, Basie!'

From then on Jim regularly helped Mrs Blackburn. Every morning he was up at dawn to rake the ash from the stove, chop firewood and lay the briquettes. Long before the water in the congs began to boil Jim had already earmarked sweet potatoes for Basie and himself, selecting those with the least blight and fungus. He saw to it that Mrs Blackburn served them the thicker rice, into which, at Basie's suggestion, he had been careful to stir the minimum of water. After their meal, when the other prisoners rinsed their tins at the latrine tap, Basie always sent Jim to fill their mess-tins with the tepid water in the potato cong. Basie insisted that he and Jim drank only this grey, pithy liquid.

Although, like everyone else, Basie was never keen for Jim to come too close to him, he clearly approved of Jim's efforts. At the end of his second week at the detention centre Basie allowed him to move his sleeping mat beside his own. Lying at Basie's feet, Jim could intercept Mrs Blackburn on her way to the kiosk.

'Always look light on your toes, Jim.' Basie lay back as Jim fanned him. 'Whatever happens, keep moving around the court. Your dad would agree with me.'

'Actually, he would agree with you. After the war you can play tennis together. He's really good.'

'Well . . . What I meant, Jim, is that I'm trying to keep up your education. Your dad would appreciate that.'

'I think he'll give you a reward, Basie.' Jim assumed that the notion of a reward would spur Basie in his search for his father. 'Once he gave five dollars to a taxi-driver who brought me home from Hongkew.'

'Did he, Jim?' At times Basie seemed unsure whether Jim was having him on. 'Tell me, did you see any planes today?'

'A Nakajima Shoki and a Zero-Sen.'

'And American planes?'

'I haven't seen those again. Not since you came, Basie. I saw them for three days and then they went away.'

'I thought they had. They must have been a special kind of reconnaissance flight.'

'To see how we all are? Where did they come from, Basie? Wake Island?'

'A long way, Jim. It must have been just about the end of their range.' Basie took the fan from Jim's hand. An elderly Australian had arrived to talk to Basie about the war. 'Go and help Mrs Blackburn. And remember to bow to Sergeant Uchida.'

'I always bow, Basie.'

Jim hovered around the conversation, hoping to catch the latest news, but the two men waved him away. Basie was surprisingly well informed about the progress of the war, the fall of Hong Kong, Manila and the Dutch East Indies,

118

the surrender of Singapore and the unbroken advance of Japan across the Pacific. The only good news in all this were the flights of American planes that Jim had seen over Shanghai, but for some reason Basie never mentioned them. He liked to talk out of the side of his mouth, telling the old Britishers about the other inmates at Shanghai Central Prison, who had died and who had been handed over to the Swiss Red Cross. Basie even sold information for small scraps of food. Mr Partridge gave him his potato for news of his brother-in-law in Nanking. Inspired by this, Jim tried to tell Mrs Blackburn about the American aircraft, but she merely sent him back to the briquettes.

Now that he felt stronger, Jim realized how important it was to be obsessed by food. Shared equally among the prisoners, their daily rations were not enough to keep them alive. Many of the prisoners had died, and anyone who sacrificed himself for the others soon died too. The only way to leave the detention centre was to stay alive. As long as he ran errands for Basie, worked hard for Mrs Blackburn and bowed to Sergeant Uchida all would be well.

Nonetheless, some of Basie's ruses unsettled Jim. On the morning Mrs Partridge died Basie learned some encouraging news about the brother-in-law in Nanking, and soon after was able to sell the old woman's hair-brushes to Mrs Blackburn. Whenever anyone died Basie would be on hand with news and comfort, though death was an elastic term for the cabin steward, open to all manner of interpretation. Jim collected Private Blake's rations for two days after he lay without moving on the store-room floor, the skin stretched across his ribs like rice-paper around a lantern. He knew that the private had died of the same fever that he and many of the prisoners had caught. But already Jim was looking at the elderly missionaries with an expectant eye, waiting for fever to recruit the old men. Once he and Basie had admitted their part in this supplementary ration scheme all guilt had gone.

Jim noticed how different Basie was from his father in this respect. At home, if he did anything wrong, the consequences seemed to overlay everything for days. With Basie they vanished instantly. For the first time in his life Jim felt free to do what he wanted. All sorts of wayward ideas moved through his mind, fuelled by hunger and the excitement of stealing from the old prisoners. As he rested between his errands in front of the empty cinema screen he thought of the American aircraft he had seen in the clouds above Shanghai. He could almost summon them into his vision, a silver fleet on the far side of the sky. Jim saw them most when he was hungry, and he hoped that Private Blake, who must always have been hungry, had also seen them.

15
On their Way to the Camps

On the day of the Englishwoman's death a fresh consignment of prisoners arrived at the detention centre. Jim was
hovering in the doorway of the women's store-room, as Mrs
Blackburn and the daughter of the old Dutchman tried to
comfort the two sons. The mother lay on the stone floor in
her drenched frock, like a drowned corpse raised from the
river. The brothers kept turning towards her, as if expecting her to give them some last instruction. Jim felt sad for
the boys, Paul and David, though he hardly knew them.
They seemed much younger than Jim, but in fact both were
more than a year older.

Jim had his eyes on the mother's mess-tin and tennis
shoes. Most of the Allied prisoners had far better shoes than
the Japanese soldiers, and he had noticed that the bodies
leaving the detention centre had bare feet. But as he sidled
into the room there was a shrill whistle from the courtyard,
and a series of barked shouts. Sergeant Uchida was working
himself up to the pitch of anger that he needed to attain in
order to issue the simplest instructions. Masks over their
faces, the Japanese soldiers began to herd from the store-
rooms everyone who could walk. A truck had stopped
outside the cinema, and its prisoners stood unsteadily in the
road.

All designs on the dead woman's tennis shoes vanished
from Jim's head. At last he would be leaving for the camps
in the countryside around Shanghai. Pushing past the two
boys, Jim dived between the guards and raced up the steps.
He lined up beside his fellow prisoners – Mr Partridge with
his wife's suitcase, as if about to take his memories of her on

a long journey, Paul and David, the Dutch woman and her father, and several of the old missionaries. Basie stood behind them, his white cheeks hidden behind the collar of his seaman's jacket, so self-effacing as to be almost invisible. He had erased himself from the small world of the detention centre, which he had manipulated for a few weeks, and would re-emerge like some marine parasite from its shell once he reached the more succulent terrain of the prison camps.

The new arrivals appeared, two Annamese women and a group of older Britishers and Belgians, the sick and elderly carried on stretchers by the Chinese orderlies. Counting their yellow eyes, Jim knew that there would soon be extra mess-tins.

His cotton mask over his face, Sergeant Uchida began to select prisoners for transport to the camps. He shook his head at Mr Partridge and kicked the suitcase in an exasperated way. He pointed to the Dutch woman and her father, Paul and David, and two elderly missionary couples.

Jim licked his fingers and wiped the soot from his cheeks. The sergeant motioned Basie towards the truck. Without a glance at Jim, the cabin steward stepped between the guards, his arms around the shoulders of the two boys.

Sergeant Uchida pressed his fingers against Jim's grimy forehead. With his constant bowing and smiling, his eagerness to run errands, Jim had been a perpetual nuisance to the sergeant, who was clearly glad to be rid of him. Then he glanced at the party of new arrivals, who stared listlessly at the cold stove, at the scum of boiled rice around the rim of the cong.

The sergeant cupped his hand around Jim's neck. With a shout muffled by his cotton mask he propelled him towards the stove. As Jim picked himself from his knees the sergeant kicked the coal-sacks, scattering briquettes across the stone floor.

Jim riddled the clinkers from the fire-box. The new arrivals wandered among the benches and took their seats facing the empty cinema screen, as if expecting a film show to begin. Basie and the Dutch couple, Paul and David, the old missionaries stood in the street behind the open army truck, watched at a distance by a crowd of rickshaw coolies and peasant women.

'Basie . . . !' Jim called. 'I'll still work for you . . . !' But the steward had lost interest in him. Already he had befriended Paul and David, inducting them into his entourage. They helped Basie as he clambered on his bruised knees over the tail-gate of the truck.

'Basie . . .' Jim riddled fiercely. He glared at the cinema screen, crossed by the first shadows of the Shanghai hotels. A Japanese soldier in a face-mask counted out a stack of mess-tins. As the injured prisoners were carried past on their stretchers Jim knew that most of the inmates of the detention centre had been sent there because they were very old or were expected to die, either of dysentery and typhoid, or whatever fever he and Private Blake had caught from the foul water. He was certain that many of the prisoners would soon die, and that if he stayed at the detention centre he would die with them. Already the Annamese women had collected the mess-tins from the soldier. They were pointing to the stove and the sacks of briquettes. When they took over the cooking of the rice and sweet potatoes they would not give Jim his fair ration. He would see the American aircraft again, and he would die.

'Basie . . . ?' Jim threw down the riddle. The last of the departing prisoners had taken their seats in the truck. The Japanese soldier by the tail-gate lowered the Dutch woman on to the wooden floor. Basie sat between the two English boys, making a toy from a piece of wire in his hand. The truck started up, moved forward a few feet and stopped. The Japanese driver shouted from his window. He waved a canvas map-wallet and slapped the metal door with his fist. The guards on the pavement shouted back, eager to close the gates of the detention centre and put their feet up in the orderly room. Then the engine stalled, and there was an instant clamour of angry voices, the soldiers and driver arguing over the destination of the truck.

'Woosung . . .' Sergeant Uchida lowered his cotton mask. His face was reddening, and drops of spittle formed on his lips, like pus forced from a wound. Already in a fury with the driver, he strode through the open gates. The driver had stepped from his cabin, unaware of the tornado about to engulf him. He dusted the map and spread it against the fender of the truck, shrugging hopelessly at the maze of nearby streets.

Jim followed Sergeant Uchida to the gates. He could see that neither the sergeant nor the Japanese driver had any idea of the whereabouts of Woosung, an agricultural district at the mouth of the Yangtze that lay beyond the northern suburbs of Shanghai. The driver gestured towards the Bund and Nantao, and climbed into his cabin. He sat passively when Sergeant Uchida pushed through the bored guards and began to scream abuse at him.

Standing beside the guards, Jim waited for Sergeant Uchida to reach the climax of his tirade, when he would be forced to make a decision. Sure enough, the sergeant searched the crowded skyline of tenement buildings and godowns, then pointed at random to a cobbled street with a disused tramline. Unimpressed, the driver cleared his throat. Wearily he started his engine and spat a ball of phlegm into the road, where it lay at Jim's feet.

'Straight on . . . !' Jim called up to him. 'Woosung – it's over there . . . !' He pointed to the street with the rusty tramlines.

Sergeant Uchida cuffed Jim on the head, bruising both his ears. He cuffed him again, bringing blood from his

124

mouth. At that moment a cloud of smoke billowed through the gates. The Annamese women had lit the stove with the rain-soaked firewood, and the smoke filled the open-air cinema, drifting across the benches as if the screen were ablaze.

Glad to be rid of Jim, Sergeant Uchida seized him in his strong hands. He swung him over the tail-gate of the truck, shouting to the Japanese guard who sat with the prisoners. The soldier dragged Jim across the laps of the Dutch woman and her father. As the truck pulled away from the detention centre, its wheels already locked in the tramlines, Jim clambered forward to the camouflaged driving cabin. He steadied himself against the pitching roof, and ignored the stream of oaths hurled at him by the driver. He raised his bloody mouth to the wind, letting the foul odours of Shanghai flush his lungs, happy to be on the way to his parents again.

16
The Water Ration

Were they lost? For an hour, as they trundled through the industrial suburbs of northern Shanghai, Jim gripped the wooden bar behind the driving cabin, his head filled with a dozen compass bearings. He grinned to himself, forgetting his illness and the desperate weeks in the open-air cinema. His knees ached from the constant swaying, and at times he had to hold on to the leather belt of the Japanese soldier beside him. But at last he was moving towards the open countryside, and the welcoming world of the prison camps.

The endless streets of Chapei ran past, an area of tenements and derelict cotton mills, police barracks and shanty towns built on the banks of black canals. They drove below the overhead conveyors of a steel works decorated with dragon-festival hoardings, dreams of fire conjured from its silent furnaces. Shuttered pawnshops stood outside the abandoned radio and cigarette factories, and platoons of Chinese puppet troops patrolled the Del Monte brewery and the Dodge truck depot. Jim had never been to Chapei. Before the war a small English boy would have been killed for his shoes within minutes. Now he was safe, guarded by the Japanese soldiers – he laughed over this so much that the Dutch woman reached out a hand to calm him.

But Jim relished the foetid air, the smell of human fertilizer from the open sewage congs that signalled the approach of the countryside. Even the driver's hostility failed to worry him. Whenever they stopped at a military checkpoint the driver would put his head out of the cabin and wave a warning finger at Jim, as if this eleven-year-old prisoner was responsible for the absurd expedition.

Watching the sun's angle, as he had done for hours in the detention centre, Jim made certain that they were moving north. They passed the ruins of the Chapei ceramic works, its kilns shaped like the German forts at Tsingtao. Its trademark stood beside the gates, a Chinese teapot three storeys high built entirely from green bricks. During the Sino-Japanese War of 1937 it had been holed by shell-fire, and now resembled a punctured globe of the earth. Thousands of the bricks had migrated across the surrounding fields to the villages beside the works canal, incorporated in the huts and dwellings, a vision of a magical rural China.

These strange dislocations appealed to Jim. For the first time he felt able to enjoy the war. He gazed happily at the burnt-out trams and tenement blocks, at the thousands of doors open to the clouds, a deserted city invaded by the sky. It only disappointed him that his fellow prisoners failed to share his excitement. They sat glumly on the benches, staring at their feet. One of the missionary women lay on the floor, tended by another prisoner, a sandy-haired Britisher with a bruised cheek who held her wrist with one hand and pressed her diaphragm with the other. The two English boys, still barely aware of their mother's death, sat between Basie and the Dutch couple.

Jim waited until Basie looked up, but the cabin steward seemed hardly to recognize him. His attention had turned to the two boys, and he had moved deftly into the vacuum in their lives. From the page of a Chinese newspaper he folded a series of paper animals, chuckling when the boys gave a weak laugh. Like a depraved conjuror, he slid his hands into the pockets of their school trousers and cardigans, searching for anything of use.

Jim watched him without resentment. He and Basie had collaborated at the detention centre in order to stay alive, but Basie, rightly, had dispensed with Jim as soon as he could leave for the camps.

The truck struck a deep gully in the cobbles, slewed across the road and came to a halt by the grass bank. They had left the northern outskirts of Shanghai and were entering an area of untilled fields and rice-paddies. Beyond a line of burial mounds two hundred yards away a canal ran towards a deserted village. The Japanese driver jumped from his cabin and bent over the front wheels of the truck. He began to talk to the steaming engine, now and then including Jim in his mutterings. He was only twenty years old, but had clearly suffered a lifetime of exasperation. Jim kept his head down, but the driver stepped on to the running board, levelled a finger at him and delivered a long harangue that sounded like a declaration of war.

The driver returned to his cabin, grumbling over his map, and Basie commented: 'Add that up any way you like and we're still lost.' Already his attention had moved from the boys to whatever advantage could be gained from their situation. 'Jim, do you know where you're taking us?'

'Woosung. I've been to the country club there, Basie.'

Basie played with his paper animals. 'We're going to the country club,' he told the boys. 'If Jim can find it for us.'

'As long as we reach the river, Basie. Then it's either east or west.'

'That's a big help. East or west . . .'

The sandy-haired Briton beside the missionary woman rose from his knees. There was a large, leaking bruise on his forehead and left cheekbone, as if he had recently been struck in the face by a rifle stock. In some pain, he settled himself on the bench. Long freckled legs emerged from his khaki shorts and ended in a pair of thonged sandals. In his late twenties, he carried no luggage or possessions, but he had the self-assured manner of the Royal Navy officers who cut such a dash at the Shanghai garden parties, thrilling the mothers of Jim's friends. He ignored the Japanese guard, talking across him as if he were a mess-boy who would soon

128

be dismissed to his quarters. Jim assumed that he was one of those tiresome Englishmen who refused to grasp that they had been defeated.

The man touched the bruise on his face and turned to Jim, whose ragged figure he appraised without comment. 'The Japanese have captured so much ground they've run out of maps,' he remarked amiably. 'Jim, does that mean they're lost?'

Jim thought about this. 'Not really. They just haven't captured any maps.'

'Good – never confuse the map with the territory. You'll get us to Woosung.'

'Can't we go back to the detention centre, Dr Ransome?' one of the missionaries asked. 'We're very tired.'

The physician stared at the abandoned paddy fields, and at the prostrate old woman at his feet. 'It might be for the best. This poor soul can't take much more.'

The truck moved forward again, trundling at a half-hearted pace down the empty road. Jim returned to his post by the driving cabin, and scanned the fields for anything that might remotely resemble Woosung. The doctor's words unsettled him. Even if they were lost, how could he want to return to the detention centre?

Jim knew that the fury of Sergeant Uchida made it unlikely that the driver would dare to turn back. But he kept a careful watch on Dr Ransome, trying to guess whether he spoke enough Japanese to demoralize the driver. He seemed to have difficulty with his sight, especially when looking at Jim, at whom he squinted in a curious way. Jim decided that he had entered the war at a later stage than Basie and himself. He had probably come from one of the missionary settlements in the interior, and had no idea of what went on at the detention centre.

But were they lost, or on course? The direction of the shadows cast by the wayside telegraph poles had barely changed – Jim had always been interested in shadows, ever since his father had shown him how to calculate the height of even the highest building by pacing out its shadow on the ground. They were still heading north-west, and would soon reach the Shanghai-Woosung railway line. Steam hissed from the truck's radiator. The spray cooled Jim's face, but the driver's fist drummed warningly against the door, and Jim knew that he was deciding when to stop and turn back for Shanghai.

Resigning himself to the wasted journey, and to their return to the detention centre, Jim studied the guard's bolt-action rifle and its imperial chrysanthemum crest. The Dutch woman pulled at his soot-stained blazer.

'Over there, James. Is that . . . ?'

A burnt-out aircraft lay on the banks of a disused canal. Wild grass and nettles grew through its wings, almost invading the cockpit, but the squadron insignia were still legible.

'It's a Nakajima,' he told Mrs Hug, pleased by this shared interest in plane-spotting. 'It only has two machine-guns.'

'Only two? But that's very many . . .'

The Dutch woman seemed impressed, but Jim had turned his attention from the aircraft. On the far side of the paddy field, hidden by the nettles, was the embankment of a railway line. A squad of Japanese soldiers rested on the concrete platform of a wayside station, cooking a meal on a fire of sticks. A camouflaged staff car was parked beside the tracks. It was loaded with coils of wire which these signals engineers were re-stringing between the telegraph poles.

'Mrs Hug . . . that's the railway to Woosung!'

As steam bathed the driving cabin, the truck had stopped. It began to reverse. Beside Jim the Japanese guard was lighting a cigarette for the return journey. Jim pulled at his belt and pointed across the paddy field. The soldier followed his outstretched arm and then pushed him on to the floor. He shouted to the driver, who tossed his map-wallet on to the seat beside him. Engine steaming, the truck strained at the camber, made a half circle and set off along the dirt track to the railway station.

Dr Ransome steadied the English boys as they slipped from Basie's grasp and swayed against the missionary woman. He helped Jim from the floor.

'Good work, Jim. They'll have water for us – you must be thirsty.'

'A bit. I had a drink at the detention centre.'

'That was sensible. How long were you there?'

Jim had forgotten. 'Quite a long time.'

'So I imagine.' Dr Ransome brushed the dirt from Jim's blazer. 'It used to be a cinema?'

'But they didn't show films.'

'I can see that.'

Jim sat back, patting his knees and beaming at Mrs Hug. The prisoners sat weakly on the facing benches, jerked to and fro like life-size puppets that had lost their stuffing. Far from reviving them, the drive from Shanghai had made them look sallow and nervous. But Jim smiled at the rusting aircraft on the canal bank. There was now no danger that they would return to the detention centre. The Japanese soldier had thrown away his cigarette and held his rifle in a military way. A signals corporal jumped from the railway platform and crossed the track.

'Mrs Hug, I don't think we'll be going back to Shanghai.'

'No, James – you must have very sharp eyes. When you grow up you should be a pilot.'

'I probably will. I have been in a plane, Mrs Hug. At Hungjao Aerodrome.'

'Did it fly?'

'Well, in a way.' Confidences given to adults often led further than Jim intended. He was aware that Dr Ransome was watching him. The doctor sat beside Mrs Hug's father,

131

whose painful breathing he was trying to help. But his eyes were fixed on Jim, taking in his stick-like legs and ragged clothes, his small, excited face. As they reached the railway line he gave Jim an encouraging smile, which Jim decided not to return. He knew that for some reason Dr Ransome disapproved of him. But Dr Ransome had not been to the detention centre.

They stopped by the railway tracks. The driver saluted the corporal and followed him to the station, where he spread his map across the cabinet of the field telephone. The prisoners sat in the warm sunlight as the corporal pointed to the drained paddies. A haze of dust rose from the untilled earth, a white veil that screened the distant skyscrapers of Shanghai. A convoy of Japanese trucks drove along the road, a brief blare of noise that merged with the distant drone of a cargo aircraft.

Jim changed benches and sat beside Mrs Hug, who supported her aged father against her breast. Two of the missionary women lay on the floor of the truck, as the other prisoners dozed and fretted. Basie had lost interest in the English boys, and was watching Jim over the bloodstained collar of his coat.

Thousands of flies gathered around the truck, attracted by the sweat and the urine running across the wooden boards. Jim waited for the driver to return with his map, but he sat on a bale of telephone wire, talking to two soldiers who cooked the midday meal. Their voices and the clicks of the burning wood carried across the steel tracks, magnified by the dome of light that enclosed them.

Jim fidgeted in his seat as the sun pricked his skin. He could see the smallest detail of everything around him, the flakes of rust on the railway lines, the saw-teeth of the nettles beside the truck, the white soil bearing the imprint of its worn tyres. Jim counted the blue bristles around the lips of the Japanese soldier guarding them, and the globes of mucus which this bored sentry sucked in and out of his nostrils. He watched the damp stain spreading around the buttocks of one of the missionary women on the floor, and the flames that fingered the cooking pot on the station platform, reflected in the polished breeches of the stacked rifles.

Only once before had Jim seen the world as vividly as this. Were the American planes about to come again? With an exaggerated squint, intended to annoy Dr Ransome, he searched the sky. He wanted to see everything, every cobblestone in the streets of Chapei, the overgrown gardens in Amherst Avenue, his mother and father, together in the silver light of the American aircraft.

Without thinking, Jim stood up and shouted. But the Japanese guard pushed him roughly against the bench. The soldiers on the railway platform sat amid the clutter of signals equipment, cramming their mouths with rice and fish. The corporal called to the truck, and the guard stepped over the missionary women and jumped from the tail-gate. He rested his rifle on the railway line and moved with his bayonet through the dried stubble of the wild sugar-cane. As soon as he had gathered sufficient kindling for the fire he joined the soldiers on the platform.

For an hour the smoke rose into the sunlight. Jim sat on the bench and brushed the flies from his face, eager to explore the railway station and the crashed aircraft near the canal. Whenever anyone moved, the Japanese shouted from the platform and pointed their cigarettes in a warning way. The prisoners had taken no rations or water with them, but there were two jerry-cans in the staff car from which the soldiers filled their canteens.

When Mrs Hug's father was forced to lie on the floor Dr Ransome protested to the Japanese. He stood unsteadily by the tail-gate, ignoring their abuse and pointing to the exhausted passengers at his feet. The bruise on his cheek had been inflamed by the sun and the flies, and had almost closed his eye. Standing there stoically, he reminded Jim of the beggars parading their wounds on the streets of Shanghai. The Japanese corporal was unimpressed, but after a leisurely stroll around the truck he allowed the prisoners to dismount. Helped by the husbands, Basie and Dr Ransome eased the old women on to the ground, where they lay in the shade between the rear wheels.

Jim squatted on the white earth, tracing the tyre patterns with a stick. How many times would each tyre have to rotate before it wore itself through to the canvas? The problem, one of a host that perpetually bothered him, was in fact fairly easy to solve. Jim smoothed the white dust and made a start at the arithmetic. He gave a cheer when the first fraction cancelled itself, and then noticed that he was alone in the open sunlight between the truck and the railway embankment.

Tended by a weary Dr Ransome, the prisoners huddled in the scanty shade below the tail-gate. Basie sat slumped inside his seaman's jacket, and he and the old men looked as dead as the discarded mannequins Jim had often seen in the alley behind the Sincere Company's department store.

They needed water, or one of them would die and they would all have to return to Shanghai. Jim watched the Japanese on the platform. The meal had ended, and two of the soldiers uncoiled a bale of telephone wire. Kicking a stone in front of him, Jim wandered towards the railway embankment. He stepped across the rails, and without a pause climbed on to the concrete platform.

Still savouring their meal, the Japanese sat around the cinders of their fire. They watched Jim as he bowed and stood to attention in his ragged clothes. None of them waved him away, but Jim knew that this was not the time to treat them to his brightest smile. He realized that Dr Ransome could not approach the Japanese so soon after their meal without being knocked down or even killed.

He waited as the driver spoke to the signals corporal. Pointing repeatedly to Jim, he delivered what seemed to be a long lecture on the enormous nuisance to the Japanese Army caused by this one small boy. The corporal laughed at this, in a good humour after his fish. He took a Coca Cola bottle from his knapsack and half-filled it with water from his canteen. Holding it in the air, he beckoned Jim towards him.

Jim took the bottle, bowed steeply and stepped back three paces. Masking their smiles, the Japanese watched him silently. Beside the truck, Basie and Dr Ransome leaned from the shadows, their eyes fixed on the sun-bright fluid in the bottle. Clearly they assumed that he would carry the water to them and share out this unexpected ration.

Carefully, Jim wiped the bottle on the sleeve of his blazer. He lifted it to his lips, drank slowly, trying not to choke, paused and finished the last drops.

The Japanese burst into laughter, chortling to each other with great amusement. Jim laughed with them, well aware that only he, among the British prisoners, appreciated the joke. Basie ventured a wary smile, but Dr Ransome seemed baffled. The corporal took the Coca Cola bottle from Jim and filled it to the neck. Still chuckling to themselves, the soldiers climbed to their feet and returned to the task of stringing the telephone wire.

Followed by the driver and the armed guard, Jim carried the bottle across the tracks. He handed it to Dr Ransome, who stared at him without comment. He drank briefly, and passed the tepid liquid to the others, helping the driver to refill the bottle from the canteen. One of the missionary women was sick, and vomited the water into the dust at his feet.

Jim took up his position behind the driving cabin. He knew that he had been right to drink the first water himself. The others, including Basie and Dr Ransome, had been thirsty, but only he had been prepared to risk everything for the few drops of water. The Japanese might have thrown him on to the track and broken his legs across the railway lines, as they did to the Chinese soldiers whom they killed at Siccawei Station. Already Jim felt himself apart from the others, who had behaved as passively as the Chinese peasants. Jim realized that he was closer to the Japanese, who had seized Shanghai and sunk the American fleet at Pearl Harbor. He listened to the sound of a transport plane hidden beyond the haze of white dust, and thought again of carrier decks out on the Pacific, of small men in baggy flying suits standing by their unarmoured aircraft, ready to chance everything on little more than their own will.

A Landscape of Airfields

As the driver filled the truck's radiator with water, Dr Ransome settled Mrs Hug on the seat beside the English boys. To Jim it seemed that the two missionary women on the floor were now barely alive, with blanched lips and eyes like those of poisoned mice. Flies swarmed over their faces, darting in and out of their nostrils. After lifting them into the truck, Dr Ransome was too exhausted to help them, and rested his arms on his heavy knees. Their husbands sat side by side and stared at them in a resigned way, as if a taste for lying on the floor was a minor eccentricity shared by their wives.

Jim leaned against the roof of the driving cabin. Aware of the gap that now separated Jim from his fellow prisoners, Dr Ransome moved forward and sat on the bench next to him. The dusty sunlight and the long journey from Shanghai had leached the pigment from his freckles. Despite his strong chest and legs he was far more tired than Jim had realized. Blood had broken through the inflamed bruise on his face, and the first pus gathered around his eye.

He bowed and made way for the Japanese soldier who stationed himself next to Jim.

'Well, we all feel better for the water. That was brave of you, Jim. Where do you come from?'

'Shanghai!'

'You're proud of it?'

'Of course . . .' Jim scoffed at the question, shaking his head as if Dr Ransome was a provincial country healer. 'Shanghai is the biggest city in the world. My father says it's even larger than London.'

'Let's hope it can stay larger – there may be one or two hungry winters. Where are your parents, Jim?'

'They went away.' Jim thought about his answer, deciding whether to invent some spoof for Dr Ransome. There was a self-confident air about this young physician that he distrusted, the same attitude shown by people newly arrived from England – Jim wondered how the British newsreels were explaining away the surrender of Singapore. He could easily imagine Dr Ransome getting into a brawl with the Japanese guards, and causing everyone trouble. Yet for all his display of public spirit, Dr Ransome had drunk more than his fair share of the water. Jim had also noticed that Dr Ransome was less interested in the dying old people than he pretended. 'They're at Woosung Camp,' he said. 'They are alive, you know.'

'I'm very glad. Woosung Camp? So you might be seeing them soon?'

'Very soon . . .' Jim gazed across the silent paddy fields. The thought of seeing his mother made him smile, an act which strained the muscles of his face. She would have no idea of all his adventures during the past four months. Even if he told her everything it would seem like one of those secret afternoons before the war when he had cycled all over Shanghai and come back with hair-raising stories he could never tell. 'Yes, I'll be seeing them soon. I want them to meet Basie.'

Basie's sallow face withdrew behind the collar of his jacket. He peered warily at the Japanese beside the railway tracks, as if suspicious of what was in store for them in these naked fields. 'I'll meet your folks, Jim.' To Dr Ransome he added, without any enthusiasm: 'I've been keeping an eye on the boy.'

'You kept an eye on me. Basie tried to sell me in Shanghai.'

'Did he? That sounds like a good idea.'

'To the Hongkew merchants. But I wasn't worth anything. He looked after me as well.'

'He's done a good job.' Dr Ransome patted Jim's shoulder. He slipped a hand around Jim's waist and felt his swollen liver, then raised his upper lip and glanced at his teeth.

'It's all right, Jim. I was trying to guess what you've been eating. We'll all have to take up gardening at Woosung. Perhaps the Japanese will sell us a goat.'

'A goat?' Jim had never seen a goat, an exotic beast of great moodiness and independence, qualities he admired.

'Are you interested in animals, Jim?'

'Yes . . . not much. What I'm really interested in is aviation.'

'Aviation? Aeroplanes, you mean?'

'Not exactly.' Casually, Jim added: 'I sat in the cockpit of a Japanese fighter.'

'You admire Japanese pilots?'

'They're brave . . .'

'And that's important?'

'It's a good idea if you want to win a war.' Jim listened to the drone of a distant aircraft. He was suspicious of the physician, of his long legs and his English manner and his interest in teeth. Perhaps he and Basie would team up as corpse-robbers? Jim thought about the goat which Dr Ransome wanted to buy from the Japanese. Everything he had read about goats confirmed that they were difficult and wayward creatures, and this suggested that there was something impractical about Dr Ransome. Few Europeans had gold teeth, and the only dead people the doctor was likely to see for a long time would be Europeans.

Jim decided to ignore Dr Ransome. He stood next to the Japanese guard, his hands warmed by the camouflaged roof of the driving cabin. As they set off towards the highway the soldiers were walking along the railway tracks, unwinding lengths of telephone wire. Were they about to launch a man-carrying kite? The furthest soldier was already lost in the haze of white dust, and his blurred figure seemed to rise from the ground. Jim laughed to himself, thinking that the soldier might suddenly soar into the sky over their heads. Helped by his father, Jim had flown dozens of kites from the garden at Amherst Avenue. He was fascinated by the dragon kites that floated behind the Chinese wedding and funeral parties, and by the fighting kites flown from the quays at Pootung, diving across each other with razor-sharp lines coated in powdered glass. But best of all were the man-flying kites which his father had seen in northern China, with a dozen lines held by hundreds of men. One day Jim would fly in a man-flying kite, and stand on the shoulder of the wind . . .

The air rushed into his watering eyes as the truck sped along the open road. Confident of his bearings, the driver was eager to deliver his prisoners to Woosung and return to Shanghai before nightfall. Jim held tight to the cabin roof, while the prisoners huddled on the seats behind him. The two missionary husbands were already sitting on the floor, and Dr Ransome helped Mrs Hug to lie under the bench.

But Jim had lost interest in them. They were now entering an area of military airfields. These former Chinese bases, which once guarded the Yangtze estuary, were being occupied by the Japanese Army and Navy Air Forces. They passed a bomb-damaged fighter base where Japanese engineers were welding a new roof on to the steel shell of a hangar. A line of Zero pursuit planes stood on the grass field, and a pilot in full flying gear strode between the wings. Without thinking, Jim waved to him, but the pilot was lost among the propellers.

Two miles ahead, beyond an empty village and its burnt-out pagoda, they were delayed by a convoy of trucks carrying the wings and fuselages of two-engined bombers. A squadron of the machines faced the afternoon sun, ready to take off and attack the Chinese armies to the west. All this activity excited Jim. When they stopped at the military checkpoint on the Soochow Road he was impatient to move on. He sat next to Basie, kicking his heels as a sergeant in the kempetai checked the list of prisoners and Dr Ransome protested about the condition of the missionary women.

Soon after, they left the highway and joined an unpaved secondary road that ran beside an industrial canal. Japanese tanks moved past, lashed to the decks of motorized lighters, while their gun crews slept on the canvas hatches. Usually Jim's imagination would have feasted on these battle vehicles, but by now he was only interested in aircraft. He wished he had flown with the Japanese pilots as they attacked Pearl Harbor and destroyed the US Pacific Fleet, or ridden in the torpedo bombers that had sunk the *Repulse* and the *Prince of Wales*. Perhaps, when the war ended, he would join the Japanese Air Force and wear the Rising Sun stitched to his shoulders, like the American pilots who had flown with the Flying Tigers and worn the flag of Nationalist China on their leather jackets.

Although his legs were exhausted, Jim was still standing behind the driver's cabin as they sped towards the gates of the internment camp at Woosung. In his mind, he had identified the Japanese aircraft of the Yangtze plain with his confidence that he would soon see his parents again. A single-engined fighter overtook them and climbed into the late afternoon sky, lifted by the golden glaze on the undersurface of its wings. Jim raised his arms and let the sun fall on the camouflage paint that stained his hands and wrists, imagining that he too was an aircraft. Behind him the Dutch woman had collapsed on the floor of the truck. She lay at the feet of her elderly father as Dr Ransome and the Japanese soldier tried to lift her on to the seat.

They crossed a wooden bridge over the arm of an artificial lake, and passed the burnt-out shell of the country club whose mock-Tudor timbers of painted cement had alone failed to catch fire. The hull of a pleasure launch lay in the shallows, its decks penetrated by reeds that advanced up the beach to the embers of the hotel.

Ahead of them a military truck was turning through the gates of a disused stockyard, through which an even greater fire had recently swept. Bored Japanese soldiers lounged outside the guardhouse, and watched a gang of Chinese labourers nailing lengths of barbed wire to a line of pine posts. Behind the guardhouse was the building contractor's store, surrounded by piles of planks and fencing timber, and a bamboo shelter where a second group of coolies dozed on their mats beside a charcoal brazier.

The truck stopped by the guardhouse, where the driver and his prisoners together gazed at this desolate site. The former stockyard was being converted into a civilian camp, but no prisoners would be interned here for months. Jim sat between Basie and Dr Ransome, annoyed with himself for assuming that his mother and father would be at the first camp they visited.

A prolonged argument began between the Japanese driver and the sergeant in charge of the camp's construction. It was clear that the sergeant had already decided that this truck and its consignment of Allied prisoners did not exist. He ignored the driver's protests and waved his cigarette in a thoughtful manner as he paced across the wooden porch of the guardhouse. At last he pointed to a patch of nettle-covered ground inside the gates, which he had apparently deemed to be a no man's land between the camp and the outside world.

Dr Ransome peered at the acres of fire-gutted stalls, a burnt-out maze through which cattle had once been steered. 'This can't be the camp. Unless they want us to build it.'

Basie's pale ears emerged from his seaman's collar. He was barely strong enough to sit upright, but could still catch the faintest scent of an opportunity. 'Woosung? There might be advantages, doctor . . . being the first people here . . .'

Dr Ransome began to help Mrs Hug from the floor, but the Japanese soldier raised the stock of his rifle and waved him back to his seat. The sergeant stood in the nettles, gazing over the tail-gate at the exhausted prisoners. The old women lay in the pools of urine at their husbands' feet. The English brothers huddled against Basie while Mrs Hug leaned on her father's knees.

Deliberately, Jim thought of his mother, and of the happy hours he had spent playing bridge in her bedroom. When the tears ran into his nose he sucked them into his parched throat. Could Dr Ransome teach himself how to cry? He looked at the glowing end of the sergeant's cigarette, and at the warm hearth of the charcoal stove in the twilight. The gang of labourers by the barbed-wire fence were walking back to their bamboo shelter.

'You're tiring everyone, Jim,' Dr Ransome warned him. 'Sit still or I'll ask Basie to sell you to the Japanese.'

'They wouldn't want me.' Jim slipped from the doctor's grasp. He knelt on the bench beside the driver's cabin. Rocking to and fro, he watched the sergeant lead the two Japanese to the guardhouse, where the soldiers were eating their evening meal. There were bottles of beer and rice wine on the wooden table, lit by a kerosene lamp. A Chinese coolie squatted by the brazier, fanning the charcoal to a white blaze, and the smell of warm fat drifted across the air.

Somehow Jim had to catch the eyes of the soldiers in the guardhouse. He knew that far from being concerned for their unwanted prisoners, the Japanese would leave them there all night. In the morning they would be too ill to move on to the next camp and would have to return to the detention centre in Shanghai.

143

The evening air settled over the burnt-out stockyards. The Chinese coolies finished their meal and sat under the bamboo shelter, drinking rice wine and playing cards. The Japanese drank beer in the guardhouse. Hundreds of stars were coming out over the Yangtze, and with them the navigation lights of the military aircraft. Two miles to the north, beyond the lines of burial mounds, Jim saw the rigging lights of a Japanese freighter heading for the open sea, its white superstructure sailing like a castle across the ghostly fields.

A foul smell rose from one of the missionary women. Her husband sat beside her on the floor, leaning against Dr Ransome's legs. Eager to catch sight of the freighter, Jim lifted himself on to the roof of the driving cabin. Sitting there, he watched the freighter slip away into the night, and then turned to the stars over his head. Since the previous summer, he had been teaching himself the main constellations.

'Basie . . .' Jim felt giddy; the night sky was sliding towards him. Losing his balance, he rolled across the cabin roof, then sat up to see the driver and the Japanese soldier stride from the guardhouse. They carried wooden staves in their hands, and Jim assumed that they were coming to beat him for sitting on the cabin. Quickly he slipped on to the floor and lay beside the Dutch woman.

The driver unshackled the tail-gate. As it fell with a clatter he rattled his stave against the swinging chains. He shouted at the prisoners and waved them from the truck. Helped by Dr Ransome, Mrs Hug and the old men lowered themselves into the nettles. Joined by Basie and the English boys, they followed the soldier towards the timber yard. The two missionary women lay on the soiled floor. They were still alive, but the driver waved his stave at Dr Ransome and beckoned him away from them.

Jim stepped across the damp floor and jumped on to the

ground. He was about to run after Dr Ransome when the driver held his shoulder and pointed to the sergeant in the guardhouse porch. He stood in the kerosene light, a small sack like a weighted cosh in his hand.

Cautiously, Jim walked up to the sergeant, who threw the sack on to the ground at his feet. Jim knelt in the deep ruts left by the truck's tyres, and treated the sergeant to his keenest smile. Inside the sack were nine sweet potatoes.

For the next hour Jim moved busily around the yard. While the prisoners rested in the timber store he relit the charcoal stove. Under the bored eyes of the Chinese coolies he fanned the embers into a flame, then fed the blaze with shavings of waste timber. Dr Ransome and the English boys brought him a bucket of water from the butt behind the guardhouse. Although Mrs Hug had been drinking from the bucket, Jim decided to wait until the potato water had cooled. Dr Ransome tried to help him with the iron cong, but Jim pushed him aside. The Eurasian women at the detention centre had taught him that potatoes cooked most quickly in shallow water under the tightest lid.

Later, before he carried the boiled potatoes to the timber store, Jim kept the largest one for himself. He sat next to Dr Ransome on the pine planks, while the missionary husbands lay in the sawdust, unable to eat. Jim regretted that they had been given even the smallest potato. At the same time, he needed these old people to survive, if they were to move on to the next camp. The Dutch woman seemed well, even if she had given her potato to the English boys. But Basie was already scanning the timber store, making an inventory of its possibilities inside his head, and if they stayed at Woosung camp Jim would never find his mother and father.

'Here you are, Jim.' Dr Ransome handed Jim his potato. He had taken a small bite, but most of the sweet pith was intact. 'It's a good one, you'll enjoy it.'

'Say, thanks . . .' He swiftly devoured the second potato.

145

Dr Ransome's gesture puzzled him. The Japanese were kind to children, and the two American sailors had befriended him in a fashion, but Jim knew that the English were not really interested in children.

He brought the pail of warm potato water for Basie and himself, and offered the pithy liquid to the others. He knelt beside the old missionary men, clicking his teeth and hoping that the sight of the Cathedral School badge would strike some religious spark in their minds and revive them.

'They don't look very well,' he confided to Dr Ransome. 'But they'll probably eat their potatoes in the morning.'

'They probably will. Rest, Jim – you'll wear yourself out looking after everyone. We'll be on our way tomorrow.'

'Well . . . there might be a long way to go.' The second potato had comforted Jim, and for the first time he felt sorry for the infected wounds on Dr Ransome's face. Returning the favour, he confided: 'If you ever go to the funeral piers at Nantao, don't drink the water.'

Jim lay on the soft sawdust, with its soothing scent of pine. Through the open doors of the timber store he watched the navigation lights of the Japanese aircraft crossing the night. After a few minutes he was forced to admit that he could recognize none of the constellations. Like everything else since the war, the sky was in a state of change. For all their movement, the Japanese aircraft were its only fixed points, a second zodiac above the broken land.

18
Vagrants

'Right . . . right . . . no . . . I mean left!'

Jim leaned through the passenger window of the cabin and shouted to the driver as the truck laboured on to the wooden deck of the pontoon bridge. The Japanese field engineers had built this temporary crossing over the Soochow Creek in the weeks following the Pearl Harbor attack, but already the bridge was coming apart under the heavy traffic. As the truck moved towards the first steel pontoon the wet planking began to splay in its worn ropes.

Posted as look-out by the Japanese driver, Jim watched the front tyre forcing the planks into the water. He had always enjoyed the sight of water rising through grilles or climbing the steps of a jetty. The brown steam washed the dust from the worn tyre, and revealed the manufacturer's name embossed on its side – befitting Jim's quest for his parents, a British company, Dunlop. The truck tilted sideways, leaning on its weak springs. Somewhere behind him a body rolled across the floor of the truck, but Jim was fascinated by the water sluicing across the dented hubcap, streaming through the wheel like the jets of a secret fountain.

'Left . . . left . . . !' Jim shouted, but the soldier at the tail-gate was already bellowing in alarm. With a weary sigh, the Japanese driver pulled on the handbrake, ordered Jim from the cabin and stepped on to the river-washed planks.

Jim crawled through the rear window on to the deck of the truck. He crossed Dr Ransome's outstretched legs and knelt on the bench, ready to take a close interest in the mounting argument between the driver and the Japanese guard.

Two hundred yards downstream the unit of field engineers

147

was raising the central span of the old railway bridge. Jim was happy to watch them at work. Most of the morning he had felt lightheaded, and the steady flow of water through the pontoons soothed his eyes. He counted his pulse, wondering if he had caught beri beri or malaria or any other of the diseases that he had heard Dr Ransome discussing with Mrs Hug. He was curious to try out some new disease, but then remembered the detention centre and the American planes he had seen over Shanghai. The previous night, when they had camped next to a pig farm run by the Japanese gendarmerie, Jim suspected that even Dr Ransome had seen the planes.

Certainly Dr Ransome did not look too well. Since leaving Woosung the wound in his face had infected the whole of his jaw and nose. He now lay on the floor of the truck, his freckled legs ominously white in the bright sun. He was asleep, but seemed to be thinking very hard about something with one half of his head. He had last spoken to Jim before their evening meal, when he made sure that Jim received the prisoners' full ration from the Japanese guard. By an enormous effort of will he had told Jim to strip and had washed his clothes in the pigs' water trough, using a piece of scented soap he borrowed from Mrs Hug.

Basie sat on the floor beside him, the two English boys asleep with their heads in his lap. The cabin steward was still conscious but had withdrawn into himself, his soft face like the flesh of a fading fruit. Often he was sick, and the floor of the truck was covered with vomit and urine which he nagged at Jim to clear away.

Mrs Hug and her father also lay on the floor, rarely speaking to each other, and concentrating on every bump in the road. Fortunately the two missionary couples had stayed behind at Woosung. Their places were taken by a middle-aged Englishman and his prim wife from the British Consulate at Nanking. They sat next to the Japanese guard at the rear of the truck, their faces drained of expression by some tragedy that had overtaken them. Between them was a wicker suitcase filled with clothing, which the driver and the guard searched every evening, helping themselves to the shoes and slippers. The couple stared without ever speaking at the landscape of paddy fields and canals, and Jim assumed that they had lost interest in the war.

Twice a day, when the Japanese stopped to make themselves a wayside meal, the guard ordered Jim to pass an earthenware water jar around the prisoners. For the rest of the time he was left to himself, free to concentrate on the task of guiding this antiquated truck towards the internment camp that held his mother and father.

For days now they had been on the road, making an erratic circuit of the countryside ten miles to the north-west of Shanghai. Jim had lost count of the exact number of days, but at least they were moving forward, and luckily the Japanese were not in any way discouraged by the worsening condition of their prisoners.

On the first day, after setting out from Woosung, a three-hour drive through the open country took them to the former St Francis Xavier seminary on the Soochow Road, one of the first prison camps established by the Japanese in the weeks after Pearl Harbor. The seminary was already filled with military personnel. All afternoon they waited behind a queue of commandeered Shanghai Transit Company buses, which together carried several hundred Dutch and Belgian civilians. Jim peered keenly through the double wire fence. Gangs of British soldiers lounged by their huts, or sat out on the assembly ground in the polished pews taken from the seminary chapel, like the congregation of an open-air cathedral. But there were no male civilians, women or children. The Japanese guards were busy taking an endless series of roll-calls, and had no time for the new arrivals hoping to be admitted. Jim stood on the seat, waving over the wire so that everyone in the camp could see him.

However, the hundreds of bored soldiers were not interested in these civilians and their Shanghai buses. Jim was relieved when they were turned away. As they set off towards Soochow the driver allowed him to sit in the front cabin. In some way this restless English boy, who had so aggravated him, now offered a small measure of security. Jim was unable to read the map, printed in Japanese characters, or understand a word of the long monologues addressed to the insect-smeared windshield. But he knelt on the front seat, clicking his teeth and leaning out of the window to watch any passing aircraft. The entire Japanese air force seemed to be on its way to attack the Chinese armies in the west.

The flat countryside by the Shanghai-Soochow road had been a war ground, and the miles of rotting trenches and rust-stained blockhouses reminded Jim of encyclopaedia illustrations of Ypres and the Somme, an immense museum of battle that no one had visited for years. The debris of war, and the flights of bombers and fighter planes, revived him. He wanted to soar like a fighting kite over the winding parapets and land on one of the massive forts built out of thousands of sandbags among the burial mounds. It disappointed Jim that none of his fellow prisoners was interested in the war. It would have helped to keep up their spirits, a task which Jim was finding more and more difficult.

In many ways, Jim liked to imagine, he was the real leader of this troupe of travelling prisoners. At times, as he carried the heavy water jar and lit the stove in the evening, he knew that he was little more than their Number Two Coolie. But without Jim to gather the firewood and boil the sweet potatoes even Dr Ransome and Basie would have gone the way of the missionary women. He noticed that after leaving the gendarmerie station at the pig farm they all

150

allowed themselves to become ill. During the night the Japanese had been beating a Chinese thief; the man's voice screamed across the water-filled paddies, shaking the dark surface. The next day everyone lay on the floor of the truck, Basie with his lungs and Dr Ransome unable to see through his infected eye.

Jim felt feverish, but he watched the Japanese planes overhead. The sound of their engines cleared his mind. Whenever his spirits flagged or he felt sorry for himself he thought of the silver aircraft he had seen at the detention centre.

The truck was moving across the pontoon bridge, man-handled by a squad of Japanese field engineers. Unable to steady himself, Jim slipped from the bench. Dr Ransome reached out weakly to hold him.

'Hang on, Jim. Stay up front with the driver – make sure he keeps going . . .'

Dozens of flies festered on Dr Ransome's face, feeding on the wound around his eye. Beside him Basie lay with Paul and David, Mrs Hug and her father. Only the English couple with the wicker suitcase full of shoes sat beside the soldier at the rear of the truck.

Jim straightened his blazer as a Japanese corporal clim-bed over the tail-gate. An angry man with wet boots, he shouted commands to the soldiers pushing the truck across the bridge. When they reached the opposite bank the soldiers walked along the water's edge to their work on the railway bridge. The corporal began to abuse the driver, clearly disgusted by the condition of the prisoners. He drew his Mauser pistol and gestured to an anti-tank ditch on the bank they had left behind.

Jim was relieved when the corporal strode back to his bridge. However ill they were, he did not want them to rest in the tank ditch. It was an effort to sit on the bench, and he was tempted to lie on the floor next to Dr Ransome, so that he could stare straight at the sky. The landscape of paddy fields, creeks and deserted villages moved past, emerging from a white haze like the milled bones of all the dead of China. The dust cloaked the cabin and bonnet of the truck, camouflaging it for the realm it was about to enter. How long had they been on the road? The lines of burial mounds were trying to trick Jim's eyes, they moved in waves towards the lumbering vehicle, a sea of the dead. The open coffins lay empty, ready to catch the American pilots who would soon fall from the air. There were thousands of coffins, enough to take Dr Ransome and Basie, his mother and father and Vera, Number Two Coolie and himself . . .

The truck had stopped, the cabin striking Jim's head. A group of huts with tar-paper roofs stood beside the road, set back from a barbed-wire fence that separated them from the embankment of a canal. Idly, Jim gazed at this small internment camp built in the compound of a ceramics factory. A pair of metal lighters had capsized at their moorings, and miniature railcars still loaded with ceramic tiles stood in the yard beside the kilns. Two of the brick warehouses had been incorporated into the camp by the barbed-wire fence that divided the factory site. Men and women sunned themselves on the steps of the wooden huts, lines of washing fluttered between the windows, a cheerful spring semaphore.

Jim rested his chin on the side panel of the truck. Below him Dr Ransome was trying to sit up. The guard jumped from the tail-gate and walked towards the entrance, where a Shanghai University bus was surrounded by Japanese soldiers. The passengers stared through the dust-stained windows. There were two nuns in black wimples, several children of Jim's age, and some twenty British men and women. Already a crowd of prisoners had gathered at the wire. Hands in the pockets of their ragged shorts, they stared silently as a Japanese sergeant boarded the bus to inspect the prisoners.

Dr Ransome was kneeling at the rear of the truck, the wound on his face hidden behind his hand. Jim stared at an Englishwoman in a frayed cotton dress who stood by the fence, her hands clasping the wire. She looked at him with the same expression that he had seen on the face of the German mother in the Columbia Road.

The bus was moving into the camp through the open gates. The Japanese sergeant stood in the passenger door, pistol in hand, waving back the crowd of prisoners. From their sullen faces it was clear that they greeted these new arrivals with little enthusiasm, more mouths to be fed from their meagre rations. Jim sat up as the truck lumbered forward to the gates. Dr Ransome fell to the floor, and was helped on to a seat by the English couple with the wicker suitcase.

Jim smiled at the woman walking along the wire. When she stretched a hand to him he wondered if she were a friend of his mother. The camp was filled with families, and somewhere among the strolling couples might be his parents. He peered at the English faces, at the gangs of boys laughing behind the Japanese sentries. To his surprise he felt a moment of regret, of sadness that his quest for his mother and father would soon be over. As long as he searched for them he was prepared to be hungry and ill, but now that the search had ended he felt saddened by the memory of all he had been through, and of how much he had changed. He was closer now to the ruined battlefields and this fly-infested truck, to the nine sweet potatoes in the sack below the driver's seat, even in a sense to the detention centre, than he would ever be again to his house in Amherst Avenue.

The truck stopped by the gates. The Japanese sergeant peered over the tail-gate at the prisoners lying on the floor.

He pushed Dr Ransome back with his Mauser, but the injured physician lowered himself to the ground, where he knelt at the sergeant's feet, catching his breath. Already the crowd of internees had begun to disperse. Hands in their pockets, the men strolled back to the huts and sat with the women on the steps.

Flies swarmed over the truck and settled on the damp pools that covered the floor. They hovered around Jim's mouth, feeding at the sores on his gums. For ten minutes the Japanese soldiers argued with each other, while the driver waited with Dr Ransome. Two senior British prisoners stepped through the gates and joined the discussion.

'Woosung Camp?'

'No, no, no . . .'

'Who sent them? In this condition?'

Avoiding Dr Ransome, they approached the truck and stared at the prisoners through the cloud of flies. As Jim kicked his heels and whistled to himself they watched him without expression. The Japanese sentries opened the barbed-wire gates, but the British prisoners immediately closed them and began to shout at the Japanese sergeant. When Dr Ransome stepped forward to remonstrate with them the British waved him away.

'Get back, man . . .'

'We can't take you, doctor. There are children here.'

Dr Ransome climbed into the truck and sat on the floor beside Jim. The effort of standing had exhausted him, and he lay back with his hand over his wound as the flies fought between his fingers.

Mrs Hug and the English couple with the wicker suitcase had waited silently through the arguments. As the Japanese soldiers returned to the camp and locked the gates Mrs Hug said: 'They won't take us. The British camp leaders . . .'

Jim gazed at the prisoners wandering across the compound. Groups of boys played football in the brick yard of the ceramics works. Were his mother and father hiding among the kilns? Perhaps, like the British camp leaders, they wanted Jim to go away, frightened of the flies and the sickness that he had brought with him from Shanghai.

Jim helped Basie and Dr Ransome to drink, and then sat on the opposite bench. He turned his back on the camp, on the British prisoners and their children. All his hopes rested in the landscape around him, in its past and future wars. He felt a strange lightness in his head, not because his parents had rejected him, but because he expected them to do so, and no longer cared.

19
The Runway

In the hour before dusk they entered an area of abandoned battlefields nine miles to the south of Shanghai. The afternoon light rose into the air, as if returning to the sun a small part of the strength it had cast to the indifferent fields. The terrain of trenches and blockhouses seemed to have sprung fully armed from Jim's head. A tank sat like a wheeled shack at the junction of the Shanghai and Hangchow roads, the sun's spotlights shining through its open hatches. The trenches hunted among the burial mounds, a maze lost within itself.

Beyond the crossroads a wooden bridge spanned a canal. Its white piles, from which the rain had leached all trace of resin, were as soft as pumice. The driver folded his map, and fanned himself with the canvas wallet, reluctant to risk his wheels on the worn timbers. Mrs Hug and the English couple sat at the back of the truck, their shadows reaching across the white beds of the drained paddy fields. Jim brushed the flies from Dr Ransome's face and patted his head. He imagined that he was one of the shadows, a black carpet lying across the tired land. A mile to the south, between the burial mounds, he could see the tailplanes of a row of parked aircraft, feathers of bone against the darkening air. Jim studied the aircraft, recognizing the plump fuselages and radial engines. They were Brewster Buffaloes, a type of American fighter that had been no match for the Japanese.

Was it here, among the burial mounds, that the American aircraft waited before taking off into his mind? However, the Japanese driver had also seen the tailplanes. He threw down his cigarette and shouted to the guard, who had jumped from the truck and was testing the rotting planks of the bridge.

'Lunghua . . . Lunghua . . . !'

The engine started, and the driver turned east at the crossroads, setting course for this distant airfield.

'We're going to Lunghua Airfield, Dr Ransome,' Jim called between his knees. The physician lay on the floor beside Basie and the Dutch woman's father, watching Jim with his single eye. 'There are Brewster Buffaloes – the Americans must have won the war.'

Jim let the warm air rush into his face. They approached the military airfield, the largest grass aerodrome that he had seen near Shanghai. There were three metal hangars, and a wooden engineering workshop built in the former car-park of Lunghua Pagoda. Dozens of aircraft were drawn up on the tarmac beside the hangars, high-performance fighters of advanced design. The three Brewster Buffaloes, their American markings painted out, sat by the edge of the field. A team of engineers with a powerful crane lifted an anti-aircraft gun to the upper decks of the stone pagoda.

The driver stopped at a checkpoint, where Japanese soldiers manned a fortified emplacement. As the sentries paced about in the dusk their corporal spoke into a field telephone. They were waved through to the perimeter road. The rutted surface had been stiffened with straw matting, churned to a pith by a convoy of vehicles loaded with building stone. A truck swayed past them with a cargo of roofing tiles torn from the tenements of the Old City.

Pairs of armed guards patrolled the perimeter road, their bayonets cutting the sombre air. Two single-engined transport aircraft were parked on the edge of the field. Accompanied by his ground crew, a Japanese pilot spoke to two fellow officers in uniform. The pilot pointed to the truck as it rattled past, and it occurred to Jim that perhaps he and

157

Basie and Dr Ransome were about to be flown from Shanghai, and that he would soon join his parents in Hong Kong or Japan.

Jim waited for the truck to stop beside the planes, but the driver pressed on to the southern perimeter of the airfield. The smooth grass fell away into a broken terrain of wild sugar cane and unlevelled earth. They crossed the dried bed of an irrigation ditch, and followed the truck loaded with roofing tiles into a narrow valley hidden between walls of nettles. Clouds of ashy white dust rose into the evening air, as the military vehicles in front of them tipped their loads of stone and rubble on to the ground. Armed soldiers and air force police guarded the valley, rifles in hand, their uniforms blanched by the dust.

Watched by the Japanese sentries, hundreds of captured Chinese soldiers in ragged tunics were carrying the tiles and cobblestones from the tip and laying the bed of a concrete runway. Even in the dusk light, and despite all the privations of the past months, Jim could see the meagre condition of these Chinese prisoners. Many were emaciated to the point of death. They sat naked in the trampled nettles, a single roof tile held in their hands like the fragment of a begging bowl. Others climbed the shallow slope to the edge of the airfield, wicker baskets laden with stones clasped to their chests.

The truck stopped by the tip. With a rattle of chains, the tail-gate fell. Led by the Japanese soldier, Mrs Hug and the English couple lowered themselves to the ground. Dr Ransome knelt by the seats, barely able to control his clumsy body.

'Right, Jim – let's get everyone to their quarters. Help Mrs Hug. Basie, boys . . .'

He stood unsteadily, but managed to lift Basie to his feet. The cabin steward's face was already covered by a layer of talc, the delicate woman's skin that Jim had first seen near the funeral piers at Nantao. Holding Jim's shoulder, he shuffled along the damp floor of the truck.

They dismounted and stood together in the cloud of white dust beside the tip. Mrs Hug sat with her father on a heap of cobbles, holding the English boys by the hands. The Chinese soldiers filled their baskets and spat on the stones. As they climbed the broken earth to the runway their chalky figures seemed to illuminate the evening air.

Around them the Japanese sentries watched without moving. Fifty feet away, on the southern slope of the valley, two sergeants sat on bamboo chairs by the edge of a pit that had been freshly dug among the nettles. Their boots and the ground at their feet were covered with lime.

Jim picked up a grey ceramic tile. None of the Japanese guards appeared to care whether they worked on the runway, but Basie already held a cobblestone in his hands. Jim followed a naked Chinese soldier towards the runway. He climbed the slope and walked across the furrowed soil. The Chinese threw down their baskets and returned to the tip. Jim laid his tile on the shallow trench filled with stones and broken bricks that ran across the airfield into the night. Basie pushed past him and dropped the cobble at his feet. He swayed in the dust, trying to brush the chalky powder from his hands.

Behind them Dr Ransome stood at the tip with Mrs Hug and the English couple. He was arguing with a Japanese soldier, who waved him towards the runway. Holding his rifle in one hand, the soldier picked a roof tile from the tip and handed it to Dr Ransome.

Jim waited by the broken stones. He stared into the dusk along the white surface of the runway. He remembered the swirling grass at Hungjao Aerodrome, and tried to imagine the slipstreams of the Brewster Buffaloes. He turned to the transport aircraft parked by the perimeter road. The Japanese pilot and the uniformed officers were walking through the grass towards the runway. They stopped on the muddy verge, laughing to each other as they inspected the work. Their buckles and polished badges shone like the jewellery of the Europeans who had visited the battlefields near Hungjao before the war.

Jim stepped into the grass, leaving the dust clouds and the lines of Chinese soldiers. He wanted to see the parked aircraft for the last time, to stand under the dark span of their wings. He knew that the Chinese soldiers were being worked to death, that these starving men were laying their own bones in a carpet for the Japanese bombers who would land upon them. Then they would go to the pit, where the lime-booted sergeants waited with their Mausers. And after laying their stones, he and Basie and Dr Ransome would also go to the pit.

The last light had faded from the fuselages of the aircraft, but Jim could smell their engines on the night air. He inhaled the odour of oil and engine coolant. Already he had begun to shut out the voices around him, the white bodies of the Chinese soldiers and the runway of bones. He shut out the young Japanese pilot in his flying suit, who was pointing at him and shouting to the sergeants beside the pit. Jim hoped that his parents were safe and dead. Brushing the dust from his blazer, he ran towards the shelter of the aircraft, eager to enfold himself in their wings.

Part II

20
Lunghua Camp

Voices fretted along the murmuring wire, carried like stressed notes on the strings of a harp. Fifty feet from the perimeter fence, Jim lay in the deep grass beside the pheasant trap. He listened to the guards arguing with each other as they conducted their hourly patrol of the camp. Now that the American air attacks had become a daily event, the Japanese soldiers no longer slung their rifles over their shoulders. They clasped the long-barrelled weapons in both hands, and were so nervous that if they saw Jim outside the camp perimeter they would shoot at him without thinking.

Jim watched them through the netting of the pheasant trap. Only the previous day they had shot a Chinese coolie trying to steal into the camp. He recognized one of the guards as Private Kimura, a large-boned farmer's son who had grown almost as much as Jim in his years at the camp. The private's strong back had burst through his faded tunic, and only his ammunition webbing held the tattered garment together.

Before the war finally turned against the Japanese, Private Kimura often invited Jim to the bungalow he shared with three other guards and allowed him to wear his kendo armour. Jim could remember the elaborate ceremony as the Japanese soldiers dressed him in the metal and leather armour, and the ripe smell of Private Kimura's body that filled the helmet and shoulder guards. He remembered the burst of violence as Private Kimura attacked him with the two-handed sword, the whirlwind of blows that struck his helmet before he could fight back. His head had rung for days. Giving him his orders, Basie had been forced to shout until he woke the men's dormitory in E Block, and Dr Ransome had called Jim into the camp hospital and examined his ears.

Remembering those powerful arms, and the quickness of Private Kimura's eyes, Jim lay flat in the long grass behind the trap. For once he was glad that the trap had failed to net a bird. The two Japanese had stopped by the wire fence and were scanning the group of abandoned buildings that lay outside the north-west perimeter of Lunghua Camp. Beside them, just within the camp, was the derelict hulk of the assembly hall, the curved balcony of its upper circle open to the sky. The camp occupied the site of a teacher training college that had been bombed and overrun during the fighting around Lunghua Aerodrome in 1937. The damaged buildings nearest to the airfield had been excluded from the camp, and it was here, in the long grass quadrangles between the gutted residence halls, that Jim set his pheasant traps. After roll-call that morning he had slipped through the fence where it emerged from a bank of nettles surrounding a forgotten blockhouse on the airfield perimeter. Leaving his shoes on the blockhouse steps, he waded along a shallow canal, and then crawled through the deep grass between the ruined buildings.

The first of the traps was only a few feet from the perimeter fence, a distance that had seemed enormous to Jim when he first crept through the barbed wire. He had looked back at the secure world of the camp, at the barrack huts and water tower, at the guardhouse and dormitory blocks, almost afraid that he had been banished from them forever. Dr Ransome often called Jim a 'free spirit', as he roved across the camp, hunting down some new idea in his head. But here, in the deep grass between the ruined buildings, he felt weighed by an unfamiliar gravity.

For once making the most of this inertia, Jim lay behind the trap. An aircraft was taking off from Lunghua Airfield, clearly silhouetted against the yellow façades of the apartment houses in the French Concession, but he ignored the plane. The soldier beside Private Kimura shouted to the children playing in the balcony of the assembly hall. Kimura was walking back to the wire. He scanned the surface of the canal and the clumps of wild sugar cane. The poor rations of the past year – the Japanese guards were almost as badly fed as their British and American prisoners – had drawn the last of the adolescent fat from Kimura's arms. After a recent attack of tuberculosis his strong face was puffy and coolie-like. Dr Ransome had repeatedly warned Jim never to wear Private Kimura's kendo armour. A fight between them would be less one-sided now, even though Jim was only fourteen. But for the rifle, he would have liked to challenge Kimura . . .

As if aware of the threat within the grass, Private Kimura called to his companion. He leaned his rifle against the pine fencing-post, stepped through the wire and stood in the deep nettles. Flies rose from the shallow canal and settled on his lips, but Kimura ignored them and stared at the strip of water that separated him from Jim and the pheasant traps.

Could he see Jim's footprints in the soft mud? Jim crawled away from the trap but the clear outline of his body lay in the crushed grass. Kimura was rolling his tattered sleeves, ready to wrestle with his quarry. Jim watched him stride through the nettles. He was certain that he could outrun Kimura, but not the bullet in the second soldier's rifle. How could he explain to Kimura that the pheasant traps had been Basie's idea? It was Basie who had insisted on the elaborate camouflage of leaves and twigs, and who made him climb through the wire twice a day, even though they had never seen a bird, let alone caught one. It was important to keep in with Basie, who had small but reliable sources of food. He could tell Kimura that Basie knew about the secret camp radio, but then the extra food would cease.

165

What most worried Jim was the thought that, if Kimura struck him, he would fight back. Few boys of his own age dared to touch Jim, and in the last year, since the rations had failed, few men. However, if he fought back against Kimura he would be dead.

He calmed himself, calculating the best moment to stand up and surrender. He would bow to Kimura, show no emotion and hope that the hundreds of hours he had spent hanging around the guardhouse – albeit at Basie's instigation – would count in his favour. He had once given English lessons to Kimura, but although they were clearly losing the war the Japanese had not been interested in learning English.

Jim waited for Kimura to climb the bank towards him. The soldier stood in the centre of the canal, a bright black object gleaming in his hand. The creeks, ponds and disused wells within Lunghua Camp held an armoury of rusting weapons and unstable ammunition abandoned during the 1937 hostilities. Jim peered through the grass at the pointed cylinder, assuming that the tidal water in the canal had uncovered an old artillery shell or mortar bomb.

Kimura shouted to the second soldier waiting by the barbed wire. He brushed the flies from his face and spoke to the object, as if murmuring to a baby. He raised it behind his head, in the position taken by the Japanese soldiers throwing a grenade. Jim waited for the explosion, and then realized that Private Kimura was holding a large fresh-water turtle. The creature's head emerged from its carapace, and Kimura began to laugh excitedly. His tubercular face resembled a small boy's, reminding Jim that Private Kimura had once been a child, as he himself had been before the war.

After crossing the parade ground, the Japanese soldiers disappeared among the lines of ragged washing between the barrack huts. Jim emerged from the damp cavern of the blockhouse. Wearing the leather golfing shoes given to him by Dr Ransome, he climbed through the wire. In his hand he carried Kimura's turtle. The ancient creature contained at least a pound of meat, and Basie, almost certainly, would know a special recipe for turtle. Jim could imagine Basie tempting it out of its shell with a live caterpillar, then skewering its head with his jack-knife . . .

In front of Jim was Lunghua Camp, his home and universe for the past three years, and the suffocating prison of nearly two thousand Allied nationals. The shabby barrack huts, the cement dormitory blocks, the worn parade ground and the guardhouse with its leaning watch-tower lay together under the June sun, a rendezvous for every fly and mosquito in the Yangtze basin. But once he stepped through the wire fence Jim felt the air steady around him. He ran along the cinder path, his tattered shirt flying from his bony shoulders like the tags of washing between the huts.

In his ceaseless journeys around the camp Jim had learned to recognize every stone and weed. A sun-bleached sign, crudely painted with the words 'Regent Street', was nailed to a bamboo pole beside the pathway. Jim ignored it, as he did the similar signs enscribed 'Piccadilly', 'Knightsbridge' and 'Petticoat Lane' which marked the main pathways within the camp. These relics of an imaginary London – which many of the Shanghai-born British prisoners had never seen – intrigued Jim but in some way annoyed him. With their constant talk about pre-war London, the older British families in the camp claimed a special exclusiveness. He remembered a line from one of the poems that Dr Ransome had made him memorize – 'a foreign field that is for ever England . . .' But this was Lunghua, not England. Naming the sewage-stained paths between the rotting huts after a vaguely remembered London allowed too many of the British prisoners to shut out the reality of the camp, another excuse to sit back when they should have been helping Dr Ransome to clear the septic tanks. To their credit, in Jim's eyes, neither the Americans nor the Dutch and Belgians in the camp wasted their time on nostalgia. The years in Lunghua had not given Jim a high opinion of the British.

And yet the London street signs fascinated him, part of the magic of names that he had discovered in the camp. What, conceivably, were Lord's, the Serpentine, and the Trocadero? There were so few books or magazines that an unfamiliar brand-name had all the mystery of a message from the stars. According to Basie, who was always right, the American fighters with the ventral radiators that strafed Lunghua Airfield were called 'Mustangs', the name of a wild pony. Jim relished the name; to know that the planes were Mustangs was more important to him than the confirmation that Basie had his ear to the camp's secret radio. He hungered for names.

Jim stumbled on the worn path, unable to control the golf shoes. Too often these days he became light-headed. Dr Ransome had warned him not to run, but the American air attacks and the imminent prospect of the war's end made him too impatient to walk. Trying to protect the turtle, he grazed his left knee. He limped across the cinder track and sat on the steps of the derelict drinking-water station. Here brackish water taken from the ponds in the camp had once been boiled by the prisoners. There was still a small supply of coal in the camp store-rooms, but the work gang of six Britons who stoked the fires had lost interest. Although Dr Ransome remonstrated with them, they preferred to suffer from chronic dysentery rather than make the effort of boiling the water.

While Jim nursed his knee the members of the gang sat outside the nearby barrack hut, watching the sky as if they expected the war to end within the next ten minutes. Jim recognized Mr Mulvaney, an accountant with the Shanghai Power Company who had often swum in the pool at

Amherst Avenue. Beside him was the Reverend Pearce, a Methodist missionary whose Japanese-speaking wife openly collaborated with the guards, reporting to them each day on the prisoners' activites.

No one criticized Mrs Pearce for this, and in fact most of the prisoners in Lunghua were only too keen to collaborate. Jim vaguely disapproved, but agreed that it was probably sensible to do anything to survive. After three years in the camp the notion of patriotism meant nothing. The bravest prisoners – and collaboration was a risky matter – were those who bought their way into the favour of the Japanese and thereby helped their fellows with small supplies of food and bandages. Besides, there were few illicit activities to betray. No one in Lunghua would dream of trying to escape, and everyone rightly ratted on any fool about to step through the wire, for fear of the reprisals to come.

The water-workers scraped their clogs on the steps and stared into the sun, moving only to pick the ticks from between their ribs. Although emaciated, the process of starvation had somehow stopped a skin's depth from the skeleton below. Jim envied Mr Mulvaney and the Reverend Pearce – he himself was still growing. The arithmetic that Dr Ransome had taught him made it all too clear that the food supplied to the camp was shrinking at a faster rate than that at which the prisoners were dying.

In the centre of the parade ground a group of twelve-year-old boys were playing marbles on the baked earth. Seeing the turtle, they ran towards Jim. Each of them controlled a dragonfly tied to a length of cotton. The blue flames flicked to and fro above their heads.

'Jim! Can we touch it?'

'What is it?'

'Did Private Kimura give it to you?'

Jim smiled benignly. 'It's a bomb.' He held out the turtle and generously allowed everyone to inspect it. Despite the gap in years, several of the boys had been close friends in

169

the days after his arrival in Lunghua, when he had needed every ally he could find. But he had outgrown them and made other friends – Dr Ransome, Basie and the American seamen in E Block, with their ancient pre-war copies of the *Reader's Digest* and *Popular Mechanics* that he devoured. Now and then, as if recapturing his lost childhood, Jim re-entered the world of boyish games and would play tops and marbles and hopscotch.

'Is it dead? It's moving!'

'It's bleeding!'

A smear of blood from Jim's knee gave the turtle's head a piratical flourish.

'Jim, you killed it!'

The largest of the boys, Richard Pearce, reached out to touch the reptile, but Jim tucked it under his arm. He disliked and slightly feared Richard Pearce, who was almost as big as himself. He envied Richard the extra Japanese rations which his mother fed to him. As well as the food, the Pearces had a small library of confiscated books which they guarded jealously.

'It's a blood bond,' Jim explained grandly. By rights turtles belonged to the sea, to the open river visible a mile to the west of the camp, that broad tributary of the Yangtze down which he had once dreamed of sailing with his parents to the safety of a world without war.

'Watch out . . .' He waved Richard aside. 'I've trained it to attack!'

The boys backed away from him. There were times when Jim's humour made them uneasy. Although he tried to stop himself, Jim resented their clothes – hand-me-downs stitched together by their mothers, but far superior to his own rags. More than this, he resented that they had mothers and fathers at all. During the past year Jim had gradually realized that he could no longer remember what his parents looked like. Their veiled figures still entered his dreams, but he had forgotten their faces.

21
The Cubicle

'Young Jim . . . !'

An almost naked man wearing clogs and ragged shorts shouted to him from the steps of G Block. In his hands he held the shafts of a wooden cart with iron wheels. Although the cart carried no load, its handles had almost wrenched the man's arms from their sockets. He spoke to the English women sitting on the concrete steps in their faded cotton frocks. As he gestured to them his shoulder blades seemed to be working themselves loose from his back, about to fly across the barbed wire.

'I'm here, Mr Maxted!' Jim pushed Richard Pearce aside and ran along the cinder path to the dormitory block. Seeing the empty food cart, it occurred to him that he might have missed the daily meal. The fear of being without food for even a single day was so intense that he was ready to attack Mr Maxted.

'Come on, Jim. Without you it won't taste the same.' Mr Maxted glanced at Jim's golf shoes, these nailed brogues that had a life of their own and propelled his scarecrow figure on his ceaseless rounds of the camp. To the women he remarked: 'Our Jim's spending all his time at the 19th hole.'

'I promised, Mr Maxted. I'm always ready . . .' Jim had to stop as he reached the entrance to G Block. He worked his lungs until the dizziness left his head, and ran forward again. Turtle in hand, he raced up the steps into the foyer and swerved between two old men stranded like ghosts in the middle of a conversation they had forgotten.

On either side of the corridor was a series of small rooms, each furnished with four wooden bunks. After the first winter in the camp, when many of the children in the uninsulated barracks had died, families with children were moved into the residence halls of the former training college. Although unheated, the rooms with their cement walls remained above freezing point.

Jim shared his room with a young English couple, Mr and Mrs Vincent, and their six-year-old son. He had lived within inches of the Vincents for two and a half years, but their existences could not have been more separate. On the day of Jim's arrival Mrs Vincent had hung an old bedspread around his nominal quarter of the room. She and her husband – a broker on the Shanghai Stock Exchange – never ceased to resent Jim's presence, and over the years they had strengthened his cubicle, stringing together a worn shawl, a petticoat and the lid of a cardboard box, so that it resembled one of the miniature shanties that seemed to erect themselves spontaneously around the beggars of Shanghai.

Not content with walling Jim into his small world, the Vincents had repeatedly tried to encroach upon it, moving the nails and string from which the bedspread hung. Jim had defended himself, first by bending the nails until, to the Vincents' horror, the entire structure collapsed one night as they were undressing, and then by calibrating the wall with a ruler and pencil. The Vincents promptly retaliated by superimposing their own system of marks.

All this Jim took in his stride. For some reason he still liked Mrs Vincent, a handsome if frayed blonde, although her nerves were always stretched and she had never made the slightest attempt to care for him. He knew that if he starved to death in his bunk she would find some polite reason for doing nothing to help him. During the first year in Lunghua the few single children were neglected, unless they were prepared to let themselves be used as servants. Jim alone had refused, and had never fetched and carried for Mr Vincent.

Mrs Vincent was sitting on her straw mattress when he

burst into the room, her pale hands folded on her lap like a forgotten pair of gloves. She stared at the whitewashed wall above her son's bunk, as if watching an invisible film projected on to a screen. Jim worried that Mrs Vincent spent too much of her time watching these films. As he peered at her through the cracks in his cubicle he tried to guess what she saw – a home-made cine film, perhaps, of herself in England before she was married, sitting on one of those sunlit lawns that seemed to cover the entire country. Jim assumed that it was those lawns that had provided the emergency airfields for the Battle of Britain. As he was aware from his observations in Shanghai, the Germans were not too keen on sunlit lawns. Was this why they had lost the Battle of Britain? Many of his ideas were hopelessly confused in a way that even Dr Ransome was too tired to disentangle.

'You're late, Jim,' Mrs Vincent told him disapprovingly, her eyes on his golf shoes. Like everyone else, she was unable to cope with their intimidating presence. Already Jim felt that the shoes gave him a special authority. 'The whole of G Block has been waiting for you.'

'I've been with Basie, hearing the latest war news. Mrs Vincent, what's the 19th hole?'

'You shouldn't work for Basie. The things those Americans ask you to do . . . I've told you that we come first.'

'G Block comes first, Mrs Vincent.' Jim meant it. He ducked under the flap into his cubicle. Catching his breath, he lay on the bunk with the turtle inside his shirt. The reptile preferred its own company, and Jim turned his attention to his new shoes. With their polished toecaps and bright studs, they were an intact piece of the pre-war world that he could stare at for hours, like Mrs Vincent and her films. Laughing to himself, Jim lay back as the hot sunlight shone through the wall of the cubicle, outlining the curious stains on the old bedspread. Looking at them, he visualized the scenes of air-battles and armadas, the sinking of the *Petrel*, and even the garden at Amherst Avenue.

'Jim, kitchen time . . . !' he heard someone call from the steps below the window. But Jim rested on his bunk. It was a long haul to the kitchens, and there was no point in being early. The Japanese had celebrated VE Day in their own way, by cutting the already meagre rations in half. The first arrivals often received less than the later ones, when the cooks realized how many of the prisoners had died or were too ill to collect their rations.

Besides, there was no obligation on Jim to help with the food cart – nor, for that matter, on Mr Maxted. But as Jim had noticed, those who were prepared to help their fellow prisoners tended to do so, and this did nothing to stop those too lazy to work from endlessly complaining. The British were especially good at complaining, something the Dutch and Americans never did. Soon, Jim reflected with a certain grim pleasure, they would be too sick even to complain.

He gazed at his shoes, consciously imitating the childlike smile on Private Kimura's lips. The wooden bunk filled the cubicle, but Jim was at his happiest in this miniature universe. On the walls he had pinned several pages from an old *Life* magazine that Basie had given to him. There were photographs of Battle of Britain pilots sitting in armchairs beside their Spitfires, of a crashed Heinkel bomber, of St Paul's floating like a battleship on a sea of fire. Next to them was a full-page colour advertisement for a Packard motor-car, as beautiful in Jim's eyes as the Mustang fighters which strafed Lunghua Airfield. Did the Americans bring out a new-model Mustang every year or every month? Perhaps there would be an air raid that afternoon, when he could check the latest design modifications to the Mustangs and Superfortresses. Jim looked forward to the air raids.

Beside the Packard was a small section that Jim had cut from a larger photograph of a crowd outside the gates of

Buckingham Palace in 1940. The blurred images of a man and a woman standing arm-in-arm reminded Jim of his parents. This unknown English couple, perhaps dead in an air raid, had almost become his mother and father. Jim knew that they were complete strangers, but he kept the pretence alive, so that in turn he could keep alive the lost memory of his parents. The world before the war, his childhood in Amherst Avenue, his class at the Cathedral School, belonged to that invisible film which Mrs Vincent watched from her bunk.

Jim allowed the turtle to crawl across his straw mat. If he carried it around with him Private Kimura or one of the guards might guess that he had left the camp. Now that the war was ending the Japanese guards were convinced that the British and American prisoners were constantly trying to escape – the last notion, in fact, to cross their minds. In 1943 a few Britishers had escaped, hoping to be sheltered by neutral friends in Shanghai, but had soon been discovered by the army of informers. Several groups of Americans had set out in the summer of 1944 for Chungking, the Nationalist Chinese capital nine hundred miles to the west. All had been betrayed by Chinese villagers terrified of reprisals, handed over to the Japanese and executed. From then on escape attempts ceased altogether. By June 1945, the landscape around Lunghua was so hostile, roamed by bandits, starving villagers and deserters from the puppet armies, that the camp and its Japanese guards offered the only security.

With his finger Jim stroked the turtle's ancient head. It seemed a pity to cook it – Jim envied the reptile its massive shell, a private fortress against the world. From below his bunk he pulled out a wooden box, which Dr Ransome had helped him to nail together. Inside were his possessions – a Japanese cap badge given to him by Private Kimura; three steel-bossed fighting tops; a chess set and a copy of Ken-

175

nedy's *Latin Primer* on indefinite loan from Dr Ransome; his Cathedral School blazer, a carefully folded memory of his younger self; and the pair of clogs he had worn for the past three years.

Jim placed the turtle in the box and covered it with the blazer. As he raised the flap of his cubicle Mrs Vincent watched his every move. She treated him like her Number Two Coolie, and he was well aware that he tolerated this for reasons he barely understood. Like all the men and older boys in G Block, Jim was attracted to Mrs Vincent, but her real appeal for Jim lay elsewhere. Her long hours staring at the whitewash, and her detachment even from her own son – she fed the dysentery-ridden boy and changed his clothes without looking at him for minutes at a time – suggested to Jim that she remained forever above the camp, beyond the world of guards and hunger and American air attacks to which he himself was passionately committed. He wanted to touch her, less out of adolescent lust than simple curiosity.

'You can use my bunk, Mrs Vincent, if you want to sleep.'

As Jim reached to her shoulder she pushed his hand away. Her distracted eyes could come to a remarkably sharp focus.

'Mr Maxted is still waiting, Jim. Perhaps it's time you went back to the huts . . .'

'Not the huts, Mrs Vincent,' he pretended to groan. Not the huts, he repeated fiercely to himself as he left the room. The huts were cold, and if the war lasted beyond the winter of 1945 many more people would die in those freezing barracks. However, for Mrs Vincent perhaps he would go back to the huts . . .

176

22

The University of Life

All over the camp there sounded the scraping of iron wheels. In the windows of the barrack huts, on the steps of the dormitory blocks, the prisoners were sitting up, roused for a few minutes by the memory of food.

Jim left the foyer of G Block, and found Mr Maxted still holding the wooden handles of the food cart. Having made the effort twenty minutes earlier to lift the handles, he had exhausted his powers of decision. The former architect and entrepreneur, who had represented so much that Jim most admired about Shanghai, had been sadly drained by his years in Lunghua. After arriving at the camp Jim had been glad to find him there, but by now he realized how much Mr Maxted had changed. His eyes forever watched the cigarette butts thrown down by the Japanese guards, but only Jim was quick enough to retrieve them. Jim chafed at this, but he supported Mr Maxted out of nostalgia for his childhood dream of growing up one day to be like him.

The Studebaker and the afternoon girls in the gambling casinos had prepared Mr Maxted poorly for the world of the camp. As Jim took the wooden handles he wondered how long the architect would have stood on the sewage-stained path. Perhaps all day, watched until he dropped by the same group of British prisoners who sat on the steps without once offering to help. Half-naked in their ragged clothes, they stared at the parade ground, uninterested even in a Japanese fighter that flew overhead. Several of the married couples held their mess-plates, already forming a queue, a reflex response to Jim's arrival.

'At last . . .'

'. . . that boy . . .'

'. . . running wild.'

These mutters drew an amiable smile from Mr Maxted. 'Jim, you're going to be blackballed by the country club. Never mind.'

'I don't mind.' When Mr Maxted stumbled Jim held his arm. 'Are you all right, Mr Maxted?'

Jim waved to the men sitting on the step, but no one moved. Mr Maxted steadied himself. 'Let's go, Jim. Some work and some watch, and that's all there is to it.'

For the past year there had been a third member of the team, Mr Carey, the owner of the Buick agency in Nanking Road. But six weeks earlier he had died of malaria, and by then the Japanese had cut the food ration to a point where only two of them were needed to push the cart.

Propelled by his new shoes, Jim sped along the cinder path. The iron wheels struck sparks from the flinty stones. Mr Maxted held his shoulder, panting to keep up.

'Slow down, Jim. You'll get there before the war ends.'

'When will the war end, Mr Maxted?'

'Jim . . . is it going to end? Another year, 1946. You tell me, you listen to Basie's radio.'

'I haven't heard the radio, Mr Maxted,' Jim answered truthfully. Basie was far too canny to admit a Britisher into the secret circle of listeners. 'I know the Japanese surrendered at Okinawa. I hope the war ends soon.'

'Not too soon, Jim. Our problems might begin then. Are you still giving English lessons to Private Kimura?'

'He isn't interested in learning English,' Jim had to admit. 'I think the war's really ended for Private Kimura.'

'Will the war really end for you, Jim? You'll see your mother and father again.'

'Well . . .' Jim preferred not to talk about his parents, even with Mr Maxted. The two of them had formed a long-standing partnership, though Mr Maxted did little to help

Jim and rarely referred to his son Patrick or to their visits to the Shanghai clubs and bars. Mr Maxted was no longer the dapper figure who fell into swimming-pools. What worried Jim was that his mother and father might also have changed. Soon after arriving in Lunghua he heard that his parents were interned in a camp near Soochow, but the Japanese refused to consider the notion of a transfer.

They crossed the parade ground and approached the camp kitchens behind the guardhouse. Some twenty food carts and their teams were drawn up beside the serving hatch, jostling together like a crowd of rickshaws and their coolies. As Jim had estimated, he and Mr Maxted would take their place halfway down the queue. Late-comers clattered along the cinder paths, watched by hundreds of emaciated prisoners. One day during the previous week there had been no food, as a reprisal for a Superfortress raid that had devastated Tokyo, and the prisoners had continued to stare at the kitchens until late afternoon. The silence had unsettled Jim, reminding him of the beggars outside the houses in Amherst Avenue. Without thinking, he had removed his shoes and hidden them among the graves in the hospital cemetery.

Jim and Mr Maxted took their places in the queue. Outside the guardhouse a work party of British and Belgian prisoners were strengthening the fence. Two of the prisoners unwound a coil of barbed wire, which the others cut and nailed to the fencing posts. Several of the Japanese soldiers were working shoulder to shoulder with their prisoners, ragged uniforms barely distinguishable from the faded khaki of the inmates.

The object of this activity was a group of thirty Chinese camped outside the gates. Destitute peasants and villagers, soldiers from the puppet armies and abandoned children, they sat in the open road, staring at the barbed-wire gates being strengthened against them. The first of these impoverished people had appeared three months earlier. At night some of the more desperate would climb through the wire, only to be caught by the internees' patrols. Those who survived in the guardhouse till dawn were taken down to the river by the Japanese and clubbed to death on the bank.

As they moved forward to the serving hatch Jim watched the Chinese. Although it was summer the peasants still wore their quilted winter clothes. Needless to say, none of the Chinese was ever admitted to Lunghua Camp, let alone fed. Yet still they came, attracted to this one place in the desolate land where there was food. Worryingly for Jim, they stayed until they died. Mr Maxted was right when he said that with the conclusion of the war the prisoners' real problems would not end, but begin.

Jim worried about Dr Ransome and Mrs Vincent, and the rest of his fellow-prisoners. How would they survive, without the Japanese to look after them? He worried especially for Mr Maxted, whose tired repertory of jokes about the country club meant nothing in the real world. But at least Mr Maxted was trying to keep the camp going, and it was the integrity of the camp on which they depended.

During 1943, when the war was still moving in Japan's favour, the prisoners had worked together. The entertainments committee, of which Mr Maxted had been chairman, organized a nightly programme of lectures and concert parties. This was the happiest year of Jim's life. Tired of his cramped cubicle and Mrs Vincent's nail-tapping aloofness, he spent every evening listening to lectures on an endless variety of topics: the construction of the pyramids, the history of the world land-speed record, the life of a district commissioner in Uganda (the lecturer, a retired Indian Army officer, claimed to have named after himself a lake the size of Wales, which amazed Jim), the infantry weapons of the Great War, the management of the Shanghai Tramways Company, and a score of others.

Sitting in the front row of the assembly hall, Jim devoured these lectures, many of which he attended two or three times. He helped to copy the parts for the Lunghua Players' productions of *Macbeth* and *Twelfth Night*, he moved scenery for *The Pirates of Penzance* and *Trial by Jury*. For most of 1944 there was a camp school run by the missionaries, which Jim found tedious by comparison with the evening lectures. But he deferred to Basie and Dr Ransome. Both agreed that he should never miss a class, if only, Jim suspected, to give themselves a break from his restless energy.

But by the winter of 1944 all this had ended. After the American fighter attacks on Lunghua Airfield, and the first bombing raids on the Shanghai dockyards, the Japanese enforced an evening curfew. The supply of electric current to the camp was switched off for good, and the prisoners retreated to their bunks. The already modest food ration was cut to a single meal each day. American submarines blockaded the Yangtze estuary, and the huge Japanese armies in China began to fall back to the coast, barely able to feed themselves.

The prospect of their defeat, and the imminent assault on the Japanese home islands, made Jim more and more nervous. He ate every scrap of food he could find, aware of the rising numbers of deaths from beri beri and malaria. Jim admired the Mustangs and Superfortresses, but sometimes he wished that the Americans would return to Hawaii and content themselves with raising their battleships at Pearl Harbor. Then Lunghua Camp would once again be the happy place that he had known in 1943.

When Jim and Mr Maxted returned with the rations to G Block the prisoners were waiting silently with their plates and mess-tins. They stood on the steps, the bare-chested men with knobbed shoulders and birdcage ribs, their faded wives in shabby frocks, watching without expression as if about to be presented with a corpse. At the head of the queue were Mrs Pearce and her son, followed by the missionary couples who spent all day hunting for food.

Hundreds of flies hovered in the steam that rose from the metal pails of cracked wheat and sweet potatoes. As he heaved on the wooden handles Jim winced with pain, not from the strain of pulling the cart, but from the heat of the stolen sweet potato inside his shirt. As long as he remained doubled up no one would see the potato, and he put on a pantomime of grimaces and groans.

'Oh, oh . . . oh, my God . . .'

'Worthy of the Lunghua Players, Jim.' Mr Maxted had watched him remove the potato from the pail as they left the kitchens, but he never objected. Crouching forward, Jim abandoned the cart to the missionaries. He ran up the steps, past the Vincents, who stood plates in hand – it never occurred to them, nor to Jim, that they should bring his plate with them. He dived through the curtain into his cubicle and dropped the steaming potato under his mat, hoping that the damp straw would smother the vapour. He seized his plate, and darted back to the foyer to take his place at the head of the queue. Mr Maxted had already served the Reverend and Mrs Pearce, but Jim shouldered aside their son. He held out his plate and received a ladle of boiled wheat and a second sweet potato which he had pointed out to Mr Maxted within moments of leaving the kitchens.

Returning to his bunk, Jim relaxed for the first time. He drew the curtain and lay back, the warm plate like a piece of the sun against his chest. He felt drowsy, but at the same time light-headed with hunger. He rallied himself with the thought that there might be an American air raid that afternoon – who did he want to win? The question was important.

182

Jim cupped his hands over the sweet potato. He was almost too hungry to enjoy the grey pith, but he gazed at the photograph of the man and woman outside Buckingham Palace, hoping that his parents, wherever they were, also had an extra potato.

When the Vincents returned with their rations Jim sat up and folded back the curtain so that he could examine their plates. He liked to watch Mrs Vincent eating her meals. Keeping a close eye on her, Jim studied the cracked wheat. The starchy grains were white and swollen, indistinguishable from the weevils that infested these warehouse sweepings. In the early years of the camp everyone pushed the weevils to one side, or flicked them through the nearest window, but now Jim carefully husbanded them. Often there was more than a hundred insects in three rows around the rim of Jim's plate, though recently even their number was in decline. 'Eat the weevils,' Dr Ransome had told him, and he did so, although everyone else washed them away. But there was protein in them, a fact that Mr Maxted seemed to find depressing when Jim informed him of it.

After counting the eighty-seven weevils – their numbers, Jim calculated, were falling less steeply than the ration – he stirred them into the cracked wheat, an animal feed grown in northern China, and swallowed the six spoonfuls. Giving himself a breather, he waited for Mrs Vincent to begin her sweet potato.

'Must you, Jim?' Mr Vincent asked. No taller than Jim, the stockbroker and former amateur jockey sat on his bunk beside his ailing son. With his black hair and lined yellow face like a squeezed lemon, he reminded Jim of Basie, but Mr Vincent had never come to terms with Lunghua. 'You'll miss this camp when the war's over. I wonder how you'll take to school in England.'

'It might be a bit strange,' Jim admitted, finishing the last of the weevils. He felt sensitive about his ragged clothes and

183

his determined efforts to stay alive. He wiped his plate clean with his finger, and remembered a favourite phrase of Basie's. 'All the same, Mr Vincent, the best teacher is the university of life.'

Mrs Vincent lowered her spoon. 'Jim, could we finish our meal? We've heard your views on the university of life.'

'Right. But we should eat the weevils, Mrs Vincent.'

'I know, Jim. Dr Ransome told you so.'

'He said we need the protein.'

'Dr Ransome is right. We should all eat the weevils.'

Hoping to brighten the conversation, Jim asked: 'Mrs Vincent, do you believe in vitamins?'

Mrs Vincent stared at her plate. She spoke with true despair. 'Strange child . . .'

The rebuff failed to bother Jim. Everything about this distant woman with her thinning blond hair intrigued him, although in many ways he distrusted her. Six months earlier, when Dr Ransome thought that Jim had contracted pneumonia, she had done nothing to look after him, and Dr Ransome was forced to come in every day and wash Jim himself. Yet the previous evening she had helped him with his Latin homework, matter-of-factly pointing out the distinction between gerunds and gerundives.

Jim waited until she began her sweet potato. After confirming that his own potato was the largest of the four in the room, and deciding not to save any for the turtle under his bunk, he broke the skin and swiftly devoured the warm pulp. When the last morsel had gone he lay back and lowered the curtain. Alone now – the Vincents, although only a few feet away from him, might as well have been on another planet – Jim pondered the jobs ahead of him that day. First, there was the second potato to be smuggled from the room. There were his Latin homework for Dr Ransome, errands to be run for Basie and Private Kimura, and then the afternoon air raid – all in all, a full programme until the evening curfew, when he would probably roam the G Block corridors with his chess set, ready to take on all comers.

The Kennedy *Primer* in hand, Jim stepped from his cubicle. The second potato bulged in his trouser pocket, but for several months the presence of Mrs Vincent had sometimes given him an unexpected erection, and he relied on the confusion to make his escape.

His spoon halfway to his mouth, Mr Vincent stared at the bulge with an expression of deep gloom. His wife gazed in her level fashion at Jim, who side-stepped quickly from the room. Glad as always to be free of the Vincents, he skipped down the corridor to the external door below the fire-escape, and vaulted over the children squatting on one step. As the warm air ruffled the ragged strips of his shirt he ran off into the familiar and reassuring world of the camp.

23
The Air Raid

On his way to the hospital, Jim paused to do his homework at the ruined assembly hall. From the balcony of the upper circle he could not only keep an eye on the pheasant traps across the wire, but also bring himself up to date on any fresh activity at Lunghua Airfield. The stairway to the circle was partly blocked by pieces of masonry that had fallen from the roof, but Jim squeezed himself through a narrow crevice worn smooth by the camp's children. He climbed the stairway, and took his seat on the cement step that formed the first row of the balcony.

The Kennedy propped on his knees, Jim made a leisurely meal of the second potato. Below him, the proscenium arch of the assembly hall had been bombed into a heap of rubble and steel girders, but the landscape now exposed in many ways resembled a panorama displayed on a cinema screen. To the north were the apartment houses of the French Concession, their façades reflected in the flooded paddy fields. To Jim's right, the Whangpoo River emerged from the Nantao district of Shanghai and bent its immense way across the abandoned land.

In front of him was Lunghua Airfield. The concrete runway moved diagonally across its grassy table to the foot of the pagoda. Jim could see the barrels of the anti-aircraft guns mounted on its ancient stone decks, and the powerful landing lights and radio antennae fixed to the tiled roof. Below the pagoda were the hangars and engineering shops, each guarded by sandbag emplacements. A few elderly reconnaissance planes and converted bombers sat on the concrete apron, all that was left of the once invincible air wing that had flown from Lunghua.

Around the edges of the field, in the deep grass by the perimeter road, lay the wreckage of what seemed to Jim to be the entire Japanese Air Force. Scores of rusting aircraft sat on their flattened undercarriages among the trees, or lay in the banks of nettles where they had swerved after crashlanding with their injured crews. For months crippled Japanese aircraft had fallen from the sky on to the graveyard of Lunghua Airfield, as if a titanic aerial battle was taking place far above the clouds.

Already gangs of Chinese scrap-dealers were at work among the derelict planes. With the tireless ability of the Chinese to transform one set of refuse into another, they stripped the metal skins from the wings and retrieved the tyres and fuel tanks. Within days they would be on sale in Shanghai as roofing panels, cisterns and rubber-soled sandals. Whether this scavenging took place with the permission of the Japanese base commander Jim could never decide. Every few hours a party of soldiers would ride out in a truck and drive some of the Chinese away. Jim watched them running across the flooded paddies to the west of the airfield as the Japanese hurled the tyres and metal plates from the salvage carts. But the Chinese always returned to their work, ignored by the anti-aircraft gun-crews in the sandbag emplacements along the perimeter road.

Jim sucked his fingers, drawing the last taste of the sweet potato from his scuffed nails. The warmth of the potato eased the nagging pain in his teeth. He watched the Chinese scavengers at work, tempted to slip through the wire and join them. There were so many new marques of Japanese aircraft. Only four hundred yards from the pheasant traps was the crashed hulk of a Hayate, one of the powerful high-altitude fighters that the Japanese were sending up to destroy the Superfortress bombers on fire-raids over Tokyo.

The long grass between the camp and the southern edge of the airfield was rarely patrolled. Jim's practised eye searched the dips and gullies in the banks of nettles and wild sugar-cane, following the course of a forgotten canal.

A second gang of Chinese coolies was at work in the centre of the airfield, repairing the concrete runway. The men carried baskets of stones from the trucks parked among the bomb craters. A steamroller moved to and fro, manned by a Japanese soldier.

The sharp whistle of its valve-gear held Jim to his seat. The gang of coolies reminded him that he too had once worked on the runway. During the past three years, whenever he watched the Japanese aircraft take off from Lunghua, Jim felt an uneasy pride as their wheels left the concrete surface. He and Basie and Dr Ransome, along with those Chinese prisoners being worked to death, had helped to lay the runway that carried the Zeros and Hayates into the air war against the Americans. Jim was well aware that his commitment to the Japanese Air Force stemmed from the still fearful knowledge that he had nearly given his life to build the runway, like the Chinese soldiers buried in their untraceable lime pit beneath the waving sugar-cane. If he had died, his bones and those of Basie and Dr Ransome would have borne the Japanese pilots taking off from Lunghua to hurl themselves at the American picket ships around Iwo Jima and Okinawa. If the Japanese triumphed, that small part of his mind that lay forever within the runway would be appeased. But if they were defeated, all his fears would have been worth nothing.

Jim remembered those pilots of the dusk who had ordered him from the work gang. Whenever he watched the Japanese moving around their aircraft he thought of the three young pilots with their ground crew who had walked through the evening light to inspect the runway.

But for the English boy wandering towards the parked aircraft the Japanese would not even have noticed the work gang.

The fliers fascinated Jim, far more than Private Kimura and his kendo armour. Every day, as he sat on the balcony of the assembly hall or helped Dr Ransome in the vegetable garden of the hospital, he watched the pilots in their baggy flying suits carrying out the external checks before climbing into the cockpits. Above all, Jim admired the kamikaze pilots. In the past month more than a dozen special attack units had arrived at Lunghua Airfield, which they used as their base for suicide missions against the American carriers in the East China Sea. Neither Private Kimura nor the other guards in the camp paid the least attention to the suicide pilots, and Basie and the American seamen in E Block referred to them as 'hashi-crashies' or 'screwy-siders'.

But Jim identified himself with these kamikaze pilots, and was always moved by the threadbare ceremonies that took place beside the runway. The previous morning, as he worked in the hospital garden, he left his sewage pail and ran to the barbed-wire fence in order to see them leave. The three pilots in their white headbands were little older than Jim, with childlike cheeks and boneless noses. They stood by their planes in the hot sunlight, nervously brushing the flies from their mouths, faces pinched as the squad leader saluted. Even when they cheered the Emperor, shouting hoarsely at the audience of flies, none of the anti-aircraft gunners noticed them, and Private Kimura, striding across the tomato plots to call Jim from the wire, seemed baffled by his concern.

Jim opened his Latin primer and began the homework which Dr Ransome had set him: the entire passive tenses of the verb *amo*. He enjoyed Latin; in many ways its strict formality and its families of nouns and verbs resembled the

189

science of chemistry, his father's favourite subject. The Japanese had closed the camp school as a cunning reprisal against the parents, who were trapped all day with their offspring, but Dr Ransome still set Jim a wide range of tasks. There were poems to memorize, simultaneous equations to be solved, general science (where, thanks to his father, Jim often had a surprise for Dr Ransome), and French, which he loathed. There seemed a remarkable amount of schoolwork, Jim reflected, bearing in mind that the war was about to end. But perhaps this was Dr Ransome's way of keeping him quiet for an hour each day. In a sense, too, the homework helped the physician to sustain the illusion that even in Lunghua Camp the values of a vanished England still survived. Misguided though this was, Jim was keen to help Dr Ransome in any way.

'*Amatus sum, amatus es, amatus est* . . .' As he recited the perfect tense, Jim noticed that the Chinese scavengers were running from the derelict aircraft. The work gang of coolies had scattered, throwing their baskets of stones to the ground. The Japanese soldier leapt from the steamroller and ran bare-chested towards the anti-aircraft emplacements, whose guns were searching the sky. Already a flicker of light came from Lunghua Pagoda, as if the Japanese were setting off a devotional firecracker. The sound of this lone machine-gun crossed the airfield, soon drowned by the complaining drone of an air-raid siren. The klaxon above the guardhouse in Lunghua Camp took up the call, a harsh rattle that drilled through Jim's head.

Excited by the prospect of an air raid, Jim peered at the sky through the open roof of the assembly hall. All over the camp the internees were running along the cinder paths. The men and women dozing like asylum inmates on the steps of the huts scrambled through the doors, mothers leaned from ground-floor windows and lifted their children to safety. Within a minute the camp was deserted, leaving

Jim to conduct the air raid alone from the balcony of the assembly hall.

He listened keenly, already suspecting a false alarm. The air raids came earlier each day, as the Americans moved their bases forward across the Pacific and the Chinese mainland. The Japanese were now so nervous that they jumped at every cloud in the sky. A twin-engined transport plane flew across the paddy fields, its pilots unaware of the panic below.

Jim returned to his Latin primer. At that moment an immense shadow crossed the assembly hall and raced along the ground towards the perimeter fence. A tornado of noise filled the air, from which emerged a single-engined fighter with silver fuselage and the Stars-and-Bars insignia of the US Air Force. Only thirty feet above Jim's head, the Mustang's wings were broader than the assembly hall. The fuselage was stained with rust and oil, but its powerful engine had the smooth drive of his father's Packard. The Mustang crossed the perimeter fence and hurtled along the concrete runway of the airfield, the height of a man's head above the deck. In its wake a whirlwind of leaves and dust boiled from the ground.

Around the airfield the anti-aircraft guns turned towards the camp. The tiers of Lunghua Pagoda crackled with light like the Christmas tree display outside the Sincere Company department store in Shanghai. Undeterred, the Mustang flew straight towards the flak tower, the noise of its guns drowned in the blare of another Mustang that swept across the paddy fields to the west of the camp. A third plane came in behind it, so low that Jim was looking down at the cockpit. He could see the pilots, and the insignia on their fuselages blackened by oil spraying from the engine exhausts. Two more Mustangs overflew the camp, and the wash from their engines tore the corrugated iron sheets from the roof of the barrack hut beside G Block. Half a mile to the east, between Lunghua Camp and the river, a second wing of American fighters swept in from the sea, so close to their own shadows on the empty paddy fields that they were hidden behind the lines of grave mounds. They rose as they crossed the perimeter of the airfield, then dived again to fire at the Japanese aircraft parked beside the hangars.

Anti-aircraft shells burst above the camp, their shadows pulsing like heartbeats on the white earth. A shell exploded in a searing flash above the assembly hall, stunning the air. Dust cascaded from the concrete roof and poured on to Jim's shoulders. Waving his Latin primer, Jim counted the dozens of shellbursts. Did the Mustang pilots realize that Basie and the American merchant seamen were imprisoned at Lunghua Camp? Whenever they attacked the airfield the fighter pilots hid until the last moment behind the three-storey dormitory blocks, even though this drew Japanese fire on to the camp and had killed several of the prisoners.

But Jim was glad that the Mustangs were so close. His eyes feasted on every rivet in their fuselages, on the gun ports in their wings, on the huge ventral radiators that Jim was sure had been put there for reasons of style alone. Jim admired the Hayates and Zeros of the Japanese, but the Mustang fighters were the Cadillacs of air combat. He was too breathless to shout to the pilots, but he waved his primer at them as they soared past under the canopy of anti-aircraft shells.

The first flights of attacking planes had swept across the airfield. Clearly visible against the apartment houses of the French Concession, they flew towards Shanghai, ready to strafe the dockyards and the Nantao seaplane base. But the anti-aircraft batteries around the runway were still firing into the air. Cat's cradles of tracer stitched the sky, threads of phosphorus knit and reknit themselves. At their centre was the great pagoda of Lunghua, rising through the smoke that lifted from the burning hangars, its guns throwing out an unbroken flak ceiling.

Jim had never before seen an air attack of such scale. A second wave of Mustangs crossed the paddy fields between Lunghua Camp and the river, followed by a squadron of two-engined fighter-bombers. Three hundred yards to the west of the camp one of the Mustangs dipped its starboard wing towards the ground. Out of control, it slid across the air, and its wing-tip sheared the embankment of a disused canal. The plane cartwheeled across the paddy fields and fell apart in the air. It exploded in a curtain wall of flaming gasoline through which Jim could see the burning figure of the American pilot still strapped to his seat. Riding the incandescent debris of his aircraft, he tore through the trees beyond the perimeter of the camp, a fragment of the sun whose light continued to flare across the surrounding fields.

A second crippled Mustang pulled away from the others in its flight. Trailing a plume of oily smoke, it rose through the anti-aircraft bursts and climbed into the sky. The pilot was trying to escape from the airfield, but as his Mustang began to lose height he rolled the craft on to its back and fell safely from the cockpit. His parachute opened and he dropped steeply to the ground. His burning plane righted itself, towed its black plume in a wavering arc above the empty fields, and then plunged into the river.

The pilot hung alone in the silent sky. His companions sped on towards Shanghai, their silver fuselages lost in the sun-filled windows of the French Concession. The hammering noise of their engines had gone, and the anti-aircraft fire had ceased. A second parachutist was coming down among the canals to the west of the airfield. A stench of burnt oil and engine coolant filled the disturbed air. All over the camp, miniature tornadoes of leaves and dead insects subsided and then whirled along the pathways again as they hunted for the slipstreams of the vanished Mustangs.

The two parachutes fell towards the burial mounds. Already a squad of Japanese soldiers in a truck with a steaming radiator sped along the perimeter road, on their way to kill the pilots. Jim wiped the dust from his Latin primer and waited for the rifle shots. The halo of light which had emerged from the burning Mustang still lay over the creeks and paddies. For a few minutes the sun had drawn nearer to the earth, as if to scorch the death from its fields.

Jim grieved for these American pilots, who died in a tangle of their harnesses, within sight of a Japanese corporal with a Mauser and a single English boy hidden on the balcony of this ruined building. Yet their end reminded Jim of his own, about which he had thought in a clandestine way ever since his arrival at Lunghua. He welcomed the air raids, the noise of the Mustangs as they swept over the camp, the smell of oil and cordite, the deaths of the pilots, and even the likelihood of his own death. Despite everything, he knew he was worth nothing. He twisted his Latin primer, trembling with a secret hunger that the war would so eagerly satisfy.

24
The Hospital

'Jim . . . ! Are you up there . . . ? Have you been hurt . . . ?'

Dr Ransome stood in the rubble on the floor of the assembly hall, shouting at the balcony. He had been exhausted by the effort of running from D Block, and his lungs rattled inside his chest. The years in Lunghua had made him seem taller, but his large bones were held together by little more than a rigging of tendons. Above the rusty beard his one sound eye had seen the top of Jim's head, white with dust as if aged by the air raid.

'Jim, I need you at the hospital. Sergeant Nagata says you can stay with me for the roll-call.'

Jim roused himself from his reverie. Uncannily, the halo cast by the burning body of the American pilot still lay over the empty fields, but he decided not to mention this optical illusion to Dr Ransome. The all-clear siren wailed from the pagoda, a signal repeated by the guard-house klaxon. Jim left the balcony and squeezed his way down the staircase.

'I'm here, Dr Ransome. I think I was nearly killed. Is anyone else dead?'

'Let's hope not.' Dr Ransome leaned against the balustrade, and fanned the dust from his beard with his straw coolie hat. Although unsettled by the air raid, he watched Jim in a weary but patient way. After the raids, when the Japanese guards began to abuse the prisoners, he was often short-tempered with Jim, as if he held him responsible. He ran his hand through Jim's hair, brushing away the powdered cement, and examined his scalp for any signs of blood. 'Jim, we agreed that you wouldn't go up there

195

during the raids. The Japanese have enough to contend with – they may think you're trying to signal to the American pilots.'

'I was, but they didn't see me. The Mustangs are so fast.' Jim liked Dr Ransome, and wanted to reassure him that all was well. 'I've done my Latin prep, doctor.'

Surprisingly, Dr Ransome was not interested in whether Jim had memorized his verbs. He strode towards the hospital, a cluster of bamboo shacks which the prisoners, in a realistic estimate of the camp's medical resources, had built next to the cemetery. The roll-call had already begun, and the pathways were deserted. Japanese guards barged through the barrack huts, breaking the last panes of window glass with their rifle butts. This precaution had been insisted on by Mr Sekura, the camp commandant, to protect the prisoners from bomb blast. In fact, it was a reprisal for the air raid, as the prisoners would know to their cost that dusk when thousands of anopheles mosquitoes rose at feeding time from the stagnant ponds around the camp.

On the steps of E Block, one of the all-male dormitories, Sergeant Nagata screamed into the face of the block leader, Mr Ralston, the organist at the Metropole Cinema in Shanghai. Behind the sergeant three guards stood with fixed bayonets, as if they expected a platoon of American marines to burst from the building. The hundreds of ragged prisoners waited patiently. As the war moved through its closing year the Japanese had become unsettled and dangerous.

'Dr Ransome, what will happen if the Americans land at Woosung?' This port at the mouth of the Yangtze controlled the river approach to Shanghai. Everyone in the camp talked about Woosung.

'The Americans probably will land at Woosung, Jim. I've always thought you should be at MacArthur's headquarters.' Dr Ransome stopped to catch his breath. He forced the air into his bony chest, staring at his reflection in the toecaps of Jim's shoes. 'Try not to think about it – you've so many other things swimming about in your head. The Americans may not land there.'

'If they do, the Japanese will fight.'

'Jim, they'll fight. As you've loyally maintained, the Japanese are the bravest soldiers in the world.'

'Well . . .' Talk of bravery embarrassed Jim. War had nothing to do with bravery. Two years earlier, when he was younger, it had seemed important to work out who were the bravest soldiers, part of his attempt to digest the disruptions of his life. Certainly the Japanese came top, the Chinese bottom, with the British wavering in between. But Jim thought of the American aircraft that had swept the sky. However brave, there was nothing the Japanese could do to stop those beautiful and effortless machines.

'The Japanese are brave,' Jim conceded. 'But bravery isn't important now.'

'I'm not so sure. Are you brave, Jim?'

'No . . . of course not. But I could be,' Jim asserted.

'I think you are.'

Although offhand, Dr Ransome's comment had an unpleasant edge. Clearly he was annoyed with Jim, as if he blamed him for the raiding Mustangs. Was it because he had learned to enjoy the war? Jim debated this as they reached the hospital. On the ground beside the worn bamboo steps was the intact cone of an anti-aircraft shell. He picked it up, curious to see if it would still be warm, but Dr Ransome took it from him and hurled it over the barbed-wire fence.

Jim stood on the rotting steps, flexing his shoes against the bamboo rods. He had been tempted to snatch the shell back from Dr Ransome. He was now almost as tall as the physician and in many ways stronger – during the past three years, as Jim grew, Dr Ransome's large body had shrunk

197

and wasted. Jim could scarcely believe his memories of the burly, red-haired man with heavy thighs and arms, twice the size of the Japanese soldiers. But during their first two years in the camp Dr Ransome had given too much of his own food to Jim.

They entered the hospital, and Jim took his place outside the dispensary with Dr Bowen – an ear, nose and throat specialist at Shanghai General Hospital – and the four missionary widows who formed the nursing staff. While they waited for Sergeant Nagata to conduct the roll-call he peered into the adjacent wards, where the thirty patients lay on their bunks. After every air raid there were a few deaths, from shock or exhaustion. The reminder that the war was nearly over seemed to encourage some people to give up the ghost. However, for those still keen to stay alive, a death was good news. For Jim it meant an old belt or a pair of braces, a fountain pen, and once, miraculously, a wristwatch that he had worn for three days before handing it over with everything else to Basie. The Japanese had confiscated all watches and clocks – as Dr Ransome said, they wanted their prisoners to be without time. During the three days, Jim had measured the time it took to do everything.

Most of the patients were suffering from malaria, dysentery and heart infections brought on by malnutrition. The beri beri patients particularly unsettled Jim, with their swollen legs and waterlogged lungs, minds so confused that they thought they were dying in England. In their last hours they were given a special privilege, the hospital's one mosquito net, and lay in this makeshift sepulchre before being consigned to the cemetery beside the kitchen garden.

As Sergeant Nagata approached the hospital, accompanied by two soldiers, Jim glanced into the men's ward. For days Mr Barraclough, the secretary of the Shanghai Country Club, had been about to die, and Jim noticed his gold signet ring. It might not be gold – nothing he offered to Basie ever was – but it would be worth something. Jim had no compunction about stealing from the dead. The only patients foolish enough to come to the hospital were those without relatives or friends willing to look after them in the huts or dormitory blocks. Apart from the fact that it contained no medicines – the small supply allocated by the Japanese had been used in the first year – the hospital rarely cured anyone. The Japanese, correctly assuming that all those who entered the hospital would soon be dead, immediately halved their food ration. Even so, Jim thought, it could take a remarkable time before Dr Ransome and Dr Bowen pronounced them officially dead. Jim knew that a large number of the extra potatoes he had eaten were dead men's rations. Dr Ransome worked hard for the sick, and Jim was sorry that recently he had seemed to lose hope.

'They're here,' Dr Ransome called out. 'Jim, stand to attention. Don't argue with Sergeant Nagata today. And don't tell him about the air raid.'

Noticing that Jim's eyes were fixed on the signet ring, he turned his head to face Sergeant Nagata as he clattered up the bamboo steps. Dr Ransome disapproved of the grave-robbery, though he was aware that Jim traded the belt-buckles and braces for food. However, as Jim quietly reflected, Dr Ransome had his own sources of supply. Unlike most of the prisoners in Lunghua, who had been allowed to pack a suitcase before being interned, Dr Ransome had entered the camp with nothing but his shirt, shorts and leather sandals. Yet his cubicle in D Block housed an impressive inventory of possessions – a complete change of clothes, a portable gramophone and several records, a tennis racquet, a rugby football, and the shelf of textbooks that had provided Jim with his education. These, like all the clothes that Jim had worn in the camp and like the magnificent golf shoes that instantly caught Sergeant Nagata's eye, Dr Ransome had obtained from the stream of patients who visited his D Block cubicle each evening. Many had nothing to give, but the younger wives always brought a modest cumshaw for whatever mysterious service Dr Ransome provided. Richard Pearce had even recognized that Jim was wearing one of his old shirts, but too late.

Sergeant Nagata stopped in front of the prisoners. The scale of the American air raid had clearly shaken him. His jaws clenched as he expressed a few drops of spittle on to his lips. The bristles around his mouth trembled like miniature antennae picking up an advance warning of the rage to come. He needed to work himself up into a fury, but the gleaming toecaps of Jim's shoes distracted him. Like all Japanese soldiers, the sergeant wore rotting boots through which his big toes protruded like immense thumbs.

'Boy . . .' He paused in front of Jim and tapped his head with the roll-sheet, releasing a cloud of white dust. He knew from Private Kimura that Jim was involved in every illicit activity in the camp, but had never been able to catch him. He waved away the dust, and with an effort uttered the only two consecutive words of English which the years in Lunghua had taught him: 'Difficult boy . . .'

Jim waited for him to go on, fascinated by the spittle on his lips. Perhaps Sergeant Nagata would appreciate a first-hand account of the air raid?

But the sergeant strode into the men's ward, shouting in Japanese to the two doctors. He stared down at the dying men, in whom he had never shown the slightest interest, and Jim had the sudden exhilarating notion that Dr Ransome was hiding a wounded American pilot. He wanted to touch the pilot before the Japanese killed him, feel his helmet and flight suit, run his fingers over the dust and oil on his goggles.

'Jim . . . ! Stop thinking . . . !' Mrs Philips, one of the missionary widows, caught him as he swayed forward, almost swooning before the image of this archangelic figure fallen among the paddies. Jim stood to attention, pretending to be weak with hunger, and trying to avoid the suspicious stare of the Japanese sentry at the dispensary door. He waited for the roll-call to end, reflecting on the likely booty attached to a dead American pilot. Soon enough, one of the Americans would be shot down into Lunghua Camp. Jim tried to decide which of the ruined buildings would best conceal his body. Carefully eked out, the kit and equipment could be bartered with Basie for extra sweet potatoes for months to come, and even perhaps a warm coat for the winter. There would be sweet potatoes for Dr Ransome, whom Jim was determined to keep alive.

He rocked on his heels and listened to an old woman crying in the nearby ward. Through the window was the pagoda at Lunghua Airfield. Already the flak tower appeared in a new light.

For another hour Jim stood in line with the missionary widows, watched by the sentry. Dr Ransome and Dr Bowen had set off with Sergeant Nagata to the commandant's office, perhaps to be interrogated. The guards moved around the silent camp with their roster boards, carrying out repeated roll-calls. The war was about to end, and yet the Japanese were obsessed with knowing exactly how many prisoners they held.

Jim closed his eyes to calm his mind, but the sentry barked at him, suspecting that Jim was about to play some private game of which Sergeant Nagata would disapprove. The memory of the air raid excited Jim. The Mustangs still streaked across the camp on their way to attack the flak tower. He imagined himself at the controls of one of the fighters, falling to earth when his plane exploded, rising again as one of the childlike kamikaze pilots who cheered the Emperor before hurling their Zeros into the American carriers at Okinawa. One day Jim would become a wounded pilot, fallen among the burial mounds and armoured pago-

201

das. Pieces of his flying suit and parachute, even perhaps his own body, would spread across the paddy fields, feeding the prisoners behind their wire and the Chinese starving at the gate . . .

'Jim . . . !' Mrs Philips hissed. 'Practise your Latin . . .'

Forcing himself not to blink, to the irritation of the Japanese sentry, Jim stared into the sunlight outside the dispensary window. The silent landscape seemed to seethe with flames, the halo born from the burning body of the American pilot. The light touched the rusting wire of the perimeter fence and the dusty fronds of the wild sugar-cane, bleached the wings of the derelict aircraft and the bones of the peasants in the burial mounds. Jim longed for the next air raid, dreaming of the violent light, barely able to breathe for the hunger that Dr Ransome had recognized but could never feed.

25

The Cemetery Garden

When the roll-call ended Jim rested on the hospital steps. Dr Ransome and Dr Bowen returned from the commandant's office and immediately shut themselves in the dispensary with the four missionary widows. Dr Ransome seemed as nervous as the Japanese. The old scar below his eye was flushed with blood. Had Sergeant Nagata slapped him for protesting at a further cut in the food ration?

Hands in pockets, Jim sauntered down the cinder track behind the hospital. He surveyed the rows of tomatoes, beans and melons in the kitchen garden. The modest crop was meant to supplement the patients' meagre diet, though many of the vegetables found their way to the American seamen in E Block. Jim enjoyed his work with the plants. He knew each of them personally, and could tell at a glance if the children had stolen a single tomato. Fortunately the long lines of graves in the adjacent cemetery kept them away. Apart from its nutritional benefits, botany was an intriguing subject. In the dispensary Dr Ransome sliced and stained the slivers of plant stems and roots, mounted them under Dr Bowen's microscope and made Jim draw the hundreds of cells and nutrient vessels. Plant classification was an entire universe of words; every weed in the camp had a name. Names surrounded everything; invisible encyclopaedias lay in every hedge and ditch.

The previous afternoon Jim had dug two fertilizer trenches for a new crop of tomato plants. Between the garden and the cemetery was a row of fifty-gallon drums which he and Dr Ransome had buried in the ground, then filled with sewage from the overflowing septic tank in G Block. A party of prisoners in the block had decanted most of the sewage into one of the drained ponds, but Jim and Dr Ransome made their own trips with bucket, rope and cart. As Dr Ransome said, there was no point in wasting anything that could keep them alive for even a few days longer. The glowing tomatoes and puffed-up melons proved him right.

Jim moved the wooden hatch from one of the drums. He waited for the thousands of flies to have the first share, then picked up the bamboo ladle with its wooden cup and began to pour the manure into the shallow trenches. He worked with the slow but measured rhythm of the Chinese peasants he had watched as they fertilized their crops before the war.

An hour later, when he had covered the manure with a layer of soil, Jim rested on one of the graves in the nearby cemetery. Various people were visiting the hospital, the block leaders and their deputies, a party of Americans from E Block, the senior Dutch and Belgians. But Jim was too tired to pester them for news. It was peaceful in the kitchen garden with its green walls of beans and tomato plants. Often he visualized staying there forever, even after the war ended.

He pushed this rustic fantasy to the back of his mind and listened to the drone of a Zero fighter warming up at the end of the runway. A single kamikaze plane was about to take off, all that the Japanese could muster as a reprisal for the American air raid. The young pilot, barely older than Jim, wore his ceremonial sashes, but the honour guard consisted only of a corporal and a junior private. Both turned away before the pilot had climbed into his cockpit, and walked back to their repair work on the damaged hangars.

Jim watched the plane rise shakily from the runway. It climbed over the camp, engine labouring under the weight of the bomb, banked towards the river and set course for the open China Sea. He cupped his hands over his eyes and followed the plane until it vanished among the clouds. None of the Japanese at Lunghua Airfield had given the aircraft the briefest glance. Fires were still burning in the hangars by the pagoda, and a cloud of steam rose from the bombed engineering sheds. Already, though, the craters were being filled by the work gang of Chinese coolies, and the scrap-dealers were scavenging the hulks of the derelict planes.

'Are you still interested in aeroplanes, Jim?' Mrs Philips asked, as she and Mrs Gilmour emerged from the hospital courtyard. 'You'll have to join the RAF.'

'I'm going to join the Japanese Air Force.'

'Oh? The Japanese . . . ?' The missionary widows tittered, still unsure of Jim's sense of humour, and pushed their wooden cart. The iron wheels rang on the stony track, shaking the body which the two women were about to bury.

Jim polished the three tomatoes he had picked from the plants. None was larger than a marble, but Basie would appreciate them. He slipped them into his shirt pocket and watched Mrs Philips and Mrs Gilmour digging the grave. Soon exhausted, the two women sat on the cart and rested beside the corpse.

He walked over to them and took the spade from Mrs Philips' worn hands. The body was that of Mr Radik, the former head chef at the Cathay Hotel. Jim had enjoyed his scholarly lectures on the Atlantic liner *Berengaria*, and was glad to repay his debt. He dug the soft soil. In one of their few acts of foresight, when they were still strong enough to do so, the prisoners had part-excavated the narrow graves. But the effort of removing a further spade's depth of damp soil was now too much for the missionary widows. The dead were buried above ground, the loose soil heaped around them. The heavy rains of the monsoon months softened the mounds, so that they formed outlines of the bodies within them, as if this small cemetery beside the military airfield were doing its best to resurrect a few of the millions who had died in the war. Here and there an arm or a foot protruded

205

from the graves, the limbs of restless sleepers struggling beneath their brown quilts. Rats had burrowed deep into the grave of Mrs Hug, the Dutchwoman who had arrived at Lunghua with Basie and Dr Ransome, and the tunnels reminded Jim of the Maginot Line he had constructed behind the rockery at Amherst Avenue for his army of lead soldiers.

He dug away, deciding to sink Mr Radik well below the ground so that the chef would not become an instant meal for the rats. Mrs Gilmour and Mrs Philips sat on the cart beside the corpse and watched without comment. Whenever he paused to rest they treated him to two identical smiles, as blanched as the flowers in the patterns of their tattered cotton dresses.

'Jim! Leave that and come over! I need you here!' Dr Ransome was shouting from the dispensary window. He had always disliked Jim digging the graves.

Hundreds of flies buzzed around the cart and settled on Mr Radik's face. With the *Berengaria* in mind, Jim continued to spade the soil.

'Jim, doctor's calling . . .'

'All right – it's ready.'

The women pulled Mr Radik from the cart. Although wearied by the effort, they handled him with the same care they had shown when he was alive. Was he still alive for these two Christian widows? Jim had always been impressed by strong religious beliefs. His mother and father were agnostics, and he respected devout Christians in the same way that he respected people who were members of the Graf Zeppelin Club or shopped at the Chinese department stores, for their mastery of an exotic foreign ritual. Besides, those who worked hardest for others, like Mrs Philips and Mrs Gilmour and Dr Ransome, often held beliefs that turned out to be correct.

'Mrs Philips,' he asked as they settled Mr Radik into his

grave, 'when does the soul leave the body? Before it's buried?'

'Yes, Jim.' Mrs Philips knelt on the ground and began to scoop the earth over Mr Radik's face. 'Mr Radik's soul has already left. Doctor's calling again. I hope you've done your Latin prep.'

'Of course.' Jim reflected on all this as he walked to the hospital. He often watched the eyes of the patients as they died, trying to detect a flash of light when the soul left. Once he had helped Dr Ransome as he massaged the naked chest of a young Belgian woman wasted by dysentery. Dr Bowen had said that she was dead, but Dr Ransome squeezed her heart under her ribs and suddenly her eyes swivelled and looked at Jim. At first Jim thought that her soul had returned to her, but she was still dead. Mrs Philips and Mrs Gilmour took her away and buried her an hour later. Dr Ransome explained that for a few seconds he had pumped the blood back into her brain.

Jim entered the dispensary and sat at the metal table facing Dr Ransome. He would have liked to take up the matter of Mr Radik's soul, but the doctor was curiously reluctant to discuss religious topics with Jim, although he himself went to the church services on Sunday morning. The scar on his face was still flushed with blood, and he was ominously busy with his tray of melted wax. Whenever he was tired, or annoyed with Jim, Dr Ransome would melt a few candles and immerse squares of old cloth in the hot liquid, then hang them up to cool. The previous winter he had made hundreds of these wax panels, which the prisoners had used to replace the broken window panes. Although the hours of work had helped to keep out the freezing winds that swept down from northern China, few of the prisoners were grateful to Dr Ransome. Still, as Jim had observed, Dr Ransome was not interested in their gratitude.

207

Jim dipped a finger in the hot wax, but Dr Ransome brusquely waved him away. Clearly his conversation with the camp commandant had upset him – he was preparing for the winter as if trying to convince himself that they would all be there when it arrived.

Taking off his shoes, Jim began to buff the toecaps. After three years in clogs and cast-offs, he enjoyed impressing everyone with these expensive leather brogues.

'Jim, it's admirable of you to look so smart, but try not to polish them *all* the time.' Dr Ransome stared heavily at the wax square. 'They unsettle Sergeant Nagata.'

'I like them to look bright.'

'They're very bright. Even the American pilots must have seen them. They probably think we have a golf course here and set their compasses to your toecaps.'

'That means I'm helping the war effort?'

'In a way . . .' Before Jim could put on his shoes Dr Ransome held his ankle. Most of the sores on Jim's legs were infected, and given the poor diet would never properly heal, but above the right ankle was an ulcer the size of a penny, engorged with pus. Dr Ransome moved the tray of melted wax from the candle-lamp. He boiled a spoonful of water in a metal pail, then drained and cleaned the ulcer with a cotton swab.

Jim submitted without protest. He had formed his only close bond in Lunghua with Dr Ransome, though he knew that in many ways the physician disapproved of him. He resented Jim for revealing an obvious truth about the war, that people were only too able to adapt to it. At times he even suspected that Jim enjoyed Latin for the wrong reasons. The brother of a games master at an English boarding school (one of those repressive institutions, so like Lunghua, for which Jim was apparently destined), he had been working up-country with Protestant missionaries. Dr Ransome was rather like a school prefect and head of rugby, though Jim was unsure how far this manner was calculated. He had noticed that the doctor could be remarkably devious when it suited him.

'Now, Jim, I'm sure you've done your prep . . .' Dr Ransome opened the Latin primer. Although distracted by the prisoners who gathered outside the huts and dormitory blocks, he stared hard at the text. Hundreds of men and their wives, many with their children, were crossing the parade ground. He began to question Jim, who continued to polish his shoes under the table.

'"They were being loved" . . . ?'

'*Amabantur*.'

'"I shall be loved" . . . ?'

'*Amabor*.'

'"You will have been loved" . . . ?'

'*Amatus eris*.'

'Right – I'll set you an unseen. Mrs Vincent will help you with the vocabulary. She doesn't mind your asking?'

'Not now.' Jim reported her change of heart matter-of-factly. He guessed that Dr Ransome had been useful with some special woman's problem.

'Good. People need to be encouraged. She may not be much use with the trig.'

'I don't need her to help me.' Jim enjoyed trigonometry. Unlike Latin or algebra, this branch of geometry was directly involved in a subject close to his heart – aerial warfare. 'Dr Ransome, the American bombers that flew with the Mustangs were going at 320 miles an hour – I timed their shadows across the camp with my heart-beat. If they want to hit Lunghua Airfield they have to drop their bombs about a thousand yards away.'

'Jim, you're a war-child. I imagine the Japanese gunners know that too.'

Jim sat back thinking this over. 'They might not.'

'Well, we can't tell them – or can we? That would be

unfair to the American pilots. As it is, the Japanese are shooting too many of them down.'

'But they're shooting them down over the airfield,' Jim explained. 'Then they've already dropped their bombs. If they want to stop them hitting the runway they should shoot them down more than a thousand yards away.' The prospect excited Jim – applied to the Japanese bases all over the Pacific area this new tactic might turn the war against the Americans and so save Lunghua Camp. He drummed his fingers on the table, imitating the way in which he had played the white piano in the empty house in Amherst Avenue.

'Yes . . .' Dr Ransome reached out and gently pressed Jim's hands to the table, trying to calm him. He submerged another cotton square in the wax tray. 'Perhaps we'll leave the trig, and I'll mark up some algebra. We want the war to end, Jim.'

'Of course, Dr Ransome.'

'*Do* you want the war to end, Jim?' Dr Ransome often seemed doubtful about this. 'A lot of the people here won't last much longer. You're keen to see your mother and father again?'

'Yes, I am. I think about them every day.'

'Good. Do you remember what they look like?'

'I do remember . . .' Jim hated lying to Dr Ransome, but in a sense he was thinking of the photograph of the unknown man and woman he had pinned to the wall of his cubicle. He had never divulged to the physician that these were his surrogate parents. Jim knew that it was important to keep alive the memory of his mother and father, in order to sustain his confidence in the future, but their faces had become hazy. Dr Ransome might not approve of the way in which he was tricking himself.

'I'm glad you remember them, Jim. They may have changed.'

'I know – they'll be hungry.'

'More than hungry, Jim. When the war does end everything is going to be very uncertain.'

'So we should stay in the camp?' Jim liked the sound of this. Too many of the prisoners talked about leaving the camp without any real idea of what would happen to them. 'As long as we stay in Lunghua the Japanese will look after us.'

'I'm not sure that they will. We've become an embarrassment to them. They can't feed us any longer, Jim . . .'

So this was what Dr Ransome had been leading towards. Jim felt a quiet tiredness come over him. His long hours spent hauling the buckets of sewage, planting and watering the crops in the hospital garden, pulling the ration cart with Mr Maxted, had been part of his attempt to keep the camp going. Yet, as he had known all along, the supply of food depended on the whim of the Japanese. His own feelings, his determination to survive, counted for nothing in the end. The activity meant no more than the movement in the eyes of the Belgian woman who had seemed to come back from the dead.

'Is there going to be any more food, Dr Ransome?'

'We hope some will come through. The Japanese can no longer feed themselves. The American submarines . . .'

Jim stared at the polished toecaps of his shoes. He wanted his mother and father to see them before they died. He rallied himself, trying to summon his old will to survive. Deliberately he thought of the curious pleasure the corpses in the hospital cemetery gave him, the guilty excitement of being alive at all. He knew why Dr Ransome disliked him digging the graves.

Dr Ransome marked the exercises in the algebra textbook, and gave him two strips of rice-paper bandage on which to solve the simultaneous equations. As he stood up Dr Ransome removed the three tomatoes from Jim's pocket. He laid them on the table by the wax tray.

'Did they come from the hospital garden?'

'Yes.' Jim gazed frankly at Dr Ransome. Recently he had begun to see him with a more adult eye. The long years of imprisonment, the constant disputes with the Japanese, had made this young physician seem middle-aged. Dr Ransome was often unsure of himself, as he was of Jim's theft.

'I have to give Basie something whenever I see him.'

'I know. It's a good thing that you're friends with Basie. He's a survivor, though survivors can be dangerous. Wars exist for people like Basie.' Dr Ransome placed the tomatoes in Jim's hand. 'I want you to eat them, Jim. I'll get you something for Basie.'

'Dr Ransome . . .' Jim searched for some way of reassuring him. 'If we told Sergeant Nagata about the thousand-yard range . . . the Japanese wouldn't shoot down any more planes, but they might give us some food . . . ?'

Dr Ransome smiled for the first time. He unlocked the medicine cabinet and from a steel cash box he removed two rubber condoms.

'Jim, you're a pragmatist. Give these to Basie, he'll have something for you. Now eat your tomatoes and go.'

The Lunghua Sophomores

'We're the Lunghua Sophomores,
We're the girls every boy adores,
C.A.C. don't mean a thing to me,
For every Tuesday evening we go on a spree . . .'

As he crossed the parade ground towards E Block, Jim paused to watch the Lunghua Players rehearsing their next concert party on the steps of Hut 6. The leader of the troupe was Mr Wentworth, the manager of the Cathay Bank, whose exaggerated and theatrical manner fascinated Jim. He enjoyed the amateur dramatics, when everyone involved was at the centre of public attention. Jim had played a page in *Henry V*, a role he relished. The costume which Mrs Wentworth had run up for him out of purple velvet was the only decent garment he had worn for three years. He had offered to wear it in the Lunghua Players' next production, *The Importance of Being Earnest*, but Mr Wentworth had declined to cast him.

'. . . We've debates and lectures too,
And concerts just for you . . .'

The rehearsal was not a success. The four chorus girls in their pierrot costumes stood on the makeshift stage of packing cases, trying to remember the song. Upset by the air raid, the women ignored Mr Wentworth and listened to the sky. Despite the hot sunlight, they rubbed their arms to keep warm.

The audience of bored internees wandered away, and Jim decided to leave the actors to it. The Lunghua Players recruited their members from the snootiest of the English families, and there was something absurd about their high-pitched voices – as affected as the rugby match which Dr Ransome, in a rare lapse from common sense, had arranged the previous winter. The teams of starving prisoners (husbands of the Lunghua Sophomores) had tottered around the parade ground in a grotesque parody of a rugby game, too exhausted to pass the ball and jeered at by a crowd of fellow-prisoners excluded from the game because they had never learned the rules.

Jim passed the guardhouse, carrying out a quick survey of the camp. A group of prisoners had gathered by the gates, waiting for the military truck which brought the daily rations from Shanghai. No official announcement had been made that the ration was to be cut, but the news had already spread through the camp.

Significantly, there were fewer Chinese beggars outside the gates. A dead peasant woman lay on the grass verge, but the disbanded puppet soldiers and out-of-work rickshaw coolies had gone, leaving behind a circle of squatting old men and a few wan-faced children.

Jim entered E Block, the men's dormitory building, and climbed the stairway to the third floor. Regardless of the weather, the British prisoners in E Block spent almost all their time in their bunks. A few were too ill with malaria to move, and lay stretched out on straw mats soaked with sweat and urine. But others still strong enough to walk lounged beside them, examining their hands for hours or staring at the walls.

The sight of so many adult men unwilling to cope with the reality of the camp always puzzled Jim, but he recovered as soon as he reached the American dormitory. He liked the Americans and approved of them in every way. Whenever he entered this enclave of irony and good humour his spirits rose.

Two of the former classrooms were occupied by the

American merchant seamen. The partition doors had been removed, and the high-ceilinged chamber was filled by some sixty men. Jim surveyed the maze of cubicles. The Britons in E Block lived in open dormitories, but each of the American seamen had constructed a small cubicle from whatever materials he could scavenge – threadbare sheets, wooden planks, straw mats and woven bamboo. Now and then a party of Americans would emerge from E Block and play a relaxed game of softball, but usually they remained in their cubicles. There they lay on their bunks and entertained a steady stream of adolescent girls, single British women and even a few wives drawn to them for reasons not very different from Jim's.

By some mechanism that Jim had never understood, the sexual activity seemed to generate an endless supply of those items that most fascinated him. This treasure had been brought into the camp by the American sailors and now circulated like a second currency – comic books and copies of *Life*, *Reader's Digest* and *Saturday Evening Post*, novelty pens, lipsticks and powder compacts, gaudy tie-pins, cigarette lighters and celluloid belts, fairground cufflinks and wild west buckles – a collection of gewgaws that in Jim's eyes had the style and magic of the Mustang fighters.

'Say, it's Shanghai Jim . . .'

'Kid, Basie's mad at you . . .'

'You want to play chess, son?'

'Jim, I need hot water and a shave.'

'Jim, bring me a left-handed screwdriver and a bucket of steam . . .'

'Why's Basie mad at Jim?'

Jim exchanged greetings with the Americans – Cohen, the softball wizard and chess fanatic; Tiptree, the large, kindly stoker who was the comic-book king; Hinton, yet another cabin steward and philosopher: Dainty, the telegraphist and premier cocksman of Lunghua – amiable men

215

whose rôles they played for Jim's benefit and constantly guyed. When they noticed him, most of them liked Jim, who in return, and out of respect for America, ran endless errands for them. Several of the cubicles were closed as the merchant seamen entertained their visitors, but the others had their curtains raised so that the sailors could lie on their bunks and observe the passing world. Two of the older seamen were racked by malaria, but they made little fuss about being ill. All in all, Jim felt, the Americans were the best company, not as strange and challenging as the Japanese, but far superior to the morose and complicated British.

Why was Basie angry with him? Jim stepped down the narrow corridor between the suspended sheets. He could hear an English woman from Hut 5 complaining about her husband, and two Belgian girls who lived with their widowed father in G Block giggled over some object they were being shown.

Basie's cubicle was in the north-east corner of the room, with two windows that gave him a clear view of the entire camp. As always he was sitting on his bunk, keeping an eye on the Japanese soldiers outside the guardhouse as he received the latest report from Demarest, his cubicle neighbour and chief henchman. His long-sleeved cotton shirt was faded but neatly creased – after Jim had washed and dried the shirts Basie would fold them in a complex, origami-like package and slide them under his sleeping mat, from which they emerged with a department-store sharpness. Since Basie rarely moved from his bunk he seemed even cooler and crisper in Jim's eyes than Mr Sekura, and in most respects the years in Lunghua had been less of a strain for Basie than for the Japanese commandant. His hands and cheeks were still soft and unworn, though with a pallor like that of an unhealthy woman. Moving around his cubicle, as if in his pantry on the SS *Aurora*, he regarded Lunghua

Camp in the same way he had viewed the world beyond it, a suite of cabins to be kept ready for a succession of unwary passengers.

'Come in, kid. Stop breathing so much, you're making Basie all hot.' Demarest, a former bar steward, spoke without moving his lips – either, as Jim believed, he had spent an earlier career as a ventriloquist or, as Mr Maxted maintained, he had passed long terms in prison.

'The boy's all right . . .' Basie beckoned Jim to sit down, as Demarest returned to his cubicle. 'There just isn't enough air for him in the whole of Lunghua. Isn't that it, Jim?'

Jim tried to control his panting – not enough red cells, according to Dr Ransome, but often he and Basie meant the same thing.

'You're right, Basie. The Mustangs took it all with them. Did you see the air raid?'

'I heard it, Jim . . .' Basie glanced darkly at Jim, as if holding him responsible for the noise. 'Those Filipino pilots must have gone to flight school at Coney Island.'

'Filipino?' Jim at last mastered his lungs. 'Were they really Filipino pilots?'

'Some of them, Jim. There are a couple of wings operating with MacArthur's outfit. The rest are old Flying Tigers based at Chungking.' Basie nodded sagely, watching Jim to make sure he appreciated his superior savvy.

'Chungking . . .' Jim was agog. This was the kind of information on which his mind feasted, even though he knew that Basie embroidered the reports for his benefit. Somewhere in the camp was a concealed radio, which had never been discovered, not because it was well hidden, but because the Japanese were confused by the false tips given by prisoners eager to collaborate. Despite all his efforts, Jim had been unable to track down the radio, which was inactive for long periods. Then Basie would supply him with news bulletins of his own describing a parallel war. Jim always pretended to be impressed, though he could rarely separate rumour from outright fiction. It was an important way of keeping them close together.

Also, there was Basie's interest in Jim's expanding vocabulary.

'You did your schoolwork today, Jim? You learned all your words?'

'I did, Basie. A lot of Latin words.' Basie was intrigued by Jim's command of Latin, but easily bored, so he decided not to recite the whole passive tense of *Amo*. 'And some new English words. "Pragmatist",' he suggested, which Basie greeted with gloom, 'and "survivor".'

'"Survivor"?' Basie chuckled at this. 'That's a useful word. Are you a survivor, Jim?'

'Well . . .' Dr Ransome had not meant the term as a compliment. Jim tried to remember another word of interest. Basie never used the words, but seemed to store them away, keeping them in reserve for a better day, as if preparing himself for a life of elaborate formality.

'Is there any more news, Basie? When are the Americans going to land at Woosung?'

But Basie was preoccupied. He rested his head against the pillow and stared at the contents of the cubicle, as if burdened by all his possessions. At first sight the cubicle seemed to be filled with old rags and wicker baskets, but it actually contained a complete general store. There were aluminium pots and pans, an assortment of women's slacks and blouses, a mah-jong set, several tennis racquets, half a dozen unmatched shoes and a king's ransom of old copies of the *Reader's Digest* and *Popular Mechanics*. All these had been obtained by barter, though Jim had never understood what Basie gave in return – like Dr Ransome, he had come into the camp with nothing.

On the other hand, it had occurred to Jim that much of

this equipment was useless. No one was strong enough to play tennis, the shoes were full of holes and there was nothing to cook in the saucepans. The cabin steward, for all his guile, was the same limited man whom Jim had first met at the Nantao shipyards, with the same clear but small view of the world. Basie's talents expanded to fill only the most modest possibilities of petty thievery around him. Jim worried about what would happen to Basie when the war was over.

'Jobs, Jim,' Basie announced. 'You set out the traps? How far did you go? Across the creek?'

'Right across the creek, Basie. I went as far as the old drill hall.'

'Good . . .'

'I didn't see any pheasants, Basie. I don't think there are any pheasants. It's too close to the airfield.'

'There are pheasants, Jim. But we need to move the traps to the Shanghai road.' He peered shrewdly at Jim. 'Then we'll have to set up a decoy.'

'We could set up a decoy, Basie.' Jim guessed that there already was a decoy – himself. The whole enterprise of setting the traps had nothing to do with catching pheasants. Perhaps one of the Americans was planning to visit Shanghai, and Jim was being used to test the escape route. Alternatively, these bored sailors might be playing a game, betting amongst each other on how far he could push the traps before being shot by the Japanese sentry in the watch-tower. Although they liked Jim, they were quite capable of gambling with his life. That was American humour of a most special kind.

He swayed with fatigue, wishing he could lie across the foot of the bunk. Basie was watching him in an expectant way. From his window he would have seen Jim at work in the hospital garden, and he was waiting for a few beans or tomatoes. Basie always demanded these tidbits, though he was generous in his own way. When Jim was younger Basie spent hours making toys for him out of copper wire and cotton reels, sewing exquisite fish flies that hung from free-floating buoys. On his birthdays it was only Basie who gave him a present.

'Basie, I brought something for you . . .' Jim took the two condoms from his pocket. Basie pulled a rusty biscuit tin from below his bunk. As he removed the lid Jim saw that the tin was packed with hundreds of the prophylactics, as the Americans called them. Once the original stock of cigarettes was exhausted, these grubby rubbers formed Lunghua Camp's main unit of currency. The number in circulation had barely fallen in three years, not because there was little sexual intercourse at Lunghua, but for the reason that the contraceptives were too valuable as units of exchange to be used for idle purposes. Playing poker, the American sailors used stacks of the condoms as chips. It was doubly ironic, as Jim had heard Dr Ransome remark, that their value continued to rise even though almost all the prisoners in the camp were either impotent or infertile.

Basie inspected the condoms, suspicious of their pristine condition.

'Where did you get these, Jim?'

'They're good ones, Basie. That's the best type.'

'Is that so?' Basie often accepted Jim's expertise in unlikely areas. 'Perhaps you were looking inside Dr Ransome's medical cabinet?'

'There weren't any tomatoes, Basie. The air raid spoiled them.'

'Those Filipino pilots . . . Never mind. Tell me about Dr Ransome's cabinet. There were medicines there, I imagine.'

'Basie, there were a lot of medicines. Iodine, mercurichrome . . .' In fact the cupboard was bare. Jim tried to remember the medicine chest in his father's bathroom, and the strange names that summed up the mysterious world of the adult body. '. . . pessaries, linctus, suppositories . . .'

'Suppositories? Lie down, Jim. You're getting tired.' Basie put an arm around Jim's shoulders. Together they gazed through the window at the crowd of prisoners waiting for the overdue ration truck from Shanghai. 'Don't worry, Jim, there'll be plenty to eat soon. Forget all this talk about the Japs cutting our rations.'

'They might do it, Basie. We're an embarrassment to them.'

'An embarrassment? Dr Ransome is worrying you with all these words. Believe me, Jim, it's going to take more than us to embarrass the Japs.' He reached under his pillow and brought out a small sweet potato. 'You eat this while I work out our jobs. When you've finished I'll give you a *Reader's Digest* you can take back to G Block.'

'Say, thanks, Basie!' Jim devoured the potato. He liked Basie's cubicle. The abundance of objects, even if they were useless, was reassuring, like the abundance of words around Dr Ransome. The Latin vocabulary and the algebraic terms were useless too, but they helped to make up a world. Basie's confidence in the future encouraged him.

Sure enough, as he licked the last pith from his fingers, saving the skin for the evening, the military truck arrived from Shanghai with the prisoners' food ration.

27
The Execution

Two Japanese soldiers with fixed bayonets stood behind the driving cabin of the truck, their thighs lost among the sacks of potatoes and cracked wheat. However, as he leaned from Basie's window, Jim could see that the ration had been halved. He was glad that some food had come, but at the same time he felt almost disappointed. A crowd of several hundred prisoners followed the truck towards the kitchens, hands in the pockets of their ragged shorts, their clogs clattering. How would they have behaved if the truck had been empty? None of the prisoners, not even Dr Ransome, seemed able to rally themselves for the last stages of the war. Jim almost welcomed the hunger, when he would see again the curious light the Mustangs had brought with them . . .

Around him the Americans were leaving their cubicles and pressing against the windows. Demarest pointed to the columns of smoke that rose from the dockyard districts of northern Shanghai. Although they were more than ten miles away, Jim could hear a hard rumble across the deserted paddy fields, a forgotten thunder that reverberated over the land long after the bombs had exploded. The sounds drummed at the windows, a vague ultimatum to the listless prisoners of Lunghua.

Jim searched the smoke clouds for any signs of American aircraft. None of the dozen serviceable Zeros at Lunghua Airfield had taken off to intercept them.

'B-29s, Basie?'

'That's it, Jim. Superfortress bombers, what we call a hemisphere defence weapon. All the way from Guam.'

'From Guam, Basie . . .' Jim was impressed by the

thought of these four-engined bombers making the long journey across the Pacific, in order to attack the Shanghai dockyards where he had spent so many happy hours playing hide and seek. The B-29s awed Jim. The huge, streamlined bombers summed up all the power and grace of America. Usually the B-29s flew above the Japanese anti-aircraft fire, but two days earlier Jim had seen a single Superfortress cross the paddy fields to the west of the camp, only five hundred feet above the ground. Two of its engines were on fire, but the sight of this immense bomber with its high, curving tail convinced Jim that the Japanese had lost the war. He had seen captured American aircrews who were held for a few hours in the Lunghua guardhouse. What impressed him so much was that these complex machines were flown by men such as Cohen and Tiptree and Dainty. That was America.

Jim thought intently about the B-29s. He wanted to embrace their silver fuselages, caress the nacelles of their engines. The Mustang was a beautiful plane, but the Superfortress belonged to a different order of beauty . . .

'Take it easy, kid . . .' Basie put an arm around his shaking chest. 'They're a long way from Lunghua. You're going to mess yourself.'

'I'm all right, Basie. The war's nearly over, isn't it?'

'That's it. Not too soon for you, Jim. Tell me, did you ever see the Hell Drivers in Shanghai?'

'Sure I did, Basie! I saw them crash right through a burning wall!'

'Okay, then. Let's calm down and get on with our jobs.'

For the next hour Jim was busy with the tasks that Basie had assigned him. First, there was water to be collected from the pond behind the guardhouse. When he had carried the bucket back to E Block, Jim set about gathering fuel for the stove. Basie still insisted on boiling his drinking water, but the shortage of fuel made this difficult. After rounding

223

up a few sticks and shreds of straw mats, Jim searched the pathways around E Block, hunting for fragments of coke embedded in the cinder track. Even the cinders gave off a surprising heat.

Having lit his stove, Jim blew on the lazy flames. He placed the pieces of coke at the neck of the clay venturi, where, as Dr Ransome had explained, the air moved most swiftly. As soon as the drinking water had boiled he decanted some grey fluid into the mess tin, which he carried upstairs and left to cool on Basie's window ledge. He collected Basie's clothes and washed the dirty shirts in the remaining water. These could be left for an hour, while he queued for Basie's rations. The male prisoners in E Block were the last to be fed each day, and the men queued at the kitchens. Jim always enjoyed the long wait for Basie's ration of cracked wheat and sweet potato, and felt himself a growing man in the company of men. The lines of sweating prisoners covered with ulcers and mosquito bites, gave off a heady odour of aggression, and Jim could understand the Japanese guards being wary of them. Much of their foul language was above his head, their brutally crude talk of women's bodies and private parts, as if these emaciated males were trying to provoke themselves by describing what they could no longer perform. But there were always phrases to be catalogued away and savoured as he lay in his cubicle.

By the time Jim returned to E Block with Basie's shirts and food ration he felt entitled to push past Demarest and sit at the foot of the bunk. He watched Basie eat the cracked wheat, flicking the weevils to and fro like a Chinese shopkeeper with his abacus.

'We worked hard today, Jim. Your dad would be proud of us. Which camp did you say he was in?'

'Soochow Central. And my mother. You can meet them soon.' Jim wanted Basie to be present at their reunion, so that the cabin steward could identify him if his parents failed to recognize him.

'I'd like to meet with them, Jim. If they're not moved up-country . . .'

Jim noticed the odd inflexion in Basie's voice. 'Up-country?'

'Well, it's possible, Jim. Maybe the Japs will move people from the camps near Shanghai.'

'We'll be out of the war, then?'

'Yes, you'll be out of the war, all right . . .' Basie hid the sweet potato among the saucepans under his bunk. He rummaged among the shoes and tennis racquets and then produced a copy of the *Reader's Digest*. He flipped through the grimy pages, which had been read a dozen times by every resident of E Block. Layers of greasy tape, stained with dried blood and pus, held the cover to the threadbare spine.

'Jim, are you still reading the *Digest*? August '41, it has some good things in it . . .'

Basie relished every moment of Jim's excitement. This elaborate teasing was part of the ritual. Jim waited patiently, well aware that Basie exploited him, setting him to work each day in return for the old magazines. These bored merchant seamen could see that he was obsessed by everything American, and in their good-natured way they kept him dangling, rationing the ancient copies of *Life* and *Collier's* that Jim needed as much as the extra sweet potatoes. The magazines fed a desperate imagination.

This unequal exchange, jobs for magazines, was also part of Jim's conscious attempt to keep the camp going, whatever the cost. The activity screened his mind from certain fears that he had tried to repress, that the years in Lunghua would come to an end, and he would find himself building the runway again. The light that emerged from the burning body of the Mustang pilot had been a warning to him. As long as he ran his errands for Basie and Demarest and Cohen, to and from the kitchens, carrying water and playing chess, Jim could sustain the illusion that the war would last forever.

Reader's Digest in hand, Jim sat on the steps outside E Block. He squinted at the sunlight, forcing himself not to glance through the pages. Groups of prisoners lounged on the balconies after their meal. The shade between the pillars was reserved for the sick internees, who squatted together like the families of beggars in the entrances to the office blocks behind the Shanghai Bund.

Next to Jim was a young man who had been a floor manager in the Sincere Company department store, and was now suffering from the last stages of malaria. His body rattling with fever, he sat naked on the cement steps and watched the Lunghua Players rehearsing their concert party. His white lips, from which all iron had long been leached, repeated an inaudible phrase.

Jim wondered how to help this skeletal figure. He offered him the *Reader's Digest*, a gesture he instantly regretted. The man clasped the magazine in his hands and crushed the pages, as if the printed words inflamed his memories. He began to sing, in a harsh but barely audible voice.

'... we're the girls every boy adores,
C.A.C. don't mean a thing to me ...'

A stream of colourless urine ran between his legs and trickled down the steps. He dropped the magazine, which Jim quickly retrieved, before the pages could be soaked. As Jim straightened the spine he heard the air raid siren sound from the guardhouse. After a few seconds, before the prisoners could run for shelter, it stopped abruptly. Everyone stared at the empty sky, expecting the Mustangs to roar in from the paddy fields.

However, the siren blast signalled an altogether different display. Four Japanese soldiers, among them Private Kimura, emerged from the guardhouse. They surrounded a Chinese coolie who pulled a rickshaw which had brought one of their officers from Shanghai. Still exhausted by the long run, the coolie plodded in his straw sandals across the bare earth of the parade ground. His head was lowered as he pulled the shafts, and he tittered in the strained way of frightened Chinese.

The Japanese soldiers strode briskly on either side of him. None of them was armed but they carried wooden staves with which they struck at the wheels of the rickshaw and at the shoulders of the coolie. Private Kimura walked behind the rickshaw and kicked the wooden seat, hurling the vehicle against the coolie's legs. At the centre of the parade ground Kimura and another soldier seized the rickshaw and propelled it forward, pitching the coolie on to the ground.

The soldiers began to saunter around the upended rickshaw. Private Kimura kicked its wheels, shattering the spokes. The others stamped on the wooden handles and snapped the shafts. Together they threw the vehicle on to its back, scattering the cushions.

The coolie knelt on the ground, laughing to himself. In the silence Jim could hear the strange sing-song that the Chinese made when they knew they were about to be killed. Around the parade ground the hundreds of prisoners watched without moving. Men and women sat in makeshift deck-chairs outside the barrack huts, or stood on the steps of the dormitory blocks. The Lunghua Players paused in their rehearsal. None of them spoke as the Japanese soldiers strolled around the rickshaw, kicking its seats and framework into matchwood. From the locker below the seat fell a bundle of rags, a tin pail, a cotton bag filled with rice, and a Chinese newspaper, the entire worldly possessions of

227

this illiterate coolie. He sat among the grains of rice scattered on the ground, and began to sing at a higher note, raising his face to the sky.

Jim smoothed the pages of the *Reader's Digest*, wondering whether to read an article about Winston Churchill. He would have liked to leave, but all around him the prisoners were motionless as they watched the parade ground. The Japanese turned their attention to the coolie. Raising their staves, they each struck him a blow on the head, then strolled away as if deep in thought. Breathlessly now, the coolie sang to himself as the blood ran from his back and formed a pool around his knees.

The Japanese soldiers, Jim knew, would take ten minutes to kill the coolie. Although they had been confused by the bombing, and the prospect of the imminent end of the war, they were now calm. The whole display, like their lack of weapons, was intended to show the British prisoners that the Japanese despised them, first for being prisoners, and then for not daring to move an inch to save this Chinese coolie.

Jim realized that the Japanese were right. None of the British internees would raise a finger, even if every coolie in China was beaten to death in front of them. Jim listened to the blows from the staves, and to the muffled cries as the coolie choked on his blood. Dr Ransome would probably have tried to stop the Japanese. But the physician was careful never to go near the parade ground.

Jim thought about his algebra prep, part of which he had already done inside his head. Ten minutes later, when the Japanese returned to the guardhouse, the hundreds of prisoners moved away from the parade ground. The Lung-hua Players continued their rehearsal. Slipping the *Reader's Digest* inside his shirt, Jim returned to G Block by another route.

Later that evening, when he had finished Basie's potato

skin, Jim lay on his bunk and at last opened the magazine. There were no advertisements in the *Reader's Digest*, which was a shame, but Jim looked at the reassuring picture of the Packard limousine pinned to the wall of his cubicle. He listened to the Vincents talking in their low voices, and to the faint whoops of their son's cough. On Jim's return from E Block he had found the boy playing on the floor with the turtle. There had been a brief confrontation between Jim and Mr Vincent, who had tried to stop him replacing the turtle in the wooden case under his bunk. But Jim had stood his ground, confident that Mr Vincent would not try to wrestle with him. Mrs Vincent watched without expression as her husband sat on his bed, staring in his desperate way at Jim's raised fists.

28
An Escape

'Is the war over again, Mr Maxted?'

All around Jim, as he waited by the kitchen doors, the prisoners were pushing aside the food carts, shouting and pointing to the gates. The all-clear siren sounded across the camp, the wail of a broken bird trying to hide from the American bombing. Arms on each other's shoulders, the prisoners watched the Japanese soldiers leaving the guardhouse. Each of the thirty men carried his rifle with fixed bayonet, and a canvas pannier holding his personal kit. Among the straw mats and kendo armour there were two baseball bats, pairs of sneakers hung by their laces, and a portable gramophone, all obtained from the prisoners in return for cigarettes, food and news of relations in other camps

'It looks as if your little friends are leaving, Jim.' Mr Maxted ran his grimy fingers between his ribs, hunting for loose shreds of skin. He squinted at them in the August sun, as if concerned that he was mislaying pieces of himself around the camp. 'I'll keep your place for you, if you want to wave to Private Kimura.'

'He knows my address, Mr Maxted. I don't like saying goodbye. They'll probably come back this afternoon when they find there isn't anywhere to go.'

Unwilling to risk his place at the head of the kitchen queue, where he and Mr Maxted had waited since dawn, Jim climbed on to the food cart. Over the heads of men in front of him he watched the Japanese file through the gates of the camp. They lined up along the road, their backs to the fire-gutted fuselage of a Japanese aircraft that lay in the paddy field a hundred yards away. The twin-engined aircraft had been shot down two days earlier as it took off from Lunghua Airfield, torn apart by the machine-guns of the Lightning fighters that rose without warning from the deserted countryside.

As he balanced on the metal cart, Jim could see Private Kimura peering uneasily at the eastern horizon, from which the fearsome American planes emerged like pieces of the sun. Even in the warm August light Kimura's face had the toneless texture of cold wax. He licked his fingers and wiped his cheeks with the spittle, nervous of leaving the secure world of Lunghua Camp. In front of him the group of Chinese peasants sat on the grass verge. They stared at the gates, which had rejected them for so many months and were now unguarded. Jim was sure that these starving Chinese, in their universe of death, were unable to grasp the meaning of an open gate.

Jim gazed at the untended space between the posts. He too found it difficult to accept that he would soon be able to walk through the gates to freedom. The soldier in the watch-tower made his way down the ladder to the guardhouse roof, his light machine-gun clipped to the webbing across his shoulders. Sergeant Nagata emerged from the guardhouse and joined his men outside the camp. Since the disappearance of the commandant in the confusion of the previous week, the sergeant had been the senior Japanese officer in the camp.

'Mr Maxted, Sergeant Nagata is going – the war *has* ended!'

'Ended again, Jim? I don't think we can stand it . . .'

During the past week, when rumours of the war's end had swept the camp every hour, Mr Maxted had found Jim's high spirits more and more tiresome. As he ran on his errands down the pathways, Jim shouted at any passers-by, waved to the prisoners resting outside the barrack huts, excitedly jumped among the graves in the hospital cemetery when the American aircraft flew overhead, all part of his attempt to cover the insecurities of the coming world beyond the camp. Dr Ransome had twice slapped him.

Yet now that the war was over he felt surprisingly calm. Soon he would be seeing his mother and father, returning to the house in Amherst Avenue, to that forgotten realm of servants and Packards and polished parquet. At the same time, Jim reflected that the prisoners *ought* to celebrate, throw their clogs in the air, seize the air raid siren and play it back at the incoming American planes. But too many of them were like Mr Maxted, staring silently at the Japanese. They seemed glum and wary, the men almost naked in their ragged shorts, the women in faded sunsuits and patched cotton frocks, their malarial eyes unable to face the glare of freedom. Exposed to the light that seemed to flood into the camp through the open gates, their bodies were even darker and more wasted, and for the first time they looked as if they were guilty of a crime.

Rumour and confusion had exhausted everyone in Lunghua. During July the American air attacks had become almost continuous. Waves of Mustangs and Lightnings flew in from the air bases on Okinawa, strafing the airfields around Shanghai, attacking the Japanese forces concentrated at the mouth of the Yangtze. From the balcony of the ruined assembly hall Jim witnessed the destruction of the Japanese military machine as if he were watching an epic war film from the circle of the Cathay Theatre. The apartment houses of the French Concession were hidden by hundreds of smoke columns that rose from burning trucks and ammunition wagons. Fearful of the Mustangs, the Japanese convoys moved only after dusk, and the sound of their engines kept everyone awake for night after night. Sergeant Nagata and his guards had given up any attempt to patrol the camp's perimeter for fear of being shot by the military police supervising the convoys.

By the end of July almost all Japanese resistance to the American bombers had ceased. A single anti-aircraft gun mounted on the upper deck of Lunghua Pagoda continued to fire at the incoming aircraft, but the batteries around the runway had been withdrawn to defend the Shanghai dockyards. In these last days of the war Jim spent hours at the assembly hall, waiting for the high-flying Superfortresses in whose silver wings and fuselages he had invested so much of his imagination. Unlike the Mustangs and Lightnings, which skimmed like racing cars across the paddy fields, the B-29s would appear without warning in the sky above his head, as if summoned by Jim's starving brain. Their rolling thunder advanced across the land from the dockyards of Nantao. A Japanese troopship leaned against the mud-flats, bombed again and again until Jim could see daylight through its superstructure.

Throughout all this, the concrete runway at Lunghua Airfield remained intact. By an heroic effort, the Japanese engineers continued to fill in the craters after each raid, as if expecting a fleet of rescue aircraft to arrive from the Home Islands. The whiteness of the runway excited Jim, its sunbleached surface mixed with the calcinated bones of the dead Chinese, and even perhaps with his own bones in a death that might have been. Impatiently he waited for the Japanese to make their last stand.

This confusion of loyalties, the fear of what would happen to them once the Japanese were defeated, affected everyone in the camp. Often there were cheers from the light-headed prisoners squatting outside the barrack huts as a stricken B-29 dropped out of its formation. Dr Ransome had been correct to predict that the food supply to Lunghua would soon end. Once a week a single truck arrived from Shanghai with a few bags of fermenting potatoes, and the

233

godown sweepings of animal feed filled with weevils and rat droppings. Fights broke out among the prisoners queuing for their small ration. Irritated by the sight of Jim waiting all day by the kitchen doors, a group of Britons from E Block pushed him aside and overturned his iron cart. From then on, he recruited the help of Mr Maxted, nagging the architect until he clambered from his bunk.

Through the last week of July they watched the Shanghai road together, hoping that the ration truck had not been attacked by a low-flying Mustang. During these hungry days Jim discovered that most of the prisoners in G Block had been quietly stockpiling a small reserve of potatoes, and that he and Mr Maxted, who had volunteered to collect the daily ration, were among the few not to have planned ahead.

Jim sat on his bunk, empty plate in hand, and watched the Vincents share a rancid potato. They nibbled at the pith with their yellowing teeth. At last Mrs Vincent gave him a small piece of skin. Was she afraid that Jim would attack her husband? Fortunately, Jim was fed from the modest reserve that Dr Ransome had accumulated from his dying patients.

But by 1st August even these supplies had come to an end. Jim and Mr Maxted roamed the camp with their cart, as if hoping that a consignment of rice or cracked wheat might materialize under the legs of the water-tower, or among the graves in the cemetery. Once Mr Maxted caught Jim looking at the wrist-bones of Mrs Hug that had emerged from her grave, as white as the runway at Lunghua Airfield.

For Jim, a curious vacuum enclosed the camp. Time had ceased to exist at Lunghua, and many of the prisoners were convinced that the war was already over. On 2 August, after the rumour that the Russians had entered the war against Japan, Sergeant Nagata and his soldiers withdrew to the guardhouse and no longer patrolled the fence, abandoning the camp to its inmates. Parties of British prisoners stepped through the wire and wandered around the nearby paddy fields. Parents stood with their children on the burial mounds, pointing to the watch-tower and the dormitory blocks as if seeing the camp for the first time. One group of men led by Mr Tulloch, the senior mechanic at the Packard Agency in Shanghai, set off across the fields, intending to walk to the city. Others gathered around the guardhouse, jeering at the Japanese soldiers who watched from their windows.

Throughout the day Jim was confused by the apparent collapse of order within the camp. He was unwilling to believe that the war was over. He climbed through the fence and spent a few minutes with the pheasant traps, then returned to the camp and sat alone on the balcony of the assembly hall. At last rallying himself, he went in search of Basie. But the American sailors no longer received their lady callers, and had barricaded the doors of the dormitory. From his window Basie called to Jim, cautioning him not to leave the camp.

Sure enough, the war's end proved to be short-lived. At dusk a motorized column of Japanese troops passed the camp on its way to Hangchow. The military police returned to the guardhouse the six Britons who had tried to walk to Shanghai. Severely beaten, they lay unconscious for three hours on the guardhouse steps. When Sergeant Nagata allowed them to be carried to their bunks they described the confused terrain to the south and west of Shanghai, the thousands of desperate peasants driven back to the city with the retreating Japanese, the gangs of bandits and starving soldiers from the puppet armies left to fend for themselves.

Despite these dangers, the very next day Basie, Cohen and Demarest escaped from Lunghua.

* * *

235

The prisoners pressed forward to the empty guardhouse, their clogs clacking on the cinder path. Buffeted by the almost naked men, Jim held tight to the handles of the iron cart. The other prisoners had abandoned their carts, but Jim was determined not to be caught out if the ration truck arrived. He had not eaten since the previous afternoon. Although the inmates were about to seize control of the guardhouse, he could think of nothing except food.

A group of British and Belgian women stood by the gates, calling through the wire to the line of Japanese soldiers in the road. Weighed down by their rifles and bedding rolls, they fretted in the August sunlight. Private Kimura gazed uneagerly at the desolate paddy fields, as if wishing he was back in the secure world of the camp.

Flecks of spittle brightened the dust around the soldiers' ragged boots. Venting the anger of years on their former guards, the women spat through the wire, shouting and jeering. A Belgian woman began to scream in Japanese, tearing pieces of faded cloth from the sleeve of her cotton dress and hurling them at the feet of the soldiers.

Jim clung to his cart, jerking the handles when Mr Maxted wearily tried to sit on the wooden shaft. He felt detached from the spitting women and their excited husbands. Where was Basie? Why had he escaped? Despite the rumours that the war had ended, it surprised Jim that Basie should leave Lunghua and expose himself to all the hazards of the countryside. The cabin steward was too cautious, never the first to try anything new or gamble away his modest security. Jim guessed that he had heard some warning message on the secret radio. He had abandoned his cubicle filled with the hard-earned treasure of years, the shoes and tennis racquets and hundreds of condoms.

Jim remembered that Basie had talked about the inmates of the camps near Shanghai being moved up-country. Was he warning him that it was time to leave before the Japanese ran amok as they had done in Nanking in 1937? The Japanese always killed their prisoners before they made their last stands. But Basie had been wrong; at that moment he was probably lying dead in a ditch after being murdered by bandits.

Headlamps flared along the Shanghai road. Wiping their chins, the women stepped back from the wire. Necklaces of spit lay on their breasts. A Japanese staff car was approaching, followed by a convoy of military trucks, each packed with armed soldiers. One of the trucks had already stopped, and a platoon of soldiers jumped down into the road and then ran across the drained paddy field beside the western perimeter of the camp. Bayonets fixed, they took up their positions facing the wire.

Silent now, the hundreds of prisoners turned to watch them. A second platoon of air force police was wading across the canal that separated Lunghua Airfield from the camp. To the east, the long bend of the Whangpoo River completed the circle with its maze of creeks and irrigation ditches.

The convoy reached the camp, headlamps reflected in the dusty spit. Armed soldiers leapt to the ground, bayonets fixed to their rifles. From the fresh uniforms and equipment, Jim could see that these security troops were a special field unit of the Japanese gendarmerie. They moved swiftly through the gates, taking up their positions outside the guardhouse.

The prisoners drew back, bumping into each other like a flock of sheep. Caught by the retreat, Jim was knocked from his cart by the crush of bodies. A Japanese corporal, a short but strongly-built man whose holstered Mauser swung from his waist like a club, seized the handles of the cart and propelled it towards the gates. Jim was about to run forward and wrestle the handles from the Japanese, but Mr Maxted gripped his arms.

237

'Jim, for God's sake . . . Leave it!'

'But – it's G Block's cart! Are they going to kill us, Mr Maxted?'

'Jim . . . we'll find Dr Ransome.'

'Is the ration truck coming?' Jim pushed Mr Maxted away, tired of having to support this ailing figure.

'Later, Jim. Perhaps it will come later.'

'I don't think the ration truck will come.' As the line of Japanese soldiers forced the prisoners across the parade ground, Jim watched the guards patrolling the wire. Seeing the Japanese again had restored his confidence. The prospect of being killed excited him; after the uncertainties of the past week he welcomed any end. For a few last moments, like the rickshaw coolie who had sung to himself, they would be fully aware of their own minds. Whatever happened, he would survive. He thought of Mrs Philips and Mrs Gilmour and their discussion of the exact moment at which the soul left the body of the dying. Jim's soul had already left his body and no longer needed his thin bones and open sores in order to endure. He was dead, as were Mr Maxted and Dr Ransome. Everyone in Lunghua was dead. It was absurd that they had failed to grasp this.

They stood on the grass verge behind the throng of prisoners who now filled the parade ground. Jim began to titter, relieved that he understood the real meaning of the war.

'They don't need to kill us, Mr Maxted . . .'

'Of course they don't, Jim.'

'Mr Maxted, they don't need to, because . . .'

'Jim!' Mr Maxted cuffed Jim, then pressed the boy's head to his emaciated chest. 'Remember you're British.'

Circumspectly, Jim eased the smile from his face. He calmed himself, then wormed his shoulders from Mr Maxted's embrace. The moment of humour had passed, but the insight into their true situation, and his sense of being apart from himself, remained. Concerned for Mr Maxted, who was dribbling an oily phlegm on to the ground before his bare feet, Jim put an arm around his bony hips. He felt sorry for the former architect, remembering their Studebaker jaunts around the Shanghai nightclubs, and sad that he should have been so demoralized that all he could do to reassure Jim was to remind him that he was British.

Outside the guardhouse, where the commander of the gendarmerie unit had established himself, the block leaders were talking to a Japanese sergeant. A wan-faced Dr Ransome, coolie hat in hand, his shoulders stooped in his cotton shirt, stood beside them. Mrs Pearce entered the guardhouse, smoothing her hair and cheeks, already giving orders to a soldier in her rapid Japanese.

The prisoners at the front of the crowd turned and ran across the parade ground, shouting to the others.

'One suitcase! Everyone back here in an hour!'

'We're leaving for Nantao!'

'Everybody out! Line up by the gates!'

'They're holding our rations at Nantao!'

'One suitcase!'

Already the missionary couples were standing on the steps of G Block, bags in hand, as if they had somehow sensed the coming move. Watching them, Jim reassured himself that the camp was only being moved, not closed.

'Come on, Mr Maxted – we're going back to Shanghai!'

He helped the weakened man to his feet, and steered him through the hundreds of running prisoners. When Jim reached his room he found that Mrs Vincent was already packed. As her son slept in his bunk, she stood by the window, watching her husband return from the parade ground. Jim could see that she had begun to shed all memories of the camp.

'We're leaving, Mrs Vincent. We're going to Nantao.'

'Then you'll have to pack.' She was waiting for him to go, so that she could be alone in the room for a few last minutes.

'Right. I've been to Nantao, Mrs Vincent.'

'So have I. I can't imagine why the Japanese should want us to go again.'

'Our rations are in a godown there.' Jim was already debating whether to carry Mrs Vincent's suitcase. New alliances needed to be forged, and Mrs Vincent's slim but strong-hipped body might well have more stamina than Mr Maxted's. As for Dr Ransome, he would be busy with his patients, most of whom would soon start dying.

'I'll be seeing my parents soon, Mrs Vincent.'

'I'm glad.' With the mildest irony, she asked: 'Do you think they'll give me a reward?'

Embarrassed, Jim lowered his head. During his illness he had mistakenly tried to bribe Mrs Vincent with the promise of a reward, but it intrigued him that she could see the humour in her refusal to raise a finger to help him. Jim hesitated before leaving the room. He had spent nearly three years with Mrs Vincent, and still found himself liking her. She was one of the few people in Lunghua Camp who appreciated the humour of it all.

Trying to match her, he said: 'A reward? Mrs Vincent, remember you're British.'

29

The March to Nantao

Like the migration of a shabby country carnival, the march from Lunghua Camp to the dockyards at Nantao began two hours later. Exhausted even before they started by the long wait, Jim watched the prisoners assemble from his place at the head of the column. Under the bored gaze of the Japanese gendarmerie, the internees stepped cautiously through the gates, the men loaded with suitcases and bedrolls, the women with bundles of ragged clothes wrapped in straw panniers. Fathers carried sick infants on their backs, while mothers steered the smaller children by the hand. As he stood behind the Japanese staff car that was to lead the march, Jim was surprised by the sight of so many possessions, which had remained under the bunks throughout the years at Lunghua.

Recreation had clearly come high on the prisoners' list of priorities while they packed their suitcases before being interned. Having spent the years of peace on the tennis courts and cricket fields of the Far East, they confidently expected to pass the years of war in the same way. Dozens of tennis racquets hung from the suitcase handles; there were cricket bats and fishing rods, and even a set of golf clubs tied to the bundles of pierrot costumes carried by Mr and Mrs Wentworth. Ragged and undernourished, the prisoners shuffled along the road on their wooden clogs and formed themselves into a procession some three hundred yards in length. Already the effort of carrying the baggage had begun to tell, and one of the Chinese peasant women seated outside the gates now clutched a white tennis racquet.

Lounging against their vehicles, the soldiers and NCOs of the gendarmerie watched without comment. Well-fed and well-equipped, these security troops so feared by the Chinese were the strongest men whom Jim had seen during the war. Yet for once they seemed curiously unhurried. They smoked their cigarettes in the hot sunlight, gazed at the few American reconnaissance planes and made no attempt to abuse the prisoners or urge them along. Two of the trucks drove through the gates and made a circuit of the camp, collecting the patients from the hospital and those prisoners in the dormitory blocks who were too sick to move.

Jim sat on his wooden case, trying to adjust his mind and eye to the open perspectives of the world outside the camp. The act of walking without challenge through the gates had been an eerie experience, and Jim had been unnerved enough to slip back into the camp on the pretext of tying his shoelaces. Reassuring himself, he patted the wooden case containing his possessions – Latin primer, his school blazer, the Packard advertisement and the small newspaper photograph. Now that he was about to see his real mother and father he had thought of tearing up the picture of the unknown couple outside Buckingham Palace, his surrogate parents for so many years. At the last moment, as a precautionary measure, he had slipped the photograph into his box.

He listened to the crying of the exhausted children. Already people were sitting down in the road, trying to shield their faces from the swarm of flies that had vacated the camp and moved towards the sweating bodies on the other side of the wire. Jim looked back at Lunghua. The terrain of paddy fields and canals around the camp, and the road of return to Shanghai, which had been so real when observed through the fence, now seemed lurid and overlit, part of a landscape of hallucination.

Jim clenched his aching teeth, deciding to turn his back on the camp. He reminded himself of their food supplies in the godown at Nantao. It was important to remain at the head of the procession, and if possible to ingratiate himself with the two Japanese soldiers beside the staff car. Jim was considering this when an almost naked figure in ragged shorts and a pair of wooden clogs shuffled up to him.

'Jim . . . I thought I'd find you here.' Mr Maxted raised his sallow face to the sun. A fine malarial sweat covered his cheeks and forehead. He rubbed the dirt from the open spaces between his ribs, as if to expose the waxy skin to the healing light. 'So this is what we've been waiting for . . .'

'You haven't brought your luggage, Mr Maxted.'

'No, Jim. I don't think I'll be needing any luggage. You must find it strange out here.'

'I don't any more.' Jim peered cautiously at the open fields, their endless perspectives broken only by the burial mounds, and at the secretive canals. It was as if these bored Japanese soldiers had switched off the clock. 'Mr Maxted, do you think Shanghai will have changed?'

A faded smile, lit by the memories of happier days, briefly eased Mr Maxted's face. 'Jim, Shanghai will never change. Don't worry, you'll remember your mother and father.'

'I was thinking of that,' Jim admitted. His other problem was Mr Maxted. Jim had come to the head of the column, partly to be first in the queue for their rations when they reached Nantao, but also to free himself from all the duties that the camp had imposed upon him. Because he was alone he had been forced to do too many jobs, in return for favours that had rarely materialized. Clearly Mr Maxted needed help, and was hoping that he could lean on Jim.

Doggedly refusing to co-operate, Jim sat on his wooden case thinking about Mr Maxted as the architect swayed beside him. His pale hands, almost worn through by the months of pushing the food cart, hung at his sides like white flags. His bones were held together by little more than his memories of the bars and swimming-pools of a younger self. Mr Maxted was starving, like many of the men and women joining the procession. But he reminded Jim of the dying British soldier in the open-air cinema.

In the ditch beside the grass verge lay the grey cylinder of a Mustang drop-tank. Looking for some way of leaving Mr Maxted, Jim was about to cross the road when a burst of hot smoke ripped from the exhaust of the staff car. The Japanese sergeant stood on the rear seat, waving everyone on. Armed soldiers were moving down the road on either side of the column, shouting at the prisoners.

There was a clatter of clogs, as if hundreds of packs of wooden cards were being shuffled and dealt. First off the mark Jim stepped forward, case in hand and shoes bright in the hot Yangtze sun. He waved to the Japanese sergeant and strode purposefully down the dirt road, his eyes fixed on the yellow façades of the apartment houses in the French Concession that rose like a mirage from the canals and paddy fields.

Guided by the swarm of flies that danced over their heads, the prisoners moved along the country road to Nantao. Across the burial mounds and ancient trench works came the sound of American planes bombing the dockyards and marshalling yards to the north of Shanghai. The thunder drummed at the surface of the flooded paddies. Anti-aircraft fire flickered against the windows of the office buildings along the Bund, and lit up the dead neon signs – Shell, Caltex, Socony Vacuum, Philco – the waking ghosts of the great international companies that had slept through the war. Half a mile to the west was the main Shanghai road, still busy with convoys of Japanese trucks and field artillery moving towards the city. The labouring noise of their engines droned like pain across the stoical land.

Jim walked at the head of the procession, trying to listen to the men and women behind him. All he could hear was the sound of their breathing, as if the experience of freedom had left them speechless. Jim ignored his own rackety breath. Despite the ceaseless activity in Lunghua, he had never undertaken a task like this shuffling walk burdened by his wooden case. For the first hour he was too concerned about Mr Maxted's exhaustion to notice his own. But soon after reaching the Shanghai-Hangchow railway line Mr Maxted was forced to stop, defeated by the shallow gradient that led up to the level crossing.

'We're climbing, Jim . . . feels like the Shanghai Hills.'

'We ought to keep going, Mr Maxted.'

'Yes, Jim . . . you're like your father.'

Jim stayed with Mr Maxted, annoyed with him but unable to help. Mr Maxted stood in the centre of the road, hands on the bowl-like crests of his pelvis, nodding at the people stepping past. He patted Jim on the shoulder and waved him forward.

'You go on, Jim. Get to the head of the queue.'

'I'll save your place, Mr Maxted.'

By then several hundred people had passed Jim, and it took him half an hour to return to the head of the column. Within minutes he had fallen back, lungs aching as he gasped at the humid air. Only the lengthy halt at a canal checkpoint saved him from having to join Mr Maxted.

They had reached an industrial canal that ran westwards from the river to Soochow. Two young Japanese soldiers forgotten by the war, guarded the sandbag emplacement beside the wooden bridge. Their faces were as pinched as those of the prisoners whose clogs dragged over the scored planks.

While the trucks edged across the rotting timbers, the eighteen hundred prisoners sat on the embankment, occupying the deep grass for a quarter of a mile. Around them

245

they settled their baggage of suitcases, tennis racquets and cricket bats. Like drowsy spectators at a rowing regatta, they stared at the algae-filled water. The current drifted past the burnt-out hulk of an armoured junk beached against the opposite bank.

Jim was glad to lie down. He felt sleepy in a feverish way, his brain irritated by the hot sun and the hard light reflected from the yellow grass. He could see Dr Ransome standing in the last of the three trucks, swaying unsteadily among the patients on their stretchers. Jim thought of his Latin prep, now a week overdue, but Dr Ransome was a hundred yards away.

Watched by the Japanese soldiers on the road above them, many of the men walked down to the water's edge. They filled their mess-tins and stood drinking together in the shallows. Jim was wary of the water, remembering the black creeks at Nantao, and the thousands of gallons he had boiled for Basie. Was there a crew of corpses in the armoured junk? Inside the iron turret, now washed by the green waters of the canal, perhaps lay the captain of this puppet Chinese naval vessel, Jim could almost see the dead blood running out into the canal, slaking the thirst of these British prisoners, on its way to nourish the roots of the rice crops raised for another generation of Chinese turncoats.

Jim opened his wooden case and took out his mess-tin. He walked down the bank between the resting women and their exhausted children. Squatting on the narrow beach, he carefully filled his mess-tin with the surface water, hoping that the algae might sustain him. He drank the tepid fluid, watching the dissolving patterns of his golf shoes in the fine sand.

Filling the mess-tin, Jim climbed the bank to his case. On his right was the wife of a Shell engineer in D Block. She lay weakly in the long grass, whose blades had already sprung through the rents in her cotton frock. Her husband sat beside her, dipping his fingers into his mess-tin and moistening her large, carious teeth with the green water.

Lying on Jim's left was Mrs Philips. It irked Jim that she had seen him drinking on the bank and decided to rest beside him. No doubt she had some little chore in mind, and would nag him about his Latin prep. Although he had left Lunghua, Jim felt imprisoned by the camp. Everyone he had ever helped was still clinging to him. He almost expected to see Basie emerge from the turret of the armoured junk and call out: 'Jobs, Jim . . .'

But Mrs Philips did not look as if she was about to set him a task. The walk from Lunghua had exhausted her. She lay in the bright grass with her wicker suitcase, all that survived of the decades she had spent in the Chinese hinterland. Her face was now the palest mother-of-pearl, as if she had been drowned and then lifted from the water on to this quiet bank. Her eyes were fixed on a remote point in the sky. Jim touched her cheeks, wondering if she was dead.

'Mrs Philips – I've brought you some water.'

She smiled at him and sipped the water, her small fists clinging to the handles of her suitcase like a pair of white mice. 'Thank you, Jim. Are you very hungry?'

'I was this morning.' Jim tried to think of a joke that would cheer Mrs Philips. 'It's air I'm short of after all that walking, not food.'

'Yes, Jim . . .' Mrs Philips opened her case. She felt inside and produced a small potato. 'There you are. Remember to pray for us all.'

'Oh, I will!' Jim bit into the potato before she had a chance to change her mind. 'I'll pay you back when we get to Nantao. All our rations are there.'

'You've already paid me back, Jim. Many times.' Mrs Philips resumed her pinpoint scrutiny of the sky. 'Could you eat the potato?'

'It was really good.' As Jim finished the potato he noticed

the old woman's eyes move fractionally. 'Mrs Philips, are you looking for God?'

'Yes, Jim.'

'Say . . .' Jim was impressed. He was keen to repay Mrs Philips' generosity, if only with a modest discussion of theology. He followed the angle of the old woman's gaze. 'Do you mean God is right above us?'

'Of course, Jim.'

'Above the 31st Parallel? Mrs Philips, wouldn't God be above the magnetic pole? You ought to look at the ground, under Shanghai . . .' Intoxicated by the fermenting potato, Jim giggled at the thought of the deity trapped in the bowels of the earth below Shanghai, perhaps in the basement of the Sincere Company department store.

Mrs Philips held his hand, trying to comfort him. Still staring at the sky, she decided: 'Nantao – then they're taking us up-country . . .'

'No . . . our rations . . .' Jim turned towards the Japanese guards. The three trucks had crossed the bridge, and he could see Dr Ransome moving among his patients with a small child in his arms. Its cries sounded through the overbright sun. The hundreds of prisoners sat in the feverish light like figures in the lurid paintings that advertised the Chinese film spectacles. The Japanese squatted beside the trucks eating a boiled rice paste which they took from their haversacks. They made no attempt to share their food with the young soldiers defending the bridge.

Up-country . . . ? There were docks at Nantao, but why would the Japanese want to move them from Shanghai? Jim watched Mrs Vincent paddling at the water's edge fifty yards away. Finding a portion of the current that satisfied her, she filled a mess-tin for her husband and child. Dr Ransome had recruited a human chain from the men sitting on the embankment below the trucks, and they passed pails of water up to the patients.

Jim shook his head, puzzled by all this effort. Obviously they were being taken up-country so that the Japanese could kill them without being seen by the American pilots. He listened to the Shell man's wife crying in the yellow grass. The sunlight charged the air above the canal, an intense aura of hunger that stung his retinas, and reminded him of the halo formed by the exploding Mustang. The burning body of the American pilot had quickened the dead land. It would be for the best if they all died; it would bring their lives to an end that had been implicit ever since the *Idzumo* had sunk the *Petrel* and the British had surrendered at Singapore without a fight.

Perhaps they were already dead? Jim lay back and tried to count the motes of light. This simple truth was known to every Chinese from birth. Once the British internees had accepted it they would no longer fear their journey to the killing-ground . . .

'Mrs Philips . . . I've thought about the war.' Jim rolled over in the grass. He was about to explain to Mrs Philips that she was dead but the old missionary was asleep. Jim studied her blanched eyes, her mouth open to reveal a broken dental plate. 'Mrs Philips, we mustn't worry any more . . .'

Headlamps flared through the dust. The gendarmerie staff car trundled along the road. Japanese soldiers strode down the bank, waving their rifles and beckoning the prisoners to their feet. The trucks at the rear of the column had started their engines. Men and women were climbing the embankment, children and suitcases in hand. Others remained in the trampled grass, unwilling to leave this placid canal.

Jim lay on his side, making a pillow of his arm. He felt drowsy after Mrs Philips' potato, and the rumble of bombing and the voices of the British wives seemed far away. He stared at the blades of grass, trying to work out the speed at which the leaves grew – an eighth of an inch each day, a millionth of a mile per hour . . . ?

Then he noticed a Japanese soldier standing in the grass beside him. All but a hundred of the prisoners had climbed the slope and formed a procession behind the staff car. Around Jim a few people lay quietly. Mrs Philips clasped her wicker suitcase, and the woman from D Block whimpered as her husband pressed his hands to her shoulders.

Grains of rice clung to the stubble around the Japanese soldier's lips. They moved like lice as he assessed Jim's condition. His expression was one that Jim had seen before, at the detention centre in Shanghai, but for the first time Jim felt unconcerned. He would remain here beside the unhurried water and help Mrs Philips to look for God.

'Come on, Jim! We're waiting for you!'

An emaciated figure tottered down the bank. Mr Maxted bowed and smiled to the Japanese soldier, as if glad to recognize him. He collapsed in the grass and pulled Jim's shoulder.

'Good boy, Jim. We're moving on to Nantao.'

'They're taking us up-country, Mr Maxted. I might stay here with Mrs Philips.'

'I think Mrs Philips wants to rest. They're holding our rations in Nantao, Jim. We need you to lead the way.'

Hitching up his shorts, Mr Maxted bowed again to the Japanese soldier and helped Jim to his feet.

The column shuffled forward, following the staff car. Jim looked back at the hundred or so prisoners left behind on the embankment. As the soldier licked the rice grains from his chin, Mrs Philips lay at his feet in the yellow grass, beside the woman from D Block and her kneeling husband. Other soldiers moved along the bank, rifles slung while they stepped among the resting prisoners. Would they later help Mrs Philips and the others to Nantao?

Jim doubted it. Shutting Mrs Philips from his mind, he

gripped his wooden case and placed his feet in the dusty imprints left by the man limping in front of him. Already Mr Maxted had fallen behind. The brief rest on the embankment had fatigued everyone. Half a mile from the bridge, by a burnt-out shell of an ammunition truck, the Nantao road turned at right angles from the canal and ran along a causeway between two paddy fields. The procession came to a halt. Watched by the Japanese, who made no attempt to hurry them along, the prisoners waited limply in the sun. Jim listened to the tired breathing. Then there was a shuffle of clogs, and the procession moved forward again.

He looked back at the ammunition truck. He was startled to see that hundreds of suitcases lay on the empty road. Exhausted by the effort of carrying their possessions, the prisoners had abandoned them without a spoken word. The suitcases and wicker baskets, the tennis racquets, cricket bats and pierrot costumes lay in the sunlight, like the luggage of a party of holidaymakers who had vanished into the sky.

Holding tight to his case, Jim increased his stride. After so many years without any belongings, he did not intend to discard them now. He thought of Mrs Philips and their talk together by the sunny canal, a setting so much more pleasant than the camp cemetery where he had usually questioned her about matters of life and death. It had been kind of Mrs Philips to give him her last potato, and he remembered his dreamy thoughts of having died. But he had not died. Jim stamped his shoes in the dust, surprised by his own weakness. Death, with her mother-of-pearl skin, had almost seduced him with a sweet potato.

30
The Olympic Stadium

All afternoon they moved northwards across the plain of the Whangpoo River, through the maze of creeks and canals that separated the paddy fields. Lunghua Airfield fell behind them, and the apartment houses of the French Concession rose like advertisement hoardings in the August sunlight. The river was a few hundred yards to their right, its brown surface broken by the wrecks of patrol boats and motorized junks that sat in the shallows.

Here, in the approaches to the Nantao district, the devastation caused by the American bombing lay on all sides. Craters like circular swimming-pools covered the paddy fields, in which floated the carcasses of water buffaloes. They passed the remains of a convoy that had been attacked by the Mustang and Lightning fighters. A line of military trucks and staff cars sat under the trees, as if dismantled in an outdoor workshop. Wheels, doors and axles were scattered around the vehicles, whose fenders and body panels had been torn away by the cannon fire.

Swarms of flies rose from the bloodstained windshields as the prisoners stopped to relieve themselves. A few steps behind Jim, Mr Maxted left the procession and sat on the running board of an ammunition wagon. Still carrying his case, Jim went back for him.

'We're nearly there, Mr Maxted. I can smell the docks.'

'Don't worry, Jim. I'm keeping an eye on us.'

'Our rations . . .'

Mr Maxted reached out and held Jim's wrist. Gutted by malaria and malnutrition, his body was about to merge with the derelict vehicle behind him. The three trucks moved past, their tyres crushing the broken glass that covered the ground. The hospital patients lay across each other like rolls of carpet. Dr Ransome stood in the last truck, his back to the driver's cabin, feet hidden among the packed bodies. Seeing Jim, he gripped the side bar of the truck.

'Maxted . . . ! Come on, Jim! Leave your case!'

'The war's over, Dr Ransome!'

Jim watched the thirty Japanese soldiers who brought up the rear of the procession. Rifles slung over their shoulders, they strolled along at a thoughtful pace. They reminded Jim of his father's friends returning from a shooting party in Hungjao before the war. Clouds of white dust rose from the trucks, hiding Dr Ransome. The first of the soldiers passed Jim, large men whose eyes were fixed to the ground. Their nostrils flickered at the scent of the urine. As they strode through the dust a fine film covered their uniforms and webbing, and reminded him of the runway at Lunghua Airfield.

'Right, Jim . . .' Mr Maxted stood up, and Jim was aware of the odour of excrement that rose from his shorts. 'Let's get you to Nantao . . .'

Holding Jim's shoulder, he hobbled forward, clogs cracking the broken glass. Unable to overtake the trucks, they moved through the clouds of dust, joining the few stragglers at the tail of the column. A number of prisoners had given up, and sat with their children on the running boards of the bombed staff cars, gypsies about to make a new life among these partly dismantled vehicles. But Jim looked down at the powdery dust that covered his legs and shoes, like the undertaker's talc blown on to the bones of a Chinese skeleton before its re-burial, and knew that it was time to move on.

By late afternoon this layer of dust on Jim's legs and arms began to glow with light. The sun fell towards the Shanghai hills, and the flooded paddy fields became a liquid chessboard of illuminated squares, a war-table on which were placed crashed aircraft and abandoned tanks. Lit by the sunset, the prisoners stood on the embankment of the railway line that ran to the warehouses at Nantao, like a party of film extras under the studio spotlights. Around them the creeks and lagoons were filled with saffron water, the conduits of a perfume factory blocked by dead mules and buffaloes drowned in its scents.

The trucks bumped forward over the wooden sleepers. Jim balanced on the steel rail, and gazed through the dusk at the brick godowns beside the jetty. A concrete mole ran across the river to a derelict lighthouse. Through their binoculars a party of Japanese soldiers examined the smoking hulk of a steel collier, which had been struck by the American bombers and beached on a sandbank in the centre of the stream. Scorched by the explosions, its bridge-house was now as black as its masts and coal-holds.

A mile downstream from the collier were the Nantao seaplane base and the funeral piers where Jim had found refuge with Basie. Wondering if the cabin steward had returned to his old hiding place, Jim steered Mr Maxted between the rails, as the prisoners followed the railway embankment to the riverside causeway. To the west of the docks, in the waters of a shallow lagoon, lay the burnt-out shell of a B-29, its tail rising into the dusk like a silver billboard advertising its squadron insignia.

Jim stared at this huge stricken plane, and sat beside Mr Maxted among the press of bodies in the dusk. Hunger numbed him. He sucked on his knuckles, glad even for the taste of his pus, then tore stems of grass from the bank and chewed the acid leaves. A Japanese corporal was escorting Dr Ransome and Mrs Pearce towards the dockyards. The wharves and godowns, which from the distance had seemed intact, had been bombed almost to rubble. The rising tide rocked the rusting hulls of two torpedo boats beached beside the mole, and stirred the corpses of the Japanese sailors lying among the reeds fifty yards from where Jim was crouching. Undeterred, several of the British prisoners walked down the bank and drank at the water's edge. An exhausted woman held her child like a Chinese mother, gripping it behind the knees as it relieved itself on the oil-stained mud, then squatted and followed suit. Others joined her, and when Jim went to drink at the water's edge the evening air was filled with the stench of defecating women.

Jim stood by the river, the wooden case at his feet. The tide swilled the white dust from his shoes. In his mess-tin the water gleamed with oil washed from the sunken freighters in Shanghai harbour. Overlapping slicks covered the surface of the Whangpoo, as if trying to smother all life from the river.

He drank carefully, then watched the water lap around his case. He had carried the wooden box all the way from Lunghua, holding tight to the few possessions that he had assembled with such effort. He had been trying to keep the war alive, and with it the security he had known in the camp. Now it was time to rid himself of Lunghua and face up squarely to the present, however uncertain, the one rule that had sustained him through the years of war.

He pushed his case on to the greasy surface. In the last moments of the dusk the dead water came alive with roses of iridescent colour. As the box floated away, like the coffin of a Chinese child, the circles of oil raced to embrace it and sent tremors of light across the river.

Jim climbed through the resting prisoners and sat down beside Mr Maxted. He handed him the mess-tin of water and then cleaned the sand from his shoes.

'All right, Jim?'

'The war must end, Mr Maxted.'

'It will, Jim.' Mr Maxted had revived briefly. 'We're going back to Shanghai tonight.'

'Shanghai – ?' Jim was unsure whether Mr Maxted was

255

delirious, dreaming of Shanghai in the way that the dying prisoners in the camp hospital had babbled of returning to England. 'Aren't they taking us up-country?'

'Not now . . .' Mr Maxted pointed through the darkness to the collier burning off the mole.

Jim watched the smoke rising from the collier's bridge and superstructure, everywhere but from its funnel. The fire in the engine-room had taken hold, and the stern of the vessel glowed like furnace coal. This was the ship that would have taken them up-country, to the killing-grounds beyond Soochow. For all his relief, Jim felt disappointed.

'What about our rations, Mr Maxted?'

'They're waiting for us in Shanghai. Just like the old days, Jim.'

Jim watched Mr Maxted sink back among the exhausted prisoners. He had made his last effort to sit upright, trying to convince Jim that all was well, that the good luck and the skill of some unknown American bomb-aimer, which had saved them from being shipped aboard the collier, would continue to watch over them.

'Mr Maxted, do you want the war to end? It must end soon.'

'It has almost ended. Think about your mother and father, Jim. The war has ended.'

'But, Mr Maxted, when will the next one begin . . . ?'

Japanese soldiers were walking along the railway line, followed by Dr Ransome and Mrs Pearce. The corporals shouted to each other, their voices drumming along the rails. A faint rain fell, and the guards waiting by the trucks put on their capes. Steam lifted from the warm rails, as the prisoners rose to their feet and clutched their small children. Voices murmured through the darkness, and wives grasped their husbands' hands.

'Digby . . . Digby . . .'

'Scotty . . .'

'Jake . . .'

'Bunty . . .'

A woman with a sleeping child on her shoulder seized Jim's arm, but he pushed her away and tried to steady Mr Maxted. The darkness and the tacky river water had made them both light-headed, and at any moment they would fall across the rails. Led by the three trucks, the prisoners left the embankment and gathered on the jetty beside the ruined godowns. A hundred of the prisoners had stayed behind on the causeway, too weary to carry on and resigned to whatever future the Japanese had prepared for them. They sat in the rain below the railway embankment, watched by the soldiers in their streaming capes.

As the column of prisoners set off, Jim realized that a quarter of those inmates who had left Lunghua that morning had fallen behind. Even before they reached the gates of the dockyard several prisoners turned back. An elderly Scotsman from E Block, a retired accountant at the Shanghai Power Company with whom Jim had often played chess, suddenly stepped from the column. As if he had forgotten where he had been for all the years of the war, he wandered across the stony yard, then walked through the rain towards the railway embankment.

An hour after nightfall they reached a football stadium on the western outskirts of Nantao. This concrete arena had been built on the orders of Madame Chiang Kai-Shek, in the hope that China might be host to the 1940 Olympic Games. Captured by the Japanese after their invasion in 1937, the stadium became the military headquarters for the war zone south of Shanghai.

The column of prisoners crossed the silent car park. Dozens of bomb craters had torn the tarmac surface, but the white marker lines still stretched through the darkness. Damaged army vehicles were parked in neat rows – shrapnel-torn trucks and fuel wagons, treadless tanks and armoured half-tracks each pulling two artillery guns. Jim stared at the pock-marked façade of the stadium. Bomb fragments had dislodged sections of the white plaster, and the original Chinese characters proclaiming the power of the Kuomintang had emerged once again, threatening slogans that hung over the darkness like the hoardings above the Chinese cinemas in pre-war Shanghai.

They entered a concrete tunnel that led into the darkened arena. With its curved stands it reminded Jim of the detention centre in Shanghai, all its dangers magnified a hundredfold by the war. The Japanese soldiers formed a cordon around the running track. The rain dripped from their capes, and lit the bayonets and breeches of their rifles. Already the first prisoners were sitting down on the wet grass. Mr Maxted dropped to the ground at Jim's feet, as if released from a harness. Jim squatted beside him, waving away the mosquitoes that had followed them into the stadium.

The three trucks emerged from the tunnel and stopped on the cinder track. Dr Ransome climbed across his patients and lowered himself from the tail-gate. Mrs Pearce stepped from the cabin of the second truck, leaving her husband and son beside the Japanese driver. Through the rain Jim could hear Dr Ransome arguing with the Japanese. Hidden under his cape, the senior sergeant of the gendarmerie watched him without expression, then lit a cigarette and strolled away to the stands, where he sat in the front row as if about to observe a display of midnight acrobatics.

Jim was glad when Mrs Pearce returned to the cabin of her truck. Dr Ransome's complaining voice, in the tones he had used so often when remonstrating with Jim over his games in the hospital cemetery, was out of place in Nantao stadium. Within a few minutes of their arrival a complete silence had come over the twelve hundred prisoners. They huddled together on the grass, watched by the guards in the stands. Dr Ransome moved through the women and children, still trying to carry out his Lunghua inspections. Jim waited until he stumbled in the dark, prompting a surly shout from a group of men.

The rain fell across the stadium, and Jim lay back and let it run across his face, warming his cold cheeks. Despite the rain, thousands of flies settled on the prisoners. Jim wiped the flies from Mr Maxted's mouth, and tried to wash his face with the rain, but they festered on his lips, picking at his gums.

Jim watched the faint breath from Mr Maxted's mouth. He wondered what he could do for him, and regretted throwing away his suitcase. Pushing the wooden box into the river had been a sentimental but pointless gesture, his first adult act. He might have bartered his possessions and obtained a little food for Mr Maxted. A few of the Japanese soldiers were Catholics, and used the Latin Mass. One of the guards in his rain-soaked cape might have valued the Kennedy *Primer*, and Jim could perhaps have arranged to give him Latin lessons . . .

But Mr Maxted slept peacefully. A grey breath emerged through the flies on his lips, and from the other prisoners nearby. An hour later, when the rain had stopped, the flashes of an American air raid lit up the stadium, like the sheet lightning of the monsoon season. As a child, safe in his bedroom at Amherst Avenue, Jim had watched the sudden glares that exposed the rats caught in the centre of the tennis court and on the verges of the swimming-pool. God, Vera agreed, was taking photographs of the wickedness of Shanghai. The noiseless glimmer of the night raids, somewhere among the Japanese naval bases at the mouth of the Yangtze, cast a damp sheen over Jim's arms and legs, another reminder of that fine dust he had first seen as he helped to build the runway at Lunghua Airfield. He knew that he was awake and asleep at the same time, dreaming of the war and yet dreamed of by the war.

Jim propped his head against Mr Maxted's chest. The rapid flashes of the air raids filled the stadium and dressed the sleeping prisoners in their shrouds. Perhaps they would all take part in the construction of a gigantic runway? In his mind the sound of the American planes set off powerful premonitions of death. Conjugating his Latin verbs, the nearest that he could move towards prayer, he fell asleep beside Mr Maxted and dreamed of runways.

31
The Empire of the Sun

A humid morning sun filled the stadium, reflected in the pools of water that covered the athletics track, and in the chromium radiators of the American cars parked behind the goal posts at the northern end of the football pitch. Supporting himself against Mr Maxted's shoulder, Jim surveyed the hundreds of men and women lying on the warm grass. A few prisoners squatted on the ground, their sunburnt but pallid faces like blanched leather from which the dye had run. They stared at the cars, suspicious of their bright grilles, with the wary eyes of the Hungjao peasants looking up from their rice-planting at his parents' Packard.

Jim brushed the flies from Mr Maxted's mouth and eyes. The architect lay without moving, his white ribs unclasped around his heart, but Jim could hear his faint breath.

'You're feeling better, Mr Maxted . . . I'll bring you some water.' Jim squinted at the lines of cars. Even the small effort of focusing his eyes exhausted him. Trying to hold his head steady, he felt the ground sway, as if he and the hundreds of prisoners were about to be tipped out of the stadium.

Mr Maxted turned to stare at Jim, who pointed to the cars. There were more than fifty of them – Buicks, Lincoln Zephyrs, two white Cadillacs side by side. Had they come to collect their British owners now that the war had ended? Jim stroked Mr Maxted's cheeks, then reached into the cavern below his ribs and tried to massage his heart. It would be a pity for Mr Maxted to die just as his Studebaker arrived to take him back to the Shanghai nightclubs.

However, the Japanese soldiers sat on the concrete

benches near the entrance tunnel, sipping tea beside a charcoal stove. Its smoke drifted between the hospital trucks. Two young soldiers were passing pails of water to a weary Dr Ransome, but the security troops seemed no more interested in the Lunghua prisoners who occupied the football field than they had been during the previous day's march.

His legs trembling, Jim stood up and scanned the parked cars for his parents' Packard. Where were the chauffeurs? They should have been waiting by their cars, as they always did outside the country club. Then a small raincloud dimmed the sun, and a drab light settled over the stadium. Looking at their rusting chrome, Jim realized that these American cars had been parked here for years. Their windshields were caked with winter grime, and they sat on flattened tyres, part of the booty looted by the Japanese from the Allied nationals.

Jim searched the stands on the north and west slopes of the stadium. The concrete tiers had been stripped of their seats, and sections of the stands were now used as an open-air warehouse. Dozens of black-wood cabinets and mahogany tables, their varnish still intact, and hundreds of dining-room chairs were packed together as if in the loft of a furniture depository. Bedsteads and wardrobes, refrigerators and air-conditioning units were stacked above each other, rising in a slope towards the sky. The immense presidential box, where Madame Chiang and the Generalissimo might once have saluted the world's athletes, was now crammed with roulette wheels, cocktail bars and a jumble of gilded plaster nymphs holding gaudy lamps above their heads. Rolls of Persian and Turkish carpets, hastily wrapped in tarpaulins, lay on the concrete steps, water dripping through them as if from a pile of rotting pipes.

To Jim, these shabby trophies seized from the houses and nightclubs of Shanghai seemed to gleam with a show-window freshness, like the floors filled with furniture through which he and his mother had once wandered in the Sincere Company department store. He stared at the stands, almost expecting his mother to appear in a silk dress and run a gloved hand over these terraces of black lacquer.

He sat down and shielded his eyes from the glare. He massaged Mr Maxted's cheeks with his thumb and forefinger, pinching his lips and hooking out the flies trapped in his mouth. Around them the inmates of Lunghua Camp lay on the damp grass, staring at this display of their former possessions, a mirage that grew more vivid in the steepening August sunlight.

Yet the mirage soon passed. Jim wiped his hands on Mr Maxted's shorts. The Japanese had frequently used the stadium as a transit camp, and the worn grass was covered with oily rags and the ash of small fires, strips of canvas tent and wooden crates. There were unmistakable human remains, bloodstains and pieces of excrement, on which feasted thousands of flies.

The engine of a hospital truck began to run noisily. The Japanese soldiers had come down from the stands and were forming themselves into a march party. Pairs of guards climbed the tail-gates, cotton masks over their faces. Helped by three English prisoners, Dr Ransome lifted down those patients either dead or too ill to continue the day's journey. They lay in the tyre-ruts that scored the grass, as if trying to fold the soft earth around themselves.

Jim squatted beside Mr Maxted, working his diaphragm like a bellows. He had seen Dr Ransome bring his patients back from the dead, and it was important for Mr Maxted to be well enough to join the march. Around them the prisoners were sitting upright, and a few men stood beside their huddled wives and children. Several of the older internees had died in the night – ten feet away Mrs Wentworth, who had played the part of Lady Bracknell, lay

263

in her faded cotton dress, staring at the sky. Others were surrounded by shallow pools of water formed by the pressure of their bodies on the soft grass.

Jim's arms ached from the effort of pumping. He waited for Dr Ransome to jump down from the hospital truck and look after Mr Maxted. However, the three vehicles were already leaving the stadium. Dr Ransome's sandy head ducked as the truck lumbered through the tunnel. Jim was tempted to run after it, but he knew that he had decided to stay with Mr Maxted. He had learned that having someone to care for was the same as being cared for by someone else.

Jim listened to the trucks crossing the parking lot, their gearboxes gasping as they gathered speed. Lunghua Camp was at last being dismantled. A marching party formed itself beside the tunnel. Some three hundred British prisoners, the younger men with their wives and children, had lined up on the running track and were being inspected by a sergeant of the gendarmerie. Beside them, on the football pitch, were those prisoners too exhausted to sit or stand. They lay on the grass like battlefield casualties. The Japanese soldiers strolled among them, as if searching for a lost ball, uninterested in these British nationals who had strayed into a cul-de-sac of the war.

An hour later the column moved off, the prisoners plodding through the tunnel without a backward glance. Six Japanese soldiers followed them, and the rest continued their casual patrol of the blackwood cabinets and refrigerators. The senior NCOs waited by the tunnel and watched the American reconnaissance planes that flew overhead, making no attempt to mobilize the prisoners in the stadium. Within fifteen minutes, however, a second group had begun to assemble, and the Japanese came forward to inspect them.

Jim wiped his hands on the damp grass and put his fingers into Mr Maxted's mouth. The architect's lips trembled around his knuckles. But already the August sun was driving the moisture from the grass. Jim turned his attention to a pool of water lying on the cinder track. He waited for the sentry to pass, and then walked across the grass and drank from his cupped hands. The water ran down his throat like iced mercury, an electric current that almost stopped his heart. Before the Japanese could order him away, Jim quickly cupped his hands and carried the water to Mr Maxted.

As he decanted the water into Mr Maxted's mouth the flies scrambled from his gums. Beside him lay the elderly figure of Major Griffin, a retired Indian Army officer who had lectured in Lunghua on the infantry weapons of the Great War. Too weak to sit up, he pointed to Jim's hands.

Jim pinched Mr Maxted's lips, relieved when his tongue shot forward in a spasm. Trying to encourage him, Jim said: 'Mr Maxted, our rations should be coming soon.'

'Good lad, Jamie – you hang on.'

Major Griffin beckoned to him. 'Jim . . .'

'Coming, Major Griffin . . .' Jim crossed the cinder track and returned with a handful of water. As he squatted beside the major, patting his cheeks, he noticed that Mrs Vincent was sitting on the grass twenty feet away. She had left her son and husband with a group of prisoners in the centre of the football field. Too exhausted to move any further, she stared at Jim with the same desperate gaze to which she had treated him as he ate his weevils. The night's rain had washed the last of the dye from her cotton dress, giving her the ashen pallor of the Chinese labourers at Lunghua Airfield. Mrs Vincent would build a strange runway, Jim reflected.

'Jamie . . .'

She called him by his childhood name, which Mr Maxted, without thinking, had summoned from some pre-war memory. She wanted him to be a child again, to run the endless errands that had kept him alive in Lunghua.

As he scooped the cold water from the cinder track he remembered how Mrs Vincent had refused to help him when he was ill. Yet he had always been intrigued by the sight of her eating. He waited while she drank from his hands.

When she had finished he helped her to stand. 'Mrs Vincent, the war's over now.'

With a grimace, she pushed his hands away, but Jim no longer cared. He watched her walk unsteadily between the seated prisoners. Jim squatted beside Mr Maxted, brushing the flies from his face. He could still feel Mrs Vincent's tongue on his fingers.

'Jamie . . .'

Someone else was calling, as if he were a Chinese coolie running at the command of his European masters. Too light-headed even to sit, Jim lay beside Mr Maxted. It was time to stop running his errands. His hands were frozen from the water on the cinder track. The war had lasted too long. At the detention centre, and in Lunghua, he had done all he could to stay alive, but now a part of him wanted to die. It was the one way in which he could end the war.

Jim looked at the hundreds of prisoners on the grass. He wanted them all to die, surrounded by their rotting carpets and cocktail cabinets. Many of them, he was glad to see, had already obliged him, and Jim felt angry at those prisoners still able to walk who were now forming a second march party. He guessed that they were being walked to death around the countryside, but he wanted them to stay in the stadium and die within sight of the white Cadillacs.

Fiercely, Jim wiped the flies from Mr Maxted's cheeks. Laughing at Mrs Vincent, he began to rock on his knees, as he had done as a child, crooning to himself and monotonously beating the ground. 'Jamie . . . Jamie . . .'

A Japanese soldier patrolled the cinder track nearby. He walked across the grass and stared down at Jim. Irritated by the noise, he was about to kick him with his ragged boot.

266

But a flash of light filled the stadium, flaring over the stands in the south-west corner of the football field, as if an immense American bomb had exploded somewhere to the north-east of Shanghai. The sentry hesitated, looking over his shoulder as the light behind him grew more intense. It faded within a few seconds, but its pale sheen covered everything within the stadium, the looted furniture in the stands, the cars behind the goal posts, the prisoners on the grass. They were sitting on the floor of a furnace heated by a second sun.

Jim stared at his white hands and knees, and at the pinched face of the Japanese soldier, who seemed disconcerted by the light. Both of them were waiting for the rumble of sound that followed the bomb-flashes, but an unbroken silence lay over the stadium and the surrounding land, as if the sun had blinked, losing heart for a few seconds. Jim smiled at the Japanese, wishing that he could tell him that the light was a premonition of his death, the sight of his small soul joining the larger soul of the dying world.

These games and hallucinations continued until the late afternoon, when an air raid at Hongkew again lit up the stadium. Jim lay in his dream-wake, feeling the earth spring below his back like the ballroom floor at the Shanghai Country Club. The flares of light moved from one section of the stands to another, transforming the furniture into a series of spotlit tableaux illustrating the lives of the colonial British.

At dusk the last march party assembled by the tunnel. Jim sat by Mr Maxted, watching the fifty prisoners form themselves into a column. Where were they going? Many of the men and women could barely stand, and Jim doubted if they could get as far as the car park outside the stadium.

For the first time since leaving Lunghua, the Japanese had become impatient. Eager to be rid of the last prisoners still able to walk, the soldiers moved across the football field. They cuffed the prisoners and pulled their shoulders. A corporal with a cotton face mask shone his torch into the faces of the dead, then turned them on their backs.

A Eurasian civilian in a white shirt moved behind the Japanese, eager to help those ordered to join the march, like the courier of an efficient travel company. At the edges of the field the Japanese guards were already stripping the bodies of the dead, pulling off shoes and belts.

'Mr Maxted . . .' In a last moment of lucidity Jim sat up, knowing that he must leave the dying architect and join the march party into the night. 'I ought to go now, Mr Maxted. It's time for the war to be over . . .'

He was trying to stand when he felt Mr Maxted grasp his wrist. 'Don't go with them . . . Jim . . . stay here.'

Jim waited for Mr Maxted to die. But he pressed Jim's wrist to the grass, as if trying to bolt it to the earth. Jim watched the march party shuffle towards the tunnel. Unable to walk more than three paces, a man fell and was left on the cinder track. Jim listened to the voices of the Japanese draw nearer, muffled by the masks over their faces, and heard the sergeant gag and spit in the stench.

A soldier knelt beside him, his breath hoarse and exhausted behind his mask. Strong hands moved across Jim's chest and hips, feeling his pockets. Brusquely they pulled his shoes from his feet, then flung them on to the cinder track. Jim lay without moving, as the fires from the burning oil depots at Hongkew played across the stands, lighting the doors of the looted refrigerators, the radiator grilles of the white Cadillacs and the lamps of the plaster nymphs in the box of the Generalissimo.

Part III

32

The Eurasian

A restful sunlight warmed the stadium. From the cloudless sky fell a squall of hail, a flurry of frozen vapour dislodged from the wings of an American aircraft three miles above the Yangtze valley. Lit by the sun, the crystals fell on to the football field like a shower of Christmas decorations.

Jim sat up and touched the hailstones, nuggets of white gold scattered on the grass. Beside him, Mr Maxted's body was dressed in a suit of lights, his ashen face speckled with miniature rainbows. But within a few seconds the hail had melted into the ground. Jim listened for the aircraft, hoping that it might launch another cascade of hail, but the sky was empty from horizon to horizon. A few of the prisoners in the stadium knelt on the grass, eating the hail and talking to each other across the bodies of their dead companions.

The Japanese had gone. The NCOs and soldiers of the gendarmerie had taken their equipment and vanished during the night. Jim stood in his bare feet on the icy grass, staring at the exit tunnel. The shallow sunlight veered against the concrete walls from the deserted parking lot. Already one of the British prisoners hobbled through the tunnel on his worn clogs, followed by his wife in her ragged dress, hands pressed to her face.

Jim waited for a rifle shot to throw the man at his wife's feet, but the couple stepped into the parking lot and gazed at the lines of bomb-damaged vehicles. Jim left Mr Maxted and walked along the running track, intending to follow them, but then cautiously decided to climb one of the stands.

The concrete steps seemed to reach beyond the sky. Jim

paused to rest among the terraces of looted furniture. He sat on a straight-backed chair beside a dining-room table and drank the warm rain-water from the polished blackwood. Below him the thirty or so prisoners on the football field were rousing themselves as if from a dishevelled picnic. The women sat on the grass, quietly straightening their hair among the bodies of their former friends while a few of the husbands peered through the dusty windows at the instrument panels of the parked cars.

More than a hundred prisoners were dead, scattered on the football pitch as if they had fallen from the sky during the night. Turning his back on them, Jim climbed through the pools of water to the top tier of the stand. Now that he had left Mr Maxted he felt guilty that he had died, a guilt in some way connected with his missing shoes. He stared at his wet footprints, and told himself that he should have sold his shoes to the Japanese for a little rice or a sweet potato. As it was, by pretending to be dead he had lost both Mr Maxted and his shoes.

Yet the dead had protected Jim, and saved him from the night march. Lying with their bodies through the dark hours, both asleep and awake, he had felt closer to them than he felt to the living. Long after Mr Maxted had grown cold, Jim had continued to massage his cheeks, keeping away the flies until he was sure that his soul had left him. During the next days he had stayed close to Mr Maxted, despite the flies and the smell from the body of the dead architect. The prisoners resting in the centre of the field waved Jim away whenever he approached. Drinking the rain-water that dripped from the furniture in the stands, he had survived on a single potato he found in the trouser pocket of Mr Wentworth, and on the rancid rice scattered towards him by the Japanese soldiers.

Jim leaned against the metal rail and looked down at the parking lot. The British couple were staring at the lines of derelict vehicles, alone in a silent world. Jim laughed at them, a harsh cough that spat a ball of yellow pus from his mouth. He wanted to shout to them: The world has gone away! Last night everyone jumped into their graves and pulled the earth over themselves!

Good riddance . . . Jim stared at the moribund land, at the water-filled bomb craters in the paddy fields, at the silent anti-aircraft guns of Lunghua Pagoda, at the beached freighters on the banks of the river. Behind him, no more than three miles away, was the silent city. The apartment houses of the French Concession and the office blocks of the Bund were like a magnified image of that distant prospect that had sustained him for so many years.

Chilled by the river, a cool wind moved across the stadium, and for a moment that strange north-eastern light he had seen over the stands returned to dim the sun. Jim stared at his pallid hands. He knew that he was alive, but at the same time he felt as dead as Mr Maxted. Perhaps his soul, instead of leaving his body, had died inside his head?

Thirsty again, Jim walked down the concrete steps, scooping the water from the tables and cabinets. If the war had ended it was time to look for his mother and father. However, without the Japanese to protect them it would be dangerous for the British to set off on foot for Shanghai.

Beyond the goal posts, a British prisoner had managed to lift the hood of one of the white Cadillacs. Watched by his companions, he bent over the engine and touched the cylinders. Jim roused himself and raced down the steps, eager to be the driver's navigator. He could still remember every street and alleyway in Shanghai.

As he crossed the athletics track he noticed that three men had entered the stadium. Two were Chinese coolies, bare-chested with black cotton trousers tied at the ankles above their straw sandals. The third was the Eurasian in the white shirt whom Jim had seen with the Japanese security troops. They stood by the tunnel, while the Eurasian inspected the stadium. He glanced at the prisoners sitting on the grass, but his attention was clearly fixed on the looted furniture in the stands.

The Eurasian carried a heavy automatic pistol tucked into the waistband of his trousers, but he smiled at Jim in an ingratiating way, as if they were old friends separated by the misadventure of war.

'Say, kid . . . You're okay?' He surveyed Jim's ragged shirt and shorts, his legs and bare feet covered with dirt and sores. 'Lunghua CAC? I guess you've had to tough it out.'

Jim stared stolidly at the Eurasian. Despite the smile, there was no sympathy in the man's eyes. He spoke with a strong but recently acquired American accent, which Jim assumed he had learned while interrogating captured American aircrews. He wore a chromium wristwatch, and the Colt pistol in his waistband was like those that the Japanese guards at Lunghua had taken from the pilots of the downed Superfortresses. His baggy nostrils quivered in the stench rising from the football field, distracting him from his scrutiny of the stands. He stepped aside for two British prisoners who hobbled through the tunnel.

'It's some set-up,' he reflected. 'Your Ma and Pa here? Looks like you could use a couple of bags of rice. Ask around, kid, if they have any bracelets, wedding rings, charms. We can work together on it.'

'Is the war over?'

The Eurasian's eyes lowered, eclipsed by some passing shadow. He rallied himself and smiled keenly. 'That's for sure. Any time now the whole US Navy is going to tie up at the Bund.' When Jim looked unconvinced, the Eurasian explained: 'Kid, they dropped atomic bombs. Uncle Sam threw a piece of the sun at Nagasaki and Hiroshima, killed a million people. One great big flash . . .'

'I saw it.'

'Kid . . .? Did it light up the whole sky? Could be.' The Eurasian sounded doubtful, but turned his eyes from the booty in the stands and began to examine Jim. For all his easy manner he was unsure of himself, as if aware that the incoming US Navy might be less than convinced by his pro-American act. He glanced warily at the sky. 'Atomic bombs . . . too bad for all those Japs, but lucky for you, kid. And for your Ma and Pa.'

Jim weighed this as the Eurasian stepped to the concrete rubbish bin by the entrance tunnel and began to root around inside it. 'Is the war really over?'

'Yeah, it's over, finished, we're all friends. The Emperor just announced the surrender.'

'Where are the Americans?'

'They're coming, kid, they have to get here with their atom bombs.'

'A white light?'

'That's correct, kid. The atom bomb, US super-weapon. Maybe you saw the Nagasaki bomb.'

'Yes, I saw the atom bomb. What happened to Dr Ransome?' When the Eurasian seemed puzzled, Jim added: 'And the people who left on the march?'

'Too bad, kid.' The Eurasian shook his head, as if regretting a small oversight. 'The American bombing, some diseases. Maybe your friend will make it . . .'

Jim was about to walk away, when the Eurasian turned from the rubbish bin. In one hand he held a pair of worn clogs which he threw on to the track. In the other he carried Jim's leather golf shoes, tied together by their laces. He was about to speak to the waiting coolies, when Jim stepped forward.

'Those are mine – Dr Ransome gave them to me.' He spoke flatly and pulled the shoes from the Eurasian's hands. Jim waited for him to draw his gun, or order the coolies to knock him to the ground. Though exhausted by hunger,

275

and by the effort of climbing the stand, Jim was aware that he was once again asserting the ascendancy of the European.

'That's okay, kid.' The Eurasian was genuinely concerned. 'I was keeping those shoes in case you turned up. Tell your Ma and Pa.'

Jim walked past the coolies and entered the light-filled tunnel. Groups of British men and women were wandering among the tanks and burnt-out trucks in the parking lot. They followed the faded marker lines, with no idea of where they were going, as if they had survived the entire war only to expire in this shabby maze. Outside the stadium the August sunlight was made even more intense by the complete silence that lay over the paddy fields and canals. A white glaze covered the derelict land. Had the fields been seared by the flash of the atomic bomb which the Eurasian had described? Jim remembered the burning body of the Mustang pilot, and the soundless light that had filled the stadium and seemed to dress the dead and the living in their shrouds.

33
The Kamikaze Pilot

Secure in his shoes, Jim stood by the concrete blockhouse that guarded the vehicles in the parking lot. The Shanghai road ran past the entrance, heading towards the southern suburbs of the city. Nothing moved in the surrounding fields, but three hundred yards away a platoon of Chinese puppet soldiers sat in an anti-tank ditch beside the road. Still wearing their faded orange-green uniforms, they squatted by a charcoal stove, holding their rifles between their knees. An NCO climbed from the ditch and waited, hands on hips, watching Jim as he stepped into the road.

If he approached them, they would kill him for his shoes. Jim knew that he was too weak to walk to Shanghai, let alone cope with all the dangers of the open road. Hidden behind the blockhouse, he set out towards the safety of Lunghua Airfield. Its western perimeter was little more than half a mile away, a terrain of nettles and wild sugar-cane covered with fuel drums and the fuselages of abandoned aircraft. Between the rusty tailplanes he could see the concrete runway, its white surface almost evaporating into the heat.

The stadium fell behind him. The road was an empty meridian circling a planet discarded by war. Jim followed the verge, stepping among the broken clogs and rags of clothing left by the British prisoners during the last yards of their march to the stadium. On either side of him were bombed-out trenchworks and blockhouses, a world of mud. On the slopes of a water-filled tank-trap, among the tyres and ammunition boxes, lay the body of a Chinese soldier, orange uniform split by his ballooning buttocks and shoulders, glistening with oily light like a burst paint-pot. A pack-horse rested beside the road, hide flayed from its ribs. Jim peered into this capacious cage, half-hoping to find a rat imprisoned within it.

He left the road when it turned eastwards to the Nantao docks. He crossed the flooded paddy fields, following the earth embankment of an irrigation ditch. Even here, a mile to the west of the river, fuel oil from the beached freighters leaked through the creeks and canals, covering the drowned paddies with a lurid sheen. Jim rested on the perimeter road of the airfield, then climbed through the wire fence and walked up to the nearest of the abandoned aircraft. Far across the airfield, below the massive flak tower of Lunghua Pagoda, were the bombed hangars and workshops. A few Japanese mechanics wandered among the wreckage, but the Chinese scrap-dealers had yet to arrive, clearly fearful of this zone of silence. Jim listened for the noise of hacksaws or cutting equipment, but the air was empty, as if the fury of the American bombardment had driven all sound from the region for years to come.

Jim stopped under the tailplane of a Zero fighter. Wild sugar-cane grew through its wings. Cannon fire had burned the metal skin from the fuselage spars, but the rusting shell still retained all the magic of those machines which he had watched from the balcony of the assembly hall, taking off from the runway he had helped to build. Jim touched the feathered vanes of the radial engine and ran his hand along the warped flank of the propeller. Glycol had leaked from the radiator of the oil cooler and covered the plane with a pink tracery. He stepped on to the wing root and peered into the cockpit, at the intact display of dials and trim wheels. An immense pathos surrounded the throttle and undercarriage levers, the rivets stamped into the metal fabric by some unknown Japanese woman on the Mitsubishi assembly line.

Jim wandered among the stricken planes, which seemed to float on their green banks of nettles, letting them fly once again inside his head. Dizzied by their derelict beauty, he sat down to rest on the tail of a Hayate fighter. He watched the sky over Shanghai, waiting for the Americans to arrive at Lunghua Airfield. Although he had eaten nothing for two days, his mind was clear.

'. . . aah . . . aah . . .'

The sound, a deep sigh of anger and resignation, came from the edge of the landing field. Before Jim could hide there was a scuffle in the nettles behind the Zero. A Japanese airman stood twenty feet from him. He wore a pilot's baggy flying overall, with the insignia of a special attack group stitched to the sleeves. He was unarmed, but carried a pine stake he had wrenched from the perimeter fence. He thrashed at the nettles around him and gazed irritably at the rusting aircraft, sucking in his breath as if trying to inspire them to flight.

Jim crouched over his knees, hoping that the faded camouflage of the Hayate would conceal him. He noticed that this Japanese pilot-officer was still in his late teens, with an unformed face, boneless nose and chin. His sallow skin and the prominent knuckles of his wrists told Jim that the schoolboy pilot was as starved as himself. Only his guttural sighs were driven by the breath of a mature man, as if on joining his kamikaze unit he had been assigned the throat and lungs of an older pilot.

'. . . ugh . . .' He noticed Jim sitting on the tailplane and for a few seconds watched him across the nettles. Then he turned away and continued his bad-tempered patrol of the airfield perimeter.

Jim watched him beating at the sugar-cane, perhaps trying to clear a space for a helicopter to land. Had the Japanese prepared a secret weapon in answer to the atomic bomb, a high-performance rocket fighter that would need a longer runway than Lunghua's? Jim waited for him to signal to the guards at the foot of the pagoda. But the Japanese was intent only on his search of the derelict aircraft. He stopped to shake his head, and Jim was reminded again of the pilot's youth. At the outbreak of war, and until a few months earlier, he would have been a schoolboy, recruited straight from the classroom to the flight training academy.

Jim stood up and walked through the nettles to the yellowing grass at the edge of the airfield. He began to follow the Japanese, fifty yards behind him, and stopped when the pilot paused to work the elevators of a damaged Zero. He waited until the Japanese moved on again, and then walked after him, making no effort to hide and carefully placing his feet in the pilot's footsteps.

For the next hour they moved around the southern edge of the airfield, the young pilot with the boy in tow. The barrack huts and dormitory blocks of Lunghua Camp rose through the heat. Far away, across the airfield, the Japanese ground-crews lounged in the sun beside the burnt-out hangars. Although aware that Jim was following him, the pilot made no attempt to summon them. Only when they came within eyeshot of two soldiers guarding a rifle pit did the Japanese stop and beckon Jim to him.

They stood together by a rusting plane that had been stripped of its wings by the scrap-dealers. The pilot sucked at the air, distracted by Jim's patient gaze like an older schoolboy forced to acknowledge an admiring junior. For all his youth, he seemed to be willing himself to the edge of an adult despair. Clouds of flies rose from the decomposing body of a Chinese coolie lying in the sugar-cane among the fuel tanks and engine blocks. The flies hovered around the pilot's mouth, tapping his lips like impatient guests at a banquet. They reminded Jim of the flies that had covered Mr Maxted's face. Did they know that this teenage pilot should have died in an attack on the American carriers at Okinawa?

For whatever reason, the Japanese made no move to brush them away. No doubt he knew that his own life was over, that the Kuomintang forces about to reoccupy Shanghai would be eager to deal with him.

The Japanese raised his wooden stake. Like a sleeper waking from a dream, he hurled it into the nettles. As Jim flinched, he reached into the waist-pocket of his flight overalls and drew out a small mango.

Jim took the yellow fruit from the pilot's calloused hand. The mango was still warm from his body. Trying to show the same self-discipline, Jim forced himself not to eat. He waited while the pilot stared at the concrete runway.

With a last cry of disgust, the pilot stepped forward and cuffed Jim on the head, waving him towards the perimeter fence as if warning him away from contaminated ground.

34
The Refrigerator in the Sky

The sweet mango slithered around Jim's mouth, like Mrs Vincent's tongue in his hands. Ten feet from the perimeter fence, Jim sat on a Mustang drop-tank that had fallen into the grass beside a flooded paddy field. He swallowed the soft pulp, and chewed at the stone, scraping away the last of the pith. Already he was thinking of the next mango. If he could attach himself to this young Japanese pilot, run errands for him and make himself useful, there might be more mangoes. Within a few days he would be strong enough to walk to Shanghai. By then the Americans would have arrived, and Jim could present the kamikaze pilot to them as his friend. Being generous people at heart, the Americans would overlook the small matter of the suicide attacks on their carriers at Okinawa. When peace came, the Japanese might teach him to fly . . .

Almost drunk on the mango's milky sap, Jim slid to the ground, his back against the drop-tank. He stared at the level surface of the flooded paddy, deciding to be serious with himself. First, could he be sure that the war was really over? The Eurasian in the white shirt had been suspiciously offhand, but he was only concerned to steal the furniture and cars stored at the stadium. As for learning to fly, a kamikaze pilot might not be the ideal instructor . . .

A familiar drone crossed the August sky, a threat of engines. Jim stood up, almost choking on the mango stone. Straight ahead, some eight hundred feet above the empty paddies, was an American bomber. A four-engined Super-fortress, it flew more slowly than any American plane that Jim had seen throughout the war. Was it about to land at

Lunghua Airfield? Jim began to wave to the pilot in the glass-domed cockpit. As the Superfortress swept overhead, its engines shook the ground with their noise, and the derelict aircraft at the edge of the landing field began to tremble together.

The doors of the bomb-bays opened, revealing the silver cylinders ready to fall from their racks. The Superfortress drummed past, the higher pitch of one of its starboard engines cracking the air. Too weak to move, Jim waited for the bombs to explode around him, but the sky was filled with coloured parachutes. Dozens of canopies floated gaily on the air, as if enjoying the August sun. The vivid parasols reminded Jim of the hot-air balloons that the Chinese conjurors sent soaring over the gardens of Amherst Avenue at the climax of the children's parties. Were the pilots of the B-29s trying to amuse him, to keep up his spirits until they could land?

The parachutes sailed past, falling towards Lunghua Camp. Unsteadily, Jim tried to focus his eyes on the coloured canopies. Two of the parachutes had collided, entangling their shrouds. A silver canister dragged its collapsed parachute and plummeted to the ground, striking a canal embankment two hundred yards away.

Making a final effort, before he had to lie down for the last time among the derelict aircraft, Jim stepped through the sugar-cane into the flooded paddy. He strode across the shallow water to a submerged bomb crater in the centre of the field, then followed its ridge towards the canal.

As he climbed the embankment the last of the parachutes had fallen into the fields to the west of Lunghua Camp. The murmur of the B-29s engines faded over the Yangtze. Jim approached the scarlet canopy, large enough to cover a house, which lay across the embankment. He gazed at the lustrous material, more luxurious than any fabric he had ever seen, at the immaculate stitching and seams, at the white cords that trailed into the culvert beside the canal.

The canister had burst on impact. Jim lowered himself down the slope of sun-baked earth, and squatted by the open mouth of the cylinder. Around him, on the floor of the culvert, was a ransom in canned food and cigarette packets. The canister was crammed with cardboard cartons, and one had broken loose from the nose cone and scattered its contents over the ground. Jim crawled among the cans, wiping his eyes so that he could read the labels. There were tins of Spam, Klim and Nescafé, bars of chocolate and cellophaned packs of Lucky Strike and Chesterfield cigarettes, bundles of *Reader's Digest* and *Life* magazines, *Time* and *Saturday Evening Post*.

The sight of so much food confused Jim, forcing on him a notion of choice that he had not known for years. The cans and packets were frozen, as if they had just emerged from an American refrigerator. He began to fill the broken box with canned meat, powdered milk, chocolate bars and a bundle of *Reader's Digest*s. Then, thinking ahead for the first time in several days, he added a carton of Chesterfield cigarettes.

When he climbed from the culvert the scarlet canopy of the parachute was billowing gently in the air that moved along the canal. Holding the cold treasure to his chest, Jim left the embankment and waded across the paddy field. He was following the ridge of the bomb crater towards the perimeter of the airfield when he heard the leisurely drumming of a B-29's engines. He stopped to search for the plane, already wondering how he could cope with all this treasure falling from the sky.

Almost at once, a rifle shot rang out. A hundred yards away, separated from Jim by the open paddy, a Japanese soldier was running along the embankment of the canal. Bare-footed in his ragged uniform, he raced past the

284

parachute canopy, leapt down the weed-covered slope and sprinted across the paddy field. Lost in the spray kicked up by his frantic heels, he disappeared among the grave mounds and clumps of sugar-cane.

Jim crouched by the ridge of the bomb crater, hiding in the few blades of wild rice. A second Japanese soldier appeared. He was unarmed, but still wore his webbing and ammunition pouches. He sprinted along the canal embankment, and stopped to recover his breath beside the scarlet canopy of the parachute. He turned to look over his shoulder, and Jim recognized the puffy, tubercular face of Private Kimura.

A group of European men were following him along the embankment, clubs of weighted bamboo in their hands. One of the men carried a rifle, but Kimura ignored him and straightened his webbing around his tattered uniform. He kicked one of his rotting boots into the water, and then walked down the slope to the flooded paddy field. He had covered ten paces when there was a second rifle shot.

Private Kimura lay face down in the shallow water. Jim waited in the wild rice as the four Europeans approached the parachute canopy. He listened to their nervous quarrelling. All were former British prisoners, barefoot and in ragged shorts, though none had been inmates of Lunghua. Their leader was an agitated young Englishman whose fists were wrapped in a pair of grimy bandages. Jim guessed that he had been imprisoned for years in an underground cell. His white skin flinched in the sunlight like the exposed flesh of a snail teased from its shell. He waved his bandages in the air, bloody pennants that signalled some special kind of anger to himself.

The four men began to roll up the parachute canopy. Despite the starvation of the past months, they worked swiftly and had soon pulled the metal canister from the culvert. They repacked its contents, lashed the nose cone in place and dragged the heavy cylinder along the embankment.

Jim watched them make their way between the burial mounds towards Lunghua Camp. He was tempted to run over and join them, but all the caution learned in the past years warned him not to expose himself. Private Kimura lay in the water fifty feet away, a red cloud unfurling from his back like the canopy of a drowned parachute.

Fifteen minutes later, when he was certain that no one was watching from the nearby paddy fields, Jim emerged from the clump of wild rice and returned to his hiding-place among the derelict aircraft.

Quickly, without bothering to wash his hands in the flooded paddy, Jim tore the key from the Spam tin and rolled back the metal strip. A pungent odour rose from the pink mass of chopped meat, which gaped in the sunlight like a wound. He sank his fingers into the meat and pressed a piece between his lips. A strange but potent flavour filled his mouth, the taste of animal fat. After years of boiled rice and sweet potatoes, his mouth was an ocean of exotic spices. Chewing carefully, as Dr Ransome had taught him, drawing the last ounce of nutrition from every morsel, Jim finished the meat.

Thirsty after all the salts, he opened the can of Klim, only to find a white powder. He crammed the fatty grains into his mouth, reached through the grass to the edge of the paddy and scooped a handful of the warm water to his lips. A rich, creamy foam almost choked him, and he vomited the white torrent into the paddy. Jim stared with surprise at this snowy fountain, wondering if he would starve to death because he had forgotten how to eat. Sensibly he read the instructions and mixed a pint of milk so rich that its fat swam in the sun like the oil on the surrounding creeks and canals.

Dazed by the food, Jim lay back in the hot grass and sucked contentedly on the bar of hard, sweet chocolate. He had eaten the most satisfying meal of his life, and his stomach stood out below his ribs like a football. Beside him, on the surface of the paddy, swarms of flies festered over the cloud of white vomit. Jim wiped the mud from the second Spam tin and waited for the Japanese pilot to appear again, so that he could repay him for the mango.

Three miles to the west, near the camps of Hungjao and Siccawei, dozens of coloured parachutes were dropping from a B-29 that cruised across the August sky. Surrounded by this vision of all the abundance of America falling from the air, Jim laughed happily to himself. He began his second, and almost more important meal, devouring the six copies of the *Reader's Digest*. He turned the crisp, white pages of the magazines, so unlike the greasy copies he had read to death in Lunghua. They were filled with headlines and catchphrases from a world he had never known, and a host of unimaginable names – Patton, Eisenhower, Himmler, Belsen, jeep, GI, AWOL, Utah Beach, von Rundstedt, the Bulge, and a thousand other details of the European war. Together they described an heroic adventure on another planet, filled with scenes of sacrifice and stoicism, of countless acts of bravery, a universe away from the war that Jim had known at the estuary of the Yangtze, that vast river barely large enough to draw all the dead of China through its mouth. Feasting on the magazines, Jim drowsed among the flies and vomit. Trying not to be outdone by the *Reader's Digest*, he remembered the white light of the atomic bomb at Nagasaki, whose flash he had seen reflected across the China Sea. Its pale halo still lay over the silent fields, but seemed barely equal to D-Day and Bastogne. Unlike the war in China, everyone in Europe clearly knew which side he was on, a problem that Jim had never really solved. Despite all the new names that it had spawned, was the war recharging itself here by the great rivers of eastern Asia, to be fought forever in that far more ambiguous language that Jim had begun to learn?

35
Lieutenant Price

By the early afternoon Jim had rested sufficiently to turn his mind from this question and eat a second meal. The warm Spam, no longer chilled by its high-altitude flight in the bomb-bays of the B-29, slipped between his fingers on to the dusty ground. He retrieved the block of jellied meat, scraped away the flies and dirt, and washed it down with the last of the powdered milk.

Chewing on a chocolate bar, and thinking about the Ardennes offensive, Jim watched a B-29 soar across the open countryside two miles to the south-west. A Mustang fighter accompanied the bomber, drifting in wide circles a thousand feet above the Superfortress, as if its pilot was bored by the chore of guarding the relief plane. A flock of parachutes sailed towards the ground, perhaps aimed at an exhausted group of Lunghua prisoners abandoned by the Japanese during their march from Nantao stadium.

Jim turned to the Shanghai skyline. Was he strong enough to walk the few, dangerous miles to the western suburbs? Perhaps his parents had already returned to the house in Amherst Avenue? They might be hungry after the journey from Soochow, and would be glad of the last tin of Spam and the carton of Chesterfields. Smiling to himself, Jim thought of his mother – he could no longer remember her face but he could all too well imagine her response to the Spam. As an extra treat, she would have plenty to read . . .

He stood up, eager to begin the walk back to Shanghai. He patted his bloated stomach, wondering if there was a new American disease that came from eating too much food. At that moment, through the branches of the trees, he saw faces turn towards him. Six Chinese soldiers strode past the derelict aircraft, following the perimeter road. They were northern Chinese, tall and heavy-boned men wearing full packs and quilted blue uniforms. There were five-pointed red stars on their soft caps, and the leader carried a machine-gun of foreign design, with an air-cooled barrel and drum magazine. He wore spectacles and was younger and slighter than his men, with the fixed gaze of an accountant or student.

At a steady pace, as if they had already covered an immense distance, the six soldiers stepped between the aircraft. They passed within twenty feet of Jim, who concealed the Spam and the carton of Chesterfields behind his back. He assumed that these men were Chinese communists. By all accounts, they hated the Americans. Seeing the cigarettes, they might shoot him before he could explain that he too had once thought seriously of becoming a communist.

But the soldiers glanced at him without interest, their faces free of that unsettling blend of deference and contempt with which the Chinese had always regarded Europeans and Americans. They walked swiftly and soon vanished among the trees. Jim stepped over the perimeter wire, searching for the Japanese pilot. He wanted to warn him of these communist soldiers, who would kill him on sight.

Already he had decided not to walk alone to Shanghai. The Lunghua and Nantao districts were infested with armed men.

He would first return to the camp, and join the British internees who had shot Private Kimura. As soon as they recovered their strength they would want to set out for the bars and nightclubs of Shanghai. Jim, with all his expertise gained in Mr Maxted's Studebaker, would be their guide.

* * *

Although the gates of Lunghua Camp were little more than a mile from him, it took Jim two hours to cross the empty countryside. Avoiding Private Kimura, Jim waded through the flooded paddy field, and then followed the canal embankment to the Shanghai road. The verges were littered with the debris of the air attacks. Burnt-out trucks and supply wagons lay in the ditches, surrounded by the bodies of dead puppet soldiers, the carcasses of horses and water buffalo. A glimmer of golden light rose from the thousands of spent cartridge cases, as if these dead soldiers had been looting a treasury in the moments before their death.

Jim walked along the silent road, watching an American fighter cruise in from the west. Sitting in his open cockpit, the pilot circled Jim, engine throttled back so that the silver machine whispered through the air. Then Jim saw that its guns were cocked, their ejection ports open, and it occurred to him that the pilot might kill him for fun. He raised the carton of Chesterfields and the *Reader's Digests*, displaying them to the pilot like a set of passports. The pilot waved to him and banked the aircraft, setting course for Shanghai.

The presence of this American aviator cheered Jim. He confidently strode the last hundred yards towards the camp. The sight of the familiar buildings, the watch-tower and barbed-wire fence, warmed and reassured him. He was going back to his real home. If Shanghai was too dangerous, perhaps his mother and father would leave Amherst Avenue and live with him in Lunghua. In a practical sense it was a pity that the Japanese soldiers would not be there to guard them . . .

As Jim reached the camp he was surprised to find that the Chinese peasants and army deserters had returned to their plot beside the gates. They squatted in the sun, staring patiently at the bare-chested Briton who stood inside the wire, a holstered pistol strapped to his bony hips. Jim recognized him as Mr Tulloch, the chief mechanic at the

Packard agency in Shanghai. He had spent the entire war playing cards in D Block, pausing once to have a brisk row with Dr Ransome for refusing to help with the sewage detail. Jim had last seen him lying outside the guardhouse after his abortive attempt to walk to Shanghai.

He now lounged against the gates, picking at an infected bruise on his lip and watching the activity on the parade ground. Two Britons were dragging a parachute canister and its canopy through the door of the guardhouse. A third man stood on the roof, scanning the countryside with a pair of Japanese binoculars.

'Mr Tulloch . . .' Jim pulled at the gates, rattling the heavy padlock and chain. 'Mr Tulloch, you've locked the gates.'

Tulloch stared distastefully at Jim, clearly not recognizing this ragged fourteen-year-old, and suspicious of the carton of cigarettes.

'Where the hell did you come from? Are you British, boy?'

'Mr Tulloch, I was in Lunghua. I lived here for three years.' When Tulloch began to wander away, Jim shouted: 'I worked at the hospital with Dr Ransome!'

'Dr Ransome?' Tulloch returned to the gates. He peered sceptically at Jim. 'Doctor shit-stirrer . . .?'

'That's it, Mr Tulloch. I stirred shit for Dr Ransome. I have to go to Shanghai and find my mother and father. We had a Packard, Mr Tulloch.'

'He's stirred his last shit . . .' Tulloch took Sergeant Nagata's key-ring from the ammunition pouch of his holster. He was still unsure whether to admit Jim to the camp. 'A Packard? Good car . . .'

He unlocked the gates and beckoned Jim inside. Hearing the clatter, the Englishman with the bandaged hands who had shot Private Kimura strode from the guardhouse. Although emaciated, he had a strong, nervous physique,

292

and a pallor that was heightened by his bloodied knuckles. Jim had seen the same chalk-like skin and deranged eyes in those prisoners released after months in the underground cells of the Bridgehouse police headquarters. His chest and shoulders were covered with the scars of dozens of cigarette burns, as if his body had been riddled with a hot poker in an attempt to set it alight.

'Lock those gates!' He pointed a bloody hand at Jim. 'Throw him out!'

'Price, I know the lad. His people bought a Packard.'

'Get rid of him! We'll have everyone with a Packard in here . . .'

'Right, Lieutenant. Hop it, lad. Look sharpish.'

Jim tried to hold the gates open with his golf shoe, and Lieutenant Price punched him in the chest with a bandaged fist. Winded Jim sat down hard on the ground beside the watching Chinese. He held on to the Spam and the carton of Chesterfields, but the six *Reader's Digests* inside his shirt spilled on to the grass and were instantly seized by the peasant woman. The small, starving women in their black trousers sat around him, each holding a magazine as if about to take part in a discussion group on the European war.

Price slammed the gates in their faces. Everything around him, the camp, the empty paddy fields, even the sun, seemed to anger him. He shook his head at Jim, and then caught sight of the Spam in his hand.

'Where did you get that? The Lunghua drops belong to us!' He screamed in Chinese at the peasant women, suspecting them of complicity in this theft. 'Tulloch . . .! They're stealing our Spam!'

He unlocked the gates, intending to wrest the can from Jim, when there was a shout from the watch-tower. The man with the binoculars stepped down the ladder, pointing to the fields beyond the Shanghai road.

Two B-29s appeared from the west, their engines droning

over the deserted land. Seeing the camp, they separated from each other. One flew towards Lunghua, its bomb doors opening to reveal their canisters. The other altered course for the Pootung district to the east of Shanghai.

As the Superfortress thundered over their heads, Jim crouched beside the Chinese peasants. Armed with the rifle and bamboo clubs, Price and three of the Britons ran through the gates and set off across the nearby field. Already the sky was filled with parachutes, the blue and scarlet canopies sailing down into the paddies half a mile from the camp.

The engine noise of the B-29 softened to a muffled rumble. Jim was tempted to follow Price and his men, and offer to help them. The parachutes had landed behind a system of old trenchworks. Losing their bearings, the Britons ran in all directions. Price climbed the parapet of an earth redoubt and waved his rifle in a fury. One of the men slipped into a shallow canal, and waded in circles through the water-weed, while the others ran along the mud walls between the paddies.

As Tulloch watched them despairingly, Jim stood up and stepped past him through the gates. The Packard mechanic loosened the heavy pistol in his holster. The sight of the falling parachutes had aroused him, and the string-like muscles of his arms and shoulders trembled in a cat's cradle of excitement.

'Mr Tulloch, is the war over?' Jim asked. 'Really over?'

'The war . . .?' Tulloch seemed to have forgotten that it had ever taken place. 'It better be over, lad – any time now the next one's going to begin.'

'I saw some communist soldiers, Mr Tulloch.'

'They're everywhere. You wait till Lieutenant Price gets to work on them. We'll park you in the guardhouse, lad. Keep out of his way . . .'

Jim followed Tulloch across the parade ground, and

together they entered the guardhouse. The once immaculate floor of the orderly room, polished by the Chinese prisoners between their beatings, was covered with dirt and refuse. Japanese calendars and documents lay among the empty Lucky Strike cartons, spent ammunition clips and the tatters of old infantry boots. Against the rear wall of the commandant's office were stacked dozens of ration boxes. A naked Britisher in his late fifties, a former barman at the Shanghai Country Club, sat on a bamboo stool, separating the canned meat from the coffee and cigarettes. He packed the bars of chocolate on the commandant's desk, and brusquely threw aside the bundles of *Reader's Digest*s and *Saturday Evening Post*s. The entire floor of the office was covered with discarded magazines.

Beside him, a young British soldier in the rags of a Seaforth Highlander's uniform was cutting the nylon cords from the parachutes. He tied the ropes into neat coils, then expertly folded the blue and scarlet canopies.

Tulloch gazed at this treasure house, clearly awed by the fortune that he and his companions had amassed. He pushed Jim from the door, concerned that the sight of so many bars of chocolate would derange the boy.

'Don't dwell on it, son. Eat your Spam in there.'

But Jim was staring at the magazines heaped on the floor at his feet. He wanted to tidy them up, and hoard them for the next war. 'Mr Tulloch, I ought to go back to Shanghai now.'

'Shanghai? There's nothing there except six million starving coolies. They'll cut off your foreskin before you can say Bubbling Well Road.'

'Mr Tulloch, my mother and father – '

'Lad! Nobody's mother and father are going to Shanghai. All those FRB dollars chasing a hundred bags of rice? Here it's falling out of the sky.'

A rifle shot rang out across the paddy fields, followed by

two more in quick succession. Leaving the naked barman to protect their treasure store, Tulloch and the Seaforth Highlander ran from the guardhouse and climbed the ladder of the watch-tower.

Jim began to straighten the magazines on the floor of the commandant's office, but the barman shouted at him and waved him away. Left to himself, Jim stepped into the cell-yard behind the orderly room. The warm Spam in his hand, he peered into the empty cells, at the dark blood and dried excrement that stained the concrete walls.

In the cell at the far end of the yard, shaded by a straw mat hung from the bars, was the body of a dead Japanese soldier. He lay on the cement bench that was the cell's only furniture, his shoulders lashed to the remains of a wooden chair. His head had been bludgeoned to a pulp that resembled a crushed water melon, filled with the black seeds of hundreds of flies.

Jim stared through the bars at the soldier, shocked that one of the Japanese who had guarded him for so many years should have been imprisoned and then beaten to death in one of his own cells. Jim had accepted Private Kimura's death, in the anonymity of the flooded paddy field, but this reversal of all the rules governing their life in the camp at last convinced Jim that the war might be over.

He left the cell-yard and returned to the orderly office. He sat behind Sergeant Nagata's desk, a luxury he had never once been allowed, and began to read the discarded copies of *Life* and the *Saturday Evening Post*. For once the lavish advertisements, the headlines and slogans – 'When Better Cars are built, Buick will build them!' – failed to touch him. Despite the food he had eaten, he felt numbed by the task of finding a way to Shanghai, and by all the confusions of the arbitrary peace imposed on the settled and secure landscape of the war. Peace had come, but it failed to fit properly.

Through the broken windows Jim watched a B-29 cross the river two miles away, searching the warehouses of Pootung for any groups of Allied prisoners. The peasants outside the gates of Lunghua ignored the bomber. Jim had noticed that the Chinese never looked up at the planes. Although they were nationals of one of the Allied powers at war with Japan, they would not share in these relief supplies.

He listened to the angry voices of the Britons returning from their foray across the paddy fields. Despite all their efforts, they had seized only two of the parachute canisters. While Lieutenant Price stood guard by the gates, rifle trembling in his hands, the others dragged the canisters into the camp. The sweat dripped from their bodies on to the scarlet silk. The remaining parachutes had vanished into the countryside, spirited from under Price's nose by the secret tenants of the burial mounds.

As large as bombs, the canisters lay on the floor in the commandant's office. The naked barman sat astride them, the sweat from his buttocks dulling the silver, while the Seaforth Highlander struck off the nose cones with the rifle butt. The men tore the cartons apart, loading their emaciated arms with cans of meat and coffee, chocolates and cigarettes. Lieutenant Price hovered among them, the bones in his shoulders shaking like castanets. He was excited and exhausted at the same time, eager to work up his irritation again and put to good use all the violence he had found within himself on beating the Japanese to death.

He noticed Jim quietly reading his magazines behind Sergeant Nagata's desk. 'Tulloch! He's here again! The boy with the Packard . . .'

'The lad was in the camp, Lieutenant. He skivvied for one of the doctors.'

'He's roaming around everywhere! Lock him up in one of the cells!'

'He isn't the talkative type, Lieutenant.' Tulloch held Jim's arm, reluctantly pulling him towards the cell-yard. 'He's walked all the way from Nantao Stadium.'

'Nantao . . .? The big stadium?' Price turned to Jim with interest, gazing at him with all the guilelessness of the fanatic. 'How long were you there, boy?'

'Three days,' Jim replied. 'Or I think it was six days. Until the war ended.'

'He can't count.'

'He must have had a good look, Lieutenant.'

'I bet he had a good look. Roaming around all the time. Boy, what did you see in the stadium?' Price treated Jim to a roguish grimace. 'Rifles? Stores?'

'Cars, mostly,' Jim explained. 'At least five Buicks, two Cadillacs, and a Lincoln Zephyr.'

'Forget about the cars! Were you born in a garage? What else did you see?'

'Just a lot of carpets and furniture.'

'Fur coats?' Tulloch interjected. 'There was no ordnance there, Lieutenant. What about Scotch whisky, son?'

Price pulled the copy of *Life* from Jim's hands. 'For God's sake, you'll ruin your eyes. Listen to Mr Tulloch. Did you see any Scotch whisky?'

Jim stepped back, keeping the silver canisters between himself and this unstable man. As if excited by the booty in Nantao Stadium, the lieutenant's hands were bleeding through their bandages. Jim knew that Lieutenant Price would have liked to get him alone and then beat him to death, not because he was cruel, but because only the sight of Jim's pain would clear away all the agony that he himself had endured.

'There might have been Scotch whisky,' he said tactfully. 'There were a lot of bars.'

'Bars . . .?' Price stepped across the cartons of Chesterfields, ready to slap Jim. 'I'll give you bars . . .'

'Cocktail bars – at least twenty of them. There might have been whisky there.'

'Sounds like a hotel. Tulloch, what sort of war did you people have here? Right, boy, what else did you see?'

'I saw the atom bomb drop at Nagasaki,' Jim said. He spoke in a clear voice. 'I saw the white flash! Is the war over now?'

The sweating men put down their cans and cartons. Lieutenant Price stared at Jim, surprised by this statement but prepared to believe it. He lit a cigarette as an American aircraft flew over the camp, a Mustang returning to its base on Okinawa.

Through the noise Jim shouted: 'I saw the *atom bomb* . . .!'

'Yes . . . you must have seen it.' Lieutenant Price fastened the bandages around his bleeding fists. He sucked fiercely on his cigarette. Gazing hungrily at Jim, he picked up the copy of *Life* and left the commandant's office. As the Mustang's engine faded across the paddy fields they could hear Price striding up and down the cell-yard, striking the doors of the cells with the rolled magazine.

Did Lieutenant Price believe that he had been poisoned by the atom bomb? Jim walked across the parade ground, looking up at the empty barrack huts and dormitory blocks. The windows hung open in the sunlight, as if the tenants had fled at his approach. The mention of the Nagasaki raid, and its confusion with the booty waiting for Price in Nantao Stadium, had calmed this former officer in the Nanking Police. For an hour Jim had helped the men to unpack the parachute canisters, and Price had not objected when Tulloch gave their young recruit a bar of American chocolate. Images of hunger and violence fused in Price's mind, as they had done during the years of his imprisonment by the kempetai.

Holding his tin of Spam and a bundle of *Life* magazines, Jim climbed the steps into the foyer of D Block. He paused by the notice boards with their fading camp bulletins and commandant's orders. In the dormitories he strolled along the lines of bunks. The home-made lockers had been looted by the Japanese after the departure of the prisoners, as if there were still something of value to be found in this rubbish of urine-stained mats and packing-case furniture.

Yet despite the emptiness of the camp it seemed ready for instant occupation. Outside G Block he looked at the baked earth, at the worn ruts of years left by the iron wheels of the food cart, pointing their way to the camp kitchens. He stood in the doorway of his room, barely surprised to see the faded magazine cuttings pinned to the wall above his bunk. In the last minutes before joining the march Mrs Vincent had torn down the curtain of his cubicle, satisfying a long-held need to occupy the whole room. Neatly folded, the curtain lay under Jim's bunk, and he was tempted to pin it up again.

A marked smell hung in the room, one he had never noticed during all the years of the war, at once enticing and ambiguous. He realized that it was the odour of Mrs Vincent's body, and for a moment he imagined that she had returned to the camp. Jim stretched out on Mrs Vincent's bunk, and balanced the tin of Spam on his forehead. He surveyed the room from this unfamiliar angle, a privilege he had never been allowed during the war. Tucked behind the door, his cubicle must have resembled one of those ram-shackle hutches which the beggars of Shanghai erected around themselves out of newspapers and straw mats. Often he must have seemed to Mrs Vincent like a beast in a kennel. It was no wonder Jim reflected as he perused a copy of *Life*, that Mrs Vincent had been intensely irritated by him, wishing him away even to the point of hoping he would die.

Jim lay on her straw mattress, smelling the scent of her body, fitting his hips and shoulders into the shallow mould she had left behind. Seen from Mrs Vincent's vantage-point, the past three years appeared subtly different; even a few steps across a small room generated a separate war, a separate ordeal for this woman with her weary husband and sick child.

Thinking with affection of Mrs Vincent, Jim wished that they were still together. He missed Dr Ransome and Mrs Pearce, and the group of men who sat all day on the steps outside the foyer. It occurred to Jim that they might also miss Lunghua. Perhaps one day they would all return to the camp.

He left the room and walked down the corridor to the rear door where the children had played. The marks of their games – hopscotch, marbles and fighting tops – still covered the ground. Jim kicked a small stone into the hopscotch

301

court and deftly flicked it around the squares, then set out on a circuit of the deserted camp. Already he could feel Lunghua gathering itself around him again.

As he approached the hospital he began to hope that Dr Ransome would be there. By the entrance to Hut 6 a rain-soaked pierrot costume of the Lunghua Sophomores lay in a muddy pool. Jim stopped to clean the Spam tin. He wiped the label with the ruff of the costume, remembering Dr Ransome's lectures on hygiene.

The bamboo shutters were lowered across the windows of the hospital, as if Dr Ransome wanted the patients to sleep through the afternoon. Jim climbed the steps, aware of a faint murmur within the building. When he pushed back the doors a cloud of flies enveloped him. Maddened by the light, they filled the narrow entrance hall, as if trying to shake off the foul odour that clung to their wings.

Brushing the flies from his mouth, Jim walked into the men's ward. The decaying air streamed down the plywood walls, bathing the flies that fed on the bodies piled across the bunks. Identifiable by their ragged shorts and flowered dresses, and by the clogs embedded in their swollen feet, dozens of Lunghua prisoners lay on the bunks like sides of meat in a condemned slaughterhouse. Their backs and shoulders glistened with mucilage, and the splayed mouths in their ballooning cheeks still gaped as if these bloated men and women, dragged from a banquet, were gripped by a ravenous hunger.

He walked through the darkened ward, the tin of Spam held tightly to his chest, breathing through the magazines cupped over his mouth. Despite their caricature faces, Jim recognized several of the prisoners. He searched for Dr Ransome and Mrs Vincent, assuming that the bodies were those of the Lunghua internees who had fallen behind during the march from the stadium. The flies festered over the bodies, in some way aware that the war had ended and

302

determined to hoard every morsel of flesh for the coming famine of the peace.

Jim stood on the steps of the hospital, looking out at the deserted camp and the silent fields beyond the wire. The flies soon left him and returned to the ward. He set out for the kitchen garden. He walked among the fading plants, wondering whether to water them, and plucked the last two tomatoes. He raised the berries to his lips, but stopped before eating them. He remembered his fears that his soul had died in the stadium at Nantao, even though his body had survived. If his soul had been unable to escape, and had died within him, would feeding his body engorge it like the corpses in the hospital?

Thinking about his last night in Nantao Stadium, Jim sat on the balcony of the assembly hall. In the late afternoon a Chinese merchant arrived at the gates of the camp, accompanied by three coolies. They carried earthenware jars of rice wine suspended from bamboo yokes across their backs. Jim watched the barter of goods take place outside the guardhouse. Wisely, Lieutenant Price had closed the door of the treasure chest in the commandant's office. Cartons of Lucky Strikes and a single parachute canopy were exchanged for the jars of wine. When the merchant left, followed by his coolies with their bale of scarlet silk, the Britons were soon drunk. Jim decided not to return to the guardhouse that evening. Lieutenant Price's white body lurched through the dusk, the cigarette burns on his chest inflamed by the wine.

From the balcony Jim gazed across Lunghua Airfield. Carefully he opened his tin of Spam. It was a pity that Dr Ransome would not be sharing it with him. As he raised the warm meat to his mouth he thought of the bodies in the hospital. He had not been shocked by the sight of the dead prisoners. In fact, he had known all along that those who fell behind during the march from Lunghua would be left to die or killed where they rested. Nonetheless, he associated the chopped ham with those fattened corpses. Each was enveloped in the same mucilage. The living who ate or drank too quickly, like Tulloch and the police lieutenant with his bloody hands, would soon join the overfed dead. Food fed death, the eager and waiting death of their own bodies.

Jim listened to the drunken shouts from the guardhouse, and the volley of rifle shots as Price fired over the heads of the Chinese at the gates. With his dungeon pallor and bandaged hands, this albino figure frightened Jim, the first of the dead to rise from the grave, eager to start the next world war.

He rested his eyes on the reassuring geometry of the airfield runway. Four hundred yards away, the young Japanese pilot walked among the derelict aircraft. Bamboo stick in hand, he searched the nettles. His baggy flying suit, lit by the evening air, reminded Jim of another pilot of the dusk who had saved him three years earlier and opened the doors of Lunghua.

37

A Reserved Room

Soon after dawn Jim was woken by the first reconnaissance flights of the American fighters. He had spent the night sleeping in Mrs Vincent's bunk, and from the windows of G Block he watched the pairs of Mustangs circle the pagoda at Lunghua Airfield. An hour later the air drops began to the prisoner-of-war camps near Shanghai. The squadrons of B-29s emerged from the hazy light over the Yangtze and cruised over the empty paddy fields with their open bomb-doors, an armada for hire of vacant limousines.

Now that the war was over, the American bombardiers seemed either unwilling, or too bored, to concentrate on their sights. Much to the annoyance of Tulloch and Lieutenant Price, they dropped their cargoes into the open fields around the camp, rolled their wings and set off in a leisurely way for home, the day's work done.

When were the American Army and Navy coming to Shanghai? From the roof of G Block Jim examined the calm surface of the river three miles to the north. No doubt the Americans were wary of sailing up the Yangtze, fearing that the Japanese submarine commanders might have decided not to surrender. But until they arrived it was too dangerous for Jim to set out in search of his mother and father. The whole of Shanghai and the surrounding countryside was locked into a zone where there was neither war nor peace, a vacuum that would soon be filled by every warlord and disaffected general in China.

After waiting for Price and his men to leave the camp in search of the parachute canisters, Jim went down to the guardhouse. The wash from the engines of the relief

Superfortress had driven the stench of rotting meat from the hospital, a pall that hung over the camp for hours. But Tulloch appeared not to notice. Once Lieutenant Price was out of the way, a spectre hunting other spectres among the burial mounds, Tulloch was prepared to admit Jim to the commandant's office. Jim helped himself to the cans stacked against the wall. He made a quick meal of Spam and powdered milk, then sat behind Sergeant Nagata's desk in the orderly room, chewing a chocolate bar and sorting out the copies of the American magazines.

Later, when Tulloch went off to abuse the growing crowd of starving Chinese outside the gates, Jim climbed the ladder of the watch-tower. He could see Price and his raiding party searching the creeks to the west of the camp. They had joined forces with a group of Allied prisoners from Hungjao, and the armed men were running along the embankments of the anti-tank ditches, firing across the flooded paddy fields.

Already it was clear that the former British internees were not the only scavengers roving the countryside. The Chinese peasants were returning to the villages they had abandoned in the weeks before the war's end. Gangs of coolies roamed the area, stripping the tyres and body panels from the burnt-out Japanese vehicles. Squads of renegade Kuomintang soldiers who had deserted to the Chinese puppet armies wandered the roads, well aware of their fate if they fell into the hands of their former Nationalist comrades but drawn towards Shanghai by the American air-drops. As Jim stood in the observation box of the watch-tower a company of these demoralized troops straggled past the gates of Lunghua. Still fully armed, in ragged uniforms from which they had torn their badges, they passed within a few feet of the solitary Packard mechanic guarding his treasure of chocolate bars and *Saturday Evening Posts*.

At noon, when Lieutenant Price appeared, dressed like a corpse in the scarlet canopy of the parachute canister dragged by his men, Jim gathered together his bundle of magazines and returned to G Block. He spent an hour sorting them into their correct order, and then set out on a tour of the camp. Avoiding the hospital, he climbed through the wire and explored the overgrown terrain between the camp and Lunghua Airfield, hoping to find the turtle which he had released in the last weeks of the war.

But the canal beside the fence contained only the body of a dead Japanese airman. Sections of Lunghua Airfield – the pagoda, barracks and control tower – were now occupied by an advance brigade of Nationalist troops. For reasons of their own, the Japanese aircraftsmen and ground crews made no attempt to escape, and lived on in the gutted hangars and workshops. Each day the Nationalist soldiers took a few of the Japanese and killed them in the waste ground to the south and west of the airfield.

The sight of this dead Japanese airman, floating face down in the canal among the Mustang drop-tanks, unsettled Jim as much as the bodies of the Britons in the camp hospital. From then on he decided to remain within the safety of the camp. He slept at night in Mrs Vincent's bed, and spent the days sampling the American canned food and chocolate, and sorting out his collection of magazines. By now he had assembled a substantial library, which he stacked neatly on the spare bunks in his room. The copies of *Time, Life* and the *Reader's Digest* covered every conceivable aspect of the war, a world at once familiar and yet totally removed from his own experiences in Shanghai and Lunghua. At moments, as he studied the dramatic accounts of tank battles and beach-heads, he wondered if he himself had been in the war at all.

But he continued to collect the magazines from the floor of the commandant's office, concealing within them a few extra cans of Spam and powdered milk, part of a long-term reserve that he had sensibly begun to stockpile. Already it was clear to Jim that the American air-drops were becoming less frequent, and sooner or later they would stop. Now that his strength had returned, Jim was able to scavenge busily around the camp and was never more pleased than when, under a bunk in D Block, he found a tennis racquet and a tin of balls.

On the third morning, as Price and his men stood with the binoculars on the roof of the guardhouse, waiting impatiently for the American relief planes, an ancient Opel truck arrived at the gates of the camp. Two bare-chested Britons, sometime Lunghua prisoners, sat in the driving cabin, while their Chinese wives and children rode in the back with their possessions. Jim had last seen the men, foremen at the Moller Line dockyards, in the stadium at Nantao, lifting the hoods of the white Cadillacs on the morning the war had ended. Somehow they had made their way to Shanghai and collected their families, who had not been interned by the Japanese. Finding themselves destitute in the hostile city, they had decided to return to Lunghua.

Already they had collected their first booty. A silver parachute canister lay like a bomb on the floor of the truck, dwarfing the dark-eyed children in their Chinese tunics. Jim watched from Basie's window in E Block, smiling contentedly as Tulloch and Lieutenant Price climbed down from the roof of the guardhouse. They strolled over to the gates but made no attempt to unlock them. A rambling argument ensued between Price and the former Lunghua prisoners, who pointed angrily at E Block, deserted now except for the fourteen-year-old boy laughing to himself at the top-floor window.

Jim drummed his fists on the concrete sill, and waved to the men and their glowering Chinese wives. After three years of trying to leave the camp they were now back at its gates, ready to take up their stations for World War III. At long last they were beginning to realize the simple truth that Jim had always known, that inside Lunghua they were free.

The gates were opening; a bargain had been struck. Lieutenant Price had taken a fancy to the Opel. Within a minute the two Britons and their families sped across the parade ground towards D Block, followed by the first Mustangs of the morning. As they soared over the camp the wash from their engines drove a foul wind through the empty buildings, a reek of offal borne on a plague of thousands of glutted flies.

The Chinese beggars sitting by the gates shielded their faces. But Jim inhaled the heady stench, shutting out his thoughts of the hospital and the dead Japanese airman in the canal beyond the wire. The time had come to forget the dead. In its way the camp was coming alive again. The days of powdered milk and chocolate bars had made him stronger, but not yet equal to the long walk back to Shanghai. Other people would be returning to the camp, and perhaps his mother and father would join him there. Even with the reduced American air-drops there would be a constant supply of food. Jim looked down at the silent kitchens behind the guardhouse, and the rusting collection of metal carts. Already he was thinking of a sweet potato . . .

His shoes rang through the empty corridors, and down the stone steps. As he raced from the foyer he heard the throbbing engine of the Opel. Tulloch and the Seaforth Highlander were loading parachute canopies and cartons of canned food over the tail-gate.

'Jim! Hold it!' Tulloch beckoned to him. 'Where do you think you're going?'

'G Block, Mr Tulloch . . .' Gasping for breath, Jim leaned against the Opel's shaking fender. In the doorway of the guardhouse Lieutenant Price was feeding cartridges into the ammunition clip of his rifle, the ritual of a man counting his secret gold. 'I want to reserve a room for my parents – they might be coming to Lunghua. I'll reserve a room for you, Mr Tulloch.'

'Jim . . . Jim . . .' Tulloch placed his hand on Jim's head, trying to steady the over-excited boy. 'It's time you found your father, lad. The war's over, Jim.'

'But the next war, Mr Tulloch. You said it's going to begin soon.'

The Packard mechanic helped Jim on to the floor of the truck. 'Jim, you need to get the last war over before you start the next. We'll give you a lift – you're going back to Shanghai!'

38
The Road to Shanghai

The truck careened from one side of the Shanghai road to the other, throwing Jim on to the agitated bundle of parachute silk. He clung to the cartons of K-rations stacked around him, and listened to Tulloch and Lieutenant Price shouting to each other above the bellows-like roar of the engine.

Through the fading camouflage on the rear window, Jim could see the policeman's bandaged hands, deliberately raised from the wheel as he allowed the speeding truck to wobble and drift from the centre of the road. The tyres reached the verge, ripping up a storm of dust and leaves. Tulloch sat in the passenger seat beside the jar of rice wine, holding the rifle through the open window. He pounded on the dented hood, as the apartment blocks of the French Concession appeared between the bomb-torn trees.

For all the dangers of Lieutenant Price's driving, Jim was glad that the two men were in such high spirits. For the first mile the lieutenant had been unable to find second gear, and they had laboured along the Shanghai road at a noisy walking pace that threatened to boil the water from the radiator. Then an air-drop at Hungjao brought back Price's driving skills. They hurtled along the farm tracks and canal embankments, following the parachutes towards the landing ground, cheered by the prospect of even more American merchandise to be sold in the black markets of Shanghai.

Others, however, had reached the treasure before them. For half an hour they trundled around the deserted paddy fields, unable to find a single parachute canister. Price waved his rifle, threatening an entire world of silent canals.

311

Fortunately, Price's anger soon abated. After returning to the Shanghai road the lieutenant steered the truck towards the body of a dead Japanese despatch rider lying beside a motorcycle. The dead man's head burst in a spray of bloodied maggots and brain tissue that drenched the roadside trees. This feat of steering put Price in an excellent mood, which Jim hoped would last long enough for him to reach Shanghai and jump from the truck at the first traffic lights.

Jim looked back at the distant rooftops of the camp. It was strange to be leaving Lunghua, but he realized that once again he had been imprisoned by the camp as he had been during the war. At a single word from Tulloch, the apparently secure world he had begun to rebuild for himself out of one small room and a few tins of Spam had collapsed at his feet.

They passed Lunghua Pagoda at the northern edge of the airfield, the barrels of its anti-aircraft guns still pointing to the sky. Jim searched the ruined hangars for any sight of the young kamikaze pilot, sorry that he had never been able to repay him for the mango. A mile to the east was the Olympic stadium at Nantao. The Chinese characters on the shell-pocked façade, celebrating the generosity of Generalissimo Chiang, rose ever more vividly above the parking lot, as if China's feudal past had returned to claim its time.

The truck swerved, skidding across the camber. On a whim, Lieutenant Price had turned on to a mud track that ran towards the stadium. Jim heard Tulloch protest, but then the wine jar was passed across the steering wheel. They sped between the first of the earth bunkers and rifle pits that guarded the former Japanese headquarters. Lines of crumbling tank ditches crossed the fields, their slopes strewn with webbing and ammunition boxes.

Jim lay back on the bale of parachute silk. He had known all along that the sight of the Olympic stadium would prove too large a temptation. Since his arrival at Lunghua Camp the group of Britons had never ceased to question him about the looted furniture in the stands. Jim had been forced to embroider his memories, in order to ensure his supplies of canned goods and magazines from the commandant's office. By now his make-believe had seized Price's imagination, and it was too late to turn back.

A hundred yards from the parking lot they left the road and stopped in a culvert between two tank-trap embankments. Price and Tulloch, both drunk on the rice wine, stepped from the driving cabin. They lit cigarettes, staring slyly at the stadium.

Price tapped the side of the truck with his rifle. In a mocking voice, he called out: 'Shanghai Jim . . .'

'Just a detour, Jim,' Tulloch assured him boozily. 'We'll pick out a case of Scotch, and a few fur coats for the girls in the Nanking Road.'

'I didn't see any fur coats, Mr Tulloch, or any Scotch. Lots of chairs and dining tables.'

Lieutenant Price pushed Tulloch aside. 'Dining tables? Do you think we came here to have lunch?' He stared at the façade of the stadium, as if its shabby chalk challenged his own pallid skin.

Jim avoided the rifle barrel aimed at his head. 'There were cupboards and wardrobes.'

'Wardrobes?' Tulloch swayed between them. 'That could be it, Lieutenant.'

'Right . . .' Price calmed himself. He touched the cigarette burns on his chest, tapping out a secret code of pain and memory. 'I told you the boy had his eyes open.'

The two men crossed the road and entered the parking lot. Price leaned against a trackless tank, and spat the prison phlegm from his lungs through an open hatch. Jim hung back among the lines of trucks, thinking of Mr Maxted. Was he still lying on the blood-stained grass? Having eaten

313

so much, Jim felt guilty, and remembered that he might have sold his shoes. For all the looted cocktail bars it contained, the Olympic stadium seemed sombre and threatening, a place of omens. Here he had seen the afterglow of the atomic flash at Nagasaki. Its white glare still lay over the road of their death-march from Lunghua, the same pale light that he could see in the chalky façade of the stadium and in Lieutenant Price's lime-pit skin.

Fanning away the flies with a copy of *Life*, Jim sat on the running board of a truck. He studied a photograph of American marines raising the flag on the summit of Mount Suribachi after their battle for Iwo Jima. The Americans in these magazines had fought an heroic war, closer to the comic books than Jim had read as a child. Even the dead were glamourized, the living's idea of the dead . . .

Two Mustang fighters flew overhead, leading a Superfortress that lumbered in from the west, its bomb doors open, ready to scatter its Spam and *Reader's Digests* across the empty fields. The engines drummed at the ground below Jim's feet, shaking the lines of derelict vehicles.

Jim lowered the magazine, and noticed that armed men were running from the entrance tunnel of the stadium, their voices drowned in the noise of the aircraft. The Superfortress ambled through the sky, but the men scattered in panic from the tunnel, as if expecting the stadium to be bombed. A bearded European in the leather jacket of an American pilot raced across the parking lot, followed by two more men carrying shotguns. A bare-chested Chinese with a pistol belt around his black trousers scuttled along at a crouch, leading a group of coolies with bamboo staves.

Pursuing them through the tunnel was a platoon of Nationalist soldiers, rifles raised to the strong sunlight. They stopped to fire at the fleeing men, letting off a ragged volley of shots. Jim opened the door of the truck and climbed into the driving cabin. Fifty feet from the entrance tunnel Tulloch lay in the white dust that had fallen from the façade of the stadium. Lieutenant Price ran past him towards the line of trucks, his face like a lantern scanning the ground. Shaking off his bandages, he leapt the perimeter wall of the parking lot and plunged into the flooded paddy field beyond the road.

The Chinese officer fired a last pistol shot at Price's splashing figure, then knelt in the stadium entrance. Rifles raised, his men approached the rusting vehicles. They made a token show of flushing out any wounded members of the raiding party, turned and retreated to the safety of the stadium. Tulloch lay dead in the sun, his blood leaking into the chalky dust.

Blue and scarlet parachutes were falling over Hungjao. Jim slid across the seat, opened the door on the far side of the cabin and slipped on to the ground. Screened by the ammunition wagons and field guns, he ran towards the perimeter wall.

Lieutenant Price had abandoned the Opel and its cargo of silks and K-rations. When Jim reached the culvert he found the truck standing alone among the anti-tank embankments. On the ground beside the passenger door a faint smoke still rose from the butt of Tulloch's last Lucky Strike.

Jim stared through the window at the instrument panel. Could he drive the vehicle to Shanghai? It was too dangerous to give himself up to the Nationalist soldiers at the stadium – they would shoot him on sight, taking for granted that Jim was a member of the raiding party.

Thinking of Tulloch, who had died before seeing the white Cadillacs of Nantao, Jim decided to walk to Shanghai. He was climbing over the tail-gate of the Opel, about to select several cans of food and copies of the *Reader's Digest*, when he heard footsteps beside the truck. Before he could turn, someone seized him by the shoulders. Hard fists punched the back of his head, and hurled him to the floor.

315

Sitting among the cartons of cigarettes, Jim felt the blood run from his nose and mouth, dripping through his hands on to the parachute canopy. He looked up at the bare-chested Chinese with the pistol belt who had raced from the stadium. He stared at Jim with the expressionless gaze he had often seen on the cook's face at Amherst Avenue before he killed a chicken. Behind him, impatient to get his hands on the truck's cargo, was a Chinese coolie with a bamboo stave.

On both sides of the culvert armed men were walking down the embankment, led by the bearded European in the leather flying jacket. Half the members of this bandit group were Chinese, some of them coolies with staves, others in Nationalist and puppet uniforms, still with their rifles and webbing. The others were Europeans or Americans, wearing an assortment of clothes and ammunition belts, holsters and Shanghai Police pouches hung over Chinese tunics. From their starved bodies, Jim assumed that most were former internees.

When the coolie raised the bamboo stave, Jim sucked back the blood and swallowed the hot phlegm. 'I'm going to Lunghua Camp . . . I'm a British prisoner.' He pointed to the south-west. Through his swollen nose his voice sounded strangely bass, as if his body were ageing in the few moments of life left to it. 'Lunghua Camp . . .'

Ignoring him, the armed men sat on the embankment and smoked their cigarettes. The European in the flying jacket paced around the truck. A coolie picked up Tulloch's cigarette butt and inhaled the smoke. Everyone watched the sky and the deserted road past the stadium. They had brought with them the slow, empty time of the prison camp. Their faces were drawn and colourless, and they seemed to have emerged from a deep lair below the ground.

'Lunghua . . .' Jim repeated. The coolie with the stave still had his eyes on him. At the smallest signal, Jim knew, the coolie would step forward and crush his skull. The bare-chested Chinese who had struck him was examining the truck, peering at the rear tyres. Hoping somehow to catch the attention of the Europeans, Jim pointed to the stadium. 'Lincoln Zephyrs – in Nantao. Buicks, white Cadillacs . . .'

'What's this talk about Cadillacs?' A small man with silvery hair and an effeminate American voice walked towards the truck, rifle slung over his shoulder. No one listened to him, and he lit a cigarette to cover the lack of response. The flame trembled in his powdered cheeks, exposing a familiar pair of wary eyes, with their sharp but modest focus.

'Basie!' Jim wiped the blood from his nose. 'It's me, Basie – Jim! Shanghai Jim!'

The cabin steward stared at Jim. After a moment's thought he shook his head in an almost formal way, as if recognizing the fourteen-year-old but no longer interested in him. He scanned the cartons of K-rations and fingered the silk of the parachute. He stepped aside to give the coolie more room to swing his stave.

'Basie!' Jim picked up the scattered magazines and cleaned the blood from their covers with his fingers. He held them up before the angry gaze of the bare-chested Chinese with the pistol. '*Life* magazine, Basie, *Reader's Digest*! I kept the latest copies for you . . . Basie, I've learned hundreds of new words – Belsen, von Rundstedt, GI Joe . . .'

39
The Bandits

The car sped along the shore of an oil-filled lagoon, past the rusting hull of a beached torpedo boat. Squeezed between Basie and the bearded Frenchman in the rear seat, Jim watched the spray leap from the wheels of the Buick. The lurid rainbows opened like peacock tails, transforming the distant office blocks of Shanghai into the towers of a paint-box city. The same gaudy light veiled the torpedo boat and cloaked the bodies of the dead Japanese lying in the shallows.

Jim tried to look over his shoulder at the receding skyline of Shanghai, but the bruises on his neck made it difficult for him to turn his head.

'Hey, boy . . .' The Frenchman struck Jim's arm with the carbine held between his knees. 'Settle down. You want some more bloody nose . . .?'

'Jim, there's no room to wrestle in here. We'll just sit quiet and learn our words.' Basie put an arm around him. 'Keep an eye on that *Digest* so you stay awake.'

'Right, Basie. I'll stay awake.'

Staying awake was all-important, as Jim knew. He propped his feet against the ammunition boxes on the floor of the car, then pinched his lips until his eyes brightened. Next to the Frenchman, against the right-hand passenger door, sat the coolie with the bamboo stave who had been about to kill Jim before Basie intervened. In the front seat beside the Chinese driver, were two Australians from Siccawei Camp.

The seven of them were packed into the mud-spattered Buick. Its windows were still adorned with the insignia and rice-paper stickers of the puppet Chinese general whose staff car this had been throughout the war. Dried vomit, blood from Jim's nose and from the wounds of injured men stained the seats. Along with the staves and weapons, the car was crammed with ammunition boxes, cartons of American cigarettes, earthenware jars of rice wine, and beer bottles into which the men continually urinated as they sped along the country roads to the south-west of Shanghai.

They came to a halt, and the oily water of the lagoon swilled around the Buick's wheels. Ahead of them was the Japanese truck carrying a dozen members of this bandit gang. The top-heavy vehicle swayed up a narrow ramp of grey bricks that led from the beach to the embankment road. It was loaded with parachute canisters, Japanese stores seized that morning from the military godowns at Nantao, and a collection of mattress rolls, bicycles and sewing-machines looted from the villages in the open country south of Lunghua.

The Buick climbed the ramp of crumbling bricks, and followed the truck through the clouds of dust that swirled from its wheels. The road ran inland from the lagoon, soon losing itself in a maze of paddy fields and canals. Jim wondered if this bandit group had any idea where it was going, a poisonous shuttle that flicked to and fro across the quilted land. Yet eight hundred yards away, along a parallel road, a second truck sped through the deserted paddies. The antique Opel captured at the Olympic stadium carried the remaining five members of the gang. They had left the seaplane base at Nantao soon after dawn, but somehow had managed to rendezvous within a few minutes of their next objective.

As the roads converged, Jim could see the bare-chested figure of the Chinese gunman with the black trousers and revolver belt. He stood behind the driving cabin, shouting commands to the coolie at the wheel. Jim feared this former officer in the Chinese puppet army, whose iron knuckles he could still feel in the bruised bones at the back of his neck. Only Basie's presence had saved him, but the reprieve might be short-lived. Captain Soong paid little attention to Basie, or to the other European members of the bandit gang, and regarded Jim as no more than a dog to be worked to death if necessary. Within an hour of his capture by the bandits, Jim was crawling among the burial mounds that overlooked a village near Hungjao, sent on ahead like a beagle to sniff out the land and draw any surprise fire. Still half stunned, the blood from his nose dripping on to the *Reader's Digest* in his hand, he waited among the rotting coffins until the shooting subsided and the bandits returned from the village with their looted bicycles, bed-rolls and sacks of rice. Recognizing that Captain Soong was the real leader of this bandit group, he had tried to make himself useful to the Chinese. But Captain Soong did not want Jim to run any errands for him. The war had changed the Chinese people – the villagers, the wandering coolies and lost puppet soldiers looked at Europeans in a way Jim had never seen before the war, as if they no longer existed, even though the British had helped the Americans to defeat the Japanese.

The trucks stopped at a crossroads. Captain Soong jumped from the Opel and strode over to the Buick. Without thinking, Basie held Jim's arm. Basie had been prepared to see him die, and only Jim's lavish descriptions of the booty waiting for the bandits in the stadium at Nantao sustained Basie's interest in him.

A tornado of dust seethed around the three vehicles as they reversed and set off along a disused canal. Within half a mile they stopped on a stone bridge above a deserted village. Captain Soong and two of his men dismounted from their truck, joined by the Frenchman in the Buick and the coolie with the stave. The Australians sat in the front of the car, drinking from a wine jar and ignoring the shabby dwellings.

Usually Captain Soong would have called Jim and sent him to ferret through the buildings, but the village was clearly abandoned, looted many times over by the bandit groups in the area.

'Are we going back to Shanghai, Basie?' Jim asked.

'Soon, Jim. First we have to pick up some special equipment.'

'Equipment you stored in the villages? Equipment for the war effort?'

'That's it, Jim. Equipment the OSS left here for us while I was working undercover with the Kuomintang. You wouldn't want the communists to get it, would you, Jim?'

Both of them went along with this pretence. Jim stared at the empty village, its single mud street divided by an open sewer. 'There must be a lot of communists here. Is the war over, Basie?'

'It's over, Jim. Let's say it's effectively over.'

'Basie . . .' A familiar thought occurred to him. 'Has the next war effectively begun?'

'That's a way of putting it, Jim. I'm glad I helped you with your words.'

'There are still a lot of words I haven't learned, Basie. I'd like to go back to Shanghai. If I'm lucky I might see my mother and father today.'

'Shanghai? That's one dangerous city, Jim. You need more than luck in Shanghai. We'll wait till we see the US Navy tie up alongside the Bund.'

'Will Uncle Sam soon be here, Basie? Every Gob and GI Joe?'

'He'll be here. Every GI Joe in the Pacific area . . .' Basie sounded unenthusiastic at the prospect of being reunited with his fellow countrymen. Jim had questioned him about his escape from Lunghua, but Basie was sly and evasive. As always, whatever happened after the escape had long since ceased to interest him. He remained the same small, finicky man worrying about his hands, ignoring everything but the shortest-term advantage. His one strength was that he never allowed himself to dream, because he had never been able to take anything for granted, whereas Dr Ransome had taken everything for granted. However, Dr Ransome had probably died on the death-march from Lunghua, while Basie had survived. Yet now, for the first time, the prospect of the treasure-store in the Olympic stadium had sprung the safety catch of Basie's caution. Jim assiduously fed the cabin steward's vision of enough wealth to return him in luxury to the United States. He assumed that Basie had heard on the camp radio of the imminent march to the killing-grounds, and had bribed a night-watchman to conceal him in one of the Nantao godowns.

Sitting beside Basie as he polished his nails, Jim realized that the entire experience of the war had barely touched the American. All the deaths and starvation were part of a confused roadside drama seen through the passenger window of the Buick, a cruel spectacle like the public stranglings in Shanghai which the British and American sailors watched during their shore-leaves. He had learned nothing from the war because he expected nothing, like the Chinese peasants whom he now looted and shot. As Dr Ransome had said, people who expected nothing were dangerous. Somehow, five hundred million Chinese had to be taught to expect everything.

Jim nursed his bruised nose, as the armed men squatted on the bridge with their jars of rice wine. Despite the years of malnutrition in the camps, few of the former prisoners bothered to eat the canned food heaped on the back of the trucks. They drank alone in the hot sun, rarely speaking to each other. Jim knew almost none of their names. At dusk, when they returned to the seaplane base at Nantao, most of them dispersed with their share of the day's booty to their hide-outs in the tenements of the Old City, reassembling the next morning like factory workers. Jim slept in the Buick parked on the concrete slipway, surrounded by the hulks of the burnt seaplanes, while Basie and the bearded Frenchman drank through the night in the pilots' mess.

The Frenchman wandered back from the village and leaned against Basie's window. 'Nothing – not even one piece of shit.'

'They could have left us that,' Basie said in disgust. 'Why don't the Chinese come back to their villages?'

'Do they know the war's over?' Jim asked. 'You ought to tell them, Basie.'

'Maybe . . . We can't wait forever, Jim. There are big guns moving up to Shanghai, about six different Kuomintang armies.'

'So it might be difficult to collect your equipment?'

'That's it. We'll go now to this communist village. Then I'll take you back to your Dad. You can tell him how I looked after you through the war, taught you all your words.'

'You did look after me, Basie.'

'Right . . .' Basie gazed thoughtfully at Jim. 'You stay with us. It would be too bad if you got yourself kidnapped.'

'Are there a lot of kidnappers here, Basie?'

'Kidnappers *and* communists. People who don't want to know the war is over. Remember that, Jim.'

'Right . . .' Trying to distract the cabin steward with some more cheerful topic, Jim asked: 'Basie, did you see the atom bomb go off? I saw the flash over Nagasaki from Nantao stadium.'

'Say, kid . . .' Basie peered at Jim, puzzled by the calm voice of this bloody-nosed boy. He took a gun-rag from the rear window-sill and wiped Jim's nose. 'You saw the atom bomb . . .?'

'For a whole minute, Basie. A white light covered Shanghai, stronger than the sun. I suppose God wanted to see everything.'

'I guess he did. That white light, Jim. Maybe I can get your picture in *Life* magazine.'

'Say, could you, Basie?'

The thought of appearing in *Life* exhilarated Jim. He wiped the blood from his mouth and tried to straighten his ragged shirt, in case a photographer were to appear suddenly on the scene. At a signal from Captain Soong, the bandits returned to their vehicles. As they left the village and set out towards the river Jim imagined his photograph among the pictures of Tiger tanks and US Marines. He had now spent four days with Basie's bandit group, and it occurred to him that his parents might think that he had died in the death-march from Lunghua. Perhaps they would be sitting by the swimming-pool at Amherst Avenue, leafing through the latest issue of *Life*, when they would recognize their son's face among the admirals and generals . . .

They were passing the eastern perimeter of Lunghua Airfield. Jim leaned across Basie and hung from the window. He scanned the creeks and paddy fields for the bodies of Japanese aircrew. The Kuomintang units which had seized part of the airfield were still killing the Japanese in batches.

'You like those airplanes, Jim?'

'I'm going to be a pilot, Basie, one day. I'll take my mother and father down to Java. I've thought a lot about that.'

'A good dream to have . . .' Basie pushed Jim aside and pointed to the derelict aircraft among the trees. 'There's a Jap pilot over there – no one's got him yet.'

Basie cocked the bolt on his rifle. Jim craned through the window, searching the line of trees. Beside the tailplane of a Zero fighter he saw the pallid face of the young pilot, lost among the upended wings and fuselages.

'He's a hashi-crashi,' Jim said quickly. 'A screwy-sider. Basie, do you want me to tell you about the stadium? There might be fur coats, I think Mr Tulloch saw them before he was shot, and hundreds of crates of Scotch whisky . . .'

Fortunately, Basie was winding up the window. A pungent grit filled the Buick. It rose from the chalky surface of the road, joining the haze of dust that climbed from the bleached fields, the tank ditches and burial mounds, the same light that Jim had seen from the Olympic stadium, heralding the end of one war and the beginning of the next.

Shortly before dusk they reached the communist town on the river two miles to the south of Lunghua. The shabby, single-storey houses huddled against the walls of a ceramics factory, like the mediaeval dwellings Jim had seen in his childhood encyclopaedias, clustering around a gothic cathedral. The domed kilns and brick chimneys drew the last of the day's sunlight towards them, as if advertising the warmth and benefit which communist rule had brought to this collection of hovels.

'Right, Jim, never mind the word-power. You're going in.'

Before Jim could place his *Reader's Digest* on the window-sill Captain Soong had flung open the door. The bare-chested officer bundled Jim from the Buick. Handling the bloody-nosed boy like a drover with a truffling pig, he propelled Jim across the road with a series of whoops and grunts, prodding him sharply with his automatic pistol. The two trucks and the Buick had stopped beside the embankment carrying the Shanghai–Hangchow railway line. Three hundred yards ahead, a spur of the line ran in a wide arc towards the ceramics works, concealing them from the town. The armed men stepped down on to the drained paddy that followed the embankment. Some opened their ammunition pouches and cleaned the breeches of their rifles. Others smoked cigarettes and drank wine from the

325

earthenware jars they placed on the hood of the Buick. Each man on his own, they stood silently in the fading light.

As the whoops and whistles of Captain Soong faded behind him, Jim trotted across the hard surface of the paddy. He pinched his nose, hoping to stop the bleeding, then let the blood smear his cheeks in the wind. With luck, any communist sentry stationed on the embankment would think that Jim was already wounded and turn his fire on the gunmen behind him.

He reached the foot of the embankment and crouched among the clumps of wild rice. He wiped the blood from their stems and licked his fingers. Already he had served his purpose. Fifty yards away, Captain Soong had crossed the paddy and was scuttling up the soft soil of the embankment. Armed with their staves, his coolies followed, accompanied by Basie and the Frenchman. Two groups of gunmen were moving across the next paddy field. The Australians and a Kuomintang deserter sat on the running board of the Buick, drinking their wine.

Jim climbed the talc-like slope. Rain had washed away parts of the embankment, and he crawled below the rusting rails and their rotting sleepers. Several sections of the line had recently been replaced, presumably by the communist troops who had made the town their base. The jetty of the ceramics factory, the railway line and the reserve of bricks in the fabric of the old kilns and chimneys, together with the proximity to Lunghua Airfield, had drawn the communist garrison to this modest backwater. According to Basie, however, they had left two days earlier, continuing their advance on Shanghai, and the town's few hundred inhabitants were undefended. Apart from their possessions, there might be stores of communist arms, and collaborators to be traded for the goodwill of the Kuomintang generals approaching Shanghai.

Concealed by the railway sleepers, Jim crouched on the

edge of the embankment. Below him lay a plain of unworked paddies, separated by a navigation canal from the patchwork of vegetable plots that encircled the town. The narrow streets were empty, but a weak smoke rose from several chimneys.

Across the river, a naval gun fired a single booming round. Two Nationalist Chinese gunboats were moored in midstream. The shell landed in the store-yard of the ceramics works, throwing up a cloud of red dust. The sound of small arms fire came from the beaches of the river to the south, where a company of Kuomintang soldiers disembarked from a wooden lighter.

Its diesels thudding, an armoured junk motored up the canal below the railway embankment. Chinese officers in smart American uniforms and steel helmets stood on the bridge, scanning the town and its vegetable plots through binoculars. The nearer of the two gunboats fired a second shell, which exploded among the grey-tiled rooftops, sending up a shower of debris. Immediately there was a flurry of movement. Like ants escaping from a broken flower-pot, hundreds of Chinese ran from the narrow alleys into the surrounding fields. Over their heads they carried bed-rolls and bundles of clothing. They raced down the pathways between the vegetable plots. An old woman in black trousers and jacket waded waist-deep in a creek beside the road, shouting to her relatives who clambered down the bank.

The motorized junk sailed along the canal, its engines drumming like fists against the wooden hull. Jim could see clearly the fresh pleats in the uniforms of the senior Chinese officers, and their elegant American combat boots. Even the platoons of private soldiers on the deck below the bridge were lavishly equipped with weapons and radios. Parked across the midships of the junk was a black Chrysler limousine, the pennant of a Kuomintang general flying from its chromium mast.

The metal barbette of an automatic cannon was mounted

in the bows of the junk. Without warning, the gunners opened fire at the town. The tracers soared over the heads of the fleeing villagers and burst against the roofs of the houses. At a signal from the bridge, the gunners swung the barrel, setting their sights on a small hamlet a few hundred yards to the west of the town. Already the first shells from the gunboats were landing on the dusty road beside the single-storey hovels. The company of Nationalist soldiers who had disembarked from the wooden lighter were now running across the paddies, hunting down the fleeing townspeople.

Then the first shell of the next salvo tripped off an immense explosion. The group of mud dwellings had vanished, sucked into the air by the boiling cloud of its own debris. The cache of detonating ammunition continued to erupt, throwing towers of smoke into the sky. On the road approaching the hamlet dozens of villagers lay among their bundles and bed-rolls, as if the inhabitants of this town had decided to spend the night sleeping in the fields.

Jim cupped his hands over his nose and mouth, trying to stop himself from shouting. He watched the plain of fire below him, the smoke-covered fields lit by the flashes of the naval guns and by the burning houses beside the ceramics factory. The kilns and chimneys glowed in the sunset as if the ancient ovens had been lit again, to be fuelled by the bodies of the villagers lying in their vegetable gardens. Jim listened to the engines of the motorized junk as it moved down the canal, an ugly heart bearing the beat of its death across China, while immaculate generals masked their eyes with binoculars, calculating their astronomy of guns.

'Basie . . .' The bandits were withdrawing from the railway line. Captain Soong and his coolies had climbed down the embankment and were returning to the trucks. 'Basie, can we go back to Lunghua?'

'Back to the camp?' The cabin steward squinted through

the dust falling from the air. He had been stunned by the concussion wave of the exploding ammunition store, and stared at the landscape below him as if waking from a dream. 'You want to go back to the camp, Jim . . .?'

'We ought to get ready, Basie. When are the Americans coming?'

For the first time Basie seemed lost for an answer. He lay back among the wooden sleepers, and then pointed to the north and gave a whistle of triumph. Ten miles away, across the sombre surface of the river, the sunlit masts and superstructure of an American cruiser had taken their place beside the office blocks and hotels of the Shanghai Bund.

40

The Fallen Airmen

All morning the sound of artillery fire had crossed the river from Pootung. A column of incendiary smoke, broader than the group of burning warehouses, leaned over the water and darkened the Nantao shore. From the front seat of the Buick parked on the mud-flat, Jim watched the flashes of gunfire in the dusty windshield. The American artillery pieces brought up by the Nationalists emitted a harsh and wet noise, as if their barrels were filled with water. Hidden from the sun, a gloomy air lay over the slack tide that swilled against the beach. The glowing barrel of the Kuomintang howitzer behind the Pootung mole flickered against Jim's knuckles as he held the steering wheel of the Buick, and lit up the conning tower of the beached submarine a hundred yards away.

Jim noticed a reconnaissance aircraft emerge from the smoke-cloud, shaking off the wisps of black vapour that streamed from its wings. A flight of three American bombers approached from the south-west. The gunfire ceased, and a torpedo boat fortified with sandbags set out across the river, ready to collect any stray canisters.

A dozen parachutes fell from the B-29s, and streaked swiftly to the ground. The canisters were loaded, not with Spam, Klim and the *Reader's Digest*, but with ammunition and explosives for the Kuomintang troops. The battalion, with its artillery support, was rooting out the last of the communist units which still hung on among the ruins of the Pootung warehouses. On the mole, the corpses of dead communist soldiers were stacked like firewood.

In the silence after the bombers had passed Jim could

hear the aching rumble of artillery barrages from Hungjao and the open country to the west of Shanghai. At least three Nationalist armies were closing around the city, jockeying among themselves for control of the airfields, dockyards and railway lines, and above all for the stocks of weapons and munitions left behind by the Japanese. Collaborating with the Nationalists, though sometimes fighting against them, were the remnants of the puppet armies, groups of renegade Kuomintang driven back to the coast, and various militia forces recruited by the local warlords who had returned to Shanghai.

Swept in front of these rival armies, like dust before a set of colliding brooms, were tens of thousands of Chinese peasants. Columns of refugees wandered the countryside, trying to shelter in the fields and looted villages, turned away from the gates of Shanghai by advance units of the Nationalist armies.

It was these refugees, the bands of starving coolies armed with knives and hoes, whom Jim most feared. Avoiding them at all costs, Basie and his bandit group stayed close to any battle that was taking place. On the eastern fringes of Nantao, between the dockyards and the seaplane base, was a no man's land of wharves, warehouses and deserted barracks which the Kuomintang militias and the peasant refugees found too near to the fighting across the river at Pootung. Here Basie and the remaining six members of the gang camped out in the bunkers and concrete forts, with little left to them but the pre-war Buick and the vague hope of selling themselves to a Nationalist general.

Now even the car was proving too obvious a target for the Kuomintang gunners.

'You sit behind the wheel, Jim,' Basie had told him as the bandits left the Buick on the mud-flat. 'Pretend you're driving this fine car.'

'Say, can I, Basie . . .?' Jim held the steering-wheel as the men stood on the black beach beside the car and prepared their weapons. Their faces flinched at the sound of the explosions that crossed the water. 'Are you going to the stadium, Basie?'

'Right, Jim. Remember those years in Lunghua – we have an investment to protect. The Nats want to take over Shanghai and keep out any foreign business interests.'

'Is that us, Basie?'

'That's you, Jim. You're part of the foreign business community. When we get back you'll have a fur coat and a case of Scotch whisky for your Dad.'

Basie stared at the ruined warehouses and the corpses stacked on the mole, as if seeing them loaded with all the treasure of the east about to be freighted back to Frisco. Jim felt sorry for Basie, and was tempted to warn him that the stadium was probably empty, stripped by the Kuomintang troops of the few valuables that had survived the sun and rain. But Basie had taken the hook and was now running eagerly towards the gaff. With luck, if he survived the attack on the stadium, he would throw away his rifle and walk back to Shanghai. Within a few days he would be a wine-waiter at the Cathay Hotel, serving with a flourish all the American officers who stepped ashore from the cruiser moored by the Bund . . .

When Basie and the men had gone, vanishing among the ruined warehouses on the quay, Jim studied the magazines on the seat beside him. He was sure now that the Second World War had ended, but had World War III begun? Looking at the photographs of the D-Day landings, the crossing of the Rhine and the capture of Berlin, he felt that they were part of a smaller war, a rehearsal for the real conflict that had begun here in the Far East with the dropping of the Nagasaki and Hiroshima atomic bombs. Jim remembered the light that lay over the land, the shadow of another sun. Here, at the mouths of the great rivers of

Asia, would be fought the last war to decide the planet's future.

Jim wiped his blood from the steering-wheel, as the shelling began again from the Pootung shore. His nose had been bleeding on and off for four days. He swallowed the blood and watched the open road that ran from the wharves towards the distant stadium. A hundred yards from the Buick, two Chinese militiamen had climbed on to the bows of the beached submarine. Rifles slung over their shoulders, they ignored the battle across the river and walked along the deck to the conning tower.

Jim unlatched the driver's door. It was time to leave, before the militiamen noticed the Buick. From the heap of cans, cigarette cartons and ammunition clips on the floor of the car he selected a chocolate bar, a tin of Spam and a copy of *Life*. When the two Chinese were behind the conning tower he stepped on to the mud-flat. Crouching below the embankment wall, he ran towards the stone ramp of a Shanghai River Police jetty. Little more than two miles to the north were the tenements and godowns of the Old City, and beyond them the office blocks of downtown Shanghai, but Jim ignored them and set out again for Lunghua Airfield.

Smoke rose from the Olympic stadium, a thin white plume fed by a single flame, as if Basie and his gang had lit a bonfire of furniture in the stands. The artillery barrages from Pootung and Hungjao had fallen silent, and Jim could hear the brief bursts of rifle fire from the stadium.

Searching for shelter, Jim left the exposed country road. He walked through the wild sugar-cane that covered the waste ground beside the northern perimeter of Lunghua Airfield. A screen of trees and rusting fuel tanks separated him from the open plain of the landing field, the ruined hangars and pagoda. Cartridge cases lay on the narrow path at his feet, chips laid in a brassy trail. He followed the straggling wire, avoiding the swarms of flies which clustered over the miniature bowers in the banks of nettles.

On either side of the pathway the bodies of dead Japanese lay where they had been shot or bayoneted. Jim stopped by a shallow irrigation ditch, in which an air force private lay with his hands tied behind him. Hundreds of flies devoured his face, enclosing it in a noisy mask. Unwrapping his chocolate bar, and fanning the flies from his face with the magazine, Jim walked through the sugar-cane. Dozens of dead Japanese lay in the nettles as if they had fallen from the sky, the members of a youthful armada shot down as they tried to fly to their home airfields in Japan.

Jim stepped over a collapsed section of the perimeter fence, and moved through the derelict aircraft that lay among the trees. Their fuselages had wept rivers of rust in the summer rain. The flies raged at the morning light, a vast anger about nothing. Leaving them, Jim set out across the grass expanse of the airfield. Inside one of the ruined hangars a group of Japanese waited in the shade, listening to the rifle fire from the stadium, but they ignored Jim as he walked across the field.

He stared at the concrete runway below his feet. To his surprise, he found that the surface was badly cracked and stained with patches of oil, scored by the marks of tyres and wheel struts. But now that World War III had begun, a new runway would soon be laid. Jim reached the end of the concrete strip, and strode through the grass towards the southern perimeter of the airfield. The ground rose to the overgrown hillocks left by the original earthworks, then shelved into the valley where the Japanese trucks had once delivered their loads of building rubble and roof tiles.

Despite the deep nettles and the hot September sunlight, the valley seemed filled with the same ashy dust. The banks of the canal were as pale as the conduit of a mortuary stream in which the dead were washed. The burst casing of an unexploded bomb lay in the shallow water, like a large turtle that had fallen asleep trying to bury its head in the mud.

Aware that the vibration of a low-flying Mustang might trip its detonator, Jim pressed on into the valley, parting the nettles with his magazine. He tossed the tin of Spam into the air, caught it with one hand, but on the second throw lost it among the reeds. Hunting about in the thick grass, he at last found it near the water's edge, and decided to eat the chopped ham before it slipped through his hands for good.

Sitting on the bank of the canal, he washed the dirt from the lid. A drop of blood fell from his nose into the water, and was instantly attacked by myriads of small fish no longer than a match-head. As a second drop struck the surface there was a violent struggle that seemed to involve entire nations of minute fish. They swerved through the water, unaware of the sunlit surface, ferociously attacking each other. Clearing his mouth, Jim leaned over and released a ball of pus from his infected gums. It fell like a depth charge among the fish, driving them into a frenzy of panic. Within a second the water was empty except for the dissolving pus.

Losing interest in the fish, Jim stretched out among the reeds and studied the advertisements in his magazine. He listened to the deeper sound of the artillery fire. The guns of Siccawei and Hungjao were louder, as the rival Nationalist armies closed their grip on Shanghai. He would eat his Spam, and then make a last effort to return to Shanghai. He was certain that Basie and the bandit gang never intended to return to the Buick, and had left him on the mud-flat to draw away any Chinese soldiers who might have followed them to the river.

In the grass nearby, a head nodded twice, approving this strategy. Jim lay rigidly, the last of the chocolate trapped in

335

his throat, startled by this intimate apparition. Someone was lying in the reeds a few feet from him, his knees almost touching the water's edge. As if trying to reassure Jim, the head nodded again. He reached out one hand and parted the grass, carefully examining the figure's face. The round cheeks and soft nose, pinched by the privations of a wartime childhood, were those of a teenage Asiatic, some villager's son come here to fish. The boy lay on his back, surrounded by a wall of grass and reeds, as if sharing a four-poster bed with Jim and quietly listening to his thoughts.

Jim sat up, the rolled magazine raised above his head. Through the swarming flies he waited for the sound of footsteps in the long grass. But the valley was empty, its bright air devoured by the flies. The figure moved slightly, crushing the grass. Too idle to stop himself, the lazing youth was sliding down the bank into the water.

With all the caution learned during the long years of the war, Jim climbed to his knees, then stood up and stepped through the reeds. Calming himself, he looked down at this dozing figure.

In front of him, wearing a bloodstained flying overall with the insignia of a special attack group, was the body of the young Japanese pilot.

41
Rescue Mission

Jim despaired. Flattening the grass with his hands, he made a small place for himself beside the Japanese. The pilot lay in his overall, one arm under his back. He had been thrown down the slope towards the canal, and his legs were caught beneath him. His right knee touched the water, which had begun to soak the thigh of his overall. Above his head Jim could see the chute of bruised grass down which he had fallen, the stems straightening themselves in the sun.

He stared at the pilot, for once glad of the swarm of flies interceding between himself and this corpse. The face of the Japanese was more childlike than Jim remembered, as if in his death he had returned to his true age, to his early adolescence in a provincial Japanese village. His lips were parted around his uneven teeth, as if expecting a morsel of fish to be placed between them by his mother's chopsticks.

Numbed by the sight of this dead pilot, Jim watched the youth's knees slide into the water. He squatted on the sloping earth, turning the pages of *Life* and trying to concentrate on the photographs of Churchill and Eisenhower. For so long he had invested all his hopes in this young pilot, in that futile dream that they would fly away together, leaving Lunghua, Shanghai and the war forever behind them. He had needed the pilot to help him survive the war, this imaginary twin he had invented, a replica of himself whom he watched through the barbed wire. If the Japanese was dead, part of himself had died. He had failed to grasp the truth that millions of Chinese had known from birth, that they were all as good as dead anyway, and that it was self-deluding to believe otherwise.

Jim listened to the artillery barrages at Hungjao and Siccawei, and to the circling drone of a Nationalist spotter plane. The sound of small arms fire crossed the airfield, as Basie and the bandits tried to break into the stadium. The dead were playing their dangerous games.

Deciding to ignore them, Jim continued to read his magazine, but the flies had swarmed from the corpses further along the creek and soon discovered the body of the young pilot. Jim stood up and seized the Japanese by the shoulders. Holding him under the armpits, he pulled his legs from the water, then dragged him on to a narrow ledge of level ground.

Despite his plump face, the pilot weighed almost nothing. His starved body was as light as the children in Lunghua with whom Jim had wrestled when he was young. The waist and trousers of his flying overall were thick with blood. He had been bayoneted in the small of his back, and again through the thighs and buttocks, then thrown down the bank with the other aircrew.

Squatting beside the body, Jim snapped the key from the Spam tin, and began to wind off the lid. Once he had eaten he would use the can to dig a grave for the Japanese. When he had buried the pilot he would walk to Shanghai, regardless of the games the dead were playing. If he saw his parents he would tell them that World War III had begun, and that they should return to their camp at Soochow.

The hot jelly of chopped ham bulged within its mucilage of melted fat. Jim washed his hand in the canal, and used the lid to cut a modest slice. He raised the meat to his mouth, but spat the fragment into the water. The greasy flesh was still alive, as if carved from the body of a breathing animal. Its lungs and liver quivered in the can, still driven by a heart. Jim cut a second slice and placed it in his mouth. He could feel its pulse between his lips, and the fear of the creature in the moments before its slaughter.

He picked the slice from his lips and stared at the oily meat. Living flesh was not meant to feed the dead. This was food that would devour those who tried to eat it. Jim spat the last shred into the grass beside the Japanese. Leaning across the corpse, he patted the blanched lips with his forefinger, ready to slip the morsel of ham into its mouth.

The chipped teeth closed around his finger, cutting the cuticle. Jim dropped the can of meat, which rolled through the grass into the canal. He wrenched his hand away, aware that the corpse of this Japanese was about to sit up and consume him. Without thinking, Jim punched the pilot's face, then stood back and shouted at him through the swarm of flies.

The pilot's mouth opened in a noiseless grimace. His eyes were fixed in an unfocused way on the hot sky, but a lid quivered as a fly drank from his pupil. One of the bayonet wounds in his back had penetrated the front of his abdomen, and fresh blood leaked from the crutch of his overall. His narrow shoulders stirred against the crushed grass, trying to animate his useless arms.

Jim gazed at the young pilot, doing his best to grasp the miracle that had taken place. By touching the Japanese he had brought him to life; by prising his teeth apart he had made a small space in his death and allowed his soul to return.

He spread his feet on the damp slope and wiped his hands on his ragged trousers. The flies swarmed around him, stinging his lips, but Jim ignored them. He remembered how he had questioned Mrs Philips and Mrs Gilmour about the raising of Lazarus, and how they had insisted that far from being a marvel this was the most ordinary of events. Every day Dr Ransome had brought people back from the dead by massaging their hearts.

Jim looked at his hands, refusing to be overawed by them. He raised his palms to the light, letting the sun warm his skin. For the first time since the start of the war he felt a surge of hope. If he could raise this dead Japanese pilot he could raise himself, and the millions of Chinese who had died during the war and who were still dying in the fighting for Shanghai, for a booty as illusory as the treasure in the Olympic stadium. He would raise Basie when he had been killed by the Kuomintang guards defending the stadium, but not the other members of the bandit gang, and never Lieutenant Price or Captain Soong. He would raise his mother and father, Dr Ransome and Mrs Vincent, and the British prisoners in Lunghua hospital. He would raise the Japanese aircrew lying in the ditches around the airfield, and enough ground staff to rebuild a squadron of aircraft.

The Japanese pilot made a small gasp. His eyes tilted, as if trying to revolve like those of the patients whom Dr Ransome revived. He was barely clinging to life, but Jim knew that he would have to leave him beside the canal. His hands and shoulders were trembling, electrified by the discharge that had passed through them, the same energy that powered the sun and the Nagasaki bomb whose explosion he had witnessed. Already Jim could see Mrs Philips and Mrs Gilmour rising politely from the dead, listening in their concerned but puzzled way as he explained how he had saved them. He could imagine Dr Ransome shrugging the earth from his shoulders, and Mrs Vincent looking back disapprovingly at the grave . . .

Jim sucked the blood and pus from his teeth and quickly swallowed them. He slipped on the damp grass and slid into the shallow water of the canal. Steadying himself, he washed his face. He wanted to look his best when Mrs Vincent opened her eyes and saw him again. He wiped his wet hands on the cheeks of the young pilot. He would have to leave him, but like Dr Ransome he had only a few seconds to spare for each of the impatient dead.

* * *

As he ran through the valley towards the camp Jim noticed that the artillery guns at Pootung and Hungjao had fallen silent. Across the airfield a column of trucks had stopped by the hangars and armed men in American helmets were climbing the staircase of the control tower. Flights of Mustangs circled Lunghua in close formation, their engines roaring at the exhausted grass. Waving to them, Jim ran to the perimeter fence of the camp. He knew that the American planes were coming in to land, ready to take away the people he had raised. By the burial mounds to the west of the camp three Chinese stood with their hoes among the eroded coffins, the first of those aggrieved by the war now coming to greet him. He shouted to two Europeans in camp fatigues who climbed from a flooded creek with a home-made fishing net. They stared at Jim and called to him, as if surprised to find themselves alive again with this modest implement in their hands.

Jim climbed through the fence and ran down the cinder track to the camp hospital. Men with spades stood in the cemetery, shielding their eyes from the unfamiliar daylight. Had they dug themselves free from their own graves? As he neared the steps of the hospital Jim tried to control his trembling. The bamboo doors opened and a swarm of flies fled through the air, their feast-days done. Brushing them from his face, over which he wore a green surgical mask, was a red-haired man in a new American uniform. In his hand he carried an insecticide bomb.

'Dr Ransome . . .!' Jim spat the blood from his mouth and ran up the rotting steps. 'You came back, Dr Ransome! It's all right, everyone's coming back! I'm going to get Mrs Vincent . . .!'

He stepped past Dr Ransome into the dark, but the physician's hands gripped his shoulders.

'Hold on, Jim . . . I thought you might be here.' He removed his mask and pressed Jim's head to his chest, inspecting the boy's gums and ignoring the blood that stained the crisp fabric of his US Army shirt. 'Your parents are waiting for you, Jim. Poor fellow, you'll never believe the war is over.'

Part IV

42

The Terrible City

Two months later, on the eve of his departure for England, Jim remembered Dr Ransome's words as he walked down the gangway of the SS *Arrawa* and stepped on to Chinese soil for the last time. Dressed in a silk shirt and tie, and a grey flannel suit from the Sincere Company's department store, Jim waited politely for an elderly English couple to make their way down the wooden ramp. Below them was the Shanghai Bund, and all the clamour of the gaudy night. Thousands of Chinese filled the concourse, jostling among the trams and limousines, the jeeps and trucks of the US military, and a horde of rickshaws and pedicabs. Together they watched the British and American servicemen moving in and out of the hotels along the Bund. At the jetties beside the *Arrawa*, hidden below its stern and bows, American sailors came ashore from the cruiser moored in mid-river. As they stepped from their landing craft the Chinese surged forward, gangs of pickpockets and pedicab drivers, prostitutes and bar-touts, vendors hawking bottles of home-brew Johnny Walker, gold dealers and opium traders, the evening citizenry of Shanghai in all its black silk, fox fur and flash.

The young American sailors pushed past the sampan men and shouting military police. They tried to stay together and fight off the crowd so eager to welcome them to China. But before they reached the first set of tram-tracks down the centre of the Bund they were swept away in a convoy of pedicabs, their arms around the bar-girls screaming obscenities at the sleek Chinese pimps in their pre-war Packards, down from the blocks in the back-alley garages of the Nanking Road.

Dominating this panorama of the Shanghai night were three cinema screens which had been set up on scaffolding along the Bund. In collaboration with the US Navy, the Nationalist general who was the military governor of the city had arranged this continuous screening of newsreels from the European and Pacific theatres, in order to give the population of Shanghai a glimpse of the world war that had recently ended.

Jim cleared the last step of the swaying gangway, and looking up at the trembling images, which were barely strong enough to hold their own against the neon signs and strip lighting on the hotel and nightclub façades. Fragments of their amplified sound-tracks boomed like guns over the roar of the traffic. He had begun the war watching the newsreels in the crypt of Shanghai Cathedral, and was now ending it below the same repetitive images – Russian machine-gunners advanced through the ruins of Stalingrad, US marines turned their flame-throwers on the Japanese defenders of a Pacific island, RAF fighters strafed an ammunition train in a German railyard. Promptly at ten-minute intervals, Chinese characters filled the screens, and vast Kuomintang armies saluted the victorious Generalissimo Chiang on his reviewing podium in Nanking. The only forces not to be celebrated were the Chinese communists, but they had been cleared out of Shanghai and the coastal cities. Whatever contribution their troops had made to the Allied victory had long been discounted, lost under the layers of newsreels that had imposed their own truth upon the war.

During the two months since his return to Amherst Avenue, Jim often visited the reopened cinemas in Shanghai. His parents recovered only slowly from their years of imprisonment in the camp at Soochow, and Jim had ample time to tour Shanghai. After calling at the White Russian dentist in the French Concession, he would order Yang to drive him in the Lincoln Zephyr to the Grand or the Cathay, those vast and cool palaces where he sat in the front row of the circle and watched yet another screening of *Bataan* and *The Fighting Lady*.

Yang was puzzled why Jim should want to see these films so many times. In turn Jim wondered how Yang himself had spent the years of the war – as a valet to a Chinese puppet general, as an interpreter for the Japanese, or as a Kuomintang agent working on the side for the communists? On the day of his parents' arrival Yang had appeared with the limousine, promptly sold the car to Jim's father and re-enrolled himself as its chauffeur. Yang was already performing in small roles in two productions of the renascent Shanghai film studios. Jim suspected that while he sat through another double feature at the Cathay Theatre the car was being rented out as a film prop.

These Hollywood movies, like the newsreels projected above the crowds on the Bund, endlessly fascinated Jim. After the dental work to his jaw, and the healing of the wound in his palate, he soon began to put on weight. Alone at the dining-room table, he ate large meals by day, and at night slept peacefully in his bedroom on the top floor of the unreal house in Amherst Avenue, which had once been his home but now seemed as much an illusion as the sets of the Shanghai film studios.

During his days at Amherst Avenue he often thought of his cubicle in the Vincent's room at the camp. At the end of October he ordered the unenthusiastic Yang to drive him to Lunghua. They set off through the western suburbs of Shanghai, and soon reached the first of the fortified checkpoints that guarded the entrances to the city. The Nationalist soldiers in their American tanks were turning back hundreds of destitute peasants, without rice or land to crop, trying to find refuge in Shanghai. Shanty towns of mud dwellings, walls reinforced with truck tyres and kerosene drums, covered the fields near the burnt-out Olympic stadium at Nantao. Smoke still rose from the stands, a beacon used by the American pilots flying across the China Sea from their bases in Japan and Okinawa.

As they drove along the perimeter road, Jim stared at Lunghua Airfield, now a dream of flight. Dozens of US Navy and Air Force planes sat on the grass, factory-new fighters and chromium-sheathed transport aircraft that seemed to be waiting delivery to a show-room window in the Nanking Road.

Jim expected to see Lunghua Camp deserted, but far from being abandoned the former prison was busy again, fresh barbed wire strung along its fences. Although the war had been over for nearly three months, more than a hundred British nationals were still living in the closely guarded compound. Entire families had taken over the former dormitories in E Block, in which they had built suites of rooms within walls of American ration cartons, parachute canisters and bales of unread *Reader's Digest*s. When Jim, searching for Basie's cubicle, tried to pull one of the magazines from its makeshift wall he was brusquely warned away.

Leaving the inmates to their treasure, he signalled Yang to drive on to G Block. The Vincents' room was now the quarters of a Chinese amah working for the British couple across the corridor. She refused to admit Jim, or open the door more than a crack, and he returned to the Lincoln and ordered Yang on a last circuit of the camp.

The hospital and the camp cemetery had vanished, and the site was an open tract of ash and cinders, from which a few charred joists protruded. The graves had been carefully levelled, as if a series of tennis courts was about to be laid. Jim walked through the empty drums of kerosene which had fuelled the fire. He gazed through the wire at the airfield, and at the concrete runway pointing to Lunghua

Pagoda. Dense vegetation covered the wrecks of the Japanese aircraft. As he stood by the wire, tracing the course of the canal through the narrow valley, an American bomber swept across the camp. For a moment, reflected from the underside of its silver wings, a pale light raced like a wraith between the nettles and stunted willows.

While Yang drove uneasily back to Amherst Avenue, annoyed in some way by the visit to Lunghua, Jim thought of the last weeks of the war. Towards the end everything had become a little muddled. He had been starving and perhaps had gone slightly mad. Yet he knew that he had seen the flash of the atomic bomb at Nagasaki even across the four hundred miles of the China Sea. More important, he had seen the start of World War III, and realized that it was taking place around him. The crowds watching the newsreels on the Bund had failed to grasp that these were the trailers for a war that had already started. One day there would be no more newsreels.

In the weeks before he and his mother sailed to England in the *Arrawa*, Jim often thought of the young Japanese pilot he had seemed to raise from the dead. He was not sure now that this was the same pilot who had fed him the mango. Probably the youth had been dying, and Jim's movements in the grass had woken him. All the same, certain events had taken place, and with more time perhaps others would have returned to life. Mrs Vincent and her husband had died on the march from the stadium, far from Shanghai in a small village to the south-west. But Jim might have helped the prisoners in the camp hospital. As for Basie, had he died during his attack on the stadium, within sight of the gilded nymphs in the Presidential stand? Or were he and Lieutenant Price still roving the landscape of the Yangtze in the puppet general's Buick, waiting for a third war to bring them into their own?

Jim had told his parents nothing of all this. Nor had he

confided in Dr Ransome, who clearly suspected that Jim had chosen to stay on at Lunghua after the armistice, playing his games of war and death. Jim remembered his return to the house in Amherst Avenue, and his mother and father smiling weakly from their deck-chairs in the garden. Beside the drained swimming-pool the untended grass grew around their shoulders, and reminded him of the bowers of nettles in which the dead Japanese airmen had lain. As Dr Ransome stood formally on the terrace in his American uniform, Jim had wanted to explain to his parents everything that he and the doctor had done together, but his mother and father had been through their own war. For all their affection for him, they seemed older and far away.

Jim walked across the quay from the *Arrawa*, looking up at the newsreels projected above the evening crowd. The second of the screens, in front of the Palace Hotel, was now blank, its images of tank battles and saluting armies replaced by a rectangle of silver light that hung in the night air, a window into another universe.

As the army technicians on their tower of scaffolding repaired the projector, Jim walked across the tramlines towards the screen. Noticing it for the first time, the Chinese stopped to look up at the white rectangle. Jim brushed the sleeve of his jacket as a rickshaw coolie blundered into him, pulling two bar-girls in fur coats. Their powdered faces were lit like masks by the weird glimmer.

However, the heads of the Chinese were already turning to another spectacle. A crowd had gathered below the steps of the Shanghai Club. A group of American and British sailors had emerged through the revolving doors and stood on the top step, arguing with each other and waving drunkenly at the cruiser moored by the Bund. The Chinese watched as they formed a chorus line. Provoked by their curious but silent audience, the sailors began to jeer at the

Chinese. At a signal from an older sailor, the men unbuttoned their bell-bottomed trousers and urinated down the steps.

Fifty feet below them, the Chinese watched without comment as the arcs of urine formed a foaming stream that ran down to the street. When it reached the pavement the Chinese stepped back, their faces expressionless. Jim glanced at the people around him, the clerks and coolies and peasant women, well aware of what they were thinking. One day China would punish the rest of the world, and take a frightening revenge.

The army projectionists had rewound their film, and an air battle started again over the heads of the crowds. As the sailors were carried away in a convoy of rickshaws, Jim walked back to the *Arrawa*. His parents were resting in the passenger saloon on the upper deck, and Jim wanted to spend a last evening with his father before he and his mother sailed for England the next day.

He stepped on to the gangway, conscious that he was probably leaving Shanghai for the last time, setting out for a small, strange country on the other side of the world which he had never visited, but which was nominally 'home'. Yet only part of his mind would leave Shanghai. The rest would remain there forever, returning on the tide like the coffins launched from the funeral piers at Nantao.

Below the bows of the *Arrawa* a child's coffin moved on to the night stream. Its paper flowers were shaken loose by the wash of a landing-craft carrying sailors from the American cruiser. The flowers formed a wavering garland around the coffin as it began its long journey to the estuary of the Yangtze, only to be swept back by the incoming tide among the quays and mud-flats, driven once again to the shores of this terrible city.

The Kindness
of Women

Contents

PART ONE

A Season for Assassins

CHAPTER ONE

Bloody Saturday

Every afternoon in Shanghai during the summer of 1937 I rode down to the Bund to see if the war had begun. As soon as lunch was over I would wait for my mother and father to leave for the Country Club. While they changed into tennis clothes, ambling in a relaxed way around their bedroom, it always amazed me that they were so unconcerned by the coming war, and unaware that it might break out just as my father served his first ball. I remember pacing up and down with all the Napoleonic impatience of a 7-year-old, my toy soldiers drawn up on the carpet like the Japanese and Chinese armies around Shanghai. At times it seemed to me that I was keeping the war alive singlehandedly.

Ignoring my mother's laughter as she flirted with my father, I would watch the sky over Amherst Avenue. At any moment a squadron of Japanese bombers might appear above the department stores of downtown Shanghai and begin to bomb the Cathedral School. My child's mind had no idea how long a war would last, whether a few minutes or even, conceivably, an entire afternoon. My one fear was that, like so many exciting events I always managed to miss, the war would be over before I noticed that it had begun.

Throughout the summer everyone in Shanghai spoke about the coming war between China and Japan. At my mother's bridge parties, as I helped myself to the plates of small chow, I listened to her friends talking about the shots exchanged on July 7 at the Marco Polo bridge in Peking, which had signalled Japan's invasion of northern China. A month had passed without Chiang Kai-shek

9

ordering a counter-attack, and there were rumours that the German advisers to the Generalissimo were urging him to abandon the northern provinces and fight the Japanese nearer his stronghold at Nanking, the capital of China. Slyly, though, Chiang had decided to challenge the Japanese at Shanghai, two hundred miles away at the mouth of the Yangtse, where the American and European powers might intervene to save him.

As I saw for myself whenever I cycled down to the Bund, huge Chinese armies were massing around the International Settlement. On Friday, August 13, as soon as my mother and father settled themselves into the rear seats of the Packard, I wheeled my bicycle out of the garage, pumped up its tyres and set off on the long ride to the Bund. Olga, my White Russian governess, assumed that I was visiting David Hunter, a friend who lived at the western end of Amherst Avenue. A young woman of moods and strange stares, Olga was only interested in trying on my mother's wardrobe and was glad to see me gone.

I reached the Bund an hour later, but the concourse was so crowded with frantic office workers that I could scarcely get near the waterfront landing stages. Ringing my warning bell, I pedalled past the clanking trams, the wheel-locked rickshaws and their exhausted coolies, the gangs of aggressive beggars and pickpockets. Refugees from Chapei and Nantao streamed into the International Settlement, shouting up at the impassive facades of the great banks and trading houses along the Bund. Thousands of Chinese troops were dug into the northern suburbs of Shanghai, facing the Japanese garrison in their concession at Yangtsepoo. Standing on the steps of the Cathay Hotel as the doorman held my cycle, I could see the Whangpoo river filled with warships. There were British destroyers, sloops and gunboats, the USS *Augusta* and a French cruiser, and the veteran Japanese cruiser

Idzumo, which my father told me had helped to sink the Russian Imperial Fleet in 1905.

Despite this build-up of forces, the war obstinately refused to declare itself that afternoon. Disappointed, I wearily pedalled back to Amherst Avenue, my school blazer scuffed and stained, in time for tea and my favourite radio serial. Hugging my grazed knees, I stared at my armies of lead soldiers, and adjusted their lines to take account of the latest troop movements that I had seen as I rode home. Ignoring Olga's calls, I tried to work out a plan that would break the stalemate, hoping that my father, who knew one of the Chinese bankers behind Chiang Kai-shek, would pass on my muddled brain-wave to the Generalissimo.

Baffled by all these problems, which were even more difficult than my French homework, I wandered into my parents' bedroom. Olga was standing in front of my mother's full-length mirror, a fur cape over her shoulders. I sat at the dressing-table and rearranged the hair-brushes and perfume bottles, while Olga frowned at me through the glass as if I were an uninvited visitor who had strayed from another of the houses in Amherst Avenue. I had told my mother that Olga played with her wardrobe, but she merely smiled at me and said nothing to Olga.

Later I realised that this 17-year-old daughter of a once well-to-do Minsk family was scarcely more than a child herself. On my cycle rides I had been shocked by the poverty of the White Russian and Jewish refugees who lived in the tenement districts of Hongkew. It was one thing for the Chinese to be poor, but it disturbed me to see Europeans reduced to such a threadbare state. In their faces there was a staring despair that the Chinese never showed. Once, when I cycled past a dark tenement door-way, an old Russian woman told me to go away and shouted that my mother and father were thieves. For a few days I had believed her.

11

The refugees stood in their patched fur coats on the steps of the Park Hotel, hoping to sell their old-fashioned jewellery. The younger women had painted their mouths and eyes, trying bravely to cheer themselves up, I guessed. They called to the American and British officers going into the hotel, but what they were selling my mother had never been able to say – they were giving French and Russian lessons, she told me at last.

Always worried by my homework, and aware that many of the White Russians spoke excellent French, I had asked Olga if she would give me a French lesson like the young women at the Park Hotel. She sat on the bed while I hunted through my pocket dictionary, shaking her head as if I were some strange creature at a zoo. Worried that I had hurt her feelings by referring to her family's poverty, I gave Olga one of my silk shirts, and asked her to pass it on to her invalid father. She had held it in her hands for fully five minutes, like one of the vestments used in the communion services at Shanghai Cathedral, before returning it silently to my wardrobe. Already I had noticed that the White Russian governesses possessed a depth of female mystery that the mothers of my friends never remotely approached.

'Yes, James?' Olga hung the fur cape on its rack, and slipped my mother's breakfast gown over her shoulders. 'Have you finished your holiday book? You're very restless today.'

'I'm thinking about the war, Olga.'

'You're thinking about it every day, James. You and General Chiang think about it all the time. I'm sure he would like to meet you.'

'Well, I could meet him . . .' As it happened, I did sometimes feel that the Generalissimo was not giving his fullest attention to the war. 'Olga, do you know when the war will begin?'

12

'Hasn't it already begun? That's what everyone says.'

'Not the real war, Olga. The war in Shanghai.'

'Is that the real war? Nothing is real in Shanghai, James. Why don't you ask your father?'

'He doesn't know. I asked him after breakfast.'

'That's a pity. Are there many things he doesn't know?'

Still wearing the breakfast robe, Olga sat on my father's bed, her hand stroking the satin cover and smoothing away the creases. She was caressing the imprint of my father's shoulders, and for a moment I wondered if she was going to slip between the sheets.

'He does know many things, but . . .'

'I can remind you, James, it's Friday the 13th. Is that a good day for starting a war?'

'Hey, Olga . . . !' This news brightened everything. I rushed to the window – superstitions, I often noticed, had a habit of coming true. 'I'll tell you if I see anything.'

Olga stood behind me, calming me with a hand on my ear. Much as she loved the intimacy of my mother's clothes and the ripe odour of my father's riding jacket, she rarely touched me. She stared at the distant skyline along the Bund. Smoke rose from the coal-burning boilers of the older naval vessels. The black columns jostled for space as the warships changed their moorings, facing up to each other with sirens blasting. The darker light gave Olga's face the strong-nosed severity of the mortuary statues I had seen in Shanghai cemetery. She lifted the breakfast robe, staring through the veil of its fine fabric as if seeing a dream of vanished imperial Russia.

'Yes, James, I think they'll start the war for you today . . .'

'Say, thanks, Olga.'

But before the war could start, my mother and father returned unexpectedly from the Country Club. With them were two British officers in the Shanghai Volunteer Force, wearing their tight Great War uniforms. I tried to join

13

them in my father's study, but my mother took me into the garden and in a strained way pointed to the golden orioles drinking from the edge of the swimming pool.

I was sorry to see her worried, as I knew that my mother, unlike Olga, was one of those people who should never be worried by anything. Trying not to annoy her, I spent the rest of the afternoon in my playroom. I listened to the sirens of the battle-fleets and marshalled my toy soldiers. On the next day, Bloody Saturday as it would be known, my miniature army at last came to life.

I remember the wet monsoon that blew through Shanghai during that last night of the peace, drowning the sounds of Chinese sniper fire, and the distant boom of Japanese naval guns striking at the Chinese shore batteries at Woosung. When I woke into the warm, sticky air the storm had passed, and the washed neon signs of the city shone ever more vividly.

At breakfast my mother and father were already dressed in their golfing clothes, though when they left in the Packard a few minutes later my father was at the wheel, the chauffeur beside him, and they had not taken their golf clubs.

'Jamie, you're to stay home today,' my father announced, staring through my eyes as he did when he had unfathomable reasons of his own. 'You can finish your *Robinson Crusoe*.'

'You'll meet Man Friday and the cannibals.' My mother smiled at this treat in store, but her eyes were as flat as they had been when our spaniel was run over by the German doctor in Columbia Road. I wondered if Olga had died during the night, but she was watching from the door, pressing the lapels of her dressing gown to her neck.

'I've already met the cannibals.' However exciting, Crusoe's shipwreck palled by comparison with the real naval disaster about to take place on the Whangpoo river.

'Can we go to the Tattoo? David Hunter's going next week . . .'

The Military Tattoo staged by soldiers of the British garrison was filled with booming cannon, thunderflashes and bayonet charges, and recreated the bravest clashes of the Great War, the battles of Mons, Ypres and the Gallipoli landings. In a sense, the make-believe of the Tattoo might be as close as I would ever get to a real war.

'Jamie, we'll see – they may have to cancel the Tattoo. The soldiers are very busy.'

'I know. Then can we go to the Hell-drivers?' This was a troupe of American dare-devil drivers, who crashed their battered Fords and Chevrolets through wooden barricades covered with flaming gasoline. The sight of these thrillingly rehearsed accidents forever eclipsed the humdrum street crashes of Shanghai. 'You promised . . .'

'The Hell-drivers aren't here any more. They've gone back to Manila.'

'They're getting ready for the war.' In my mind I could see these laconic Americans, in their dashing goggles and aviator's suits, crashing through the flaming walls as they answered a salvo from the *Idzumo*. 'Can I come to the golf club?'

'No! Stay here with Olga! I won't tell you again . . .' My father's voice had an edge of temper that I had noticed since the labour troubles at his cotton mill in Pootung, on the east bank of the river. I wondered why Olga watched him so closely when he was angry. Her toneless eyes showed a rare and almost hungry alertness, the expression I felt on my face when I was about to tuck into an ice-cream sundae. One of the communist union organisers who threatened to kill my father had stared at him in the same way as we sat in the Packard outside his office in the Szechuan Road. I worried that Olga wanted to kill my father and eat him.

'Do I have to? Olga listens all the time to French dance music.'

'Well, you listen with her,' my mother rejoined. 'Olga can teach you how to dance.'

This was a prospect I dreaded, an even greater torture than the promise of unending peace. When Olga touched me, it was in a distant but oddly intimate way. As I lay in bed at night she would sometimes undress in my bathroom with the door ajar. Later I guessed that this was her way of proving to herself that I no longer existed. As soon as my parents left for the golf club my one intention was to give her the slip.

'David said that Olga –'

'All right!' Irritated by the ringing telephone, which the servants were too nervous to answer, my father relented. 'You can see David Hunter. But don't go anywhere else.'

Why was he frightened of Shanghai? Despite his quick temper, my father easily gave in, as if events in the world were so uncertain that even my childish nagging carried weight. He was too distracted to play with my toy soldiers, and he often looked at me in the same firm but dejected way in which the headmaster of the Cathedral School gazed at the assembled boys during morning prayers. When he walked to the car he stamped his spiked golf shoes, leaving deep marks in the gravel, like footprints staking a claim to Crusoe's beach.

Even before the Packard had left the drive, Olga was reclining on the verandah with my mother's copies of *Vogue* and the *Saturday Evening Post*. At intervals she called out to me, her voice as remote as the sirens on the river buoys at Woosung. I guessed that she knew about my afternoon cycle rides around Shanghai. She was well aware that I might be kidnapped or robbed of my clothes in one of the back alleys of the Bubbling Well Road. Perhaps the terrors of the Russian civil war, the long journey with her parents through Turkey and Iraq to this

16

rootless city at the mouth of the Yangtse, had so disoriented her that she no longer cared if the child in her charge was killed.

'Who did your father let you see, James?'

'David Hunter. He's my closest friend. I'm going now, Olga.'

'You have so many closest friends. Tell me if the war begins, James.'

She waved, and I was gone. In fact, the last person in Shanghai I wanted to see was David. During the summer holidays my schoolfriends and I played homeric games of hide-and-seek that lasted for weeks and covered the whole of Shanghai. As I drove with my mother to the Country Club or drank iced tea in the Chocolate Shop I was constantly watching for David, who might break away from his amah and lunge through the crowd to tap me on the shoulder. These games added another layer of strangeness and surprise to a city already too strange.

I wheeled my cycle from the garage, buttoned my blazer and set off down the drive. Legs whirling like the blades of an eggbeater, I swerved into Amherst Avenue and overtook a column of peasants trudging through the western suburbs of the city. Refugees from the countryside now occupied by the Chinese and Japanese armies, they plodded past the great houses of the avenue, their few possessions on their backs. They laboured towards the distant towers of downtown Shanghai, unaware of everything but the hard asphalt in front of them, ignoring the chromium bumpers and blaring horns of the Buicks and Chryslers whose Chinese chauffeurs were trying to force them off the road.

Standing on my pedals, I edged past a rickshaw loaded with bales of matting, on which perched two old women clutching the walls and roof of a dismantled hovel. I could smell their bodies, crippled by a lifetime of heavy manual work, and the same rancid sweat and hungry breath of all

17

impoverished peasants. But the night's rain still soaked their black cotton tunics, which gleamed in the sunlight like the rarest silks on the fabric counters in the Sun Sun department store, as if the magic of Shanghai had already begun to transform these destitute people.

What would happen to them? My mother was studiously vague about the refugees, but Olga told me in her matter-of-fact way that most of them soon died of hunger or typhus in the alleys of Chapei. Every morning on my way to school I passed the trucks of the Shanghai Municipal Authority that toured the city, collecting the hundreds of bodies of Chinese who had died during the night. I liked to think that only the old people died, though I had seen a dead boy of my own age sitting against the steel entrance grille of my father's office block. He held an empty cigarette tin in his white hands, probably the last gift to him from his family before they abandoned him. I hoped that the others became bar-tenders and waiters and Number 3 girls at the Great World Amusement Park, and my mother said that she hoped so too.

Putting aside these thoughts, and cheered by the day ahead, I reached the Avenue Joffre and the long tree-lined boulevards of the French Concession that would carry me to the Bund. Quick-tempered French soldiers guarded the sand-bagged checkpoint by the tramline terminus. They stared warily at the empty sky and spat at the feet of the passing Chinese, hating this ugly city to which they had been exiled across the world. But I felt a surge of excitement on entering Shanghai. To my child's eyes, which had seen nothing else, Shanghai was a waking dream where everything I could imagine had already been taken to its extreme. The garish billboards and nightclub neon signs, the young Chinese gangsters and violent beggars watching me keenly as I pedalled past them, were part of an overlit realm more exhilarating than the American comics and radio serials I so adored.

Shanghai would absorb everything, even the coming war, however fiercely the smoke might pump from the warships in the Whangpoo river. My father called Shanghai the most advanced city in the world, and I knew that one day all the cities on the planet would be filled with radio-stations, hell-drivers and casinos. Outside the Canidrome the crowds of Chinese and Europeans were pushing their way into the greyhound arena, unconcerned by the Kuomintang armies around the city waiting to attack the Japanese garrison. Gamblers jostled each other by the betting booths of the jai alai stadium, and the morning audience packed the entrance of the Grand Theatre on the Nanking Road, eager to see the latest Hollywood musical, *Gold-Diggers of 1937*.

But of all the places of wonder, the Great World Amusement Park on the Avenue Edward VII most amazed me, and contained the magnetic heart of Shanghai within its six floors. Unknown to my parents, the chauffeur often took me into its dirty and feverish caverns. After collecting me from school, Yang would usually stop the car outside the Amusement Park and carry out one or other of the mysterious errands that occupied a large part of his day.

A vast warehouse of light and noise, the Amusement Park was filled with magicians and fireworks, slot machines and sing-song girls. A haze of frying fat gleamed in the air, and formed a greasy film on my face, mingling with the smell of joss-sticks and incense. Stunned by the din, I would follow Yang as he slipped through the acrobats and Chinese actors striking their gongs. Medicine hawkers lanced the necks of huge white geese, selling the cups of steaming blood to passers-by as the ferocious birds stamped their feet and gobbled at me when I came too close. While Yang murmured into the ears of the mahjong dealers and marriage brokers, I peered between his legs at the exposed toilets in the lavatory stalls and at the

19

fearsome idols scowling over the temple doorways, at the mysterious peep-shows and massage booths with their elegant Chinese girls, infinitely more terrifying than Olga, in embroidered high-collared robes slit to expose their thighs.

This Saturday, however, the Great World was closed. The dance platforms, dried-fish stalls and love-letter booths had been dismantled, and the municipal authorities had turned the ancient building into a refugee camp. Hundreds of frantic Chinese were forcing their way into the ramshackle structure, held back by a cordon of Sikh police in sweat-stained khaki turbans. Like a team of carpet-beaters, the Sikhs lashed at the broken-toothed peasant farmers with their heavy bamboo staves. A burly British police sergeant waved his service revolver at the monkey-like old women with bound feet who tried to push past him, their calloused fists punching his chest.

I stood on the opposite sidewalk, listening to the sirens sounding from the river, a great moaning of blind beasts challenging each other. For the first time I guessed that war of a kind had already come to Shanghai. Buffeted by the Chinese office clerks, I steered my cycle along the gutter, and squeezed past an armoured riot van of the Shanghai Police, with its twin-handled Thompson machine-gun mounted above the driver's cabin.

Breathless, I rested in the doorway of a funeral parlour. The elderly undertaker sat among the coffins at the rear of the shop, white fingers flicking at the beads of his abacus. The clicks echoed among the empty coffins, and reminded me of the superstition that Yang had graphically described, snapping his fingers in front of my nose. 'When a coffin cracks, the Chinese undertaker knows he will sell it . . .'

I listened to the abacus, trying to see if the coffins gave a twitch when they cracked. Soon a lot of coffins in Shanghai would be cracking. The old man's fingers flicked faster as he watched me with his vain, dreamy eyes. Was he adding up all those who were going to die in Shanghai, trying to reach my own number, somewhere among the cracking coffins and clicking beads?

Behind me a car horn blared into the crowd. A white Lincoln Zephyr was forcing its way through the traffic, hemmed in by the rickshaw coolies and refugees clambering into the entrance of the Amusement Park. David Hunter knelt on the rear seat beside his Australian nanny, blond hair in his eyes as he squinted at the pavement. Forgetting the coffins and the clicking abacus, I pushed my cycle along the gutter, aware that David would see me once the traffic had cleared.

An air-raid klaxon sounded from one of the office buildings, overlaid by a heavy, sustained rumble like a collapsing sky. A shouting coolie strode towards me, bales of firewood on a bamboo pole across his shoulders, from which the veins stood out like bloated worms. Without pausing, he kicked the cycle out of my hands. I bent down to rub my bruised knees, and tried to reach the handlebars, but the rush of feet knocked me to the ground. Winded, I lay among the old lottery tickets, torn newspapers and straw sandals as the white Lincoln cruised past. Playing with his blond fringe behind the passenger window, David frowned at me in his pointy way, unable to recognise me but puzzled why an English boy in a Cathedral School blazer had chosen this of all moments to roll about in a filthy gutter.

The klaxon wailed, keening at the sky. Chinese office workers, women clerks and hotel waiters were running down the Nanking Road from the Bund. An immense cloud of white steam rose from the Whangpoo river behind them, flashes of gunfire reflected in its lower surface. Around it circled three twin-engined bombing planes, banking as they flew through its ashen billows.

A squadron of Chinese aircraft were bombing the

21

Idzumo and the Japanese cotton-mills at Yangtsepoo, little more than a mile from the Bund across the Garden Bridge. The boom of heavy guns jarred the windows of the office buildings in the Thibet Road. A tram clanked past me towards the Bund, its passengers leaping into the road. High above them, on the roof of the Socony-Vacuum building, stood a party of unconcerned Europeans in white tennis clothes, binoculars in hand, pointing out details of the spectacle to each other.

Had the war really started? I was expecting something as organised and disciplined as the Military Tattoo. The planes lumbered through the air, as if the pilots were bored by their targets and were circling the *Idzumo* simply to fill in time before returning to their airfield. The French and British warships sat at their moorings near the Pootung shore, signal lights blinking softly from their bridges, a vaguely curious commentary on the bombing display down-river.

Mounting my cycle, I straightened the handlebars and brushed the dust from my blazer – the officious junior masters at the school liked to roam the city in their spare time, reporting anyone untidily dressed. I set off after the empty tram, steering between the polished rails. When it neared the Bund the conductor dismounted, swearing at the driver and waving his leather cash bag. The tram's warning bell clanged at the empty street, watched by groups of Chinese clerks pressing themselves into the doorways of the office buildings.

A water-spout rose from the choppy waves beside the bows of the *Idzumo*, hovered for a second and then surged upwards in a violent cascade. Arms of hurtling foam punched through the air and soared high above the radio aerials and mast-tops of the ancient cruiser. A second squadron of Chinese bombers swept in formation down the Whangpoo, midway between the Bund and the Pootung shore, where my father's cotton mill lay behind a veil of greasy smoke. One of the planes lagged behind the others, the pilot unable to keep his place in the formation. He rolled his wings from side to side, like the stunt pilots at the aerobatic displays at Hungjao Airfield.

'Jamie, leave your bike! Come with us!'

The white fenders of the Lincoln Zephyr had crept behind me. David's Australian nanny was shouting to me, her arms stretched across the shoulders of the nervous Chinese chauffeur. Steadying her straw hat with one hand, she waved me towards the car. Nurse Arnold had always been easy-going and friendly, so much more pleasant to me than Olga, and I was surprised by her bad temper. David had recognised me, a gleam of triumph in his eyes. He brushed the blond hair from his forehead, aware that he was about to make the first capture of our marathon game of hide-and-seek.

The *Idzumo* was laying smoke around itself. Scrolls of oily vapour uncoiled along its bows. Through the sooty clouds I could see the tremble of anti-aircraft fire, the sounds lost in the monotonous drone of the Chinese bombers.

'Jamie, you stupid . . . !'

I pedalled away from them into a wall of noise and smoke. Glass was falling from the windows of my father's building in Szechuan Road. Office girls darted from the doorways, their white blouses speckled with fine needles. My front wheel jolted over a piece of masonry shaken loose from a cornice. While I straightened the pedals a low-flying bomber veered away from the Japanese anti-aircraft fire. It flew above the Bund, exposed its open bombing racks and released two bombs towards the empty sampans moored to the quay.

Eager to watch the water-spouts, I mounted my cycle, but a pair of powerful hands gripped my armpits. A uniformed British police sergeant whirled me off my feet. He kicked away my cycle and crouched by the steps of the

Socony building. As he held me against his hip the metal hammer of his revolver tore the skin from my knee.

Exploding debris burst between the hotels and department stores of the Nanking Road and filled the street with white ash. A wave of burning air struck my chest and threw me to the ground beside the sergeant. Chinese office workers with raised hands ran towards us through the billows of dust, blood streaming from their foreheads. One of the stray bombs had fallen into the Palace Hotel, and the other into the Avenue Edward VII beside the Great World Amusement Park. The buildings in the Szechuan Road rocked around us, shaking a cascade of broken glass and roofing tiles into the street.

Beside the kerb a matronly Eurasian woman stepped from her car, blood running from her ear. She touched it discreetly with a silk handkerchief as the police sergeant propelled me towards her.

'Keep him here!' He jerked my shoulders, as if I were a sleeping doll, and he were trying to wake me. 'Lad, you stay with her!'

When he ran towards the Nanking Road the Eurasian woman released my hand, waving me away and too distracted to be bothered with me. Blood seeped down my leg, staining my white socks. Looking at the thin trickle, I noticed that I had lost one of my shoes. My head felt empty, and I touched my face to make sure that it was still there. The explosion had sucked all the air from the street and it was difficult to breathe. Gesturing to me in an absent way, the Eurasian woman wandered through the debris, wiping the dust from her leather handbag. The blood ran from her ear as she stared at the broken glass, trying to recognise the windows of her own apartment.

Far away, police sirens had begun to wail, and an ambulance of the Shanghai Volunteer Force drove past, the glass spitting under its tyres. I realised that I was deaf, but everything around me was deaf too, as if the world could no longer hear itself. Two hundred yards from the Great World Amusement Park I could see that most of the building had vanished. Smoke rose from its exposed floors, and an arcing electric cable sparked and jumped like a swaying firecracker.

Hundreds of dead Chinese were lying in the street among the crushed rickshaws and burnt-out cars. Their bodies were covered with white chalk, through which darker patches had formed, as if they were trying to camouflage themselves. I walked among them, tripping over an old amah who lay on her back, pouting face covered with powder, scolding me with her last grimace. An office clerk without his arms sat against the rear wheel of a gutted bus. Everywhere hands and feet lay among the debris of the Amusement Park – fragments of joss sticks and playing cards, gramophone records and dragon masks, part of the head of a stuffed whale, all blanched by the dust. A bolt of silk had unravelled across the street, a white bandage that wound around the lumps of masonry and the mislaid hands.

I waited for someone to call to me, but the air was silent and ringing, like the pause after an unanswered alarm. I could no longer hear my feet as they cracked the blades of broken glass. I walked back to the Hunters' Lincoln Zephyr. The chauffeur stood in his pallid uniform by the open driver's door, brushing away the dust that covered the windshield. David sat alone in the back, hands pressed to his mouth. He ignored me and stared at the torn seat-cover with fixed eyes, as if he never wanted to see me again.

I looked through the broken windows at Nurse Arnold, who was lying across the front seat. Her hair fell across her face, forced by the explosion into her mouth. Her hands were open, white palms exposed, displaying to any passer-by that she had washed them carefully before she died.

*

Later, when he visited me in Shanghai General Hospital, David asked me about the blood on my leg. Curiously, this was the only blood that he had seen on Bloody Saturday.

'I was wounded by the bomb,' I told him.

I had begun to boast in a small way, but more truthfully than I realised. One thousand and twelve people, almost all Chinese refugees, were killed by the high-explosive bomb that fell beside the Great World Amusement Park. As everyone constantly repeated, proud that Shanghai had again excelled itself, this was the largest number killed by a single bomb in the history of aerial warfare. My own trivial injury, caused by the police sergeant's revolver, numbered me among the thousand and seven who were wounded. Although not the youngest of those injured, I liked to think that I was No. 1007, which I firmly inked on my arm.

Months of fierce fighting took place around the International Settlement before the Japanese were able to drive the Chinese from Shanghai, during which tens of thousands of soldiers and civilians were to perish. But the Avenue Edward VII bomb, dropped in error by a Chinese pilot, had a special place in the mythology of war, a potent example of how mass death could now fall from the air.

At the time, as I rested in my bed at Shanghai General, I was thinking not of the bomb beside the Amusement Park, but of my army of toy soldiers on the floor of my playroom. Even as the rescue workers of the Shanghai Volunteer Force carried me to their ambulance through the dusty streets I knew that I needed to rearrange their battle lines. I had seen the real war for which I had waited so impatiently, and I felt vaguely guilty that there were no models of dead Chinese in my boxes of brightly painted soldiers. Now and then my ears would clear for a brief moment, and the eerie sounds of Japanese artillery drum-

26

ming at the hospital window seemed to call to me from another world.

Within a few days, however, my memories of the bombing had begun to fade. I tried to remember the dust and debris in the Szechuan Road, but the confused images in my head had merged with the newsreels I had seen of the Spanish civil war and the filmed manoeuvres of the French and British armies. The fighting in the western suburbs of Shanghai veiled the window with curtains of smoke which the autumn winds drew aside to reveal the burning tenements of Nantao. The nurses and doctors who tested my ears with their tuning forks, Olga and my school-friends, my mother and father on their evening visits, were like actors in the old silent films that David Hunter's father screened for us against his dining-room wall. The bomb that destroyed the Amusement Park and killed more than a thousand people had become part of those films.

It was three months before I could go back to Amherst Avenue. Artillery shells from the rival Chinese and Japanese howitzers at Siccawei station and Hungjao were passing over the roof of our house, and my mother and father had moved to an apartment in the French Concession. The battle for Shanghai continued around the perimeter of the International Settlement, shaking the doors of our apartment and often jamming the elevator. Once Olga and I were trapped for an hour in the metal cage. She, who was usually so silent, spent the time delivering a torrent of words at me, well aware that I could hear not a single one. I often wondered if she was accusing me of starting the war, though in Olga's eyes that would have been the least of my crimes.

In November the Chinese armies began to withdraw from Shanghai, retreating up the Yangtse to Nanking. They left behind them the devastated suburbs, which the Japanese occupied, ringing the International Settlement with their tanks and machine-gun posts. We were then safe to return to Amherst Avenue. While my parents talked to the servants I ran up to my playroom, eager to see my army of toy soldiers again.

The miniature battle of Shanghai had been swept aside. Broken soldiers lay scattered among my train set and model cars. Someone, perhaps Coolie or Number 2 Boy, had used my *Robinson Crusoe* as an ash tray, stubbing his half-smoked cigarettes into the cover as he watched nervously from the windows. I thought of reporting him to my father, but I knew that the servants had been as frightened as I was.

I gathered the soldiers together and later tried to play with them, but the games seemed more serious than those that had filled the playroom floor before Bloody Saturday. When David and I set out our rival armies it worried me that we were secretly trying to kill each other. Thinking of the severed hands and feet I had seen outside the Amusement Park, I put the soldiers away in their box.

But at Christmas there were new sets of soldiers to take their place, Seaforth Highlanders in khaki battle-kilts and Coldstream Guards in bearskins. To my surprise, life in the International Settlement was unaffected by the months of fighting around the city, as if the bitter warfare had been little more than a peripheral entertainment of a particularly brutal kind, like the public strangulations in the Old City. The neon signs shone ever more brightly over Shanghai's four hundred nightclubs. My father played cricket at the Country Club, while my mother organised her bridge and dinner parties. I served as a page at a lavish wedding at the French Club. The Bund was crowded with trading vessels and sampans loaded with miles of brightly patterned calico which my father's printing and finishing works produced for the elegant Chinese women who thronged the Settlement. The great import-export houses of the Szechuan Road were busier than before. The radio stations broadcast their American adventure serials, the bars and dance halls were filled with Number 2 and Number 3 girls, and the British garrison staged its Military Tattoo. Even the distant war between Japan and Chiang Kai-shek continued in the hinterland of China the roulette wheels turned in the casinos, spinning their dreams of old Shanghai.

As if to remind themselves of the war, one Sunday afternoon my parents and their friends drove out to tour the battlegrounds in the countryside to the west of Shanghai. We had attended a reception given by the British Consul General, and the wives wore their best silk gowns, the husbands their smartest grey suits and panamas. When our convoy of cars stopped at the Keswick Road check-point I was waiting for the shabby Japanese soldiers to turn us back, but they beckoned us through without comment, as if we were worth scarcely a glance.

Three miles into the countryside we stopped on a deserted road. I remember the battlefield under the silent sky, and the burnt-out village near a derelict canal. The chauffeurs opened the doors, and we stepped on to a roadway covered with pieces of gold. Hundreds of spent rifle cartridges lay at our feet. Abandoned trenchworks ran between the burial mounds, from which open coffins protruded like drawers in a ransacked wardrobe. Scattered around us were remnants of torn webbing, empty ammunition boxes, boots and helmets, rusting bayonets and signal flares. Beyond rifle pits filled with water was an earth redoubt, pulverised by the Japanese artillery. The carcase of a horse lay by its gun emplacement, legs raised stiffly in the sunlight.

Together we gazed at this scene, the ladies fanning away the flies, their husbands murmuring to each other, like a group of investors visiting the stage-set of an uncompleted war film. Led by my father and Mr Hunter, we strolled towards the canal, and stared at the Chinese soldiers floating in the shallow water. Dead infantrymen lay everywhere in the drowned trenches, covered to their waists by the earth, as if asleep in a derelict dormitory.

Beside me, David was tittering to himself. He was impatient to go home, and I could see his jarred eyes hidden behind his fringe. He turned his back on his mother, but the dead battlefield surrounded him on every side. Deliberately scuffing his polished shoes, he kicked the cartridge cases at the sleeping soldiers.

I cupped my hands over my ears, trying to catch the sound that would wake them.

CHAPTER TWO

Escape Attempts

All day rumours had swept Lunghua that there would soon be an escape from the camp. Shivering on the steps of the children's hut, I waited for Sergeant Nagata to complete the third of the day's emergency roll-calls. Usually, at the first hint of an escape attempt, the Japanese sentries would close the gates with a set of heavy padlocks – a symbolic gesture, as David Hunter's father remarked, since anyone planning to escape from Lunghua hardly intended to walk through the front gates. It was far easier to step through the perimeter wire, as I and the older children did every day, hunting for a lost tennis ball or setting useless bird-traps for the American sailors.

Symbolic or not, the gesture served a practical purpose, like so much of Japanese ceremony. Closing the gates was a sign to any Chinese collaborators in the surrounding countryside that a security alert was under way, and told the few informers within the camp – always the last to know what was going on – to keep their eyes open.

However, the gates hung slackly from their rotting posts, and the sentries stamped their ragged boots on the cold earth, even more bored than ever. Almost all the Japanese soldiers, like Private Kimura, were the sons of peasant farmers, so poor that they regarded Lunghua, with its two thousand prisoners and its unlimited stocks of cricket bats and tennis rackets, as a haven of affluence. The unheated cement dormitories at least received an erratic supply of electric power, an unimagined luxury for the Japanese peasant.

I whistled through my fingers, trying to attract Kimura's attention, but he ignored me and gazed at the Chinese beggars waiting patiently outside the gates for the scraps that never came. As if depressed by the untended paddy-fields, Kimura frowned at the steam that rose from his broad nostrils. I imagined him thinking of his mother and father tending their modest crops in a remote corner of Hokkaido. Neither of us had seen our parents during the years of the war, though in many ways Kimura was more alone than I was. In the panic after the Japanese seizure of the International Settlement I had been separated from my mother and father when we left our hotel on the Bund. Nonetheless, I was confident that I would see them again, even if their faces had begun to fade in my mind. But Kimura would almost certainly die here, among these empty rice fields, when the Japanese made their last stand against the Americans at the mouth of the Yangtse.

I lined my fingers on his shaven head, as if aiming Sergeant Nagata's Mauser pistol, and snapped my thumb.

'Jamie, I heard that.' A tall, 14-year-old English girl, Peggy Gardner, joined me at the doorway, her thin shoulders hunched against the cold. She nudged me with a bony elbow, as if to make me miss my aim. 'Who did you shoot?'

'Private Kimura.'

'You shot him yesterday.' Peggy shook her head over this, her face grave but forgiving, a favourite pose. 'Private Kimura is your friend.'

'I shoot my friends too.' Friends, surprisingly, made even more tempting targets than enemies. 'Besides, Private Kimura isn't really my friend.'

'Not half. Mrs Dwight thinks you're an informer. Why do you have to shoot everyone?'

Sergeant Nagata emerged from D Block, scowling over his roster board, the British block commander behind him. Peggy pushed me against the door and forced my hands into my back. Glaring suspiciously at every blade of grass, Sergeant Nagata would not appreciate serving as my practice target. I leaned against Peggy, glad to feel her strong wrists and smell the cold, reassuring scent of her body. She was always trying to wrestle with me, for reasons I was not yet ready to explore.

'Why, Jamie? You've shot everyone in Lunghua by now. Is it because you want to be alone here?'

'I haven't shot Mrs Dwight.' This busybodying missionary was one of the English widows who supervised the eight boys and girls in the children's hut, all war-orphans separated from parents interned in the other camps near Shanghai and Nanking. Rather than make sure that we had our fair share of the falling food ration, Mrs Dwight was concerned for our spiritual welfare, as I heard her explain to the mystified camp commandant, Mr Hyashi. For Mrs Dwight this chiefly involved my sitting silently in the freezing hut over my Latin homework – anything rather than the restless errand-running and food-scavenging that occupied every moment of my day. To Mrs Dwight I was a 'free soul', a term that contained not a hint of approval. Spiritual well-being seemed to be inversely proportional to the amount of food one received, which perhaps explained why Mrs Dwight and the other missionaries considered their pre-war activities in the famine-ridden provinces of northern China such a marked success.

'When the war's over,' I said darkly, 'I'll ask my father to shoot Mrs Dwight with a real gun. He dislikes missionaries, you know.'

'Jamie . . . !' Peggy tried to box my ears. A doctor's daughter from Tsingtao, she was a year older than me and pretended to be easily shocked. As I knew, she was far more protective than Mrs Dwight. When I was ill it was Peggy who had looked after me, giving me some of the younger children's food. One day I would repay her. She ruled the children's hut in a firm but high-minded way, and I was her greatest challenge. I liked to keep up a steady flow of small outrages, but recently I had noticed Peggy's depressing tendency to imitate Mrs Dwight, modelling herself on this starchy widow as if she needed the approval of an older woman. I preferred the strong-willed girl who stood up to the boys in her class, rescued the younger children from bullies, and had a certain thin-hipped stylishness with which I had still to come to terms.

'If your father's going to shoot anyone,' Peggy remarked, 'he should start with Dr Sinclair.' This vile-tempered clergyman was the headmaster of the camp school. 'He's worse than Sergeant Nagata.'

'Peggy . . . ?' I felt a rush of concern for her. 'Did he hit you?'

'He nearly tried. He always looks at me in that smiley way. As if I was his daughter and he needed to punish me.'

Only that afternoon one of the ten-year-olds had come back to the hut with a stinging red forehead. Our real education at the Lunghua school came from learning to read Dr Sinclair's moods.

'Did you tell Mrs Dwight?'

'She wouldn't listen. Just because they're kind to us, they think they can do anything. She's more frightened of him than I am.'

'He doesn't hit everybody.'

'He'll hit you one day.'

'I won't let him.' This was idle talk, and my next Latin class could prove me wrong. But so far I had avoided the clergyman's heavy hands. I had noticed that Dr Sinclair left alone the children of the more well-to-do British parents. He never hit David Hunter, however much David tried to provoke him, and only cuffed the sons of factory foremen, Eurasian mothers or officers in the Shanghai Police. What I could never understand was why the parents failed to protest when their children returned to their rooms in G Block with ears bleeding from the clergyman's signet ring. It was almost as if the parents accepted this reminder of their lowly position in Shanghai's British community.

Bored with it all, and deciding to show off in front of Peggy, I picked up a stone from the step and hurled it high into the air over the parade ground.

'Jamie, you're in trouble! Sergeant Nagata saw that . . .'

I froze against the door. The sergeant was standing on the gravel path twenty feet from the children's hut. As he stared at me he filled his lungs, his face bearing the weight of some slow but vast emotion. However complicated the British at Lunghua seemed to me, there was no doubt that Sergeant Nagata found them infinitely more mysterious, a stiff-necked people whose armies in Singapore had surrendered without a fight but nonetheless acted as if they had won the war. For some reason he kept a close watch on me, as if I were a key to this conundrum.

Why he should have marked out one 13-year-old boy among the two hundred children I never discovered. Did he think I was trying to escape, or serving as a secret courier between the dormitory blocks? In fact, most of the adults in the camp shied away from me when I loomed up to them, eager to play blindfold chess or offer my views on the progress of the war and the latest Japanese aerial tactics. My nerveless energy soon tired them and, besides, I was forever looking to the future. No-one knew when the war would end – perhaps in 1947 or even 1948 – and the internees coped with the endless time by erasing it from their lives. The busy programme of lectures and concert parties of the first year had been abandoned. The internees rested in their cubicles, reading their last letters from England, roused briefly by the iron wheels of the food carts. Mrs Dwight was not the only one to see the dangers of an overactive imagination.

'Jamie, look out . . .' Mischievously, Peggy pushed me

through the doorway. I stumbled on to the gravel, but Sergeant Nagata had more pressing matters on his mind than a head-count of the war children. Slapping his roster-board, he led his entourage back to the guard-house. I was sorry to see him go – I enjoyed squaring up to Sergeant Nagata. There was something about the Japanese, their seriousness and stoicism, that I admired. One day I might join the Japanese Air Force, just as my other heroes, the American Flying Tigers, had flown for Chiang Kai-shek.

'Why isn't he coming?' Disappointed, Peggy shivered in her patched cardigan. 'You could have escaped – think what Mrs Dwight would say. She'd have you banished.'

'I am banished.' Not sure what this meant, I added: 'There might be an escape tonight.'

'Who said? Are you going with them?'

'Basie and Demarest told me.' The American merchant seamen were a fund of inaccurate information, much of it deliberately propagated. As it happened, escape could not have been further from my mind. My parents were interned at Soochow, far too dangerous a distance to walk, and the British in charge might not let me in. They were terrified of being infected with typhus or cholera by prisoners transferred from other camps.

'I would have gone with them, but Basie's wrong.' I pointed to the guard-house, where Private Kimura was saluting the sergeant with unnecessary zeal. 'They always close the gates when Sergeant Nagata thinks there's going to be an escape.'

'Well . . .' Peggy hid her pale cheeks behind her arms and shrewdly studied the Japanese. 'Perhaps they want us to escape.'

'What?' This struck me with the force of revelation. I knew from the secret camp radio that by now, November 1943, the war had begun to turn against the Japanese. After the attack on Pearl Harbor and their rapid advance across the Pacific, they had suffered huge defeats at the battles of Midway and the Coral Sea. American reconnaissance planes had appeared over Shanghai, and the first bombing raids would soon follow. Along the Whangpoo river Japanese military activity had increased, and anti-aircraft batteries were dug in around the airfield to the north of the camp. Lunghua pagoda was now a heavily armed flak tower equipped with powerful searchlights and rapid-fire cannon. The Korean and Japanese guards at Lunghua were more aggressive towards the prisoners, and even Private Kimura was irritable when I showed him my drawings of the sinking of the *Repulse* and the *Prince of Wales*, the British battleships sent to the bottom of the South China Sea by Japanese dive-bombers.

Far more worrying, the food ration had been cut. The sweet potatoes and cracked wheat – a coarse cattle feed – were warehouse scrapings, filled with dead weevils and rusty nails. Peggy and I were hungry all the time.

'Jamie, suppose . . .' Intrigued by her own logic, Peggy smiled to herself. 'Suppose the Japanese want us to escape, so they won't have to feed us? Then they'd have more to eat.'

She waited for me to react, and reached out to reassure me, seeing that she had gone too far. She knew that any threat to the camp unsettled me more than all the petty snubs. What I feared most was not merely that the food ration would be cut again, but that Lunghua camp, which had become my entire world, might degenerate into anarchy. Peggy and I would be the first casualties. If the Japanese lost interest in their prisoners we would be at the mercy of the bandit groups who roamed the countryside, renegade Kuomintang and deserters from the puppet armies. Gangs of single men from E Block would seize the food store behind the kitchens, and Mrs Dwight would have nothing to offer the children except her prayers.

I felt Peggy's arm around my shoulders, and listened to

her heart beating through the thin wall of her chest. Often she looked unwell, but I was determined to keep her out of the camp hospital. Lunghua hospital was not a place that made its patients better. We needed extra rations to survive the coming winter, but the food store was more carefully locked than the cells in the guard-house.

As the all-clear sounded, the internees emerged from the doorways of their blocks, staring at the camp as if seeing it for the first time. The great tenement family of Lunghua began to rouse itself. Listless women hung their faded washing and sanitary rags on the lines behind G Block. A crowd of children raced to the parade ground, led by David Hunter, who was wearing a pair of his father's leather shoes that I so coveted. As he moved around the camp my eyes rarely left his feet. Mrs Hunter had offered me her golfing brogues, but I had been too proud to accept, an act of foolishness I regretted, since my rubber sneakers were now as ragged as Private Kimura's canvas boots. The war had led to a coolness between David and myself. I envied him his parents, and all my attempts to attach myself to a sympathetic adult had been rebuffed. Only Basie and the Americans were friendly, but their friendliness depended on my running errands for them.

Mrs Dwight approached the children's hut, her fussy eyes taking in everything like a busy broom. She smiled approvingly at Peggy, who was holding a crude metal bucket soldered together from a galvanized-iron roofing sheet dislodged by the monsoon storms. With the tepid water she brought back from the heating station Peggy would wash the younger children and flush the lavatory.

'Peggy, are you off to Waterloo?'

'Yes, Mrs Dwight.' Peggy assumed a pained stoop, and the missionary patted her affectionately.

'Ask Jamie to help you. He's doing nothing.'

'He's busy thinking.' Artlessly, with a knowing eye in

my direction, Peggy added: 'Mrs Dwight, Jamie's planning to escape.'

'Really? I thought he'd escaped long ago. I've got something new for him to think about. Jamie, tomorrow you're moving to G Block. It's time for you to leave the children's hut.'

I emerged from one of the hunger reveries into which I often slipped. The apartment houses of the French Concession were visible along the horizon, reminding me of the old Shanghai before the war, and the Christmas parties when my father hired a troupe of Chinese actors to perform a nativity play. I remembered the games of two-handed bridge on my mother's bed, my carefree cycle rides around the International Settlement, and the Great World Amusement Park with its jugglers and acrobats and sing-song girls. All of them seemed as remote as the films I had seen in the Grand Theatre, sitting beside Olga while she stared in her bored way through *Snow White* and *Pinocchio*.

'Why, Mrs Dwight? I need to stay with Peggy until the war's over.'

'No.' Mrs Dwight frowned at the prospect, as if there was something improper about it. 'You'll be happier with boys of your own age.'

'Mrs Dwight, I'm never happy with boys of my own age. They play games all the time.'

'That may be. You're going to live with Mr and Mrs Vincent.'

Mrs Dwight expanded on the attractions of the Vincents' small room, which I would share with this chilly couple and their sick son. Peggy was looking sympathetically at me, the bucket clasped to her chest, well aware of the new challenge I faced.

But for once I was thinking in the most practical terms. I knew that I would be easily dominated by the Vincents, the morose amateur jockey and his glacial wife, who

39

would resent my presence in their small domain. I might try to bribe Mrs Vincent with the promise of a reward for being kind to me, which my father would pay after the war. Unhappily, this choice carrot failed to energise the Lunghua adults, so sunk were they in their torpor.

If I was going to bribe the Vincents I needed something more down to earth, the most important commodity in Lunghua. Ignoring Mrs Dwight, I seized my cinder-tin from beneath my bunk, shouted a goodbye to Peggy and set off at a run for the kitchens.

Spitting in the cold wind, the glowing cinders seethed across the ash-tip behind the kitchens. Naked except for their cotton shorts and wooden clogs, the stokers stepped from the steaming doorway beside the furnace, ashes flaming on their shovels. Now that the evening meal of rice congee had been prepared, Mr Sangster and Mr Bowles were raking the furnace and banking the fires down for the night. I waited on the summit of the ash-tip, enjoying the sickly fumes in the fading light, while I watched the Japanese night-fighters warming up at Lunghua airfield.

'Look out, young Jim.' Mr Sangster, a sometime accountant with the Shanghai Power Company, sent a cascade of cinders towards my feet. The ashes covered my sneakers and stung my toes through the rotting canvas. I scampered back, wondering how many extra rations had helped to build Mr Sangster's burly shoulders. But Mrs Sangster had been a friend of my mother's, and the horseplay was a means of steering the most valuable cinders towards me. Small favours were the secret currency of Lunghua.

Two other cinder-pickers joined me on the ash-tip – the elderly Mrs Tootle, who shared a cubicle with her sister in the women's hut and brewed unpleasant herbal teas from the weeds and wildflowers along the perimeter fence;

40

and Mr Hopkins, the art master at the Cathedral School, who was forever trying to warm his room in G Block for his malarial wife. He poked at the cinders with a wooden ruler, while Mrs Tootle scraped about with an old pair of sugar tongs. Neither had the speed and flair of my bent-wire tweezers. A modest treasure of half-burnt anthracite lay in these cinder heaps, but few of the internees would stir themselves to scavenge for warmth. They preferred to huddle together in their dormitories, complaining about the cold.

Squatting on my haunches, I picked out the pieces of coke, some no larger than a peanut, that had survived the riddling. I flicked them into my biscuit tin, to be traded when it was full for an extra sweet potato or a pre-war copy of *Reader's Digest* or *Popular Mechanics*, which the American sailors monopolised. These magazines had kept me going through the long years, feeding a desperate imagination. Mrs Dwight was forever criticising me for dreaming too much, but my imagination was all that I had.

As I knew, criticising everyone else was a full-time British occupation. Sitting on the ash-tip, while Mrs Tootle and Mr Hopkins scratched at the spent clinkers in their doomed way, I looked down at the camp. The British had nothing to which they looked forward, unlike the Americans, whose world was always filled with possibilities. Every American was an advertisement for confidence and success, like the vivid pages in the *Saturday Evening Post*, while every Englishman was a sign saying 'tres-passers prosecuted'. One day, my father had told me, I would go to school in England. Already I feared that the England I visited after the war would be a larger version of Lunghua camp, with all its snobberies and social divisions, its 'best' families with their strangled talk of 'London town' brandished about like the badges of an exclusive club, a club I would do my best to avoid joining.

The last heat faded from the cinders below my feet. The night air was chilled by the flooded paddy fields and the maze of creeks and canals around Lunghua. I watched the exhaust of the Japanese fighters, warming myself with the thought of their powerful engines. Mr Hopkins had wandered away from the ash-tip, carrying his few coals back to his invalid wife, but Mrs Tootle still stabbed at the dead clinkers. There was an evening curfew at Lunghua, but the Japanese made little effort to enforce it. In the unheated huts and cement buildings of the former teacher-training college the internees went early to bed, assuming that they had ever got up in the first place. Mrs Dwight and the missionary ladies were used to my roving the adult dormitories with my chessboard, gathering the latest rumours of war.

I slid down the slope towards Mrs Tootle and selected three choice pieces of coke from my tin.

'Jamie . . . I can't take those.'

'You keep them, Mrs Tootle. Tell your sister I gave them to you.'

'I will . . .'

A cup of herbal tea already brewing in her mind, she drifted off into the darkness. I felt sorry for her, but I needed her out of the way. When I was alone on the ash-tip, screened from the camp buildings by the kitchen roof, I crawled across the cinder slope to the brick wall of the annex.

Here was stored Lunghua camp's food supply for the coming week – sacks of polished rice and cracked wheat, and straw bales of grey sweet potatoes. Crouching by the rear wall of the annex, I reached inside my jacket and withdrew a crude knife I had fashioned from a broken Chinese bayonet. All but two inches of the blade were missing when I found the weapon in a disused well behind the camp hospital, but I had honed it into a useful tool. During the hours I spent on the ash-tip, waiting for the next consignment of spent coals, I had noticed that the mortar surrounding the brickwork was little harder than dried mud. Either the Japanese engineers responsible for equipping Lunghua camp had never known that they were being cheated by the Chinese contractors, or they had not expected the war to last more than a few months before America sued for peace.

Selecting the lowest course, I scraped at the mortar, the sound of the blade lost in the rumble of engines at the airfield. Within ten minutes I had loosened the first brick. Carefully, I withdrew it from the wall, slid my fingers into the dark space and touched the coarse straw sacking of a bale of sweet potatoes.

The next two bricks fell into my hands, as if the entire wall of the annex was about to collapse. They lay beside me, like gold bars in the darkness. Later I would return them to the wall, using the white coal-dust as a substitute mortar. With any luck I would be able to revisit the food store without arousing the suspicions of Mr Christie, a former manager of the Palace Hotel, who guarded these mildewed potatoes and warehouse sweepings with fanatic zeal. If Mr Christie had his way, the food reserves of Lunghua camp would be larger than the Sincere Company's department store, and all the internees would be dead.

I pulled the bricks from the soft mortar, steadily enlarging the aperture. The distant lights of the airfield threw silhouettes of the perimeter fence-posts on to the wall above my head. A straw sack filled most of the opening, but in the sweeping searchlight I could see the airless interior of the store-room, a mysterious inner world like the dwarfs' cottage in *Snow White*. The heavy sacks slumbered against the walls, and their comforting bulk reminded me of a family of dozing bears. My few doubts about stealing the food were forgotten. Already I thought of crawling into the store-room and sealing the wall behind

43

me. Peggy and I would sleep there, out of the cold, safe among the great drowsing sacks . . .

A signal flare exploded in the night sky. Its amber light trembled in a halo of white smoke. It fell slowly towards the open ground between the perimeter fence of the camp and the airfield boundary, reflected in the surface of a flooded paddy field.

Without thinking I stood up, my shadow leaping across the wall of the annex. Fifty feet from me four figures were caught by the intense light, their orange faces like lanterns in the darkness. Two of the men had already climbed through the wire, and a third knelt with one leg through the sagging strands. They shouted to each other above the spitting flare, and the man caught in the wire tore off his shirt and stumbled through the grass towards the paddy field. His shirt hung on the wire like a ragged flag.

Torches veered across the ground on both sides of the fence. Armed Japanese soldiers stood in the deep grass between the perimeter fence and the airfield. Already the would-be escapers had stopped and were waiting for the Japanese to approach them. The fourth figure stood by the wire, and began to disentangle the tattered shirt. When he looked up I recognised the blond hair and pinched face of David Hunter.

The signal flare fell into the paddy field and was swallowed by its black surface. Taking my chance, I scrambled from the ash-tip and darted past the rear door of the kitchens. I tripped over my cinder-tin, scattering the precious coke, and stumbled into a torch-beam that filled my face. Rifle raised, Private Kimura blocked the path leading to the children's hut, the night mist rising from his nostrils. Beside him stood Sergeant Nagata, the beam of his torch tapping my head as he watched his men round up the escaping prisoners. When they had been knocked to the ground, Sergeant Nagata beckoned me to him. I waited for him to slap me, but he stared into my face as if he had difficulty in recognising me, and found it scarcely conceivable that I, of all the internees in Lunghua, should want to escape.

Later we sat on one side of the wooden table in the guardhouse. The Japanese soldiers stood against the wall, their boots covered with wet grass. The camp commandant, Mr Hyashi, roused from his quarters in the staff bungalows, paced up and down, doing his best to control himself. A former diplomat at the Japanese Embassy in London, he was a small and precise man of painstaking nervousness, the only Japanese civilian in the camp and as frightened of Sergeant Nagata as any of the prisoners. Long pauses interrupted his interrogation, as he formulated the necessary phrases in his laboured English.

Bored by this time-wasting, Sergeant Nagata strolled behind us, slapping our heads at random. My ears rang, as they had done after the bomb in the Avenue Edward VII. I was sure we would soon be too deaf to understand Mr Hyashi's halting questions.

At one end of the wooden bench, his chest and face bruised by the rifle stocks, was a 29-year-old Londoner called Mariner. After being discharged from the Shanghai Police for robbing a rickshaw coolie he had become a foreman at the Shell terminal, and had scarcely stirred from his bunk since entering the camp. Beside him were the Ralston brothers, stable lads who had come out from England to work at the Shanghai racecourse. They joked nervously with David Hunter, who sat between them with his head lowered, blond hair streaked with blood.

Why David, with his caring parents, should have tried to escape from Lunghua puzzled me, and clearly puzzled Mr Hyashi.

'You walked . . . through the . . . fence?' He pointed at Mariner. 'You?'

45

'We didn't walk, no. We *climbed* through the fence,' Mariner explained half-facetiously. 'You know, stepped like . . .'

The older Ralston inclined his head, dripping blood on to my arm, and said in a stage-whisper: 'I knew I got these cuts somewhere.'

Both Ralstons tittered, and Sergeant Nagata stepped behind them and slapped their heads with his hard fist. They fell forward across the table, dazed but still smiling in a cracked way, and unable to hear Mr Hyashi's next question for which they were punched again.

I frowned at David, warning him to keep a straight face, but he was caught up by the Britishers' horseplay. Without thinking, David began to titter with them, tears streaming across his cheeks. He avoided my eyes, as if he was glad to be caught and was prepared to be punished. Like the Chinese, they laughed because they were frightened, but to Mr Hyashi and Sergeant Nagata they were being deliberately insolent in a peculiarly British way, never more arrogant than when they had blundered into defeat.

Baffled by them, Mr Hyashi took up his position at the head of the table, forced to preside over this deranged meeting for which his diplomatic training at the Foreign Ministry in Tokyo had not prepared him. He stood a few inches from me, and I could feel him trembling as Sergeant Nagata slapped the laughing Ralstons. I was so frightened that I, too, wanted to laugh, but already I was wondering what would happen when the sergeant discovered my attempt to break into the food store.

Mr Hyashi gazed down at me, noting my lowered eyes. Relieved to find one small point of sanity, he placed his unsteady palm on my head, as if to reassure himself that I was real.

'You not . . . trying to escape?'

'No, Mr Hyashi.'

'Not?'

'Mr Hyashi, I like Lunghua camp. I don't want to escape.'

For the first time Mr Hyashi raised his hand to restrain Sergeant Nagata. 'Not escaping. Good.' He seemed immensely relieved.

The older Ralston leaned against me, his eyes dazed by the blows. 'Look after yourself, lad. You're on your own here.'

'Everyone in Lunghua . . .' Mr Hyashi began, as if addressing the assembled camp. He searched for a phrase, and then let the air leak from his lungs, visibly resigned that he would never master this strange language and its stranger people. Covered in blood, Mariner was lying across the table, but the Ralstons were still uncowed, ready to provoke the Japanese and force them to do their worst. I admired them for their courage, as much as I admired the Japanese. I never understood why the only brave Britishers were the ones I was never allowed to meet, while the officers my mother and her friends danced with at the Country Club had surrendered without a shot at Singapore.

Mr Hyashi pointed to me, and turned a wavering fore-finger towards the door. Five minutes later I was back in the children's hut, regaling Peggy and an astonished Mrs Dwight with the saga of my attempted escape.

On the following day the first American daylight raid took place over Shanghai. Flying from airfields near Chung-king, Fortress bombers attacked the dockyards at Yangtsepoo. At last the war was coming home to the Japanese. As they strengthened the anti-aircraft defences of Lunghua airfield all concern for the escape attempt was forgotten. After a night in the guard-house cells the three men returned to convalesce on their bunks in E Block. A shocked David Hunter, his face still bruised, watched me

47

from the window of his parents' room, refusing to wave back to me as I stood on the parade ground.

To my relief, no-one learned of my attempt to break into the food store. The Japanese cemented the bricks into the wall, assuming that the escaping prisoners had tried to supply themselves with rations for their long cross-country walk to the Chinese lines four hundred miles away.

To anyone who would believe me, I pretended that I had joined the escape party at the last moment. Mrs Dwight expected nothing less, but Peggy shook her head over my boasts in her kindly, sceptical way. She knew that I was too wedded to Lunghua to want to leave it, that my entire world had been shaped by the camp, and that I had found a special freedom which I had never known in Shanghai.

One day war would end, but for the time being I was busy learning to cope with the stony couple whose room I shared. Around my bunk I constructed a small hutch, where I tried to recreate the peaceful interior of the food-store. Sitting on the ash-tip as Mr Sangster tossed the evening's coals at my feet, I waited for the American bombs to set fire to the sky, and thought of the white dust and the cracking coffins in the Avenue Edward VII.

Below me the fresh mortar marked the outline of a secret door into an interior world. Far from wanting to escape from the camp, I had been trying to burrow ever more deeply into its heart.

CHAPTER THREE

The Japanese Soldiers

Everyone was shouting that the war had ended. Prisoners leaned from their windows, waving to each other across the parade ground and pointing to the sky. Peggy Gardner and a delegation of missionary women gathered outside the guard-house and peered through the door at Sergeant Nagata's ransacked desk. I stood by the open gates of the camp, looking at the dusty road that followed the long arm of the Whangpoo river towards the south. The August sky was veiled by layers of haze that enclosed the empty landscape like an immense mosquito net. Threads of cloud ran through the pearly light, stitching the sky together. Vapour trails left by the American reconnaissance planes dissolved over my head, the debris perhaps of gigantic letters spelling out an apocalyptic message.

'What do they say, Jamie?' Peggy called to me. 'Is the war really over?'

'Ask Sergeant Nagata. I'm going to the river.'

'Sergeant Nagata's not here any more. You can go back to Shanghai now.' She plucked at the patches on her dress, sorry to see me leave but not yet sure that I had the necessary nerve. 'If you want to . . .'

'I'll come back tonight. Wait for me at the hut.'

For all the excitement, no-one was in any hurry to evacuate the camp, as Peggy had noticed. For days we had listened to rumours that the Americans had dropped a new super-bomb on Japan, destroying the cities of Nagasaki and Hiroshima. Some of the prisoners even claimed to have seen the bomb-flash. The squadrons of B-29s had broken off their attacks on Lunghua airfield, but armed Japanese soldiers still waited by the anti-aircraft guns.

One morning we woke to find that Mr Hyashi and the guards had vanished, slipping away under the cover of the night curfew. We stood by the perimeter wire, like children abandoned by their teachers and unsure whether to leave the classroom.

All day we watched the Shanghai road, expecting a convoy of American vehicles to speed towards us out of the dust, though everyone knew that the nearest Americans were hundreds of miles away on the island of Okinawa. Bored by this stalemate, a few men from E Block stepped through the wire and stood in the deep grass. Staring at the silent air, they seemed oddly self-conscious, as if they had forgotten who they were.

Showing off to Peggy, I climbed through the fence behind G Block and walked towards a burial mound two hundred yards from the camp. I mounted the stairway of rotting coffins, with their small skeletons asleep under quilts of silky mud. Standing in the overbright air, I signalled to Peggy as she pressed against the wire, breathlessly waiting for me to be shot. I could see the burnt-out hangars and cratered runways of Lunghua airfield, surrounded by the wrecks of fighter aircraft, and the unchanged skyline of Shanghai that had formed the horizon of my mind for the past three years. Despite myself I kept glancing over my shoulder at the camp, seeing the cement buildings and wooden huts for the first time from this strange perspective.

By leaving the camp I had stepped outside my own head. Had the atom bombs in some way split the sky, and reversed the direction of everything? I felt uneasy in the open air, a tempting target for some brooding Japanese sentry. I jumped down from the coffins, leaving my ragged footprints in the soft quilts, and ran to the safety of the wire. Ignoring Peggy's angry eyes, I went back to G Block and lay behind the curtain of my cubicle, glad for once to hear Mr Vincent's voice, complaining to his wife about the failure of the allied authorities to notify us properly of the war's end.

But did I want the war to end? The next day, when the Japanese guards returned to Lunghua, I felt secretly relieved. Already there were signs that life in the camp was breaking down. Led by the Ralston brothers, a gang of men had tried to break into the kitchens, while others had looted the guard-house. The food-stocks were almost exhausted, and our daily ration was down to a bowl of congee. The American bombing raids had imposed a kind of order, which both the prisoners and their guards had respected. Now the sky was empty and exposed, a house without its roof.

Fortunately, the Japanese commandeered the guard-house and posted sentries outside the kitchens. But the soldiers were pale and uneasy, and Private Kimura avoided my eyes, aware now that he would never see his family again. Even Sergeant Nagata was subdued, waving me away when I hovered around the guard-house, trying to think of something to encourage him. He sat stiffly at his rifled desk, and ignored the English and Belgian women who stood outside his window in their tattered cotton dresses, screaming abuse at him until necklaces of spit glistened on their breasts.

At last came the Emperor Hirohito's broadcast, calling on his armies to lay down their weapons. At the time I laughed aloud at this. No Japanese would ever surrender. As long as he had a bayonet and grenade, or a rifle with a single round, he would fight to the end. Like everyone else, I took for granted that the Japanese forces in China would make their last stand against Chiang Kai-shek and the Americans at the mouth of the Yangtse, well within sight of Lunghua.

But the first American reconnaissance planes appeared in the sky, cruising a few hundred feet above the camp, and the anti-aircraft guns at the airfield remained silent.

Sergeant Nagata and his men, who had only returned to Lunghua in the hope of finding food, once again abandoned us, marching off into the night. The next day at noon, the two Shanghai Water Company engineers who had operated the clandestine radio throughout the war placed the battered bakelite set on the balcony above the entrance to F Block. Then at last we heard the recorded victory speeches of Truman and MacArthur.

So, I told myself, the war had ended. But as I stood by the open gates I was still not convinced. The missionary women had wandered away, and Peggy gave a last hopeless shrug and went back to the children's hut, leaving me to hover between the rotting posts. Everything within the camp was unchanged, but beyond the fence lay a different world. The wild rice growing by the roadside, the blades of sugar cane and the yellow mud of the abandoned paddy fields were touched by the same eerie light, as if they had been irradiated by the bomb dropped on Nagasaki, 400 miles across the China Sea. The drowned canals and the grave-mounds, the forgotten ceramics works by the river, looked like an elaborate stage-set. I stepped forward, but the curving ruts which the supply truck had cut into the earth steered me back into the camp.

I knew, though, that it was time to leave. My mother and father would soon return to our house in Shanghai, and I wanted to meet them while there was still a faint chance that they remembered me. Shanghai was eight miles away, across a silent terrain of rice fields and deserted villages. In my pockets were a bottle of water that Peggy had boiled for me and a sweet potato I had saved. Settling them into my khaki shorts, I stepped through the gates on to the open road.

I set off along the dusty verge, trying to fix my eyes on the Shanghai skyline. Within the barbed wire another day in Lunghua was unfolding. The war might have ended, but the women worked over their washing and the men lounged on the entrance steps to the dormitory blocks. David Hunter and a group of younger children played one of their hour-long skipping games, jumping together as David whipped the ground under their feet, as always carried away by his wild humour.

Outside the children's hut Peggy sat with one of the four-year-olds, teaching him to read. I called to her, but she was too engrossed in the book to hear me. Peggy's parents would take weeks to travel from Tsingtao, and I would be back to look after her. If Lunghua was my real home, Peggy was my closest friend, far closer now than my mother and father could ever be, however hard the missionary women tried to keep us apart. We often quarrelled, but in the dark times Peggy had learned to rely on me and control my leaping imagination.

I passed the kitchen garden behind the hospital, with its rows of beans and tomatoes. Peggy and I had grown them to eke out our rations, fertilising the ground with buckets of nightsoil that we hoisted from the G Block septic tank, the only useful product of the Vincents' existence. Mrs Dwight stood on the hospital steps, lecturing a young Eurasian whose father had been chauffeur to the Dean of Shanghai Cathedral. A reluctant orderly at the hospital, he would once have deferred meekly to Mrs Dwight, but I could see from his bored stare that he was no longer impressed by her moralising talk. British power had waned, sinking like the torpedoed hulks of the *Repulse* and the *Prince of Wales*, and he could choose to become a Chinese again. As David's father often reflected during our chess games, the Japanese attack on Pearl Harbor had marked the first revolt by the colonised nations of the east against the imperial west. Shanghai, which had endured throughout the war, might have changed more than I realised.

Leaving the road, I turned my back on the camp and

stepped into the deep grass that ran towards the canal marking the southern perimeter of the airfield. A cloud of mosquitoes rose from the stagnant water, greeting me as if I were the first person to enter this empty world. Dragonflies hunted the lacquered air, swerves of electric blue reflected in the oil leaking from a bombed freighter at Nantao.

A sunken Japanese patrol-boat lay in the canal, its machine-gun pointing skywards from the armour-plated turret. Already sections of the wooden decking had been chopped into firewood by the returning Chinese villagers. Strafed by the American Mustangs before the crew could take cover, the craft was dissolving into the soft mud of the canal bottom. Only the Japanese soldier lying face down in the shallow water was still himself, the brass buckles of his canvas webbing polished by the stream. I stood on the bank above him and watched the water lift the hairs from his scalp. I could see each of the ulcers on his neck, and the swollen stitching of his coarsely woven shirt. Water-beetles raced between his fingers, sending shimmers of light into the air, as if this dead soldier was tapping the underside of the surface and sending out some last message.

The canal turned to join the Whangpoo half a mile away. I left the bank and strode through the waist-high grass towards the circular rim of a flooded bomb crater. A white snake swam through the milky water, exploring this new realm. Beyond the crater was the boundary road of the airfield, roofless hangars standing beside the bombed engineering sheds.

Caught by the last of the American air-raids, a Chinese puppet soldier lay by the embankment of a single-track railway line. Bandits had looted his body, stripping his pockets and ammunition pouches, and he was surrounded by scraps of paper, pages from his pass-book, letters and small photographs, the documentation of a life he might have laid out beside himself as he waited to die.

Envying him all these possessions, I climbed the earth embankment, a spur of the Hangchow–Shanghai railway which ran towards the north-west, losing itself in the misty light. I strode between the polished rails as they hummed faintly in the heat, adjusting my step to the wooden sleepers. I searched for Lunghua camp, but its familiar rooflines had vanished. An intense light, more electric than solar, lay over the derelict fields, as if the air had been charged by the energy radiated by that sombre weapon exploded across the China Sea. I stared at my hands, wondering if I had been affected, and tasted the tepid water in my bottle. For the first time it occurred to me that everyone in the world outside Lunghua might be dead, and that this was why the war was over.

Half an hour later, when I had walked a further mile into the haze, I approached a small wayside railway station. It stood beside the track with a modest waiting room and ticket office, faded time-tables hanging in the air. Sitting on the concrete platform were four Japanese soldiers. They were fully armed, rifles beside them, and wore canvas webbing and ammunition pouches over their shabby uniforms. A unit of field infantry, they were perhaps waiting for their orders at this rural station, orders that would now never come. They had cooked a simple meal on a makeshift stove, using strips of wood torn from the walls of the waiting room, and were resting in the mid-day heat.

Smoking their handmade cigarettes, they watched me walk towards them between the rails. I slowed my step, unsure whether to make a detour around the Japanese. Below the embankment was an anti-tank ditch partly filled with water, in which lay a dead water-buffalo. The carcase of this docile beast was somehow reassuring, and I stopped to catch my breath before sliding down the embankment.

Then I noticed that one of the Japanese had raised his hand. I stared back at him, my feet slipping in the soft earth. I decided not to make a run for it – there was nowhere to go, and the Japanese would shoot me without a moment's thought. Walking up to the platform, I stopped by the private soldier who had beckoned to me. Grunting to himself over the last of his meal, he squatted beside his rifle. With his heavy workman's hands he was coiling the telephone wire which he had cut from the wooden pole above the station.

Sitting with his back to the telephone pole, hands tied behind him, was a Chinese youth in a white shirt and dark trousers. Bands of wire circled his chest, and he breathed in empty gasps. His quick mouth and composed eyes reminded me of the clerks who had worked for my father before the war. He seemed out of place on this rural railway platform, unlike the soldiers and myself. The Japanese corporal lashing him to the telephone pole tightened the cords as if to anchor him firmly to this desolate terrain.

The Chinese choked, his throat knotting while he fought for air. Trying to ignore him, I faced the soldier coiling the wire. All my experience of the Japanese had taught me never to comment on anything they were doing, nor to take sides in any dispute involving them. I told myself that the Chinese was an important prisoner, and that they had tied him up before taking their afternoon sleep.

One of the older soldiers was already dozing in the shade of the waiting room, head on his knapsack. The other sat by the stove, carefully reaming out the mess-tins. Their faces were empty of all feeling, as if they were aware that the war had ended but knew that, for them, this meant nothing.

Only the first-class private coiling the wire showed any interest in me. I guessed that they had been up-country, fighting the Kuomintang armies, and had seen few Europeans. Their food rations would have been as meagre as those in Lunghua, but the private's broad temples were still fleshy, his cheekbones swollen like a boxer's at the end of a hard-fought bout. He flicked his lips with a blackened finger and cleared his throat in a forced way, as if releasing to the air a stream of thoughts that no longer concerned him.

Exhausted by the long walk, I leaned against the platform, unsure whether to risk eating my sweet potato. The corporal securing the Chinese youth to the telephone pole was a short, starved man with a war-hardened face. As soon as I touched my pockets he began to watch me in a hungry way. The smells of burnt fat from the stove made my head swim, and I drew the water bottle from my trousers.

With a brief grunt, the private put out his hand. I released the cap, took a quick gulp and handed the bottle to him. He drank noisily, spoke to the corporal and passed the bottle back to me, disappointed that it contained nothing stronger than water. He tossed the coil of wire on to the platform beside the prisoner, and then turned his attention to me. A wistful smile appeared on his roughened lips, and he pointed to the sun and to the sweat staining my cotton shirt.

'Hot?' I said. 'Yes, it's the atom bombs . . . you know the war's over? The Emperor –'

I spoke without thinking. The only sound in the silent landscape, marooned in its haze, came from the Chinese. As another coil of telephone wire encircled his chest he tried not to breathe, and then began to pant rapidly, his head striking the wooden pole. His eyes were loosening themselves from his face. The corporal knotted the wire and tightened the noose with a wristy jerk. Drops of bloody saliva fell from the youth's lips, staining his white shirt. He looked at me, and gasped a word of Chinese, like a warning shout to a dog.

The first-class private scowled knowingly at the sun,

urging me to drink. He appeared to be busy with his own thoughts, but every few seconds his eyes fixed on a different point in the surrounding fields. He was watching the drained paddy beside the embankment, the burial mound at its north-west corner, the stone footbridge across a canal. Did he know that the war was over, that his Emperor had called on him to surrender? Among the canvas packs and ammunition boxes piled against the waiting room was a field radio only issued to specialist troops. Perhaps they had heard that the war was over, but this simple statement, so meaningful to civilians far from the front line, meant nothing to them. Within a few weeks the American forces would reach Shanghai, and the Chinese armies they had fought for so many years would take control of this derelict realm in which they waited, their minds already far beyond any future in store for them.

I decided to eat my sweet potato while I still had the chance. The private watched me approvingly, brushing a fly from my shoulder. His ragged uniform was a collection of tatters held together by the straps of his webbing, from which the smell of sweat emerged in almost intact layers. While I ate the potato skin he pointed to a piece of pith that clung to the back of my hand, and waited until I returned it to my mouth.

As he smiled at me in his simple way I felt an uneasy sense of pride. Despite myself, I admired this Japanese soldier, with his swollen temples and bruised face. He was no more than a labourer, but in his way he had risen to the challenge of the war. His heavy shoulders, marked by patches of eczema and scores of flea-bites, were bursting through the fabric of his shirt, his chest restrained like an animal by the canvas webbing. He was one of the few strong men I had met, completely unlike the officers in the British forces and most of the adults in Lunghua. Only Mariner and the Ralston brothers would have been a match for this Japanese warrior.

I finished the potato and wiped my fingers on my lips, watching the sweat running from his neck into the hollows of his collar bones. I wished that I had learned enough Japanese from Private Kimura to explain that the war was over. The Chinese prisoner on the platform was now scarcely able to breathe, his ribs crushed by the coils of telephone wire. Bruises filled with congested blood stared from his forehead. Tired by the effort of knotting the heavy wire, the corporal tossed the cable on to the concrete floor and strolled stiffly along the platform.

The private's fingers flicked at his lips, tapping a message to himself. He grimaced over some memory bothering him like a mosquito. Deciding to take the risk, I slid my clasp knife from my hip pocket. With the blade closed, I offered it to the private, hoping that he would want to test the blade, and might cut the telephone wire binding the Chinese prisoner.

But the blade was of no interest to him. He cut away a canvas flap that hung from his ragged boot, and turned his attention to the clasp. He smiled at the cowboy motif carved into the mother-of-pearl handle. His thick fingers traced out the ranch-hand in stetson and high-heeled boots, and the twirling lasso that resembled the telephone wire he had been coiling at his feet.

The railway lines hummed in the heat, a sound like pain. The Chinese slumped against the pole, his neck so flushed that it was almost blue. He raised his head and looked at me in a fevered way, as if we were fellow passengers who had missed our connection. He was four or five years older than I was, his hair cut neatly in a way that Mrs Dwight had always urged on me. Was he a Kuomintang agent, one of the thousands in Shanghai, or an office clerk working for the Japanese occupation authority who had fallen foul of the kempetai?

The corporal stepped on to the track and gathered sticks for the fire. I searched the railway line, hoping that an

American patrol might be approaching. From the moment I left Lunghua all the clocks had stopped. Time had suspended itself, and only the faraway drone of an American aircraft reminded me of a world on the other side of the pearly light.

The private gestured to me to empty my pockets. The corporal stood at the end of the platform, relieving himself on to the track. The drops of urine hissed as they struck the rail, sending up a fierce cloud of yellow steam. The corporal walked back wide-legged to the Chinese prisoner. He had cut his hands on the wire, and shook his head ruefully as he bent down and picked up the coil, ready to return to his work.

Hurriedly I dug into my pockets and handed my tie-pin to the private, hoping that the silver buckle might distract the corporal. The private's gaze brightened again as he examined the worn image of a long-horn cow. With his thumb-nail he cleared away the flaking chrome, then placed the pin against the brass clip of his ammunition pouch. Keen to display his new insignia, he shouted over his shoulder, puffing up his chest. The corporal nodded without expression, too busy with his cumbersome knots. He wrenched at the wire, spreading his legs like a rancher trussing a steer.

The private returned the tie-pin to me, catching sight for the first time of the transparent celluloid belt looped through the waist-band of my cotton shorts. This belt, which I had nagged out of one of the American sailors, was my proudest possession. In pre-war Shanghai it would have been a rarity eagerly sought after by young Chinese gangsters.

As I released the buckle the private stared at me cannily. I guessed that he was weighing in his mind the small duplicity represented by this transparent belt, virtually invisible against my khaki shorts. He inspected the belt, holding it up to the light like the skin of a rare snake, and tested the plastic between his strong hands. He blew through the crude holes that I had gouged, shaking his head over my poor workmanship.

'Look, you keep the belt,' I told him. 'The war's over, you know. We can all go home now.'

By the telephone pole the Chinese had ceased to breathe and I knew that he would soon be dead. The corporal worked swiftly, coiling lengths of wire around the Chinese and knotting them with efficient snatches of his wrists. The youth's arms were pinned back by the wire, but his hands tore at the seat of his trousers, as if he were trying to strip himself for his death. When the last air left his crushed chest he stared with wild eyes at the corporal, as though seeing him for the first time.

'Listen, Sergeant Nagata . . .'

The belt snapped in the private's hands. He passed the pieces to me, well aware from my trembling that I had willed myself not to run away. His eyes followed mine to the second telephone pole at the western end of the platform, and the wire that looped along the embankment. The resting soldiers lay against their packs, watching me as I rolled up the celluloid belt. One of them moved his mess-tin from the stream of urine crossing the concrete from the heels of the Chinese. None of them had been touched by the youth's death, as if they knew that they too were dead, and were matter-of-factly preparing themselves for whatever end would arrive out of the afternoon sun.

A hooded rat was swimming around the carcase of the water buffalo in the anti-tank ditch. Despite the sweet potato, I felt light-headed with hunger. The haze had cleared, and I could see everything in the surrounding fields with sudden clarity. The world had drawn close to the railway station and was presenting itself to me. For the first time it seemed obvious that this remote country platform was the depot from which all the dead of the war

61

had been despatched to the creeks and burial mounds of Lunghua. The four Japanese soldiers were preparing us for our journey. I and the Chinese whom they had suffocated were the last arrivals, and when we had gone they would close the station and set out themselves.

The corporal tidied the loose coils of wire, watching me as I steadied myself against the platform. I waited for him to call me, but none of the Japanese moved. Did they think that I was already dead, and would continue my journey without their help?

An hour later they let me go. Why they allowed a 15-year-old boy to witness their murder of the Chinese I never understood. I set off along the track, too exhausted to stride between the sleepers, waiting for a rifle shot to ring out against the steel rails. When I looked back, the station had faded into the sunlit paddy fields.

The railway line turned towards the north, joining the embankment of the Shanghai–Hangchow railway. I slid down the shingle slope, walked through a deserted village and set off towards the silent factories on the western outskirts of the city. As I neared Amherst Avenue I recognised the cathedral at Siccawei and the campus of Chiao Tung University, the wartime headquarters of the puppet army raised by the Japanese.

I pressed on through the quiet suburban roads, past the tree-lined avenues of European houses, with their half-timbered gables and ocean-liner facades. Groups of Chinese sat on the steps, waiting for their owners to return from the camps, like extras ready to be called to the set of an interrupted film production. Time was about to get off its knees. But for a few moments Shanghai, which I had waited so patiently to revisit, had lost its hold on me.

On the next day, August 14, I at last saw my parents again. Throughout the war our house had been occupied by a general of the Chinese puppet armies. A single unarmed soldier was standing guard when I reached the front steps after the long walk from Lunghua. He made no attempt to resist as I pushed past him, and vanished half an hour later. I wandered stiffly around the silent house, with its strange smells and musty air. There were Chinese newspapers on my father's desk, and a Chinese dance record on the turntable of the gramophone, but otherwise not a carpet or piece of furniture had been disturbed, as if the house had been preserved in a quiet bypass of the war. Even my toys lay at the bottom of the playroom cupboard, my *papier mâché* fort and Great War artillery guns. Holding them in my hands, I could hardly believe that I had ever played with them, and felt vaguely sorry for the small boy who had taken them so seriously.

The refrigerator was filled with bowls of boiled rice and the remains of the last meal which the puppet general had interrupted before he discarded his uniform and disappeared into the alleys of the Old City. I helped myself to the cold noodles and pickled pork, startled by the taste of animal fat, and drank the dregs of rice wine in the stone jars. Exhausted, I sat on the verandah and stared at the jungle of the garden and the drained swimming-pool, which had been used as a garbage tip.

Slightly drunk, and with my stomach painfully stretched by this huge banquet, I roved around the house. I lay on my mother's mattress, smelling the general's sweet hair oil, and stared at the imposing bathrooms, like white cathedrals, that I had forgotten how to use. I was trying out my past self, but it seemed too small and confined for me, like the toys in the playroom cupboard. I fell asleep in my father's armchair in the panelled study. The heavy leather furniture and dark walls reminded me of the food-store at Lunghua which I had dreamed of sharing with Peggy.

At noon the next day my parents arrived, in a taxi

covered with the yellow dust of the Lunghua road. They had driven to the camp hoping to collect me. Smiling cheerfully, they embraced me as if we had been separated for no more than a few days. Did they really recognise me? I was happy to be with them, but we were like actors playing parts presented to us at short notice. We played the roles of parents and son, and in a few days were word-perfect and genuinely glad to be together. I remembered my mother's voice, and her mouth and cheeks, but her eyes belonged to an older woman who had never known me.

Meanwhile, life in Shanghai resumed without a pause, as if the war had never occurred. Yang, the chauffeur, and most of the servants reappeared, and I almost expected Olga to arrive and tell me that it was time for bed. Sitting in my uneasy new clothes at my parents' dinner parties, I began to remember the Shanghai of my childhood. My parents entertained their old French friends, rich Chinese businessmen and officers of the American occupation army. I listened to the talk of the latest London and Broadway plays, real estate values in Hong Kong and California, and the flood of antiquities which impoverished Chinese families were releasing on to the market.

The war had already been absorbed into the extraordinary history of Shanghai, along with the Avenue Edward VII bomb, the Japanese attack on the city and the years of brutal occupation. The assets of the Axis powers, the Japanese cotton mills and the German engineering works, were swiftly appropriated and put to use. The great trading houses opened their doors. The port of Shanghai was crammed with freighters unloading merchandise for the department stores of the Nanking Road. Thousands of bars and nightclubs lit the afternoon sky. American servicemen swarmed ashore, an army of war embraced by an even more disciplined army of peace, the Chinese pimps and their massed ranks of White Russian, Chinese and Eurasian prostitutes, who welcomed them eagerly as they stepped on to the Bund.

But from all this activity I felt set apart, as if I had landed in an unfamiliar future. So much had happened that I had not yet been able to remember or forget. There were too many memories of Lunghua that were difficult to share with my parents. Over breakfast my father and I talked about our experiences, as if we were describing scenes from the films showing in the Shanghai theatres. My sense of myself had changed, and I had mislaid part of my mind somewhere between Lunghua and Shanghai.

Strangest of all, Japanese soldiers were still patrolling the streets of Shanghai. As Yang and I drove in the puppet general's Buick to a garden party at the British Consulate I pointed to the Japanese sentries in faded uniforms, standing with their long rifles on the steps of the Mayoral Office. Yang sounded his horn, forcing the Buick through the pedicab drivers, beggars and office clerks, shouting to the Japanese to clear the way. I stared at the faces hidden under their peaked caps, hoping to recognise the first-class private and the corporal I had left behind on the railway platform.

Other Japanese sentries, at the request of the American and Kuomintang authorities, guarded key government buildings around the city. My father told me that the Free French occupying Indo-China had recruited units of the Japanese army in their fight against the communist Viet Minh. For all this, whenever I saw the armed Japanese I thought of the isolated railway station in the countryside south of Shanghai. I almost believed that the Japanese soldiers guarding the city were preparing the bar-keepers, prostitutes and American servicemen for a longer journey that would soon set out from that rural platform.

The first of a long series of war crimes trials were held in October, and the senior Japanese generals who had ruled Shanghai during the war were charged with an endless catalogue of atrocities against the Chinese civilian population. Almost in passing, we heard that the Japanese had planned to close Lunghua and march us up-country, far from the eyes of the neutral community in Shanghai. But for the sudden end of the war, they would have been free to dispose of us, and only the atomic bombs had saved our lives. The pearly light that hung over Lunghua reminded me forever of the saving miracle of Hiroshima and Nagasaki.

Once a week I visited the camp, where several hundred of the British internees were still housed. They survived on the rations parachuted by B-29 Superfortresses identical to those that had bombed Nagasaki. The dead and the living had begun to interbreed. As Yang drove south along the Lunghua road I searched the paddy fields for any sign of the railway station, expecting to see its platform crowded with new arrivals.

I tried to explain all this to Peggy, while she waited for her parents to sail from Tsingtao. I gave her the presents of clothes that I had bought at Sincere's, the latest American lipsticks, nylon stockings and a box of Swiss chocolates. I was happy to be with her again in the children's hut, watching her try on her new make-up. Through the rouge and lipstick a vivid woman's face appeared, more beautiful than all the prostitutes at the Park Hotel. I wanted to embrace her and thank her for everything she had done for me, but we knew each other too well. Already I felt that she had begun to free herself from the camp, and that we would soon grow apart.

Casually, I described the death of the young Chinese. When I finished, hiding my feelings behind a liqueur chocolate, I realised that I had made him sound like myself.

'Jamie, you should never have gone.' Peggy settled a small child into its cot. 'We did try to stop you.'

66

'I had to go back to Shanghai. You know, I was really looking for Sergeant Nagata . . .'

'Those soldiers might have killed you.'

'They didn't need to – I wasn't ready for them.'

'Jamie, they didn't touch you! You walked away from them.'

'I suppose I did – I keep thinking I should have stayed. Peggy, they wouldn't have hurt me.'

Already she could see that I was disappointed.

At the end of October, as I left the Cathay Hotel after lunch with my mother, I shared a taxi with two American navy pilots who were trying to find the Del Monte Casino. I guided the Chinese driver to the Avenue Haig, only to find that the casino had been ransacked by the Japanese in the last days of the war. As we left the taxi, looking at the shattered windows and the broken glass on the steps, I noticed David Hunter hailing the driver from the lobby of Imperial Mansions, a run-down apartment building across the street in which several brothels operated.

David, like me, was dressed in a pale grey suit and tie, which he wore in the faintly shifty way shared by all the former Lunghua boys, as if we had been released after serving a sentence at a corrective institution. At times we would meet every day, but often I would do my best to avoid him. He had recovered from Sergeant Nagata's slaps on the evening he tried to escape, but his swerves of dangerous humour exhausted me. Often I saw him on the steps of the Park Hotel, staring in a strained, smiling way at the Eurasian women waiting for the Americans. Once he lured a suspicious 14-year-old Chinese prostitute into his father's Studebaker, which he borrowed to take us to the jai alai stadium. In the car-park she squatted expertly across David's lap, embroidered gown around her waist, shouting over her shoulder at the Chinese chauffeur. Dazed by her energy and nakedness, I let David order me into the night air, but twenty minutes later, when the chauffeur and I returned, she was kicking David in a fury of Chinese obscenities and trying to escape through the passenger window. David was laughing generously, his hands on her waist, but under his ruffled pale hair the flush of his cheeks resembled the bruises left by Sergeant Nagata's hand.

I listened to my feet cracking the broken glass outside the Del Monte. Deciding to give David the slip, I left the American pilots with their taxi and stepped into the entrance of the casino. Gilt chairs lay heaped against the walls of the foyer, and the red plush curtains had been torn from the windows. Like chambers in an exposed dream, the gaming rooms were flooded with sunlight that turned the dance floor into the scene of a traffic accident. A roulette table lay on its side, gaming chips scattered around it, and the gilded statue of a naked woman with upraised arms that supported the canopy of the bar had fallen across a collapsed chandelier, a princess frozen in a jewelled bower.

A Chinese waiter and a young European woman were straightening the overturned chairs and brushing up the plaster that had fallen from the ceiling. As I walked past them the woman turned and followed me, pulling my arm.

'James! They said you were back! You remember your Olga?'

Olga Ulianova, my pre-war nanny, pinched my cheeks with her sharp fingers. Unsure whether she had recognised me, she felt my shoulders, running her brightly varnished nails over the lapels of my suit.

'Olga, you really scared me. You haven't changed.' I was glad to see her, though time seemed to be running in all directions. If I was three years older, Olga was both in her early twenties and late thirties. A procession of faces had been let into the bones of her face, layers of paint and experience through which gleamed a pair of pointed and hungry eyes. I guessed that she spent her days fighting off American sailors in the backs of the Nanking road pedicabs. Her silk suit was torn around the armpit, exposing a large bruise under her shoulder blade, and a smear of lipstick marked the strap of her brassiere. As she looked me up and down I knew that she had already dismissed my own experiences of the war.

'So . . . such a smart suit. Mr Sangster said you had a good time in Lunghua. I guess you miss it.'

'Well . . . a little. I'll take you there, Olga.'

'No, thanks. I heard enough about those camps. All those dances and concerts. Here it's been real hell, I can tell you. The things my mother had to do, James. We didn't have the Japanese looking after us.' She sighed headily, swayed by the memory. She was sober, but I guessed that for the past three years she had been slightly drunk.

'Do you work here, Olga? Are you the owner?'

'One day. Bars, hotels, sing song parlours, everywhere. Believe me, James, these American boys have more money than Madame Chiang . . .'

'I hope they give you plenty, Olga.'

'What? Well, we won the war, didn't we? Tell me, James, is your father still rich?'

'He definitely isn't.' The thought of money had rekindled her waning interest in me. 'He's been in Soochow camp all through the war.'

'He can still be rich. Take it from me, you can find money anywhere. Just look hard enough and give a big pull.'

She wiped the lipstick from her teeth, appraising me anew. Already I felt aroused by Olga, as confused as ever by her changes of temper. In every sense she was more wayward and exciting than the women in Lunghua. Before the war, when I undressed, she had glanced at my naked

69

body with the off-hand curiosity of a zoo-keeper being shown a rare but uninteresting mammal. I took for granted now that no male body would rouse even a flicker of interest. Yet her eyes were sizing me up as if she were about to place a large physical burden on my shoulders.

'I can see that you're still a dreamer, James. I'm thinking about your father. He can make a good investment right now, while the Americans are here. There's a small restaurant in the Avenue Joffre, only six tables . . .'

She stepped forward on her high heels, stumbling across the cut-glass pendants of the chandelier. She steadied herself, holding my arm in a strong grip. Her hip pressed against mine, trying to remind me of something I had forgotten. A potent scent of sweat and powder rose from her shabby dress, a quickening odour that I had noticed in the women's huts at Lunghua.

I let her lean against me as we walked across the dance floor, our shoes breaking the glass. A rush of ideas filled my head as she worked her thigh into my leg. The war had accelerated everything, and I felt that I was surrounded by moving trains all beyond my reach. I wanted to have sex with Olga, but I had no idea how to approach her, and I knew that she would enjoy laughing at my gaucheness.

At the same time, something more than shyness held me away. Part of her attraction was the thought of going back to my childhood, but if I was certain of anything it was that I was no longer a child, and that the games of hide-and-seek through the streets of pre-war Shanghai were over forever. Being brought up by servants, supposedly the gift of privilege, in fact exposed a child to the most ruthless manipulation, and I had no wish to be manipulated again, by sex or hunger or fear. When I made love for the first time it would be with Peggy Gardner.

I listened to the pendulum-like motion of the waiter's broom. Olga's free hand had slipped under my jacket and was pressed against my abdomen. She was hesitating, as

70

if aware that she might find herself cast again as my governess, reminded of her parents' penury in their pre-war tenement and the boring hours she had spent looking after this little English boy with his cycle and free-wheeling imagination.

From the hollows of Olga's neck and the enlarged veins in the skin of her breasts I guessed that she had eaten as little as I had in the past three years. I put my arm around her shoulder, suddenly liking this tough young woman with her rackety ideas. Only the first-class private at the railway station had looked at me so intently. I wanted to tell Olga about the dead Chinese, but already the lost Japanese patrol was moving into the rear of my mind.

'Are you going back to England, James?'

'After Christmas – I'm sailing on the *Arrawa* with my mother.' This troopship, a former refrigerated meat carrier, would repatriate the British nationals in Shanghai. 'My father's staying on here.'

'He'll stay? That's good. I'll talk to him about my restaurant. Will you study in England?'

'If I have to.' On an impulse, I said: 'I'm going to be a doctor.'

'A doctor? That's very good. When I'm sick you can look after me. It's your turn now.'

As I left, promising to introduce her to my father, Olga said: 'Now you can play hide-and-seek in the whole world.'

A week after Christmas I left Shanghai for ever. Some six hundred former internees, mostly women and children, sailed for England in the converted meat carrier. My father and the other Britons staying behind in Shanghai stood on the pier at Hongkew, waving to us as the *Arrawa* drew away from them across the slow brown tide. When we reached the middle of the channel, working our way through scores of American destroyers and landing craft,

71

I left my mother and walked to the stern of the ship. The relatives on the pier were still waving to us, and my father saw me and raised his arm, but I found it impossible to wave back to him, something I regretted for many years. Perhaps I blamed him for sending me away from this mysterious and exhilarating city.

When the last of the banks and hotels faded into the clouds above the Bund I carried my suitcase to one of the men's mess rooms. At night we slung our hammocks across the open decks where the refrigerated carcases of New Zealand meat had hung. In the darkness the hundreds of sleeping bodies swayed together like sides of lamb packed in canvas.

After our evening meal I returned to the stern rail, almost alone on the deck as the *Arrawa* neared the entrance to the Yangtse. Shanghai had vanished, a dream city that had decided to close itself to the world. The rice fields and villages of the estuary stretched to the horizon, with only the sea to separate them from the nearest landfall at Nagasaki.

The *Arrawa* paused at Woosung, readying itself to join the great tide of the Yangtse as it flowed into the China Sea. As we waited on the swell, edging closer to the eastern bank of the Whangpoo, we drifted past a large American landing craft beached on the shore. A tank-landing vessel scarcely smaller than the *Arrawa*, its flat prow lay high on the streaming mud-flat, as if it had been deliberately beached on this isolated coast. The *Arrawa* was in no danger of striking the craft, but a signal lamp flashed from its bridge. American military police patrolled its decks, their weapons levelled as they waved us away.

A fetid stench floated on the air, as if vented from an exposed sewer filled with blood. Leaning from the stern rail, I saw that the hold of the landing craft was filled with hundreds of Japanese soldiers. They sat packed together in rows, knees pressed against each other's backs. All were in a bad way, and many lay down, crushed by the mass of bodies. They ignored the *Arrawa*, and only a group of handcuffed NCOs turned their eyes towards the ship.

A loudspeaker barked from the bridge of the landing craft, and the American guards shouted at the British officers in the wheel-house. Clearly the *Arrawa* had appeared at an inconvenient moment. The Japanese armies in China were being repatriated, but I wondered how this large body of men, almost a brigade in strength, would ever survive the three-day voyage to the Japanese mainland.

Then, on a cliff above the mud-flats, another group of armed soldiers caught my eye. Hundreds of Kuomintang infantry, in their peaked caps and leggings, bayonets fixed to their rifles, stood on the grass-covered slopes, waiting for the *Arrawa* to move away.

A siren thundered over my head, almost splitting the funnel. Its echoes hunted the vast brown swells of the Yangtse. We steered ahead, the single propeller churning the water and sending its spray into my face. The forward ramp of the landing craft was being lowered from the prow, and the first Japanese soldiers were stumbling on to the mud-flat.

PART TWO

The Craze Years

CHAPTER FOUR

The Queen of the Night

Women dominated my years at Cambridge – fellow medical students, the cheerful Addenbrookes nurses I took drinking on the Cam and the moody demonstrators in the Physiology Department, forever polishing their cracked nails behind the jars of embryos – but none more than Dr Elizabeth Grant. During my first term at the university I saw her naked every day, and I knew her more intimately than any other woman in my life. But I never embraced her.

I remember the October morning in the Anatomy Department when I first met Dr Grant. With the hundred freshmen joining the medical school, I took my seat in the amphitheatre for the welcoming address by Professor Harris, the head of anatomy. I sat alone in the topmost row, marking my distance from the other undergraduates. Exempt from military service, and rugby fanatics to a man, they were mostly the sons of provincial doctors who in due course would take over their fathers' practices. Already I was depressed by the thought that in forty years' time, when I needed their help, it would be these amiable but uninspired men who held my life in their hands. But in 1950 I knew nothing about medicine, and had yet to learn that inspiration and amiability played next to no part in it.

Professor Harris entered the theatre and stood at the podium. A small, puckish Welshman, he gazed at the tiers of beefy young men like an auctioneer at a cattle market. He spotted me sitting alone under the roof, asked for my name and told me to put out my cigarette.

'Come and join us – there's no need to be standoffish. You'll find we need each other.'

He waited as I crept red-faced to the seats below. Despite the humiliation, I admired Harris. He and his brother, both now eminent physicians, had been born to a poor Swansea family, and each had worked for six years to support the other until he qualified. Despite the late start, Harris had rapidly propelled himself to the professorship of anatomy at Cambridge. His idealism and lack of privilege struck me as unique in the university, and I identified myself closely with him. Needless to say, the privileges of my own childhood escaped me altogether.

Welcoming us to his profession, Harris took us through a brief history of medicine from the days of Vesalius and Galen, stressing its craft origins and low social standing – only in the present century, in response to the emotional needs of his patients, had the physician's status risen to that of the older professions, and Harris warned us that in our own lifetimes its status might fall. In China, I remembered, physicians were paid only while their patients enjoyed good health. The payments were suspended during illness and only resumed when the treatment succeeded.

Lastly, Harris stressed the importance of anatomy as the foundation stone of medicine, and warned that a small number of us would be unable to face the long hours of dissection. Those repelled by the sight of a cadaver should call on him privately, and would be assigned to other degree courses.

How many did? None in my own year. I can remember the sudden silence, and uneasy jokes, as we entered the dissecting room, part nightclub and part abattoir, with an illuminated ceiling of frosted glass. Waiting for us, lying face up on the dissection tables, were some twenty cadavers. Steeped in formaldehyde, they were the colour of yellow ivory. More than anything else, the richness of their skins marked out the dead, as if their personalities had migrated hopefully to the surface of their bodies. Every kind of blemish stood out in the harsh light, moles and operation scars, warts and faded tattooes, an amputated big toe and a pair of supernumerary nipples on the barrel chest of a cadaver with a prize-fighter's physique. Each body was an atlas recording the journeys of an entire life.

I took my place at the glass-topped table assigned to me, and set out my dissection manual and instruments. Already I noticed a few curious stares. Alone among the cadavers, mine was that of a woman. For purposes of dissection, the human body was divided into four sections: thorax and abdomen; head and neck; arm; and leg. Each would occupy a term, and be dissected by a team of two students. I knew no-one at the medical school whom I could partner, apart from Peggy Gardner, now in her final year at Cambridge, and decided to select a cadaver at random. Then, scanning the list of numbers I noticed that one was identified as '17F'. Without hesitating, I wrote my name alongside.

Sure enough, I found myself sitting beside the bald head of a strong-shouldered woman who had died in her late middle age. Fine blonde hairs rose from her shaved eyebrows, lips and pubis, and her face had the firm set of a headmistress or hospital matron. In most respects she was indistinguishable from the male cadavers – her breasts had subsided into the fatty tissue of her chest wall, while the genitalia of the males had shrivelled into their groins – but she was already an object of attention. Most of the students had spent the war in their boarding schools relocated far from the bombed cities, and had probably never seen a naked body, let alone that of a mature woman.

Only Peggy Gardner was unimpressed, when she entered the dissecting room and found me working with my partner, a Nigerian dentist in his thirties, who was taking an anatomy degree.

'There's a lot more work there,' she said reprovingly. 'You'll have to cut away all the fat before you reach the fascia.'

'It was the luck of the draw.' Embarrassed, I added: 'For some reason I got the Queen of the Night.'

'Rubbish. And that's awfully flippant, Jamie. You're still trying hard to be different. You haven't changed since Lunghua.'

'Peggy, that sounds like a death sentence.'

I may not have changed, but Peggy had transformed herself from the thin-shouldered 16-year-old who had sailed to England with me on the *Arrawa*. I remembered how she had started to mimic the fine-stitched mannerisms of the widowed Mrs Dwight. Peggy had spent her first years in England in a world without men. Behind her handsome stride I could see the self-confident spinsters who had taught Peggy at her boarding school near Brighton. Stylish but well-buttoned, she sailed through the young demonstrators who tried to flirt with her.

But Peggy, at least, seemed at home in England, which for me was a zone of transit between my past life in China and a future that, annoyingly, showed no signs of arriving. I was marooned in a small, grey country where the sun rarely rose above the rooftops, a labyrinth of class and caste forever enlarging itself from within. The English talked as if they had won the war, but behaved as if they had lost it. My years at school had made me realise how much I was an outsider – the other boys were friendly, but left me alone, as if they found me threatening in some undefined way. I thought all the time of going back to Shanghai, but that escape route had closed in 1949 with Mao Tse-tung's takeover of China.

Soon after arriving at Cambridge I invited Peggy to my rooms at King's, with their windows on to the noisy, organ-weary chapel. Happy to see her again, I watched her stalk around my sitting-room, shaking her head over the Magritte and Dali reproductions on the mantelpiece, and the novels by Camus and Boris Vian. I remembered our days together in the children's hut at Lunghua when she had carefully explained, in at least twelve stages, the right way to sew a button on to my shirt. Sensible housewifery could hold any demons at bay, any hunger.

'Why do you read all this stuff? You aren't going to the Sorbonne. Nobody's heard of them here.'

'Peggy, they haven't heard of anything in Cambridge. The dons are only interested in their damned madrigals and getting on to the Brain's Trust. The whole place is fake gothic pageant with a cast of thousands of bicycles.'

'It isn't gothic and it isn't a fake.' Peggy turned the novels face down on to the mantelpiece, clearly worried for me. 'When they built King's Chapel it was more modern than Corbusier, and stood for something weird enough even for you to believe in. Go to the Cavendish – Rutherford split the atom there.'

'You make it sound like Anne Hathaway's cottage. I have met E. M. Forster – he tottered into the Provost's sherry party yesterday. Whiskery old gent with sad eyes, like a disappointed child-molester.'

'Good.' Peggy nodded approvingly. 'At last you're meeting the real King's. Did he put his hand on your knee?'

'I waited, but no luck. The real King's, all right. If you listen carefully you can hear the choir-boys sobbing. That's why they play the organ all day long.'

'You're too old for him, that's all. Those Addenbrookes nurses are more your line. They'll completely corrupt you . . . all this brave talk about psychoanalysis.'

'Psychoanalysis? If I talk about it ever, it must be to myself. Here they see it as a rather strained kind of mittel-European joke.' I stared through the window at the

American tourists outside the chapel. 'Yesterday I saw a Chevrolet in the Psychology Department car-park – it must be the only Chevvy in Europe. God, it made me think of Shanghai and all those Americans.'

'Why? Stop thinking about Shanghai and Lunghua. It's all over.'

'I don't think about it, actually. But it isn't over.'

Peggy took my shoulders, as if we were back in the children's hut and she was warning me not to provoke Sergeant Nagata. 'Jamie, try to remember – you're here, in England.'

'Yes . . . in a weird way Lunghua was a small version of England. I used to wonder why no-one tried to escape.'

'Where would they have escaped to?'

'That wasn't it. Lunghua reminded them of home. Remember all those signs? "Waterloo Station", "Piccadilly Circus", "The Serpentine"? That was a stagnant pond that gave everyone malaria.'

'It kept people's spirits up. Besides, you've forgotten that some people did escape. You were the one who wanted the war to go on forever. While David and the Ralstons were trying to break out, you were trying to break in. People thought it was very funny.'

'The food store? So everyone knew? I wanted us to live there forever. Hansel and Gretel, I suppose. God, I loved you so much . . .'

But when I placed my hands on her waist, trying to thank her for all she had done in Lunghua, she slipped away from me. I sat down in my armchair, as the organ blared insanely from the chapel, thinking of the elderly lechers who had made Peggy's last year in the camp such a trial. Something about my books and reproductions disoriented her; perhaps she feared that Cambridge might be dismantled like the Tsingtao of her childhood. The French novels and my feigned world-weariness were not merely frivolous and adolescent, but dangerous, like my decision

82

to dissect a female cadaver. Peggy had been my first love, but sadly not my first lover. She had known me too closely in Lunghua, washing and feeding me when I was ill, and sharing too much emotional stress, to want us to come together again.

During the following weeks, as I began to dissect the dead woman, I realised that my decision had been correct. I took part in undergraduate life, getting drunk on the river with the Addenbrookes nurses, playing tennis with my fellow Kingsmen, but in every other sense the university remained a foreign city. Sometimes I would wake in my rooms, roused by one of the endless voluntaries, and be unable to remember where I was. Then I would smell the faint traces of human fat and formalin on my hands and think of the woman in the dissecting room. I imagined her lying on the darkened table, as deep as pharaoh in her dream of death. Her calm presence presided over the cadavers and students alike. Exposing herself to young men with knives in their hands, she set a kind of order on my memories of the dead Chinese and Japanese I had seen during the war.

As the four student teams began to dissect this unknown woman, opening flaps of skin in her limbs, neck and abdomen, she seemed to undress in a last act of self-revelation, unpacking herself of all the mortal elements in her life. Sitting beside her, I pared back the skin of her shoulder, dividing the muscles and exposing the nerves of her brachial plexus, the strings that had once moved her arms as she caressed her husband, brushed her hair, cradled her child. I tried to read her character in the scars beneath her chin, traces perhaps of a car accident, the once broken bridge of her strong nose, and the mole on her right temple which she may have disguised with a handsome blonde wave. Pretending to read my Cunningham, the dissection handbook whose pages were now stained by the

83

dead woman's skin, I stared at her matronly hips, and at the callouses on her left fingers, those of an amateur cellist . . . ? As we opened the doors of her body, students and demonstrators working on other cadavers would pause behind us, drawn to this solitary woman among the dead men. She alone was treated to none of the lewd dissecting room humour.

Hoping to identify her, I talked to the assistants in the preparation room, and learned only that she had once been a physician. Almost all the cadavers were those of doctors who had donated their bodies before their deaths – it moved me to think that these dying men and woman had bequeathed themselves to the next generation of doctors, a great testimony to their spirit.

Aware of her hold over me, and eager to get out of Cambridge for a few hours, I bought a Triumph motorcycle and began to ride into the flat countryside to the north of the city, a realm of fens and water-courses that vaguely resembled the landscape around Shanghai. Behind the hedges lay forgotten wartime airfields, from which the bombing offensive against Germany had been launched, but there were new and larger bases where nuclear bombers were parked in their fortified dispersal bays. American military vehicles patrolled the runways, and the stars and stripes flew from the flagstaffs by the gates. Chryslers and Oldsmobiles cruised the country lanes, sudden dreams of chromium, driven by large, pensive men and their well-dressed wives, who gazed at the surrounding fields with the confident eyes of an occupying power. From their closely-guarded bases they were preparing England, still trapped by its memories of the Second World War, for the third war yet to come. Then the atomic flash that I had seen over Nagasaki would usher these drab fields and the crumbling gothic of the university into the empire of light.

*

Every afternoon, as I left the dissecting room, I passed the blue Chevrolet parked outside the Psychology Department, owned perhaps by some visiting Nobel Prizewinner from Harvard or MIT. Admiring the car, and the Stan Kenton gramophone record on the rear shelf, I noticed a windshield sticker inviting volunteers to take part in a new experimental project. Almost all the department's volunteers were medical students, who could be counted on to walk the treadmills with electrical leads taped to their chests, and ride exercise bicycles without gagging into the mouthpieces.

I hesitated before pushing back the swing doors of the designated office, wondering if I would rather spend the afternoon with one of the physiology demonstrators and her cracked nails. A lecturer knelt on the floor, hard at work repairing an electric coffee percolator. He ignored me until he had finished, and handed the machine to a tall, dark-haired schoolgirl in her late teens who was standing beside the secretary's desk.

'Good . . . Coffee first, psychology second.' Looking up at me, he asked: 'Another victim? We need all the volunteers we can get. Miriam, fill out his death certificate.'

Already I had recognised the rising star of the Psychology Department, Dr Richard Sutherland, presumably the owner of the Chevrolet and the Stan Kenton record. More like a film actor than a Cambridge don, he was a handsome Scotsman with a shock of red hair that he combed out to maximum effect. He wore basketball sneakers, tartan shirt and jeans, clothes only seen in Cambridge on off-duty American servicemen. On the wall behind him were the wooden propeller of a Tiger Moth, a New Jersey licence plate and a framed photograph of himself with von Neumann. Sutherland had taken his doctoral degree at Princeton, and it was even rumoured that he had appeared on television, inconceivably fast behaviour for a Cambridge academic.

He cast an affable eye over me, as if he already had a serviceable grasp of my motives. 'You're a first-year med . . . ? How did I guess? The formalin – you all smell like Glasgow undertakers. Let me show you what we're testing.'

Watched by the schoolgirl's approving but arch eyes, he took me rapidly through the experiment, which would test the persistence of after-images in the optical centres of the brain.

'You'll find it fascinating – you can actually see the brain working – assuming you medicos have a brain, something Miriam inclines to doubt. First we'd like you to fill out this questionnaire. We need to get an idea of your psychological profile. Do introverts have more persistent after-images than extroverts? Nothing personal, we don't need to know if you lusted after your grandmother.'

'She lusted after me.'

'That's the spirit. Miriam, take over, he's ready to confess.'

'I'm looking for the thumbscrew, Dr Richard.'

Sutherland lifted an American ski-jacket from the door-peg. 'Miriam's in the sixth form at the Perse School, she's helping out while my secretary has a baby. See you after my lecture.'

He left us while Miriam took me through the questionnaire. She read out the entries in a mock-solemn voice, strong eyes watching me without expression as I fumbled over my replies. Her fingers played with the beads of her bracelet, as if adding up her first impressions of me. A modest score, I guessed. Despite the school uniform, she was only a year younger than me, and in complete command of the office, handling the bulky folders like an experienced book-keeper. Her loosened school tie, creased tunic and the laboratory stain on her cotton shirt gave her a kind of dishevelled glamour. Had she just left the unmade bed I could see in the inner office? Already I wondered if she and Dr Sutherland were lovers.

Only when she checked the details of my birth in China did she properly notice me for the first time.

'Shanghai? Were you there during the war?'

'I was interned by the Japs. Do you know Peggy Gardner?'

'Of course – we're all in awe of her.'

'She was in the same camp.'

'Peggy? How strange. Why doesn't she talk about it?'

'Nothing very much happened.'

'I can't believe that. How long were you and Peggy there?'

'Three years. I never think about it.'

'Perhaps you should.' Using an American ball-point pen shaped like a silver rocket ship, she checked off my entries, eyebrows raised as her fingers flicked through the beads. 'Then you came to England and went to the Leys School – I can imagine how you felt about that.'

'It was fine. Just like the camp, only the food was worse.'

'God, I know, school food. I refuse to eat ours. I practically led a riot last week.' She lowered her voice. 'I only come here for Richard's chocolates. He calls me his Hershey bar girl.'

'Why do you work for him?'

She picked at the stain on her tunic, showing off her breast for me. 'I used to hang around here after school – it's easily the most interesting department. I go to a lot of lectures – Leavis, Ryle, Leach. Richard's are the best. One day he gave me a lift in his car.' She smiled at the memory.

'You're going to read psychology here?'

'No fear! I've spent enough time in Cambridge. My

father's the bursar at Fitzwilliam Hall. I want to be a cocktail waitress in New York, or live on a desert island with three strange men. Anything to get out of here.'

'I have a motor-bike. Why don't you?'

'I will!' Aware that I might be sceptical, she said with some pride: 'I tried to join the RAF. Richard's taken me up in his Tiger Moth and says I have a real flair for flying. The RAF had the nerve to turn me down, something about the lack of toilet facilities in the V-bomber force. Jesus, if I can fly a plane I can learn to pee in a milk bottle.'

'Well . . . Professor Harris says anatomy is the basis of everything.'

'He's right. So why are you doing medicine?'

'I've forgotten already. I thought that I wanted to be a psychiatrist.'

'But why? What do you need to cure? Something to do with the war?'

I hesitated, unsettled by this bright schoolgirl and her shrewd questions. 'That might be true. I haven't found out yet.'

'Well, you will.' She spoke with a robust confidence in me. 'And now you're cutting up your first corpse. Treat him with respect.'

'Of course. In fact, it's a woman.'

'A woman?' She whistled through a chipped tooth. 'You're my first necrophile.'

'In a way, that's not far from the truth.'

'Go on. This is being secretly recorded.'

'Nothing. You can get very close. It turns into a sort of weird marriage.'

'Hold on! Professor Harris is going to be bailing you out of the local clink.' She leaned back and put her feet on the desk, revealing her long legs and the white skin of her thighs through the holes in her black school stockings.

88

'So?' I asked.

'Instead of the dead, why don't you try the living?'

In her teasing way, this intelligent schoolgirl had seen through my undergraduate banter and realised that I was still preoccupied by wartime events that now seemed to be reimposing themselves on the calm Cambridgeshire landscape. The students poled their punts on the Cam, talked endlessly in the coffee houses and debated the issues of the day at the Union, mimicking the tones of the House of Commons. Meanwhile, on the airfields that ringed the university, American bombers were massing for a final nuclear countdown.

On Sunday afternoons I drove Miriam on my motorcycle to Cambridge airfield, where we watched Richard Sutherland circle the field in his Tiger Moth. Later I took Miriam out to the great American bases at Lakenheath and Mildenhall, and we walked together through the November wind to stare at the nuclear bombers. Once we came across a run-down British air-base where World War II Liberators sat in parking bays far from their hangars. As Miriam kept watch, I climbed through the wire and approached one of the unguarded bombers. I swung myself through the ventral hatch into the equipment-cluttered fuselage. As the wind drummed at the bomber's hull and flexed its heavy wings I imagined myself taking off towards the east.

'Jim, you're trying awfully hard to get arrested,' Miriam told me when we returned to King's. 'Where is your father now?'

'He's still in China.'

'You won't feel at home until he comes to England.'

'He's stuck in Shanghai for a while. The communists put him on trial. Luckily, he'd read more Marx and Engels than the peasant judges, so they let him off.'

'There's a moral there . . .' Miriam took my arm as we

stood by the fire, running her eye along the surrealist reproductions. 'Ernst, Dali, the Facteur Cheval . . . they're your real syllabus. Don't let Peggy Gardner rubbish them. Hang on to your imagination, even if it is a bit lurid.'

'Miriam . . .' I had heard this too often at school. 'The world *is* lurid. You've never had to rely on your imagination, thank God.'

'Any moment now, he's going to start tunnelling . . .'

I had described my attempt to break into the food-store at Lunghua, which Miriam thought comical but oddly touching. Already I was infatuated with this quick-witted schoolgirl, with her bold gaze and outrageous enthusiasms. At times she would lose interest in me, preoccupied with some grudge against one of the women teachers at the Perse, or after the endless rows with her mother about her drinking in the undergraduate pubs. The proctors had complained to her father that Miriam had been seen in a punt with a crowd of Trinity men, threatening them with a pint of beer in each hand.

Every moment with her produced some surprise. She told me that the optical experiments devised by Richard Sutherland were no more than a blind, part of a larger test to determine the psychological profiles of students who volunteered to take part in medical experiments. Research workers had always assumed that casually recruited volunteers formed a typical cross-section of the student population.

'But that isn't true. Richard says that the only ones who apply are either aggressive extroverts or neurotic introverts.'

'And where are the sane ones?'

'They never apply. They're either getting drunk or necking on the river.'

'Call Professor Harris . . .' We were lying in bed together, and I searched below the sheet. 'Where does that leave me?'

Miriam pressed my head to the pillow and brushed the hair from my eyes. 'Jim, you're a war criminal.'

'What?'

'Or you think like one. Richard and I were talking about you.'

'Another bogus test . . .'

'Listen, if you take away the war you behaved just like a schizophrenic child. Richard has a patient whose son was schizophrenic. He spent twenty years quietly trying to kill himself. It's all he wanted to do.'

'And?'

'I forget. Anyway, you aren't going to kill yourself. I need you for at least the next three weeks.' She sat up on one elbow, laying her right breast on my chest, and drew lines with her fingernail around her nipple. 'Tell me, is it strange to dissect a woman? You say she's the only one there.'

'Speak softly, she's the queen of the dead.'

'I know she's my biggest rival. Can you imagine dissecting me? Where would you start?'

Smiling, I turned to face Miriam, drawing back the frayed sheets so that the firelight warmed her broad hips and rib-cage. 'I don't know . . . in a way, dissection is a kind of erotic autopsy. We could start with the cervical triangle, save me having to wring your neck . . .' I kissed the small mole under Miriam's chin, savouring the taste of her mother's perfume. 'Or a nasal re-section, you have been getting a little toffee-nosed . . .' I pressed my tongue into her nostril with its scent of decayed lavender until she snorted with laughter. 'Or what about an augmentation mammoplasty, not really necessary in your case . . .' I ran my lips from the musky sweet hollow of her armpit to her full breast with its heavy nipple. Veins ran below the white skin, asps waiting to sting a princess. I tasted the skin of her breasts, hunting for the scent glands, running my tongue against the hard pippin of her nipple. I moved down to her abdomen. 'Your navel smells of oysters . . .'

'Wait a minute. You haven't dissected the abdomen yet.'

'The only tool I need here is a slice of lemon.'

'So this is what you get up to in the DR. My mother always warned me about unqualified doctors . . .'

I embraced her, pressing my lips against her nipple. The only women I had made love to, apart from David Hunter's Chinese girl-friends in Shanghai, were the middle-aged landlady and her daughter who ran the small hotel in west London where I had stayed during my mother's return to the Far East, and a Cambridge prostitute who thought I was an American serviceman posing as an undergraduate, a shrewd guess in the circumstances. With Miriam, sex for the first time brought with it a sense of the future. I hoped that she and I would make love many other times, and that an unlimited store of affection lay waiting for us in some bonded warehouse of the heart.

Miriam's fingers were snipping across my chest, scissoring at my breast-bone. She tapped down to my stomach, by-passing my navel with an elegant swerve, and with a cry caught my testicles in a lobster's claw. Laughing, I raised her thigh and placed it across my hip. She sat astride me and rested her vulva against my penis, teasing me as she held the tip between her labia. I entered her vagina, needing her so much that I could happily have dissected her. I imagined a strange act of love performed by an obsessed surgeon on a living woman, in a deserted operating theatre in one of those sinister clinics in the Cambridge suburbs. I would kiss the linings of her lungs, run my tongue along her bronchi, press my face to the moist membranes of her heart as it pulsed against my lips . . .

'Jim . . .' Miriam paused, a forefinger on my nose. 'What are you thinking about?'

'It's probably illegal.'

'Well, stop . . .'

I held her tightly, forgetting the dissecting room and its cadavers, the nuclear bombers and the November fens.

Soon after, Miriam returned to her Trinity friends and her work for Richard Sutherland. She was unsettled by my obsessive visits to the American bases, and aware that I was still ensnared in a past from which I made little effort to free myself. She realised, too, that I was under the sway of a woman whose body I knew even more intimately than her own. Concerned for me, she tried to make me talk about Shanghai and the war, and even asked another medical student to smuggle her into the dissecting room, ready to confront her rival. But I cared for Miriam too much to risk exposing her to the past.

So, in her wise and kindly way, she kissed me against the mantelpiece, formally turned my surrealist paintings to the wall, and with a friendly wave closed the door of my rooms behind her.

I was sorry to see her leave, but she was right in thinking that a strange duel was taking place between herself and the dead physician who had begun to dominate my waking hours in Cambridge. Through the milky eyes of this silent woman I felt that I was joined once again to the Shanghai I had left behind, but which I still carried with me like a persistent dream that gripped my shoulders. Inside my head hung the facades of the Bund and the Nanking Road. When I looked from the windows of the Anatomy Library at the flat Cambridgeshire countryside, with its American air-bases and their glowing vision of a third world war, I could see the abandoned paddy fields near Lunghua. The railway lines that carried me back to Cambridge after my weekend visits to London seemed to lead to the small country station where the four Japanese soldiers still waited for me.

Without speaking to me, the woman doctor on her glass

table had identified herself with all the victims of the war in China, and with the young Chinese clerk I had seen murdered against the telephone pole. By dissecting her, exploring her body from within, I felt that I was drawing closer to some warped truth which I had never been able to discuss with anyone since sailing from Shanghai on the *Arrawa*. Its refrigerated meat-holds had carried a secret cargo back to England. I had left Shanghai too soon, with a clutch of insoluble problems that post-war England was too exhausted and too distracted to help me set aside.

The British had known their own war, a conflict with clear military and political goals, so unlike the war in China. They had coped with its unhappy memories and their reduced status like the adults in Lunghua camp. Over the rubble of bombed streets and the deflated hopes of a better world they had imposed a mythology of slogans, a parade of patriotic flags that sealed the past away forever, far from any searching eye.

Even the ex-servicemen I met in London bars, who had experienced real combat during their years in the British forces, seemed to have taken part in a different war, a bloody pageant not too far removed from the Military Tattoos which one or two of them, bizarrely, had helped to stage in Shanghai. But war, which had widowed and maimed so many of them, had never touched their imaginations. In Shanghai, from 1937 to the dropping of the atom bombs, we had been neither combatants nor victims, but spectators roped in to watch an execution. Those who had drawn too close had been touched by the blood on the guns.

I tried to shut my eyes, dozing in the cramped flats of the hard-drinking physiology demonstrators, but the past endured. More and more, the cadavers in the dissecting room reminded me of the severed limbs I had seen in the Avenue Edward VII.

On the last Thursday in November I drove out to Cambridge airfield. I knew that Miriam often skipped her sports afternoon at school, and sneaked away to watch Richard Sutherland practise aerobatics in his Tiger Moth. As I guessed, she was waiting in the Chevrolet when I arrived, running the car's powerful heater. Cheerily, she waved me towards her, and threw open the passenger door. Glad to be with her again, I sat next to her in the car, listening to the exhilarating drone of aircraft engines.

Comfortable in her untidy school uniform, Miriam held my cold hands. Her breasts trembled as the antique biplane flew over the car park, propeller wash drumming at the Chevrolet's windshield.

'So, how's everything in the dissecting room?' she asked. 'There must be some news from the dead.'

'I'm still working on the arm – I'd like to get away from the place, but it has a kind of hold . . .'

'Jim, have you thought of giving up medicine?'

'Not yet. This is my first term. I'll wait until I've finished the head and neck.'

'That might be too late. See your tutor, say that you want to read English.'

'After medicine? Why bother? *Gray's Anatomy* is a far greater novel than *Ulysses*.'

'It's making you worse, not better. Cutting up all those bodies – it reminds you of the war.'

'Miriam . . .' I squeezed her shoulders reassuringly. 'Real bodies don't look like dissecting room cadavers. They look like the living – that is what's so strange.'

'I want to help, Jim. But there's nothing I can do.'

'Maybe not.' I watched Richard step from the Tiger Moth and stride towards us in his yellow flying suit. 'I'll take up flying.'

'Good – then you can teach me. I need to fly!'

She kissed me and stepped from the car, holding Richard's helmet as I straddled the Triumph. We made a

95

curious trio, the aviator, the schoolgirl and the medical student. Richard watched me with his friendly actor's smile. Thinking of Miriam's American underwear, I wondered if this spunky young woman had been his gift to me, part of another experiment. He was always glad to see me, asking about the war in a casual but faintly prurient way, as if I were some kind of laboratory specimen exposed to too many images of violence. Sometimes in his office, while I waited for Miriam to finish her typing, he would watch me turning the pages of *Life* magazine with its graphic photographs of the Korean War. Despite all this, I liked him for his energy and openmindedness, for Miriam and for his American car. He and his sister had been evacuated to Australia before the London blitz, and he had sprung free from the Sydney suburbs, a man with no past and only the present.

'Jim – Miriam says you're going to take up flying. Come out next week and I'll give you a spin. You can try some circuits and bumps.'

'Thanks, Richard. You trust me at the controls?'

'Of course.' Once, to his irritation, Miriam and I had overtaken him on the Triumph as he flew along the Newmarket road. 'By the way, you've been to Lakenheath? The big American base?'

'A few times.'

'He goes every weekend.' Miriam took my arm, pressing her cheek to my leather jacket, as if trying to read the wind in its bruised seams. 'Jim will be the first to know when the war comes.'

'Absolutely. I've always taken that for granted. Jim, there's a chance of visiting the base, part of some Anglo-American community project, so that we don't feel left out when armageddon begins. Come along – we might wangle a look at a nuclear bomber.'

'I'll pass, Richard.' I guessed that I was being tricked into another experiment, and remembered the term 'imposed psychopathy' that he had used in the lecture I attended. He had moved around the podium like an actor delivering Hamlet's soliloquy, ignoring the twenty students in the front rows of the auditorium and addressing himself exclusively to me as I sat high at the back under the fanlights, deliberately smoking under the 'no smoking' sign. Yet already he was appealing far beyond the empty seats, to a greater audience he had glimpsed from the air.

He watched me encouragingly while I kick-started the Triumph's heavy engine. Miriam waved as I drove between the parked aircraft.

'See you tonight, Jim! You can take me to a flick. And keep away from that woman!'

However, it was that dead woman doctor who set me free. As the weeks of dissection continued, the teams of students cut away the superficial muscles of their cadavers and reached the underlying bones. For convenience, each body was then divided into its constituent parts. The Nigerian dentist and I detached the woman's arm from her thorax, and stored the limb in one of the wooden chests at the end of the dissecting room.

Arriving one morning, I was surprised to find that she was without her head. I hunted the tables, and at last found the head at the bottom of a storage cabinet. It lay among a dozen detached heads, the name-tags of their students stitched through their ears. The advanced stages of dissection had pared away the skin of her face and the flaps of facial muscles, so that each muscle layer folded back like the page of a book. I held her head in my hands, looking into the eyes still set in the dissected orbit. Someone nudged my arm, and the book of her face fell open to reveal her hungry bones and notched teeth, warning me away.

The doctor demonstrating the female urino-genital system asked the students at our table to detach the remaining arm and legs, and soon only the thorax and abdomen remained. The womb, fallopian tubes and pelvic basin were displayed like a miniature stage set, a boudoir framed by the curtains of the abdominal muscles. The unneeded blood-vessels and nervous tissue were discarded into a scrap pail. I tied together her shoulder blade and arm bones, and attached my name to her identification tag. I held her dissected hand, whose nerves and tendons I had teased into the light. Its layers of skin and muscle resembled a deck of cards that she waited to deal across the table to me.

On the last day of term she had gone. The tables were cleared, and the assistants polished the glass tops. When we returned after Christmas a new set of cadavers would lie under the overlit ceiling, and we would begin the dissection of a second body part.

Searching for a scalpel I had mislaid, I stepped into the preparation room, where the chief assistant was tying together the bones of each cadaver. Later they would be individually cremated or interred. Little more than clutches of gristle and joint, they lay on the work-benches like the remains of so many Sunday roasts.

I scanned the benches, and recognised a familiar hand tied with a stout string to her ribs and hip bones. Together, they made up a parcel that might have slipped into a small suitcase. I read the name tag: *Dr Elizabeth Grant*. This dead physician had not only offered her body for dissection, but had reduced herself to a heap of fatty sticks as if deliberately dissolving whatever power she held over me.

I threw my gown into the laundry basket, emptied my locker and set out to find Miriam. If I needed to woo her from Richard Sutherland I would buy an American car, take up flying, cast myself as her Lindbergh, ready to fly the Atlantic with nothing but a packet of sandwiches and my own will.

CHAPTER FIVE

The Nato Boys

As always, the sound of engines in the morning sent the slipstream racing through my mind long before I steered the Harvard from the parking apron. Snow lay across Moose Jaw airfield, draped like overnight laundry on the windsocks and the grilles of the landing lights. But the sky was a crystal summer blue, lit by needles of high-altitude ice, the flying weather of which we trainee pilots had dreamed as we waited among the dog-eared magazines in the flight room.

For four days the Saskatchewan fogs had put an end to all flying, and now every serviceable Harvard at the Nato training base was on the apron. The ground crews moved along the line of aircraft with their battery carts. The signal lamps flashed in a green fever from the control tower, and the first planes taxied towards the runway. As each engine choked and stuttered into life another layer of sound stiffened the air, the bull-throated roar of exhausts and intakes. The windows of the Canadian officers' mess and the cadet barracks trembled with the noise of propeller steel setting its edge against the wind.

A ground crew moved their battery cart under my starboard wing. Muffled like arctic explorers in oilskins, goggles and ear-muffs, they plugged their cable into the starter motor. I completed the take-off check, signalled to them through the canopy and pressed the worn brass ring of the ignition button.

The heavy engine snuffled and kicked, the cylinders trying to clear their throats, and the propeller threw a slice of wet ice across the windshield. The blades lurched in unwieldy staggers against the air. I cracked the throttle, increasing the fuel supply to the carburettors, and felt the harness pulling at my shoulders as the cylinders fired together. The slipstream whirled the ice from the windshield and buffeted the yellow wings and tailplane, jarring the control column against my knees. An organ loft of noise filled the aircraft and reached out to the frozen deserts of Saskatchewan, driving everything from my mind. As I waited for the battery cart I had been thinking of my overdue letters from Miriam, the drunken brawl earlier that week at the Iroquois Hotel in Moose Jaw and the penalty hours cleaning aircraft in the hangar, and the fifty dollars I owed David Hunter for stripping the second gear from his Oldsmobile. But all this was forgotten when the engine came to life and the Harvard thrust itself against the brake pedals.

To my left Captain Hamid of the Turkish Army moved from the apron. He scowled at the odour in his open face mask, remembering the unspeakable ham and egg breakfasts in the mess. He steered his Harvard with a heavy hand, forcing the plane to left and right like a stupid horse on a parade ground. But I could eat the breakfasts and take the eventless winter wheatlands in my stride. Behind me a sharp-tempered Frenchman urged me on, flicking his flying gloves against the windshield. Harvards were taking off and making right-hand circuits of the airfield, solo trainees and student pilots with their instructors in the back seat, the junior air arm of Nato preparing itself for the even colder and more crowded high-altitude space above the north German plain. Within hours of my first solo I had decided to transfer to Bomber Command after my jet training. I saw myself at the controls, not of this antique World War II trainer, but of a nuclear, delta-winged Vulcan as it sped over the marshy forests of Byelorussia armed with pieces of the sun . . .

'Air Force two niner niner one . . .' A Canadian flight controller leaned against the tower windows, watching me through field glasses. Behind me a line of Harvards waited their turn to reach the runway, engines aimed at the back of my head.

'Moose Jaw tower, this is Air Force –' A crackle of squawks interrupted me. However clearly I spoke, trying to disguise my English voice and assume a Canadian accent, the RCAF flight controllers deliberately made their intercom messages as garbled as possible, venting all their irritation with the Nato training programme. The French, Norwegian and Turkish pilots, despite the hours spent in the English language classes, had virtually no idea what their instructors were saying to them. World War III could have broken out and ended before we disentangled ourselves and climbed through the babel of the Canadian skies.

Aligned at the foot of the runway, I waited for the tower's final signal, and eased the throttle to its maximum setting. Released from its brakes, the Harvard lumbered forward like a short-sighted rhino, hunting for every crack in the worn concrete. At full throttle, the engine seemed to tear itself from the fuselage spars, and I waited for the elderly craft to disintegrate at the end of the runway. But the Harvard had trained generations of American fliers. I pushed the stick forward to raise the tail off the ground. At 70 knots I drew back on the column and the aircraft rose comfortably into the air, its broad wings breasting the thermals that rose from the heated runways. I climbed to three thousand feet, trimmed the elevators and set the engine for cruise. The winter fields of southern Saskatchewan, its frozen lakes and empty highways, stretched to the horizon. Beyond Saskatoon, the vast wildernesses of northern Canada extended to the planet's edge, touched only by the aurora borealis and the condensation trails of military jets surfing on the upper limits of the atmosphere. Here the great radars of the Norad chain and the Russian defence system bayed at each other like lions staked to the ice.

Loosening my harness, I listened to the steady drone of the engine and watched the white land shift beneath me. Officially, I was to practise stalls and spins, and navigate a course to Swift Current before returning to Moose Jaw, but like most of the trainee pilots I had no intention of following my instructions. The evening at the Iroquois had left me with a two-day hangover and an infected shoulder bite. Neither would be helped by being thrown around thousands of feet of overlit air. As always, I went up into the sky to calm myself, to think of Miriam, to rest and to dream.

Flying, which had obsessed me since the war years in Shanghai, had brought me to this remote town in the Canadian west. I had left Cambridge after two years, completely cured of any need to become a doctor. Despite the Cavendish laboratory, the university was excluded from the more urgent world of the American nuclear bombers flying from their Cambridgeshire airfields, readying themselves for the final global war. The Berlin Airlift, the Korean War, a re-arming Europe belonged to a realm I had seen born over the paddy fields of the Yangtse estuary. Dr Elizabeth Grant had freed me from my dreams of the dead, but a far greater army of casualties was preparing itself for the planetary dissecting room.

I sat with Miriam in the Cambridge cinemas, compulsively watching the newsreels of the hydrogen bomb-tests. The sight of these immense explosions at Eniwetok stirred and enthralled me, and often I had to steady my trembling hands to avoid frightening Miriam. The mysterious mushroom clouds, rising above the Pacific atolls from which the B-29s had brought to Nagasaki the second day of apocalypse, were a powerful incitement to the psychotic imagination, sanctioning everything. Fantasies of nuclear war fused forever with my memories of Shanghai, reminding me of the white dust in the Avenue Edward VII, down which I had walked like a child straying into a preview of the future.

Working as a copywriter for an advertising agency in London, I thought constantly of the pioneers of aviation – Lilienthal and the Wrights, Lindbergh and even little Mignet, who ended his days in poverty, camping in disused hangars under the wing of his beloved Flying Flea. In my mind all the romance and ascensionist myths of flight were linked to weapons of destruction and the greater possibilities that lay beyond them.

At a reunion of Shanghai friends at the Regent Palace Hotel, I saw David Hunter for the first time since our arrival at Southampton in 1946. Despite the seven years he had scarcely changed, eyes under his pale fringe still watching the doors and windows as if he had just escaped from a penal institution. After a few years of working for his father, an import-export agent in the City, he had been a tennis instructor, a trainee actor and even, briefly, a Jesuit novice. We began to see each other for lunch, drawn together by that sense of an unresolved past which we shared. He was nearly always drunk, but at the same time almost pedantically sober, unable to make sense of his own life but certain about the right course for mine. When his face was flushed with gin I could see the bruises rising through his skin.

'Psychiatry wasn't right for you, Jim,' he told me frankly, waving aside an entire career. 'You'd have spent all your time analysing yourself.'

'Why? I didn't know there was anything to analyse.'

'You could have fooled me, dear sport. Your patients would never have left the waiting room.' David glanced at me in the same irritating and knowing way that Richard Sutherland had sometimes watched me in his office at the Psychology Department, as if waiting for some sudden

103

insight into my character. 'Tell me, do you still think about Shanghai?'

'Less than I used to. We might as well forget it – Shanghai's forgotten us.'

'Unsettling, that. Strange city, but it does have a kind of claim on us. All those poor bloody Chinese. What was Cambridge like?'

'I didn't see that much of the place. It's a glorified academic gift-shop for American universities, where they can buy some quaint little professor for a few dollars. You need to be a tourist or an au pair girl to get the most out of it.'

'I took a course of lessons at the flying school. For some reason I wanted to go crop-spraying in British Guiana. It's curious the delusions one has.' David shook his head at himself. 'A girl and I went on the river in a punt. Cambridge seemed a good place to be.'

'The Americans have their nuclear bases there. Advanced jets sit on the runways loaded with hydrogen bombs, while huge quartermaster-sergeants cruise the country lanes in their Chryslers, looking for turkey farms.'

'Nuclear bases – I imagine you spent a lot of time hanging around them?'

'A little. Better than singing madrigals every hour of the day and night, or pretending to be Rupert Brooke.'

'Only in a way. You should have gone to Yale – though I wouldn't put it past them to be singing madrigals there as well.' David stared at his hands, holding them up as if he had just discovered a new weapon. 'You know, we ought to join the American air force. You'd look great in a USAF uniform, Jim, driving around Cambridge in a Chrysler. It's really what you've always wanted to do. You could lay all the girls who haven't already been laid by the boys in USAF uniforms. Jim, *think* about it.'

'David, I am thinking about it. It's quite an idea – in fact, the first new one I've heard for years.'

'And not just for the girls . . .' David steadied his cutlery, glancing around the tables as if he wanted to straighten all the knives and forks in the restaurant. He was smiling at me with the excited but reassuring eyes I remembered from our afternoons in Shanghai, when he invited the wary Chinese bar-girls to the apartment he rented from a Russian dentist in Imperial Mansions. As usual, he had soon provoked these young prostitutes into abusing him. Sex, for David, was as close as he could get to that terrifying evening in the guard-house with Sergeant Nagata and Mr Hyashi.

A career as a military pilot offered an even more direct entry to the realm of violence for which we hungered. For both of us the war years in Shanghai still set the hidden agendas of our lives. David dreamed of violence, in his concerned and thoughtful way, while I was looking for a means of recreating the pearly light I had seen over the rice-fields of Lunghua beside the railway station, and which seemed to hover so promisingly over the American air-bases near Cambridge.

During the next weeks we met again and talked around the possibilities of a flying career. I was bored by my job as a copywriter, and there were fewer weekend visits to Cambridge now that Miriam was working for her history of art degree. Still the mutinous sixth-former, she had become one of the star turns of undergraduate life, scandalising the first-year men with her powerful motorcycle, acting in a pornographic play by Apollinaire that the proctors had banned, smuggling boyfriends overnight into her room at Girton. She was always happy to see me, fiercely holding my shoulders as if ready to marry me that afternoon. But she was waiting for me to come to terms with the war and find my real compass bearing.

Flying in the American bomber force, now readying itself for a nuclear attack on the Soviet Union, seemed to fulfil all those dreams, a make-or-break challenge that would force me to face myself. However, the US Embassy, in a misguided fit, declined to recommend us for pilot training. David was stunned by the rejection, remonstrating with the polite but weary officials, who clearly regarded us as complete madmen and strongly urged us to join the RAF.

'No Chrysler for you, Jim, more like some gravel-rash MG.' David patted my shoulder as we stood outside the RAF recruitment office in Kingsway, after enlisting on short-service commissions. 'But at least you'll get a ringside seat at World War III.'

Needless to say, this shrewd guess summed up my real reasons for joining the RAF. During our three months of basic training at RAF Kirton in Lincolnshire, as we learned the rudiments of meteorology, scaled hangar walls on assault courses and fired submachine-guns at the rifle range, I never once lost my belief that at last the real elements of my life were coming together. I was preparing myself, in the most practical way, for the third world war which had already begun at Nagasaki and Hiroshima, and whose first instalments were the Berlin crisis and the Korean war. Somewhere over the skies of central Europe armageddon would wake me from my dreams.

As it happened, we fledgling pilots were sent, not to a front-line base in West Germany, but to one of the remotest corners of the world, RCAF Moose Jaw in Saskatchewan. As part of the Nato agreement, the aircrews of its European members received their flight training in Canada. We crossed the Atlantic in the *Empress of Britain*, a pre-war liner of the Canadian Pacific fleet, sitting under the baroque ceilings of the vast state-rooms. Miriam drove her motorcycle up to Liverpool to see me off, and stared with awe at the magnificent gilt furniture and attentive stewards, as if I were going off to some strange and lavish war in which every private soldier travelled to the front in his own Rolls-Royce. When she embraced me on the gangway she had clearly taken for granted that she would never see me again. I waved from the rail long after the Liver building had dropped below the horizon.

Surviving the Atlantic, a subarctic realm of vertical seas, deranged ice and voracious sea-birds, we landed at Montreal, and began a pleasant, month-long acclimatisation period at a Toronto air-base, being prepared for the social and psychological hazards of a waffle-and-turkey lifestyle that David and I eagerly embraced. Even the endless hours of propaganda and VD films -- which carried the message that the entire female half of the human race was dedicated to infecting us – failed to cool our pleasure at being in north America.

At last, after a four-day train journey from Toronto, we arrived at Moose Jaw, Saskatchewan. We stepped from the train with our suitcases and stared at the small prairie town, a mixed group of suspicious Turks, stoical Norwegians, hungover Britishers and impatient Frenchmen.

'I wish Miriam could see this.' I gazed at the immensity of the Saskatchewan plain. 'Where does it end? This is the wrong planet.'

'If visitors from outer space ever land on earth they will choose this place,' David reflected gloomily. 'Moose Jaw, Saskatchewan, will remind them of home.'

But Moose Jaw was more interesting than we realised. Beyond the 49th parallel were the great cities of the American mid-west. The re-arming United States of the Eisenhower years enjoyed a confidence and prosperity unknown in Europe. Fleets of baroque vehicles soared along its highways, as if a race of interplanetary visitors were landing on a recreational visit. On our second day David bought a used Oldsmobile, and we began to take long drives in any direction. The Canadians were a hospitable and tolerant desert people, living on the edge of a wilderness of snow and permafrost. Winnipeg, Regina and Saskatoon were cities of the northern desert, Samarkands of ice. At the end of every street there were white horizons of emptiness. My mind leapt, expanding to fill the void . . .

A shadow veered across the Harvard, darkening its wings. I woke as a blare of engine noise drummed at the canopy. A pilot of the French training flight swept past in a shallow dive, so close that the torque from his propeller almost rolled the Harvard into a high-speed stall. I secured my harness, put out the cigar I was smoking and prepared for a chase, when a second Frenchman dived past my starboard wing, climbing away into a steep half-spiral that would put him back on to my tail. The two planes had crept behind me as I cruised over the snow-covered wastes of Deer Lake, listening to the country music broadcast from a Medicine Hat radio station.

For the next five minutes we hauled the ageing trainers around the sky in a mock dog-fight, and only scattered when a dual-control Harvard with a Canadian instructor in the rear seat sped towards us from the south. Deer Lake was out of bounds, while mock air-battles and unauthorised low-flying were court martial offences. The mink-farmers of Saskatchewan, a powerful political lobby, were our sworn enemies, and their farms were marked on our maps like so many German ball-bearing factories in World War II. We liked to overfly their farms, so low that the angry farmers were unable to photograph our identification numerals, engines so loud that the frantic beasts tore down their cages and scattered to the safety of the snow.

However illicit, these air games helped to sustain us. The Frenchmen swung away to the south-west, heading towards Medicine Hat, and the Canadian instructor set off after me. I took for granted that he was shouting at me over the R/T, but my tanks were lighter by fifty gallons and I soon pulled away from him. Gradually he fell behind, then gave up and returned to Moose Jaw.

Scanning the snow-covered wilderness, I searched for a railroad line or highway that would give me my bearings. I was now some 70 miles to the north-west of Moose Jaw, above a featureless terrain of snow-covered lakes. Under the needle-like sunlight the snow had begun to melt, and the pools of darker water resembled bowls of black sherbet. A mile to starboard a grain silo rose from the white plain, like a silver sculpture erected beside the embankment of a railway line. I turned towards it, one eye on my fuel gauge, following the Harvard's shadow across a curious turtle-shaped lake. In one of its arms I saw a submerged structure that resembled a sunken cabin with a flat yellow roof.

Or a Harvard trainer lying inverted in fifteen feet of water? Too short of fuel to make another circuit of the lake, I followed the railroad spur towards Swift Current and set course for Moose Jaw. But as I faked the navigation course on my knee I was thinking of the Turkish pilot, Captain Artvin, who had disappeared two months after our arrival.

Of all the Nato trainees, the Turks were the most unhappy. Older and more senior than the young Canadian instructors, they mustered no more than a few words of English between them. They pooled their pay and bought a second-hand Ford from a Moose Jaw dealer, only to find that there was nowhere to go. They sat silently around the mess tables in their green, American-style uniforms, gold bars gleaming on their shoulders, as the blizzards swept horizontally past the windows. When the snow ceased they stared at the watery skies and the triple suns, as if these optical illusions produced by the vast mists of ice crystals were a signal to some desperate action.

Unable, perhaps, to cope with this arctic world of snow and mirages, Captain Artvin had disappeared on a training flight. Every Canadian instructor took to the air and searched the wintry landscape within a 100-mile radius. His fellow Turks refused to assist the enquiry, but none showed the slightest surprise. Curiously, Artvin had taken with him all his possessions, his spare uniforms, his newly purchased electric razor and American radio. Everyone assumed that Artvin had defected to the Russians, but I was convinced that he had simply had enough of RCAF Moose Jaw and decided to fly home.

But the captain's Harvard was never found. Had he managed to land on isolated airfields in Alberta and the North-West Territories, refuel with the help of Soviet sympathisers and somehow make his way across Alaska to the Bering Strait? It seemed unlikely, and I preferred to think that Captain Artvin had set off towards the east, ignoring his fuel gauges, and flown on into his own dream.

'Artvin? Poor bugger,' David commented when I told him of the possible sighting. The submerged cabin with its yellow roof had certainly resembled a Harvard. 'Are you going to report it?'

'Naturally. "Sorry, Group Captain, just happened to be over Deer Lake, all these damned Canadian lakes look the same, you know . . ."'

'What about the Turks?'

We were changing out of our flying suits, and David passed me the bottle of bourbon he kept in his parachute locker. I watched Captain Hamid stowing his boots, overall and helmet in the same neat way that I imagined Artvin packing his radio and electric razor. These impressive and over-controlled men reminded me of the Japanese, hovering perpetually on the edge of a mental crisis. The Danes and Norwegians were self-contained, the British blurry with drink, in the air as on the ground. The French, for their part, were forever staging mutinies, refusing to obey

110

their senior officers until the French military attaché flew in from Ottawa and arranged some concession that briefly calmed them down. North American cooking, the waffles and turkey drumsticks and jugs of milk were a constant intellectual challenge.

But it was these sombre Turks who would run amok one day. As we sat together in the meteorology theatre during our current affairs classes, watching the propaganda newsreels and the endless VD films with their demonstrations of how to soap and wash the male genitalia after intercourse, I expected the Turks to seize all the weapons in the armoury and slaughter the English-speaking world to a man.

'Tell the Turks?' I reflected. 'That might not be good for the nerves. I don't want to wake up and find my testicles inside my mouth.'

'I'm glad you've still got testicles, dear sport. It's Friday night and we're heading for the Iroquois.' David took a sip from his bottle, scarcely bothering to disguise it from a Canadian instructor who walked past. 'Hard cheese on Artvin. He didn't make it to Mother Russia after all.'

'I don't think he was trying. He didn't defect to the Soviets.'

'So what was he doing?'

'He was flying home. He'd had it here.'

'Well, he didn't get very far.'

'Far enough.'

'Jim?' David was about to hand me the bourbon, but put the cork into the bottle. 'What did that mean? I can see the Lunghua look in your eye.'

'There's no Lunghua look.'

'Artvin's sitting upside down in fifteen feet of iced water. That isn't flying home.'

'It's a figure of speech – people create their own mythologies.'

'You should have sung more madrigals. Never mind,

we're off to the Iroquois tonight.' David steadied himself against me. Completely sober for a fleeting moment, he said: 'When you fuck Yvette and Brigid promise me you'll think of Miriam . . .'

Four hours later I lay on a bed in the Iroquois Hotel, my hands gripping the candlewick bedspread. The room rotated around me like a slowly precessing gyroscope. Beyond the room a larger carousel circled in a clockwise direction, carrying the elderly hotel and its shabby ceilings, the noise from the bar downstairs, the streets of Moose Jaw with their filling stations and hardware stores, and beyond those the snow-covered fields and the old bison slumbering by the railroad creek in their overcoats of wallows mud. For some reason I was at the centre of this rotating system, which had begun to tilt, as if banking into a power dive. I was flying the world . . .

'Jim, are you still with us?' David was calling to me through the glare of the bedside lamp. 'Oh, my God! Don't look at him . . .'

I was trying to open the pillow case, needing desperately to be sick. My trousers lay on the floor beside the bed. Too dazed to think, I vomited into them. Tears welled from my nose and eyes as shreds of turkey and bourbon streaked with blood lay inside the vent like a rancid haggis.

'Jesus, what a spectacle,' David exclaimed from somewhere behind me. 'I hate to say it, girls, but there's no sight more disgusting than the British officer class with its pants down. It was men like him who did the dirty on us at Singapore. No wonder the Japs slapped their faces . . .'

I dropped the trousers to the worn purple carpet and rested against the quilted headboard, stained with the hair-oil of a thousand anonymous salesmen. The room had steadied itself, and I could see David lying naked on the next bed, laughing in his happy but slightly crazed way at the two young women who knelt across him, taking turns to suck his penis. In a firm baritone he sang:

'With his mixture rich and his carb heat cold
He got the highest pressures on his manifold . . .'

One of the women was a strong-shouldered blonde, naked except for the silk stockings rolled down to her ankles. The other, kneeling with the grubby soles of her feet towards me, wore a black slip around her waist. It rode over her buttocks, which David parted with his left hand as he fondled the dark hair and pink combs of her vulva.

'God, yes, Yvette, yes . . . watch those teeth, for Christ's sake, this isn't a lunch counter. I'm going to have to take a leak. Jesus, that stink . . .'

The women ignored him and continued their efforts over his flagging erection, all the while keeping up a brisk conversation about a local beauty parlour that had spurned their custom. I could feel the bites on my penis, and the pain in my anus where an untrimmed finger-nail had almost stripped away the mucous membrane. I vaguely remembered having sex with the blonde girl, Yvette, while David played one of his odd little games in the bathroom, urging Brigid to slap his buttocks with the soles of her high-heeled shoes as he dropped dollar bills into the toilet.

Friday night at the Iroquois was taking its familiar course. First there were two hours of forced drinking in the bar crowded with Nato trainees and railroad workers, our shirts soaked with the beer that swilled across the counter. Then we took Brigid and Yvette to the two rooms on the second floor. As usual, I was so drunk that I could scarcely separate the floor from the walls. Flat surfaces, some carpeted and others with lamps and switches bolted to them, were forever veering at me and striking my face.

For reasons clear only to David, we always had sex in

the same room – he needed to watch and to be watched. Brigid sat across me, wearing her little slip like a masonic apron, steering my penis inside her with one hand as she squeezed my testicles with the other. Yvette at last made me come while she lay on her back, breast held to my mouth as she forced her finger into my anus. In turn, David liked me to watch him on the adjacent bed. His eyes would be fixed on mine in a curiously innocent and trusting way. Shoe-marks flushed his thighs, and Yvette sat across him, smearing my semen from her vulva on to the pillow. His hands thoughtfully massaged the stretch-marks of her heavy abdomen. One evening he had taken photographs which no-one in Moose Jaw would develop. The flash lights irritated the women's eyes, but in the sudden glare their faces, so empty of expression when they had sex, at last came alive, and I saw two blue-collar housewives who had ditched their husbands and aspired to the most bourgeois of lives.

'You Nato boys sure need your liquor,' Yvette opined. She grimaced as David carried my trousers into the bathroom. 'How come they ever let him into the air force?'

'It's all part of the communist conspiracy,' David explained. He began to wash out the trousers in the hand-basin, picking at the shreds of turkey. 'Don't you listen to Senator McCarthy? Nato is a plot to overthrow the US of A. We're so busy fighting each other we'll have no time to take on the Russkies.'

'I can believe that. It beats me you're ever fit to climb inside those airplanes.'

'Yvette, let me tell you. A few drinks make those old tubs really sit up. Jimmy boy's planning to start World War 3 on his own.'

'Looks like he's already finished.' Brigid, the dark-haired girl in the black petticoat, sat on the bed beside me. Her small, detergent-chafed hands, with their smell of lipstick, semen and rectal mucus, ran across my forehead, trying to find a surviving personality. A flicker of concern crossed her eyes, and then faded into the vast indifference that separated her from all men. Her small, bony face had the seriousness of a determined child's. She helped me into the bathroom and watched without comment as I sat on the edge of the bath, washing my face in the basin. David had rinsed out my trousers and hung them over the radiator. When I finished she stood in front of the mirror and began to bathe her breasts, trying to soap away the marks left by David's teeth.

I led her into the spare bedroom and sat beside her on one of the beds. Music drummed through the wall, shaking the Victorian dresser. Looking at Brigid's reflection in the full-length mirror, I realised that she was pregnant. I lifted her petticoat and stared down at the plump curve of her abdomen. I held her breast, almost expecting to feel the milk gathering inside its heavy globe, then gently touched her stomach.

'Hey, you're too young for that stuff.' She pushed me away. 'It's okay to fuck me but anything else is off limits.'

'Don't worry.' It had not occurred to me that sexual games could be played with an unborn child. 'How many months are you, Brigid?'

'The doctor thinks four, but I say five.'

'That's good. What about the father? Does he know?'

'What father?' She glanced at me as if I had not yet learned the facts of life. 'She doesn't have a father.'

'It could be a boy.'

'It's a girl.' She spoke with complete certainty, then lay on the bed and raised her knees to expose her vulva. I knelt in front of her, drawing her buttocks onto my thighs, and eased my penis into her vagina, moved by the thought of sharing this private space with her unborn infant. For the child's sake, I hoped it was not a son.

'Just take your time. You won't hurt her.'

Who was the father – one of the Danes or Norwegians,

or some Canadian railroad worker waiting for her in the trailer town behind the grain elevators?

'Did Captain Artvin ever come here?'

'Who's that again?'

'Artvin – the Turkish pilot who disappeared.'

'They all disappear, believe me. I went with some of the Turks. Yvette likes them, but I couldn't get to them. What did this one look like?'

'I never met him. He took off one day and flew away.'

'Sounds like a great idea. Next time he can ask me to go with him.' She held my scrotum, drawing on my testicles. 'Come on, baby, more now . . . that's it, push for momma . . .'

Later I lay beside her, gazing at the curve of her abdomen. One day soon, a midwife would be using similar words to her. Accepting that I had no prurient interest, she let me raise the petticoat and put my hand on her skin. I was surprised by the size of the child. Now and then a small tremor moved the surface, as if it recognised my hand.

'You come from England?' Brigid asked. 'I always wanted to visit there. Maybe I'd see the king and queen.'

'The king died. But I've seen them – they came to my college.'

'On the level?'

'Sure. A big limousine pulled up and four little people stepped out, the king and queen and the princesses. They looked as if they were landing on the Earth for the first time.'

'That's something. Did you really get to meet them?'

'Almost . . .' As an undergraduate prank I had taken off my academic gown and laid it in a pool of water under the wheels of the approaching Daimler. Describing the incident, I realised that I had impressed Brigid at long last. When I entered her body she saw me as working for

116

her, doing my bit to help the unborn child, but now I was more than 20 Canadian dollars.

In the next room David and Yvette were asleep. I was glad that David had calmed himself and was able to embrace Yvette without needing some elaborate ruse. Flying, and these matter-of-fact women with their direct view of the world, had settled him.

Brigid lay on her side and pressed my hand to her abdomen. 'It doesn't bother you?'

'I used to be a medical student.'

'Then you know about it. Yvette says it's going to be hard in the last months. You can attract the wrong kind of guy.'

I was massaging the small of her back, in a way I imagined young husbands caring for their pregnant wives. I felt the child stir, as if woken by the music. The likelihood of Captain Artvin being the child's father was remote, but something bound them together in my mind. Assuming that Artvin was dead, and that I alone knew his resting place, as a fellow pilot I had some notional responsibility for this infant. I tried to think of Miriam, but her letters had become more and more infrequent.

'Tell me, Brigid, would you like to go to England?'

'Sure. I could meet the queen – you can introduce us.'

'I mean it. I have enough money.'

'So?'

'So we go together. You can stay with me there.'

'Together?' She turned from me and lay on her back, moving my hand from her abdomen. She pulled down the black slip.

'Why not?' I waited for her to reply. 'You think I'm too young?'

'Just a little. You Nato boys . . . you're going to be flying around with your atom bombs, making the world a safer place. Let's get to sleep while there's still time left . . .'

*

117

Her coolness hurt, however naïve my drunken scheme seemed in the uneasy light of the next day's hangover. A week later, flying over Deer Lake, I tried to remember the position of the drowned Harvard. Somewhere to the north-west I had seen the turtle-shaped lake, but it had vanished into the featureless landscape. Warmed by the late February sunlight, the surface ice was beginning to melt, and the lakes were changing shape as the snow retreated to the original shorelines. Abandoning my navigation exercise, I flew back and forth across the white land, past the isolated water-towers and grain elevators.

An hour later, when I found the Harvard, I had almost run out of fuel. The turtle lake had become a long ellipse, one of a cluster of small lakes separated by yellowing meanders. Algae covered the fuselage, but I could see the blurred numerals on its wing. Circling the lake at 500 feet, I fixed its map position – once the lake warmed in the early spring, a month before we moved to the jet school at Winnipeg, I would rent an inflatable dinghy and show the Turks where their comrade was buried. I hoped that they would decide to leave him in the lake, sealed away from the world in his cocoon of algae, still embarked on his solitary flight.

Twenty miles from Moose Jaw the fuel tanks were empty. By luck I found an empty stretch of road between two deserted wheatfields. At the last moment, as I came in to land, I saw the fencing posts beneath their upholstery of snow. The Harvard touched down in a storm of icy mud that sluiced across the silent fields. It lost its starboard wing-tip, then ground-looped and careened to a halt in the ditch beside the road.

Fifteen minutes later a mink-farmer in a slush-covered Cadillac drove up as I sat stunned in the cockpit. He stared calmly at the blood leaking from my helmet, and drew on his cigarette with his hard lips. At last he raised his window and rolled away. I learned later that he had never contacted the airfield, perhaps hoping that I would freeze to death behind my cracked windshield.

The senior Canadian officers hearing my case openly admitted their bafflement. I had been seen over Deer Lake, but they were puzzled that I had managed to consume the Harvard's ample reserves of fuel. They had already decided that I should cease training and be returned to England, but they examined and re-examined my flight plan, suspecting that I had been navigating a secret course of my own.

Did they think that I might be planning to defect, and was rehearsing the same escape flight made by Captain Artvin? In a sense they were right, as David was well aware. He made no attempt to intervene on my behalf, knowing that it was time for me to leave the air force. Whatever mythology I constructed for myself would have to be made from the commonplaces of my life, from the smallest affections and kindnesses, not from the nuclear bombers of the world and their dreams of planetary death. By revealing the location of the lost Harvard I might have persuaded them to alter their decision, but I had seen enough of the RAF. I wanted to forget Shanghai and the Avenue Edward VII and the flash of the Nagasaki bomb, and there was a simple way of doing so.

I would never lead the Moscow run to the Third World War. The unborn child in the Iroquois Hotel had given me my new compass bearing. Miriam had written to say that she had taken a job on a Fleet Street newspaper, and I wanted to be with her again and be amazed by her American underwear. I was sorry to leave David, endlessly driving the long roads of Saskatchewan in his second-hand Oldsmobile, but he was happy now and had his own destinations. Flying had helped to free him from the past, and already he talked of leaving the RAF at the end of his initial engagement period and becoming a commercial pilot. For the time being he was right to stay in Moose Jaw and do his best to cheer up the Turks. The Nato boys would stage their mutinies and fill the bar of the Iroquois, while the VD films played in the meteorology theatre and Captain Artvin continued his long flight home.

CHAPTER SIX

Magic World

'Shall we go to Magic World?' I asked the children.

'Magic World! Yes!' Four-year-old Henry was already at the gate, rattling the iron catch. He shouted to the neighbours' dozing retriever: 'Polly, we're going to Magic World!'

Three-year-old Alice skipped down the path, admiring her shiny shoes. 'Magic World, Magic World . . . !'

Miriam leaned against the door while I hunted for sunglasses in the clutter of toys and unread bills on the hall stand. She waved to the children, smiling at them as if she would never see them again and wanted to remember this moment forever. When we returned from the walk Alice and Henry would have changed in a hundred small and marvellous ways, leaving their present selves somewhere in the woods. Parents were nostalgic for every second of these lost lives.

'Keep an eye on them.'

'They'll keep an eye on me. We'll be gone for an hour – you're sure nothing's going to happen before then?'

'I don't know . . .'

In the last month of her pregnancy time seemed to slow for Miriam, stretching her smallest gesture – a hand raised to ease her heavy breasts, the lipstick drawn absent-mindedly across her mouth. She was moving into the timeless realm of the child in her womb; mother and child would begin life together. She pressed against me, knowing that I liked to feel the warm bulk beneath her smock, and lightly patted my penis.

'Just making sure you have everything you might need on the walk.'

'Sh . . . Midwife Bell will hear you. She disapproves enough of me already.'

'She adores you. Without you she'd be out of a job.'

I embraced Miriam, breathing the familiar heady scents of baby talc, basil, gloss paint and washing powder that clung to her smock. On its hem was a brown potty stain left by one of the children, taking its place among the countless stains and smells of our little house, a realm of soft armpits and swollen nipples in which I had spent an entire life.

'Rest, now. Don't start rebuilding the bedroom.'

'Bring me back some magic.'

With a last wave, I latched the gate and set off with Henry and Alice down the sun-filled street. Polly the retriever had decided to join us. He trotted beside Alice, now and then detouring to quiz and spray a lamp-post. The modest houses in Charlton Road sat in their quiet suburban gardens, but seeing them through the dog's and the children's eyes transformed the rose bushes and rockeries, the freshly painted front doors and forgotten roller skates. They became more vivid, as if aware that Polly and the children would soon forget them, and were urging themselves more brightly into existence. Our own house was as modest as the others – my salary as assistant editor of a scientific journal barely matched the small mortgage – but Miriam, Henry and Alice turned it into an endless funfair of noise and cheer. Behind other doors in Charlton Road were other Miriams. Young wives and their children strolled the streets of Shepperton and played in their gardens like agents of an exuberant foreign power.

The number of children always surprised me – this small Thames-side town was a life-engine. When we reached the end of Charlton Road we had already collected a sandy-haired boy on a tricycle, two ten-year-old girls and the infant daughter of the local builder. The splash meadow was filled with children playing on the grass and fishing for minnows along the reedy banks of the stream. I could almost believe that the bright summer frocks, fishing nets and children's voices were a dream conjured from this placid stream asleep beneath the willows.

Alice and Henry ran towards the bank, where two mothers kept watch on a park bench. I took off my tennis shoes and walked in bare feet through the cool pelt of the meadow. Beyond the willows lay the calm surface of a gravel lake, its giant excavator rising like the gantries at Cape Canaveral.

Water surrounded Shepperton – the river, the gravel lakes and the reservoirs of the metropolitan water board whose high embankments formed the horizon of our lives. Once I told Miriam that we were living on the floor of a marine world that had invaded our minds, and that the people of Shepperton were a new form of aquatic mammal, creatures of a new *Water Babies*.

'You're Tom, the poor sweep,' she told me, as if placing me for the first time. 'Poor Tom . . .'

'And who are you – Mrs Do-as-you-would-be-done-by?'

'I don't think so, somehow. More like Mrs Do-as-you-would-like-to-do-with . . .'

But we were all water babies. Alice was shrieking at the green slime that Henry flicked with a stick from the stream. I showed them a dead water-beetle, but they were more interested in an aerosol paint-can that floated between the reeds. It still held some of its propellent gas, and Henry fired a burst of spray at a dragon-fly that veered too close.

Trying to repaint the air, we moved through the willows to the water-splash that crossed the road. The water ran clear over the worn pebbles, but cars taking a short cut to Shepperton often stalled there. The exasperated drivers would look up to find a beaming audience of mothers and their children curious to see what they would do next. It

123

was here that the water-splash sequence from *Genevieve* had been filmed. Whenever Miriam and I watched the scene of the stranded antique car we could see ourselves, Henry and Alice out of shot as we leaned on the polished rail of the footbridge.

Led by the retriever, we set off along the upper arm of the stream, collecting more children on our way. The rectangular stages of Shepperton film studios rose above the trees. Their presence dominated the town as much as the marine world of the reservoirs. Many of the programmes we watched on television were filmed in the streets of Shepperton, and its leafy avenues stood in for locations all over England. In Henry's intense four-year-old mind, Shepperton had begun to colonise the whole country.

These confusions of image and illusion gave Shepperton its special charge, as if true reality rested in the merging of the two. Next door to us lived a married couple whose daughter was a minor television actress. Twice a week the children watched her appear in one of their favourite series, and sometimes would turn from the screen to see her in Charlton Road, stepping from her car on a family visit. Henry and Alice would rush out to greet her, taking for granted that her real character lay somewhere between her fleeting street-self and the far more solid broadcast figure on the screen. Many of our neighbours worked as extras in feature films made at Shepperton studios, and I sometimes felt that Miriam and I were playing our parts in some happily chaotic sitcom whose script we extemporised as we went along.

The children squatted on the edge of the gravel lake and stared at a submerged motor car resting on the sandy bed. The lake had been stocked by a local fishing club, and rainbow trout swam through the open windows. These drowned cars never failed to intrigue Alice and Henry.

'Henry, where's the car going?' Alice asked.

'Going a long way,' he told her. 'Going to China.'

Miriam had explained that a hole dug deep enough in our garden would emerge somewhere in China. The gravel pit was the largest lake that Henry had ever seen, and he often tried to convince me that it was this hole that went all the way to Shanghai. Once when I dived into the lake he watched me as if I were about to set off forever to the world of my childhood.

'Daddy, are you going to swim to China now?'

'Well, it's too far to swim before tea. Let's go to Magic World instead.'

I waited for Polly to round up the children and led them towards a screen of fir trees. Mattresses and rusting bicycles lay among the pine cones, and we followed the dark path to an enclosed meadow behind the film studios. The sunlight played by itself on the knee-deep grass, and the children ran ahead of me, their faces bobbing like lanterns.

Standing in the grass was a collection of stage props abandoned by the companies shooting television commercials. A candy bar the size of a small car lay in the sun, its papier-mâché wrapper peeling from the wooden frame. Beside it were a detergent pack my own height, its plywood sheeting warped by the rain and sun, and a fibreglass ketchup bottle painted in red enamel. Canvas peeled from the shampoo sachets and toothpaste tubes, but this never dismayed Alice and Henry. They ran squealing through the grass, fascinated as ever by the magnified versions of the objects that made up their domestic world.

Pride of place in their affections was taken by a ten-feet-high replica of a pink toilet roll. On earlier visits Henry had pulled back a flap of the rotting canvas, and through this small door the children crawled one by one. I could hear them shrieking with delight at this notion of a toilet roll large enough to live in. They waved their arms

125

through the canvas, shouting to Polly, who was frantically trying to nose his way into the dim interior.

'Let's have a party!' someone shouted.

'Party, party . . .' Alice was skipping inside the giant roll, eyes on her shiny shoes in case they vanished from her feet.

I lay back in the grass, thinking contentedly that there would soon be another child to dance in this enchanted meadow. I was glad that our third child would be born here, as much from the stream and the splash-meadow as from Miriam's womb. Her first labour, at the nearby maternity hospital, had been over before I returned home, expecting to be called the next day. Our huge son, solemn as any alderman, was asleep in his mother's arms when I reached the ward. But the infants were separated from their mothers for long periods of the day, bellowing together in their cribs behind a heavy door, and Miriam vowed to have her future children delivered at home, in our own bed.

So we conceived and slept beside the growing Alice as she came to term, and made love an hour before the labour began. Miriam lay back on her own pillows, hands grasping the headboard with its erratic reading light, surrounded by the wardrobe and her familiar clothes, her mother's photograph and her friends' flowers and greetings cards on the dressing-table. In this warm midden with its utter lack of hygiene she had swiftly given birth to Alice as I stood weeping behind the capable shoulders of Midwife Bell. That night we slept together with Alice in her cot beside us, as Polly the retriever nosed the dustbin, snuffling for the placenta in its parcel of newspaper. The next day Miriam was up to welcome her friends and see me off to work.

Not only was I glad that our child would be born in Shepperton, but I almost believed that I too had been born there. The past had slipped away, taking with it my

126

memories of Cambridge and Canada, of the dissecting room and the snow deserts of Saskatchewan, and even of Shanghai. The warm light over Shepperton reminded me of the illuminated air that I had seen over the empty paddy fields of Lunghua as I walked along the railway line, but the light that filled the splash-meadow came from a kinder and more gentle sun. The children Miriam had borne and the others who played by the stream had taken the place of the dead Chinese lying in the Lunghua creeks and canals.

For the first time I was living in an endless present that owed nothing to the past. The skies over Shepperton were crossed by airliners taking package tourists to the holiday beaches of Corfu and the Costa Brava. Soon the whole planet would be on vacation. At Cape Canaveral, the Americans were readying themselves to fly into space. On television we watched Richard Sutherland reporting from the space centre, the Florida sun gleaming through his blow-dried hair. He was now a presenter of popular science programmes, one of the new breed of media academics who taught the world to feel at ease with itself. His upbeat commentaries dovetailed perfectly with the commercials for candy bars and fabric conditioners. Past and future had been annexed into a present as depthless and cheerful as a child's colouring book.

I woke in the sleepy heat of the meadow grass, aware that the children were fighting inside the toilet roll. A light aircraft soared overhead, its propeller catching the sun. A single-engined Piper, it had flown from the west, where Fair Oaks airfield lay in the woodland beyond Chertsey. It turned in a wide circle above the studios, flaps lowered as if the pilot were trying to land in this secret meadow.

The children broke off their quarrel. Alice ran to me as I knelt in the grass and hid in my shoulder.

'Is that a bad plane, Daddy?'

As always, I was surprised by her shrewdness. She had

127

seen me frowning at the aircraft and its camera pylon mounted behind the passenger door.

'No, it's a good plane – it might bring you a present.'

Henry sat against my knee, pushing Alice's hand from my chin. 'Daddy, has it got a bomb?'

'A bomb? Who would want to bomb Shepperton?'

'Uncle David might. He has a bomb, Daddy. He told me.'

'Not any more. Besides, he's much too fond of you and Mummy. Home, everybody . . .'

David Hunter came to see us that afternoon. He had left the RAF at the end of his short-service commission, after active service against the terrorists in Kenya and a last tour flying the Vulcan nuclear bomber. 'Think, Miriam,' he liked to remind her, 'if that Turk hadn't defected to the Russians, your husband and I could have dropped the first hydrogen bomb on Moscow. How does it feel to be married to a man who might have started World War 3?'

His scatty charm still protected him, but he had the edginess of a man who expected the past to come up behind him and tap him on the shoulder with some absurd but nagging inquiry. For a year he had drifted along the fringes of private aviation, and then bought a small company specialising in aerial photography. He would be away for months, photographing industrial complexes in Brazil or hotel developments in the Seychelles. For the past week he had been based at Fair Oaks, making a cine-film of the pre-war Brooklands motor-racing circuit.

As rootless as ever, he never ceased to be amazed by my quiet domesticity, suspecting that I had repressed a large part of my true nature. Aware that Miriam felt uneasy at any talk of Shanghai, he rarely referred to our war years together.

He arrived with presents for the children, a bottle of whisky for me which he promptly opened and began to drink, flowers for Miriam and lavish compliments she was too delighted to resist.

'Why are pregnant women so erotic? Tell me, Miriam. In my bones I know we'll get married one of these days.'

'There's a queue forming,' Miriam warned him. 'Richard Sutherland, Henry, Jim . . . You'll have to fight your way down the aisle.'

'God, woman, I'm kneeling by the altar.' He placed his hands on Miriam's smock. 'It must be due any moment – if it comes this afternoon, can I watch?'

'Only if you can prove that you're the father.' Miriam loved his attentions, as she loved those of other men, revived by their compliments far more than by mine. She had always been a flirt, but five years of marriage and children made the lightest flirtation seem a serious business. To a mother of two children, sex was all or nothing. I knew that sometimes she longed to get away, to live on her desert island with three strange men – though with husband and children tucked into a decent pension in the next bay – and that she encouraged my writing as a way of being adventurous by proxy. I dimly guessed that one day she would have affairs and this second childhood would be over. I had learned that a woman could love her husband and children but still feel restless enough to want to leave them.

As we stumbled around the broken toys in the garden, David came to the point.

'I'm off to Hong Kong at the end of the month. All expenses paid. We're filming a housing project in Kowloon for a Chinese developer.'

'What a plum. There are lots of old Shanghai hands you can look up.'

'I'll avoid them. I want to go up to Shanghai itself.'

'Think of me as you stroll down the Bund.'

'As it happens, I wondered if you'd like to come?'

129

'To Hong Kong?'

'Shanghai, mostly. You could take a month's leave. We need to go back and see the place for ourselves.'

'David, I can't. Even if I wanted to, there are Miriam and the baby. You'll find someone in Hong Kong.'

'No, thanks. Those old Shanghai hands, and all that talk of tiffin and mah-jong and how many servants they had – nothing to do with what really happened. That's why you and I should go.'

'Nothing did happen.'

'For a start, Jim, we happened. That railway station you were always talking about in Moose Jaw. We ought to find it for you.'

'That was a killing. Sad for the Chinese, but it meant nothing.'

'You used to say he was trying to tell you something. You need to get away from this – it's potty botty doo-doo all the day . . .'

'David, it's the only time I've been happy.'

'But you shouldn't be too happy, Jim.'

After David had gone I mentioned his offer to Miriam.

'David's a fool!' She thumped her saucepan on to the kitchen table, where the children had set up a miniature replica of their Magic World. 'You haven't flown for years. He'd have you killed the first time you tried to take off.'

'He doesn't want me to fly. He needs me to go to Shanghai with him, walk the streets where we played hide-and-seek. Sometimes I think he's still playing there by himself. He's like those old Shanghai hands he hates so much.'

Miriam knew that I had no intention of going, but held my shoulders reassuringly. 'Dear, forget about it – you've put all that behind you.'

'One day I might write about the war – it would help to have been there.'

'It won't. If you don't go back anything you write will be far more true. When I visit Mother and Dad in

Cambridge I look around the house and can't believe I was ever a child there. It's like a film set with these two old actors . . . even they can't remember the script.'

Later, in bed, when the children were asleep and the old retriever had barked at the moon for the last time, I massaged Miriam's tired shoulders. Strange scents hovered over her ears and armpits, quickening odours of hormones rising and falling, overrunning each other's cycles. I touched her tender nipples, damp with some secretion I remembered from her earlier confinements.

'Tasty?' Miriam asked, finishing the glass of wine that helped her to sleep.

I touched my fingers to my lips, savouring the racy flavours, closer to the taste of her vulva than to the milk massing within her breasts.

'Colostrum . . . in fact, men don't like the taste of their wives' milk.'

'Good news for baby. Nature's way of making sure he gets his share. Have you tried anyone else's milk?'

'No . . .' I thought of the pregnant whore at Moose Jaw who had wanted to meet the queen. 'Ask your friends at the clinic for a sample.'

'Midwife Bell would love that.'

'Tell her we're going into the dairy business. Mother's Pride Milk Products. Slogan: "Putting Shepperton's breasts to work."'

'"Butter freshly churned from mother's milk." Oh, my God, yoghurts and milk-shakes. Jim, think . . .'

'We'd have a range of cheeses, flavoured by cigarette brand, lipstick and toothpaste . . .'

'Policemen's wives would give a sturdy goat-like cheese.' Miriam loved her flights of fantasy, and had a healthy interest in the more wayward possibilities of human anatomy and physiology; she had always seen the mischief and humour in the surrealists. Shepperton bored

131

her a little, and she liked to provoke its domestic norms. As the secretion from her nipples moistened my hands she extemporised happily: 'Vegetarians would make bland and mimsy cheeses, West End actresses over-ripe Camembert, queens and princesses a high royal Stilton . . .'

'We'll stage a cheese-tasting for all our friends . . .'

'I can just see Peggy Gardner!' Miriam sat up, smothering her laughter in her pillow, abdomen heaving, the baby riding a roller-coaster of snorts and guffaws.

Fifteen minutes later her labour began.

'We'll make you tidy, dear. We want baby to find a nice bedroom.'

Midwife Bell moved expertly around the room, stirring up the dust and old talc as she ran a damp towel over the dressing-table. She hung Miriam's maternity smocks in the wardrobe like a theatrical dresser stowing away unwanted costumes at the end of a season. Beneath the bed she found a one-legged teddy bear and a child's potty, ancient contents fossilised in place, and handed them to me with a refined grimace. She had arrived after midnight, soon after Miriam had finished her bath, but insisted on shaving and bed-washing her again. She changed the sheets as Miriam lay on the bed, employing a series of complex folds like a conjuror demonstrating a trick of large-scale origami.

Now that mother and bedroom met with Midwife Bell's satisfaction, the child could be born. On the bedside table were her instrument case, gloves and gas cylinder, everything except the legendary hot water, not a drop of which had I ever been asked to boil.

Disturbed by the noise, Alice had begun to cry in her sleep. Henry woke and shouted at her, rocking his cot against the wall. Miriam lay quietly, her large eyes on Mrs Bell's composed face, waiting for her next contraction. I went off to settle the children, played a small word-game with Alice that she enjoyed and then handed Henry his comforter, an ancient baby blanket that was a universe of friendly smells.

By the time I returned to the bedroom Miriam's contractions were coming every other minute. Nightdress rolled back to her breasts, she filled her lungs with deep, measured breaths as Mrs Bell sat beside her, listening to the child's heartbeat with her stethoscope.

'You can hold your wife's hand – I know she'd like that . . .'

I pressed Miriam's fingers. She smiled briefly, but I could see that she had already withdrawn from me. Only the midwife and the child were properly in the room with her. She moistened her lips, staring at the shadowy ceiling and the frayed lampshade on the headboard, as if this was the only delivery that had ever taken place, the primeval birth from which all life had sprung. As Miriam released my hand I felt that she and Midwife Bell had returned to a more primitive world, where men never intruded and even their role in conception was unknown. Here the chain of life was mother to daughter, daughter to mother. Fathers and sons belonged in the shadows with the dogs and livestock, like the retriever growling at Midwife Bell's unfamiliar car from the window of my neighbours' living room.

Nonetheless, I was glad that Miriam had overruled Mrs Bell and insisted that I be with her during the delivery. Richard Sutherland, for all his sense of the modish, had squeamishly declined to be present when Miriam half-jokingly invited him to watch the birth. He claimed that the ordeal of a woman in the *extremis* of labour, exposing her genitalia and gasping with pain, unconsciously mimicked the act of rape and diminished the wife in her husband's eyes, as if he had witnessed her assault by an invisible stranger. Not for nothing did the world's oldest

133

cultures segregate women during confinement, preserving the mystery of the wife's body.

By contrast, I felt my closest to Miriam during these last minutes. Everything bonded me to her: the sweat on her thighs, the mole above her navel, her freckles and pearly stretchmarks, the shaved skin of her pubis and the bright petals of her labia, her engorged clitoris with its endearing leftward tilt, the childhood riding scars on her knees and the spots on her bottom, the damp talc gleaming on her breasts and shoulders.

She farted lustily, and reached up to grip the headboard. Midwife Bell averted her nose, but the air was heavy with the smell of anaesthetic gas.

'We'll be waking the whole street if we go on like that. Push again now, dear. Baby's ready. Push harder . . .'

Miriam frowned at the headboard, concentrating as she waited for the next contraction. Panting, she clenched her fists.

'God Jesus! My piles are killing me . . . !'

I knelt down and placed my hand between her buttocks, pressing my fingers against her swollen anus. The bloated lining of her rectum ballooned outwards, and I pushed the spongy cushion into her anus, then held it there as the last contractions came.

'One last push, it's coming now, another push for the head . . .'

Miriam's vulva had expanded and the crown of a minute head had appeared between her legs. The black hairs were moist and neatly parted, as if a thoughtful nature had groomed the child for its first appearance in this world.

'Push now, we're almost there . . .'

The whole face had emerged, a high forehead, miniature nose and mouth, and closed eyes, streamlined as if by time, by the aeons that had preceded this child down the biological kingdom. Waking into the deep dream of life, it seemed not young but infinitely old, millions of years entrained in the pharaoh-like smoothness of its cheeks and its ancient eyelids and nostrils. Its lips were composed, as if it had patiently endured the immense journey across the universe to this modest house with its waiting mother.

Suddenly it was young again; in a last rush of fluid a pink and hairless puppy bundled itself into Midwife Bell's arms. As the tears wept from my eyes I felt Miriam's fingers grip my hands. The dawn light was filling the spaces between my neighbours' roofs. After a few hours away from me, Miriam had returned and was a wife again.

Miriam slept during the morning, the baby girl in the wicker-work cot beside her. At noon Midwife Bell called, bathed the baby and pronounced herself satisfied, as if willing to accept the formal entry of our child into the mundane world of time and space. Before leaving, she handed Miriam her make-up case, hair brush and mirror. Midwives sat close to the fire, busy with their washings and breaking of the waters, drawing life into the light. By contrast Miriam's local physician, Dr Rogers, with his jovial humour and misplaced advice, resembled a light-headed tour guide searching none too confidently for the sacred spring.

Alice and Henry crept into the bedroom and inspected the baby, curious but faintly disapproving.

'Will she stay with us?' Alice asked.

Miriam laughed at this. 'Don't you want her to stay?'

'I might . . .'

Henry was more interested in the remnants of the midwife's equipment, the foil caps, spare swabs and mouthpiece. Miriam sat up and hugged them tightly. Later I drove them to spend the afternoon with local friends of Miriam, and they were already planning games and initiation ceremonies for their new sister. Seen through my sleepless eyes, Shepperton had changed. The air was more vivid, as if the town was being lit for some large-budget production at the film studios. The women sitting under the driers at the hairdressers, the cashiers behind the counter at the bank, resembled extras recruited to play the roles of ordinary suburbanites. At any moment the action would begin, and I would find that I had a walk-on part and lines of dialogue I had forgotten to learn.

When I returned home Miriam called to me from the bedroom. She had put on a fresh nightdress, combed her hair, and rouged and powdered her face. The slash of lipstick on her mouth was a pennant flying proudly above the debris of this quiet room.

I looked down at the baby. She had changed yet again, more puckered and more alive, her lips moving while she slept, as if she were trying to remember a message entrusted to her by the unseen powers of creation. Within a few hours she had recapitulated her roles, from archaic messenger to slippery water sprite baptised in her mother's caul, and then a dreamy swaddling whose skin flinched at the light and air.

'Lucy?' I suggested.

'Yes . . . Lucy.' Miriam beckoned me to the bed. 'You must be exhausted. Come and lie down for an hour.'

I undressed and lay beside her, my hand against her shoulder. The faint, smothering odour of anaesthetic gas clung to the pillows, and I felt myself drifting back into the heady night from which Lucy had emerged.

'Hold me . . .' Miriam pressed my hands to her waist. She lowered the neck of her nightdress and exposed her breasts, their swollen nipples already quickened by the baby's lips. She pushed back the sheet and drew the nightdress to her hips, reached down and held my penis in her hand. Knees in the air, she smiled as I massaged her feet and calves, and caressed her thighs.

'Come into me . . .'

Lying on my side, I gently entered her vagina. Already

136

its walls had contracted, and it held me in a firm embrace.

Lucy stirred, her larynx clicking. Miriam smiled at her, her hands on my shoulders as I moved softly within her. Life-magic breathed over us, over the sleeping child, over everything in the sunlit town.

CHAPTER SEVEN

The Island

I was swimming strongly, four hundred yards from the beach at Santa Margarita, when I saw the Estartit ferry steering towards me. Loaded with holiday-makers on their way to Cadaques and the Dali mansion at Port Lligat, it cut through the dark water where the Bay of Rosas met the open sea. Bolts of foam jumped from its bows and swept the passenger rail, cooling the legs of the German and Scandinavian girls gazing through their sunglasses at the lizard-backed hills.

A yacht passed me, its main-sail only inches from the water. A middle-aged French couple sat on the side-decking in their yellow life-jackets, watching me in a sceptical way. A pedalo driven by two teenage boys was as far from the beach, but I was well beyond the limit of most holiday swimmers. I had set out to swim across the bay from Santa Margarita, little more than a mile in all, but the French pair clearly took for granted that I was not going to make it.

Ignoring them, I swam on through the black, sunlit water, now and then glancing at the balcony of our apartment. After breakfast I had announced my decision to challenge the bay, and the children had been seized by the vastness of the project.

'Daddy, that's at least . . . seventeen lengths!' Alice cried, thinking of the public swimming pool near Shepperton.

'More like a hundred,' I told her. 'Or two hundred, if I swim back.'

'Two hundred! Daddy, you're making up fibs again . . .'

An impromptu arithmetic lesson followed, one of the

few in which they had ever taken an interest. They watched me walk into the water, convinced that their father would never return. I could see them on the beach below the apartment, sitting in a row on the rubber inflatable, arguing over my exact position. I waved to them, and saw Miriam, in sun hat and black bikini, wave back, then a semaphore of little arms. My heroic status was guaranteed at least until tea-time.

I pressed on towards the cape, carried to the west by the strong counter-clockwise current that circled the bay. The Estartit ferry was less than a hundred yards away, turning towards the quay at Rosas where it would collect its last batch of sightseers. The helmsman stood behind the open windows of the bridgehouse, surveying the pedalo-filled waters like a hunter at a turkey-shoot. He noticed me trailing my small wake, and then altered course straight towards me.

Was he drunk? I waited for him to spin his wheel, but the bars of his moustache were fixed on me like the arms of a range-finder. The ferry captains of the Costa Brava had been deranged by the endless tourists, like the waiters and taxi-drivers, hovering all summer on the edge of a mental explosion. An isolated swimmer impaled on his bows would be no more than a butterfly on a windshield. The ferry sped towards me, the dull murmur of its propeller carried through the water. Switching to my fastest crawl, I swam at right angles to the vessel's path. Passengers were leaning on the forward rail, waving to me as if I were determined to kill myself.

The ferry passed within a dozen feet, a clamour of engine noise and clinking beer bottles, its wash sending a cloud of diesel fumes into my face. Exhausted, I lay in the rocking wake. The beach was six hundred yards away, and a row of unfamiliar hotels faced me across the water. Our apartment house had moved along the bay, and Miriam and the children were lost behind the lines of umbrellas and beached pedalos. The current had carried me beyond the concrete mole that marked the end of the Santa Margarita beach. Already I could see the undeveloped shoreline of Ampuriabrava, an area of grass-covered dunes, creeks and mosquito inlets.

Giving up any hope of swimming across the bay, I rested on the current, and began the long swim to the empty beach. The concrete mole cut off my sight of Santa Margarita, and I wondered if Miriam had seen me apparently disappear under the ferry's lethal bows.

Twenty minutes later, when I reached the beach, I was too tired even to crawl. I lay in the shallow water, my hands resting on the corrugated sand, my face nudged by the curious waves. A speedboat swept past, two men towing a 15-year-old girl on water-skis. They soared away, leaving behind a blare of pop music.

Untouched by the feet of holiday-makers, the white sand was like fluffed sugar. I stepped out of the water and sank into its soft quilt. I had nearly been chopped into bloody fillets under the critical gaze of hundreds of tourists clutching their Dali guide-books. Somewhere beyond the mole there was the sound of the inflatable's outboard. Miriam had seen me, and was speeding towards the shore.

She expertly beached the craft as Henry jumped onto the sand.

'Are you all right?' Miriam knelt beside me. 'What are you doing here? I'm married to a madman.'

Henry scowled at me. 'Is he dead?'

'He's pretending awfully hard.'

'Being dead must feel like this.' I sat up, glad to see the sun. 'It was like trying to cross the Styx – a ferryman almost ran me down.'

'What a nerve! We'll report him to the Guardia Civil.'

'They're probably in league.'

'How many lengths did you swim?' Henry asked.

'About a thousand.' I leaned against Miriam, resting

my chafed chin against her sea-cool shoulder. 'What about Alice and Lucy?'

'They're with the Nordlunds – they spotted you from their balcony. Henry, we'll get Daddy back to the boat.'

'Hold on – let's explore a little. This is some sort of island.'

'A real desert island, Daddy? With cannibals?'

'Definitely cannibals . . .'

We had come ashore on a long sandbar, separated from the dunes of Ampuriabrava by an arm of shallow water. Some fifty yards wide, the sandbar followed the curve of the bay, rising in a series of grass-covered hillocks. As we walked along the firmer ground we passed the remains of a rusting shack. Wine bottles, an old portable radio and a bicycle wheel lay half-buried in the sand beside this terminal hut. In the hollows between the dunes small fires had been lit during the winter. Across the inlet the scrubland of creeks and inlets extended as far as the Figueras road, but already property developers' signs stood by their marker posts, announcing a new resort complex of hotels, marinas and apartment houses.

As we strolled along, my arm around Miriam's waist, Henry rushed back to us through the long grass.

'There's a Wendy house! It's got a door and windows – and guess what? A real toilet!'

'A Wendy house with a toilet.' Miriam took his hand. 'Are you sure?'

'Yes – I used it!'

At the western end of the island the dunes rose twenty feet above the beach. An old sea-wall had collapsed into the inlet, and the stones had been carried ashore. Standing on a makeshift patio was an ornately gabled cabin that had once been an Edwardian bathing machine, and had probably served for years as a chicken coop in some Rosas back garden. A tattered parachute canopy hung from a trellis of wooden poles and formed a shaded verandah.

141

I pushed back the cabin door and glanced at the interior. There was a rudimentary kitchen with a stone sink, bottled gas cooker and chemical toilet. Sand covered the wooden floor, blown through the weather-boarding.

Miriam lay back in a wicker chair below the canopy, while Henry and I set out to explore the dunes. We found burnt-out fireworks, beer cans and even, mysteriously, an old portable typewriter. When I carried it back to the patio Miriam nodded approvingly.

I sat beside her and blew through the sandy keys. 'Well, I guess I'm ready to start work. It's not quite the Villa Mauresque, but so what . . .'

'Good for you.' Miriam closed her eyes, listening to the waves. 'It's lovely here – who owns all this stuff?'

'Local beatniks? Nothing's locked and everything's broken.'

'That sounds more like Shepperton. I always thought we were Shepperton's beatniks without realising it.'

'We still are.' I rested my feet on the typewriter, all notions of work already forgotten. 'I hate to mention it, but the apartment is going to cost us a fortune in dilapidations.'

'I'll talk to Señor Robles. He'll understand.'

'So you always say. This time, put on your best show.'

'I will – I think he likes looking at my breasts.'

'It's his sinister little secretary you'll have to talk to. I hope she likes your breasts.'

'Maybe she does . . .' Miriam began to rub ointment into my blistered shoulders, her eyes turning towards Santa Margarita. Recently she had become intrigued by the admiring glances of other women. The admiration of her own sex existed on a higher and more intense plane than anything men could offer, like the romantic rivalries of sisters. Together, women formed a conspiracy of glances entirely exchanged behind the backs of their menfolk.

'We'll bring the girls tomorrow,' Miriam said. 'I want them to see this – it's like something straight out of television.'

'Miriam? What a thing to say . . .'

'Tell me, why don't we get our own place here? You've always said you wanted to live in Spain.'

'We will, one day.'

'Hemingway, Gaudi, Bunuel . . . you could work here, they're more your world.' Miriam turned my face towards her and pressed a finger between my eyes. 'Face it, dear, you're never going to feel at home in England.'

'Is that true? I feel at home in Shepperton.'

'Not even in Shepperton. You've been in England for eighteen years and you still look as if you've stepped off the wrong train.'

'Perhaps I need to go back to Shanghai. I should have taken up David's offer.'

'No, not Shanghai. You've finished with all that, thank God. Spain might give you just the jolt you're waiting for.'

'Am I waiting for a jolt?'

'Yes – like a rabbit in a Skinner box. You're getting bored with that one damned lever. Look how you come alive at those third-rate bull-fights in Figueras.'

'That's tourist Spain. What about schools?'

'They have schools here. The Spanish may be mad, but they're literate. Think about your parents – they went out to China.'

'But they took a piece of Surrey with them. Spain would be a much bigger challenge. For you, anyway.'

'Balls. We've got to get you out of England . . . you've found a small strangeness where you're comfortable, and that's dangerous. Anyway, Dali's here at Port Lligat. We might meet him.'

'And the mysterious Gala, his weird.'

Miriam bent down as if to kiss me, and bit my ear. She held a speck of blood on the tip of her tongue, and left it

143

between my lips. 'Jim, you need to meet more weird women. A tussle with Señor Robles's secretary would do you a world of good. I might even arrange it.'

'I wouldn't know what to do.'

'Dear, you would do nothing – she'd quietly take your brain apart like a neurosurgeon. Poor love, I'll protect you . . .'

She pulled my head on to her lap, with its scents of sea-salt, baby lotion and perfume borrowed from Mrs Nordlund. We watched Henry wading in the water beside the sea-wall. He lifted a stone and carried it across the patio, where the first flight of a simple staircase had been laid. He smoothed out a new shelf and carefully laid the stone, then surveyed his work with a child's pride.

'I'm coming, Henry!' Miriam pushed me aside and leapt up. She waded into the water and began to help Henry with the stones. I lay back under the awning, watching her assemble this modest stairway that in her mind already led to a new life. Eight years of marriage and three children had failed to dent her enthusiasms. From our earliest days she had always pushed me along, giving up holidays so that I could finish a book, taking the children to London Zoo to allow me a few hours of peace. Her confidence in me had never wavered, even during the time of endless rejection slips. She hid bank statements, quietly borrowed money from her mother and Dick Sutherland. In many ways she had remade me. I owed her everything, my children, my first published books, my refound confidence in the world.

But change would soon come, and I wondered if I was equal to it. She had taken part in the Shepperton Players' open-air performance of *As You Like It*, playing a spirited Rosalind like a feminist agitator. Already she talked of going back to her career in journalism. Watching her move impatiently around her kitchen, bored with the endless meals, I could see the mature and strong-willed woman in her forties that she would become. In a sense she would leave me far behind her, a problematical Peter Pan whose pockets were filled with a strange yellow earth . . .

For the moment she had set her heart on Spain. I guessed that Señor Robles had already shown her one of his villas in the hills above Rosas and Cadaques. The Dalis might prove to be more demanding neighbours than Miriam realised, but I was happy to see her revelling in the attentive gaze of the melancholy Spaniards as she strode around the supermarkets of Rosas in her black bikini. An economy of pleasure and possibility was about to rule our lives.

A new Europe had sprung up along the beaches of the Mediterranean, in effect a linear city 3000 miles long and 300 metres deep, that stretched from Gibraltar to Glyfada Beach beyond the eastern suburbs of Athens. The old Europe had shed its past, its hierarchies and snobberies. Here in this classless realm Lancashire typists shared bar tables with Stockholm accountants and Danish truck-drivers. The beaches of Spain were Europe's California, or at least its Florida. I liked its marina culture, its endless highways and apartment houses. This was the future that President Kennedy and the space race had helped to create, a residential zone laid down in advance for the science parks and high-technology projects yet to come.

In many ways there was something almost lunar about the white hotels, haunted by criminals running hash from north Africa, stealing antiquities or on the run from Scotland Yard. After the sombre light of northern Europe, the peculiar geometry of these overlit apartments seemed to lead us into a more abstract world where emotions were leached away. Even sex became more stylised. In the afternoons, while the children slept through the heat, Miriam and I would drink white wine in the kitchen. When she was pleasantly drunk, she liked to make love in the bathroom, taking up her positions against the mirrors and white enamel like a perverse gymnast. She watched me without expression, as if we were having sex in a space capsule hundreds of miles above the earth, conceiving the first of a new race of astronauts.

After a year on the Costa Brava we would be totally decorticated, with that blankness of mind I could see in the faces of package tourists after only a week. Before leaving England we had seen Hitchcock's *Psycho*, and the English secretaries in their bikinis behaved like so many Janet Leighs who had decided not to take that crucial shower but could no longer remember where they had left their lives.

'Jim, stir a leg!' Miriam called to me, arms covered with wet sand. 'While we're slaving away he's lying there like a pasha. Tomorrow we'll bring the dinghy here – the girls are going to be really impressed . . .'

Building this simple flight of steps was Miriam's touching way of showing that she was serious about settling in Spain. Every morning the five of us set off in the inflatable, taking with us a picnic for the day. As I repaired the awning, stitching the ragged parachute silk, Miriam and the children cleared out the cabin and swept the patio. In the afternoon, after cold chicken and sangria, we dozed in the shade or swam with the children from the stone steps. The water-skiers sped across the bay, portable radios gleamed on the beach at Santa Margarita, and the mad ferryman aimed his bows at any passing swimmer.

A week later, when we landed on the island, new arrivals had occupied our beach hideaway. A small Citroën loaded with suitcases and camping gear had crossed the shallow water of the inlet and was parked on the sand. A bearded man and a young woman with a black shingle were swimming from Miriam's jetty, watched by a tall, naked man

146

in his forties with shoulder-length hair, a book in one hand and a pipe in the other.

Uncertain, the children stopped by the car. Henry pointed to the sticker pasted to the rear fender above the French licence plate: 'Happiness is overtaking a 2CV'.

'What's a 2CV?'

'A kind of car – let's say hello.'

'Why is happiness overtaking it?'

Alice peered through her fringe and took Miriam's hand. 'Are they the cannibals? Is Daddy going to fight them?'

'Of course not. It's probably their house.'

The car was packed with bottles of Spanish wine, loaves of bread, and a clutch of paperbacks by Kerouac, Henry Miller, Ginsberg and William Burroughs. Lashed incongruously to the roof rack was an expensive pigskin suitcase covered with the labels of New York and Chicago hotels. Had they stolen the case from some distracted traveller at Perpignan station? As the naked man waved his pipe at the children I was visualising a new breed of beach criminal, reading *On the Road* or *Howl* as he slid the tourist's purse from her handbag.

The bearded man in the water was calling in French to the children. The door of the bathing machine opened and a blonde-haired young woman with an ivory-white skin came out to greet us. She wore high-heeled beach shoes and the bottom of a cream bikini. Her face had a look of slightly shop-soiled elegance, as if she had neglected herself for too long in some intimate way. When she smiled the sunlight shone against a set of immaculate American teeth, from which the left canine was missing, bridged by an inferior piece of English dentistry. But she had a rangy manner that I immediately liked.

'Hello . . . I thought some little pixies had been cleaning the kitchen.' She swept Lucy into her arms and held the startled girl to her shoulder. 'Are you a pixie?'

147

'No! Mummy . . . !'

'I think you are. You've been scrubbing and dusting and polishing . . .'

She chattered on in a pleasant New England voice as the pipe-smoker ambled up to us. The children stared at him open-mouthed, even more intrigued by the star-shaped scars across his abdomen and thigh than they were by his penis and scrotum. I guessed that he had been badly wounded during the war.

Seeing that we were English, he introduced himself: 'Peter Lykiard. You're from London? Good. I teach at Regent Street Poly.' He pointed to the couple in the water. 'Robert and Muriel Joubert, from Nanterre. And this is Sally Mumford, one of my American students. She's probably going to steal your children.'

'I'm definitely thinking about it.' The young woman lowered Lucy to the ground and welcomed us into the shade. With a cheerful flourish she produced a jug of sangria, tapas and cigarettes. The French couple sunned themselves on the patio, their naked bodies inspected by the children with the measured eyes of experienced anthropologists. They had seen Miriam and me naked every day of their lives, but a different anatomy, however small the distinctions, held a universe of intriguing possibilities.

Sharing our hamper and wine cooler with this amiable crew, we sat drinking under the parachute canopy as Lykiard explained that he came down to Ampuriabrava every summer – though this, sadly, would be the last. The property developers' bulldozers would soon level the site.

'This island will vanish, literally turn into cement. They'll up-end the beach into half a mile of hotels and apartment houses.' He pointed to the pine posts like so many gibbets which the surveyors had staked into the dunes. 'There's a model of the whole complex in Gerona. They plan to consolidate the waterways with promenades of boutiques and bars, then sell off the housing plots to

148

all those Dusseldorf dentists. Three years from now the place will be a film set, with a series of mock-antique Catalonian villages along the speed-boat canals.'

'Miriam wants us to settle here – she thinks it would be good for my imagination.'

'I can't see that there'd be anything left for your imagination to do. In fact, it's hard to visualise the lifestyles of these sober-sided Rhinelanders once they've set up their beach-head. When bourgeois life meets surrealism head on we know who wins.'

Children's squeals came from the beach, where Henry's sandcastle was holding out against the ferry-boat's bow-waves. Sally was on her hands and knees, constructing an elaborate double bed of damp sand with bolsters and eiderdown, under which she tucked a delighted Lucy and Alice. I dozed while Miriam helped Lykiard and the Jouberts to unload the car. Lykiard worked in his unhurried way, pausing to refill his pipe and read a page or two of the books packed below the seats. Watching him put a friendly hand on Miriam's waist, I realised how bourgeois we had become, with our rented flat, estate car and loyal inflatable bounding behind us on its trailer. Even our attempt to clean the bathing hut had shown the same bijouising suburban strain. I had always smiled at my parents for taking an intact piece of Surrey with them to Shanghai, but Miriam and I were in the same export business. The real trapeze artists and dare-devils on the scene were the Dusseldorf dentists.

At dusk the first marijuana smoke began to overlay the warm air, pricking at the children's nostrils. Sorry to leave, we gathered our things together and piled them into the inflatable.

'Bye-bye, pixies, come again tomorrow,' Sally told the children as they sat in their life jackets. 'We'll do some more cleaning. We've got to dust and polish the whole beach – just look at this untidy sand . . .'

Miriam winced, but I warmed to this excitable American girl. She waded out into the water, the smoke from her loose-packed cigarette sending its scent into the evening. Holding it aloft in one hand, she tugged at the inflatable with the other. As we motored away I could see her generous, ironic smile following us across the waves.

'God, I feel so square,' Miriam told me as she gazed around our apartment, pastis in hand. '"Do some more cleaning" – that was a dig at me.'

'In a friendly way.'

'Am I square?'

'My depraved and respectable wife?' I pressed her reassuringly against the refrigerator. 'Miriam, the Jouberts work at a left-wing lycée, and he teaches modern literature at a fashionable polytechnic. They drive a 2CV and smoke pot. What could be more square than that?'

'You're avoiding the point.' Miriam finished off the pastis and stared at the sand-bar beyond the mole, a pale smudge along the shore of Ampuriabrava. The blazing driftwood fire we had left behind was a faint ember. 'Let's buy some pot.'

'Okay – I know you're dying to be arrested by those handsome Spanish cops. Remember, Lykiard and his chums don't have children.'

'That amazes me – they look as if they're at it hard enough. Do you think they sleep with each other?'

'Who cares? They're probably all celibate.'

'In a way, I care . . .' Miriam nodded briskly to herself, mind already set on an urgent recovery project, the retrieval of those possibilities that marriage and motherhood had consigned to some cul de sac. I often caught her staring at herself in the bathroom mirror, as if she sensed that her entire life, her husband and children, were a detour from the main road.

Every morning we returned to the island, leaving the

crowded beach at Santa Margarita with its haze of sun-oil and deodorant that formed an almost visible micro-climate. We berthed the inflatable on the sand below the headland, and joined the others under the tattered para-chute awning. In the afternoon the French couple, keen bird-watchers, put on their saris and prowled the creeks and dunes of Ampuriabrava, sketch-pads and camera at the ready. Sally swam with Henry and the girls, while Miriam helped Lykiard to extend the patio, carrying stones from the sea-wall.

Watching Sally, I was surprised by her unforced pleas-ure in the children. She was forever down on her knees with them, devising games and conspiracies, mysterious errands that sent them darting off into the sand-grass. Miriam told me that her father was the owner of a Boston department store, and that she had achieved the distinc-tion, rare for a rich man's daughter, of being expelled from both her private school and exclusive women's col-lege. She had set off for the Mediterranean, crewing the yachts of her father's friends, and had come to England to meet the Beatles. Self-consciously a free spirit, she seemed deliberately to neglect herself, living on nothing but tapas, sangria and pot. I sensed that in some way she wanted to revenge herself on her own body.

Miriam also told me, in her most casual voice, that Sally slept with both Lykiard and Joubert, a piece of infor-mation that she swallowed whole and was digesting at her leisure. But it was only when we drove to Barcelona to see Cordobés and Paco Camino that she recognised the raw edge of Sally's mind and her uncertain grip on the world.

Leaving Lucy and Alice in our apartment with the Jou-berts, the rest of us set off in our car. In honour of Cordobés, we sat in the primo barreras and bought thimbles of fundador to toast the Beatle of the bullring

151

who scandalised the traditionalists with his bizarre stunts and reckless bravery. Henry sat between Sally and myself, clutching a huge plastic bull with a penis and scrotum, Sally whispered to me, larger than his own.

One of the early bulls, disoriented by the jeers and shouts of the tourist crowd, jumped the barricade and ran past us, spraying us with his saliva, ragged horns inches from our hands. Henry clutched his model bull, awestruck by the inflamed eyes of this violent and terrified creature, but Sally sprang to her feet and slapped its dung-smeared haunches. She was wearing a pale silk dress, and her excited sweat stained the bodice and armpits. She gripped Henry's hand, whistling and shouting as she worked herself up, while the band blared and the crowd screamed at every pass of the cape. When the banderilleros savaged the bull's shoulders with their ribboned darts she rose to her feet with a strange throaty cry, like a mad-woman in an abattoir.

Embarrassed by herself, she fell quiet when a handsome torrera, in elegant black jacket and flared breeches, fought a bull on horseback in the Portuguese manner. A commanding, strong-nosed woman with the maquillage of a glamorous bank-manager, she glared threateningly at the audience and noticed Sally standing at the barrera. The two women gazed at each other across the noise and the smell of blood and the reek of fundador. Time and again the torrera was about to be caught by the veering bull, but always accelerated away as the horns brushed the flanks of her horse. During one stand-off, while the bull choked on its tongue, bathed in blood and rage, she sat ramrod straight in her saddle a dozen feet from us. Sally and I could hear the stream of obscenities, the insults to the bull's testicles and paternity, spitting from the mouth of this imposing horsewoman.

When she dismounted to kill the exhausted beast, she first fed saliva from her scarlet lips onto the tip of her sword, making plain that she was advancing on the bull as more than a mere man, and that her saliva was the semen with which she would impregnate the creature as she struck it dead at her feet.

Dazed by the fundador and the screams of the crowd, I was trying to visualise how one would even dare to approach this terrifying figure, let alone have sex with her. But Sally had already decided. Sweat soaking her armpits, she gripped the wooden rail, and stared at the horse-woman as if she recognised all the headmistresses of her New England childhood. I expected her to rip away her silk dress, leap the barricade and mount the horse with her white legs, arms clasping the torrera's waist as they galloped out of the arena.

While Cordobés was in the ring I forgot Sally, and mar-velled with Miriam and Lykiard at this handsome street-fighter, part gangster and part film-star. As Lykiard pointed out to us through the hoots and applause, however close the bull charged the boy never moved his feet. For all his theatrical strutting and open insults to the decorum of the bullring, he took immense risks with his own life. After exhausting his second bull he began to play the fool, humiliating the gasping beast that staggered towards him, drenched in blood. As it stood on its shaky forelegs, Cordobés knelt with his back to the bull, its horns only inches from his shoulder blades, arms outstretched to catch the approving roars of the arena, which the older Spaniards were already leaving in disgust.

When he retired from the ring, through the delirium of the European and American tourists, I saw Sally clam-bering between the seats, her dress half-torn from her back. An hour later we found her in the mêlée around the bullfighter's black Mercedes, her make-up bruised, being pushed about by the jeering chauffeurs and bodyguards. Lykiard and I carried her to my car, watched by a shocked little Henry who offered her his bull. When we lifted her into the back seat she struck at us with her hard fists, still gripped by her unsatisfied need for some kind of violent climax to the afternoon. Miriam managed to calm her, holding her hands and wiping the streaks of mascara from her chin. The two women sat side by side, like sisters returning from a deranged funeral.

In the traffic back to Gerona I watched the flush in Sally's cheeks fading through the rear-view mirror. She sat in her torn silk dress, a delinquent schoolgirl caressing the coarse hide of Henry's plastic bull, forcing her lips together as she swallowed the aftertaste of some toxic emotion.

'I like her American spunk,' Miriam decided when we returned to the apartment. 'She knows what she wants, and goes out and gets it. Of course, she's completely mad.'

'Maybe she's completely sane – for people like Sally that amounts to the same thing.'

'Jim, she wanted to fuck those bulls! Never mind Cordobés and the chauffeurs. I bet they caught her trying to cut off the testicles. What do they do with them, anyway?'

'They're some kind of delicacy. Why don't you try a pair? We'll find a good restaurant in Gerona.'

'I might . . .' Miriam stared in a determined way from the balcony. 'Sex is a branch of gastronomy – the best cooks make the best lovers. Every woman soon discovers that.'

I could see the 2CV trundling across the sand-dunes of Ampuriabrava. Sally was standing in the open roof behind Lykiard, the tatters of her silk dress floating like pennants between the poles of the property developers, an eager fury touring a field of gibbets.

Miriam put her arm around me. 'She's strange, but I like her. Do you wish you'd married someone like that?'

'I did.'

154

'I'd like to help her. She needs to have a child.'

'Only I can help her there.'

'You're going to be busy with Señor Robles's secretary, remember. Tomorrow could be tricky.'

I embraced Miriam, glad that Sally had charged her imagination. 'Dear, you always wanted to live on a desert island with three strange men.'

However, by the next day Sally's sunny humour had returned. She knelt on the sand by the bathing hut, straw horns tied to her head as Henry made passes with a beach towel. While Miriam fed Alice and Lucy, I took a handful of black olives and a bottle of beer, and walked into the scrub-covered dunes. I sat down in one of the hollows, trying to work out my route across the bay. Thinking of Cordobés and the maimed beasts waiting for the sword, I imagined a startled tourist on a pedalo crossing a wake stained with blood. Long after the ferry left for Cadaques, its waves rolled against the beach, as if Poseidon himself were reminding me of my close escape.

Smoking a cigarette, Sally climbed through the grass towards me. She still wore the straw horns around her white hair.

'Time for a rest.' She slumped down beside me. 'Jesus, I'm pooped. You and Miriam . . . there must be a knack.'

'Tell us if you find it – we've been exhausted since 1957.'

She sailed the straw horns into the air. 'They're wonderful, take it from me. Everything turns into a party. I wish my childhood had been so much fun.'

She spoke wistfully, and flicked at the hair blowing into her eyes, almost trying to set the loose ends alight with her cigarette. Endlessly patient with Henry, Alice and Lucy, she was short-tempered with her own body, as if it had failed like a thoughtless child to respond to the problems on its mother's mind. She had chewed her nails to the quick, and her left nipple was raw and tender. A faint chemical odour rose from the gusset of her bikini, a hint of stale spermicidal jelly, and I guessed that she had been too distracted to change her cap for a few days. She helped herself to an olive from my hand.

'Where's your apartment? I can't see it today.'

'Next to the hotel with the sign . . . if some developer hasn't moved it. We should have come straight here with a couple of tents.'

'It's great. I like Gozo best – Circe's island, I drank from her spring. And Ruanda. Last year I was going to live with the Watusi.' She patted the sand on her legs, as if readying herself for some husband painted in white dust. 'Miriam told me that you come from China.'

'Years ago. I've settled in England now.'

'Do you like it?'

'It takes getting used to.'

'That could be a good thing. Maybe you need to feel like a refugee.'

'What about you?'

She grimaced through the smoke, a gleam of American teeth. 'I keep waiting . . . there aren't too many stars in the east these days. Sometimes I think that everywhere is pretty much the same. Miriam says you want to buy some pot?'

'Only if you have any to spare. She feels we're getting too bourgeois.'

'It's good for sex . . .' Sally was lying on her side, her breast touching the bottle of beer in my hand. I could see the tender nipple magnified through the pale green glass. She passed her cigarette and watched as I took a draw on the loosely packed hemp and tobacco. The children were hidden behind the headland, Miriam was working on the patio, and the empty beach would give us all the warning we needed as we lay within the dune grass. Sally took another olive from my palm, her lips briefly sucking my thumb. She was waiting for me, but I felt curiously gauche, as if I were effectively a virgin with no experience of

156

women. During the eight years of our marriage I had been faithful to Miriam, and knew her body far more closely than I knew my own. Another woman's body was an unfathomed mystery, let alone another woman's emotions and needs.

'Well, back to the monsters.' Sally stood up, brushing the sand from her thighs. She smiled quickly, erasing the offer of herself without any resentment, and strode down to the beach.

I followed fifty yards behind her, pausing to wash the guilty sweat from my face. I was surprised to find that I was shaking with irritation at myself – I was loyal to Miriam, though a little less loyal than I had realised.

When I reached the cabin the Jouberts were stepping from their Citroën, loaves of bread in their arms, more tapas and cheap wine from the bodega. Lykiard was holding a biology class for the children, who stood in a line, gazing fixedly at the lizard in his hand as Sally pulled a face over his shoulder.

The bow wave of the Estartit ferry struck the beach. Miriam strode across the patio, about to rinse the swimsuits in the sea. She skipped down the steps, stumbled and missed her footing on the polished stones. Her right leg skewed sideways, and she fell heavily on the staircase.

The crack of her head against the stone made everyone turn. When I reached the steps she was lying half-stunned, eyes staring at my face as if she no longer recognised me. Her leg was twisted under her hips, blood running from a deep graze on the ankle.

Lykiard was beside me, warning the children away with the lizard, which he threw into the sea. I lifted Miriam onto her side, trying to feel the broken bone. Still stunned, she held on to my shoulder and sat up, her face small and pale, inhaling shallow breaths.

'My, that was a knock.' She spoke flatly. 'Silly fool, where was I going?'

'Love, are you all right? Your leg . . .'

'Hurts like hell. Don't worry, Lucy. Mummy was silly and fell over. God, my head – I shouldn't have laid all those steps . . .'

Sally and I helped her back to the patio and settled her in the wicker chair. Miriam was shivering with the shock, her hair matted to her scalp, as she held Henry's hand. I tried to calm her trembling shoulders while Sally cleaned the ankle wound with a tampon soaked in mineral water. She turned to kiss Henry, and I saw the swollen bruise above her right ear, pushing against the unbroken skin.

Lykiard had put on his jeans and sandals. He spoke quickly to the Jouberts and brought out a bottle of fundador, but Miriam waved it away. She was reassuring the children, her face as small as theirs, her eyes staring at the staircase as if she had mislaid part of herself on the damp steps.

'I'd take her back to your flat,' Lykiard suggested. 'We'll drive the kids in the car. She'll be more comfortable in the dinghy.'

Sally and the Jouberts helped me to lift Miriam into the inflatable. We pushed off, leaving our hamper and beach equipment on the sand, where the waves were already soaking the towels. Miriam waved to the children climbing into the back of the Citroën, her awkward hands gripping the sides of the inflatable. During the short journey the sea air seemed to revive her, and she smiled at me confidently, raising her damp eyebrows to apologise. But she collapsed when I pulled the dinghy on to the beach, and had to lie down among the lines of parasols and the watching sunbathers until she recovered her breath.

She was strong enough to walk to the lift, but when I opened the door to the flat I sensed that only half of her mind recognised it. I called the bureau for the telephone number of a local doctor, and Miriam wandered on to the balcony, blinking at the crowded beach.

An hour later, when the Spanish doctor arrived, she was lying on our bed, smiling wanly at the sound of the children on the Nordlunds' balcony. The doctor examined her in a slow but scrupulous way. Afterwards he patted me encouragingly and spoke in Spanish to Lykiard. The practicante, a visiting male nurse, would keep Miriam under observation until the doctor called again that evening.

While the practicante sat beside Miriam in the bedroom I went into the kitchen and prepared the children's supper, then carried the tray to the Nordlunds' apartment. When I returned, the practicante was on the telephone. He spoke to the doctor, and then told me to be calm while he summoned an ambulance. I went into the bedroom and held Miriam's shoulders. She had lost all feeling from her left leg and arm, and was moving in and out of a shallow consciousness, smiling in a faint way as she seemed to recede from herself. She frowned at me with one side of her face, touching her numbed body with a small hand.

When the ambulance arrived I was already dazed with panic. The driver and his attendant were trying to assemble the collapsible wheelchair. While they argued with each other I lifted Miriam from the bed and carried her in my arms to the elevator. Her eyes stared vaguely at the falling lights of the floor buttons, and her body was cold, as if she had spent hours in the sea. We eased her into the ambulance, waving away the tourists returning from the beach, watched by the expressionless children on the Nordlunds' balcony.

Miriam could no longer see them. I heard the rear doors close behind me, and saw Lykiard smiling stiffly with a fist clenched in encouragement. I crouched on the jump seat behind the attendant as he secured Miriam under the blanket and readied his oxygen cylinder. We sped along the Figueras road, siren wailing, and began to swerve in and out of the traffic. I massaged Miriam's calves, trying to feel the pulse in her legs. The oxygen from the mask had driven the sweat from her face, which seemed as small as Lucy's at the moment of birth. Only her right eye was focused, moving across the lace curtains on the windows of the ambulance. She was forcing herself to breathe, but her rib-cage had collapsed.

We stopped behind a bus that blocked the road to the bullring. The attendant opened the rear doors and remonstrated with the driver, who slowly reversed out of our way. We reached the hospital ten minutes later, as the last crowds dispersed from the football stadium. The flower-sellers by the ticket office were wrapping up their unsold blooms, and the news vendors were taking down their metal racks. But by then Miriam was already dead.

CHAPTER EIGHT

The Kindness of Women

The kindness of women came to my rescue, at a time when I had almost given up hope. Within a few weeks of her death I discovered that I had lost not only Miriam but all the women in the world. An unbridgeable space separated me from Miriam's friends and the women I knew, as if they had decided to isolate me within a carefully drawn cordon. Later I realised that they were standing at a distance, in the nearby rooms of my life, waiting until I had faced my anger at myself. Then they came forward and did everything to help me. The kindness of women and the affection of my children steered me safely through those first long months.

During our final days in Rosas, as the Nordlunds helped me to pack, I looked down from the balcony at the tourists stretched out on the beach, playing their parts in the eerie imitation of reality that life had become. The sun shone on the same parasols and pedalos, but everything had changed. In the hours since Miriam's death the entire female race had mutated into a different species. The women eating their gambas in the beach restaurants avoided my eyes, talking among themselves as they licked their red-stained fingers. When I cashed the last of my traveller's cheques I noticed that the bodies of the women queuing at the counter had lost their scent. Even Mrs Nordlund, with her determined smile and affection towards the children, stared at me with the gaze of a relief worker from a foreign country.

Only Señor Robles's German-speaking secretary was still herself. Checking the inventory, she peered into the darkened bedroom, clearly assuming that here Miriam had died at my hands. She opened the mirrored cabinet in the bathroom and ran her fingers along the tooth glasses.

'Nix kaputt?'

'Kaputt nix.'

She glanced at me in that way I would come to resent, a mixture of curiosity and distance, like a spectator at the scene of a crime. I wanted to take her wrists and raise her elbows so that I could inhale the scent of her armpits, press my fingers into her natal cleft. I disliked this cock-sure young woman enough to have sex with her while the children waited in the car with the Nordlunds. I wanted to prove that at least one woman still existed. But she moved away from me to the hallway, and took the stairs rather than be alone with me in the elevator. In her mind my wife's death had let a rapist loose upon the world.

Rosas and the lizard-ridged rocks of Cape Creus fell behind us as we set off for Figueras and the French border. The resort beaches of the Costa Brava, the hotels and cafés slid past through a dream more lurid than any of Dali's paintings, a vision of the world's end seen in terms of polluted sand, the stench of sun-oil and terraces of over-exposed flesh. We passed the entrance to the munici-pal cemetery at Figueras, and the long corridor of cypresses leading to the whitewashed walls and the ornate porticos of the family tombs. Miriam was buried in the adjacent Protestant cemetery, a flowerless boneyard where a few anti-clerical Spaniards rested under modest stones beside an English youth drowned in a yachting acci-dent. Looking back for the last time, I turned north towards the Pyrenees, France and home.

The children sat behind me, playing compulsive games all the way to the Channel. Henry was too stunned to speak, but Alice and Lucy soon took charge. Already they were more concerned for me than they were for them-selves. Mile after mile, they helped me with the road maps and chose hotels for our overnight stops, and kept a careful watch on the whisky bottle I held between my thighs. Their good sense and cheer laid the foundation on which we rebuilt our lives together.

During the drive I could only remember my last moments with Miriam and the burial service at the cemetery. Nature had committed a crime against my young wife and her children, and I felt a deep, confused anger not merely at myself, for bringing Miriam to Rosas, but at the vine-covered hills, the plane trees and the grazing cattle. An hour after she died a fierce peace had come over Miriam as she lay in the emegency room at Figueras hospital. Her head was flung back, her chest braced upwards, and her lips gaped in a rictus that exposed the livid muscles of her mouth and throat. Her jaw thrust itself at me from the blue skin, teeth set in a scream of death. Steadied by Nordlund, I walked to the cathedral-like Figueras undertakers. We moved through the lines of ornate gothic coffins that resembled pews facing a profane altar of black marble headstones. Thinking of Miriam, it seemed only fitting that she should be consigned to the earth in a casket like a prop from a horror film.

But later that evening, when I returned to the hospital, a complete change had come over her. All the pain and fear of her last moments, as her stricken brain collapsed inwards upon itself, had passed. Her face had relaxed, and her skin was soft and white again. A nurse had combed her hair for me, and her cheeks and lips were as small and neat as a little girl's, giving me a last glimpse of her vanished childhood.

At the burial service the next day, the coffin was wheeled on its cart into the Protestant cemetery. The iron rims rang across the dusty rubble. The children stood beside me in their best party clothes, and I hoped that they would never hear the rage of death below the coffin lid. The young Spanish clergyman abandoned his broken English and spoke in a thick Catalan, once banished by

General Franco, whose dark consonants were the language of the dead which Miriam would now be speaking. Sally Mumford stood with Lykiard and the Jouberts. None of them could look at me. Smoking her reefer, Sally stared at the graves as if she expected the stone lids to be flung back and the angry occupants to leap out and seize us.

The grave-diggers bent over their spades. The first stones struck the lid like a fist beating against a door. Nordlund handed a spare spade to me and I cast two blades of the nutty soil into the grave. Together we walked from the cemetery and drove through the football crowds, as if leaving a crime behind us.

After three days to cross a country and a sea, we returned to Shepperton. The long French roads helped me to straighten the perspectives of my mind. The past, on which I had turned my back on the day of my marriage, had rushed up and now stood behind me. Miriam's death joined me once again to all those nameless Chinese who had died during the Second World War. I remembered the dusty dead beside the crushed motor-cars in the Avenue Edward VII, and the straining jaw of the Chinese clerk at the rural railway station, first rehearsals for an afternoon at Figueras. Images of the bone-white paddy fields came back to me, like the pearly light that lay over Lunghua after the explosion of the atom bomb at Nagasaki. Kennedy had outstared Khrushchev during the Cuban missile crisis, but American bombers were still parked under the flat skies of Cambridgeshire, and the kingdom of light waited to be born from those concrete aprons among the fens.

Miriam's sister, Dorothy, and her husband were waving cheerfully by the gate when we arrived home. They had treats and surprises for the children, a cold roast lunch fit for a wake, and bottles of wine open on the table. I was grateful to them and held Dorothy tightly in my arms. But the echo of Miriam's bones in her sister's face, and the Cambridge crispness in her voice, made me feel that I and the children had returned to a parallel world that tried too hard to mimic its original.

While the children opened their presents I left Dorothy and Brian and climbed the stairs. The untidy rooms, strewn with toys and clothes, with favourite teddy bears rejected at the last minute, fixed the exact moment of our departure four weeks earlier. I stood by Miriam's dressing-table, looking down at the clutter of hairbrushes and cosmetics, and a discarded tube of the previous summer's suntan oil with its broken cap. Her finger-prints were set in the film of talc that covered the glass top, the ghost of her mouth in the red smear of a crushed tissue.

I opened the centre drawer, crammed with old phone bills, tampons and school reports, faded brassieres held together with safety pins, and her faithful Dutch cap, like an unreliable family servant, for years the home of the spare car keys. I tipped the waste-basket onto the floor, and sifted through the hair balls and tubes of contraceptive jelly, the torn suspender belt and fishnet stockings that she liked to wear at parties and later vamp around the bedroom. I lifted the stocking to my lips, smelling the scent of Miriam's thighs, the same body scent that rose from the pillows and greeted me when I opened the wardrobe on to the racks of her dresses. Her hundred presences filled the house like a chorus of ghosts.

I needed to let them go. I opened the windows and watched the clouds of talc and dust drift through the air, repatriating themselves to Figueras. In the garden the children were chasing their old toys while Brian mowed the lawn. Alice was rearranging the furniture in the tree-house, casting out the cardboard tables and chairs as if spring-cleaning before the arrival of a new domestic regime. Henry had found a still-inflated party balloon and was trying to stamp on it, while Lucy tested the swing, taking it up to a wild new altitude.

Watching them, I felt the first smile cross my lips. I knew that the children were braver than I was – during the long drive home they had never once mentioned their mother, the first of the many unspoken pacts which we made in the coming months. I sat on the bed, as the scents of Miriam's body floated on the summer air.

Dorothy was carving the cold roast in the kitchen. She was three years older than Miriam, the more serious sister, a partner in a firm of Cambridge solicitors. At our wedding she had smiled and shaken her head as I kissed the bride, clearly doubting whether I would ever be a match for the high-tempered Miriam.

I drank a tumbler of duty-free whisky, and hesitated before pouring another. Dorothy pressed my hand, refilling the glass.

'Go on – you've earned it. That must have been the most tremendous drive.'

'We were totally lost near Poitiers. I can tell you, Henry's French saved the day. For one moment I thought of turning back.'

'You should have done. No, what am I saying?' Dorothy checked herself, surprised by her tongue. 'Brian wondered if you were going to move?'

'From Shepperton?'

'From this house, at least – you ought to make a fresh start somewhere.'

'No . . .' I watched Alice and Lucy vigorously cleaning the tree-house. A flurry of leaves was followed by an old stuffed toy, loyal companion of years, that plunged head-first to the newly mown grass. Women were ruthless from an early age, and needed to be. 'We've made a fresh start. It's best if we stay here and face things.'

'You'll keep the children?'

'Of course. It was part of the deal.'

'It's quite a challenge. Brian and I could have the girls.'
'Thanks, but no. We'll stick it out together.'

After lunch, when Brian had taken the children to Chessington Zoo, Dorothy and I began to tidy the rooms. As we put away the scattered toys and clothes I had the sense that we were scene-shifters changing a set of props. Everything tilted at an unfamiliar angle. Even Dorothy's resemblances to her sister, the echo of Miriam's broad cheekbones and small hands, strong walk and determined hips, made me feel that we were extras rehearsing a scene to be played by others.

'Would you like me to do the bedroom?' Dorothy was staring at the cluttered dressing-table and wardrobe. 'Heavens, it's sad. Jim, throw it all away. Clear everything out. Give the clothes to the jumble people.'

'I will, don't worry. I need a little longer. It's all that's left.'

'It isn't.'

Dorothy held my shoulders, trying to pull me back into the present. I put my hands on her waist, desperate to embrace her. After the spectral women of Rosas beach, Dorothy with her firm hips and comforting breasts was wholly alive. I pressed my hands to her shoulder blades, searching for the familiar contours that Miriam had trained me to recognise. Dorothy stiffened and moved away from me, unsettled by my trembling hands. Then she leaned against me, pressing her cheek to mine, calming my agitated face.

'All right. We'll go into Henry's room.'

'No . . . stay here. In Miriam's bed.'

Trying to control myself, I untied her apron and slipped my hands beneath her shirt, feeling the smooth skin of her back and her strong ribs. I sat on the untidy bed, the sheets still marked by the creases of the last night before the holiday, and placed my head against her thighs.

Dorothy stood calmly in front of me as I undressed her, palms lightly on my cheeks, running her fingers into my mouth as I tasted their scent. An unfamiliar mole marked the skin of her left shoulder, but for a moment I could believe that she was Miriam. I kissed her labia and then sat her on my knees, caressing her vulva as if I had parted its lips on countless afternoons in this bedroom of a loving husband. When I pressed my mouth to her nipples she smoothed away the sweat on my forehead, and pushed me back onto Miriam's pillow.

For these few minutes her duty to her dead sister's children overrode her loyalty to her husband. She knelt across me, adjusting her knees to my heavier torso. Exhausted and over-excited, desperate for this kindly woman, I tried to press my limp penis into her vulva. Smiling in a distant but reassuring way, Dorothy took it from my fingers and began to massage the head between her hands. She forced a little spit onto her finger-tips and moistened the mouth of her vagina. She eased my penis into her, glanced through the window at a passing car and put her breast to my mouth, looking down at me like a wet nurse caring for a neighbour's feverish child. When I came, and sank back onto the pillow, she lay beside me and held my diaphragm until my breathing had steadied. I let my fingers into her vulva and tasted the sweet moisture, making sure that I would remember it in the empty months ahead.

She waited until I was ready and passed my clothes to me. Without speaking, she began to tidy the dressing-table, lining up the cosmetics and hairbrushes, and polishing the finger-smeared mirror. I gratefully embraced her before she left the bedroom for the last time.

From that afternoon I was celibate for nearly a year. Although the children and I often visited Dorothy and her husband, I never again made love to her. She had met her obligations to her dead sister, calming the widowed husband and reminding him that Miriam endured within our affection and shared memories. Greeting us, Dorothy would hold me briefly, keeping alive the link between her lost sister and the women I would know in the future.

But much as I needed other women, I found it impossible to approach them. My friends were careful to invite me to their parties, but a chasm of time and pain separated me from the women I met. Tongue-tied and clumsy, I moved past them in a daze of sexual desire.

Once, standing among the coats in David Hunter's bedroom, I found myself alone with one of his flying-club groupies, the young widow of an RAF sergeant killed in Cyprus. I guessed that he had assigned her the job of bringing me back to life. As David stood guard in the corridor, and pretended to discuss the Mercury space flights with an aviation journalist, she leaned against the door and drew me on to her thighs. I held her small shoulders as if she were one of my daughters, frightened after a fall in the garden. I pressed my cheek to her mouth, and felt her lips in my ear, teeth biting at the lobe. When I failed to respond she slipped her hand below the waist of my trousers, fingers probing between my buttocks. She tugged at my shirt and palpated me as she would have soothed a wounded lover. She waited patiently for my erection, but then gave up with a shrug, kissed me cheerfully on the forehead and slipped through the door.

Had nature, through long trial and error, decided that I had failed as both husband and father, and banished me before I could do any further damage? Certainly, many people thought that I should not be looking after the children. But Henry, Alice and Lucy were all I had to believe in, and I was sure that I could make them happy. We cooked in the crowded kitchen, following the girls' outlandish recipes, argued over television and did our homework together. With longer memories of his mother, Henry was sometimes sad, and in the evenings I carried the TV set into my study and sat with him on the sofa, an arm around him while he quietly watched his favourite comedy programmes. One evening at last I heard him laugh.

Every day was an Aladdin's Cave of schemes and enthusiasms. Alice and Lucy, seven and four, soon took charge of everything, deciding when we should go shopping or visit friends, whether I needed a rest from them or if it was time to hold a party. Already they were sizing up the mothers of their school-friends, urging me into little flirtations and blithely waving aside the minor problem of their husbands. I collected them from school in the afternoons and felt a thrill of relief when they clambered noisily into the car, as if we had been separated for months.

What they most resented was any hint that there was something freakish about our family. Too many people, swayed by folk wisdom or modish child psychology, took for granted that the loss of their mother was a wound from which they would never recover, and that no father, however loving, could ever take the mother's place. Even Peggy Gardner, now a paediatrician at Guy's Hospital in London, seemed to hold this view. Whenever she visited Shepperton she gazed tolerantly at the untidy rooms cluttered with the children's drawings and projects, as if the confusion reflected the deep crisis within this stricken family.

Peggy had never married, despite a long line of men-friends and an easy knack with children. Miriam had vaguely distrusted her, aware that Peggy was the first woman I had ever needed and that our relationship went far beyond the possibilities of sex. At the same time she was curious to see behind the handsome self-control that Peggy showed to the world. Bourgeois life had claimed Peggy – good sense, tolerance and understanding had totally corrupted her.

Six months after our return from Spain she called in to see us on the way back from a child-care conference in Bristol. Still in her professional mode, briefcase in hand, she sat smilingly on the sofa while Lucy made room for her. Surrounded by Lucy's full parade of dolls and bears, arranged in meticulous order of seniority, Peggy faintly resembled a stuffed toy herself. As always, I could see that my motherless children reminded her of our days together in Lunghua.

'That's nice, Lucy.' Peggy beamed at the row of dolls. 'I'm in the middle of a lovely little family.'

'You're not in the family,' Lucy warned her. 'But you're the oldest.'

'And the wisest,' I added.

Lucy straightened a battered kangaroo. 'Mrs Roo's much wiser – she told Daddy's fortune.'

'And what was that, Lucy?'

'He's going to live for a hundred years.'

'That's wonderful. I think he's going to live forever.'

'No,' Lucy said, her eyes fixed on mine. 'He won't live forever. But nearly forever . . .'

When Lucy had gone, Peggy smiled at the contingent of battered but cheerful dolls as if it were a model of my own family.

'Lucy's a dear – they all are. You've done an amazing job. How on earth do you manage to write?'

'They go to school.'

'But when they're home? It's a perpetual riot.'

'I like it.' I felt myself being pushed into a familiar corner. 'Some writers listen to Vivaldi. I like to hear my children playing. There's nothing abnormal in that.'

'It seems to work. You've been very brave.'

'Peggy!' Irritated, I pulled the glass of wine from her hand. 'For God's sake, men are capable of loving their children.'

'Not the ones I see at Guy's.'

'Men have never been given a chance. Every social convention you can think of is against them, believe me.'

'I do – but conventions are hard to change.'

'Women don't want them changed. It takes only one hand to rock a cradle, and they want that hand to be theirs.'

'The women I see are making a run for the nursery door.'

'Are they? Most women think it's wrong of me to look after the kids myself. They feel it's unnatural. Even you do.'

'It is unusual.'

'Look at men on a beach, where they're allowed to play with their children. You'll see all the care and affection in the world, while the women are busy fussing over their damn mascara.'

'I'll think of you here as on the beach.' Peggy sipped her wine, surveying the posters on the wall, wild drawings of aircraft on fire, dropping their nuclear bombs. 'How's Henry doing?'

'He's getting better. He's much happier. We read and play a lot together. I try not to go out too often.'

'You must get out sometimes.'

'I've been out. It looks pretty much the same old scene. Every day here is a new adventure.'

'Even so, you can't spend all your time mothering the children.'

I sat down on the sofa and took Peggy's hand. 'Peggy, I'm not "mothering" the children. I can't take Miriam's place, and I won't try to.'

'You still miss her – I can see that.'

'Of course . . . there are so many things I wish I'd done for her. In many ways I was a lousy husband.'

'At least you loved her. You should think about her as much as you want.'

'I do. Take it from me, the death of a wife is all about

172

sex. I keep dreaming about her in a weird way – walking around the bedroom in Rosas, or in the bullring at Barcelona. Dreams full of blood and dead bulls. I even saw her in Lunghua, strolling along the railway line to that little station. In some peculiar way she was involved with that. All those meaningless deaths that mean everything.'

'Do you think you'll marry again?'

'Not many women would marry a man with three children. Whenever I see a couple together in their car I really resent them. Almost as if they were to blame.'

Peggy put her hand on my arm. I looked at her capable fingers, unchanged since the days at Lunghua. During my fevers in the children's hut she had talked to me in her sensible schoolgirl's voice, trying to explain away the eerie visions of delirium. I felt the enlarged knuckle of her wrist, the condyle chipped when I darted into the hut and drove the door against her hand.

In the nursery the children were arguing over the Monopoly board, Alice delivering a magisterial lecture on the significance of passing Go. Henry was insisting on circling the board counter-clockwise. Peggy smiled, still holding my hand, but when I touched her thigh she pushed me away.

'Peggy . . .'

'I know. Deep in the underwear something stirred. I have to go.'

'Stay the night. Why not?'

She picked up her handbag. 'I'm due back at Guy's. Besides, those dreams are just for you . . .'

I waited while she said goodbye to the children. Had she guessed that I would be impotent and decided to spare my feelings? We had been too close to each other in Lunghua, forced into a child marriage that revealed too many flaws and limits.

She held my hand through the window of her car, one of the first Japanese imports, an engagingly odd choice.

'You're fine – the children have looked after you wonderfully. I've talked to Alice and Lucy and they're going to make sure you go out more often.'

I watched her drive erratically away. Of course she was right: it was the children who were bringing me up. They had come to terms with the past far more quickly than their father. I had emptied the wardrobes of Miriam's clothes, but I sometimes noticed that prying little fingers had teased the hem of a skirt through the lid of the suitcases where I stored them. One afternoon, while repairing the fence, I was aware that the children were unnaturally quiet. Climbing the stairs, I saw them in my bedroom. They had found Miriam's wedding dress, which Alice now wore, tottering on Miriam's high-heeled shoes as Lucy played a bridesmaid holding the train. Henry wore my old panama hat and dinner jacket. Bursting with glee, they paraded around the bed, bowing and curtseying through a mock marriage ceremony. Then Alice stretched out on the bed and closed her eyes, while Lucy and Henry folded the bedspread around her, solemnly laying her to rest.

Watching them without a word, I crept down the stairs, knowing that they had recovered. An hour later the dress had been carefully returned to the suitcase. A few flecks of confetti shaken loose from its hems lay on the bedroom carpet beside my slippers.

My own recovery took longer, delayed by the well-meaning refusal of almost everyone to refer to Miriam's death. A gentle conspiracy existed among my friends and publishing acquaintances, as they feigned not to notice that Miriam had vanished through a window of time and space. This silence reminded me of the cruel childhood game in which we pretended, without telling him, that one of our friends no longer existed – the poor victim would be ignored, stared through, excluded from any games. I envied the elaborate mourning rituals of the Chinese, the public wailing of the widow on which Europeans so looked

174

down. Watching the national mourning of a stricken America after the assassination of President Kennedy, I almost envied his bereaved wife. Every moment of her grief was endlessly replayed and anatomised on television. Her husband's death, like the murder of his assassin, was recapitulated in slow motion, frame by numbered Zapruder frame. She wore her blood-spattered skirt like a scream of rage at the world that had widowed her.

One evening, after eleven months of unbroken celibacy, I was taken on a tour of Soho's strip clubs by a London publisher then living in New York. The worst kind of Manhattanised Englishman, he wolfed down his sole and Chablis, and then dragged me from one back-street club to the next. At first I tried to slip away from him, but I was curious to see my own reactions. On minute boudoir stages the young strippers worked through their routines, smiling in their overlit way at the wan-faced men who packed the narrow seats. Caressing their breasts and buttocks, masturbating as they exposed their vulvas for a ritual few seconds, they mimicked the audience's lust in routines as formalised as the aircraft emergency drills rehearsed by air hostesses in the minutes after take-off. I waited for them to arouse me, but the strippers seemed to parade their sexual possibilities with all the fervour of anatomy demonstrators in a dissecting-room taking their students through the urino-genital system.

'How long since you had a woman, Jim?' the publisher asked.

'A long time.'

'Well, come on then. Cheer up.'

He told me that this tour of Soho clubs was our appetiser before we booked into an exclusive Westminster brothel he had been recommended by a British criminal whose memoirs he was editing. But I knew that he was too drunk to do more than go back to his hotel. Watching him as he gazed at a cobra-eyed teenager stroking her anus with a forefinger, I guessed that it was this stylisation of sex that most appealed to him, not the act itself. The atrocity exhibition was more stirring than the atrocity.

When I left him at the door of his taxi he put a heavy hand on my shoulder, searching for some insight into my sad condition.

'Perhaps, Jim, you just don't like girls any more . . .'

I walked away from him under a cinema marquee advertising the first of the *Mondo Cane* films, bogus documentaries that cunningly mixed fake atrocity newsreels with genuine footage of human oddity. Next to the marquee was a newspaper billboard promoting a special supplement devoted to the Kennedy assassination, with a grainy enlargement of the Zapruder frame that recorded the last moments of the stricken President. Near Piccadilly Circus a group of CND members were canvassing support for an anti-nuclear rally to be held in Trafalgar Square. A well-nourished young woman pressed a leaflet into my hand bearing a photograph of a simulated nuclear attack, which showed hundreds of volunteers lying down together in a placid high street.

Fantasies of apocalyptic death fuelled the imaginations of these comfortable suburbanites. I was thinking of a different atomic bomb, which many of the Lunghua prisoners claimed to have seen above Nagasaki, the bomb that had saved our lives. In the rancid glare of the music arcades, as the hips of the young street-walkers shook to Trini Lopez, I could almost believe that a third World War might have saved Miriam, and that the war to come after that might resurrect her from her grave. A secret logic that I had yet to explore seemed to connect her death with the dead in the Avenue Edward VII, as if the unconscious needs of the human race could only be fulfilled in an obliterating sexual apocalypse, replayed in an infinity of slow-motion photography. Fragments of deranged dreams veered across the night air above the raucous neon.

The lurid glare still hung in my eyes as I walked the children to the school gates the following morning. When I returned to my car I began to chat to a mother of two boys in Lucy's class. We discussed the costumes for the children's Christmas party which she was helping to design. Keen to show me the patterns, she invited me for coffee at her nearby home.

As we sat at her kitchen table she explained that she and her husband had separated, but told me that he still brought his laundry home. Something about this admission seemed to amuse her. Without much prompting she added that they made love in the kitchen while the washing machine completed its cycle.

'Domestic routines survive everything,' I commented. 'I like that. It's rather touching.'

'Isn't it . . .' Coming to the point, she switched on the washing machine. 'By the way, you haven't anything that needs washing?'

'No . . . except this handkerchief.'

'It looks a bit grubby. Let me do it for you.'

While the machine circled and the white flag of my handkerchief waved to us from its drowned world, I sat her on the kitchen table, scarcely smaller than the strip-club stages. Her knees were held tightly against my hips by her short leather skirt. Her hands rested on my chest, as if she were measuring me for a new life on which I was about to embark. I was grateful to her for the unforced references to Miriam, whom she had known well, and for taking the lead so expertly. She had realised that only a frivolous approach, as divorced from real feeling as the Soho clubs and marquee signs, could ever have reached me.

Her fingers lowered my zip, and I said: 'I hope something happens . . . it's been a long time.'

'Three weeks? Or three months?'

'Eleven months.'

'Time for a baby. Let's see what we can do about that.'

She unbuttoned my shirt and pressed her hands against my diaphragm. 'Heavens, you're tense . . . deep breaths, now.' She laughed cheerfully, amused by herself. 'Still, at least we've met before. These days you have sex straight away and the wooing starts later.'

'I'll woo you.'

'Good. Something does seem to be happening. Now, can you remember what to do next?'

That night I dreamed of Miriam for the last time. I was walking down Shepperton High Street on my way to the shops when I saw her by the traffic lights at the crossroads. She was as young and beautiful as I ever remembered her, and I was filled with a deep sense of love for her, and relief that we would meet again. I was glad that the nightmare of the past months was over and that we would be reunited with the children in our little house. I called to her as she strode confidently across the road, her skirt swinging at her knees. She looked back, recognising me with a cheery smile, and walked on. I called to her again, but she strode past the shops, and I saw her disappear among the cars and pedestrians.

Waking from the dream, I listened to my children sleeping in their rooms. I lay in the darkness, and knew that Miriam had set me free.

CHAPTER NINE

Craze People

'We'll take the pixies with us! You can't leave them behind!'

With a noisy swoop Sally Mumford lifted Lucy into the air and held the excited six-year-old against her shoulder, while gathering Alice and Henry to the folds of her floor-length dress.

'Sally . . .' I tried feebly to protest. 'They're too young for a pop concert. And I'm too old.'

'Rubbish! We're going together. We won't listen to him, will we?'

'No!' they yelled.

'Right! Coats and scarves, and ear-plugs for Daddy. I'll make a picnic for us, if I can find anything in that mouldy fridge . . .'

Sally had taken charge. As always, I watched her with unstinted admiration as she rolled her skirt around her thighs, exposing her long white legs. She squatted, scowling, in front of the open refrigerator. Out came salami, brie, two bottles of white Burgundy.

'Right. That's us. Now, what do you feed the monsters?'

'Beans on toast and all that jazz.'

'Too much of a fiddle. They can have salami.'

'They hate salami.'

'They'll love it! Washed down with a glass of wine? It's their first pop concert.'

'And mine.'

'Good. I'm going to get you out of here more often.' Sally licked and dabbed, making a quick survey of the refrigerator. She waved a cheese-tipped forefinger at me, flecks of cole slaw on her brightly painted mouth. 'Jim, you're spending too much time in Shepperton. It's like living on a small planet miles from anywhere. I'm moving you back to Earth.'

I loved to watch her, whether she was fuelled by amphetamines or plain American sass. She and Peter Lykiard had arranged to call for me, but Lykiard had left separately for the open-air concert, near Brighton on the south coast. The Arts Laboratory, of which Lykiard was now exhibitions director, was to stage a number of prose and poetry readings during the intermissions, and Sally had persuaded me to take part, against my better judgement. I found it impossible to resist her swerves of enthusiasm and good cheer.

'You'll enjoy it – Burroughs will be there.'

'The great man. But what do I read?'

'Anything. One of your sado-masochistic romps should go down a treat. The audiences are very conventional.'

'So am I. Sally . . .'

But nothing could stop her. As we drove away from Shepperton towards the south-east I felt my usual pang of uneasiness at leaving the Thames-side town. Sally was right – in the two years since Miriam's death the familiar gardens and water-meadows had come to my rescue, but at something of a price. I went up to London more often, but the quiet streets with their bricky villas, presided over by the film studios, formed the reassuring centre of my mind. Through the tranquil TV suburbs moved a light as serene as any Stanley Spencer had seen at Cookham.

At the same time, I was grateful to people who lured me away from it. Lykiard and Sally had arrived unexpectedly on the doorstep six weeks earlier. They carried presents and a cheery welcome for the children, who had almost forgotten them, and a bottle of Japanese whisky for me which Sally was opening as she stepped through the door. Lykiard wanted me to write the catalogue notes to an exhibition of Kennedy assassination photographs, but this was little more than the pretext for their visit.

I was happy to see them both, even though their island hideaway had been the setting for Miriam's fatal accident. Watching Sally whooping around the children, I realised how strong a memory she had left me of herself. Casually she filled the nursery with scented smoke that had the children's nostrils flicking like butterfly wings. She regaled them with baffling word games, concocted elaborate family histories for the tribe of plastic trolls that were their latest craze, scandalised them with media gossip from the television world where she now worked as a news pro- gramme researcher. Anyone within range was treated to her eccentric comments on the Viet Nam war, Carnaby Street fashions, the latest outrage committed by President Johnson and the British police. She was full of anecdotes about Dali, whose entourage at Port Lligat she had pen- etrated, and his voyeuristic delight in watching young couples have sex, without making clear whether she altogether disapproved.

Only when her last amphetamine tablet began to wear off would she become scratchy and silent, rubbing the coolness from her eyes until she could take her handbag and a glass of water upstairs to the bathroom. But I always looked forward to seeing her. She excited me in the way that Miriam had done, and I envied Lykiard his close hold over her wayward imagination.

The 1960s were tailor-made for them. In his office at the Arts Laboratory the pipe-smoking Lykiard logged onto his wall-charts the latest outburst of psychedelia, the newest drug craze or exhibition of concept art, like a contented meteorologist registering a summer of unexpected cyc- lones. Exhibitions of Viet Nam atrocities, posters advertis- ing a self-mutilating cabaret performer or an Artaud revival moved beneath his tolerant eyes as if he had put aside all emotion or even, conceivably, not yet experi- enced this rare condition. For him the end of the world,

the imminent nuclear armageddon against which pro-
testors marched on every weekend, would merely be the
ultimate happening, the audience-storming last act in the
theatre of cruelty.

Sally, at least, still kept her feelings, though jammed
into the wrong pigeon-holes in her mind. She thrived on
the volatile landscape of the mid-60s, which made a virtue
of psychic damage. Mediated by the TV documentaries
which she helped to edit, the civil wars in Algeria, Viet
Nam and the Congo became a never-ending group catharsis, a psychological life-support system into which she
could plug between her amphetamine highs. Trying to sort
all this out had brought her to Shepperton. In Sally's mind,
a near-addicted Scotch drinker blessed with an ox-like
liver and three children seemed a model of almost church-
going rectitude. Once she had offered me her flat tin of
amphetamine tablets, but then quickly withdrew them as
if tempting me with the fruit of the second forbidden tree.

How could I manoeuvre her away from Lykiard? Her
large, ramshackle apartment in an expensive Bayswater
block was a museum of unmet needs. Dusty photographs
of her mother, sitting stiffly in the garden of some private
mental clinic near Boston, hung side by side with stills of
jack-booted parade-ground troops from *Triumph of the
Will*.

'Gorgeous men . . . just *so* glamorous,' Sally commented wistfully, settling her icy heroes next to a magazine profile of Israeli kibbutz sentries, her other sexual
dream. She attended Ouspenski seminars, had taken a
parachute jump at Elstree Flying Club, loathed her
department-store tycoon father, yet treasured her schoolgirl letters from him and wore his old silk smoking jacket
as a dressing-gown, inhaling the ancient odours of sweat
and tobacco like healing balm. Naively, I asked if they
had committed incest. 'I wish we had,' she mused nostal-

gically. 'Jesus, I wanted him to – I know what a deprived childhood really means . . .'

All the way to Brighton she played happily with the children in the back of the car. Was she, I wondered hopefully, trying to make herself one of my daughters? After ten years of Miriam's level commonsense it was difficult to hunt the zig-zag contours of Sally's mind. The Hell's Angels guarding the entrance to the concert site were wearing her beloved black leather and death's head insignia, but she gave them scarcely a glance.

We parked behind a tower of steel scaffolding high enough to launch a space-vehicle, and walked through the buses and location vans to the performers' canvas tent. Lykiard was holding court with his Arts Laboratory groupies – intense young women, concept artists all, with the intimidating stares of gangsters' molls. Anyone over thirty was a race enemy, and having three children instantly marked me down for retribution. Sally's presence gave me a temporary laissez-passer, to be revoked, I was made to feel, at the slightest betrayal of such bourgeois inclinations as wanting an ice-cream for the children or a hygienic lavatory. Lykiard informed them that I would read a text celebrating the perverse sexuality of President Kennedy's widow, and there was a momentary flicker of interest behind the heavy shades, soon replaced by a stony hostility. Class assumptions and exclusivities survived strongly amid the rock amplifiers and Warholiana.

Between the sudden bursts of rock music, as the engineers wired their circuits, the children were whispering to Sally.

'Me too,' Sally agreed. Entrusting the picnic hamper to Lykiard, she spotted a sign behind the stage, on which was printed 'Free Toilet'. An arrow pointed towards a wood of beech trees. Like characters in a Magritte painting, people wandered in a dislocated way among the trees, whose trunks steamed with urine. Burroughs hovered briefly into view, as formal as an undertaker in his natty suit.

I watched Alice and Lucy daintily pick their way through the moist grass after Sally, who had gathered up her long skirts. Henry was happily spraying every tree, and accidentally sprinkled the boots of a Hell's Angel too stoned to notice. Already the counter-culture was a revelation beyond all their childhood dreams.

Lykiard showed me his time-table and the ramp of wooden planks that led to the upper of the two stages. I gazed uneagerly at the tower of steel scaffolding.

'Is this thing going to hold together? If one bolt snaps we'll all be launched into orbit.'

'I think that's the idea. It may be our only chance. Let's face it, middle-aged America has hijacked the Apollo programme. Men older than your bank manager will land on the Moon.'

'But is it going up or down?' Trying to steady my nerves, I bought a whisky at the bar, then found that the plastic cup contained nothing but a brown stain.

'It isn't dirty,' Lykiard explained. 'That's your measure of whisky. Smoke pot, but don't buy any here. You'll find capitalist exploitation at its most ruthless.' He pointed to the seats in the VIP enclosure below the stage. 'Despite appearances, the old class structures survive intact. The best seats are reserved for the pop aristocracy – promoters, record company executives, TV people and the music press. Behind them we get the pop world's middle class, all those well-brought-up girls from the suburbs who just come for the day. But down at the bottom, as ever, is the proletariat of the drug culture . . .'

Strolling through the fringes of the crowd, we reached a wide ditch that marked the edge of the field rented from a local farmer. Groups of shabby young men and a few sallow girls were camping in the ditch. Most of them had spent the night there, sleeping among the tree roots in makeshift tents of tarpaulin. Smoking their joints, they were cooking on small stoves from which a sweet pine-smoke rose into the air. They reminded me of the Chinese peasants I had seen clinging to life in the irrigation ditches of wartime Shanghai. One of them offered me a skillet of gruel. I squatted under the tarpaulin and ate the spicy oatmeal, sharing the plastic cup of wine I had taken from the picnic hamper.

Later, as I recovered from my reading, I lounged beside Sally and the children on the grassy slopes behind the concert stage. The entire terrain of trees and meadows resembled the aftermath of some harmless and cheerful Waterloo. Bodies lay in the long grass, singly and in pairs, as if they had fallen on the field of battle, while the survivors sat in their square below the stage, many of them wearing the scarlet tunics, gold braid and epaulettes of the classic English regiments. I envied them all their mastery of make-believe. I had wasted my own youth dissecting cadavers and training to be a military pilot, trying to match myself against the realities of the post-war world. But the 1960s had effortlessly turned the tables on reality. The media landscape had sealed a technicolor umbrella around the planet, and then redefined reality as itself.

Drowsy on the warm wine, I thought of myself on the swaying platform above the crowd, bellowing into the erratic microphones. Giant fragments of amplified prose had toppled away through the air like sections of a glacier. No-one had heard a word. My dreams of Mrs Kennedy's sexuality had boomed across the placid downs, unsettling the grazing cattle a dozen fields away.

'It was a surrealist joke – on me,' I told Sally, shutting my eyes to the humiliation of it. 'Not the kind that Duchamp or Tzara would approve of . . .'

'You were wonderful. Wasn't he, pixies?'

'Yes!' Their eyes were opening to a new world far richer than anything Shepperton could offer.

'Sally, the whole thing was absurd.'

'So? Nothing matters any more. Jackie Kennedy, Viet Nam, flying to the Moon – they're just TV commercials.'

'And what are they selling?'

'Everything you need – pain, fun, love, hate. You can make anything mean anything. Only the pixies matter.'

She seemed restless with me, smoking an endless series of joints that left her eyes blunted. Wine bottle in hand, she spent the afternoon striding around in her long gown, her neck and breasts turning pink in the sun, blonde hair like a white whip that she flicked from one shoulder to the other. The festival, which celebrated nothing except itself, already bored her. She wandered away from us, and an hour later I found her in a quiet field beyond the car park. She was running with a family of horses, a black mare and two foals, driving them round and round the field, her hands happily slapping their haunches, her eyes lit with some memory of childhood.

When she demanded that we visit the beach at Brighton I discovered what had unsettled her. Searching for Lucy in the performers' tent, we saw Lykiard and one of his concept artists lying in a deck-chair behind the bar. Ignoring Sally, they embraced each other, and both seemed to hide behind the single pair of sunglasses. Sally stared at them, the pink flush fading from her breasts. She took Lucy's hand and walked along the bar, scattering the paper cups with their brown stains.

Fortunately, she cheered up as soon as we left the festival behind and reached the beach. The incoming tide and strong black waves put an ironic gleam into her eyes. We parked on the hard shoulder above the beach and watched the waves splinter themselves against the wooden breakwater.

'Right!' Sally opened the door. 'I'm going for a swim.'

'Sally . . . the sea's too strong.'

'I'll tell it to behave . . . it's just a big puppy.'

I followed her across the shingle, as she kicked off her shoes and strode to the water's edge. The foam seethed at her feet, delighted to greet this beautiful and deranged young woman. I expected her to strip, but she stepped straight into the water, bare feet feeling among the stones. The waves smothered her legs, the sodden fabric of her dress clinging to her knees.

'Sally!' Henry had stepped from the car, model aircraft forgotten in his hand. The girls' little faces pressed to the windscreen.

Sally strode out as a larger wave launched itself at the breakwater. The violent black jelly slid around her, clasping her waist, and the undertow dragged at her feet. She was up to her armpits in the foam, her legs trapped by the weight of drenched fabric. She let the next wave carry her towards the shore, and stood unsteadily in the racing surf, waving to me with an apologetic grin. She was knocked from her feet in the surging water, pulled down and carried into the breaking maw of a huge channel roller.

Warning Henry to stay by the car, I ran into the water, stunned by the wave as it struck my thighs. Wading out, I jumped chest high through the next roller and swam towards Sally as she lay helplessly on the surface. I seized her shoulders and held her against my chest, stood up and pulled her to the shore.

She sat exhausted on the shingle, teeth chattering while the foam seethed its disappointment against her feet, as if the sea were laying its eggs and hoping she would fertilise them. The shoulder straps of her dress had broken, and the bodice was around her waist, exposing the icy skin of her torso covered with shreds of sea-weed. Washed from her eyes, her make-up ran in blue stains down her cheeks. Her nose and chin were smaller, shrunk by fear and the cold, and she stared at the waves tugging at the train of her dress like a child remembering a drowning at sea.

Passers-by were watching us from the promenade. I

covered Sally with my jacket and helped her back to the car and the silent, astounded children. Sally sank gratefully into the front seat.

'Well,' she said to the children, brushing away the flecks of sea-weed. 'How many lengths did I swim?'

Later that evening, when the children were asleep, Sally sat on the sofa among the stuffed toys, her good humour returned. During our silent drive she had slumped against the door inside my jacket, eyes fixed on the sodden dress between her feet. At the time I wondered if this had been a half-hearted suicide attempt, prompted by the glimpse of Lykiard in the deck-chair, or perhaps a bravura piece of exhibitionism by which she hoped to regain the centre of the stage. But when I mentioned Lykiard she scarcely recognised his name. Her near-drowning had been nothing more than an impulsive Channel dip.

Wearing my dressing-gown, she breathed the fumes rising from a tumbler of hot whisky. When I sat beside her among the stuffed toys she laid her head on my shoulder.

'Are the pixies asleep? I didn't mean to frighten them.'

'They're fine. They think you went for a swim.'

'I did! Until right at the end. When you reached me I was thinking what it would be like.'

'Drowning?'

'Those last moments before the end . . . I had the strange feeling they would go on forever.' She pulled away from me and stared hard at a stuffed toy. 'I want to live my whole life like that.'

'Sally, you do . . .'

She opened my palm and carefully read its lines, then slipped it under the lapel of the dressing-gown and placed it on her breast. Despite the hot bath her skin still smelled strongly of brine. A depraved and innocent Miranda had been washed ashore on the island of Shepperton. When I caressed her breast she smiled at me in a conspiratorial way, as if we were two lubricous children in a tree-house.

'My nipples aren't very sensitive – probably less than yours.'

She watched me as I undressed her, curious to see how I would discover her body, beckoning me towards her with a ready smile. When I stroked her clitoris she lay back with her legs wide, her face between the soft toys. She took my fingers and moved them to her anus, rhythmically pumping her rectum like a soft accordion.

'Don't bother to fuck me. Just bugger me.'

She knelt on the carpet, her chest and shoulders across the cushions. Spitting on her fingers, she pushed the saliva into her anus with one hand, testing my penis with the other. I hesitated to enter her, nervous of tearing her scarred anus, but she pressed my penis into her, adding more spit between the gasps of pain. When I was fully inside her she at last relaxed, and her rectum was as soft as the vagina of a child-bearing woman. She buried her face among the teddy bears and brought her wrists behind her back, inviting me to force them to her shoulder blades. I moved carefully, trying to control her prolapsing rectum, gently forcing her arms as she wanted, picking the hairs from her mouth as she shouted to me, an eager, desperate child.

'Bugger me, daddy! Beat me! Pixie wants to be buggered!'

From that moment Sally Mumford became my guide to a new world. At the start she seemed keen to make a new life for us all in Shepperton, to be the wife and mother we had left among the Spanish cypresses. Part big sister and part friendly witch, and capable in the children's eyes of unlimited amazements, Sally brought all her good cheer and wayward flair to our suburban retreat. I tried to calm and steady her, as she relived her childhood like an exciting roller-coaster ride. Despite playing the role of her father, I felt surprisingly dependent on her, and hoped that I could give her the happy childhood that she was helping to give to my own children.

At the same time I knew that I could learn so much from her. Sally was a true child of the 1960s, and my guide to the secret logic that I saw unfolding. After years of domesticity in my marooned suburb by the Thames I had stepped into the middle of a decade that had started without me. I had woken from a dream of the Second World War into an England that seemed like the aftermath of the third.

In this overlit realm ruled by images of the space race and the Viet Nam war, the Kennedy assassination and the suicide of Marilyn Monroe, a unique alchemy of the imagination was taking place. In many ways the media landscape of the 1960s was a laboratory designed specifically to cure me of all my obsessions. Violence and pornography provided a kit of desperate measures that might give some meaning both to Miriam's death and the unnumbered victims of the war in China. The demise of feeling and emotion, the death of affect, presided like a morbid sun over the playground of that ominous decade, to which Sally seemed to hold a key. The brutalising newsreels of civil wars and assassinations, the stylisation of televised violence into an anthology of design statements, were matched by a pornography of science that took its materials, not from nature, but from the deviant curiosity of the scientist.

At an Arts Laboratory party launching an exhibition of work by a fashionable woman artist – a display of used sanitary towels – I proudly introduced Sally to Dick Sutherland, who had left Cambridge and now led a research team at the Institute of Psychology. In the hard months after our return from Spain he had been a generous friend. Often he drove to Shepperton in the evenings with bottles of bourbon and the latest traveller's tales from

Cape Kennedy, Tokyo or Los Angeles. 'You'll bounce back,' he told me confidently. Television had kept him young. Roaming around the world with his BBC crew, he was one of the first of the airport thinkers, always available to give an executive-lounge interview.

Sally took to him instantly, and Dick could see that she was everything I needed: wayward, affectionate and perverse. When he invited us to visit his laboratory I remembered that I had first met Miriam while volunteering to take part in a bogus experiment. True to form, Dick was still playing games with illusion and reality. He took us on a tour of his laboratory, charmed Sally with a series of well-rehearsed optical tricks and paradoxes, all the while keeping up his smoothly practised patter. His real talent, I realised, was to make all those he met feel that they were on a television programme.

Dick's infatuation with television made him as much a true citizen of the 1960s as Sally and Peter Lykiard. He was fascinated by the way in which television theatricalised everything while anchoring it firmly to the domestic and mundane. Since leaving Cambridge he had jettisoned his own past and begun to float free into this electronic realm that, like a kindly sky, taught the audience to admire itself. In an unguarded moment, he told me of his childhood in Scotland, the son of a stony Edinburgh architect and his devout Presbyterian wife. Wartime evacuation to relatives in Australia had opened his eyes to the charms of a beach culture where affection and approval came, not from within the family, but from the world around it.

Not surprisingly, Dick had never married. Without the ever-present autocue and monitor screen, a close relationship would have seemed a little unreal. But his awareness of his own flaws made him an astute psychologist, and he was an endless fund of ideas, many at my expense. The house in Shepperton always intrigued him.

'You've been to Jim's place in Shepperton, Sally?'

'Of course. It's a shrine.'

'Absolutely. Freud's primal cave furnished with wall-to-wall carpeting and a million years of love. In the long run, suburbia will triumph over everything, though it's hard to tell if the suburbs are a city's convalescent zone or a kind of petting zoo. In fact, they may be where a city dreams – Jim's like a sleeper poised at the onset of REM sleep. But before he wakes, let me show you round the lab. Nothing is quite what it seems, rather like reality in a way . . .'

In a darkened lecture theatre a volunteer panel of housewives, secretaries and off-duty firemen stared at the photographs of unnamed men and women projected onto a screen, trying to identify which were murderers and which victims.

'In fact, they're photos of the previous panel,' Dick whispered to Sally. 'People have remarkably strong prejudices about certain facial characteristics. The smallest cues convince them that they're looking at a child rapist or a Gestapo killer.'

In the laboratory next door a second group of volunteers were completing a confidential questionnaire about the effect of violent newsreels on their sex lives.

'Of course, there's no influence at all,' Dick assured us, 'and the footage we show them is much less violent than we tell them it's going to be. What's interesting, though, is that most people assume it does improve their sex lives. Everyone says there's too much violence on TV but secretly they want more.'

'So, thanks to TV, everything is the opposite of what it seems?' I commented.

'It does look like it.' We had returned to Dick's office, and he lay back in his chair, sneakers on the desk, letting Sally admire his long legs and actor's profile. 'It's obviously true in politics. We've studied the TV commercials put out by Governor Reagan of California. You can see that all this fierce right-wing stuff is the complete opposite of his reassuring body language. But people believe the body language – generally we've summed a person up long before he opens his mouth. We think Reagan knows this, thanks to his Hollywood experience. His whole political career is one long reaction shot with an irrelevant voice-over, as you can prove by deleting the sound-track and asking people to guess what he's saying. They trust the friendly sportscaster manner. On the other hand, once he's sitting in the Governor's mansion in Sacramento he has his mandate . . .'

'You're saying that the Fuehrer shouldn't have ranted and raved but come on like . . . the cowardly lion?'

'Exactly. The totalitarian systems of the future will be docile and subservient, and all the more threatening for that. Though there'll always be a place for out-and-out madness. In some way, people need the notion. The agnostic world keeps its religious festivals alive to meet the vacation demands of its work-force. By the same token, when medical science has conquered disease certain mental afflictions will be mimicked for social reasons – I'd put my bets on schizophrenia. It seems to represent the insane's idea of the normal.'

'And not the other way around?'

'Probably not – a disease that flatters our vanity has a huge advantage, like most venereal complaints.' Dick turned to the film projector behind his desk. 'Speaking of schizophrenia, we've been going through some wartime German film stored in the basement. One of the cans is a Waffen SS instructional film on how to build a pontoon bridge.'

Sally almost swooned at this. 'God, that's so weird – it just says everything . . .'

'Doesn't it?' Pleased by her attention, Dick reluctantly lowered the blind, uneager to put himself in the shade.

'Perhaps we could show it at the Arts Lab? I'd be happy to introduce it.'

We sat sipping wine in Dick's darkened office, surrounded by American licence plates and photographs of him at the controls of his Cessna, while the SS film fluttered through his projector. Was the film yet another fake? It looked convincingly real, and Sally held tight to my arm, mesmerised by the strong, white-skinned young men goodnaturedly singing their work-songs. Dick smiled to himself through the flickering light, murmured into the telephone when a BBC producer called, and watched Sally approvingly. He seemed glad that I had become the lover of this rapt and aroused young woman, and well aware of the rich and fierce sex we would have that evening as Sally replayed the film in her mind.

When we left he confided: 'She's right for you, Jim. Just what you need.'

Although Sally depended on me, in most respects I was her pupil, and the most important lesson she taught me came at the New Year's Eve party that she held at her flat in Bayswater. For some reason the place always unsettled me, filled with the debris of Sally's past, like those abandoned houses in wartime Shanghai where clock-time had been suspended for a little too long, and one returned to be confronted by the invisible stranger of one's younger self. I strolled around the Persian carpets stained with wine and cigarette ash, past the sofas with their unwashed covers reeking of stale incense, and thought of my children asleep in Shepperton as the middle-aged baby-sitter read her travel guide to British Honduras.

Yet the next day Sally would be washing Alice's hair and helping Lucy to stitch a miniature wardrobe for her trolls. Now she reeled about, amphetamines in her left hand, between the Marat/Sade posters and the blown-up photographs of Diane Arbus dwarves, shrieking at Peter

Lykiard as he arrived with a po-faced Japanese artist who had recently filmed their buttocks.

Sally proudly held my arm, hiccuped and left a fleck of vomit on my shoulder. She recovered with a flourish, cleared her mouth into a glass of wine and kissed me happily on the lips.

'Jim, I've found some wonderful *crêpe-de-chine*! Lucy's going to adore it . . .'

She careened away, swinging from shoulder to shoulder like a gymnast on the overhead rings.

Shortly before midnight, remembering the baby-sitter, I decided to leave for Shepperton. Searching for Sally, I pushed my way through the noise and smoke. Couples embraced among the unwashed dishes in the kitchen, and a party within a party was taking place as six guests camped on Sally's double bed. Two acolytes of the Japanese artist were taking a shower together in Sally's bathroom. I searched the other bedrooms and the second bathroom, filled with her friends' art school lumber, and then glanced into her little dressing-room.

When I reached the door Peter Lykiard asked me for a cigarette, clearly trying to distract me, as if I were a child about to stray into the adults' bedroom.

'Sally's busy, Jim – before I forget, I wanted to ask you about this Waffen SS film. Dick Sutherland is keen to do a presentation . . .'

Pushing past him, I opened the door. Sally was sitting on the quilted seat of the laundry basket, her skirt raised to her waist. Her bare legs were crossed around the hips of a young Spanish photographer whom we had met briefly at the Arts Laboratory. His unzipped trousers had slipped around his thighs, and his strong hands had pulled down the bodice of Sally's dress to expose her breasts. With their awkward and almost abstract movements, he and Sally seemed to be rehearsing a pornographic circus turn

195

in which they somehow swapped their clothes during an intense sex act. As he sucked at her right breast Sally kissed his forehead, her strong legs drawing his penis into her. Seeing me, she held the Spaniard's shoulders and gave me a frank and happy smile.

While I drove back to Shepperton I thought of Sally's affection for me, and her thousand kindnesses towards the children. Deep affection and the most casual disloyalty coexisted, separated by that tolerant smile. I remembered seeing the Vincents making love in their tired way on Sunday afternoons in Lunghua, and Mrs Vincent's knowing eyes when she saw me watching her through my curtain. I could almost believe that Sally had deliberately exposed herself to me, urging me to take the next step in my unsentimental education. I had been drawn to Sally because she offered a key to this strange decade, but the only stable element in Sally's world was instability. By isolating my emotions, by separating feeling from action, I might perhaps even learn to enjoy Sally's infidelities.

I thought of her near-drowning at Brighton beach, when she had allowed me to bring a second wife back from the waves. I could still feel the sombre power of the dark rollers striking my thighs and chest as I waded into the deep water where death ran, and the black foam through which I had dragged her on to the shingle.

Images of pain and anger floated free, like the billboards advertising the endless deaths of the murdered President, messages of violence and desire that alone could assuage the bereaved.

I sped on past the oncoming headlights, crossing the moonlit Thames to where Shepperton lay asleep in my children's dreams.

CHAPTER TEN

The Kingdom of Light

'Think of LSD as the kaleidoscope's view of the eye.'

While Dick spoke I sat in my study by the open French window, looking down at the glass of water in my hand and the sugar cube exposed beside the BBC tape-recorder. A sinister glitter rose from the foil wrapper.

'Dick, are we ready?' I asked over my shoulder. 'This is starting to feel like a suicide attempt.'

'Give me a moment – you *are* going to heaven . . .' Dick adjusted the tripod of his cine-camera, aiming its ferocious little lens at my face. Already I resented the camera, staring at me like a deformed robot. Summer light filled the garden, playing among the broken toys and the clothes-line with its waving pyjamas – the usual cheerful mess that I had offered to clear away. But Dick had been adamant that I change nothing.

Sipping at the water, I noticed the collapsed wigwam which Alice and Henry had built from an old tartan blanket and the cucumber frame. Banished from its dark interior for some breach of childhood protocol, Lucy had demolished the wigwam with her pedal-car. The others had threatened a terrible revenge, forgotten the moment that Cleo Churchill and her daughter Penny arrived at the front door. Friends of Dick, they would take the children down to the river while he and I embarked on a trip of our own, a short safari across the width of my skull.

'Dick, the garden's a mess – I ought to clear it up. Let's face it, your TV audience isn't going to be on acid.'

'Just what the ratings need. I'll suggest it to the BBC. They can put a gift-pack in *Radio Times*.'

The four children were shouting in the hall, clamouring

for ice-cream, comics and bubble-gum wrappers. Cleo Churchill put her head around the door and grimaced cheerfully.

'There's a riot brewing. I'll have to leave you to it.'

'That's fine, Cleo. Jim's eager to go. Give us a couple of hours.'

'Two hours? You ought to be filming me.' She frowned at the camera and microphone, the blood-pressure kit and my straight-backed chair. 'Jim, it looks genuinely weird – are you going to be all right?'

'Don't worry. Dick's monitored a lot of trips.'

'Even so. Never trust the ferryman.'

I could see that she disapproved, taking the view that there were more than enough adult excitements in the world; the experiment that Dick and I were about to make with my brain chemistry was a boy's game scarcely different from those that Henry played in the garden, when he lit a cigarette stub inside the wigwam, or exploded a box of matches. Cleo, with her quick smile and shy glamour, was an editor of children's books whom I sometimes saw at Dick's parties. Aware, a little uneasily, of her concern, I guessed that she was worried about more than Dick's credentials. As she withdrew her hand reluctantly from my shoulder she glanced from the perspiration on my face to the untidy study and garden. Beyond any thoughts about the wisdom of experimenting with LSD was a thirty-second guess at my character and whatever flaws this potent hallucinogen might expose.

'Okay . . .' Dick set a dial on his aviator's watch and started the tape-recorder. 'It's 15:05 on June 17, 1967 . . .'

Meeting Cleo's warning eyes, I placed the sugar cube on my tongue and let it rest there in a small show of defiance. As the children flung back the front door and rushed towards the gate I hesitated for a last moment. When Cleo had gone, slamming the door after her, I swallowed a mouthful of water.

'Right,' Dick told me. 'You'll feel something in about half an hour, so sit back and relax. We can play chess.'

'I'll look at the garden.' I could usually beat Dick at chess, but this was one game he would enjoy losing, as the pieces turned into dragons. I listened to the children's shouts fading down the street, followed by Cleo's strong, cheerful voice. Herself a single parent, she had implied that I was stepping out of character, a responsible father taking this questionable drug, still legally available in England, though there had been frequent calls to have it scheduled.

I stared at the toy-cluttered garden, a moraine of happy memories that the past three years had deposited on this suburban plot. The glacier had moved on, Miriam sleeping calmly within its deeps. The children had almost forgotten their mother, something I had tried to prevent, mistakenly. If they remembered her it was on other levels, in their good humour, resilience and confidence in unearned affection.

Strangely, Miriam had begun to recede even from me, while at the same time standing out more clearly in my memory. She seemed like the statue of a madonna suspended above the nave of a cathedral, rising into the air as I stepped away from her. The perspective lines of my life still led back to Miriam, but I owed a great deal to the women I had known since her death, above all to Sally Mumford, who had helped me to face head-on the pressures of pain and obsessive sexuality. Curiously, Sally's open infidelities had helped to ease my memories of Miriam, as if her death had been an infidelity of a special kind.

However, Dick had not been keen on having Sally present when he offered to supervise my LSD experiment. Her sudden swerves of mood, her muddled enthusiasms, might derail the hallucinatory locomotive. Eager to make the experiment, and explore the locked doors of consciousness, I agreed that Cleo Churchill should look after the children. The amphetamines and drinamyls I had sometimes taken seemed less mind-altering than the average double Scotch, but Dick assured me that LSD was pushing against the limits of the brain.

I remembered his presentation to the head of the BBC's science programmes, as he outlined the projected series in which I would take part. Confident as always that he held his audience's attention, he had prowled around his display charts of brain sections and ECG readings like a pitchman selling the human brain to a party of intrigued visitors from another planet.

'The central nervous system is nature's Sistine Chapel, but we have to bear in mind that the world our senses present to us – this office, my lab, our awareness of time – is a ramshackle construct which our brains have devised to let us get on with the job of maintaining ourselves and reproducing our species. What we see is a highly conventionalised picture, a simple tourist guide to a very strange city. We need to dismantle this ramshackle construct in order to grasp what's really going on. The visual space we occupy doesn't actually coincide with the external world. Shadows are far deeper than they seem to us; the brain softens out the sharp contrasts so that we can analyse them more clearly – otherwise the world would be a mass of zebra stripes . . .

'Consciousness is the central nervous system's brave gamble that it exists, an artefact that allows it to make its way around the internal and external environments. In fact, we're beginning to think that time itself is a primitive psychological structure that we've inherited from the distant past, along with the appendix and the little toe. Yet we're totally trapped by this archaic structure with its minutes and hours trailing after each other like a procession of the blind. Once we get hold of a more advanced notion of time – let's say, time perceived as simultaneity

– we reach the threshold of a far larger mental universe . . .

'Why do the dying think they're floating through tunnels? Under extreme pressure, the various centres in the brain which organise a coherent view of the world begin to break down. The brain scans its collapsing field of vision, and constructs out of the last few rings of cells what it desperately hopes is an escape tunnel. Right to the end the brain is trying at all costs to rationalise reality – whether it's starved of input or flooded with sensory data it builds artificial structures that try to make sense of the world. Out of this come not only near-death experiences but our visions of heaven and hell.'

Everyone had been intrigued, but the BBC declined to buy the series.

'Dr Sutherland,' the head of science programmes had commented, 'your description of the dying brain rather resembles the BBC . . .'

'Dick, my watch has stopped.'

'Let me see. No, it's 3.45.'

'It must be later than that . . .'

I stared at the motionless second hand, and tried to work the winder. My fingers felt as cool and sensitive as a jeweller's, but I had the sudden notion they belonged to someone else. The second hand moved again, then halted for a further indefinite moment. A deep ruby light filled the garden, as if the sun had begun to overheat. I leaned forward, almost falling from the chair, and peered at the vivid cyanide blue of the sky.

'Sit back and relax.' Dick stood behind me, reassuringly holding my shoulders. 'There'll be a little retinal irritation to start with.'

'Dick, I'm moving in and out of time.'

'That began some while ago. Look at the garden and

see what you make of the colours – they're probably drifting down the spectrum.'

I pushed Dick's hands away, and wondered if he was playing another of his devious games. He had always been strongly competitive, and envied me both Miriam and my China background. There was a sly look on his face which I remembered seeing in his office at Cambridge, like that of a fisherman who had hooked an unexpected catch and was just out of reach of his gaff.

The spools of the tape recorder were turning, but I noticed that they were spinning towards each other. Assuming that this was another piece of antiquated BBC equipment, I waited for the unravelling tape to loop into the air. The black plastic case had separated from the frame, but before I could warn Dick he had stepped away from me to his camera.

Colours were floating free from the surfaces around me. The summer air had become a translucent prism and the blades of uncut grass were touched by a layer of emerald light. The giant Russian sunflowers that I had grown for Alice and Lucy wore crowns of gold that drew them towards the sky. A haze of dense ruby air suffused the foliage of the cherry trees. The scarlet paintwork of Lucy's pedal car was separating from the battered metal, a glowing carapace that some skilful technician had painted on the air, and which I wanted to press down onto the rusty shell.

The untidy garden glowed with chemical light. The apple tree and its tree-house formed a chalet-sized cathedral, its branches a stained-glass window in which the broken toys were set within their own haloes. The dragon-patterns of the Chinese carpet under my feet, the shaggy bark of the pear tree scored with Henry's initials, the creosoted panels of the fence were releasing the light trapped within themselves. The green veil of every leaf and stem, the scarlet of Lucy's car, were detachable skins below which the real leaf and car were waiting to be discovered. The sunlight and its generous spectrum were gaudy pennants celebrating the unique identity of the smallest stone and twig. Refracted through the prism of their true selves, the leaves and flowers were glowing windows in the advent calendar of nature.

'Jim, look towards the camera . . .'

Dick sat in the armchair beside me, the tape recorder on his lap. Its spools still turned in opposite directions, but none of the tape had become entangled. As the light in the garden grew more intense I was struck by the remarkable lustre of Dick's hair – some over-eager make-up girl at the studios had fitted him with a shoulder-length toupee of copper fleece. Light coursed through its filaments, and I wanted to warn Dick that his viewers would see every fevered mole and freckle in his cheeks. The blood raced through the enlarged capillaries, turning his hands and face into a set of inflamed maps.

Stifled by the seething room, I stood up and stepped through the French window. I walked across the garden, my feet sinking through the electric haze that lay over the grass. The stones in the rockery shone like gems set in jeweller's velvet, and the soil in the flower-beds was warm with the glow of compost giving life to itself.

My arms and legs were dressed in light, sheathes of mother-of-pearl that formed a coronation armour. I looked down at the simple headstone that marked the grave of Henry's Dutch rabbit, waiting for the creature to reconstitute itself from its own bones and lollop through the glowing grass. In the waking dream of this illuminated garden, time and space no longer pressed their needs. The contingent world was rearranging itself, and serial time was giving way to simultaneity, as Dick had promised, where the living happily consorted with the dead, the animate with the inanimate.

I waited for Miriam to appear among the trees. She

would walk in this garden again, while Alice and Lucy played with their younger selves and I met the youthful husband I once had been. I looked back at the house, but Dick had vanished, and his camera stood on its tripod beside my empty chair. Charlton Road ran through a nave of light towards the river, and I assumed that Dick had gone to collect the children, telling them of their new playmates waiting for them at home.

I followed the pathway around the house. The silver envelope of my car floated in the drive like a tethered blimp. My neighbour approached with her elderly retriever, whose frayed coat and white muzzle glowed like a lion's. Shepperton lay before me, a town of matadors and their families dressed in their suits of light. The traffic moved down the high street, the cars exchanging their vivid auras. A helicopter crossed the river, its blades throwing silver spears at the great elms.

I crossed the road by the war memorial and entered the riverside park. In the distance, under the willow trees, my children were playing with balloons they had bought at the sweet-shop. Globes of painted air hovered between their hands. Behind them a young woman walked through the forest. Her blonde hair floated among the leaves, shedding haloes on to the ground at her feet. Breathless, I was struck by the grace of her walk, as she calmed the trees with a gesture and settled the starlings with a smile. With her unguarded beauty, she reminded me of a princess in the jewelled caverns of Gustave Moreau. I waved to her, hoping that she would touch me with the same calm grace, but she was following the children towards the river.

Losing my way in the overlit foliage, I sat down on a bench and stared at the unmoving hands of my watch. The world paused as time held its breath. The light was now so intense that it bleached all colour from the foliage of the elms. The grass around me was a carpet of milled glass, the trees hung with pendants of ice carved from the crystallised air. My eyes were exhausted by the whiteness of the world. Alice and Lucy ran towards me, figures in an over-exposed film, all expression blanched from their faces as they played in their snow palace.

The river was a glacier of opal, moving past frosted banks. If time stood still, the water would fail to break under my feet. I walked towards it, ready to step on to its corrugated surface, aware of Cleo Churchill warning me away with her Moreau smile. She was pulling at my arm, but I knew that we could cross the river together and rest with the children in the meadow facing the park.

I called soundlessly to Alice and Lucy, who stared at me in a puzzled way, as if they had forgotten that I was their father. Then Dick Sutherland was running through the trees towards me, holding my shoulders and guiding me away from the water. I sat with him on the white grass, while the doors of the sun closed around me.

Three hours later I lay in my bedroom, a pillow under my back, and my neck aching from the strain of staring at the sky. An interior dusk had settled over everything. The garden was sombre now, the muted colours locked away within the trees and flowers, as if depressed after their brief freedom. I tried to shield my inflamed eyes from the sunlight reflected off the passing cars. My entire nervous system was irritable and exhausted, and I could neither sleep nor rest. After rescuing me from the river, Dick had driven me back to the house and left me to recover while Cleo cooked an evening meal for the children.

Distracted by a call from a TV producer, Dick had allowed me to slip away to the park. Already I regretted taking part in the experiment. Dick's carelessness, whether deliberate or not, had nearly led me to drown myself. Annoyingly, he was far more interested in my messianic attempt to walk on water than in my vision of

Shepperton as a solar garden, a sleeping paradise waiting to be woken from every stone and leaf.

Trying to steady my mind, I stared at the bedroom ceiling. Whenever my gaze lingered for more than a few seconds a festering sore appeared in the old plaster, as if my eyes were transmitting a virulent disease, a Gorgon-stare that turned a minute insect stain into a throbbing infection. Soon the suppurating plaster was covered with a plague of boils. Trying to recapture their paradise vision, the optical centres of my brain were misreading the smallest cues in the play of light across the quiet room.

I covered my eyes and listened to the children enjoying an impromptu party with Cleo and her daughter. Their voices calmed me, but when I moved my hand I saw that flies covered every inch of the room. Their trembling wings seethed on the sheets and pillows, cloaking my hands in black mittens. Trying to drive them away, I touched my scalp and found that a piece of my skull was missing. The tips of my fingers dipped into the soft tissues of my brain . . .

Hearing my cry, Cleo left the children and ran up the staircase. She sat on the bed and placed my hands in her lap, shaking her head over the afternoon's folly. Looking up at her concerned face, I could still see the nimbus of light that had followed her through the riverside trees. I remembered the benediction she had bestowed on every starling and blade of grass.

'Jim . . . shall I telephone Richard? I ought to ring your local doctor.'

'No – but call Peggy Gardner. I'll come out of it soon.' The last person I wanted around was Miriam's sometime physician, still under the thumb of Midwife Bell and ready to cast doubt on my fitness as a parent. Short cuts to paradise and shamanistic visions belonged to the dubious realm of back-street abortions and nutmeg addiction. I moved my hands gingerly to my scalp, relieved that my

206

skull was intact. 'My fingers are so sensitive – I thought I'd pushed them into my brain. Are the children all right?'

'They're fine – I've invented a new game for them. They think you've got sunstroke.'

'I have! That intense light – for a few seconds this afternoon I saw . . . heaven and hell.'

'That *must* be one of Richard's overdoses.' There was a hint of criticism, as if she were well aware of Dick's ambiguous experiments. 'I hope it was worth it.'

'Yes . . . yes, it was.' I held her hand, waiting as the termites faded into the walls. Somewhere inside my head Cleo was still walking through the riverside forest, waiting for me to join her in the palace of light. Its doors stood ajar among the homely elms. In that paradise vision all her shyness had gone, she no longer hid her eyes behind her long hair and ever-ready smile. 'It went to pieces at the end, but I saw something I'd never seen before, a dream of . . .'

'The real world?'

'All the real worlds. Everything was its original self . . .' Trying to explain myself, I reached out and touched her hair. 'I told Dick that you looked like an archangel.'

She moved my hand from her cheek, frowning at my foolhardiness. 'That should do wonders for my career. I hope you repeat that on the programme.'

'I will.' I raised myself and sat uncomfortably on the bed beside her. I wanted to embrace Cleo's broad hips. One day she and I would make that river crossing together. 'Cleo, tell me – was there any film in the camera?'

'I assume so – why?'

'People are easier to control when they think they're going on television. It's just Dick . . .'

'Perhaps you've been too trusting – but I imagine he understands you.'

She paused at the door, looking at me as if aware for

the first time of my real motives for embarking on this risky expedition across my head.

If Cleo was prepared to put aside her doubts, Peggy Gardner was resolutely disapproving. During the next days I prowled the garden, staring at the sunflowers and the broken toys, as I tried to understand why the light had left them. The whole of Shepperton was drab and inert, exhausted by the effort of briefly becoming its real self. While the children were at school I walked down to the river, searching the trees for any sign of Cleo's presence. As the sunlight pierced the foliage I caught hints of that magic glade where she had walked with the birds, dressed in light.

'You've let a Trojan horse into your mind,' Peggy told me, mustering a show of sympathy. 'What were you really trying to do?'

I conducted the air, thinking of a reply. '"Place the logic of the visible at the service of the invisible . . ." It was stranger than I expected – I was actually looking inside my own head.'

'But, Jamie dear – we already know what's there. It's obvious to anyone who's read a few pages.'

'Shadows on the wall. Dick was right – I was watching the brain at work, seeing it assemble pieces of time and space into a workable dream of life.' I pointed to the walls of my study and the sunlit garden. 'All this is just as much a stage-set as anything in Shepperton Studios.'

'And what happens when you move the stage-sets out of the way?'

'To be honest, I don't know yet.'

'You're going to try again?'

'In a month or two. Dick is keen to film me.'

'Mad . . . all this for a television programme?'

'I'm humouring him there. It's hard to describe the

intense light, the sense that one's about to witness some huge revelation.'

'But what?'

'I'll find out. The same light lay over Lunghua on the day the war ended.'

'It never ended – for you.'

Peggy stood in the open doorway with her back to the garden, looking at me in the same kindly and tolerant way I remembered from the children's hut, when I had outlined some madcap method of finding food for us. The light touched her strong shoulders and the handsome hips I had never held. In a real sense we knew each other too well. Sex was for strangers, and as soon as one ceased to be a stranger desire died. Miriam had always been careful to keep part of herself veiled from me. Perhaps one day Peggy and I would become strangers to each other, as we grew older and apart . . .

The light shifted, a retinal veer. For a moment I saw Peggy suspended in the air above the pear tree, angel of our suburb. I imagined this spinsterish doctor in her sensible woollen suit and court shoes, positioned at various points above the rooftops of Shepperton.

'Are you all right?' Peggy was staring at my eyes. 'You were miles away. What about the children – is Sally going to look after them?'

'Dick's asked a friend of his, Cleo Churchill. She brought her daughter and slept on the sofa. She's more level-headed – I think he's frightened that Sally might –'

'Poor Sally. You people use each other like deviant children.'

I kissed Peggy fondly, watched her drive away, and then helped the children with their homework and prepared our lunch. Deviant adults? The reproof stung, however much I reminded myself that Peggy's stance of responsibility and good sense was more at odds with the world than

209

she realised. She might care for her deprived and abused infants, but she had never loved a child of her own, with all that love entailed. Spectres stalked the little garden of her house in Chelsea. It was not only in my mind that the four Japanese soldiers still waited at their wayside railway station for a train that would never come, as trapped by time as we were. War was the means by which nations escaped from time. Peggy and I and those Japanese soldiers had been marooned on that island platform, waiting for another war to set us free. They had tormented the Chinese to death in the hope that cruelty alone would release the mainspring of war.

Three weeks later, on another warm summer afternoon, I sat in my chair by the open French window. Dick's camera, with or without its film, sat on its tripod. While Cleo readied the children for a picnic, Dick was talking to his agent on the telephone, still in high hopes of selling his brain series to a regional channel.

At Dick's suggestion we had transformed the overgrown garden into a model of bourgeois family life. The children's toys sat on the grass like exhibits at a church fete. Rescued from the darkest cupboards, an older generation of bears and koalas sat in a circle like geriatric patients allowed to take the sun. The girls' brightest frocks, washed and ironed, hung from the clothes line, and Henry's bull-fight poster, listing his name with those of Cordobés and Paco Camino, was pinned to the pear tree.

Hearing the children shouting by the gate, I left my seat and walked around the side path. Cleo was lifting a picnic basket through the kitchen door.

'Are you coming with us? Good.' She greeted me with a smile of surprise. She disapproved of Dick's experiments, and clearly thought I was being manipulated by him.

'No.' I helped her with the basket. 'I wish I was. We're starting in a moment.'

She brushed her hair from her cheeks, deliberately showing me her strong face. 'I hope you're all right. Last time . . .'

'There was something wrong with the dose. Don't worry. I'll see you as an archangel again.'

'See me as I am.' She stopped by the car and rested the picnic basket on the hood. Earlier she had helped Dick to set out the children's toys on the grass, striding uneasily around the garden on her strong legs like the reluctant member of a demolition squad. 'Why don't you come with us? You're the last person who needs to experiment with himself.'

'Cleo, I promised Dick . . .'

Lucy skipped up to me, showing off her shiny belt. 'Daddy, are you coming?'

'Come on, Daddy,' Henry chimed in. 'We're going to Magic World.'

'Daddy, go on.'

Cleo hefted the basket onto her strong hip, leaving me to make my own decision. 'I've heard a lot about Magic World.'

'I hope it's still there. Old film props from TV commercials.'

'That sounds like fun. A lot more real than Dick's nonsense.'

I held the gate for her, and watched the children charge off towards the water-meadow, followed by the old retriever. Were they trying to recruit Cleo into their lost childhood, finding again that idyllic dream for which I was searching with LSD? I remembered the pale, spectral children who had gazed at me beside the river, as if watching me from the other side of death.

Alice held the retriever's collar, smiling as she waited hopefully for me to join her.

211

'You're right.' I took the basket from Cleo's hand. The warm scent of her body was more vivid than anything even LSD could contrive. 'Dick can find someone else. We'll bring a couple of bottles and see you at the splash in a few minutes . . .'

Hallucinations sang on the summer¯ air, skipping towards the water meadows and the magic glade by the film studios.

CHAPTER ELEVEN

The Exhibition

The idea of staging an exhibition of crashed cars came to me in 1969 after the road accident near Fair Oaks airfield in which Sally and David Hunter were involved. Luckily, neither of them was hurt in any way, but the strange circumstances of the accident, and the behaviour of the witnesses, seemed to spring straight from the special logic of the Sixties. The exhibition at the Arts Laboratory, which intrigued some visitors and outraged a great many more, summed up so many of my obsessions at the time, and clearly foretold the car crash that nearly killed me three months later. Right until its end, the decade continued to unravel its lurid mythologies.

Sally, still determined to prise me away from Shepperton, had bought tickets for the Fair Oaks air show, where David was taking part in a formation flight of vintage Tiger Moths. Alice and Lucy were too frightened by the exploding exhausts to come with us, and were spending the day with Cleo Churchill and her daughter. Generous as ever, Sally insisted on a special treat for Henry. When she arrived he was assembling a model aircraft in the nursery, surrounded by his own air display of World War II fighters, exquisite replicas that seemed to contain more detail than their originals.

'Come on, Henry! I'll ask David to give you a spin around Shepperton.'

'Well . . . David's scary. Will Neil Armstrong be there?'

'He sent his apologies – he had to go back to the Moon.'
Sally squeezed Henry's American football helmet, a gift

from Dick Sutherland, over her white hair. 'Henry, I'm going to be the first woman astronaut.'

'Wow . . . ! A woman?'

'Hard to grasp, isn't it? One giant step for womankind, that's what we need.' When Henry went off to change, Sally soared around the model planes, blowing smoke from her Moroccan Gold through the silver propellers. 'They're so perfect, like hatched Fabergé eggs. The world's filling up with broken plastic, and little Henry sits here by himself, putting it all together again. That's the sort of thing you should write about.'

'I do, Sally. It's practically my only theme.' Glad to see her, I held her restless hips. 'Sally . . . you're five miles high before the wheels leave the ground.'

'This is your captain speaking.' She placed her scarred forearms with their medley of sampler scents on my shoulders. 'The plane now crashing on Shepperton is the Mumford Express . . .'

She was still wearing the football helmet when we set off for Fair Oaks airfield. Her visits to Shepperton, though less frequent, always calmed Sally. She landed like an eccentric Victorian balloonist, tethered to the ground by the children's affection for her. But once we left its gentle gravity she began to soar away. Blonde hair streaming through the open roof, she lay with her arms out of the window, waving to the extras leaving the film studios. The glowing end of her loosely-packed cigarette blew a train of sparks into the rear seat and set fire to the ear of a faithful koala. As Henry choked, Sally lunged over the seat and slapped at the smoking embers. She shouted to the young policeman guiding traffic into Fair Oaks, who gazed in awe at her mini-skirt riding over her ice-pale buttocks.

When we reached the car park she noticed a television crew filming the air display. Sally pulled off the helmet and assumed the hard-eyed stare of her favourite amphetamine shades, gazing in a ravaged way at the parked planes and the handsome pilots. The anti-Viet Nam protest marches and scuffles with police, the drug busts and cooling-off trips to New York, had given her a terminal Manhattan tremor, part permanent jet lag, part overdose of heroin and time. Like so many others at the end of the 60s, that ten-year pharmaceutical trial, she thought of the media landscape as a life-support system, force-feeding a diet of violence and sensation into her numbed brain.

But sometimes I felt that it was Sally and a few thousands like her who supported the decade, which ruthlessly tapped their fraying nervous systems for the last pulse of energy and excitement. The carousel was spinning ever faster, driven on by Sally as she rode her exhausted unicorn. I hated the needle arms, but loved to see her sweep into Shepperton with presents for the children and endless King's Road talk. She was happy to camp for hours with Alice and Lucy in their garden tent, bake and ice a birthday cake for a long-serving teddy. Later, when the children were asleep, she lay back on the sofa with her heels in the small of my back, almost strangling me as she seized some slipping memory of her father that I had helped to return to her.

She would dress quickly and forget me, rushing into the night with shouts about a party, too impatient to burden herself with any needs of mine. A little deflated, I was usually relieved to see her go. I was nervous of the empty syringes I found in the lavatory cistern. Worryingly, she stole money from the children, as if trying to take back part of the affection she had given them. Alice and Lucy were too fond of Sally to care. When I tried to lend her money she waved her cheque books at me, and I realised that she needed to steal the small coins from the girls' purses. The carousel had tricked her into thinking that nothing mattered but its speed.

'Sally, sweet . . . Jim, she got you out of that little

Alcatraz of yours.' David stood glamorously by his Tiger Moth in a white flying suit, adjusting a fire extinguisher. He embraced Sally, treated me to a friendly but cool smile, and placed the extinguisher in my hands with a gesture implying that I might soon need it. 'Let's go, Henry – we'll sneak off and bomb Shepperton . . .'

'Say, can we, David? Let's bomb my school.'

I had guessed for some time that Sally was seeing him. They shared nothing in the way of temperament or interests – David loathed hippies and bikers, and would try to run them down – but they could map their wayward needs on to each other.

Henry and I paused to peer at a Mignet Flying Flea, little more than an aerial skateboard, and Sally strolled towards the Tiger Moth, which David flew in a vermouth commercial. She peeled away her silk scarf as if they were about to make love under its wing. When he greeted Sally, David's eyes were filled with the easy humour he had turned upon the Moose Jaw whores. He held her to his shoulder, pressing her blonde hair to his lips, while giving Henry a cheery wave. Within minutes Sally was wearing a Bomber Command jacket, and an antique helmet and goggles, a fetishist's dream of a white-haired woman in flying leather. As she stood on tip-toe and kissed David, her crutch ruled the airfield.

Sally clung to his arm, glad to test this dangerous man. When they took off together in the Tiger Moth, David made a formal circuit of the airfield, and I sensed that he was exposing her to the entire air show, a naiad of the air he had brought down from the clouds. After they landed he lifted her from the cockpit, formally introducing her to the mortal earth. Sally's face was white with cold, her nose and lips as pointed as an arctic bird's, the wind still blowing through her roused eyes. The sky behind her was a dream of heroin. I wanted to stay with them, fearing that

216

Sally might incite David to some mad piece of stunt flying, but he avoided my eyes.

David and I had seen less of each other in recent years. I liked him for his disruptive spirit and off-hand charm, and his fondness towards the children – Henry's entire passion for aircraft had been carefully instilled by David, who spent endless afternoons driving him to remote light airfields. But David had taken Miriam's death badly – far from forgetting her, he felt her loss more strongly as time passed. Sometimes he looked at me as if he thought that I was responsible for her death, and that he alone was keeping her memory alive. A week before the Fair Oaks air show he came up to me in a Soho restaurant, where I was having lunch with an American journalist, and stood silently by our table, ignoring my invitation to join us. While the waiters brushed past him he stared into my face, at last recognising me for what I was. I wondered if he was going to hit me, but he touched my shoulder without speaking and walked back to his friends.

Outwardly he was still the wise older brother, understanding my entire character and motives. He had never read anything of mine, saying that there was no need to – we had already lived through the most important story inside my head. His sense of humour had become more eccentric, almost mimicking the surrealists I admired so much. The increasing numbers of Japanese tourists who visited London he regarded as a conscious attempt to provoke him. Giving me a lift back from the premiere of *2001: A Space Odyssey* ('. . . a Pan-Am instructional film for space-hostesses,' was his comment), he stopped his Jaguar in Belgrave Square and smilingly watched one of the high stucco houses. I assumed that he had tracked down the home address of a favourite TV comedian, but as it happened this was the Japanese embassy. When some luckless attaché emerged, probably on the way to a British Council seminar on cultural relations between our countries, David raced the engine and hurled the Jaguar at the elderly Japanese, almost throwing him across the bonnet. To David this had been a lighthearted joke, which would have lost none of its point if he had killed the man. 'I have to remind myself of Shanghai,' he shouted as we cornered through Knightsbridge at speed. 'I'm starting to forget it . . . the damn thing is, there's nothing else to remember.'

Fortunately, his service in the RAF had given him a support network of ex-military pilots, one of the strongest in the world. He was now an aircraft dealer, selling French two-seater helicopters to pop stars and style-conscious business tycoons. But his real passion was saloon-car racing at Brand's Hatch. He had twice been banned for dangerous track manoeuvres, the same dangerous driving to which he treated every suburban dual carriageway. He drove in a deliberately careless way, as if trying to express a casual nothingness. Cut off from his past in China, which both of us had begun to forget, and with no roots in England, he watched the few real elements in his life abandon him as his parents died and war-time friends retired to Australia and South Africa.

Concerned for David, I wanted to help him, just as I wanted to steer Sally away from her needles, but I was too busy with the children. When they strolled arm in arm towards the flying-club bar I began to follow them, and felt Henry tug at my arm. He had the sense to know that we should leave them alone, and was far more interested in the lines of vintage flying machines drawn up on the grass, each a conjuring trick to trump the wind. Glad to be together, we spent the afternoon roaming the air show.

At the end of the day, when we returned to the car-park, David's Jaguar and Sally had gone. I assumed that David had given her a lift to her flat in Bayswater. The scent of her body still filled the interior of our car, imprinted on the seat beside me like an almost visible photograph of affection and desire. I thought of her as we pushed through the traffic returning to London. Tailbacks blocked both lanes, and warning beacons flashed from the roof of a police cruiser parked on the grass verge.

Two cars had collided in the approaches to Chertsey Bridge, and windscreen glass speckled the road. We moved forward, waved on in a theatrical way by a police patrolman, as if we were film extras late for the day's shooting. Through the oncoming traffic I could see the first of the damaged cars, a London taxi carrying two Japanese air stewardesses and their suitcases. Watched by a police sergeant, the cab driver was examining his crushed headlights and radiator grille. The young Japanese women stood beside him, squinting at the English sunlight in an almost guilty way.

I recognised the second car, and the white leg extended to the road through the open passenger door. David's silver Jaguar lay slewed across the road, its chromium bumper twisted into the right wheel housing. Sally and David sat together in the front seat. Neither had been hurt, but the Jaguar's windscreen had burst, covering the passenger compartment and the roadway with nuggets of glass. Sally lay back, her thighs spread, one hand resting on David's arm. She was looking down at the glass that covered their laps, which neither of them made any attempt to brush away. Watching them, I was struck by their self-conscious pose, like dancers arrested in an audience-catching flourish at the end of their performance. They were uninterested in each other's well-being, but only in the postures they assumed within the cabin of the Jaguar, as if they were memorising for future use the exact geometry of Sally's exposed thighs and the ribbed leather of the upholstery, the precise angle between David's crutch and the jut and rake of the steering wheel.

The police sergeant spoke to them through the window,

but they ignored him, staring in a rapt way at their own hands. They seemed almost to be rehearsing themselves for a performance to come, some even more elaborately staged collision. There was no trace of shock in Sally's face, but a thin smile that was faintly sexual in its self-regard.

The traffic crept towards the bridge, but I stopped the car and opened my door, ready to offer my help before the ambulance arrived.

'Daddy . . . !' Henry warned. 'The policeman's shouting at you!'

A fist drummed on the roof over my head. I acknowledged the patrolman's signal, waved encouragingly to Sally and David and rejoined the queue crossing the bridge. A few pedestrians stood at the kerb, staring idly at the damaged cars. They stepped back, making room for a more appreciative audience that had now arrived. Spectators returning from the air show were leaving their cars in a side-street and in the car-park of a riverside pub. They gathered around the Jaguar, inspecting the damaged bodywork and the pattern of tyre-marks scored into the road with the practised eyes of enthusiasts judging a display of aerobatics. Two cine-cameras recorded the scene, and the police made no attempt to stop them, so impressed were they by the knowledgeability of this sympathetic audience. Yet no one made the smallest effort to help Sally and David, and a man in a flying jacket even protested when an ambulance appeared on the scene and the attendants lifting Sally from the Jaguar blocked the view-finder of his expensive camera. As I watched, a new street theatre had been born.

During the next weeks, as I drove through central London, I noticed the same thoughtful gaze in the people who gathered at street accidents, as if the secret formulas of their lives were exposed by these random collisions.

Office-workers on their way to lunch, drivers unloading delivery vans, stared at the damaged cars that materialised out of the passing traffic in a fanfare of ringing metal and sounding horns. An attentive audience would invariably form, calmly inspecting the stricken vehicles.

Often I stopped my car and walked through the crowds, struck by the spectators' quiet and measured response. Only ten years earlier everyone would have been pulling with their bare hands at the broken bodywork and crushed roofs, trying to free the injured occupants. Born out of an ecology of violence, acts of numbing brutality now ruled the imaginative spaces of their lives, leaching away all feeling and emotion. Perhaps, in their thoughtful communion with the crashed car, they were trying to come to terms with the televised disasters and assassinations that enfolded their minds, and doing what they could to restore a lost compassion.

Where this perverse logic might lead I grasped for the first time when Sally drove me to the opening of the Arts Laboratory at its new premises in Camden Town. Usually I was wary of being a passenger in Sally's spirited but erratic MG, and always found an excuse to prevent her driving the children. On this evening, however, she was surprisingly sedate, driving well within the speed limit and keeping a steady eye on the rear-view mirror. Anxious for her, I wondered if she were still recovering from the collision after the air show.

'I didn't feel a thing,' she told me, clearly disappointed. 'I didn't even see it happen. Suddenly we were sitting there with all this glass and these huge policemen. Not even a scratch – I really feel cheated.'

'You could have gone through the windshield.'

'Jim, it was a bump! You would have enjoyed it. David pulled the wheel over without thinking.'

'I can't believe that . . .' At the foot of Chertsey Bridge the Japanese stewardesses had stood blinking in the sun-

221

light like hostages tied to a target. 'I bet he knew exactly what he was doing.'

'No, that's David. He felt like a shunt. I don't know why the Japanese were there.'

'Sally, he'll kill you.'

'Great! I might like that . . .' We had stopped on the Westway flyover, and the traffic lights flared across Sally's sallow face and its wild smile. Seeing that she had shocked me, she pressed my hand to the steering wheel. 'Don't worry, David wants to get himself killed, he isn't interested in me. He's always trying to hit other cars. Every shunt reminds him of something – the war, I guess. You never talked about your camp, Jim. Did he have a bad time, physically?'

'Physically, nothing happened to him at all.'

'And what about you – mentally, maybe?'

'Sally, that was long, long ago.'

'Not for him. Car crashes bring it all back for David. They mean for him what bull-fights mean for everyone else – sex and death . . . Jim, you didn't mind me going off with him? He's your oldest friend, in a way it's not like my picking someone you didn't know.'

'I suppose that's true . . .'

'I love the pixies. They helped me to grow up. And you. Now you're writing all the time, and I'm so busy with things . . .' She spoke softly, as if to herself. 'Everyone changes, and we're always moving away from each other. Just for once I wish we could all stand still and remember the way things were. There's so much happening, and I want to be part of it all. I want to live everyone's dreams, be right inside them . . .'

'Sally, you are. But –'

'Jim, I'll always let you fuck me.'

She brushed her ungroomed hair, aware that I might not always want to. Her fingers fiddled with her scarred upper lip, where she had been punched by a casual lover,

222

an evil-tempered underground film-maker. Looking at her, as she bravely tried to draw herself together, I realised how much she had lost any centre to her life. Shepperton had been the axis of her carousel, where she had warmed herself by the cheerful calliope she had helped to play with my children; but she had moved away to the whirling lights and the rushing air far out on the rim. I was too dull for her, too immersed in the children's games and homework, too steeped in the tumblers of whisky and soda that cheered me and calmed the world, a trade-off that Sally found too limiting. She needed the world to rush up to her like the waves seething around her waist at Brighton beach.

We drove on, crossed the Marylebone Road and strayed into the maze of old commercial properties off Camden High Street. As Sally fumbled with the rear-view mirror, I sensed that she had deliberately lost her bearings, as if waiting for someone to find us. I searched the skyline of derelict buildings. The Arts Laboratory had moved into a one-time pharmaceutical warehouse; its open concrete decks were the perfect setting for its brutalist happenings and exhibitions, its huge ventilation shafts purpose-built to evacuate the last breath of pot smoke in the event of a drugs raid.

As we turned into a one-way street I saw headlights flash from a waiting car parked in a slip-road. It moved towards us, accelerating with the roar of a supercharged engine. I forced the wheel over while Sally stamped at the brake pedal, but the car had swerved past us, its wind-screen pillar clipping the mirror from a parked van. In the rush of speed and danger I recognised the silver Jaguar and its deformed fender. Without pausing, it careened out of the one-way street and headed into the night.

'Sally – pull off the street. He may come back.'

Sally lay against the head-rest, white hair across her face like a lace of death, stunned by the moment of violence that had opened and closed with the roar of a furnace door. In the darkness the broken mirror rang for a last time against a fender. Depressing the clutch with my foot, I started the stalled engine and steered the car into the loading bay of a disused warehouse.

We sat in the silence, listening to the distant moan of the Jaguar's engine as it hunted the streets, a lover's cry in the night.

'Was that David?' I asked. 'Sally, did you see him?'

'He'll be back.' Sally held my arm. 'He was trying to warn you.'

'How long has he followed you around?'

'Only sometimes. Then I follow him.' She pressed her hand over mine as I gripped the steering wheel. 'It's a game of hide-and-seek. We pretend to crash into each other. Keep out of his way, Jim – once he said you were really Japanese . . .'

She sat in the darkness, looking at the faded sign on the wall beside us, advertising sets of Edwardian crucibles and alembics. She had spread her thighs, imitating her posture in David's car after the Chertsey Bridge collision. She was sedated and aroused at the same time, adrift within a dream of violence and desire.

'It's snug here. Car crashes always . . . Jim, you'll have to . . .'

She took my hand and placed it between her thighs. The cotton gusset was damp with moisture that soaked her skirt, a fluxus brought on by the swerving Jaguar. Arching her back, she pulled the G-string down to her knees, and kicked it away among the pedals. She steered my hand to her vulva, settling my ring-finger over her clitoris, and spread her arms across the back of the seat, as if reclining in the car after a spectacular accident. When I caressed her thighs, trying to soothe the needle ulcers on her veins, she followed my fingers with her own,

224

searching for the outlines of the wounds that would set their seals into her white skin.

'Jim, one day we'll be in a crash together. I'd like that . . . think about it now for me.'

She moved diagonally across the seat and raised her thighs to expose her anus, caressing her vulva with her forefinger. I embraced her tenderly, thinking of the years we had spent together. I remembered her running with the horses in the field near the pop festival, her white hair lifting among the horses' tails, her eyes flushed with thoughts of her childhood.

I knelt on the floor of the passenger well, aware of the dashboard panel gleaming against my shoulder, the instrument binnacle jutting forward in the darkness. The stylised interior of the car embraced Sally as intensely as any lover. When my penis entered her vulva she took my hips in her hands, holding me so that only the glans lay between her labia. She pulled the black shoulder straps from her dress, and lowered the bodice to free her breasts.

When I caressed them she watched me in an expressionless way, as if she wanted to be violated by a machine. She held my head a few inches from her nipple, tracing out a sign on her breast, the diagram of an undreamed mutilation. She was exposing herself not to me but to the designers of her car, to David Hunter, whose proxy I had become, and to the unknown man who had shaped her childhood. Her fingers scratched at my chest, trying to draw the bandages from a wound, and she tapped her nipple like a nurse drawing blood from a vein. When I came she pressed her breast to my mouth, as if returning to me all the blood that I had lost in the sex-death that filled her dreams.

We lay together as David's Jaguar hunted the streets, a beast pursuing its strange courtship. When the headlamps flared against the walls of the warehouses Sally pressed her head to my shoulder. Sucking her infected arms, she

225

clung to my chest, afraid that she might leave me and run towards the oncoming light.

My exhibition of crashed cars was held for four weeks at the Arts Laboratory, and throughout that time came under continuous attack from visitors to the gallery. One of the few who wholeheartedly approved was Peter Lykiard. When, at Sally's urging, I suggested the exhibition to him, he instantly accepted the project.

'Excellent, Jim . . . in its way, emotional minimalism at its purest. Warhol would approve.'

In fact, my intentions were the exact opposite. For me, the crashed car was a repository of the most powerful and engaged emotions, a potent symbol in the new logic of violence and sensation that ruled our lives.

In my catalogue notes I wrote: 'The marriage of reason and nightmare which dominates the 1960s has given birth to an ever more ambiguous world. Across the communications landscape stride the spectres of sinister technologies and the dreams that money can buy. Thermonuclear weapons systems and soft-drink commercials coexist in an uneasy realm ruled by advertising and pseudo-events, science and pornography. The death of feeling and emotion has at last left us free to pursue our own psychopathologies as a game . . . "Crashed Cars" illustrates the pandemic cataclysm that kills hundreds of thousands of people each year and injures millions, but is a source of endless entertainment on our film and television screens.'

Contrary to expectations, setting up the exhibition presented few problems. The automobile graveyards of north London were a treasure house of exhibits, the outdoor store-rooms of a technological Louvre. In a Hackney breaker's yard we selected a telescoped Peugeot and a Mini that had rolled down a motorway embankment, whose grass was still growing in its roof sills.

By chance, we found a Lincoln Continental that closely

226

resembled the open-topped limousine in which President Kennedy had met his death. This huge American car had been involved in a massive front-end collision that had driven the radiator grille deep into the engine compartment while leaving the remainder of the car in virtually pristine condition.

Without doubt it was this crushed Lincoln that excited the strongest reactions. The immense black car sat under the clear gallery lights, surrounded by the barest white walls. Although none of the cars would have prompted the slightest concern had they been parked in the street outside, or a moment's grief over the tragic fate of the occupants, within the gallery they became the focus for nervous laughter and angry comment. Visitors who wandered into the gallery and found the cars unexpectedly in front of them began to titter to themselves or swear at the vehicles.

These responses confirmed all my suspicions of everything that an aberrant technology was threading through our lives. Further testing the audience, I hired a topless young woman to interview the guests at the opening party on closed-circuit television. She had originally agreed to appear naked with her microphone, but on seeing the cars decided that she would only bare her breasts – an interesting response in its own right.

Needless to say, all this provoked the guests beyond endurance. No gallery opening in my experience had ever degenerated so quickly into a drunken brawl. Egged on by Sally and David Hunter, the guests poured wine over the cars, tore off the wing mirrors and began to break the few intact windows. David leapt around the gallery, supervising the mayhem in high good humour. His restless hands hardly left the damaged cars, as if he had at last found his natural habitat.

Towards the evening's end the party took an uglier turn. Sally was nearly raped in the rear seat of the Continental by an over-boisterous tableau sculptor for whom she was

227

mimicking the postures of the President's widow. Carried away by the excitement, David urged the topless girl to interview her during the heat of the assault.

'Sally, this is live TV! Tell the viewers how you feel!' David dragged the camera-man after him, snatched the microphone and rammed it through the passenger window into Sally's enraged face. 'Over to you, Sally! Let's have a commentary in your own words . . .'

By the time Cleo Churchill and I had rescued Sally the party was spilling into the street, the guests searching for an even larger exhibition. Straightening her torn dress, Sally lunged at the drunken sculptor with her shoe and hobbled away on a broken heel through the scattered wine-bottles. She grimaced at the image of herself on the television screen and disappeared with a cry into the night.

'Is Sally safe?' Cleo avoided the wine dripping from the roof of the Lincoln, and slammed the passenger door with relief. 'You've proved something, Jim – though I don't know what. Was it worth it?'

'As an experiment? I think so.' I knew that she disapproved of the exhibition, and had gamely come along to give me support. 'At least they never stopped looking at the cars, which is more than you can say for most gallery openings. Dick Sutherland wants to film all this for his new series. When he gets back from the States they'll stage the party again at the Television Centre, with studio extras playing the guests.'

'Heaven forbid . . . Don't let him use you all the time.' Unsettled by the violent evening, Cleo wiped the wine from her hands. She pointed to the monitor screen transmitting a picture of the empty gallery. 'You're on TV now – isn't that enough?'

'Broadcast TV, Cleo – Dick feels the idea deserves an audience of millions.'

'I thought it had one. You know, out in the streets, the real thing?'

'Cleo, this is the real thing . . . But I'm glad you came. Can I give you a lift home?'

'Jim, dear, I think not. This is one evening when I wouldn't trust your driving . . .'

Cleo stood in front of the camera, using the screen as a mirror as she checked the wine stains on the sleeves of her dress. The electronic colours had separated slightly, and reminded me of my acid vision when I had seen Cleo robed in a train of light as she strolled through the trees beside the river. My Moreau princess, who turned the starlings into peacocks and calmed the air with her graceful hands. I wanted to invite her to Shepperton again, drawn by her intelligence and forthright mind.

But Cleo was nervous of me, aware that I was doggedly following a dangerous logic of my own. If death had outstared life, which the world seemed to believe, I could rest my case. In a desperate sense Miriam would be alive again, Kennedy would drive triumphantly through Dealey Plaza, the casualties of the Second World War would rest in their graves and a Chinese youth at a rural railway station would at last have conveyed his desperate message to me.

The exhibition ran its four-week course. During this time the cars were continually abused by outraged visitors. A hare krishna sect stormed into the gallery and threw a tin of white paint at the Lincoln. Meanwhile Sally and David continued their courtship, hunting each other across the city in the same way that David and I had once played hide-and-seek in the streets of Shanghai, a game too important to be brought to an end.

On the evening that the exhibition closed I was driving back to Shepperton along the Hammersmith flyover, when I saw Sally's MG speeding down the exit ramp in front of me. I had spent the afternoon at the gallery, supervising the removal of my battered exhibits, whose distressed condition – they were covered with paint and graffiti, their seats soaked in urine – shocked the hardened car-breakers when they arrived with their tow-truck. At first they refused to accept the vehicles, their eyes opened to the barbarities of modern art. The cars might be destined for the compactor and the blast furnace, but as they dragged them into the street they were already cleaning them protectively.

While I drove along the flyover I wiped the last of the white paint from my hands, and watched Sally's sportscar speeding through the traffic, a defective tail-light winking at the dusk. In the past, whenever I saw her on the roads to the west of London, I was sure that she was on her way to Shepperton. Now I guessed that she was off to see David at Fair Oaks airfield, and for a moment I felt a small part of that loss I had known after Miriam's death. Sally at least would smile at me again; we would make love and remain as fond of each other as ever. But the last things she wanted were sympathy and affection. She needed David's unresolved aggressions, and his outbursts of erratic humour when he would slap her face for her if she played the difficult child.

Beyond Twickenham the traffic began to open out. As we passed the rugby stadium Sally moved into the fast lane, forcing an overtaking car to brake. Headlights flared against the bounding tail of the MG, and Sally pushed a derisive finger through a tear in the canvas hood, sending a shower of embers from her cigarette into the night air. Reluctantly, she moved over to allow the faster car to pass her, then swerved back into his slipstream, her headlamps flooding the driver's mirror.

Left behind in a line of slower cars, I waited until we reached the next roundabout, accelerated past an idling truck and set off after Sally. She glanced in the rear-view mirror, and I wondered if she had seen me, but she was repairing the make-up to her eyes and lips.

I thought of her with David, making love on his air bed, as she had often told me, under the wings of his Cessna in the silent hangar. A reverie of jealousy and desire filled my mind, regret that I had lost Sally to this winged man, anger at myself for being so prudishly afraid of her needle ulcers and thieving . . .

Escaping from my hands, the car leapt across the road and touched the tail of the MG. Our fenders locked as we careened along the carriageway. Startled, Sally crouched away from the wild headlights and the hurtling mass of the car that had leapt out of the night. Cigarette in her mouth, she pulled away to my left, overran the soft shoulder and then swerved in front of me as she lost control of the small steering wheel.

Trying to avoid a collision, I braked sharply into the fast lane. As the car veered to the right I felt a front tyre burst and deflate. The wheel wrenched itself from my hands. The car side-slipped across the dual carriageway, and the flattened tyre struck the central reservation, hurling the vehicle onto its side. It demolished an illuminated traffic sign, rolled on to its back and carried on along the on-coming lane.

Hanging from my seat belt, I saw the asphalt rush past a few inches above my face, a ceiling of racing gravel lit by my headlights. The windscreen exploded in a burst of glass chips. The roof collapsed, and the rear-view mirror struck my forehead.

The car had stopped, and lay in the centre of the oncoming lane a hundred yards beyond the demolished traffic sign. I listened to the wheels spinning in the night air. Around me cars were slowing, horns competing with each other. Already I could smell the fuel dripping from the engine on to the glass-covered road. Drivers were running from their cars towards me. I switched off the engine and tried to free myself, but the collapsed roof had locked the door into its frame. Fuel pooled against the window as a dozen people rocked the car, trying to loosen the door. A man's fist drummed against the pillar. I wound down the window, released my seat belt and sank on to the warped ceiling.

Hands seized my shoulders and dragged me from the cabin. Stunned by the blow to my head, I lay on the grass verge as a crowd gathered around my car. I could still see the rushing asphalt in the glare of headlights, as if death itself were speeding towards me, passing a few inches above my eyes.

An ambulance man knelt beside me, frowning over his first-aid kit. He seemed uninterested in me, and complained to the driver about some missing piece of equipment. A police vehicle, its beacon flashing, stopped within thirty feet of my car, which a group of young men were rocking from side to side. Two teenage girls in party frocks looked down at my face, moving from one dance slipper to the other on the cold night grass. They hummed the melody of a recent pop song, gazing at me as if I were a drunk at a party who had fallen at their feet.

A cigarette lighter flared in the night air. Before I could speak Sally Mumford pushed between the girls. Drawing protectively on her cigarette, she peered over the head of the ambulanceman, and lowered the lighter flame to my face, curious to see the driver of the car which had nearly killed her.

Four months later, in the last days of the 1960s, I stood with the cheering crowd in a disused soccer stadium in east London, watching the battered saloon cars of a demolition derby lumber around the muddy track. In the centre of the arena, helmet on her hip, Sally stood in white jeans and a crimson rally driver's tunic. She was shouting angrily at David Hunter, now out of the race and resting behind the wheel of his demolished car. As Sally urged him on, whistling through her broken teeth, he lay back in his silver suit and stretched his arms, gazing contentedly at the rusty impacts around him.

Watching these desultory collisions, I remembered my own crash and the exhibition at the Arts Laboratory. I still assumed that the exhibition had been designed to test the psychology of its audience, but David took for granted that its sole purpose had been to incite myself. Was my accident, in which I was lucky not to be killed, an attempt to die in an erotic death-pact with Sally?

David had suggested as much, when he and Sally visited me in Roehampton hospital. Looking up from my bed at this deteriorated couple, of whom I was so fond, I realised that I had exploited them in the same way that Dick Sutherland and Lykiard had exploited me. I wanted to help them, but the insane roller-coaster of the Sixties had seized our lives and swept us headlong between its screaming rails.

The last cars on the circuit heaved against each other like the bored bison wallowing in the mud-pit beside the railroad bridge at Moose Jaw. I thought of the hell-drivers in Shanghai before the war, and the spectacular collisions staged by the casual Americans. Across the years their spirit seemed to hover over this modest track, and over the greatest of all motorised tragedies, Kennedy's death by motorcade. I could still remember individual frames of the Zapruder film, endlessly anatomised on television and in a thousand magazine exposés. Had the events in Dealey Plaza been no more than the most elaborate of a series of staged accidents prefigured on that Shanghai race-course of my childhood?

Chilled by the winter air, the spectators shuffled their feet on the wooden stands. Nostrils quickened in the drifting smoke and engine fumes. The advertised highlight of the afternoon was the recreation of a spectacular road accident, a multiple collision on a Manchester overpass in which a dozen vehicles had been involved.

As a curtain-raiser, there would be a women's event, and the crowd moved forward for a closer view. Sally and a group of women drivers, all in striped silk jackets, faces made up like streetwalkers, were gripping the roof sills of their cars and sliding their legs through the drivers' windows. The spectators, heavy men in leather coats, pushed past me to the rail. They settled their hands deep in their pockets. They had only come for the women's event, a figure-of-eight destruction course filled with jolting impacts, when every penis in the arena would be clenched within a hand.

CHAPTER TWELVE

In the Camera Lens

'A film festival,' Dick Sutherland remarked over our third rum collins at the Copacabana Palace Hotel, 'gives you a fair idea of what the future will be like.'

'Beautiful but unapproachable women, frazzled men, and a million dreams held together by hype?'

'That sort of thing. Lang's *Metropolis* re-shot in Las Vegas. It's not that illusion takes the place of reality, but that out-and-out hallucination takes the place of illusion. Activities of the human brain it's needed the whole of evolution to control are here let out to play. I love it.'

'Dick, I thought you might. And what about our congress of science films?'

'The same thing applies. In many ways, more so.' Dick smiled knowingly, always happy when he could provoke me. 'Sooner or later, like everything else, science is going to turn into television.'

'Does that sound sinister?'

'Very. Exciting, though. What's that idea you're always trotting out . . . ?'

Dick liked me to repeat this weather-worn prophecy of mine whenever his confidence flagged or he found himself in a place where no one recognised him, the ultimate in sensory deprivation for the TV personality.

'I forget . . . that you might be responsible for the first major scientific discovery to be made on television?'

'That's it. It could happen here. Rio is a total media city.'

From the air-conditioned bar he gazed contentedly at the procession of giant floats that moved along the Avenida Atlantica advertising the star film of the festival,

Stanley Kubrick's *2001*. Through the crowded traffic edged a fleet of silver space craft, resembling the demonstration models of an interplanetary nightclub. In their abbreviated foil space-suits, the crews of hip-rolling young women flashed cocktail-waitress smiles at the crowds of tourists. For some reason, only the beggars and cripples squatting outside the beach hotels bothered to watch them. Waves of amplified music rose above the clamour of police sirens and the cries of lottery salesmen. Two light aircraft flew above the beach, and towed pennants advertising rival film attractions. Challenging them, giant fragments of 'Also Sprach Zarathustra' drummed against the facades of the hotels and rolled out to sea to wake Poseidon himself.

The carousel disappeared into the din and haze, instantly forgotten. Apart from Dick and the families of beggars, no one had paid any attention to the floats. Everything in Rio was dominated by the beach. This was no strip of basking sand on the Mediterranean model but a linear, open-air city in its own right, filled with thousands of sunbathers, kite and watch salesmen, ice-cream vendors and marauding beggar troupes, and a complete league of football teams playing on almost full-sized sand-pitches. No one swam. The morose Atlantic breakers hurled themselves against the Richard Strauss crescendos, wave for wave, daring the film executives and festival organisers to match their epic reach.

As Dick and I had noticed soon after flying in from London, Rio happily embraced the film festival and at the same time completely ignored it. Everywhere the crowds jammed the movie theatres, and the hotel terraces were packed with television crews, starlets and producers. Fleets of limousines and buses ferried the delegates from one lavish embassy party to another, while gangs of prostitutes and their pimps so packed the streets of Copacabana that they squeezed out any hope of finding a customer.

But the city absorbed all this, as if the illusory visions of the festival scarcely matched the vastly greater illusion of Rio itself, a city that reminded me of pre-war Shanghai in so many ways, but a Shanghai of tiled sidewalks ruled by the most confident and beautiful women in the world. Watching the bored policemen white-washing the wind-screens of illegally parked cars, I could almost believe that they were protecting the drivers from a blinding glimpse of this extraordinary sex.

And above all this were the people of the favelas, the shanty towns crowding the dozens of large hills that rose from the streets of Rio. Where the poor and destitute of most cities occupied its nether regions, in Rio they lived up in the sky, coming down from the clouds to exhibit their undernourished and crippled children and pluck at the tourist sleeve. Had these impoverished people found the door to heaven open one morning, taken possession of its misty peaks and discovered too late that they had been tricked by those with their feet on the firmer ground far below? 'On you it looks great,' I heard a film executive remark to a beggar woman, carrying a bony child asleep on her dry breast, who dared to raise her withered arm to him outside the Copacabana Palace.

However, it was easy for Dick and me to buy off our consciences with a few conference cruzeiros, and perhaps equally naive. The gangs of confident pickpockets and the cripples viciously defending their pitches against any rivals reminded me again of Shanghai, with its rich beggars pro-tected by their bodyguards. Shanghai, too, had been a media city, perhaps the first of all, purpose-built by the west as a test-metropolis of the future. London in the 1960s had been the second, with the same confusions of image and reality, the same overheating.

In Rio fiction and reality still played their games. At a party given by the American Embassy we found ourselves in a reception line shaking hands with the crew of the

Starship *Enterprise*, a group of grey-haired actors like venerable morticians. Famous faces surrounded us, older and unsuccessful impersonations of themselves. Struggling to make small talk to a producer's wife, I felt that I, too, was an impostor, masquerading as myself in an unconvincing way. I was grateful for the light-show and the amplified music that raised all conversation to an unintelligible shout.

Rescuing me, Dick pushed through the throng and seized my arm. 'Jim – come and meet Fritz Lang . . .'

He plunged into the press of dinner jackets towards a group of some twenty guests gazing down at what seemed to be the scene of a small accident. An elderly man in an oversize tuxedo sat on a straightbacked chair turned sideways to the wall. He slumped in the chair like an abandoned ventriloquist's dummy, buffeted by the noise and music, the light show dappling his grey hair a vivid blue and green. He looked infinitely weary, and I thought that he might have died among these garish film people. When I shook his hand, and briefly told him how much I admired his films, there was a flicker of response. An ironic gleam flitted through one eye, as if the director of *Metropolis* had realised that the dystopia he had visualised had come true in a way he had least expected.

Lang's resigned humour came to mind as we finished our rum collins at the Copacabana Palace and set off for the congress hall where the festival of scientific and documentary films was being held, an adjunct to the main festival which the organisers had decided to sponsor as a tribute to Kubrick's science fiction epic. A crowd of film fans pressed around us when we climbed into a taxi, and Dick momentarily brightened until we realised that almost all of them were pickpockets, brothel touts and voodoo pitchmen.

'Hey, mister, you want voodoo? Real good voodoo?'

'Mister, you want to watch a guy fuck a chicken?'

'Only ten years old, mister. Real clean girls.'

We shut the windows on a forest of arms. 'Well, Dick,' I asked. 'Do you? It's not exactly your everyday BBC wildlife film.'

'Wait and see – you may be surprised, Jim. Even you.'

Offering Dick my moral support, I sat in on his lecture and the panel discussions which he chaired, fascinated as ever by the sight of him working his audience like a seasoned music hall trouper. Yet his performance seemed oddly subdued, as if he were trying to shrug off the repertory of television mannerisms he had cultivated so carefully since the Cambridge days. Now and then, as he acknowledged the audience's laughter, he glanced at them in the same weary way that Fritz Lang had accepted my handshake. Rio was filled with old actor-managers trapped within their images of themselves.

Dick's laboratory at the Institute of Psychology was now little more than a public relations bureau, and Cleo told me that he had secretly borrowed bench-space in a colleague's lab so that he could return to original research. Sometimes he would sit there for an hour, in this shrine to his younger self, unable as yet to come up with an original project. Then he would return to his own laboratory and become the reluctant fugleman of popular psychology, feeding news of the latest breakthroughs to his coterie of TV producers. I admired Dick, and regretted that I had always encouraged him to think of the media world as his true laboratory. Sometimes, when I asked him about his own research, he became almost testy.

Later, wandering around the wide corridors where the out-of-competition films were screened, I was surprised by the variety of documentary films being produced, only a fraction of which would ever reach the general public. Zoos, schools of dentistry, agricultural research stations, international hotel chains, hairdressing colleges, and a consortium of undertakers and embalmers all had active film units.

In the glowing half-light the shirt-sleeved delegates stood by the lines of monitor screens, watching studies of the nose-wheel housing of the Boeing 707, the stress-fractures of ice-hockey players, the life-cycle of the cane-toad, the architecture of brothels. As I turned from a close-up of an exposed nasal septum to another about the curing of sable skins the two seemed to merge in my mind. Were all these films moving in their reductive way towards the same undifferentiated end? Drained of emotion and value-judgement, the lens of the scientific camera anato-mised the world around it like a patient and pensive voyeur.

The medical and psychological films showed the process most clearly at work. In the competition section of the festival I watched Dick introduce the afternoon's pro-gramme on the theme: 'Aversion therapy – desensitisation in the perception of sexual imagery'. The three films described work in Sweden, Japan and the United States with habitual sex offenders, in which these doomed and gloomy men were exposed to endless images of their notional victims – small children, vulnerable women, racial targets and fellow sex-offenders. Doses of emetic drugs, surges of electric current, noise and other aversive conditioning supposedly turned the subjects against the objects of their desire.

As the succession of harrowing images passed by, I looked away from the cinema screen to the members of the audience. For the most part documentary film makers and professional psychologists, they gazed at the screen with the same steady eyes and unflinching expressions of the men in the Soho porn theatres, or the fans of certain kinds of apocalyptic science fiction. Whenever the crimi-nal subjects winced with pain or vomited into their sick-basins, ripples of appreciation would move across the audience at some particularly striking camera angle or expository close-up, as the Soho patrons might have applauded a telling crutch shot or elegant anal penetration.

Later, when we returned to our hotel on Copacabana Beach and our first frozen daiquiri of the evening, I said to Dick: 'I need this. We should have gone to the voodoo. That was quite an afternoon.'

'Gruelling stuff?'

'I was watching the audience. The future may be like a film festival, but which one? Yours, or the one at this end of the beach? They had the eyes of tourists at a death camp, the kind of tourists who keep going back.'

'We've shocked you, Jim – that was worth coming to Rio for.' Delighted to catch me out, Dick glanced at me slyly over his glass. The rivalry between us, which for reasons of his own he had always encouraged, had become more open in Rio. 'It's interesting that scientific films unsettle you more than hard-core porn.'

'But pornography is really very chaste – it's the body's unerotic dream of itself. Your films come straight from the psychopathic ward. Imagine how you'd react if you found them in the film-library of a sex-criminal.'

'So . . . ? Take a set of surgical instruments – innocent in an operating theatre, but in Myra Hindley's handbag? You're seeing them out of context.'

'Nothing is seen in context any more. Switch on your TV set, Dick, and you find a murdered prime minister, a child eating a candy bar, Marilyn lifting her skirt – what sort of scenario is the mind quietly stitching together?'

'It might be interesting to know. Tell me.'

'One of Cleo's fashion magazines showed some models prancing about in front of a blow-up from the Zapruder film – the Kennedy assassination as a fashion accessory?'

'Of course. In the future everyone will need to be a film critic to make sense of anything.'

241

'Not a psychologist?' His remark surprised me. 'Surely, you . . . ?'

'No, I think the psychologist has had his day . . .'

Dick stared coolly across the crowded terrace of the Luxor, at the relaxing delegates and the photographers waiting by the lobby in hope of a passing celebrity. Despite his success that afternoon he seemed dissatisfied, as if he accepted that the epoch of popular television, in whose secure playground he had thrived, would soon be replaced by a harsher and more open world, an ever-changing media landscape in which fame was as transitory as a may-fly. Like an astronaut unable to tether himself to the Moon's surface, he longed for a stronger gravity. The need for attention had sent him bounding ever higher through the airless dust of celebrity, and there was nothing now to pull him down. He often asked me about the children's school results, glad to hear of their success, and clearly envying me my family ties. He had never married, and his women-friends moved through his life like game-show panellists, cheerful, optimistic and unremembered. Even their fascination with Dick was never enough.

'Dr Sutherland – we saw your interview. Without doubt, the most handsome psychologist in Rio . . .'

An avuncular voice hailed Dick across the terrace. Señor Marcial Pereira, a leading film critic on a Rio news-paper, approached our table, accompanied by two of Copacabana's ambling beauties. He recognised Dick from the interview he had given the previous evening on a local T.V. station. He joined us at our table with his companions, who surveyed us with the eyes of empresses. Like all the women in Rio, they were filled with such character, elegance and hot beauty that only some inexplicable over-sight had prevented them from achieving Hollywood careers.

'We have a party tonight, in my apartment at Ipanema,'

Pereira told us. 'A festival car will collect you at ten. Each day we must relax a little more. I leave you with my actress friends – Carmen and Fortunata. They are most anxious to meet visiting Englishmen.'

When he had gone the women settled themselves at our table, eyes conferring as they swiftly surveyed the crowded terrace. Both wore the same loose silk frocks that revealed their thighs and shoulders. They were scarcely older than my daughters, with an equal command of the space around them. Carmen's dark hair sprang from a sharply sloping profile that was part Portuguese and part Indian. Her forehead was perpetually creased, as if she were fretting over some misplaced clue to the world. Her friend, Fortunata, a passive, heavy-breasted blonde, was waiting for the signal to leave, but Dick, excited by the heady body scent of the two women, was already ordering drinks and practising his pidgin English.

'You live in Rio? Here?'

'On the beach? No.' Carmen was ticking off Dick's television smile, his gold medallion and credit cards. 'São Paulo. We come for the festival.'

'Like us. We come from London – in England.'

'London, oh . . . Carmen and I go to London.' Fortunata stared down some Carnaby Street vista inside her head, at the end of which stood the Beatles and the Rolling Stones. She spoke wistfully, as if unsure whether Carmen would agree.

'Rio is much better,' Dick assured her. 'Many beautiful women. Like you two.'

'Yes . . . many women in Rio.' Carmen sounded like a commodities dealer in a slow market. 'You prefer beautiful women?'

'Of course. Especially in Rio.'

'You're an actress?' I asked. 'Have you made any films?'

'Yes. I act in films. With Fortunata.'

She spoke matter-of-factly. I assumed that we were with

243

two São Paulo prostitutes visiting Rio on a speculative trawl. I waited for Dick to realise that there was only one way to impress them. Carmen was strumming at the table top with one hand, while the other flicked at her shoulder strap. She was exposing her breast to me, at the same time letting the hem of her silk dress ride up her thigh.

I remembered Marilyn Monroe's early years on the fringes of prostitution. I had shaken hands with the great Fritz Lang and with the crew of the Starship *Enterprise*, but this stony-faced beach whore would be my real contact with the international film industry. Perhaps she had appeared in TV commercials advertising dog-food or a valet-parking service.

I looked up from her breast. Dick was ready for me to make the first move. Since our arrival at Rio airport he had scarcely taken his eyes from the women who strolled along the sidewalks of this extravagant city, but I knew that the idea of sex always excited him more than the event. He needed me to complete the circuit of desire and fulfilment. For years I assumed that he and Miriam had been lovers at Cambridge, a suspicion she had always denied but Dick had subtly encouraged.

Carmen was flicking at her shoulder strap, like a bored guitarist trying to think of a tune. Fortunata primly smoothed her skirt with the broad hands of a docile child.

'Where do you stay?' I asked. 'Here in Copacabana?'

'We go to our apartment.' Carmen pointed to a nearby side-street. 'You have American dollars? One hour, two hours . . .'

'Dick? Money for time? Shall we go?'

'Of course. Money is the original digital clock . . .'

We left the Luxor and set off through the crowds in the Avenida Atlantica, past the beggars and jewellery salesmen, the nightclub touts with their waiting taxis. Carmen led the way on her long legs. She stepped into the traffic when we reached the side-street, avoiding the hundreds

244

of pimps standing on the pavement, each with his woman. Prostitution powered Rio, provided its engine. When I first walked down this side-street on the evening of our arrival I had been struck by the charm of these countless couples talking amiably on the wide pavements, a tribute to the marital bliss of this benign city. But the husbands were touting their wives' wares, like so many bales of cloth. Freelancers and festival-hunters such as Fortunata and Carmen had to run the hazards of the traffic-filled roads.

We dodged through the passing limousines and entered the lobby of a huge block of low-rent apartments. Beside the annunciator buttons hundreds of mail slots ranged like all the addresses in hell. A minute elevator carried us to an upper floor where a low-ceilinged corridor ran forever into the gloom past dozens of doors. The perspiring tenants lounged outside their cramped apartments. Children played under the dim light, and a damp corridor life survived like fungi in a cavern. Men in vests and undershorts leaned against the walls, mothers dressed their daughters' hair, old women worked at trestle tables.

At the door of her apartment Carmen turned, hand on key, and peered at me. During the short walk from the hotel she had forgotten my face. She waited for a curious old man to drift away.

'Okay, now we see. Fifty dollars.'

'That's a lot.'

'For two. As long as you like. Afterwards we go to Señor Pereira's party in Ipanema.'

'Fine by you, Dick?' He already had his arm around Fortunata while I searched for my wallet. He was romping playfully with her, as he did with my daughters.

Carmen stuffed the notes into her purse, and opened the door on to a crowded room. Three middle-aged women and a small child were working at a trestle table, surrounded by piles of plastic sacks. They were producing cheap mementoes for the film festival, stitching cardboard-backed photographs of film stars into gilt *papier mâché* frames, assembling festival kites from ready-made components which they snatched from the sacks. Hundreds of belt buckles with movie motifs, *2001* lapel badges and other geegaws lay in open cardboard boxes on the shabby sofa, lined up in rows by the methodical child. Bags of spare components filled the small kitchen and were piled around the lavatory in the bathroom.

'Wait a minute . . .' I turned to Dick. 'Let's go back to the hotel.'

'No.' Carmen tugged my arm with surprising force. She pointed to the bedroom of the apartment. 'We go in – it's just for us.'

A woman with a stapling machine glanced at us without interest, and drove a staple through the forehead of Elvis Presley. As Carmen unlocked the door I assumed that she and Fortunata rented the room during the day. Beyond the double bed, unwashed windows looked out on to the rear balconies of a vast apartment block, more low-rent housing in this city where the poor were pushed away into the sky. Every balcony was crammed with bird-cages and cardboard cartons, washing lines and abandoned furniture.

'Okay – nice time now.'

Carmen tried to close the door, but Dick and I were staring uneasily at the room. The rumpled sheets were stained with sweat and lipstick, the pillows covered with a blue glaze of mascara and vaginal jelly. Underwear hung across the pine dressing table, and on the floor beside the bed were a dozen paper tissues, each crushed around a smear of phlegm. Impassively surveying this scene was a small cine-camera on a tripod. Nearby, boxes of Kodak film were stacked on the wall unit.

'Jim, you'll catch something . . .' Dick frowned at me, turning towards the door. He held Fortunata by the waist, but his interest in the escapade had cooled. His eyes had retreated behind his handsome face, and he seemed to have aged since setting out from the hotel. The cheap cine-camera threatened him in a way he had never known at the BBC Television Centre, with its soft and accommodating lenses. I was surprised to find him so obviously out of his element, and wondered why he had urged me into the hands of these two prostitutes. Perhaps he hoped to see me humiliated in some small way that would do no damage to our friendship but would leave him in the dominant position.

Behind us, the stapling machine stamped through the faces of the film stars. Undisturbed by our presence, the women hunched over their table, now and then snapping at the child. An old man in a vest wandered into the apartment, tried to remember something, and faded into the corridor.

'Jim, we need another room, we can't all . . .'

'Yes . . .' Fortunata brightened up, drawing Dick towards the bed. 'It's nice . . . all together.'

Pointing to the women in the sweat shop, I said to Carmen: 'Ask the women if we can use their room – just for an hour.'

'They must work, it's very busy.'

'I'll give them ten dollars. They deserve a rest. Tell them to go to the movies.'

'Sure. I tell them.'

Carmen spoke to the women, who together peered at me, baffled by this show of modesty. They downed tools, stowed the money into a shared handbag and moved into the corridor. As Carmen closed the door I saw them leaning against the dingy wall outside the apartment, lighting their cigarettes as they waited for us to finish.

Dick had pushed a tray of film badges onto the floor and sat back on the sofa cushions with Fortunata, who had slipped the shoulder straps of her dress. With a thin smile he pretended to admire the weight and curvature of her heavy white breasts, like a greengrocer assessing a new variety of albino melon. When Fortunata flicked at her extruding nipples with little gasps I shut the bedroom door.

Carmen stepped out of her high-heeled shoes and hung her dress on the wardrobe, brushing the silk with house-wifely concern. Using her free hand, she reached out and expertly released my belt buckle.

'Okay. It's very nice.'

I undressed beside her, aware of her jollying me along. Time, not money, dominated the prostitute's life. To enjoy sex with them required a special knack of its own. A teenage girl with a cat in her arms was watching me from a balcony thirty feet away. While I drew the curtain Carmen took a spermicide dispenser from the dressing-table drawer. Screwing it into the open tube, she squeezed three inches of jelly into the dispenser. She lifted a leg onto the bed, parted her labia with her fingers and eased the shaft into her vagina. She pressed the plunger, with-drew the dispenser and wiped her fingers on the sheet.

Waiting for her, I turned the camera and pointed the lens towards the bed.

'You like for me to make a film?' Carmen asked.

'You'll film us here?'

'It's good, for four minutes. Only one hundred dollars. Perhaps you show your girl-friend. Or your wife.'

'My wife?'

'Yes! It's popular, it's really good.'

I sat on the bed, staring at my reflection in the camera lens. Beyond the bedroom door I could hear Dick laugh-ing as he chased Fortunata around the work-room, and the women in the corridor shouting to the straying child. By comparison, the bedroom was a stage set. This earnest young prostitute, the stained sheets and the tissues with which she had wiped her clients' semen from her vulva, an enticing spoor for future customers, together seemed like film props. The presence of the camera transformed and even dignified this seedy bedroom.

As we lay together on the waxy sheets I asked: 'Have you been in other films?'

'Sure! Many films . . .' She screwed up her face, dismissing the bedside camera with a contemptuous wave. She held my limp penis in both hands, tugging lightly at my scrotum. 'I make many films – I'm acting for real director.'

'That's good.' I could guess the kind of studio. 'For Señor Pereira, maybe?'

'Señor Pereira . . . ugh!' She grimaced at the mention of the film critic. 'His films . . . not clean!'

I moved the hair from her fierce forehead, admiring her determination. 'You'll work for other directors. You'll be a star one day.'

'Yes . . .' Ignoring the doubts in my voice, she licked her fingers and smoothed her eyebrows, gazing fiercely at the future that lay beyond the walls of this rented bedroom. As she searched her lips for a small sore, the muscles of her arrow-shaped face were set with a touching confidence.

She noticed me lying beside her and returned to work, shaking her head over my feeble erection. She took her left breast and teased out the nipple, tapping it with her sharp nails until it grew erect. Raising it to my mouth, she pressed the warm body of the breast against my nose and chin, placed my hand against her buttocks and steered my fingers down to her anus, pushing the tip of my ring-finger into the soft pad. She reached down to the root of my penis, searching for my prostate. When my penis came to life she nodded encouragingly, made sure that my eyes stayed on her breasts and my fingers on her anus. With her strong arms she turned me on to my back and squatted

249

across my hips, sitting on her haunches so that the only part of her body to touch me was her vulva.

Like a fisherwoman at an angling hole, patiently waiting for a bite, she moved about on her heels, the tip of my penis between her labia. At last, when the rake of both penis and pubis had matched to her satisfaction, she settled down and let my penis enter her vagina. She bobbed away energetically, glancing briefly at herself in the dressing-table mirror, and now and then blowing the hair from her eyes.

I held her strong thighs, aware that she was working as hard as the older women assembling their trinkets. All of us, myself certainly included, were working to make the film festival a success. Even the empty camera in whose lens we were reflected had helped to shape our sex act. As she smoothed her eyebrows Carmen was measuring her profile against the lens, preparing herself for the even more elaborate sex films in which she would appear. Lying between her thighs, I was little more than an extra recruited from the hotel terraces of Copacabana. When she raised herself, teasingly holding the tip of my penis between her breasts, I almost felt that we were extemporising a small variation on a fixed routine.

With its passive and unobtrusive despotism, the camera governed the smallest spaces of our lives. Even in the privacy of our own homes we had all been recruited to play our parts in what were little more than real-life commercials. As we cooked in our kitchens we were careful to follow the manufacturer's instructions, as we made love in our bedrooms we embraced within a familiar repertoire of gestures and affections. The medium of film had turned us all into minor actors in an endlessly running day-time serial. In the future, airliners would crash and presidents would be assassinated within agreed conventions as formalised as the coronation of a tsar.

When I came, my cheeks pressed to the spermicidal

pillow, Carmen nodded matter-of-factly. She took her breasts from me, and disengaged her vulva from my penis, a technician turning off a life-support system. Her body shining with my sweat, she stepped from the bed and opened the door into the next room, where Dick and Fortunata were playfully throwing the plastic mementoes at each other. Dick, I noticed, had not undressed.

Carmen watched them bleakly and closed the door. She plucked a tissue from the carton on the dressing table. With a jerk of her thumb, she confided: 'He no fuck.'

Deftly she scooped my semen from her vulva, wiped a streak from the inside of her thigh, then crushed the tissue and threw it carefully on to the floor below the camera, a small offering to this one-eyed inquisitor.

Later that evening, I saw Carmen under the lens of a very different camera. As promised, the festival limousine arrived at the Luxor to take us to Pereira's party at Ipanema. Another guest, a Dutch film distributor, shared the car with us. He and Dick kept up an animated commentary as we drove down Copacabana Avenue, pointing to the movie theatres besieged by the eager crowds, the gangs of whores and pimps striding arm in arm through the flashing strobes, and the passing tourists stunned by the sight of the Rio police holding up six lanes of traffic while they knocked about some pickpocket or parking offender.

Throughout dinner Dick had been in unflagging good humour, while I felt vaguely depressed. Missing the children, I telephoned Cleo Churchill, who had volunteered to look after them while we were away. I spoke to each of them in turn, thrilled to hear their voices telling me of the day's triumphs and excitements, a model aircraft lost in the river and a tame squirrel in the garden. Listening to them, I wanted to put the receiver down and head for the airport. Cleo spoke last, reassuring me that all was

251

well and that the children scarcely remembered me.

'Don't hurry, back – they're having the time of their lives. I hope you and Dick are thoroughly misbehaving yourselves.'

'I am, but Dick's been too busy giving TV interviews. Everyone agrees he's the sexiest psychologist in Rio.'

'And in London – bring him back in one piece.'

I remembered Dick romping in the women's work-room, and Fortunata with the medallions of Jane Fonda and Bardot clipped to her nipples, Robert Redford's face pressed to her pubis. Dick would look but not touch. Yet I was depressed and he was in ebullient form. A certain reserve now marked his attitude to me, as if I had failed an important test. I had always been reluctant to appear on television, a shyness that amused him and which he put down to an old-fashioned strain in my character. Clearly I was too bound to the mundane, to the contingent realities of a wife, children and desire, to the fear of death and the anguish of space-time. Dick had side-stepped all these, accepting that the electronic image of himself was the real one, and that his off-screen self was an ambitious but modest actor who had successfully auditioned for a far more glamorous role. He might interview Carmen and Fortunata, but he would never break the spell by touching or needing them.

Watching as he enjoyed himself in the limousine, I guessed that he was the forerunner of an advanced kind of human being. If one day the world became a film festival, its inhabitants would all resemble Dick Sutherland. Television had made him impotent; but perhaps its real role, in evolutionary terms, was to depopulate an over-crowded planet. The camera lens was our way of disengaging from each other, distancing ourselves from each other's emotions. Looking out from the limousine at the veering, over-exuberant streets, it occurred to me that everyone in Rio was having, not a good time, but the image of a good time.

Except, unmistakably, at Señor Pereira's party. The terrace and reception rooms of the duplex apartment seemed to rotate like a satellite nightclub in orbit over Rio, filled with lavish buffet tables, roulette wheels and a light-show. Hundreds of guests danced to a maracas band, celebrating new year's eve in the year 2000. Elderly bankers who seemed to be impersonating distinguished film extras, sleek Rio gangsters more handsome than any film star, and fashionable property tycoons looking like expensive call-boys mingled with a lower echelon of film agents, journalists and television executives who formed the proletariat of the super-rich.

Above the cocaine voices and firework display on the terrace, I shouted to the Dutchman: 'This party must have been going on since last year's festival. Rio film critics live in some style.'

'Pereira is much more than a film critic. He has a stake in a local TV station, all sorts of businesses and even his own production company.'

Just what Pereira's film company produced I saw later that evening. Dick was dancing with the most glamorous woman at the party, somewhere between sixteen and sixty, whose costume had ransacked a Las Vegas casino. The Dutchman and I had fallen in with an American casting director and her husband, who were imagining the impossible task of casting the party's guests from the world's stock of supporting actors. After a buffet supper together we went in search of Dick.

Outside the disco in the dining-room I caught sight of a familiar stocky blonde climbing the stairs to an upper floor.

'You know Fortunata?' the Dutchman asked. 'She's trying to get into Pereira's films.'

'Can't she act? What's the problem?'

253

'No, she's stupid, but she can act – that's the problem. His films need obvious amateurs. They employ a new kind of realism.'

A glass verandah fronted the upper floor of the duplex. Guests thronged the rail, looking out over the sea towards the lights of Copacabana, the Sugar Loaf and the great illuminated Christ of Corcovado. But Fortunata had turned into a small corridor that led past a kitchenette and bathroom into the rooms at the rear of the duplex. A uniformed security man stood by a locked door, talking to one of Pereira's gangster friends. He let Fortunata through, pointing out some defect in her make-up. When she smiled at me, snapping her compact, he assumed that we were with her and beckoned us forward.

We had entered a private suite within the duplex. An office equipped with desks and filing cabinets served as temporary storage space for the furniture moved from the rooms used for the party. Film equipment, lights and silver umbrellas stood in the corner with a set of stage props – two plastic sofas, a roll of turquoise nylon carpet and a tawdry bedspread, like the decor of a cheap motel.

Fortunata opened the rear door and stepped into the corridor beyond, where powerful, ice-white lights flooded through an archway. Two men in tuxedos and a woman in a ball-gown with a drink in her hand were staring into the lights. Fortunata joined them, frowning as a dog barked in pain and its handler shouted angrily.

When the dog calmed itself, whimpering plaintively, Fortunata stepped into the room. Over the Dutchman's shoulder I could see the dim faces of a film crew through the harsh lighting. Guests in evening dress leaned against the walls, watching as Pereira signalled to his cameraman. He gestured impatiently at the sound engineer who crouched forward with a boom microphone, trying to pick up the dog's pathetic barks. The nervous German Shepherd was being alternately comforted and abused by its handler, a small, shirt-sleeved man in his sixties with a pencil moustache. The glaring lights, the soundman's nervous thrusts and the handler's fingers fondling its testicles had unsettled the large dog. It tugged at its leash, eager to go home, paws slithering on the tiled floor.

In front of the dog the crew had assembled a miniature film set, a garish double bed with a quilted headboard, a cheap dressing table and a red plastic lamp. Kneeling on the floor beside the bed was a naked woman, muttering to herself as she moved from one tired hand to the other. The fierce lights had bleached all the tones from her skin, which seemed like the latex on an inflated dummy. When she shook her long hair and glared angrily at Pereira I recognised Carmen's arrow-like profile. The dog struggled against its handler and she slapped her hand on the floor, shouting some obscenity in Portuguese. Pereira tried to calm her, but she stared at him with unconcealed distaste, as if regretting that she had been persuaded against her better judgement into an ill-considered career-move with this incompetent producer.

The dog's ears pricked forward, its nose scenting Carmen's exposed buttocks. The handler warbled into its ears, one hand massaging its penis, the other pushing its bushy tail from his face. With a look of mock resignation, Carmen glanced at the spectators along the wall. There were nods of sympathy, heads shaken over the incompetence of the handler and his beast's lack of virility.

The sound engineer moved forward with his microphone, and the cameraman adjusted his eye-piece. The lights intensified, blanching out the faces of the spectators. The dog approached, paws slipping on the floor, the handler steering it by the testicles. Carmen raised one palm and brushed away an annoying piece of grit, then stared self-critically at the black pool of her shadow.

*

Three days later I stood on the steps of the conference centre, waiting to say goodbye to Dick Sutherland before catching the flight back to London. I had missed him when the audience dispersed after the televised panel discussion he had chaired. Giving up, I was about to walk to my taxi when I saw him emerge from the building with Señor Pereira. The film critic spoke effusively, thanking Dick for his presentation to camera and the few words of Portuguese he had memorised.

In the doorway behind Pereira, her silk dress lit by the TV monitors and their scientific films, Carmen was practising her English with one of the women simultaneous translators. Pereira saluted Dick, and she strode up and smilingly took the film critic's arm. Together they stepped into a waiting car.

'Dick, I'll see you in Shepperton. Carmen seems happy – I thought she loathed Pereira.'

'She did. But she feels her career is taking off – apparently she's made some film with a dog. Pereira wanted to show me the rough cut. It's been a big hit with the distribution people.'

'Lassie come home, all is forgiven . . .'

'Is that the title? I'll give it a miss.'

'I would, Dick.'

Dick gazed at the statue of Christ on Corcovado. He squared his shoulders, not unhopefully, measuring himself against the TV ratings of the ultimate media personality. Along Copacabana Beach the salesmen were flying their festival kites above the heads of the footballers, hawking their movie-star lapel badges and belt buckles. The beggar woman from the favelas and her crippled child were hiding among the limousines outside the Copacabana Palace Hotel, ready to startle an unwary film executive. In the air-conditioned corridors of the conference centre the scientific films filled the monitor screens with their close-ups of nose-wheel housings, nasal septums and pain-registers, a vast dormant pornography waiting to be woken by the magic of fame.

CHAPTER THIRTEEN

The Casualty Station

Mental asylums, like the prisons they resemble, are so often burdened with the least appropriate names. As I drove through the gates of Summerfield Hospital I wondered who had christened this sombre Victorian pile. Immense red-brick walls like a perpetual headache rose to the shabby eaves, broken by barred windows that had never been cleaned, as if to protect the patients from the gloomy micro-climate that hovered over this forgotten corner of south London. Faded lawns struggled in the shadows of the tall fir trees, but on my visits to David Hunter I had never seen even one of the two thousand patients taking the air.

Anyone, I found, could drive through the gate-house without being stopped, and the endless internal roads that wound past the great buildings gave the impression that Summerfield was open to the world. In fact, the gate-house, like the dead lawns and the visitors' car-parks, was part of a decoy. The central enclave of the asylum, the citadel of the insane, remained securely sealed within itself. From the windows of David's ward, through one clear pane that had replaced the original frosted glass, I could see the internal courtyards attached to the high-security wings. Into these bleak stone pits, walls topped by steel claws, the deeply insane were occasionally released to stare in their haunted way at the mystery of the open air. Puzzlingly, the exercise yards were all of different shape, some triangular, others rectangles or gnomons, with small recesses that served no conceivable purpose, as if they together formed a jigsaw of a fractured mind, to be completed before a patient's release.

Two vehicles occupied opposite corners of the car-park, breaking that companionable rule by which drivers arriving at an empty car-park place themselves alongside each other. Most of the patients, I noticed, were visited only by the poorer of their friends and relatives, who had to make the long walk from the gate-house and were too tired to do more than sit and listen. A signpost pointed to the short-term wards – 'Narcissus', 'Rosemary', and 'Hyacinth'. Carrying my chessboard and a bag filled with fruit, aviation magazines and newspapers, I set off towards the entrance lodge. As always, however hard I tried to repress the sensation, I felt that I was arriving with my luggage to begin my own stay at Summerfield. These impassive buildings possessed a moral authority far more intimidating than the tired psychiatrists who worked within their wards.

While the superintendent checked my name against the roster I rattled the chessboard, and guessed that it would soon be lighter by a piece. The battered chess-sets at Summerfield had lost half their men. In his matter-of-fact way, David explained that these destitute patients, often abandoned by their families, possessed nothing, and would treasure a stolen piece like a precious doll. Usually, as I sat in the day-room with David, one of the old men he had befriended would be staring at his private pawn on an open board. A former accountant at the Church Commissioners, he had tried to suffocate his invalid wife. After an hour of thought he would at last embark on a cautious move.

Closing the board at the end of my visits, David always palmed one of the pieces, usually the black bishop, which he had identified with me. This was partly to irritate me, and partly to ensure that I played with no one else. While I searched for him I could hear his gentle voice outside the women's ward, as he gallantly steered one of the old women towards the lavatories. He greeted me cheerily, closing the lavatory door.

'I hope she knows what to do,' he confided. 'Most of the time she just stands there, trying to remember her daughter. She calls it her memory box . . .'

Affable and good-humoured as ever, he surveyed the day-room, looking for something new to tell me. Patients in dressing-gowns sat on the leather chairs, talking to their subdued relatives. On the sofa beside us a young woman lay with her knees pulled up to her chin, lost in her deep sleep of largactil. Her open eyes were tilted into their upper lids, as if she were trying to see something inside her skull. At the dispensary hatch a line of patients queued for their thimbles of tranquilliser.

'They'll bring some tea in a moment.' David leafed through the aviation magazines, and held my arm, glad to see me. His confinement had brought us together. 'It's good of you to come – how are the kids?'

'They're blooming, passing all their exams. Henry's built an aircraft for you – the Wright Flyer. Alice and Lucy wanted to come with me.'

'Not a good idea, actually.' David tore at an orange and treated me to a knowing smile. 'They can visit you, Jim, when it's your turn.'

I let this pass, and watched another of the older women, wearing nothing but a faded nightdress, carry a vase of daffodils to the window-ledge. She held the flowers to the light, introducing them to the sun.

'It's restful here,' I commented. 'All the sunlight, and these sleeping women. You could be in a private hotel on the south coast.'

'Of a rather special kind, dear sport.'

'I know – it always amazes me that they let the men and women wander around together.'

'No one's got pregnant yet.' David stared at the young woman asleep on the sofa beside him, the hem of her nightdress around her plump calves. As he set out the chessboard I noticed that the black king had failed to appear, a modest penalty I had incurred. 'Besides, the medical staff trust us completely. For them, we're the normal ones. They know our names and faces and little ways of doing things. It's you people who seem genuinely weird.'

'We probably are.'

David hunched over the chessboard, watching me through the pieces. He was waiting for me to catch up with my real self. He regarded my visits to Summerfield as an educative process; gradually I would accept my responsibility for the events that had brought him to this grim institution. At the end of my visits, when he accompanied me to the staircase, he clearly expected me to decide to stay. I would move into a spare bed in Hyacinth ward and our games of chess would continue until all the pieces had been stolen from the board.

'Have you seen Sally yet?' he asked off-handedly. 'I think she'd like to hear from you.'

'We talked on the telephone – she's staying in Scotland with some rich woman-friend of her father's, while they try out this new methadone treatment. She sounded a lot calmer.'

'She ought to go back to the States. I can see her strolling around Haight-Ashbury . . .' His hand was trembling over the board, as he fixed his eyes on some wayward dream of the past. When I reached out to reassure him, touching his wrist, he pulled away from me, and I saw that he had replaced the black king.

'David, all that's over now – the GIs are back from Viet Nam, and Nixon's gone to China.'

'I know. Thank God I'm here, everything's so earnest. You'll miss Viet Nam.'

'Will I? Why?'

'All those newsreels every night? I used to wonder why

you never came back to Shanghai with me. You didn't need to – they started the Viet Nam war for you instead.'

'I wasn't ready to go back.' I watched the old accountant hovering over his solitary pawn. 'It would have been too much like returning to the scene of a crime.'

'I know what you mean, Jim. I looked for that little railway station of yours.'

'On the Hangchow-Shanghai line?' I tried not to sound sceptical. 'I'm surprised you never told me.'

'Well . . . Miriam had died. You had enough things on your mind. Anyway, the damned taxi-driver couldn't find it. Those tourist guides are doing their best to turn Shanghai into a riddle.'

'It's probably gone, I shouldn't worry. Let's play some chess – black or white?'

'No, it's there.' David ignored my raised hands, his eyes fixed on mine. 'It's marked on the Greater Shanghai Transit Company map. And inside your head.'

'Not any more.'

'No? Your crashed cars exhibition – no one realised it, but that's what you were staging there.'

'At a few removes.'

'At no removes. Jim, I understand . . .'

Not for the first time he had linked his own last accident to my exhibition, implying that I had served as the catalyst for his erratic driving. But, if anything, the exhibition had been inspired by David. I remembered him hunting the streets of London, driving in the same dangerous way that he had practised for the first time on the long, straight road from Moose Jaw to the air-base. At the demolition derbys in the shabby stadiums of east London he and Sally had willed themselves towards death.

One-way streets excited them to play a desperate roulette. Late one evening, two years after the exhibition, David had driven the wrong way down the westward lane of the Hammersmith flyover, headlamps flashing as he forced the oncoming cars against the safety rail. A middle-aged cellist and her husband, confused by the siren of the pursuing police car in the parallel carriageway, had failed to stop in time. The wife had been killed over her steering wheel, and only David's deranged behaviour after his arrest, and his active RAF service in Kenya, had saved him from a manslaughter charge.

Under a section of the Mental Health Act he had been sent, first, to the special custody unit at Rampton, and then to Summerfield for observation. Six months later, as he crouched with his largactil shudders in this sunlit room filled with entranced and grumbling women, the memory of the cellist's death still pushed at the door of his mind. I felt nothing but concern for him and his younger self, now the same age as Henry, who had emerged from his Japanese camp into the post-war world. David had understood my needs but failed to read his own. He had tried, hesitantly at first, to recreate the cruelty he had known in war-time China, not realising that the post-war world was only too keen to do this for him. The psychopath was saint.

When I first visited him at Summerfield he had said, setting out the rules of our relationship: 'Remember, Jim – all I did on the flyover was what you did in your exhibition . . .'

Now the casualties of the Sixties were coming home, to the veterans' hospitals, the mental institutions and private clinics. In a drawing-room above a cold Scottish lake Sally Mumford was measuring out her days in methadone. When I telephoned her she sounded flat but rested, unlike the confused and hyper-irritable woman who had arrived at Shepperton one evening two months earlier, needing my help but refusing to speak to me. Fortunately the children had been away, staying with their aunt. I tried to sleep on the sofa as Sally spent the night weeping and striding around the empty bedrooms, ransacking the cupboards for old toys which she stuffed into her bag.

The next day she allowed me to take her to our family doctor, who referred her to an American physician at the London Clinic. She then moved to a specialist nursing home on the Thames near Marlow, one of those private prisons in which the rich, with the connivance of the medical profession, confine their elderly or embarrassing relatives. When I visited her there she was calm and sedated, smiling from a waking sleep as she spoke of our first meeting on the sand-island near Rosas ten years earlier. She seemed a child again, the kindly and generous young woman who had come to the help of my own children when they most needed her. Only when I mentioned Dick Sutherland did she frown and turn away from me.

Dick, alone, had made a triumphant exit from the Sixties. As I guessed, science and pornography at last made their long-awaited rendezvous under the lens of his laboratory camera. His successful TV series on the paranormal – ESP, astrology and telekinesis – was sold to an American network and brought him to the attention of a progressive New York magazine tycoon who had recently founded an institute of sexual research. On its governing body sat many of the gurus of the counter-culture – evangelists for LSD, trend-hunting neurologists, zen philosophers and Marxist popularisers. With much fanfare, the tycoon announced that the institute would continue the pioneering work of Masters and Johnson, Kinsey and Havelock Ellis.

At first, its researchers devoted themselves to scientific films of heterosexual intercourse, using the latest fibre-optic technology and miniaturised body-orifice TV cameras, all in pursuit of the white whale of modern sexology, the female orgasm. Soon, however, as graphic stills from these exploratory films were published in the parent company's magazines and pushed the circulations to record heights, the research broadened to include more wayward forms of sexual activity. The institute was discreetly relocated in London, avoiding the scrutiny of the US Justice Department and any possible threat to the professorial tenure of its academic board-members.

Dick became the institute's scientific director at its new headquarters, in a former hotel overlooking the Regent's Park canal. Here, under the neutral gaze of the rostrum camera, a recruited force of volunteers had explored every legal permutation of lesbian, homosexual and heterosexual intercourse. The cans of undeveloped film were air-freighted to the magazine offices in New York, and selected stills appeared beside the gate-fold nudes with Dick's scientific commentary.

When I mildly suggested to Dick that he was producing something indistinguishable from pornography he had readily agreed.

'Except for one thing – our aim is to analyse, not arouse. Think of this vast human activity, common to the whole biological kingdom, and you realise that surprisingly little is known about it. What actually happens when a woman fellates you? Do you know, Jim?'

'Dick, you make me doubt it . . .'

'Well, what more is there to say?'

'But why do I need to know?'

'Because sex is the last great frontier.' Dick had gestured at the horizons of Regent's Park like Cortez grasping the immensity of the Pacific. 'One thing we can say for certain about the future of sex – there's going to be a lot more of it. Already we can see that new forms of social structure will emerge to cope with the sexual imagination. What you and everyone else think of as the pornographic mind may well allow us to transcend ourselves and, in a sense, the limits of sex itself.'

'Your new series should be fascinating, Dick.'

'You've already heard about it? Good.'

I hadn't, but I saluted him ungrudgingly. Thinking of our journey to Rio, I realised that the evening with Carmen and Fortunata had been his brave attempt to step down from the television screen into a lost world of emotion and desire. He had discarded the image of the hoodlum scientist – part rock star, part Robert Oppenheimer – that had sustained him since his Cambridge days. Out went the leather jackets and gold medallions, in came tweed suits and woollen ties. He was at ease with me now, happier and more confident, at last engaged on the original research that had always eluded him, and unaware that he himself was the victim of a bogus experiment.

But Sally had been hurt. Along with the other volunteers who worked at the institute, she had been beguiled by Dick's evangelical ardour. She told me that she had been amazed by the unedited films screened for the volunteers in the institute viewing theatre, of the cathedral-like interior of her own vagina, moisture beading on its cavernous walls like jewels dripping in a grotto. As she lay with her laboratory partner, a remote-controlled camera recorded the involuntary movements of her facial musculature, the flushing of her breasts and abdomen, the skin tremors on the backs of her thighs.

Seeing these abstracted portions of herself had led to a growing numbness, a fading sensitivity of her skin to pain and feeling, as if her nervous system had been connected, not to the familiar nerve endings of her hands and lips, but to the screen in Dick's viewing theatre. She would turn the pages of the men's magazines in the waiting room before the laboratory sessions and find detached parts of her anatomy between the covers, the moist escarpment of her pubis like a remote mountain range viewed from the window of an airliner.

A progressive dismemberment of herself was taking place, until she reached the point where she expected to find the skin of her breasts and thighs stretched across an advertising billboard or upholstering the seats of a modish nightclub. When, like most of Dick's volunteers, she dropped out of the programme, she never fully reintegrated herself, and would wander the streets in her heroin daze searching for the lost parts of her face and lips.

Soon after, the Home Office became interested in the institute, and its work was suspended. Across the Atlantic, the magazine tycoon announced that the sexual revolution was over, and that he had donated the miles of cine-film to the Kinsey Foundation. Leisure industries represented the wave of the future, and investment would be moved to new vacation sites in Hawaii and the Caribbean. Sex, with every regret, was left to fend for itself.

The set-back was a blow to Dick. As he admitted in a moment of surprising frankness, he had naively hoped that the institute's original work would be accepted for what it was. He knew that his reputation in the scientific community had been damaged, and that the doors of most laboratories would be closed to him. Trying to help him, I introduced him to an interested publisher, and at my suggestion Dick quickly wrote the text of a pop-up guide to human psychology. Later, reading through this colourful best-seller, which seemed to have strayed from the back of a cornflakes packet, I was struck as always by Dick's shrewdness, intelligence and wit. Since its sales far exceeded those of my own books, Dick could continue to patronise me in his friendly way. I was still his gauche student, making the coffee in his laboratory and allowed to flirt with his secretary.

But had the rat in the Skinner box always controlled the experimenter? When I thought of David Hunter, of Dick and Sally, I sometimes wondered what part I had played in plotting the course of their lives, steering them towards goals that I had set many years earlier. I had never consciously manipulated them, but they had accepted their assigned roles like actors recruited to play

267

their parts in a drama whose script they had never seen.

Peggy Gardner had no doubts about my responsibility. I visited her small Chelsea house after seeing David remanded in custody at the magistrate's court, hoping that she might later testify as a character witness. She sat away from me in a straight-backed chair, surveying me as if I had been at the wheel of the Jaguar and she were a police psychiatrist called to give her assessment.

'Poor David. The last of your troupe. First Sally, then Dick . . .'

'Dick? I've had nothing to do with him.' I lowered my tumbler of whisky with such force that I cracked the enamel of her blackwood table. 'Peggy . . . ?'

'That tawdry institute, and all those TV programmes.'

'He's an actor at heart, who happened to stray into psychology. Dick's . . . a shaman for the TV age.'

'For years you've been encouraging him to buy all those American cars, telling him – what was it, some nonsense? – that he'd make the first scientific discovery on television. How could he resist?'

'He never wanted to resist. Can't you remember him at Cambridge?'

'I tried to avoid him. He was always so attentive and flattering.'

'He was just waiting for television to come along.'

'He was waiting for you.' Peggy paced over to the mantelpiece and stared at me through the mirror, as if the reversed image might give a clue to my sinistral dreams. 'Sometimes I think he set up that bogus experiment just to meet you.'

'He didn't know I existed.'

'Someone like you. Obsessed with the Third World War, your head full of all those American bombers and Lunghua . . .'

'I never talked about them.'

'You didn't have to! You were desperate for violence!

268

It made sense of everything, but you needed television to fill the air with it, play all that horror and pain over and over again. That really excited Dick. He gave you Miriam as the only way of holding on to you.'

'Isn't that a little callous? He'd have found his way to television if he'd never met me.'

'The Viet Nam war, the Kennedy assassinations, the Congo, those ghastly *ratissages* . . . they might have been invented for you.'

'Peggy, that makes me sound like a war criminal.'

'Miriam used to say you were. And you love your children.' Peggy pressed her hands against the mirror, touching the secure glass. 'Before we left on the *Arrawa* you took me to a film in Shanghai, about an American aircraft carrier . . .'

'*The Fighting Lady* – a collection of newsreels.'

'I thought you might get carried away in the dark, but I needn't have worried. Your mind was up there, moulded against that screen. I was so amazed I couldn't stop watching you.'

'It was the only film in Shanghai. Anyway, I was fascinated by flying.'

'You told me you'd seen it ten times!'

'The Americans brought it with them, and gave us all free tickets. I had nothing else to do.'

'Nothing else? In the whole of Shanghai? You'd been locked up for three years and all you wanted to do was sit in the dark and watch those suicide pilots crashing into American ships?' Peggy turned from the mirror, ready to face me. 'Tell me, you know that Dick has a copy of that film?'

'I think he does.'

'You know he does. Miriam told me that you used to watch it together in his garage at Cambridge.'

'Once or twice. Dick had a pilot's licence and I'd flown

in Canada. Besides, it's a remarkable film – those American pilots were brave men. And the Japanese.'

'Of course they were. No braver than the Russian pilots or the British pilots. What the Americans had was more style and more glamour.'

'Like everything American. So?'

'And that's exactly what you've always needed – glamorised violence. That terrible afternoon on the railway line near Siccawei – you'd seen dozens of atrocities by then.'

'We all had. That was Shanghai.'

'But for once you were too close. A part of it actually happened to you. All those car crashes and pornographic movies, Kennedy's death, they're your way of turning it into a film, something violent and glamorous. You want to Americanise death.'

'Peggy . . .' She had spoken with surprising force. Patiently, I followed her as she carried the drinks tray into the kitchen. 'As a matter of interest, Dick's institute did come up with some original research. I never watch pornographic films, and I've had a single car crash in my entire life. You have one every year.'

'I know. You live in Shepperton and you've brought up three wonderful and happy children. How, I don't know.'

I leaned against the refrigerator, looking around the little kitchen with its elegant spice jars and expensive French saucepans, so different from my own, where scarcely a piece of crockery matched and half the glasses had been given away at filling stations. Peggy's house was a boudoir designed for the charm and excitement of men. She had been through many affairs, but had kept herself untouched by them. There were no holiday photographs to remind her of the men who had taken her to Florence and San Francisco, shared villas over the years with her at Vence and in the Lot. Not a masculine gift stood on the immaculate desk in her office.

She had never married, as if afraid that she might bear

a daughter who would one day grow to be twelve and remind her of the years of separation from her parents. Curiously, the one person who had helped to sustain her had never been allowed to share her bed, and was the person whom she continued to reprove and reproach in the way she had done when I played pranks in the children's hut.

'And what about you, Peggy?'

'Me?' She stowed the glasses in the dishwasher. 'Are you trying to recruit me into your repertory company?'

'I was thinking of the dedicated paediatrician who's never dared to have a child.'

'I've left it a little late.' She dried her hands and placed them forbearingly on my shoulders. 'Besides, I had you. I think I looked after you rather well.'

'You still do – is that why you became a paediatrician?'

'Christ, don't say that!' Without thinking, she slapped my mouth, then caught herself and winced at my bruised lips. 'Oh, damn – there's blood on your teeth. Jim, I didn't mean to upset you over Miriam . . .'

I kissed her, for the first time since we sat alone together in the circle of the Grand Theatre in the Nanking Road. I could feel her tongue tasting the blood in my mouth. The scent of her body had changed, and her greying hair reminded me of her mother's as she stepped from the American landing craft after the journey from Tsingtao. I placed my hands around her, feeling for the thin bones of the girl I had known in Lunghua. The soft arms against my chest were those of another woman.

Then I felt her shoulder blades, and the strong ribs of the hungry twelve-year-old who had firmly lifted me from my sick-bed. I slipped my hands around her waist, touching the familiar broad crest of her pelvis. Kissing her again, I ran my fingers along the shy chin that had lengthened as the war progressed, always set to one side as she pondered my latest scheme for finding food. She smiled at me in the kitchen mirror, trying to apologise for my bruised mouth. I gently raised her upper lip with my fore-finger, feeling a rush of memory and affection for her worn but still even teeth, now marked with my blood.

'It's stopped bleeding.' She slipped between my hands. 'Jim, you're not demonstrating the skeleton to a class of freshers – let's move upstairs.'

She drew the curtains, folded back the bedspread and began to undress at a leisurely pace, neatly hanging her clothes on the chair beside the wardrobe. I expected her to be shy, but she was staring proudly at her handsome body in the mirror. Still smiling to herself, she stood in front of me as I struggled with my cufflinks, and massaged away the pressure lines below her breasts. She held in her stomach, hiding her plump abdomen and teasing me with the reminder of a very different body that had once hung from these bones.

Sitting on the bed in front of her, I placed my hands on her hips and began to kiss the small freckles on her abdo-men, and the spiral scar whose pearly silver curved around the small of her back and ended below her appendix. This marked her kidney operation ten years earlier, the Anderson-Hinds resection of the renal pelvis. When I col-lected her from the Middlesex Hospital she had walked unsteadily with me down Charing Cross Road, and in the medical section at Foyles I had bought for her the sur-geon's monograph, the book of her operation. I felt the eroded surface of the scar, trying to catch up with the thousand small bumps and bruises her body had known. I could see her clasping the monograph as we stepped from the bookshop, smiling at me with all her hot temper and exasperation.

I held her tightly, sucking back the blood from my mouth, unsettled as if I were embracing a sister. She calmed me with a hand, and began to caress my chest as we lay together, settling the movements of my diaphragm.

Decades of need and dependence surged from me to her breast as I held it to my mouth. I moved her knee on to my hip and eased myself between her legs, wishing that we had once conceived a child together.

She wiped my blood from her nipple and raised it to her lips. 'Quiet blood . . . that's good, Jim. Now I can remember . . .'

I moved inside her, in that deep interior embrace, glad that I could no longer feel her bones.

'Peggy . . . I wanted to do this thirty years ago.'

'Poor boy, you couldn't have managed it then.' She kissed my forehead, cleaning her lips and leaving a damp bow of blood that I could feel on my skin. 'This is the last time – you'll have to wait another thirty years.'

'I'll wait . . .'

I rested within her as she began to make love on her own. Her eyes watched her breasts as they rose and fell, and she touched her nipples to excite herself and then steered my fingers to her pubis, letting herself into some reverie of lust as private as a dream. Her mind was far away, beyond this little house and the King's Road rooftops. She gazed at her strong ribs against my chest. Her brisk interrogation in the sitting-room had been her devious courtship of me, and the blood in my mouth allowed me to play the sick child again. For a few moments we were lying on my bunk in the children's hut. In her roundabout way she was making her own return to the war, to her first desire for me. Now that her parents had died, she and I had taken their place and we were free to go back to Shanghai. Once again we were 12-year-olds who had made a small marriage of need among the rags and malarial straw.

When we had dressed she straightened my tie and jacket, brushing away a fleck of dandruff in a wifely way. She said

273

goodbye on the doorstep and kissed me robustly, sending me out into the world.

'Talk to David's lawyer,' I reminded her. 'He'll telephone you.'

'I'll see what I can do – I can tell the magistrate he was abused by the Japanese.'

She embraced me for a last time in front of the passers-by. A window into our childhoods had opened and closed.

'Tea-time – thank God.' David sat up, our chess game forgotten. 'The biscuits are good here, the best in Summerfield.'

Pushed by a tall Jamaican nurse, the trolley bearing the tea-urn advanced towards the polished table, on which some forty cups and saucers were laid out in ranks. Five minutes earlier, a barely perceptible movement of patients had begun. Dressing-gowns fastened, spectral figures appeared from the lavatories and dormitories. Other patients stood up without a word and drifted away from their relatives, pausing to shake the shoulders of the sedated men and women asleep in their chairs. None dared to approach the table, waiting as the nurse, with much officious rattling of the tea urn, set out the biscuit plates.

'It's kind of you to come, Jim.' David held my arm, but the black king had temporarily left the board. 'To be honest, I don't get too many visitors.'

'David, I'm glad to come. Peggy and I are doing everything we can. We're trying to get you released as an out-patient.'

'The old Shanghai firm – never escape from that. It's interesting here – I thought it might give you a few ideas.'

'It has . . .'

Beside us, the young woman with the plump calves and everted eyes slept in her deep largactil stupor, unaware

274

of the wraith-like figures advancing past her. They froze whenever the nurse glanced imperiously over her shoulder, as if all the ordeals of their lives obliged them once again to play a childhood game. Still unaware of the tea-urn, the elderly woman in the nightdress was laying a row of daffodils along the strip of carpet that separated the recess of the bay window from the rest of the day-room. Watching her, I tried to guess at the significance of this floral threshold, perhaps a gateway through which her lost children might one day appear.

'Doreen! Stop messing with those daffs!' The nurse banged the lid of the tea-urn, glaring at the row of dripping flowers taken from their vases. 'Now help me with these teas.'

Reluctant to leave her handiwork, Doreen began to line the cups beside the urn. David leaned back in his armchair, stretching towards the tea trolley, as if about to put his hand up the skirt of this imposing Jamaican woman. He was looking at the tray of biscuits, his hand moving to and fro like the head of a cobra. Every eye in the ward was fixed on him, and even the drowsing young woman had straightened her eyeballs to watch him.

'Doreen, you're getting behind.' The nurse stepped forward, her massive legs putting an end to David's dream. Doreen was holding a cup filled with tea, eyes fixed on the brimming liquid. She stared at the trembling surface, clearly struck by the unbearable contrast between the infinitely plastic fluid and the polished hardness of the table. She held the cup at arm's length, unable to bear the contrast between these opposing states of geometry. At last, testing a desperate hypothesis, she inverted the cup in a defiant gesture.

'Doreen . . . !' Tea was splashing everywhere, soaking the biscuits and racing across the table to pour in a steaming torrent on to the carpet. The nurse indignantly turned off the tap, her skirt and starched apron damp with the flying drops. 'Doreen, why did you do that?'

'Jesus told me to.' Doreen spoke matter-of-factly. She gazed happily at the mess before her, pleased that she had been able to resolve these irreconcilable natures. Her moment of insight had seemed divinely inspired.

'Get to your room!' The nurse bore down on her. She seized Doreen's wrist and elbow, and pitchforked her violently across the floor, shaking the old woman so severely that I feared she would break an arm. No blows were struck, but a dose of corporal punishment was being administered. Doreen stumbled to the carpet, and I rose from my seat to help her, ignoring the outraged nurse and the shocked stares of the relatives. Doreen's body was as light as a child's. She clung to her injured arm, sobbing to herself. When I left her at the door of her dormitory she stared at the rows of deserted beds, and spoke to them plaintively: 'Jesus *told* me to . . .'

After saying goodbye to David I made my way down to the lodge, glad to see the empty lawns and the car-park. 'Twenty-nine, thirty, thirty-one,' David had counted as he returned the pieces to the box. He locked the catch and added: 'Thirty-two.' He smiled at me, fully aware of the game we were playing. Find the key was David's game, but he had never found it, and the search had led him to Summerfield, while Doreen had found her own in a moment of faith and imagination. I thought of this simple woman protecting herself from the world with her cordon of flowers, solving a pressing mystery of time and space with a brave gesture.

I gave my name to the orderly and stepped into the sunlight. In a curious way I felt that I was being discharged from Summerfield. David and all the patients in this Victorian asylum had put their heads together, trying to solve the puzzle from whose board an essential piece had been stolen.

I walked to my car, across the damp asphalt that never dried after the night's rain. Before I started the engine I made a note to visit David in the following fortnight and to bring daffodils for Doreen. Summerfield fell behind me, an empty labyrinth hoarding its exits and entrances.

PART THREE

After the War

CHAPTER FOURTEEN

Into the Daylight

The telephone call from Sally Mumford surprised me. Four years after returning to America for good – she had sent farewell postcards from Berkeley, California, and a retreat somewhere in Idaho – she was in England again, with a young husband, a small daughter and a house in the Norfolk countryside. In a cheerful, almost matronly tone she told me that she had been back for six months, squirrelled away in what sounded suspiciously like a hippy commune left over from the Sixties. She had invited David to visit them and suggested, on hearing of his life-time driving ban, that I come too and give him a lift.

'We have a goat, I grow beans and cauliflowers and bake our own bread. You'll be amazed!'

My heart couldn't decide whether to sink or soar.

The trip, three weekends later, got off to a confused start. David failed to appear as agreed in the lobby of the Heathrow Penta Hotel, delayed by a late flight from Brussels. After waiting for an hour I headed towards the North Circular, wondering if David shared my second thoughts. I was glad to be seeing Sally again, at last with a child of her own and expecting her second – or so she had seemed to mention in an earth mother's vague afterthought, as if she now intended to be permanently pregnant for the rest of her life.

But the thought of returning to an intact piece of the Sixties was as daunting as trying to re-enter the previous weekend's hangover. Eight years after the decade's end there were all too many Sixties casualties still around, a walking wounded like the veterans of an unpopular war, who had no compunction about nagging at the public conscience. They clung to the fringe-life of provincial universities, edited books on the occult or alternative lifestyles, or sat entombed in remote offices of the BBC, always ready to waste a lunch-hour with talk of programmes on some 19th century herbalist or forgotten friend of the Pre-Raphaelites.

The dream of the Sixties lay dead in their eyes, and probably in my own, along with the hopes for a millennial world of peace and harmony – hopes, curiously, that had been propelled aloft by the cruel excitements of the post-Kennedy era and a million drug overdoses. My children had set off for their universities, leaving a vacuum in my life that would never be filled. The house in Shepperton was like a warehouse discarded by the film studios, along with the plywood candy bars and toilet roll of Magic World. The old toys and model aircraft that crammed the cupboards were the props of a long-running family sitcom which the sponsors, despite its high ratings and loyal audience, had decided to drop.

The sense of being pulled out of the schedules pressed on me as I mooned around the empty bedrooms, looking at the old holiday snapshots lying in the debris. Wiping away the dust, I stared at these pictures of the girls cutting a swathe through the Greek and Spanish waiters, Henry arm-wrestling with a captain of pedalos and learning to water-ski. I missed our shared childhood that had once seemed to go on forever. When they came home on their brief visits – eerily like cast reunions – I knew that I was the last of us to grow up. They accepted adult life, while I was still thinking of our happy days watching the televised Moon-landings and Miss World contests, anachronisms that belonged to a vanished decade.

As I left London I ran deeper into the past than Sally's commune near Norwich. I could have chosen a more easterly route, avoiding Cambridge altogether, which I had not visited for twenty years. But the old university town, where I had first met Miriam and Dick Sutherland, was worth a detour, if only to see if my mixed feelings towards the place had survived intact.

Fortunately, any uneasy memories were forgotten in the roar of heavy traffic that filled the approaches to the city. Cambridge had expanded into a complex of industrial and science parks, ringed by monotonous housing estates and shopping precincts. At its centre, like the casbah in Tangier, was the antique heart of the university, a stop-over for well-disciplined parties of Japanese tourists stepping from their TV-equipped German buses. As an undergraduate I had prayed for a new Thomas Cromwell who would launch the dissolution of the universities, but mass tourism had accomplished this, overwhelming the older European universities as it would soon destroy Rome, Florence and Venice.

I parked my car near the backs, crossed the Cam and joined a column of Japanese as they wound through King's. Undergraduates lolled in their punts like bored film extras hoping to catch a producer's eye. Dons with their faux-eccentric manners posed outside the chapel with the self-consciousness of minor character actors, waiting as a Spanish TV crew set up its lights. The spirit of the Disney Corporation and the ethos of the theme park hovered over the gothic stone. Listening to a tour-guide's commentary, I waited to be told that the entire chapel was a fibre-glass, tourist-resistant replica, and that the original structure was now in the more enlightened care of the Ford Foundation in some warehouse on Long Beach.

The Cambridge of old, of Rutherford, Keynes, Ryle and Crick, had long since departed to the American universities that had superseded it, leaving behind a TV academia with its eyes on its script-consultancy fees. Meanwhile, the more real world that I had first glimpsed on my motor-cycle rides still existed. Away from the tourist cameras and the posing dons presided the enduring realities of American power. Beyond the hedges and the chain-mail fences the nuclear bombers stood at the ends of their runways, guarantors of the civilised order upon which the university so preened itself.

Hearing the sound of American engines, I turned off the road near Mildenhall as a huge bomber swept over the trees. A car passed me, carrying an off-duty American airman and his family. They wore civilian clothes when they ventured from their bases, like the keepers at a nature reserve maintaining a discreet watch on their unpredictable charges. I parked in a narrow lane and stared through the perimeter fence at the worn concrete beside the nuclear weapons silos. The unsung and unremembered cement was more venerable than all the primped and polished stone of the university. The runways were aisles that led to a more meaningful world, gateways of memory and promise.

'Jim! You haven't changed . . . you should have warned me!'

'Sally . . . ? Dear, you've –'

'*I've* changed. My God, yes!'

She embraced me fiercely, arms strengthened by tethering goat, child and husband. Her hair was cut short, swept back to reveal a plump, cheerful face that might have belonged to Sally's sensible younger sister, married to a Philadelphia surgeon. Her skin gave off a rainbow of scents that set my mind reeling back to the first years of marriage – baby lotion, disinfectant, kitchen herbs, a recently potted geranium, warm breasts and armpits, topped up with a dab of best perfume brought out to greet the occasion.

I put down my presents and surveyed her fondly, amazed by the sight of this robust Anglo-American housewife. She was only three months pregnant, but seemed to have doubled her weight, a handsome, strong-legged woman with a warm flush of a complexion.

Surrounded by this pleasant farmhouse overlooking the tidal mud-flats of the river, I had the feeling that I had strayed into another film set. A few minutes earlier, driving up the rutted farm-track towards an old metal barn, I had expected to find an encampment of teepees, with a troupe of former account executives and record industry drop-outs picking the fleas from their caftans as they mumbled mantras and smoked their pot. But the farmhouse, with its Chinese carpets and deep sofas, seemed more like a dream of the Eighties. Even its coffee table was stocked with genuine coffee-table books and not with highbrow biographies. Its comfortably lived-in air and children's toys heaped in a corner might have starred as the backdrop to a wholemeal bread commercial.

'Well, what do you think?' Sally was watching me with a look of her old mischief.

'Sally, it's bliss – I'm thrilled for you. It certainly isn't what I expected.'

'Of course it isn't. But do you recognise it?'

'In a way. Don't tell me it's been on television?'

'I hope not. Think hard.' When I gave up, she cried triumphantly: 'It's just like Shepperton!'

'Where? My old dump?'

'Yes! Don't look so stunned. I thought of you and the pixies when we furnished it.'

'Sally . . . I can't believe it. So all along I was a complete suburbanite without realising it.'

'Of course you were. If you're going to bring up children there's only one way to go about it.'

'Yes . . . the children decide that, all right. I can't wait to see little Jackie.'

'She's a love, I'd die without her. Edward's bringing her back from a kiddies' party.'

'And Edward too.'

'You'll be impressed. He's years younger than me but he's so mature. Sometimes I think he's my father.'

'I'm glad . . .' She had spoken without any thought of the past, as if all memories of her Bayswater flat and the stock-car tracks of east London had vanished forever. 'Sally, it's wonderful here.'

'I've bought the whole package – station wagon, big dogs, sheep-skin jackets, church fetes. I should have moved in with you years ago. Now, tell me about the pixies.'

She poured tea, happily showing off her mother's silver tea-set. We settled back on the sofa and brought each other up to date. She had met Edward, a physics lecturer at the University of East Anglia, while he was on a year's sabbatical at Berkeley. I imagined Sally as one of the morose, chain-smoking ex-hippies sitting on the kerb along Telegraph Hill, but in fact she had been the manager of a small bookshop, and had begun to settle down long before meeting her husband. Watching her, I felt that the past years had slid away down some chute in her mind. She was young again, confident of herself and the world, the sunlight and this cheerful, untidy room. In her middle thirties she had been able to rendezvous with the 18-year-old self she had last seen at Idlewild airport in 1962, catching a plane to Europe.

Another Sally Mumford had gone off to join the Sixties, had taken too many overdoses and fallen into the doubtful company of arts administrators, TV psychologists and impresarios of car crash exhibitions. Happy for her, I listened as she described Jackie's latest crazes. At the same time, I wondered how long all this would last, whether it was another momentary fantasy, a dream that would founder when it struck the first hard wave . . .

A battered Volvo estate car had turned into the drive, rolling in the deep ruts. A boyish-looking man with a shock of pale hair and strong footballer's shoulders stepped from the car. He opened the rear door, released a harness and swung out a little girl in a party frock.

'They're here. Just look . . .'

Eyes bright with pride, Sally beckoned me to the door. She hoisted Jackie on to her shoulder, rubbed noses and quizzed her about the party. She kissed her husband, who greeted me pleasantly but warily. When we followed Sally and her daughter into the sitting-room he told me that David Hunter was due at Norwich station within an hour.

'I'll collect him from the station, and we'll join you at our site – we're digging out a wartime Spitfire. Sally thought you'd be interested.'

'I am – my son should have come along.'

Sally had mentioned that Edward was a member of a local group of aircraft enthusiasts, excavating the remains of old planes that had come down in the estuary. Photographs of the aircraft stood on the mantelpiece – an ancient Heinkel and a wingless Messerschmidt encrusted with peat being lifted by crane from a mud-flat. An almost intact Hurricane had pride of place. Edward and his team posed beside it with the curator of an aircraft museum to whom they had donated the Battle of Britain fighter.

But there were more important matters at hand than these forgotten aircraft. I took Jackie's present from my bag and handed the box in its bright tissue and ribbon to the serious-faced little girl. I thought affectionately of the hundreds of hours that Sally had happily given to my own children. Jackie stood beside her mother, now and then raising her arms stiffly to remind herself of her taffeta dress, watching me with her sweet but empty smile. Her prominent knees and elbows, the hands that flexed so sharply that their palms touched her wrists, and her toneless face made me realise that the clouded mind of this handicapped child would never be aware of the loving home that Sally had created for her.

Already I regretted the over-elaborate toy I had bought, a model kitchen with battery-powered lights and cooker far beyond Jackie's grasp. She seemed almost to understand this, as Edward set out the toy on the coffee table and connected the batteries. She stared at her father with her trusting, fixed smile, as if she were crossing the world at a slight angle to the rest of us. Now and then she reached out in a tentative way, and then gravely withdrew when Sally held her hands, a child of nature who would forever play alone in a twilit garden walled by shadows she could never touch.

Throughout our cheerful lunch Sally beamed fondly at her daughter. Pouring the wine, Edward reminisced about his year at Berkeley, and their meeting, quite by chance, when Sally's car broke down on the Bay Area Bridge. I was sure that this decent and responsible man had never even speculated that his life would have taken a different turn had he chosen not to drive to San Francisco on that particular morning. Watching them, I was confident that this loving house was not a facade. If anything, the daughter had strengthened the family, and Sally's dream would endure.

The tide had begun to run through the estuary, slipping between the mud-flats. Stranded by the falling water, sailing dinghies sat above us on the draining pedestals of silt. A cabin cruiser creaked against its mooring line, waking from its deep riverine sleep into the open air. When we set off in the rowing skiff the last of the tidal water ran into the channel, carrying away the reflection of the house.

I lay back comfortably among the cushions while Sally pulled on the oars, scarcely glancing over her shoulder as she navigated expertly through the maze of waterways. Two hundred yards from the house we left the main channel of the river and entered a parallel realm of small islands and tributary streams. Edward and Jackie had driven to the railway station at Norwich, and would join us at the excavation site, which we could reach more easily by boat.

'Where are we?' Sally rested on the oars and shielded her eyes from the gleaming mud. 'They only dig at low tide. If you can manage to stand without falling in, try to spot a church spire. It should lean to the left.'

'I see it.' I stared across a lake of grass. An entire air force could have disappeared into this world of forgotten creeks. 'There's some kind of crane on a barge.'

'Norfolk Lighterage. One of the directors is an aircraft buff.' Sally pulled away with strong arms, knees spread beneath her swelling abdomen. Her smock rose in the shifts of air to reveal her long brown legs. Minute pearls of scar tissue were all that remained of her old needle ulcers.

'What sort of plane is it? Are they sure it's a Spitfire?'

'Edward thinks so – because of the engine. Usually that's all there is left. You'll be impressed, Jim.'

'It could be a Mustang . . . that used a British engine.'

Watching the mud-flats slide past, I listened to the plash of Sally's oars, and wondered why Sally was so keen that David and I visit the excavation site. I thought of the Mustangs that had strafed the airfield next to Lunghua camp, and the downed pilots hunted by the Japanese soldiers in their dilapidated trucks. In some ways the banks of mud reminded me of the Whangpoo and the crashed aircraft lying by the irrigation ditches.

'I'm beat.' Sally decked the oars and let the skiff drift on the water. 'Time for my rest.'

'I'll take over.'

'No. Too risky. It's good for me, anyway.'

Taking my hand, she left her seat, stepped along the trembling boat and sank beside me on to the cushions. She wiped away the sweat that matted her blonde hair to her forehead. We drifted on the ebbing water, sealed off from the world by the wild grass and the slopes of silky mud.

'That sounds like Jackie.' Sally raised her head to the warning hoot of a disturbed water-fowl in the reeds. 'No, too far.'

'She's gorgeous, Sally . . . you're very lucky.'

She leaned her head against my shoulder and held my hand, tracing my palm-lines with a cracked finger-nail as if to remember my strange life. 'She's great. Edward adores her. She's getting on really well at the remedial classes and made masses of friends.'

'And she'll have company soon. Is it a boy or girl? You can choose these days.'

'No, thanks! I don't want to know. Boy or girl, *it's* going to decide.' She pressed my hand to her belly, and chortled when I felt the child kick. 'Beware of pregnant women, Jim. You've spent a lot of time with them.'

'I loved every minute – let me know if you ever get bored with Edward.'

'I won't get bored.' She closed my hand around my life-line. 'Do you remember when Miriam was pregnant?'

'I never knew her when she wasn't. Believe me, she was twice your size.'

'Happy to hear it. I'm going to be thrice my size. Do you think I've changed?'

'Completely. David's going to be amazed.'

'It was time to change. For you, too, Jim. Those were wonderful years, but . . . I keep looking at Edward and little Jackie and I'm so glad. We must have been very, very sane to act so crazily and get away with it.'

'Not everyone did.'

'Like David? I know.'

'You'll be surprised. David's a lot better – he runs his air-freight company in Brussels. He and his girl-friend are trying to adopt an Asian child . . .'

'David's dead.' Sally dropped her hand into the water. 'I heard it in his voice. He died years ago.'

'That's unfair. And it's not true – you could say that about me. Peggy Gardner frequently does . . .'

'No – everyone knew what you were looking for. But David? Still, I'm glad he's all right.' She smiled to herself, avoiding my eyes. 'I tried to call Dick Sutherland – we keep seeing him on a children's programme. He's Jackie's favourite doctor.'

'He's the same matinee idol he always was. People who go on television never grow old – or they grow old in a different way. Some sort of kidney trouble has slowed him down; he wants to give up TV and become a serious psychologist again.'

'Hey, you always said that television was serious! Don't tell me Dick's started to think for himself. I used to feel that he was totally under your thumb . . . Now, tell me about yourself. All those books?'

'There's nothing to tell – that's the problem. I spent the whole of my adult life with children. Suddenly, when I'm fifty, there's this colossal vacuum. Mothers feel the same way. Nature hasn't provided a contingency plan – or, as Dick would say, nature's contingency plan is death.'

'Rubbish. You're not going to die. Not this afternoon, anyway. Besides, you've got the children, even if they're not at home. It must be a bit of a relief – how you coped with teenage girls I'll never know.'

'I always did exactly what they told me. Actually, fathers can be better mothers than you think. It's mothers who make a hash of their teenage daughters – some of Alice's and Lucy's friends went through hell.'

'Well, think about it – all these young men ringing the bell, daughters on the pill, the poor mother finds she's practically running a brothel. No wonder Peggy disapproved of you. Besides, she wanted to keep you forever in that awful hut . . . but Miriam would have been proud of Henry and the girls. Do you still think about her?'

I drew my name on the surface of the water. 'Now and then – the damned thing is I've started to forget what she looked like. Sometimes I try to remember her and it's like watching someone else's home movie. I know I shouldn't say that. Memories of the people you love are supposed to last forever, but often they're the first to go . . .'

Sally moved my hand to her breast. She held it there for a moment, and then placed it on her lap. The women I had loved were saying goodbye. We lay together in the sun, as the water carried us through the clicking reeds.

The diesel tapped against the deck plates of the lighter, sending its smoky exhaust into the clear estuary air. Cables unwound from the winch and the crown block descended from the sky. Sally and I sat in a saddle of dry sand between two hillocks of grass, the picnic hamper open in front of us. Still wearing her party frock, Jackie squatted between her mother's legs, smiling in her straightfaced way at the swaying boom of the crane.

Below us, in the bed of the drained creek, Edward and his team were digging out the last silt from the fuselage of the entombed aircraft. Sections of flat steel piling had been driven into the bed, forming the walls of a metal chamber. Their interlocked edges held back the silt from the remains of the aircraft six feet below the surface. When the estuary flooded, the excavation site filled with water, which drained away at low tide and allowed the team a brief two hours to resume their patient work.

I stood up and searched for any sign of David, who had become bored with the slow preparations. Delighted to see Sally again after so many years, and bemused by her transformation from Sixties hippy into career housewife, he happily played hide-and-seek with little Jackie among the dunes. He ignored the excavation site, clearly disapproving of this morbid interest in old war wrecks.

'It's like your bloody car crash exhibition – Jim, you really started something there . . .'

'David, hold on. They were digging these planes out during the war.'

'Maybe – the next thing they'll be hiring Olympia, and laying out the debris of a 747 for everyone to pick over . . . You could help to arrange an Arts Council grant.'

Morosely, he wandered off to a small inn four hundred yards across the mud-flats where the cars were parked. Since leaving Summerfield he had become almost puritanically strict towards himself and the world, with all the zeal of the recent convert. I sensed that he disapproved of his entire past life, and felt that he was responsible, not only for having spent his childhood in Shanghai, but for my being born there as well. No penance could atone for this historical crime; a logic triggered in that cruel city had led inevitably to the death of the woman cellist on the Hammersmith flyover.

Leaving Sally, I strolled to the edge of the sand-cliff and looked down into the pit. Buckets of silt were being hoisted from the watery bed, and Edward stood knee-deep in the dark ooze, ready to hose away the last debris from the engine and canopy of the aircraft. Most of the wings and tail were missing, lost when it plunged into the creek, but I could see the typical nose-heavy bulb of a single-engine World War II fighter.

As it emerged for the first time into the daylight everyone fell silent. Edward hosed the intact canopy, watched by the small group of locally recruited workmen and the two-man crew of the lighter. Even after nearly forty years it was easy to imagine the immense force with which this stricken machine had plunged into the creek. The exposed engine block, a black bull's head of unrecognisable metal, was a fossil of pain. We waited for it to give its last cry as Edward hosed the silt from the valve-jacket and propeller boss. His boyish face revealed a clear-eyed seriousness that must have swept everything from Sally's heart when he parked behind her on the Bay Area Bridge and changed the flat tyre of her VW.

A warped propeller blade appeared, bent into a graceful arc. Edward wiped the mud from his arms and chest. Leaning against one of the ladders lowered into the pit, he ran his hands over the engine, searching for the carburettors and exhaust ports. Behind us, David had left the inn and was wandering across the mud-flat, a tray loaded with beer glasses in his hands, attention distracted by a child with a large dog.

'It's a Spitfire,' someone said. One of the excavation team, a Norwich surgeon, turned and gave a thumb's up to Sally and nodded encouragingly at me. I waved to David, who approached through the grass, watching the froth on the glasses. Edward was hosing away the mud from the top of the fuselage, exposing the cockpit canopy and the ragged metal plates where the tail had been torn away. He was frowning at something he had discovered, and turned off the hose, shaking his head to himself.

There was a shout, followed by a further moment of silence as everyone stared into the pit. The Norwich surgeon signalled to the lighter-men, and the diesel ceased its tapping. The workmen stepped closer to the pit.

'What is it?' Sally asked. 'Is Edward all right?'

'He's fine. The canopy's closed.'

'And? Does that matter?'

'The pilot's probably still in there.' I lowered my voice. 'If he'd baled out the canopy would have shattered on impact.'

'Dear God.' Sally grimaced, holding tight to her daughter as David arrived with the tray of drinks. 'Jim, I'm sorry, we shouldn't have come. I thought you and David might –'

'No . . .' I touched her shoulder, trying to calm her. 'I'm glad we did.'

'What's going on?' David stepped past us, and made his way down to the site. 'Is someone hurt?'

'No, but . . .'

I followed him to the edge of the pit. Pints of ale were passed round, but no-one drank. Wrenches in hand, Edward and the surgeon straddled the fuselage, like sailors unfurling a shroud. The canopy, its black panes intact, lifted without any effort, revealing a solid mass of ancient silt moulded to the glass and windshield.

I waited as buckets of water were lowered, and the suction hose drew off the liquefied silt. David stood beside me, face set, sipping his pint. His fair hair raced across his forehead in the breeze, a frantic semaphore. I watched his lips tasting the malty foam. White beads clung to the fine scars, miniature balloons celebrating these residues of his accident.

Dials had appeared in the cockpit, their last readings registered after all these decades. The trim wheels and throttle mounting emerged, a few fragments of blackened leather and the pilot's harness straps.

'The cockpit's empty – he must have baled out,' I said to David, but he shook his head and put his glass into my free hand. Edward was pulling at a leather parcel, bound by rotting straps, that lay below the seat on the floor of the cockpit, perhaps a spare parachute left behind by the pilot.

Reaching into the cockpit, Edward eased the parcel on to the seat and applied water and suction hose. Calling to him, David pushed through the watching workmen. He climbed over the steel palings and stepped on to a ladder, still wearing his grey worsted suit. One of the workmen pointed to the mud that already smeared his trousers, but David ignored him and sank to his knees in the wet silt that filled the bottom of the excavation pit. Arms inside the cockpit, he helped Edward to release the contents of the leather parcel. I realised that they were holding the remains of a flying suit, jacket and helmet. Already I could see the notched teeth and nasal bones of a small skull. Without thinking, I sipped at David's beer, surprised by its coldness.

They buried Pilot Officer Pierce two weeks later, in the churchyard below the tilting steeple, within sight of the creek into which he had plunged on a June morning 38 years earlier. His grave lay among the worn memorial stones of the local villagers, and of six RAF aircrew who had been interred during the war. None of Pierce's relatives was present; the only surviving member of his family was an elderly cousin living in New Zealand, but the RAF provided the honour guard that attended the burials of recently discovered wartime aircrew, and two former pilots from his squadron made the journey to attend.

Standing behind these elderly men, their blunt and polished medals on their dark lapels, I found it difficult to believe that P.O. Pierce, had he parachuted safely from his Spitfire, would now be over sixty. The small skeleton in the leathery parcel of his flying suit seemed to be that of a teenage boy, some child pilot who had bluffed his way into a wartime fighter base.

I remembered how Edward and the Norwich surgeon had laid the flattened parcel on the wet floor of the excavation pit, beside the exposed mass of the Merlin engine. As they carefully prised away the mummified leather they found a few small bones, a shoulder blade and several ribs, scarcely enough to constitute a grown man. Wearing his mud-drenched suit, David had climbed into the cockpit and sat in the pilot's seat, searching with his hands through the silt on the floor of the fuselage.

As he felt under the instrument panel and between the brake pedals, I imagined him at the controls of this Spitfire, sitting on its grass airfield somewhere in southern England in 1940. Had he or I been a few years older we would have returned to England to fight in the war, and our bones might well have been brought to light by these weekend archaeologists. I thought of the crashed Japanese and Chinese planes at Hungjao aerodrome, and of how as a ten-year-old I had often climbed into the cockpit of a forgotten fighter lying in the long grass. I had played with its rusty controls at about the same time as Pilot Officer Pierce sat in his Spitfire at the bottom of this Norfolk creek.

With luck, the burial of his bones had laid to rest more than one young pilot. David had been reluctant to leave the excavation pit. Sitting in the cockpit, his arms black with mud, he had looked up at the daylight as if newly born into the fresh air of the Norfolk estuary from the deep memories of decades. He stood beside me through the service, wearing his RAF uniform for the first time in twenty years. Head back in the light breeze, he was smiling and handsome again, mouth working in the ironic way I remembered from the japes of our childhood. He had looked at the Lunghua commandant, Mr Hyashi, with the same insolent grimace.

I worried that he might create a scene, but I realised later that his real recovery dated from that chance moment when he had returned with the tray of drinks across the mud-flats. He had brought with him a friend from the aviation world, a burly South Korean who had once been a JAL pilot and now worked at London Airport. I was puzzled why David should have invited this impassive, middle-aged executive all the way to a modest churchyard in Norfolk, but it then occurred to me that a retired

Korean pilot was as close as David could come to asking a Japanese to witness the interment of all his resentments of the past forty years.

CHAPTER FIFTEEN

The Final Programme

From the start, everyone I knew felt uneasy at the very thought of Dick Sutherland's last television project. Cleo Churchill urged me not to take part – the proposed documentary struck her as ghoulish in the extreme, pandering to the exhibitionist strains in Dick's character. More tolerant of Dick, and admiring his courage, I had tried to sidestep his invitation for different reasons. In later years, countless similar programmes were to be shown on television, and the making of these films became part of the therapeutic process by which the dying prepared themselves for their deaths. But in 1979 the idea of an explicit filmed record of the last weeks running up to one's death seemed virtually pornographic.

However, as I pointed out to Cleo, the film satisfied the logic of Dick's life. He had only felt fully alive on television, and in a macabre way would only be fully dead if his last weeks, and even the moment of his death, took place under the camera lens. A BBC producer had already shown an interest in the project, and a format had been devised which would incorporate Dick's film into a documentary series about the taboos surrounding this most unmentionable of topics.

'Taboos?' Cleo scoffed at the word, when we talked it over at her publisher's office, careful to separate herself from me behind a barricade of wholesome children's books. 'He's actually going to make a snuff movie. Jim, he's staging a sex-death in which he's raped out of existence by the whipped-up emotions of all those peak-time viewers. And you're going to take part?'

'Cleo . . . that's unfair. Think beyond the film. Aldous

Huxley took LSD as he died – perhaps this is Dick's way of coping with a challenge he can't face. The film will probably never be shown, and I dare say he knows that.'

'But do you know it? Piffle!'

Three weeks earlier, after an exhausting struggle against his thyroid cancer, Dick had discharged himself from hospital. A make-up girl preparing us for a late-night discussion programme had first noticed the goitre. I remembered waiting to take Dick's chair in front of the mirror, and how he sat surrounded by all the lights and cosmetic jars, his throat bobbing as the make-up girl pointed out his enlarged Adam's apple. He caught my eye in the mirror, as if aware that a dimension had entered the script for which all his years in television had never prepared him.

He was subdued during the recording, though outwardly his confident and charming TV self. I thought, unkindly, that it took only this modest swelling, probably a cyst or mild iodine deficiency, to touch his one vulnerable point – his own body. As he smiled and spoke to camera his familiar repertory of gestures and mannerisms suddenly seemed like so much decorative armour breaking loose from a stumbling warrior. When I drove him home to Richmond, before going on to Shepperton, he was already complaining about his sore throat, almost needing to punish his body. I knew he had been slightly ill during the past year, and urged him to see his doctor.

Soon after, Dick entered hospital for observation, passing into the paradoxical world of modern medicine, with all its professional expertise, ultra-high technology and complete uncertainty. As Dick pointed out on my first visit to Kingston Hospital, the qualities traditionally ascribed to patients – self-delusion, a refusal to face the truth, irrational hope and a despair born of underlying pessimism – in fact were those of their doctors.

'You have to realise,' he whispered to me when a nurse

had declined to answer a direct question about his suspected cancer, 'that the first and most important job of medical science is to protect the profession from the patients. We unsettle them and make them feel vaguely guilty. We ask questions they know they can't answer – the one thing they really want us to do is go away, or pretend that there's nothing wrong with us. What they like best of all is to admit us to hospital and then hear us say we feel fine, even if we're at death's door.'

Despite the prospect of exploratory surgery, Dick had already recovered his spirits. He flirted with the nurses and tamed the formidable senior sisters, promising them parts in his next TV series. But the reductive and grinding logic of hospital life began to take its toll, and he was astute enough to see behind the facade of ward-level optimism.

'The nurses are amazingly sunny,' I commented. 'I feel as if I ought to climb into the next bed.'

'Not a good idea, on the whole. Remember, they're like hostesses in a nightclub who know the customers aren't going to enjoy the floorshow.' Dick leaned against the big pillows, his keen eyes scanning the ward. 'It's interesting that the higher you move up the professional ladder the more depressed the doctor becomes. Your local G.P. and the junior housemen are reasonably cheerful – they can pass on the serious decisions. But as you meet the senior consultants you find this deepening gloom, because they realise there's almost nothing they can do to help you. Serious cancers are the worst thing they have to face – they remind them of how helpless medicine really is.'

But Dick's good humour had passed when I next saw him. He had woken after surgery in acute pain, unable to swallow and convinced that another throat had been transplanted into his own. Lowering the loose cotton dressing, he showed me the wound running from ear to ear, held together by a score of metal clips and covered with dried blood. He was discharged three days later, and within a week returned to the specialists to learn the results of the biopsy.

Far from clarifying the real nature of his condition, the operation had only served to confuse it. A specialist had eventually seen Dick, and embarked on an enthusiastic account of the educational benefits of TV medical programmes. Dick described, with grim relish, how his use of the word 'cancer' was met with a silent rebuke, followed by a disquisition on the meaninglessness of the term in the context of modern medicine. At last, as an afterthought, the specialist recommended the complete excision of the thyroid gland, reassuring Dick that he would re-open the old scar, and so preserve his neck for the TV cameras.

'The remarkable thing,' Dick confided to Cleo and myself, 'is that no-one will tell me I have cancer. It's as if they want to hide the news from themselves, just when I've been able to face it. Now I feel almost guilty. A brain tumour with lots of secondaries in the lungs and liver would have been the decent thing . . .'

Cleo and I admired Dick's courage and humour, which sadly deserted him after the second operation. The complete removal of his thyroid lowered his metabolism, and he became lethargic and dispirited, despite the large doses of calcium. His appearance radically changed. A long pointed jaw jutted from his eroded neck, and we both noticed that he no longer glanced at himself in the hand-mirror that a nurse had given him.

When we arrived he stared at us as if we belonged to an alien species and his true companions were his fellow-patients in the ward. I sensed that he regretted his own self-delusions, of which the greatest had been his apparently sincere attempt to discover the truth about his cancer. This was a bluff that had now been called. His attitude to the nursing staff had also changed. All irony and humour had gone, and he was far more docile and cooperative, like a rebellious prisoner at last accepting the unwritten rules of an institution.

Exhausted by the radiation therapy, Dick lay against his pillows, his bald head covered by the NASA baseball cap that Cleo had found in his computer room at Richmond. He had lost interest in himself, and neither the nurses nor the registrar to whom we spoke seemed to have any clear idea of his real condition. Concerned with its own needs, the hospital moved in a parallel world to that of its patients.

After three weeks of radiation therapy, Dick learned that the last of the malignant tissue had yet to be eradicated. He was now completely hairless, and no longer bothered to wear his NASA cap or conceal his ravaged neck. Leaning on my arm, he walked with difficulty to the ambulance that would take him to what, in a moment of brave but tired humour, he described as the 'Caesar's Palace of cancer therapy' – the Royal Marsden Hospital to the south of London.

As it happened, this ultra-modern hospital might well have been a hotel-casino on the Las Vegas strip. Its airy corridors were hung with Pop art posters, and Dick was given a ward to himself, with telephone, television and disposable toilet. In fact, this room was an isolation cell, in which he was imprisoned for nine days, watched by the geiger counter above his bed, until he had excreted the last of the radioactive iodine. When he spoke to us on the telephone, as Cleo and I stood by the lead-glass windows under the warning neon sign, his voice seemed to lift from a tape played at wavering speeds. The nurses who entered his room to take his blood and urine samples wore heavy gloves and protective overalls, and left him as quickly as they could, like conspirators setting a lethal device with the shortest of fuses.

Despite some success in eradicating the tumour, malig-

nant cells had rooted themselves in his spine and liver.
Too weak to bear any further treatment at the Marsden,
Dick was returned by ambulance to Kingston Hospital and
the chemotherapy ward of last resort.

Here, left to recover and without medication, he began
to improve. I felt a surge of affection for him as he rallied
himself, sitting up in bed to try on his new wig, shuffling
along the landings with us as he craned through the
windows for a distant view of the river and his Richmond
house, even asking Cleo about her publishing career.
When he was strong enough to submit to chemotherapy
he would be moved to a sterile room which would give his
depressed immune system the best chance of fighting off
any passing infection.

Making sure that the nurses were elsewhere, he showed
me briefly into the small, sterilised cell that was being
prepared for him, a cubicle stripped of all furniture and
fittings that might harbour bacteria, with a sealed door
and windows, and a ventilation system that resembled a
midget submarine's. Eerily, the screen of a TV set was set
into the wall behind a thick glass plate, as if even television
was withdrawing from Dick.

'Cosy, isn't it?' Hunched inside his dressing gown, Dick
straightened his wig and beckoned me away. 'Just the
place to take your last view of the world. Did you notice
the TV screen? Like a retina seen from the rear.'

'Dick, come on . . .' I held his arm as he hobbled away,
aware how much stronger he was, like a wiry and determined old man. 'You're so much better – you may never
move there. I can feel it.'

'I can feel it, all right . . .' He let me help him on to a
settee in the patients' day-room, then pulled up a wooden
chair for me. As he stared around the room I realised
how much he had changed. He had lost all illusions about
himself – he had always enjoyed being recognised in
public, but no-one now, neither the nursing staff nor his

fellow-patients, remembered the handsome presenter-psychologist who had fronted so many popular science programmes. Dick appeared not to care. To show his indifference to his earlier self, he had selected an oversize golden wig, almost a caricature of his sandy hair.

'You'll have time to read,' I commented. 'Cleo has the keys to your house, she can pick anything you want from the shelves.'

'No – I'm too busy watching everyone here.' He pulled my arm and whispered: 'You have to admire people. Most of them are far worse off than me – yards of gut cut out, half their jaws gone, ribs and God knows what. Yet they look like film extras ready to play a party scene.'

'Perhaps you should bring a camera in here?'

'It's a thought. In fact –' Dick glanced at me, as if recognising me for the first time. 'They say factory production always goes down after a film-crew visit. Here I'd expect the opposite effect. Perhaps there are too many TV screens in hospitals and too few cameras. Jim, tell me about Cleo and the children. It's good to see you, by the way.'

My suggestion had taken root. He was rallying himself, trying to be interested in our inconsequential world. Looking at his long, jutting jaw, I sensed his gathering will, if not to survive, at least to impose himself on whatever time was left to him.

The following Sunday, when I visited the hospital, I learned that he had discharged himself and returned home.

'It looks as if I have three or four months, possibly six,' Dick explained as we sat in his computer room. '*Omnibus* and *Horizon* are both very interested . . .'

'Dick, are you sure?'

'They'll set up the lights and equipment for me, and some kind of static video camera we can talk into. The idea is to show what actually happens as we approach the end, and break through all the taboos and preconceptions. No high-flown stuff about life and death, but as close to our ordinary talk as we can get. We'll start with something easy to get the ball rolling, the ten best films ever made, our last trips to New York, Chomsky versus Skinner. Most of it will be taped down here, but we'll move upstairs towards the end . . .'

He spoke in a confident and matter-of-fact way, sitting comfortably at his desk as if he were back in his old office at the Institute of Psychology. I was impressed by his easy command of his situation – he had found a role for himself, which I considered to be quietly heroic, but which he saw as merely the most interesting way of using the time left to him. He had lost even more weight, and wore a high-collared shirt and silk scarf to cover his chin. A smaller and neater wig allowed him, in a certain light, to resemble his former self, but I felt once again that he had begun to reject the affable and good-humoured personality I had known for so many years.

Altogether he had made a marked recovery from the months of medical treatment. Was he enjoying one of those periods of remission that give false promise to the victim or, as I still hoped, had he made a genuine return to health? As for his macabre documentary, at its worst this was a last gamble that his own survival would invalidate the project. Or, perhaps, having rid himself of all illusions in the radio-iodine room at the Marsden, he was now free to choose whatever maverick notion he needed to fill his last days.

As we soon learned, the improvement in Dick's condition was a brief upward tremor on a steadily downward graph. The specialists at the Marsden had arranged with Dick's doctor in Richmond to provide the drugs that would hold back the metastasising tumours. Now the cure, rather than the disease, would kill him. The cancer would not spread, but the increasing doses of chemotherapy would destroy his immune system, so that the smallest respiratory infection would turn into a fatal pneumonia.

But Dick was beyond the reach of these ironies. He was conserving what strength was left to him in order to carry out an important psychological experiment that would test his audience as much as himself. During our first recorded conversation, a trial run of the equipment, I found it difficult to speak at all, as if my throat was trying to mimic Dick's ravaged larynx. Our second appointment was cancelled when I developed a heavy head cold. But Dick was insistent; for reasons of his own he had decided that I should be the moderator, in part because I had first suggested the documentary to him, but also because he wanted to involve me directly in his death.

Sitting in his study as we prepared for the first episode, I regretted raising the idea. When Dick at last settled behind his desk I could see that he was almost exhausted by the effort of calming himself for the interview. The youthful actor-psychologist had become a shrunken and wounded old man, visibly fading under his powdered wig, and I hoped that the BBC team would pull the plugs on the entire spectacle. But everything was now grist to television's mill, like the razor-toothed rollers in abattoirs that stripped the last shreds of gristle from the bones of a carcase.

While we waited for the sound engineer to check his levels, I noticed that Dick had taken down the California licence plates on the walls of his study, the Cocoa Beach beer mats and Cape Kennedy press badges. During the course of our interviews more of these snapshots of his past were to disappear, as if he were consciously dismantling a carefully constructed myth of himself.

But when he spoke to camera he soon rallied.

'. . . Many people have left detailed accounts of how they ended their lives, from the Greek Stoics to the Jewish doctors in the Warsaw ghetto who kept careful records of how they starved to death. In the past, of course, everyone knew what happened when a human being died – relatives sat around the death-bed, doing their best to comfort the dying, and most people died in their homes. Today, though, death is something we experience for the first time when it happens to us . . . most people die in hospital, surrounded by machines, and watching someone die, especially a person very close, is more than we can face. Why? What is it about death that so unsettles us? In this series we're going to look at death through the eyes of a single dying person – me. I'm Dr Dick Sutherland. Three months ago my doctor told me that . . .'

While Dick rested from his introduction, I noticed the digital desk clock recording the date, September 23, 1979. The green rice-grain letters blinked through the minutes and hours, unmoved by the camera or Dick's commentary. He sat in a deck-chair in the bathroom while the director and the series producer discussed the few fluffs and verbal slips. They decided that, given the nature of the documentary, these would only enhance its authenticity, despite the problems they posed for the dubbing of foreign-language versions sold abroad. My own role, thankfully, was limited to asking Dick a number of general questions about his state of mind.

'. . . How do I really feel? Does the thought that all this is going to end in two months' time – as it happens, before the last episode of my favourite TV series – throw me into a complete panic? Do I walk around all day with a feeling of terror, like a victim in a horror film? Surprisingly, the answer is no. If anything, I feel cool and detached, as if all this is happening to someone else. The brain seems to have developed a way of standing back from itself, like a locomotive uncoupling the carriages behind it. To tell the truth, the biggest problem faced by the dying is how other people feel, especially their friends. There's a real sense in which the dying have to die twice, once for themselves, and once for their friends . . .'

Did Dick believe this? His sister and her husband, a retired Dundee accountant, had moved into the house to look after him, but they were unobtrusive, sensitive and reassuring. As I drove home it occurred to me that Dick had many acquaintances but virtually no close friends other than myself. Did he resent my concern for him and my visits to his hospital bed? Or were the friends for whom he had to die the invisible TV audience that had invested its admiration in him for so many years and now needed to be placated?

But all sense of an audience had gone by the time of our second interview. The first recording had left me light-headed. Unable to work, I roamed from room to room. Time seemed dislocated, like an endless afternoon in a strange city. When I arrived at Richmond, an hour early, Dick scarcely seemed to recognise me, and consulted his diary as if to remind himself. During the recording he sat stiffly at his desk with a brave if bleak smile, and described his activities in the past week, which seemed, eerily, to resemble my own.

I noticed that more mementoes had left the walls, the ticket stubs of the Rio premiere of *2001* and photographs of himself with the American astronauts at the Houston Space Center. I guessed that he was clearing away these remnants of the past twenty years so that he could return to his youth. Steadied by the camera, he reflected on his Scottish childhood and his wartime schooldays in Australia, where he and his sister had been evacuated.

'. . . Thinking about the Japanese during the first years of the war was rather like thinking about death. Everyone in Australia was vaguely frightened of the Japanese soldiers and knew they were approaching, but no one had ever seen one. Of course, our idea of the Japanese was a complete caricature – very different from your case, Jim, as a boy in wartime Shanghai. You knew exactly what the Japanese were like, and you'd also seen a great deal of death. Looking back, how do you think that affected you?'

I watched the sound engineer's tape-deck turning, and looked up to find Dick watching me with surprisingly clear eyes, his long jaw raised to reveal his ravaged neck.

I replied clumsily: 'I did see a lot of dead people – as you'd expect during a war. In some ways I think it was very corrupting . . .'

'Go on – you say corrupting, but how exactly?'

'Well . . . it wasn't the dead who were devalued, but the living. Our expectations of life were lowered.'

'Is that because they were too high in the first place?' Before I could reply, Dick continued in a last surge of breath: 'Perhaps we have exaggerated ideas about life, expectations that we see are unrealistic only as it draws to an end? It may be that we've allowed life and death to become polarised, when they're really much closer to each other than we realise. As I get nearer to my own death the distance seems to shrink . . .'

After the recording Dick held my hand in a friendly but absent-minded way. He walked stiffly into the dining-room, which overlooked his high-walled garden. Had he begun to forget me, along with the beer mats and the American licence plates? Yet his apparently impromptu question had made a telling point, addressed more to me than to the television audience, a brief but acute inquiry into my own motives and character.

The days between our recordings seemed to lengthen, as if I were applying some unconscious brake to time in an attempt to hold back the approaching end. A different man was emerging through Dick's wasted features, far more self-reliant than the television performer he had seduced himself into becoming. At our third and fourth interviews he spoke to camera in a short-breathed and almost impatient tone, describing his pleasure in the everyday world around him, in the garden and fish pond, his sense of triumph at winning the affection of his neighbours' cat. But these pleasures seemed as abstract as the moves in a chess-game. I guessed that he was entering a realm where, seeing everything with absolute clarity, he no longer cared to be distracted by pleasures of any kind.

Our fifth recording was cancelled, and I assumed that Dick had decided to end the series. But his sister told me that he had briefly returned to the Marsden, to be introduced to a new regime of drugs that would stabilise a secondary tumour in his knee. By now, two months after discharging himself, he breathed with continuous effort, his diaphragm forced into his rib-cage by the enlarging lobes of his liver. On the day of our interview his sister and I knocked on his bedroom door, unable to get a reply. We entered to find the French windows open to the cool November air. Dick was sitting in his woollen dressing-gown at the bottom of the garden, staring at the house without noticing us. I had seen the same fixed eyes in my neighbours' golden retriever when it had crept into the garden to die. Only when Dick rose from his deck-chair and stepped slowly towards us did time begin again.

Without any greeting, he led me to his computer room, where a small editing suite had been installed. Before the arrival of the BBC crew Dick began to run through the film of our earlier conversations. Shifting the clips of film with his impatient fingers, he stared at himself as he addressed the camera. Until then I had been glad that the TV screen was helping to ease his last days. The medium that had trivialised his scientific career had appeared to come to his rescue, but now its magic had dimmed.

The BBC crew arrived, and we could hear their lowered voices in the hall. Usually their appearance provided Dick with a slight lift, and the expression would return to his face like a bucket drawn from a dark well. But he ignored them, staring at the empty screen of the editing machine.

I touched his arm, thinking that he had lost consciousness, but his eyes were alert.

'Dick, they're here . . .'

'You can tell them to wait.' He gestured dismissively at the screen. 'The producer's lost his nerve – he wants to change the "direction" of the series. Can you believe that? A little late in the day. Bring in other topics, what do I now think of abortion? Abortion – do-it-yourself genocide . . . He didn't like that.'

He laughed thinly, massaging his knee through his pyjamas.

'Dick, can you walk? I'll bring the wheel-chair.'

'No – it's just down the hall. The surgeon at the Marsden talked about a prosthetic limb. The wonders of modern prosthetics, dear God – the castration complex raised to the level of an art form. He explained that they're close to "understanding" disease – they don't realise that they're soon going to be overwhelmed by an epidemic of *imaginary* diseases. The one thing we treasure most is a corrupt version of ourselves.' He held my wrist, aware that I was trembling. 'Now, this experiment . . . Someone else will have to take over. Perhaps one day, who knows . . .'

These were the last words that Dick spoke to me. He stood up and stepped quietly into his bedroom with a backward wave of the hand. He closed the door, leaving me to apologise to the film crew. He had spoken matter-of-factly of our 'experiment', and I realised that he had taken part in the documentary with one end in mind. The series had been a desperate stratagem that alone might have saved him. He had literally put his faith in my ironic prophecy that he would make the first great scientific discovery on television, and had gambled against all logic that the scientific discovery would be his recovery from inoperable cancer.

What was to have been our last interview never

occurred. When I arrived at the house a fortnight later an ambulance was parked outside. In the hall were Dick's local doctor and the district nurse, his sister and her husband, all lit by the glare of the television lights through the door of Dick's bedroom. He was to have taped his last reflections on his life before being taken to hospital, but it was clear that he was now too exhausted to speak. The producer had persuaded the reluctant doctor to allow a last shot of Dick lying on his bed in the dining-room, beside the dark mahogany table and its straight-backed chairs, a scene set for a tribunal.

Standing in the doorway behind the cameraman, I waved to Dick as he lay with the oxygen mask over his face, a glucose drip in his arm, a catheter draining into a glass flagon under the bed. He no longer wore his wig, and his face seemed to have been sucked into the mask, as if his wasted body was about to drain away down these encircling tubes, their coils like the telephone wire looped around the chest of the young Chinese on the railway platform.

CHAPTER SIXTEEN

The Impossible Palace

A funfair was visiting Shepperton. As I walked along the river I could see the chromium-panelled caravans through the trees, driving into the park beside the war memorial. There were trucks loaded with dodgem cars and sections of merry-go-rounds, a dismantled dream that these taciturn circus folk reassembled each weekend in one of the small towns of the Thames Valley, reminding the inhabitants of a forgotten corner of their imaginations. Already the children playing by the river bank had left the water. Whooping to their mothers, they ran towards the park, where the dozen vehicles were drawn up in a circle, a magic fortress that only children could storm.

I remembered how Alice and Lucy would ride their unicorns side by side, sixpenny treats that bought a fortune of excitement as they moved up and down, ribbons flying, arms clasped around the unicorns' necks, wide eyes cutting the air. Henry would sit stiffly in his silver aeroplane, embarrassed at being too large for the cockpit, then stand up like a stuntman and grip the leading edge of the wing, a lordly, three-year-old Lindbergh.

I strolled through the trees, almost expecting to see them waiting for me by the entrance to the funfair. They had left for the start of the university summer term, but in my mind they were always playing in the park. Alice's bright eyes, a swirl of Lucy's white frock, Henry's excited shout at some new idea, conjured themselves from the eddies of air and light. Generously, the park released its hoarded treasures. Stirred by the summer wind, the great elms were shedding their memories. I shielded my eyes from the sun and looked up at the shifting hampers of foliage, searching for a troupe of children perched on the branches, younger selves of the housewives and office workers of Shepperton. Perhaps I would see my own youthful self, bony cheeks under a strange haircut, whom I scarcely recognised in our snapshot albums.

As if cued by these memories, a young man in a pin-striped business suit and tie was standing in the car park beside his Triumph sportscar, watching me as he folded back the canvas hood. I followed the children towards the caravans in the centre of the park, not quite able to make out his expression, though he seemed to recognise me. From its licence plate I realised that his Triumph was twenty years old, the same age and model as the car that Dick Sutherland had once let me drive.

Chattering to herself, a neighbour's daughter overtook me. When she held my hand, urging me towards the fun-fair, the young man left his Triumph and began to walk in a deliberate way towards me. Was he a friend of Alice and Lucy? There was an edge to his jaw that reminded me again of the photograph of myself before my marriage. As the elms stirred over our heads, dappling the hair of the child pulling at my hand, I had the absurd notion that this young man was myself. He was calling to me, a hand raised in warning.

'I say – are you the parent . . . ?'

I turned to greet him, and bumped into the girl's older sister, who had followed us from the river. I helped to pick up her bucket and spade that I had knocked onto the grass, but by the time we had exchanged apologies the young man had returned to his car. He locked the canvas hood, avoiding my eyes as he stepped into the driver's seat. I guessed that he had seen me following the children, too old to be a parent and too young to be a grandfather, and suspected that I might have some illicit interest in them.

I watched him drive away, exhaust roaring as he

swerved past the war memorial and the crowded lunch-hour pubs. When he had gone I felt that I had narrowly missed meeting myself.

This sense of an imminent rendezvous somewhere in Shepperton had been growing within me during the six months since Dick Sutherland's death. I woke each morning, looking forward to the day's work, buoyed by the warm spring light and by a mysterious elation that had overtaken me. I had expected to be depressed by Dick's death, an ordeal made all the more harrowing by the uncompleted documentary, but I felt an immense sense of release. The air outside the crematorium was so bright and pungent that I scandalised Cleo Churchill by searching the chimneys for any signs of combustible flesh.

The non-denominational service, with its recorded organ voluntary and mock-solemn trappings, had resembled the rites of a new religion still in its development stages, an effect only stressed by the large contingent of television producers who were present. Behind their heavy shades, forever dreaming of 12-part series, they perhaps saw Dick as a mana-personality for the age of global TV. We were attending the funeral of someone who, with the shrewdest foresight, had already interred himself within the film archives of the BBC.

I had taken care to grieve for Dick while he was still alive, aware that repeats of his old programmes would soon be returning to our screens. Much as I disliked the documentary film in which we had taken part, I was grateful to Dick for choosing me as his interviewer. By demystifying his own death he had freed me from any fears of my own. For the first time since the birth of my children I felt that I was wholly done with the past and free to construct a new world from the materials of the present and future.

Time itself, bundling us headlong towards destinations of its own choice, had begun to loosen its grip. A day would last as long as I chose. Leaving my typewriter, I could spend an hour watching a spider build its web. On my walks by the river I stood among the elms and waited for time to calm itself, listening to its measured breath as it settled itself over the forest. I recognised the mystery and beauty of a leaf, the kindness of trees, the wisdom of light. My small house, the domestic streets and gardens glowed with the same vivid air I had seen during my experiment with LSD, and in that unending summer when Henry, Alice and Lucy had been born.

At the entrance to the funfair, while their mothers gossiped and searched their handbags, the children waited impatiently by the ticket booth. They rushed squealing towards the merry-go-round, leaving behind the solitary, copper-eyed son of the Pakistani newsagent. He watched me shyly as I bought our tickets and darted away to join the others.

The carousel was turning, and the children shrieked as the ancient calliope chuntered out its brassy tune. Horses and unicorns rose and fell. Small hands tugged at the horses' manes, pig-tails streamed in the air and cries of alarm gave way to frowns of deep seriousness.

Watching them sail by, I stepped closer to the rotating canopy. The lights swirled past, borne on the jangling music that drew memories from the wind, a dream of my own children when they had ridden these shabby unicorns. A two-year-old boy solemnly piloted the miniature aircraft, too frightened to cry, eyes charged by the steaming hoots of the calliope.

As I gazed at this enchanted scene, the carousel seemed almost stationary, preserved forever in a single moment. For the first time I could see beyond the little riders, through the silver forest of spiral pinions and the rotating mirrors above the calliope. Everyone I had known was riding the unicorns, Miriam and Dick Sutherland, a teenage Sally Mumford, boyish David Hunter. I stepped forward, waiting for an empty mount . . .

'Jim! Look out! What are you doing?'

A wooden pillar struck my hand. The carousel whirled past in a rush of noise and light, a raucous tumbril of chipped paint and peeling gilt. I fell backwards, steadied by two men watching their sons. A woman's firm arms held me as I stumbled across the veering air.

'Jim – you nearly fainted!' Cleo Churchill pressed my cheeks, concerned eyes peering into my face. 'I thought I'd find you here. You looked as if you were trying to climb on board . . .'

Sunlight filled the garden below the windows of my study, cheering the brambles and elders that crowded the edges of the lawn.

'I'm glad you don't drive like that . . .' Cleo brought two tumblers of gin and ice from the kitchen. 'Jim, tell me – were you trying to join the children?'

'Not really . . .' I managed to laugh at myself, and massaged my bruised hand. The rosy glow of angostura suffused the gin like a bloodstream glimpsed through a butterfly's wing. The carousel owner and his muscular sons had ordered me away, suspecting that I was up to no good. 'I'd forgotten the thing was moving – a trick of the sun. It turned the carousel into a kind of stroboscope . . .'

'Well, I believe you . . . try not to stop any speeding cars – I'd hate having to explain that to Lucy and Alice.'

The fan on the mantelpiece was turning, and the reflected sunlight through her blonde hair reproduced this curious effect. The same aura hovered over Cleo's bare shoulders as over every leaf in the garden. I was sorry to have worried her – for months she had been telling me that I was marooned in Shepperton, and the accident at the funfair must have seemed to her like another of my attempts at internal escape.

318

Old friends by now, we had never become lovers – in a boozy and reflective mood I had once described this to her as a technical omission, to which she had replied with a raised eyebrow, a shrewd smile and silence. But we had been separated by our shared friendship with Dick. Our different perspectives on this remarkable but ambiguous man had kept us apart, along with a certain wariness that Cleo felt towards me. Now that Dick had gone we had only ourselves, that shock of recognition sensed at so many funerals, and the cue to so many realignments.

I wanted to embrace her, but I found it difficult to get to grips with anything around me, the realm of desire and even the world of everyday objects. Cleo's sensitive hands and shy lips, the leaves in the drive, the rainbows on the windshield of my car, had all become idealised versions of themselves. The housewives shopping in Shepperton High Street, the extras leaving the film studios, the children on the carousel had been transformed by Dick's death. Distanced from their everyday selves, they seemed to hover beyond the contingent world of time and space, exiled from the paradise of the ordinary.

I stood by my desk, where Cleo had placed two heavy manila envelopes. They contained those mementoes of Dick which his sister had offered to us. While Cleo watched from the safety of her glass of gin, I drew out the California licence plate, the fading photographs of Dick in the cockpit of his weekend Cessna, posing alongside astronauts and space scientists at the 1960s Cape Kennedy. There were coasters from the Tropicana Motel in Hollywood, chips from a Las Vegas casino, and name tags of forgotten psychological conferences.

I arranged them in chronological order, as far as I could remember. The photographs and mementoes were clips from the film of his life, in which he had been both star and director. The artless vanity of the young Richard

Sutherland only prompted my affection for him. I was glad that he had died quietly and without pain, in the deep peace of the hepatic coma.

Cleo wiped her eye, taking my arm. 'It's like a shrine. The bones of a saint. Are you going to keep everything?'

'I don't think we need to. Let's each of us take just one thing.'

I was looking at the sunlit sky over Shepperton, and remembering how Dick had talked about our perception of time. If our sense of time was an archaic mental structure, one we had inherited from our primitive forbears, perhaps Dick had made a first move towards dismantling it?

Cleo leaned across the desk, sunlight on the pale crown of her scalp. She was one with the children of the carousel, motionless but forever moving past me. I had scarcely touched her, aware of the distance she had set between us, but I put my hands on her shoulders, embracing her in the light.

Later, Cleo watched me while I undressed her in the bedroom, her hands on my forehead, as if watching my temperature.

'We don't want you to explode. I'm glad we came upstairs – those beer mats are a bit unnerving. Like that terrifying film the two of you made.'

'Poor man, he was trying to pull off a miracle. I saw him edit the thing, moving pieces of himself back and forth, trying to solve a jigsaw. He was literally editing his own life.'

'Are you going to edit me?'

I kissed her strong wrists as she tried to pull them away from me. 'Absolutely. All arguments and disagreements will be wiped from the tape. Left profile only to be shown –'

'But I like my right profile – it has more intellectual integrity . . .'

'– flattering glances to be stressed, with deferential pauses . . .'

'God, I never *stop* being deferential . . . !' She helped me with the zip. 'Is this part of the editing?'

'Absolutely.' I carried the zip down to the base of her spine and let the dress fall forwards from her shoulders on to the floor. 'Think of it this way – I'm really dressing you, but you're seeing the film run backwards.'

'So it's all the fault of the projectionist? If only I'd told my mother that . . .'

She reached out and adjusted the wings of the dressing-table, then opened the wardrobe door so that its full-length mirror multiplied our reflections. Satisfied, she glanced at me slyly to see if I approved.

'I feel at home,' I commented. 'It's like *The Lady from Shanghai*.'

'What have I done? She got shot!'

We stood naked together, surrounded by the images of ourselves, lovers who had found each other during an orgy in a house of glass. Naked couples stood around us, immersed in themselves, half-hidden behind the doors. We were watched by the lenses of a dozen cameras, multiplied and dismantled at the same time. I held Cleo's breasts in my hands, touching the blue veins that ran past her broad nipples, and caressed away the pink grooves left by the wiring of her brassiere. I kissed a small scar in her armpit, relic of a childhood I had never known, and ran my lips through the shoal of silver stretch-marks, like seeds of time spilled across her abdomen by Ceres herself as she sowed her fields. She held my penis in her hands, rolling it gently between her palms, her fingers drawing on my scrotum. Phallic corridors receded from us, an erotic labyrinth in an impossible palace. When I kissed Cleo's

321

nipples a battalion of lovers bent their heads. I sat on the bed as she knelt on the carpet between my knees, her forearms resting on my thighs. She took the head of my penis in her mouth, touching the tip of my urethra with her tongue, then sank deeper to hold the shaft between her teeth, biting lightly on the swollen muscle.

I drew her beside me, kissing her thighs and hips. With her firm hands she pressed my shoulders to the pillows and knelt astride me, long hair falling across my chest. I lay back, happy to share Cleo with the mirrors, but she stretched out and kicked the wardrobe door with her heel. The house of glass vanished into the cupboard, a collapsing concertina of light.

'Just you and me, Jim . . . I think that's all we can manage now . . .'

She returned to the pillows and lay beside me, brushing the hair from her eyes, knees raised in the air as I caressed her vulva. Engorged with blood, her labia rose like coxcombs around her clitoris. My fingers parted the mottled crests and moistened the stiffened nub. I soothed the hot pad of her anus, pushing back the soft upholstery of a small pile. Lying beside her, I masturbated her affectionately. When a sudden fluxus drenched the sheet she gasped at the ceiling and bit my shoulder, embarrassed by herself. She rested for a few breaths, held my hips and drew me between her legs.

Watched by a single mirror, we made love through the afternoon. As I lay deep within her, I was certain that this act of sex would endure far beyond these summer hours. Time had refused to yield to Dick Sutherland, a Janus locked within his own relentless self-regard. Cleo had been right to seal away those silver screens. With every glance in the mirror a small part of us died. Images of ourselves formed the real walls of our lives. The tyranny of the lens shored its fragments against us, an infinity of recorded selves that shut out the world beyond. I held

322

Cleo tightly, trying to fuse the scent of her body into my skin. One day we would find the key to the mirror, and enter it together.

At the end of September, Cleo telephoned me from her office to say that the documentary on Dick's death would be shown on television.

'I thought they'd scrapped it,' she said, sounding unsettled. 'Are you going to watch?'

'No.' I knew that she had always disapproved of the film, suspecting that Dick had invited me to take part as a means of binding me to him forever. 'We'll remember Dick when he was alive.'

'Good. I feel a lot better. Let's take a boat for the weekend and sail up to Henley. You haven't been out of Shepperton for months.'

This was literally true. Cleo had been happy to leave London at the weekends, cook in my third-world kitchen, and drink double gins in the gardens of the riverside pubs. Sitting with her at the water's edge, as she tore up her sandwiches and threw pieces to the aggressive swans, I felt more contented than I had been for twenty years. Sally had given birth to her second child, a healthy daughter, and bombarded us with invitations. Peggy Gardner's surprise marriage to an architect young enough to be her son (a fourteen-year gap, Cleo noted, Peggy's age when I had left the children's hut in Lunghua), and the orphaned Malaccan boy whom David and his Belgian wife had adopted, together convinced me that the past had been laid to rest.

Before we collected the rented cabin cruiser Cleo asked the marina operator to remove the miniature TV set in the saloon. Filled with riverside gin, we would be sleeping soundly when the late-night documentary was transmitted. As we moved through Shepperton lock, Cleo at the helm, I stood beside her with my arm around her waist.

'Cleo, we've never done this before. Why?'

'Why, indeed? You've been a prisoner in Shepperton.'

'We'll stop at Cookham and see if it's changed.'

'Not Cookham – and it won't have changed.'

'Why not?' I was surprised, knowing that she admired Spencer's visionary paintings. 'You always liked Cookham.'

'Too many angels dancing in the trees. Be honest, do you really want to hear Christ preaching again at the regatta?'

'We'll have lunch at Runnymede. We can visit the Kennedy Memorial.'

'Do I approve of *that*? I'll think about it . . .'

These talismanic zones disturbed Cleo. She distrusted their hold on me, for the soundest reasons. My decision not to watch Dick's documentary struck her as a promising first step in my rehabilitation, a return to the contingent world. I looked back at Shepperton, at the great elms in the park by the war memorial, at the film studios and the riverside hotels, receding from me like the Bund at Shanghai.

'Jim!' I felt Cleo gripping my arm. 'Relax, the place will still be there when you get back.'

'I know. I'll get a drink for us.'

'We don't need a drink. You always behave as if Shepperton only exists thanks to an act of will on your part.'

Laughing, I embraced her, almost sending the cruiser into the bank. 'Cleo, I dream the place . . .'

'And a wonderful dream, too. Alice and Henry and Lucy. Now and then, though, wake up.'

'I will . . .'

Two hours later we moored at Runnymede and walked across the meadow towards the hills that rose through the woods. In a sentimental gesture, a British Prime Minister had bequeathed an acre of soil to the American nation, and the limestone monolith of the memorial to John F. Kennedy overlooked the site of Magna Carta. During the Viet Nam war the memorial had been continually defaced and vandalised, and on one occasion cracked by a bomb.

Arm in arm, we climbed the pathway towards the memorial. The crack that divided the limestone was freshly cemented. Ancient graffiti had left their blurred traces in the face, overlaid by slogans and swastikas aerosolled in day-glow paints. Litter and beer cans were strewn about the site, and the remains of a takeaway meal in silver foil had been pushed under the memorial stone. Fifty feet away, partly concealed by a magnolia shrub, a middle-aged man with a shock of pale grey hair was copulating with a twenty-year-old woman. Trousers loosened around his waist, he lay between her raised legs, moving in hurried spasms as if urged on by the presence of this morbid stone.

Cleo lowered her gaze and frowned at the litter. 'Doesn't anyone ever clean the place? You'd think Kennedy was completely forgotten.'

'I suppose he is – in a way, that's a good thing.'

I thought of the role that Kennedy and his assassination had played in my own life, and how his televised images had shaped the imagination of the 1960s. Stills from the Zapruder film had seemed more poignant than a Grunewald crucifixion. Now only the graffiti endured, like the bird-droppings on the statues of Victorian generals and statesmen in the squares of London.

We walked down to the gate and crossed the meadow to the car-park beside the jetty. Groups of people leaned against their cars, watching a family recover a motor-boat from the river. A father and his teenage daughter manoeuvred a two-wheel trailer down a stone ramp. When they had submerged the trailer in the shallow water the father released the speed-boat from its mooring by the bank and steered the craft on to the metal cradle. Above them, on the ramp, his wife sat at the controls of their car, waiting to tow the trailer from the water. A younger daughter sat behind her, eating an ice-cream and engrossed in a comic.

The current pulled at the speed-boat, trying to draw it into the centre of the stream. The father struggled with the metal cradle as his wife raced her engine, watching him through the rear-view mirror. When he signalled, she engaged bottom gear and edged up the ramp in a blare of noise and exhaust. The tow-rope tightened and the trailer moved forward, its tyres emerging from the water. But the speed-boat had floated away, and the man shouted to his wife, who switched off her engine. Oblivious of all this, the girl in the rear seat read her comic, now and then remembering to lick her ice-cream.

A youth in swimming trunks strode down the ramp and helped the man to pull the speed-boat on to the trailer. The wife reversed a few feet, releasing the tension in the rope. As Cleo and I boarded our cruiser they were fastening the craft to its cradle. The wife restarted her engine, released her hand-brake before engaging gear, and fumbled with the controls when the car rolled backwards down the slope. Everyone began to shout in warning, and the car-park attendant left his ticket booth and remonstrated with the hapless driver.

'What's going on?' Cleo asked, as I waited to cast off. 'Are they driving into the river?'

'It's starting to look like it . . .'

The car's rear wheels had disappeared below the water. Flustered by the attendant and the shouts of the onlookers, the woman had lost control of the car. The girl in the rear seat cried out and lifted her feet from the water covering the floor. Her mother opened the driver's door, allowing her impatient husband to take the controls. But as she stepped into the shallow water there was a shout from the young man in the swimming trunks.

Buoyant now in the deeper current, the speed-boat had

floated into the stream, dragging the trailer with it and pulling the car down the ramp. People were leaving their parked vehicles, cups of tea forgotten in their hands. Two men waded into the river and gripped the door pillars of the car, trying to hold it against the current.

'Cleo, wait here!'

As I stepped into the water I could see the white-faced child screaming in the rear seat, the water already up to her armpits. Trying to reach her, the mother floundered into the river, the skirt of her cotton dress floating into her face. Her husband seized her arms and pulled her on to the ramp. Already exhausted, he plunged into the water, face below the surface as he tried to disconnect the tow-rope.

I gripped the left-side door pillar, trying to reach the girl, who held the ice-cream over her head. Her shoulders were covered by the water, and she screamed at her mother, surrounded by loose tissues and aerosol containers, road-maps and cigarette stubs that had risen from the ash-trays and glove-pockets.

Before I could seize the child, the car began to tilt to one side, dragged back by the speed-boat. Everyone was shouting as the water swilled over the roof, a white spiral of ice-cream floating on the surface. Knocked from my feet, I found myself swimming beside the father as he fought his way to the speed-boat. He released the metal catches on the cradle and the craft swung away across the stream, bumping into the hull of a passing cabin cruiser whose crew stared at us from their sun deck, glasses of wine in hand.

Finding our footing, we pushed the car on to the stone ramp. The father pulled open the door, releasing the last of the water, only to find that the rear seat was empty. He plunged through the water beside the bank, slapping the waves with his hands as he searched for his daughter, but the car-park attendant had found her lying on the floor below the steering wheel.

Cleo joined me as they laid her on the wet grass.

'Dear God – do you know any first aid?'

'No, but I think . . .' The cold river-water streamed from my chest and legs. When the attendant lifted the child, her body hung from his hands like a dead rabbit, her eyes unfocused, her blue arms trailing across the grass. The sobbing mother smoothed the child's hair, and the attendant began to move her arms rhythmically across her chest. Soon tired, he lowered his face to her blanched cheeks, trying to detect her breath, and then resumed his to and fro motion as if exercising a doll.

Stunned by the suddenness of the tragedy, Cleo was weeping into her hands. I held her head against my shoulder. Trying not to look at the child, I searched the Windsor road, hoping to see a passing ambulance. A coach loaded with Middle East tourists sped past, but too late it occurred to me that at least one doctor would have been among the party.

Fifty feet away, a tall man in hiking boots strode along the footpath, approaching us at a brisk pace. He carried a bulky haversack on his shoulders, and his bare knees brushed aside the long grass. Between his heavy beard and the hair that crowded his forehead was a narrow face with red-rimmed eyes, as if he had spent too much of his hiking holiday reading in an unlit tent. A paperback guide-book to Eton and Windsor protruded from the pocket of his tartan shirt, and he seemed more interested in finding the historic site of Runnymede than in this tragedy on the river-bank.

As he neared us, he caught sight of the little girl. Before anyone could speak he slipped the haversack onto the ground, asked a middle-aged couple to keep an eye on it, and stepped through the circle of onlookers. He ignored

328

the sobbing mother and knelt on the grass, taking the arms of the inert child from the exhausted attendant.

His bony fingers moved like a conjuror's over the child. He lifted her shoulders, so that her head fell back, forced apart her jaws with his thumb and with a deft hooking movement of his forefinger released some obstruction in the back of her throat. One hand held her ribs and the other compressed her diaphragm. Instantly there was a gush of water from the child's mouth. Carefully smoothing his beard, he bent down and placed his lips over her mouth and nose. He began to breathe slowly but strongly, stopping to pump the child's breastbone. As he worked, the crowd of some thirty people was silent around him.

'She's breathing . . . oh, my God.' Cleo's fingernails had torn the fabric of my shirt. The girl was coughing. She choked and spat out the water in her lungs and windpipe. The bearded man watched her calmly with his blood-shot eyes, then sat her up with his strong hands and steadied her breathing. The girl gasped at the air, and her eyes focused on the circle of people. She leaned against her distraught mother, coughed and rubbed her nose, sucking great gasps of air over her swollen tongue.

Two cars had backed to the edge of the stone ramp, the drivers discussing the fastest route to the hospital at Windsor. As the water streamed from her cotton dress, the mother carried the child to the nearer of the cars. Cleo smiled at me through the tears that blurred her mascara. Everyone followed the child, but I was watching the bearded man who had saved her. He made sure that the child was breathing comfortably in the car, then slipped through the crowd and reclaimed his haversack, thanking the couple who had placed it on their card-table. Before the convoy left the car-park he had already resumed his walk along the bank.

*

We passed him an hour later, striding towards Windsor. I wanted to thank him, which no-one had managed to do, but I found it difficult to come up with the right words. I steered the cruiser close to the bank and reduced speed so that we kept pace with him. He strode along in his heavy boots, checking some detail on his map. On his tartan shirt I could see the dry stain of the ice-cream that he had expressed from the child's stomach. I guessed that he was a school-master or civil servant, but I knew that he might just as well be a ship's purser or a day-release psychiatric patient. The heavy knapsack cut into his narrow shoulders, but he seemed unconcerned by the weight. Tied to the back of the knapsack was a pair of drying socks that I had not seen before and which I assumed he had washed in the river soon after saving the child.

Cleo waved to him, and he gave her a friendly but quick smile, lengthened his stride and moved away from us. He was enjoying his holiday and preferred his own company. Cleo's contingent world, the bare knees and the ice-cream stain and the drying socks, moved past the cabin cruiser and the dozing swans. I had thought of asking him who he was, but I realised that, for all practical purposes, I already knew.

CHAPTER SEVENTEEN

Dream's Ransom

Guests were arriving in fancy dress, for a party of a very special kind. Hundreds of vehicles lined the quiet Buckinghamshire lane, and as I searched for a parking space I was overtaken by a studio van carrying two Marie Antoinettes, a pirate chief and a trio of Roman senators. Their rouged cheeks and painted lips gave them a look of plague victims on their way to a fever hospital.

My dream of Shanghai had materialised, like all dreams, in the least expected place, among the imposing houses built around the golf course at Sunningdale, little more than a fifteen-minute drive from Shepperton. I had lived for thirty years within sight of the studios, but had never stepped inside the huge sound-stages, and was unprepared for the scale of a major Hollywood production. A genie had sprung from the pages of my novel, and was busily conjuring the past into life, working with an extravagance more than a match for the original Shanghai.

The city of memory whose streets I had redrawn within the limits of the printed page had materialised in a fusion of the real and the super-real. Memory had been superseded by a new technology of historical recovery, where past, present and future could be dismantled and reshuffled at the producer's whim.

I had set out from Shepperton at seven that morning, expecting to find a small location crew at the Sunningdale mansion. Rented by the film company, the house would play the part of my childhood home in Amherst Avenue. Much of the film had already been shot in Shanghai, where the banks and hotels along the Bund stood unchanged since the Communist seizure of the city in 1949. But the houses in Amherst Avenue were semi-derelict, turned into tenement apartments crammed with Chinese families and makeshift offices. No. 31 Amherst Avenue now contained the New China Electronic Import and Export Agency. Its drive was overgrown, its rotting window-frames were supported by bamboo scaffolding, and the swimming-pool had been roofed over to provide a damp-proof warehouse.

Fortunately, a reasonable replica of Amherst Avenue lay to hand on the other side of the world, a few miles from the studios at Shepperton. These handsome, half-timbered mansions, built in the 1930s beside the golf course, had served as the models for the houses which the British émigrés like my parents had built in the suburbs of Shanghai – houses whose Tudor exteriors were themselves facades, hiding American bathrooms, kitchens and air-conditioning.

There was something odd in the notion that the home of a near-neighbour could serve so plausibly as my childhood house, as if these Thames Valley towns formed part of Greater Shanghai. While I followed the studio van carrying the party of costumed extras I looked up at the familiar mullioned windows and realised how shrewd an eye the art director had brought to his job. He had convincingly recreated the exotic city of memory from materials far nearer to me than I cared to accept.

In place of the small location crew that I expected, a fleet of vehicles had taken over this quiet corner of Sunningdale. At first sight the scene resembled the evacuation of London – dozens of trailers sat in the surrounding fields, huge marquees stretched their canvas over miles of duckboard, double-decker coaches, restaurant buses and lavatory trailers were parked in lines, generators drummed at the cold morning air, sending their current through a maze of cables to the location three hundred yards away. A private police force controlled the traffic, and a bus service ferried cast and crew from the trailers and make-up vans.

Not one house, I discovered, but four of the mansions had been rented by the film company, each contributing a segment of my childhood home – one provided a drained swimming-pool, another the reception rooms and lawn where the fancy dress party on the eve of Pearl Harbor would be held, while the third and fourth would recreate the kitchen, dining-room and my own bedroom. Later that day, as I walked around the site, I stared through the windows of the mansions around the golf course, wondering what other segments of my childhood were hidden among the bridge tables and billiard rooms.

I parked my car on the edge of a commandeered tennis court, and watched a team of scene-shifters unloading the 1930s props – Chinese screens, art deco lamps, tiger-skin rugs and white telephones. All these technicians, I realised, from the barber who had given me a period short-back-and-sides, to the carpenters, lighting specialists and costume designers, were working to construct a more convincing reality than the original I had known as a child.

The clock of my life had come full circle, in all sorts of unexpected ways. In a kindly gesture, the director had invited me to play the part of a guest at the costume party. Grateful to him, I had accepted with all the nervousness of a passenger volunteering to parachute from an airliner. A benign conspiracy was already in motion. Many of my neighbours had worked for years as part-time extras, and had been hired to play internees at Lunghua Camp. Only the previous afternoon, leaving the wine store in Shepperton High Street, I was greeted by the mother of a girl who had gone to the same school as Lucy and Alice.

'Jim, I've just heard. We're in the camp together! Tim Bolton and the Staceys are going to be there . . .'

Not only the mother but her daughter, now 25, would play a Lunghua prisoner. I almost believed that I was dreaming, and that my sleeping mind was recruiting my Shepperton neighbours into the narrative of the dream.

Walking home, I wondered why I had come to live in Shepperton in the first place. Thirty years earlier, Miriam and I had picked the town at random, but perhaps I had known even then that one day I would write a novel about Shanghai, and that it might well be filmed at these studios, using my own neighbours as extras and the nearby mansions that had inspired the houses in Amherst Avenue. Deep assignments ran through our lives; there were no coincidences.

'Jim, you made it!' One of the American producers waved to me through the electricians and lighting men who were moving in and out of the house. She held my arm, as if suspecting that I might lose my nerve and escape. 'We weren't sure if you were going to turn up.'

'How could I miss it? I don't mind saying, Kathy, it feels pretty strange . . .'

'I bet it does. It's a good thing you decided against coming to Shanghai with us. How does the house look?'

'Uncanny.' White pigeons released during the shooting of the children's party the previous day still strutted on the lawn, and a security man sent them fluttering into the roof. 'I should have bought it 30 years ago.'

'Then you'd have had nothing to write about. And we wouldn't be here . . . We're shooting the party in about an hour, so you'll have to change. The dresser's waiting for you upstairs.'

'I need a disguise . . .'

While we spoke I became aware that a three-man film crew was quietly recording our exchange for a documentary about the production, a film within a film that took its place in the corridor of mirrors. This sense of illusions trapped within illusions persisted as I entered the large bedroom on the first floor. Here the principal actors were changing into their costumes, a cheery group whom I recognised from scores of films and television plays. Their faces seemed oddly different, but when they put on their

334

make-up they grew more real. By contrast, I felt an impostor inside my John Bull costume of red tail-coat, top hat and Union Jack waistcoat.

Later, in the long drawing-room overlooking the garden, I stood with the party guests in a virtual replica of the house at Amherst Avenue. On the table beside me were copies of *Time* and *Life* dated December 1941, a week before the Japanese attack on Pearl Harbor, and I almost expected the white telephone to ring with a warning that we should leave on the next passenger steamer for Singapore.

Standing with a glass of whisky in my hand, I felt curiously like one of the intruders who sometimes gate-crashed my parents' parties – Axis agents posing as real estate dealers, professional bridge-players with a sideline in morphine, ex-nightclub hostesses on the look-out for my mother's jewellery box – whom Boy and Number 2 Boy would escort firmly to the door. I waited for my parents to appear and ask me to leave, failing to recognise me in this caricature costume.

'Hello . . .' An engaging 12-year-old with a slim face and mature eyes stood in front of me, wearing Turkish slippers, spangled vest and trousers. He introduced himself confidently:

'I'm you . . .'

As he extended his hand I could see him doubting if this overweight figure could ever have resembled himself.

'. . . and we're your mum and dad!'

An attractive couple in their early thirties, he in pirate costume, she dressed as a milkmaid, greeted me laughingly. While we spoke the lights filled the drawing-room with a powerful glare. The dream was about to dream itself. The camera crew were ready for a tracking shot through the party. After talking to each other about the threat of war, the guests would say their goodbyes and

335

step through the hallway into the drive, where a second camera would record our departure.

The director came up to me with a friendly word.

'All set, Jim?' He nodded encouragingly. 'Just relax – put a hand on your hip. You look as if you know how to hold a glass of whisky.'

'I've had a little practice – but that's as far as it goes.'

'What about a line of dialogue? You can give yourself one right now.'

I stared at him, too tongue-tied to even say my name. He patted me reassuringly and walked back to the monitor. Everyone fell silent and the camera began to turn. I felt myself drifting into a trance, trying to imagine this line of dialogue missing from my earlier life, which I had spent my entire career trying to define.

Followed by the camera, we moved towards the hall. Lights were shining in the driveway, reflected from the polished roofs of the cars into which we would step. Drawn up on the raked gravel were a Buick roadster of the 1930s, a high-roofed Packard like my parents' car, a black gangster's Chrysler with running boards and white-wall tyres, and a 1940 Lincoln Zephyr convertible. Beside them stood Chinese chauffeurs in pre-war Shanghai uniforms, caps under their arms as they opened the rear doors for the departing guests.

Staring at the scene, I tried to focus my eyes on the camera and the watching crowd beyond the gates. I stepped into the rear seat of the Packard, remembering in time to remove my top hat. The actor playing my chauffeur closed the door and took his seat behind the wheel. As the cars moved across the drive between the departing guests I felt that I was being carried away from this quiet Buckinghamshire lane, across another world and another time to the Shanghai of half a century earlier, towards the lights of the Bund and the department stores of the Nanking Road, through the French Concession to the tramline

336

terminus at the end of the Avenue Joffre, to the barbed-wire checkpoints that led to the western suburbs and the high-gabled house where a small English boy played with his German toys, surprised by the white pigeons that had taken shelter on his roof.

The cabin stewards cleared away the last drinks before we landed, moving nimbly through the debris of the 12-hour flight from London. Sitting beside Cleo in the front row, the cockpit of the 747 far above us, I peered over her shoulder at the north-east suburbs of Los Angeles. Vast highways busy with cars stretched across the sun-filled landscape, covered by a yellow haze as if the sand had begun to evaporate from the desert.

'Swimming-pools . . .' Cleo pointed below. 'Thousands of them. When the rains fail these people will survive. How do you feel?'

'Fine. I'll recover. As if I've taken too many amphetamines.'

'You have. Don't worry, you'll land in about three days, when it's all over.'

'I hope so. It's a long way to go to a movie.'

'But what a movie.' In fact, neither of us had seen the film. 'It's a shame you're in fancy dress – no-one will recognise you.'

'It's hardly a major role.'

'Rubbish – it's modest, but crucial.'

'Cleo, I may have been edited out altogether.'

'Of course you haven't! How could they?' she huffed, indignant at the very idea. 'You're the only one who was really there.'

'I'm not sure that's true – I think the actors felt that I was the odd man out, the only one who wasn't real. Most of them had been back to Shanghai.'

'You could have gone with them.'

'I know, but I hadn't the nerve. I wasn't ready to face

337

everything again – I've spent my whole life trying to sort it out. This is the right way to go back to Shanghai, inside a film. In a sense they started shooting it fifty years ago . . .'

The world premiere would be held in three days' time, at a theatre in Westwood. Seatbelt fastened, I waited as the plane turned over the sea and swept in across the idle waves. Despite the long flight from London, and what I had said to Cleo, I felt remarkably at ease. I looked down at the deserted beaches, with their isolated palms standing on the edge of the Pacific Ocean that I had last seen in 1946. I had never visited Los Angeles, but it seemed right that my childhood should meet its end in this desert city whose limitless imagination had re-mythologised the past and invented the future.

An hour later we rolled along the San Diego freeway in the studio car, looking at the landscape of Los Angeles that neither of us had seen before, but which was instantly familiar. Thousands of films and television series had installed an intact replica of the city in our minds, far more accurate than the preposterous beefeater and pearly queen image conveyed by the British tourist board. Vaguely garish bungalows and store-fronts stretched for miles under the tangle of overhead wires, a terrain of ticky-tack and painted glue fading in the sun, as if the entire city was a dusty film set waiting to be refurbished in some as yet to be financed production. I loved every inch of it, and felt instantly at home.

Then, as we left the freeway and joined Santa Monica Boulevard, I saw the first anomaly, a jarring intrusion from another level of reality. A billboard the size of a tennis court stood beside the road, advertising the film we had come to see, my own name below those of the producers and director. For a moment the dream had woken and summoned its sleeper.

Identical signs reared over the rooftops of Los Angeles, and even over Sunset Boulevard, where another writer,

Joe Gillis, had become entangled in the Hollywood dream. In our hotel I switched on the television set to find commercials for the film filling the screen with low-flying Mustangs, a real Shanghai burning again as Japanese soldiers marched down the Bund and my boyhood self was swept up in a panic of coolies and office clerks. Arm in arm, Cleo and I stared from our terrace at the billboard over Wilshire Boulevard. My past had escaped from my head and was clambering across the rooftops like some doomed creature in a Forties monster movie.

Happily, the irony of all this was not lost on Cleo.

'How did Sinbad get the genie back in the bottle? Think.'

'God knows – some piece of low cunning, I suppose.'

'You've spent years writing about the media landscape, and now it's escaped and stood you in the palm of its hand.'

'I'll rent a car tomorrow. We'll find the real Los Angeles.'

'Dear, wake up. This *is* the real Los Angeles.'

The next morning we set out on a circuit of this mysterious city. Entire districts sat in the musty sunlight like intact fragments of television episodes, as strangely familiar as the revisited streets of one's childhood. Far from being the youngest, Los Angeles was the oldest city of the 20th century, the Troy of its collective imagination. The ground-courses of our deepest dreams were layered into its past among the filling stations and freeways.

On the day before the premiere, while Cleo was visiting English friends in Santa Barbara, the reception desk rang to say that a Mrs Weinstock had called to see me. Assuming she was a local journalist, I asked the desk-clerk to send her up to our suite. Moments later, I opened the door to find a handsome American woman in her middle sixties, strikingly dressed in a Persian lamb coat and silk hat. Her commanding eyes rose instantly to the challenge when I failed to recognise her.

'James, you're too busy to remember me?' She stepped forward, in a heady aura of perfume and expensive fabrics. She seized my shoulders and pressed my face to her smooth cheeks. 'Olga! Olga Ulianova from Shanghai!'

'Olga . . . ?' I was pinned against the television screen by my childhood governess, who had materialised from the Hollywood sky like the billboards and TV commercials. 'Olga . . . I can't believe it . . .'

'So you'd better start now.' She glanced around the suite, taking in every detail of the books on the table, Cleo's clothes hanging in the bedroom, the open suitcases and presentation photographs. As she sized me up, deciding that no more than a few seconds' inspection was needed, I tried to remember the edgy young woman I had last seen in the Del Monte nightclub. Despite the years, her features were almost unchanged, the lips as cutting as ever, the hectic eyes carrying out an inventory of my clothes, self-confidence, integration into the real world. But her face wore a curious mask, as if a child's cheeks, nose and chin had been slung from her temples, through which glared the penetrating eyes and sharp teeth of an old woman.

'You haven't changed, James. Not even a little. You're still riding your pedal-bike.' She smiled shrewdly, slipping her coat across a chair. 'But now you remember me?'

'Olga, yes . . . I'm still amazed to see you. Did the studio arrange this?'

'The studio? Everything isn't a film, James. My daughter and I are staying with our friends in Van Nuys, so I thought, let's see how my James is.'

'I'm glad you did. But you got out of Shanghai?'

'Of course! Once the Americans left. Believe me, James, I'm not designed for communism. I'm living in San Francisco for many years now . . .'

'And you're married . . . ?'

'Mrs Edward R. Weinstock – my husband is a nose and throat surgeon, very influential.' She nodded darkly, scrutinising with only marginal approval a photograph of Cleo and myself. 'But you were nearly a doctor yourself? I read an interview – I couldn't understand . . .'

'I gave it up after a couple of years – I wanted to be a writer.'

'A writer?' Her nostrils twitched doubtfully, as if only the plushness of this Beverly Hills hotel suite prevented her from criticising a disastrous career-move. She was wearing an expensive gown with a gleaming lamé thread that she might have worn to the opening of a Las Vegas casino, but as she turned to and fro on her rapier heels I found myself glancing under the arms for the tell-tale tear. I remembered the brief glimpse of her breast that had so dazed my adolescent mind. Despite her expensive hair and jewellery, there was still something slatternly about Olga, as if her body was a disposable tool to be used as necessity dictated. I thought of her in post-war Shanghai, a tank-trap full of vodka, lying in wait for the young American servicemen.

'So this film, James. Is it good?'

'I'm sure it is. They say it's his best. I haven't seen it yet.'

'You haven't?' This was clearly a serious omission, one I should have rectified before signing the film contract or, more sensibly still, before writing a line of the book. She shook her head, as if I was still the odd little boy who had cycled all over Shanghai in search of a war. 'Anyway, it's a big help for your career. You were always telling stories. Your poor mother didn't know what was coming next . . .'

'This is the only book I've written about Shanghai – for some reason, it took a long time.'

'Too much to forget, people don't realise . . . the things I could tell about Shanghai. You and I should write a

341

book, James, a real best-seller. My ideas and your –'

'One is enough, Olga. I might write a sequel about my life in England.'

'England?' Doubtfully, Olga sniffed her Scotch. 'Is it so interesting? I read about your wife – that's sad for you.'

'That was a long time ago. I'll treat you to lunch, Olga, and you can bring me up to date.'

'Listen, it's never long enough. When my mother passed away . . .' As an afterthought, she added: 'My second husband died. An English dentist in Hong Kong, so I understand.'

On our way to the rooftop restaurant she held my arm in a genuine show of sympathy, evoked almost entirely by her feelings of pity for herself. Responding to the attentions of the restaurant, she was soon as animated as a teenager, showing off her smooth cheeks and trimmed nose. The young Olga I remembered, whose body I had tried to glimpse as she undressed in the bathroom, seemed to beckon across the years from this ageing but still glamorous woman. She spoke with scarcely a pause for breath about her years in Hong Kong and Manila, battling her way to the top of the social hill as husbands died under her like horses under a cavalryman at Austerlitz.

When we returned to the suite she said: 'James, your book made a lot of interest in San Francisco – many people from Shanghai are living there. Perhaps you could give a talk to us. You could say I was your family's friend. Maybe in the diplomatic service . . .'

'Olga, I'd like to, but even writing about Shanghai was difficult enough.'

'Of course. I know your feelings. We were always close, James. You never told your mother about those things I took – the silver and the jade horses . . . I always wanted to thank you for that.'

'Olga, I never knew.'

'Maybe you forgot. They had so much, and my parents

342

were hungry every day. My father lost all his hope, sitting in that little room. It's lucky he died before the war came. My mother forgave me – women understand – but a father? Never . . .'

Olga held my arm, the scent of her hair, throat and breasts overrunning my senses. She stood beside me, staring at the mansions of Beverly Hills as if seeing the vanished facades of Amherst Avenue. I remembered how, forty years earlier, I had felt her strong hip pressed against mine as we stood in the glass-strewn ballroom of the Del Monte nightclub. During the dark days at school in England I had often thought of Olga. We would have made love on one of the roulette tables if I had been less intimidated by her, and particularly if I had offered a short cut to my father's office.

I embraced this exotic female chimera, with her dream's ransom of a face-lift. Her body was even older than mine, but her face was that of the White Russian teenager who had first looked after me.

She smiled to herself, perhaps amused by the memory of some childish exploit in the garden at Amherst Avenue.

'And your friend, James?' Her fingers loosened my tie and shirt. She ran her nails across my chest, making sure that my nipples were still there. 'Is she back soon?'

'Not till tomorrow – she's gone to see publishing people she knows in Santa Barbara. Olga, this has nothing to do with her.'

'Publishing? Then it's okay . . .' She raised her face in front of me, a small screen on which was projected the image of a young woman.

I wondered why she had bothered to see me – perhaps out of pride, and to remind me that she could still dominate my life. Certainly, she would have felt no debt of honour for stealing from my parents before the war. But she knew that we were both victims in our different ways of western rule in Shanghai, which my parents represented

343

for her. We had once been wounded and corrupted by Shanghai, in so far as children could be corrupted, and by making love in this California hotel we would prove to each other that the wounds had healed.

'Good . . . you know, James, I never waited long for a man. This could be a bad example for me . . .'

She held my wrists in the same firm grip she had used half a century earlier to steer me towards the bathroom. Standing beside the bed, she closed the wardrobe mirrors so that no reflection of her back would reach my eyes. She began to undress me as if preparing me for a party, her fingers never leaving my skin as they moved around my body.

Delaying herself deliberately, she stood against me, playing the moody governess unsure whether to accord some trivial privilege to her charge. I kissed her affectionately, glad that she had come through and was happily married to her influential surgeon.

The film of our life rushed backwards through the projector, devouring itself as it hunted for some discarded moment that held the key to our earliest selves.

On our final day in Los Angeles, a week after the film premiere, Cleo and I decided on a last visit to the ocean. Waiting for our car, we stood in the entrance of the hotel, looking up at the black skyscrapers of Century City a few hundred yards away. This cluster of sightless towers emerged through the low-rise sprawl of the city like a harsh, obsidian Manhattan.

Cleo stared at the razor cornices, and gave a shiver. 'Is it all going to look like this when we come back? Please, God . . . what sort of heaven circles those spires?'

'None I want to wake into. But face it, Cleo – modernism is the gothic of the information age. Dreams sharp enough to bleed, and no doubts about man's lowly place in the scheme of things. Let's head for the beach . . .'

Venice, by contrast, was ramshackle and comforting. An intact fragment of the Sixties survived along its promenades. The wide sands stretched past roller-skaters and muscle-builders, break-dancers and beggars posing as Viet Nam psychos. Its modest stands were hung with flower-power T-shirts and mystic jewellery. Driftwood fires were burning on the sand beside the shelters which the groups of hippies had erected. The sea seemed far away, a glimmer of waves along the horizon, as if the Pacific had decided to withdraw for the day. I could almost believe that we were walking on the bed of a fossil sea, with ancient cigarette ends, ball-point pens and beer cans embedded in its scarred surface, all that remained of some earlier race.

I slipped my arm around Cleo's waist, happy to be with her and glad that we would be going together to New York. The premiere had been a great success, presented with effortless Hollywood professionalism, like a vast good-natured hallucination – the hundreds of limousines, revolving searchlights and sealed-off streets lined with red carpet and security guards. The audience of film actors seemed to have absconded from reality for the evening, ambling down the aisles of the theatre with their sable coats and pop-corn cartons.

As it happened, my small role had been edited out of the finished film, much to my relief, though I survived as a brief blur seen as the camera followed my younger self playing with his model aircraft. But this seemed just, like the faint blur which was all that any of us left across time and space. Besides, the film had served a deeper role for me – seeing its masterly recreation of Shanghai had been the last act in a profound catharsis that had taken decades to draw to a close. All the powers of modern film had come together for this therapeutic exercise. The puzzle had solved itself; the mirror, as I had promised, had been broken from within. In my mind the image had fused with its original, enfolding it within its protective wings. Looking at the great hotels along the Bund, unchanged after fifty years, I could almost believe that my memories of Shanghai had always been a film, endlessly played inside my head during my years in England after the war.

'They're launching some kind of ship.'

Cleo pointed to the crowd of people at the water's edge. A caterpillar tractor backed across the sand, pushing a trailer loaded with a bizarre sailing vessel. A single mast rose above a cabin that resembled a thatched hut. As we approached across the sand we could see that the hull was built entirely of papyrus reeds, bound together at stem and stern like the handle of a wicker shopping bag.

A square-rigged sail floated from the mast, bearing a half-familiar red emblem.

Cleo stopped and squinted through cupped hands.

'It's Heyerdahl's papyrus ship – *Ra*. We published the book.'

'I thought it sank in the Atlantic . . .'

'He must be trying to cross the Pacific. Jim, you ought to volunteer. It's the original slow boat to China.'

'I don't think it's an original of anything . . .'

Crew-men knelt in the shallow waves, examining the underside of the craft. We stepped through the children and dogs playing in the water around the tractor. The mock-papyrus superstructure, assembled from moulded plastic and fibre-glass, was bolted on to a sturdy steel hull.

'It's the replica of a replica.' Cleo laughed at herself for being taken in. 'They must be using it in a film.'

'It looks like a real ship, though. If they're making a TV commercial they'll need something more seaworthy than Heyerdahl's original. This one's going somewhere.'

'Jim, now's your chance to get aboard.'

A black labrador ambled through the waves, licking our hands and ready to shake its coat over us. I patted its

346

head, admiring the easy expertise of the American crew. A man in swimming trunks and straw hat filmed the launch with a hand-held video-camera. At least this vessel would not sink, and a trial cruise among the weekend yachts of Marina Del Rey might uncover more truths about the performance of crew and vessel than its original's abortive mock-voyage across the Atlantic.

I thought of Olga, sailing serenely through the lobby of the Beverly Hilton after we said goodbye. As she pressed her cheeks against my own I kissed for the last time the face of my childhood governess. That youthful and ageless mask was her true self, which time had stolen from her, the innocent and unlined face she had never been allowed to know as an adolescent.

The war had postponed my own childhood, to be rediscovered years later with Henry, Alice and Lucy. The time of desperate stratagems was over, the car crashes and hallucinogens, the deviant sex ransacked like a library of extreme metaphors. Miriam and all the murdered dead of a world war had made their peace. The happiness I had found had been waiting for me within the modest reach of my own arms, in my children and the women I had loved, and in the friends who had made their own way through the craze years.

The waves struck sharply at our ankles. A strong wind was gusting across the beach, and the papyrus craft had broken free from its crew. With only the camera-man aboard, fumbling at the mast as he ducked the swinging boom, the craft confidently rode the waves. The launch crew leapt through the deeper water, pulling on the mooring lines but unable to restrain the boisterous vessel. The replica of a replica it may have been, but it was buoyant and well-founded, more than capable of taking on the sea and setting its own course across the Pacific, with only its shanghaied camera-man as crew, perhaps ending with a last triumphant heave on the beaches of Woosung.

'New York tomorrow. Then home to the children.' Cleo held my arm tightly as we walked back to our car, past the hippies and the fragrant beach fires, embers glaring in the freshening air. 'Tell me – when they show the film in London, will they put back your little cameo?'

'I hope not.' I watched the papyrus craft, cresting the breakers that rolled in from the Pacific, its bows set towards the China shore. 'Cleo, think where that might lead . . .'